For
Doctor
Maxwell

06/24/16

Nina Cooper

The Casebook of
Monsieur Lecoq

The Casebook of Monsieur Lecoq

The Orcival Murder
File 113

by
Emile Gaboriau

translated and introduced by
Nina Cooper

A Black Coat Press Book

Acknowledgements: Thanks to Charles Griggs, with appreciation for reading the Introduction. Thanks to Kitty Werner for helping reintroducing the character of Monsieur Lecoq to the contemporary English-reading public.

Visit our website at www.blackcoatpress.com

TABLE OF CONTENTS

Introduction

'Tis morning, but no morning can restore What we have forfeited. I see no sin: The wrong is mix'd. In tragic life, God wot, No villain need be! Passions spin the plot: We are betray'd by what is false within. Excerpt from "Love's Grave"

— George Meredith (1828–1909)

Emile Gaboriau is frequently credited with creating the modern detective story with his "roman judiciaire" and his detective Monsieur Lecoq, precursor of Sir Arthur Conan Doyle's Sherlock Holmes.

He was born in Saujon in the Charente-Maritime region of France on November 9, 1832. After a short period as an apprentice to a notary and a second class infantry man in Africa, he settled in Paris to begin life as a writer. He contributed short articles and popularized historical articles on French royal mistresses to various newspaper "feuilles," insertions in newspapers appearing over a period of months. Once the "feuilles" had completed their run in newspapers, they were published as 400 to 500 page novels. He worked as secretary and sometimes as a ghost writer to Paul Feval, the most popular "feuilletoniste" of the period and the author of the famed series of crime novels, The Black Coats.[1] He became well known when Alphonse Millaud published *The Lerouge Affair* in his newspaper, *Le Soleil*. The novel launched Gaboriau as a major "feuilletoniste," and led to the Monsieur Lecoq series featuring one the eponymous characters,

The novels in the Monsieur Lecoq series are: *L'Affaire Lerouge* (1866), *Le Crime d'Orcival* (1867; translated here as The Orcival Murder), *Le Dossier No. 113* (1867; tr. here as *File 113*), *Les Esclaves de Paris* (1868) and *Monsieur Lecoq* (1869 [2]).

Gaboriau's novels, particularly the plot of *File 113*, illustrate in many ways the lines above from George Meredith, Gaboriau's contemporary. Although Meredith's poem in its entirety does not totally fit, it does apply to parts of all of Gaboriau's novels, in that "Passions spin the plot." That is not to say that Gaboriau's novels have no villains and no sinners. They have, indeed, a plethora of both, of all sorts, and few achieve redemption. Villains use poison in *File 113*

---

[1] Available from Black Coat Press.
[2] Available from Black Coat Press, ISBN 978-1-934543-31-3.

and in *The Orcival Murder*; newborns conceived in love, but out of wedlock, and snatched from their sorrowing mothers, help spin the plots in *File 113*, and in Volume II of *Monsieur Lecoq*; blackmailers and extortionists are essential to the plots in *File 113*, in *Baron Trigault's Vengeance*, as well as in *The Slaves of Paris*. These are only a few of the most villainous. Violence, lies, adultery, duplicity, murder, including fratricide and attempted parricide, falsely exchanged or abandoned sons and stolen birthrights, and ever more sins and villainies, find a place in Gaboriau's novels, as they do in many contemporary detective stories, television series, and often even in real life.

Gaboriau drew on the forty years of slow evolution of the crime story, following Poe in the United States, and writers such as his amanuensis Paul Féval, Eugène Sue, Alexandre Dumas the elder, Pierre-Alexis Ponson du Terrail and Honoré de Balzac in France, writing popular literature for the masses. He worked as a secretary and sometimes as a ghost writer for Féval, who, at the time, was the most famous of those *feuilletonistes*. He initially submitted his first novel, *The Lerouge Affair*, to a newspaper with a limited circulation, *Le Pays,* where it ran from September 14 through December 7, 1865. His friend Alphonse Millaud, editor and publisher of *Le Soleil,* a better-known newspaper with a wider circulation, was also publishing at the time stories by Alexandre Dumas, the elder, and *Toilers of the Sea*, by Victor Hugo. He read the novel and decided to republish it in an expanded version in *Le Soleil*, where it ran from April 18 through July 2, 1866. The success of *The Lerouge Affair* earned Gaboriau a contract from Alphonse Millaud's uncle, the publisher and banker, Moïse Millaud. Millaud signed Gaboriau to a long-term contract to write exclusively for his major newspaper, *Le Petit Journal.* Founded in 1863, it was the first popular newspaper directed toward the man-in-the-street who could, thanks to the Industrial Revolution, afford to pay five centimes for an issue. The newspaper was also apolitical, and therefore could avoid both the government's restrictions on freedom of the press, and the government's tax. (*Le Petit Journal* existed longer than any other newspaper of its kind in France, running from its creation in 1863, until its demise in 1944.)

Ernest Mandel, a Trotskyite and theorist for the Fourth International, in his work *Delightful Murder: A Social History of thee Crime Story*, equates the rise of the interest in detective fiction to interest in the popular press and the *feuilletonistes*. He wrote:

> *The rising preoccupation with crime is best exemplified by Thomas De Quincey's* "On Murder Considered as one of the Fine Arts," *which appeared in 1827. In his 1827 essay, he actually insisted upon the delectation with murder and speculation about whodunit among 'amateurs and dilettantes,' thereby opening the way to Edgar Allen Poe, Gaboriau and Conan Doyle. He also initiated the link between popular journalism and writing about murder, which would involve Dickens, Poe, Conan Doyle and so many other*

crime story writers, up to Dashiell Hammett, E. Stanley Gardner and other contemporaries.[3]

This evolution of popular literature, contributed to by the *feuilletonistes,* had reached its maturity by the 1860s in France. At first, *feuilletoniste* publications were considered hardly respectable, and read by only the lowest class of society. However, the weekly publications of nerve-tingling stories soon created another type and level of reader. For the first time, the man-in-the-street had access to popular written fiction. One of the results of a new reading public was a change in the way the man-in-the street viewed the police. Prior to the advent of the *"roman judiciaire,"* the police had a long-standing bad reputation among the citizenship. Frequently using criminals and prostitutes as informers, and often recruiting policemen from among the criminals, their reputation had to be changed before they could become heroes of romance. In *Au Bonheur du Feuilleton* (q.v.), stressing the necessity of changing the role of the policeman in the view of the masses, Marie-Françoise Cachin says:

> *To leave infamy he had to exist as a personality, as an actor, as an author, clearly recognizable in the space of a text. To bring this about, it was necessary to present the police as an honorable activity, useful work without ambiguity in the symbolic and social re-evaluation of a profession. Such a process couldn't take place without the press...The space given to the feuilleton is evidently at the heart of this process.*

She ends her analysis by remarking on the present-day role of the policeman: *"There are no longer any feuilletons, but for the police, always looking for legitimacy, it's through other feuilletonesque means, that of television series, that the process continues today."*[4]

The popular press brought about not only a new, more middle-class reader, but also a totally new type of fiction in France. When in 1866, *Le Petit Journal* printed as *feuilleton* installments Gaboriau's novel, *The Lerouge Affair,* it was the first *roman judiciaire,* the modern detective story. In that novel, Lecoq is still a novice policeman, assistant to Gévrol, a superior officer in the Sûreté, the French National Police, less intelligent than he and jealous of the young policeman's abilities. Gévrol will recur in Lecoq's life to thwart Lecoq's ambitions when he can.

---

[3] Marie-Françoise Cachin, et al. "Au Bonheur du Feuilleton: Naissance et Mutations d'un Genre (Etats Unis, Grande Bretagne, XVIII–XX siècles)," Paris: Editions Crane, Créaphis, 2007. pp. 149–150.
[4] Ernest Mandel, *Delightful Murder: A Social History of the Crime Story,* Minnepolis: The University of Minnesota Press, 1984.

Lecoq's first investigation involves the death of a widow in a small village outside Paris. The widow Lerouge, a somewhat mysterious newcomer to the village community, is an unlikely candidate for murder. A young, new, Investigating Magistrate, representing the French National Police, the Sûreté, calls in an amateur detective, Père Tabaret, a sometimes consultant for the police in unusually difficult cases. Tabaret is called by his associates "Tireauclair," the one who brings things to light. Lecoq meets his superior in analytical ability and continues as his disciple.

Gaboriau obviously did not at first intend Lecoq to be a major character. In *The Lerouge Affair*, he is ancillary to Tabaret, an armchair detective, who will later appear as his mentor. Tabaret, as a retiree who had also recently received a sizeable legacy, collected anything he could find on crime, criminals, and police procedure. After several years, his knowledge became as vast as his library. He hesitatingly offered his free services to the Rue de Jérusalem, the Sûreté headquarters. He wasn't immediately accepted; but after performing menial tasks, while also unobtrusively utilizing his skill in both inductive and deductive logic, he proved his worth, and became the best and most knowledgeable person in the Sûreté. He was able to elucidate situations and deduct facts, which earned him the name of *Tire-au-Clair*, the one who brings things to light. He stirred up jealousy by working without a salary, even occasionally paying himself for the necessities of an investigation, and finally made one mistake. His active detective career ended; he became a source of information and instruction for Lecoq and others.

In *The Lerouge Affair*, Lecoq is on the margins of crime, talented both as a would-be major criminal, and as a young man gifted with the ability to logically analyze crime scenes and facts. In the next novel, he is a successful member of the Sûreté, and his tainted past is not mentioned; and in *Monsieur Lecoq*, it is explained away. Père Tabaret does not appear in *The Orcival Crime*, but Lecoq refers to him as his "master" as he works out the details of this next crime. In the third novel, *File 113*, he needs Tireauclair's help to give him the necessary confidence to pursue unraveling the crime and its motive. By the time Gaboriau has reached *File 113*, his detective is head of a Sûreté department, has perfected his art of disguise and his modus operandi, seeking the solution to the present crime in the events of the past.

A primary technique Gaboriau used in the *Monsieur Lecoq* series allowed him to keep producing breathtaking adventures, which made up many months' contributions to *Le Petit Journal,* and later turned into 400, and more, page novels. This technique, the extended flashback, varied somewhat from novel to novel. *The Orcival Murder* is divided about half and half between the crime and the flashback, laying the foundation of the causes of the crime in the first part of the novel. In *File 113*, the same technique leaves the present to return to the past, in Chapter 12 of the 25 chapters, coming back to the present only at the last two chapters. To give the story a spectacular finish, *Monsieur Lecoq* brilliantly explains the relation of the past to the present, and sees the criminal fittingly punished, and himself justified. In *Monsieur Lecoq*, the flashback takes up all of Volume II, "The Honor of the Name," except for the last few pages, and could stand alone as a separate novel.

A second important technique of Gaboriau, one he shared with Sir Arthur Conan Doyle's Sherlock Holmes, is attributing to Lecoq a mastery of the art of disguise. Lecoq perfects this art to the point that his real personality, physique and facial expression are not known, even to his fellow employees in the Sûreté. The only telling feature he cannot change is his eyes, and to disguise those he, when acting as the head of a department in the Sûreté, wears gold-rimmed spectacles. Sometimes he is a middle-aged, fat red-headed man; at other times he is a youngish man, but far removed from his actual physique and facial appearance. Gaboriau explains how Lecoq is able to maintain multiple personalities so successfully. In *The Orcival Murder* he says:

"You could never tell when he was acting. How could you know; he didn't always know himself. This great artist, passionate about his art, had practiced feigning all the movements of the soul, just as he had accustomed himself to use all kinds of costumes."

In most of the Lecoq series, Gaboriau does not use the omniscient narrator point of view. The reader must know only what Lecoq knows, and only the facts as he discovers them. If Lecoq makes a mistake, or is wrong in an assumption or a deduction, the reader must follow and be thrown off the trail also. Avoiding the omniscient narrator point of view is essential, particularly in Volume I, "The Investigation," of *Monsieur Lecoq*, where he is wrong or distrusts himself and is chastised by Père Tabaret, leading to Volume II, and connecting Volumes I and II. To maintain this technique, Lecoq must have a secondary character, a foil, like Sherlock Holmes' Dr. Watson. In *Monsieur Lecoq*, it is the old drunkard who has no name except that of his favorite drink, Absinthe. In *File 113*, he is contrasted with, and seconded by, the ambitious Sûreté agent Fanferlot, nicknamed the Squirrel, and the man accused of theft, the bank teller Prosper Bertomy.

Lecoq appears in only five novels of Gaboriau's extensive work. After Gaboriau's death, Fortuné du Boisgobey, then a popular *feuilletoniste* and novelist, added two more volumes to *Monsieur Lecoq*'s fictitious life: *The Old Age of Monsieur Lecoq* and *The Nabob of Babour: A Sequel to The Old Age of Monsieur Lecoq*.

Although they shared some 19th century prejudices as well as literary techniques, Gaboriau's novels in the Lecoq series, did not, unlike Conan Doyle's Sherlock Holmes, avoid a passionate love interest for the detective and leave that to lesser characters. Indeed it is, in all the novels, one of the "passions" that "spin the plot." Even the logical *Monsieur Lecoq* is not free from its illogical, passionate hold.

Women characters, those who motivate the passion, are not always the stereotypes of the Victorian era. They are sometimes strong women, and often villainous. The fatal attraction of Berthe for her lover in *The Orcival Murder*, and her hold on two men, causes the damnation of all three. Diane de Laurebourg in *The Slaves of Paris*, incites her lover to attempted parricide. The Comtesse de la Verberie in *File 113*, lacks all maternal tenderness, but holds wells of greed and self-interest. A more virtuous woman, Mademoiselle Madeleine in *File 113*, uses to her advantage the hold she has on the villain because of his irrational, all-consuming passion for her. At other times they are "betrayed by what is false within," as is Marie Anne, in *Monsieur Lecoq*. Beloved by three men, she chooses one and prepares for her own destruction. Madame Fauvel in *File 113*, is not strong enough to avoid her first mistake, nor strong enough to extricate herself from its repercussions twenty-six years later. Others, like Marie de Puymandour in the *The Slaves of Paris*, are pawns in loveless marriages made by families to secure position and fortune.

Children conceived out of wedlock, a major sin in the Victorian era, are central to the plot of novels in the Lecoq series. The result of illicit affairs functions in different ways in the various novels, but the plot doesn't move forward without them. The common woman, never to be married or respectable, has her own place in the plots, as for example, Nina Gypsy in *File 113* and Jenny Fancy in *The Orcival Murder*. The innocent girl, seduced and abandoned, even if left reluctantly, adds another dimension, as in *File 113*, and in *The Orcival Murder*.

Men in Gaboriau's Lecoq series usually contrast with the detective unfavorably, even though they are sometimes sympathetic characters. They are frequently stupid, like Old Man Absinthe or the old Baron de Sairmeuse in *Monsieur Lecoq*; or jealous, like Inspector Gévrol in *Monsieur Lecoq*; or weak and unable to control their lives like Prosper Bertomy in *File 113*, and Norbert de Chamdoce in *The Slaves of Paris*, and Trémorel in *The Orcival Murder*. The last two characters fit the description Gaboriau gives of Trémorel. *"He was one of those weak men who flee from the reasons for situations, who, rather than take precautions while there is still time, let themselves be foolishly driven into a corner by circumstances."* But the most dangerous are the totally wicked and depraved who will stop at nothing to attain wealth, power, or the woman who inspires their passion, those like Daumon in *The Slaves of Paris*, and Louis de Clameran in *File 113*.

Although doctors and investigating magistrates receive sympathetic treatment, only two characters are a match for Lecoq: Père Tabaret (*Tire-au-Clair*) and the Marquis de Sairmeuse. These two, his equals, or at times, his superiors, accurately estimate Lecoq's intelligence and his character; one, Père Tabaret, remains his helpful friend, and the other becomes his sometimes mysterious friend, as in *File 113*.

Careful readers will note that Gaboriau is at times careless with dates, facts, and ages. A major character in *Monsieur Lecoq* is given three different birthdates. Another is both born an only child, and had a brother. A major character in *File 113* is frequently said to be twenty or twenty-four, the age necessary for the plot at that point; but facts from the opening of the plot make him about thirty, somewhat old for his important role as a charming, handsome, and very young man. A minor character begins the story as Albert, but mid-way becomes Abel. These careful readers may forgive Gaboriau these minor discrepancies, due, possibly, to the urgency of meeting newspaper deadlines. The casual reader may not notice them.

Tarascon and the Rhône River Valley, where Gaboriau spent part of his childhood, are used as background in several novels. His description of the countryside and the peasants there are some of his best, and some are unforgettable. The opening scene of Volume II of *Monsieur Lecoq*, in the village church square, and the scenes involving the peasants' revolt, show Gaboriau's talent for storytelling, his twists in the plot, and his interesting, and sometimes beautiful imagery. He describes the outskirts of fashionable Paris in *The Orcival Murder*, and the palatial St. Germain neighborhood of the 19th century, as well as the dens and slums of Paris of the same era in *Monsieur Lecoq*. His night scenes in Paris contrast interestingly with those in the Rhône Valley in the day.

It is reported that Gaboriau, after reading Flaubert's *Madame Bovary*, predicted his own success, but linked it to the appearance of a new level of readers and the firm establishment of the one-*sou* newspaper. And what would he have written had he lived, not in the 19th Century, but in the 21st, with access to modern communication technology, not to mention television soap operas, and Hollywood as well as Bollywood?

Nina Cooper

THE ORCIVAL MURDER

Chapter I

The 9th of July 18**, a Thursday, Jean Bertaud, called La Ripaille, and his son, well known in Orcival for living by poaching and pilfering, got up about 3:00 a.m. to go fishing at daybreak. Carrying their tackle, under the shade of acacia trees, they went down the charming road which can be seen from the Evry station and which leads from the town of Orcival to the Seine. They went to their boat, usually moored some fifty meters upstream from the iron bridge, alongside a meadow joining Valfeuillu, the beautiful property of the Count de Trémorel. Coming to the edge of the river, they put down their fishing equipment and Jean LaRipaille got into the boat to empty out the water. While bailing out the water with an experienced hand, he noticed that one of the rowlocks of the old boat, worn by the oar, was about to break.

"Philippe," he shouted to his son, who was busy disentangling a casting net which a fishing warden would have found to have too tight a mesh, "Philippe, try to find me a piece of wood to repair our rowlocks."

"Right away," Philippe answered.

There wasn't one tree in the meadow. So the young man started toward the Valfeuillu Park only a few feet away. And paying very little attention to Article 391 of the Penal Code, he jumped the wide ditch which enclosed Monsieur de Trémorel's property. He intended to cut a branch from one of the old weeping willow trees which at that spot dipped their weeping branches over the water.

He had hardly taken his knife out of his pocket, while glancing about him with the uneasy look of the poacher, than he let out a stifled cry.

"Father! Eh! Father!"

"What is it?" The old poacher answered without looking up.

"Father, come quick," Philippe continued, "in the name of Heaven, come quickly!"

From the hoarse voice of his son, Jean La Ripaille knew that something extraordinary had happened. He stopped scooping out water and, worry helping him, in three leaps he was in the park.

He too remained dumbfounded in front of the spectacle which had terrified Philippe. Stretched out on the river bank among the rushes and the water lilies was the cadaver of a woman. Her long flowing hair was spread out among the water grasses. Her tattered grey silk dress was soiled with mud and blood. The entire upper part of the body was plunged in the shallow water and her face was buried in the mud.

Philippe, whose voice trembled, murmured, "A murder."

"That's for sure," answered La Ripaille in an indifferent voice. "But who can that woman be? It almost looks like the Countess."

"We'll soon see," said the young man.

He took a step toward the cadaver. His father stopped him, holding him by the arm.

What are you going to do, for Heaven's sake?" he asked. "You should never touch the body of a murdered person without the law."

"Do you think so?"

"Certainly! There are penalties for that."

"Then, let's go inform the mayor."

"To do what? The people around here don't have it in for us enough? Who knows but what they would accuse us."

"Nevertheless, Father..."

"What! If we went to tell Monsieur Courtois, he would ask us how and why we found ourselves in Monsieur de Trémorel's park to see what was happening there. What does it matter to you that someone murdered the Countess? The body will be found without you... Come on, let's leave."

But Philippe didn't budge. His head bowed, his chin in the palm of his hand, he was thinking.

"We have to tell," he declared in a firm tone. "We aren't savages. We'll tell Monsieur Courtois that we saw the body while skirting the banks of the park in our punt."

The elder La Ripaille resisted at first, then seeing that his son would go without him, he appeared to give in to his entreaties. They again jumped over the ditch, and, leaving their tackle on the prairie, they started in all haste to the house of Monsieur the Mayor of Orcival.

Situated five kilometers from Corbeil on the right bank of the Seine, twenty minutes from the Evry station, Orcival is one of the most delightful villages of the Paris suburbs in spite of the infernal etymology of its name.[5] The noisy and plundering Parisian who, more destructive than the locust, lays waste to the fields on Sundays, hadn't yet discovered its pleasant countryside. The depressing odor of frying in the little dinner-dance restaurants hadn't overpowered the perfume of the honeysuckles. The echoes had never been frightened by the refrains of boaters and the blaring of the cornets in the public dance halls.

Nestled lazily on the gentle slopes of a hill bathed by the Seine, Orcival

---

[5] Not to be confused with the Orcival in the Puy-de-Dôme department in Auvergne in central France.

has white houses, delicious shady areas, and a new bell tower which is its pride. Vast country estates, kept up at great expense, surround it on all sides. The weather vanes of twenty chateaux can be seen from its highest point. On the right are the huge trees of Mauprévoir and the pretty little castle of the Countess de la Brêche. Across, on the other side of the river, there is Mousseaux and Petit-Bourg, the former Aguado domain, which has become the estate of a famous carriage maker, Monsieur Binder. Those beautiful trees on the left belong to the Count de Trémorel. That beautiful park is the Etiolles Park, and in the distance, very low on the horizon, is Corbeil. That immense building, whose roof rises higher than the great oaks, is the Darblay mill.

The mayor of Orcival lives at the top of the village in one of those houses that can be dreamed of with 100,000 pounds of income. Formerly a maker of canvas cloth. Monsieur Courtois courageously entered commerce without a *sou* and after thirty years of relentless labor he retired with an income of a full 4,000,000. At that time, he intended to live peacefully with his wife and his daughters, spending the winter in Paris and the summer in the country. But, then, suddenly he became nervous and agitated. Ambition came gnawing at his heart. He performed a hundred services in order to be forced to accept being mayor of Orcival. And, much against his will, he accepted the position, as he will tell you himself. That office of Mayor was at the same time his joy and his despair. Apparent despair, real and private joy. He was in good form when, his forehead clouded with worries, he cursed the cares of power. He was in better form when as head of the municipal body he triumphed, his stomach girded with the golden tasseled sash of office.

Everybody was still asleep at the Mayor's house when the Bertauds, father and son, came banging the heavy door knocker. After a short wait, a servant, three-fourths awake, half clothed, appeared at one of the windows on the ground floor.

"What's the matter, you rascals?" he asked in a bad-tempered voice.

La Ripaille didn't think it the proper time to take note of an insult that his reputation in the community only too well justified.

"We want to talk to Monsieur le Maire," he answered. "And it's terribly important. Go wake him, Monsieur Baptiste. He won't scold you."

"Do I get scolded, me!" Baptiste grumbled.

Nevertheless, it took ten good minutes of negotiations and explanations for the servant to make a decision. Finally, a little fat, red-faced man, very unhappy to have been torn out of bed so early, appeared before the Bertauds. It was Monsieur Courtois. It had been decided that Philippe would speak.

"Monsieur le Maire," he began, "we've come to tell you a great misfortune. It's for sure that a crime has been committed at Monsieur de Trémorel's house."

Monsieur Courtois was a friend of the Count. At that statement he became whiter than his shirt.

"Ah! *Mon Dieu!*" He stammered, incapable of controlling his emotion. "What's that you're telling me?"

"Yes, we've seen the body, a little while ago, and as real as you are. I believe it's that of the Countess."

The worthy mayor lifted his arms toward heaven with a totally wild-eyed expression.

"But where? But when?" he asked.

"A little while ago, where we were skirting the end of the Park to go take up our nets."

"This is horrible!" the good Monsieur Courtois kept repeating. "What a misfortune! Such a worthy woman! But that isn't possible. You must be mistaken. I would have been told..."

"We certainly saw it, Monsieur le Maire."

"Such a crime, in my jurisdiction! Well, you were right to come. I'm going to get dressed in two seconds and we'll run... That is...no...wait."

He seemed to think a minute and called out:

"Baptiste!"

The servant wasn't very far away. His ear and his eye alternately glued to the door's keyhole, he was listening and looking as hard as he could. At his master's voice, he had only to stretch out his arm to open the door.

"Monsieur called me?"

"Run to the Justice of the Peace," the Mayor told him. "There's not a second to lose. It's a matter of a crime, of a murder perhaps. Tell him to come quickly, very quickly. And you others," he said, addressing the Bertauds, "wait for me here. I'm going to put on a jacket."

The Orcival Justice of the Peace, Père Plantat, as he was called, was a former Melun lawyer. At fifty, Père Plantat, to whom everything had been as successful as could be wished, lost in the same month his wife, whom he adored, and his sons, two charming young boys, one age eighteen, the other twenty-two.

These losses, one after the other, brought low a man that thirty years of prosperity had left without a defense against misfortune. For a long time they feared for his sanity. Just the sight of a client coming to trouble his sorrow in order to tell him stupid stories concerning their self-interest exasperated him. Therefore, people were not surprised to see him sell his practice at half-price. He wanted to be at home with his grief, with the certainty of not being distracted from it.

But the intensity of regrets diminishes and the malady of idleness arrives. The position of Justice of the Peace of Orcival was vacant. Père Plantat applied for it and got it. Once he was Justice of the Peace, he was less bored. That man, who thought his life was over, undertook to become interested in the thousand different causes that came to be pleaded before him. He applied all the strength of a superior intelligence, all the resources of a mind eminently clever enough to disentangle the false from the true among all the lies he was forced to hear.

In addition, he stubbornly insisted on living alone, despite the exhortations of Monsieur Courtois, claiming that all social contact tired him and that an unhappy man was a spoil-sport. The time left from his legal duties he consecrated to an unparalleled collection of petunias.

Misfortune, which modifies personalities, either for good or bad, had made him, apparently, very self-centered. He claimed to be no more interested in the things of life than a blasé critic is to stage settings. He liked to show off his profound indifference for everything, swearing that a rain of fire falling on Paris wouldn't even make him turn his head. To touch him seemed impossible. "What does that matter to me!" was his invariable refrain.

Such was the man who, a quarter of an hour after Baptiste's departure, arrived at the house of the Mayor of Orcival.

Monsieur Plantat was tall, thin, and nervous. There was nothing remarkable about his appearance. He wore his hair short. His restless eyes seemed always to be looking for something. His nose was very long and thin as the blade of a razor. His mouth, so fine in the past, was deformed since his sorrows. His lower lip had sunken in and gave him the deceptive appearance of simplicity.

"What's this about someone murdering Madame de Trémorel?" he asked as he neared the door.

"At least that's what these men here claim," answered the Mayor, who had just reappeared.

Monsieur Courtois was no longer the same man. He had had time to pull himself together somewhat. His face was trying to express a majestic coldness. He had soundly criticized himself for having lacked dignity by showing his trouble and his sadness in front of the Bertauds.

"Nothing should affect a man in my position to this point, " he had told himself.

And, although terribly agitated, he forced himself to be calm, cold, impassive.

Père Plantat himself was that way naturally. "This is perhaps a very unfortunate accident," he said in a tone of voice he forced himself to render perfectly disinterested, "but, as a legal issue what is that to us? Nevertheless, we have to go see what it's all about without delay. I've alerted the Gendarme Brigadier, who will join us."

"Let's go," said Monsieur Courtois. "I have my official sash in my pocket."

They left. Philippe and his father went ahead, the young man in a hurry and impatient, the old gloomy and preoccupied.

At each step, the Mayor let out some exclamation.

"Can you believe that," he murmured. " A murder in my commune, a commune where, in the memory of man, there hasn't been any crime committed at all."

And he gave the two Bertauds a suspicious look.

The road which led to the house—in the countryside they said chateau— of Monsieur Trémorel is rather unattractive, encased as it is by wall a dozen feet high. On one side it's the park of the Marquise de Lanascol, on the other the large garden of Saint-Jouan.

The comings and goings had taken time. It was almost 8:00 a.m. when the Mayor, the Justice of the Peace, and their guides stopped in front of the iron gate of Monsieur Trémorel.

The Mayor rang the bell. The bell is very big. Only a little five- or six- meter sanded courtyard separated the iron gate and the house. However, no one came. Monsieur le Maire rang louder, then louder still, then with all his strength. In vain.

In front of the iron gate of Monsieur de Lanascol's chateau, situated almost across the road, a groom was standing, busy cleaning and polishing the bits of a bridle.

"It won't do any good to ring, Messieurs," that man said. "There's nobody at the chateau."

"What do you mean, no one?" the Mayor asked, surprised.

"I mean," replied the groom, "that only the masters are there. All the household staff left yesterday evening by the 8:40 p.m. train to go to Paris to attend the wedding of the former cook, Madame Denis. They're supposed to come back this morning by the first train. I myself was invited..."

"Grand Dieu! interrupted Monsieur Courtois, "Then the Count and the Countess were alone last night?"

"Absolutely alone, Monsieur le Maire."

"That's horrible!"

Père Plantat seemed to be becoming impatient with this dialogue.

"Let's go," he said. "We can't spend eternity at this door. The gendarmes aren't coming. Let's send for the locksmith."

Philippe was already getting ready to rush off when they heard songs and laughter at the end of the road. Five people, three women and two men appeared almost immediately.

"Ah! There's the chateau staff," said the groom, whom that morning visit seemed unusually to intrigue. "They must have a key."

On their side, the servants, seeing the group stopped in front of the iron gate, were quiet and came forward quickly. One of them even began to run, thus outstripping the others. He was the Count's personal valet.

"Do you gentlemen wish to speak to Monsieur le Comte?" he asked, after having greeted the Mayor and the Justice of the Peace.

"We've rung five times as hard as we could," said the Mayor.

"That's surprising," said the Count's valet. "Because Monsieur is a light sleeper! After all that, he may be out."

"Poor people!" Philippe cried out. "Someone murdered them both!"

These words sobered up the chateau servants, whose gaiety showed the very reasonable number of toasts drunk to the happiness of the newlyweds.

Monsieur Courtois himself seemed to study the attitude of the older Bertaud.

"Murder!" murmured the Count's valet. "It was for the money, then. They would have known..."

"What?" demanded the Mayor.

"Yesterday morning the Count received a very large sum."

"Ah! Yes, a big sum," added a chamber maid. "There were bank bills as big as that. Madame even told Monsieur that she wouldn't sleep a wink that night with such an immense sum in the house."

There was silence. Everyone looked at each other with a frightened air. Monsieur Courtois himself was thinking.

"What time did you leave yesterday evening?" he demanded the servants.

"At 8:00 p.m. We put the dinner hour forward."

"All of you left together?"

"Yes, Monsieur."

"You didn't separate from each other?"

"Not one minute."

"And you all came back together?"

The servants gave each other an unusual look.

"All of us," answered a chambermaid who had a loose tongue. "That is to say, no. There was one of us who left us on arriving at the Lyon train station in Paris. That was Guespin."

"Ah!"

"Yes, Monsieur. He dashed off in his direction, saying he would rejoin us in the Batignolles, at Wepler's where the wedding took place."

Monsieur le Maire gave a big shoulder nudge to the Justice of the Peace, as if to suggest he pay attention, and continued to interrogate.

"And this Guespin, as you call him, did you see him again?"

"No, Monsieur. I even asked news of him, uselessly, several times during the night. His absence seemed suspicious to me."

Evidently, the chamber maid was trying to show superior intelligence. In a little while she would have talked about premonitions.

"This servant, has he been with the household a long time?" Monsieur Courtois asked.

"Since Spring."

"What were his qualifications?"

"He was sent from Paris by the Gentil Jardinier employment agency to take care of the rare flowers in Madame's greenhouse."

"And did he know about the money?"

And the servants again gave each other very meaningful glances.

"Yes! Yes!" They all responded at once. "We all talked about it a great deal among ourselves in the servants' hall."

The chamber maid, an easy talker, added: "He even told me, speaking just to me: 'Just think that the Count has in his secretary what would make all our fortunes!'"

"What kind of man is he?"

That question absolutely shut off the servants' talkativeness. Not one dared speak, knowing that the least word might serve as the basis for a terrible accusation.

But the groom from the house across the road, eager to get mixed up in that affair, didn't have these scruples at all.

He answered: "Guespin, he's a nice fellow, and someone who's been around. *Dieu de Dieu!* does he know some stories! He knows everything, that man does. It seems he was rich in the past and if he wanted to…but *Dame!* he likes an easy job. And what's more, he's a party-goer like nobody else, a billiard ace, don't you know!"

While listening to these depositions, or to speak more accurately, this gossip, with one ear, apparently distracted, Père Plantat was carefully examining the wall and the iron gate. He returned to the conversation at this point the interrupt the groom.

"That's really enough of this," he said, to the great scandal of Monsieur Courtois. "Before going on with this interrogation, it would be well to look into the crime, if, however, there is a crime, which hasn't been proven. Whoever among you has a key, open the gate."

The Count's valet had the key. He opened the gate and everyone one moved into the courtyard. The gendarmes had just arrived. The Mayor told the Brigadier to follow him and placed two men at the gate with orders to let no one enter or leave without his permission.

Only then did the Count's valet open the door to the house.

Chapter II

If there had been no crime, at least something very extraordinary had taken place in the Count de Trémorel's house. The impassive Justice of the Peace must have been convinced of that at his first step into the vestibule. The glass door leading into the garden was wide open, and three of the panes were broken into a thousand pieces. The pathways of canvas oilskin which ran from door to door had been ripped up, and on all the white marble tiles could be seen large drops of blood. At the foot of the stairway was a stain bigger than the others, and on the last step a splatter hideous to see.

Very little made for such spectacles, for a mission such as that he had to fulfill, honest Monsieur Courtois felt faint. Fortunately, he drew strength very far from his character from the feeling of his own importance and dignity. The more the preliminary investigation of that affair seemed difficult to him, the more he intended to direct it well.

"Take us to the place where you saw the body," he ordered the Bertauds.

But Père Plantat intervened.

"It would be wiser, I believe," he objected, "and more logical, to begin by going through the house."

"All right, yes, in fact, that was what I was thinking," said the Mayor, clinging to the advice of the Justice of the Peace as a drowning man clings to a plank.

And he had everyone leave, with the exception of the Brigadier and the Count's valet, who was to serve as a guide.

"Gendarmes!" he shouted again to the men on guard in front of the gate. "Watch to see that no one leaves, keep anyone from coming into the house, and above all let no one go into the garden."

When they came to the landing of the second floor:

"Tell me, my friend," the Mayor asked the Count's valet, "do your masters sleep in the same bedroom?"

"Yes, Monsieur," the servant answered.

"And where is their bedroom?"

"There, Monsieur."

And at the same time as he answered, the valet stepped back, frightened, pointing to a door whose upper panel bore the imprint of a bloody hand.

Drops of sweat like pearls glistened on the poor Mayor's forehead. He too was afraid. He remained upright with great difficulty! Alas! Power imposes terrible obligations. The Brigadier, an old soldier of the Crimean War,[6] visibly

---

[6] The Crimean War (Oct.1853-Febr.1856) was a conflict in which Russia lost to an alliance of France, the United Kingdom, the Ottoman Empire, and Sardinia.

moved, hesitated.

Only Père Plantat, as tranquil as if in his own garden, kept his coolness and looked at the others stealthily.

"A decision has to be made nevertheless," he pronounced.

He went in. The others followed him.

The room they entered showed nothing very unusual. It was a boudoir, the walls hung with blue satin, furnished with a divan and four armchairs upholstered with the same fabric as the walls. One of the armchairs was turned over.

They passed into the bedroom

The disorder of that room was horrifying. There was not one piece of furniture, not one piece of bric-a-brac which didn't show signs that a terrible, enraged fight without mercy had taken place between the murderers and the victims.

In the middle of the bedroom, a little lacquered table was turned over and scattered all around were morsels of sugar, silver-gilt teaspoons, and the debris of broken porcelain.

"Ah!" said the valet, "Monsieur and Madame were having tea when the scoundrels entered!"

The bric-à-brac from the mantel piece had been thrown to the floor. The clock when it fell had stopped at 3:20 p.m. The lamps were spread out near the pendulum; the globes were in pieces; the oil ran everywhere.

The bed canopy had been torn down and covered the bed. Someone must have clung desperately to its drapery. All the furniture was turned over. The stuffing of the armchairs had been hacked by blows from a knife and the stuffing was coming out in places. They had broken open the secretary. Its broken shelf hung by its hinges; the drawers were open and empty.

"The mirror of the armoire was in pieces; in pieces a charming Boule chiffonier; the work table broken, the vanity table turned over.

And everywhere there was blood, on the carpet, along the wall covering, on the furniture, on the drapes, and, above all, on the drapery of the bed canopy.

Evidently the Count and the Countess de Trémorel had defended themselves valiantly and for a long time.

"The scoundrels!" stammered the poor Mayor. "The scoundrels! This is where they were massacred."

And remembering his friendship for the Count, forgetting his importance, throwing off the mask of the impassive man, he wept.

Everyone was losing his head somewhat. But the Justice of the Peace during this time was busy making a minute search. He made entries in his notebook; he visited the least recesses of the bedroom.

When he had finished.

"Now," he said, "let's look somewhere else."

Elsewhere the disorder was similar. A band of infuriated mad men or of criminals gone mad, had certainly spent the night in the house.

The Count's study in particular had been turned upside-down. The murderers hadn't even taken the trouble to force the locks; they had worked with hatchet blows. They must certainly not expect to be heard, because they must have had to strike terribly hard to break open the massive oak desk. The books from the library were on the floor, *pêle-mêle.*

Neither the drawing room nor the smoking room had been respected. The settees, the chairs, the sofas had been torn apart as if someone had stuck swords through them. Two extra bedrooms, bedrooms reserved for

friends, had been turned upside down.

They went up to the third floor.

There, in the first room they went into, they found themselves facing a trunk that had already been attacked by a wood-cutting ax, but not opened, that the Count's valet recognized as belonging to the household.

"Now do you understand," the Mayor said to Père Plantat. "It's evident there were a number of the murderers. The murder committed, they spread throughout the house looking everywhere for money they knew to be there. One of them was here busy hacking into this trunk when the others down below put their hands on the money. They called to him. He hurried down, and judging any more search useless, he left that hatchet here."

"I can see the thing as if I were there," agreed the Brigadier. "The first floor, that they went into next, hadn't been touched. The crime committed, however, the valuables picked up, the murders felt the need to relax. They found the remains of supper in the dining room. They devoured all the left-overs in the buffets. On the table beside eight empty bottles— bottles of wine or liqueurs— were lined up five glasses."

"There were five of them," the Mayor murmured.

With willpower, excellent Monsieur Courtois had recovered his usual self-control.

"Before going to pick up the cadavers," he said, "I'm going to send word to the *Procureur Impérial* of Corbeil. In an hour we'll have an Investigating Magistrate who'll finish our painful task."

A gendarme was given the order to hitch up the Count's tilbury and to leave in all haste.

Then the Mayor and the Judge, followed by the Brigadier, the Count's valet and the two Bertaud's made their way toward the river.

The Valfeuillu Park is very vast, but it extends right and left. It's hardly two hundred feet from the house to the Seine. Stone baskets of flowers are interspersed throughout a beautiful green lawn. You follow one of two pathways to go around the lawn to reach the edge of the water.

But the criminals hadn't followed the pathways. Cutting across the shortest way, they had gone over the lawn. Their traces were perfectly visible. The grass was trampled and stamped down as if someone had dragged some heavy burden across it. They saw something red in the middle of the lawn. The Justice of the Peace went to pick it up. It was a house shoe that the Count's valet recognized as having belonged to the Count. Further on they found a white scarf that the servant swore he had often seen around his master's neck. That scarf was stained with blood.

Finally they came to the edge of the water under those weeping willow trees from which Philippe had wanted to cut a branch and they saw the cadaver.

At that spot the sand had been deeply burrowed into, plowed up, so to speak, by feet looking for a solid footing. There, everything indicated, the supreme fight had taken place.

Monsieur Courtois understood all the importance of those footprints.

"Don't let anyone go forward," he said.

And, followed only by the Justice of the Peace, he approached the body.

Although they couldn't make out the face, the Mayor and the Justice of the Peace recognized the Countess. Both had seen her wear that gray dress trimmed with blue lace.

Now, how did she get there?

The Mayor supposed that having succeeded in escaping the hands of the murderers, desperate, she had fled. They had followed her and they had caught up with her there. They had struck her the last blows and she fell, never to rise again.

That version explained the footprints of the fight. It would then have been the Count's cadaver that the murderers had dragged across the lawn.

Monsieur Courtois was speaking with animation, trying to get through his impressions to the mind of the Justice of the Peace. But Père Plantat was scarcely listening. He might have been thought to be a hundred leagues from Valfeuillu. He responded only with monosyllables: "yes, no, perhaps."

And the good Mayor was taking a lot of trouble. He came, went, took measurements, inspected the terrain minutely.

There wasn't more than a foot of water at that spot. A bank of silt, on which grew clumps of gladiolas and some thin water lilies, sloped gently from the edge to the middle of the river. The water was clear; the current negligible. The smooth and glossy silt could be easily seen.

Monsieur Courtois was at that point in his investigations when he appeared suddenly struck with an idea.

"You, LaRipaille," he shouted, "Come forward."

The old poacher obeyed.

"So you said, that it was from your boat that you saw the cadaver?" questioned the Mayor.

"Yes, Monsieur le Maire."

"Your boat, where is it?"

"Over there, moored at the prairie."

"All right, take us there."

For all those present, it was obvious that order greatly impressed the fellow. He trembled and turned pale under the thick weather-beaten layer deposited on his cheeks by the rain and the sun. They even caught a look, which seemed menacing, thrown toward his son.

"Let's go," he finally answered.

They were going to return to the house when the Count's valet suggested going across the ditch.

"That would be much quicker," he said. "I'll run look for a ladder that we can put across it."

He left and a minute afterwards reappeared with his improvised footbridge. But, just as he was about to put it across,

"Stop!" the Mayor shouted to him. "Stop!"

The prints left by the Bertauds on both sides of the ditch had just jumped out at him.

"What's this?" he asked. "Evidently someone has gone across here, and not long ago. These footprints are very fresh."

And, after several minutes' examination, he ordered the ladder placed further away. When they came near the boat:

"Is there the place you tied up your boat this morning to take up your nets?"

"Yes, Monsieur."

"Then what did you use?" the Mayor continued. "Your casting net is perfectly dry. That boat hook and those oars haven't been in the water in more than 24 hours."

The worry of the father and the son became more and more apparent.

"Do you persist in your claims, Bertaud? And you Philippe?" the Mayor insisted.

"Monsieur," stammered the young man, "we've told the truth."

"Really!" continued Monsieur Courtois in an ironic tone of voice. "Then you'll explain to the proper authorities how you were able to see something from a boat that you haven't been in. Ah! *Dame!* You can't think of everything. It can be proved also that the body is placed in such a way that it's impossible, do you understand me, absolutely impossible, to see it from the middle of the river. Then, you'll still have to explain what those tracks are that I saw, there on the grass, which go from your boat to the place where the ditch was jumped several times by several persons."

The two Bertauds lowered their heads.

"Brigadier," ordered the Mayor, "in the name of the law, arrest these two men and prevent all communication between them."

Philippe seemed about to be sick. As for Old La Ripaille, he just shrugged and said to his son:

"*Hein!* That's what you wanted, wasn't it?"

Then, as the Brigadier led away the two poachers and shut them up separately guarded by his men, the Justice of the Peace and the Mayor went back into the Park.

"With all that," murmured Monsieur Courtois, "no trace of the Count."

It was a matter of picking up the body of the Countess. The Mayor sent someone to find two planks that they put on the ground with a thousand precautions and thus they could work for the investigation without erasing the precious prints.

Alas! Was that really the woman who had been the beautiful, the charming Countess de Trémorel? Was that really the fresh, laughing face, those beautiful, expressive eyes, that fine and witty mouth? Nothing, there remained nothing of her. The swollen face was nothing more than a gaping wound soiled with mud and blood. A part of the skin of the forehead had been torn off with a fist-full of hair. The clothes were in shreds.

The monsters who had killed the poor woman had certainly been maddened by furious drunkenness. She had received more than 20 knife blows. She must have been struck with a cudgel, or rather with a hammer. They had kicked her, dragged her by her hair! In her clenched left hand was a fragment of ordinary, grayish cloth, probably torn from the clothing of one of the murderers.

While going forward with these dismal observations and taking notes for his verbal testimony, the poor Mayor felt his legs give way so much that he was forced to lean on the impassive Père Plantat.

"Let's carry the Countess to the house," ordered the Justice of the Peace. "Later we'll see about looking for the cadaver of the Count."

The Count's valet and the Brigadier, who had returned, had to call for the assistance of the servants who had remained in the courtyard. At the same time, the women rushed into the garden. There was then a terrible concert of cries, tears, and oaths.

"The scoundrels! Such a good woman! Such a good mistress!"

One could certainly see, on that occasion, that Monsieur and Madame Trémorel were adored by their servants.

They had just placed the body of the Countess on the billiard table on the ground floor when someone told the Mayor of the arrival of the Investigating Magistrate and a Doctor. "Finally!" murmured good Monsieur Courtois. And in a lower voice he added: "The most beautiful medals have a reverse side."

For the first time in his life, he had just seriously cursed his ambition and regretted being the most important person in Orcival.

Chapter III

The Investigating Magistrate assigned to the Corbeil tribunal was at that time a remarkable magistrate, Monsieur Antoine Domini, since called to high functions. Monsieur Domini was a man of some forty years-old, well-built, gifted with a fortunately expressive face, but serious, too serious. He seemed to incarnate the solemnity, sometimes a little rigid, of the legal profession. Penetrated with the majesty of his functions, he had sacrificed his life to them, refusing the simplest distractions, the most legitimate pleasures. He lived alone, went out seldom, rarely invited friends, not wishing, he said, that the failings of the man might tarnish the sacred character of the judge and diminish the respect that was due him. That last reason prevented him from marrying, although he felt himself made for family life. Always and everywhere he was the magistrate, representing it, convinced right to fanaticism of what there is the most venerable in the world: justice. Having a naturally gay disposition, he had to watch himself especially carefully when he wanted to laugh. He had wit, but if a clever word or a joking phrase escaped him, you can be sure he paid penance for it. It was really body and soul that he gave to his profession and nobody could have brought more conscientiousness to fulfilling what he considered his duty. But, too, he was more inflexible than others. To argue about an article of the legal Code was in his eyes a monstrosity. The law spoke. That was sufficient. He closed his eyes, stopped his ears, and obeyed.

From the day an investigation began, he no longer slept. He must arrive at the discovery of the truth and nothing else mattered to him. Nevertheless, he wasn't considered a good Investigating Magistrate. To fight against an accused man with cunning seemed repugnant to him. To lay a trap for a scoundrel was, he said, unworthy. Finally, he was stubborn, but stubborn to the point of folly, sometimes right to absurdity, right to denying there was sunshine in the middle of the day.

The Mayor of Orcival and Père Plantat had risen hurriedly to rush to meet the Investigating Magistrate. Monsieur Domini greeted them gravely, as if he had never before met them, and presented to them a man of some sixty years who had come with him.

"Messieurs," he said, "Doctor Gendron."

Père Plantat shook hands with the doctor. Monsieur le Maire gave him his most officially gracious smile.

The fact is that Doctor Gendron was well known in Corbeil and in all the Department. He was even famous, despite the proximity of Paris. A physician of more than usual ability, loving his art and exercising it with passionate wisdom, Doctor Gendron, however, owed his fame less to his knowledge than to his life style. They said of him: "He's one of a kind." They admired his affectations of independence, skepticism and plain speaking.

He held office hours between five and nine o'clock in the morning, summer and winter. Too bad for anyone those hours bothered. There wasn't at all, *Dieu Merci!* a shortage of doctors. After 9:00 a.m., "*Bonsoir,*" that was the end of the day. Nobody, no more doctor. The doctor was doing his own work; the doctor was inspecting his wine cellar; the doctor had gone up to his laboratory, near the attic, where he cooked-up strange ragouts. In public they said he was looking for some chemical industrial secrets to increase still more his 20,000 pounds of retirement income, a not very worthy activity.

And he let them talk, because the truth was that he was busy working with poisons. He was perfecting a system he had invented which would recover all the traces of the alkaloids which, to that date, escaped analysis.

If his friends reproached him, even in joking, for getting rid of sick people in the afternoon, he became angry and very red.

"*Parbleu!*" he answered. "I find you superb! I'm a doctor four hours a day. I'm hardly paid but by a fourth of my patients; therefore, that's three hours I give every week to humanity that I despise and to philanthropy. Let each one of you give as much and we'll see."

But Monsieur le Maire of Orcival had made the newcomers pass into the drawing room where he had set himself up to direct the verbal testimony.

"What a misfortune this crime is for my commune," he was saying to the Investigating Magistrate. "What shame! Now Orcival is losing its reputation."

"I know nothing about it, or almost nothing," answered Monsieur Domini. "The gendarme who came to get me was poorly informed."

Then Monsieur Courtois recounted at great length what he had learned from his preliminary investigation, not forgetting the minutest details, dwelling on the admirable precautions that he had thought he should take. He told how the Bertaud's attitude had immediately aroused his suspicions, how he had caught them at least in the very act of lying, and how, finally, he had decided to have them arrested.

He was standing, speaking in an emphatic tone, his head thrown back, listening to himself, and drawing out his sentences. And at every moment the words: "We, the Mayor of Orcival," or "after that," going back over his discourse. Finally, he expounded on his functions, and the pleasure of speaking somewhat made up for his worry.

"And now," he concluded, "I've just ordered the most painstaking searches which will, without a doubt, lead us to recovering the cadaver of the Count. Five men that I pressed into service and all the household servants are scouring the park. If their searches are not crowned with success, I have fishermen at hand who will sound the river."

The Investigating Magistrate was silent, simply nodding his head from time to time in sign of approval. He studied, he weighed the details communicated to him, already building a plan of investigation in his head.

"You've acted very wisely, Monsieur le Maire," he said finally. "The misfortune is immense, but I believe as you do that we are on the trail of the guilty persons. These poachers that we hold, that gardener who hasn't reappeared must be implicated in some way in this abominable crime."

For several minutes, Père Plantat had been hiding, both well and poorly, or rather, poorly more than well, signs of impatience.

"The unfortunate thing is," he said, "that if Guespin is guilty, he wouldn't be stupid enough to come back here."

"Oh! We'll find him before we leave Corbeil," answered Monsieur Domini. "I've sent a telegraph to the Prefecture of Police in Paris to request an agent from the Sûreté. And he'll be here shortly, I imagine."

"While waiting," the Mayor suggested, "Perhaps you would like, Monsieur, as Investigating Magistrate, to visit the scene of the crime."

Monsieur Domini started to stand up, but immediately sat down again.

"In fact," he said, "nothing should be seen before the arrival of our agent. But I would certainly need information about the Count and the Countess of Trémorel."

The worthy Mayor triumphed again.

"Oh! I can give you that," he answered quickly, "and better than anyone else. Since their arrival in my commune, I was, I may say, one of the best friends of Monsieur the Count and Madame the Countess. Ah! Monsieur, what charming people! And excellent, and affable, and devoted."

And at the memory of all the qualities of his friends, Monsieur Courtois felt certain tightness in his throat.

"The Count de Trémorel," he began again, "was a thirty-four-year-old man, a handsome fellow, intelligent right down to the end of his fingernails. He sometimes had bouts with melancholy, during which he didn't wish to see anyone. But ordinarily he was so friendly, so polite, so obliging. He knew so well how to be noble without being haughty that everyone in my commune respected and adored him."

"And the Countess?" the Investigating Magistrate asked.

"An angel! Monsieur. An angel on the earth! Poor woman you're going to see her mortal remains shortly, and you certainly won't guess that for beauty she was the queen of the countryside."

"Were the Count and the Countess rich?"

"Certainly! Between the two of them they must have had more than 100,000 francs of income. Oh! Yes, a great deal more, because for the last five or six months, the Count, who didn't have the aptitude for farming of that poor Sauvresy, had been selling land to get cash."

"Had they been married a long time?"

Monsieur Courtois scratched his head. That was the way he called up his memory.

"*Ma foi*," he answered. "It was in the month of September last year. It's been just ten months since I married them myself. That poor Sauvresy had been dead a year."

The Investigating Magistrate stopped taking notes in order to give the Mayor a surprised look.

"Who is this Sauvresy you're telling us about?" he questioned.

Père Plantat, who had been furiously biting his nails in his corner, apparently a stranger to what was going on, stood up quickly.

"Monsieur Sauvresy," he said, "was the first husband of Madame de Trémorel. My friend Courtois overlooked that fact..."

"Oh!" rejoined the Mayor in a wounded tone, "it seems to me that in the present situation..."

"Pardon!" the Investigating Magistrate interrupted. "It's just such a detail that can become valuable, even though foreign to the case and even insignificant at first."

"Hum!" grumbled Père Plantat, "insignificant, foreign!..."

His tone at this point was so unusual, his manner so equivocal that the Investigating Magistrate was struck by it.

"Don't you share, Monsieur," he asked him, "the opinions of Monsieur le Maire in this account of the de Trémorel couple?

Père Plantat shrugged.

"Me, I have no opinion. I live alone," he replied. "I see no one. What do all these things matter to me? However..."

"It seems to me," exclaimed Monsieur Courtois," that nobody could know better than I do the history of people who were my friends and under my administration."

"Then in that case," Père Plantat answered dryly, "you're telling it badly."

And as the Investigating Magistrate pressed him to explain, he began quickly to speak, to the great shock of Monsieur Courtois, thus rejected to second place, sketching in broad outline the biography of the Count and Countess.

"The Countess de Trémorel, born Berthe Lechaillu, was the daughter of a poor little village schoolteacher.

"Her beauty, when she was eighteen-years-old, had been famous everywhere for three years. But as all the dowry she had was her big blue eyes and admirable blond hair, lovers—that is to say lovers for the right reason—seldom presented themselves.

"On the advice of her family, Berthe had already resigned herself to "*coiffer* Sainte Catherine, never to marry, be an old maid, and look for a position as an elementary school teacher—a sad situation for such a beautiful girl. Then the heir to one of the richest estates in the countryside saw her and fell in love with her.

"Clement Sauvresy had just turned thirty. He no longer had any family and possessed an income of almost 100,000 pounds in beautiful and good property absolutely free of encumbrance. That is to say that he better than anyone had the right to take a wife that pleased him.

"He didn't hesitate. He asked for Berthe's hand, got it, and one month afterward he married her at high noon, to the great scandal of the incredulous heads in the country, who went about repeating:

'What madness! What's the good of being rich if you don't double your fortune by a good marriage!'

"About a month after the marriage, Sauvresy had put workers at Valfeuillu and in no time he had spent there, in repairs and in furnishings, the bagatelle sum of 30,000 *écus*.

"It was at this beautiful property that the couple chose to spend their honeymoon. They found themselves so comfortable there that they set themselves up there permanently, to the great satisfaction of all those who were connected to them. They kept only a small apartment in Paris.

"It seems Berthe was one of those women who are born just to marry millionaires. Without any worry or embarrassment, she moved without transition from the poor school room, where she helped her father, to the superb drawing room of Valfeuillu. And when she did the honors of her chateau for all the aristocracy in the region, it seemed she had never done anything else her whole life. She was able to remain simple, pleasant, while at the same time taking on the tone of the highest society. She was loved."

"But it seems to me," interrupted the Mayor, "that I didn't say anything different, and it's not really worth the trouble..."

With a gesture, the Investigating Magistrate, made him be quiet and Père Plantat continued.

"People also loved Sauvresy, one of those hearts of gold, that doesn't even want to suspect evil. Sauvresy was one of those men with healthy beliefs, with stubborn illusions. Doubt never brushed his eagle wings. Sauvresy was one of those who, even so, believe in the friendship of their friends, in the love of their mistress.

"This young household should have been happy. It was. Berthe adored her husband, that honest man who, before saying a word of love to her, had offered her his hand.

"Sauvresy himself demonstrated a cult-like devotion to his wife that some people found almost ridiculous.

"Moreover, they lived in a grand style at Valfeuillu. They entertained a great deal. When autumn came, the numerous bedrooms for friends were all occupied. The carriages were magnificent.

"Finally, Sauvresy had been married for two years when one evening he brought one of his former intimate friends from Paris, a comrade from secondary school whom people had often heard spoken of, Count Hector de Trémorel.

"The Count came to stay for several weeks at Valfeuillu, he announced. But the weeks rolled by, then months. He stayed.

"People were not surprised. Hector had had a more than tumultuous youth, filled with boisterous debauchery, duels, betting with bookmakers, love affairs. He had thrown a colossal fortune to the winds of his fantasy. The relatively calm life at Valfeuillu must have seduced him.

"In the first days, people told him often: 'You'll soon get enough of the country.' He smiled without answering. People then thought, and rather justly, that become relatively poor, he didn't very much care about parading his ruin among those whom his splendor had dazzled.

"He was rarely absent and then only to go to Corbeil, almost always on foot. There he registered at the Belle Image hotel, the best one in the village, and there he met, as if by chance, a young lady from Paris. They spent the afternoon together and separated at the hour of the last train."

"*Peste!*" grumbled the Mayor. "For a man who lives alone, who doesn't see anybody, who, for nothing in the world, would be interested in other people's affairs, it seems to me that our dear Justice of the Peace is rather well informed."

Obviously, Monsieur Courtois was jealous. How could he, the most important person in the commune have been absolutely ignorant of these rendez-vous! His bad temper again increased when Doctor Gendron answered:

"*Peuh!* All of Corbeil gossiped about that a while back."

Monsieur Plantat's lips moved in a way that signified: "I know still more things." However, he continued without comment.

"The Count's moving in changed absolutely nothing to the routine at the chateau. Monsieur and Madame Sauvresy had a brother, that's all. If at that time Monsieur Sauvresy made several trips to Paris, that was because he was taking care of his friend's affairs, as everyone knew.

"That delightful existence lasted a year. Happiness seemed to have been established absolutely forever under the shade trees of Valfeuillu.

"But alas! It happened one evening, returning from a hunt in the marshes, Sauvresy found himself feeling so sick that he was obliged to go to bed. They called a doctor, who was none other than our friend Doctor Gendron. Pleuropneumonia was the diagnosis.

"Sauvresy was young, strong as an oak. There were no serious worries at first. Two weeks later, in fact, he was up and about. But he wasn't careful and had a relapse. He got better again, at least almost.

"A week later there was another relapse, and so serious that it could be seen the sickness would be fatal. It was during that interminable sickness that Berthe's love and de Trémorel's affection were most manifest.

"No sick man was ever cared for with such solicitude, surrounded with so many proofs of the most pure and absolute devotion. He had his wife or his friend at his bedside night and day. He had hours of suffering, never a second of worry.

"To all those who came to visit him at this time, he said, he kept repeating, that he had come to bless his sickness.

"He said to me, 'If I hadn't fallen sick, I would never have known how much I was loved.'

"He said the same thing to me a hundred times," the Mayor interrupted. "He repeated them to Madame Courtois and to Laurence, my oldest daughter."

"Naturally," Père Plantat continued. "But Sauvresy's illness was one of those against which the knowledge of the most experienced doctors and the most assiduous care fail.

"He assured people he didn't suffer enormously, but he grew visibly weaker. He was no longer anything but the shadow of himself.

"Finally, one night about two or three o'clock in the morning, he died in the arms of his wife and his friend.

"He had kept full use of his mental faculties right up to the end. Less than an hour before he died he wanted all the servants of the chateau to be awakened and come in. When they were all assembled around his bedside, he took his wife's hand, placed it in the hand of the Count de Trémorel, and made them swear to marry each other when he was no more.

"Berthe and Hector began by protesting, but he insisted in such a way as to make a refusal impossible, begging them, repudiating them, claiming that their refusal would poison his last moments.

"What's more, the thought of the marriage of his widow and his friend seemed to preoccupy him to an unusual degree at the end of his life. In the preamble to his will, dictated the evening of his death to Monsieur Bury, the Orcival notary, he formally stated that their union was his dearest wish. He was certain of their happiness and he knew his memory would be piously kept."

"Monsieur and Madame Sauvresy had no child?" the Investigating Magistrate asked.

"No, Monsieur," answered the Mayor.

Père Plantat continued:

"The sorrow of the Count and the young widow was immense. Monsieur de Trémorel most of all appeared absolutely desperate. He was like a mad man. The Countess closed her doors to everyone she liked most, even to the Courtois ladies.

"When the Count and Madame Berthe reappeared, they had changed so much they were scarcely recognizable. Monsieur Hector in particular had aged twenty years.

Would they keep the oath made at Sauvresy's death bed, an oath everyone knew about? People asked that with so much more interest since they admired the profound sorrow for a man, born remarkable, who truly merited it."

The Investigating Magistrate stopped Père Plantat with a nod of his head.

"Do you know, Justice of the Peace, if the rendezvous at the Belle Image hotel had stopped?"

"I presume so, Monsieur. I believe so."

"And me, I'm almost certain," confirmed Doctor Gendron. "I remember having heard talk—everybody knows everything at Corbeil—about a noisy argument between Monsieur de Trémorel and the pretty lady from Paris. After that scene, they were not seen any more at the Belle Image."

The old Justice of the Peace smiled.

"Melun isn't at the end of the world," he said, "and there are hotels in Melun. With a good horse, you can get quickly to Fontainebleau, to Versailles and even to Paris. Madame de Trémorel might have been jealous. Her husband had first-class trotters in his stables."

Was Père Plantat expressing an absolutely disinterested opinion? Was he slipping in an insinuation? The Investigating Magistrate looked at him closely in order to be sure, but his face expressed nothing but a profound calm. He was telling that story as you would tell any other, no matter which.

"I'll ask you to continue, Monsieur," Monsieur Domini said.

"Alas!" Père Plantat took up again, "Nothing is eternal here below, not even sorrow. I, more than others, can say that. Soon to the tears of the first days, to the violent despair of the Count and Madame Berthe, there followed a reasonable sadness, then a gentle melancholy. And a year after the death of Sauvresy, Monsieur de Trémorel married his widow."

During this rather long story, the Mayor of Orcival had, at many points, shown signs of great irritation. Finally, he could no longer control himself.

"Certainly, those are exact details," he exclaimed. "They couldn't be more exact, but I wonder if they've gotten us one step further toward the question which concerns us all—to find the murderers of the Count and the Countess."

At these words, Père Plantat fixed his clear and intense gaze on the Investigating Magistrate as if to search the depth of his conscience.

"These details were indispensable to me," answered Monsieur Domini, "and I find them very clear. These rendezvous in a hotel impress me. One never knows to that extremes jealousy may lead a woman."

He stopped abruptly, probably looking for a connection between the pretty Parisian woman and the murderers. Then he began again:

"Now that I know the de Trémorel 'couple' as if I had lived closely with them, let's get to the actual facts."

Père Plantat's shining eyes suddenly became dull. He moved his lips as if he wanted to speak. However, he was silent.

Only the Doctor, who hadn't stopped studying the old Justice of the Peace, had noticed the sudden change of expression.

"The only thing left for me to know is how the new spouses lived," said Monsieur Domini.

Monsieur Courtois thought that he owed it to his dignity to take the floor from Père Plantat.

He answered quickly: "You want to know how the new spouses lived. They lived in perfect agreement. Nobody in my commune knows it better than I, who was on an intimate footing with them...intimate. The memory of that poor

Sauvresy was a tie of happiness between them. If they liked me so much, it was because I often spoke about him. Never a cloud, never a word. Hector—that's what I called this dear and unfortunate Count— had for his wife the attentive cares of a lover, the exquisite considerations, which husbands, in general, I'm afraid to say, too quickly lose the habit."

"And the Countess," asked Père Plantat in a tone too naïve not to be ironic.

"Berthe!" the Mayor retorted—"She allowed me to call her that in a fatherly way—Berthe! I wasn't afraid to hold her up as an example many, many times to Madame Courtois. Berthe! She was worthy of Sauvresy and Hector, the two most worthy men that I ever in my life encountered."

And seeing that his enthusiasm surprised his listeners somewhat:

"I have my reasons for expressing myself in this way," he continued more softly. "And I don't at all fear to express myself so before men whose profession, and, still more, whose character guarantees me discretion.

Sauvresy did me a great service in my life…when I had my hand forced to become Mayor. As for Hector, I believed him so well turned away from the errors of his youth, that, having believed I saw that he was not indifferent to Laurence, my elder daughter, I thought about a marriage. It was so much more suitable because, if Hector de Trémorel had a great name, I was giving my daughter a rather considerable dowry to guild almost any escutcheon. Only events changed my projects."

The Mayor would have continued singing the praises of the "spouses Trémorel" for a long time, and his own at the same time, if the Investigating Magistrate hadn't started to speak.

"I've decided," he said. "From now on, it seems to me..."

He was interrupted by a loud noise coming from the vestibule. It seemed to be a fight and the shouts and the curses reached the drawing room.

Everyone got up.

"I know what it is," said the Mayor. "I know only too well. They've just found the cadaver of the Count de Trémorel."

Chapter IV

The Mayor of Orcival was wrong.

The drawing room door opened suddenly and there, held on one side by a gendarme, on the other by a servant, was a man, apparently of a slight build, defending himself furiously and with strength one wouldn't have suspected.

The fight had already been going on for some time and his clothes were in the most frightful disorder. His new frock coat was torn, his tie dangled in shreds, his collar button had been snatched off and his open shirt showed his naked chest. His hair was disheveled and his long black hair fell pell-mell across his face, which was contracted by terrible agony. In the vestibule and in the courtyard could be heard the furious shouts of the chateau servants and the curious—there were more than a hundred of them—that the news of the crime had brought together in front of the gate, impatient to know and, above all, to see.

That enraged crowd was shouting:

"That's him! Death to the murderer. That's Guespin! There he is!"

And the miserable man, taken by immense fright, continued to struggle.

"Help!" he shouted in a hoarse voice. "Help me! Let me go. I'm innocent!"

He had grabbed hold of the drawing room door and he couldn't be made to go any further.

"Then push him," commanded the Mayor, whom the intense anger of the crowd reached little by little. "Push him!"

That was easier to order than to do. Fear gave Guespin enormous strength.

But the Doctor, having had the idea of opening the second side of the French doors to the drawing room, the miserable man lacked something to hold onto and he fell, or rather he rolled to the feet of the table on which the Investigating Magistrate was writing.

He stood up again immediately and his eyes looked for a way out. There not being any, because the windows as well as the door were blocked by the curious, he let himself fall back into a chair.

That unfortunate man was the image of terror at its highest. The bluish marks of the blows he had received in the fight stood out in his livid face. His pale lips trembled and he moved his jaws up and down, as if searching for a little saliva for his burning tongue. His abnormally large eyes were full of blood and expressed the most terrible bewilderment. Last of all, his body was shaken by convulsive spasms.

That spectacle was so frightening that the Mayor of Orcival thought that it could be used as a high moral example. Turning toward the crowd, pointing out Guespin, and in a tragic tone he said:

"That is the face of crime!"

The others, however, the Doctor, the Investigating Magistrate, and Père

Plantat, exchanged surprised looks.

"If he's guilty," muttered the old Justice of the Peace, "why the devil did he come back?"

It took some time to get the crowd removed. The Brigadier of the gendarmerie was only able to do so with the help of his men. He then came back in to stand beside Guespin, judging that it would not be prudent to leave such a dangerous criminal alone with unarmed people.

Alas! He was scarcely to be feared at this moment, the poor man. A reaction had set in. His overextended strength weakened like a flame put in a handful of straw. His overly tense muscles became limp and his prostration resembled the effects of an excess of brain fever.

During this time, the Brigadier was giving an account of events.

Some servants from the chateau and from neighboring houses were talking in front of the gate, recounting the crimes of the night and Guespin's disappearance the evening before when suddenly they saw him coming at the end of the road, with an unsteady walk and singing at the top of his lungs like a drunken man.

"Was he really drunk?" asked Monsieur Domini.

"Dead drunk, Monsieur," answered the Brigadier.

"Then that would be the wine that was left for him and that would explain everything," murmured the Investigating Magistrate.

The Brigadier, for whom Guespin's guilt didn't seem to leave the shadow of a doubt, continued:

"When they saw the scoundrel, François, the valet of the departed Monsieur le Comte, and the servant of Monsieur le Maire, Baptiste, who were there, dashed to meet him and took him into custody. He was so drunk that, not knowing anything, he thought they were joking with him. The sight of one of my men sobered him up. Just then one of the women shouted at him—'Thief! You were the one who murdered the Count and the Countess last night!' At that he became paler than death. He stopped, open-mouthed, as if struck dead, you might say! Then suddenly he started to fight so vigorously that if I hadn't been there he would have escaped. Ah! he's strong without looking it, the villain!"

"And he didn't say anything?" Père Plantat asked.

"Not a word, Monsieur. His teeth were so clenched in rage that he couldn't even say 'bread,' I'm sure. Finally we got him. I searched him and this is what I found in his pockets: a handkerchief, a pocket knife, two small keys, a scrap of paper covered with numbers and signs and an address for the Forges de Vulcain department store. But that wasn't all."

Looking at his auditors, the Brigadier struck a pose. He was preparing his effect.

"That wasn't all. While they were bringing him in, he tried to get rid of his money holder in the courtyard. Fortunately I was watching and I saw the act in time. I picked up the money holder that had fallen into a clump of flowers near the door and here it is. Inside there's a hundred franc note, three *louis*, and seven francs in change. Now, yesterday the scoundrel didn't have a *sou*."

"How do you know that?" asked Monsieur Courtois.

"*Dame!* he borrowed twenty-five francs from François, the Count's valet, who told me. He said it was to pay his share of the wedding."

"Let somebody go get François," ordered the Investigating Magistrate.

And as soon as the valet appeared he asked him curtly:

"Do you know if Guespin had any money yesterday?"

"He had so little, Monsieur," the valet answered without hesitating, "that during the day he asked me for twenty-five francs, saying that if I didn't lend them to him, he couldn't go to the wedding. He didn't even have enough to pay for the train ticket."

"But he could have had some savings, a hundred franc bill, for example, that he was reluctant to get changed."

François shook his head with an incredulous smile.

"Guespin isn't a man to have any savings," he stated. "Women and cards eat up everything. No later than last week, the owner of the Café du Commerce came to make a scene about what he owed and even threatened him with going to the Count."

And seeing the effect produced by his deposition, the valet added as a sort of correction:

"It isn't as I had anything at all against Guespin. I've always considered him, right up to today, as a good fellow, although liking dirty jokes too much. He was a little proud, considering his up-bringing..."

"You may go," said the Investigating Magistrate, cutting short Monsieur François' evaluation of Guespin.

The Count's valet left.

During this time, Guespin had come round little by little. The Investigating Magistrate, Père Plantat, and the Mayor were curiously watching his facial expressions, that he couldn't have been thinking about composing while Doctor Gendron was holding his wrist and counting his pulse.

"Remorse and fear of punishment," murmured the Mayor.

"Innocence and the impossibility of proving it," responded Père Plantat in a low voice.

The Investigating Magistrate took in these two exclamations, but he didn't react to them. He hadn't formed what he believed and he, the representative of the law, the deliverer of punishment, didn't want his feelings to be prejudiced by words.

"Are you feeling better, my friend?" Dr. Gendron asked Guespin.

The unhappy man nodded affirmatively. Then, after having thrown around him the anxious glances of a man who measures the precipice from which he's fallen, he passed his hand over his eyes and asked:

"Something to drink."

They brought him a glass of water and he drank it in one gulp with an expression of inexpressible voluptuousness. Then he stood up.

"Are you now in a state to answer me?" demanded the Investigating Magistrate.

Trembling at first, Guespin had gotten control of himself. Leaning on the back of a piece of furniture, he stood in front of the Investigating Magistrate. The nervous trembling of his hands had lessened. Blood was coming back into his cheeks. While he was answering, he repaired the disorder of his clothes.

"You know the events of last night?" the Investigating Magistrate began. "The Count and the Countess de Trémorel were murdered. You left yesterday with all the servants of the chateau. You left them at the Lyon railway station about 9:00 p.m. You now come back alone. Where did you spend the night?"

Guespin lowered his head and stayed silent.

"That's not all," the Judge continued. "Yesterday you were without money. The fact is well known. One of your comrades has just confirmed it. Today they found in your money holder a sum of one hundred and sixty francs. Where did you get that money?"

The unfortunate man's lips moved as if he wanted to answer. A sudden thought stopped him. He didn't speak.

"Another thing," the Judge continued. "What is that card from a hardware store which was found in your pocket?"

Guespin made a desperate gesture and murmured: "I'm innocent."

"Please note," the Investigating Magistrate said quickly, "that I haven't yet accused you. You knew that during the day the Count had received an important sum of money."

A bitter smile puckered Guespin's lips and he answered:

"I know very well that everything is against me."

The silence in the drawing room was profound. The Doctor, the Mayor and Père Plantat, seized with passionate curiosity, couldn't move. That's because there is nothing in the world more moving than these duels without mercy between justice and the man suspected of a crime. The questions may seem unimportant, the responses ordinary. Questions and responses hold terrible innuendoes, the least gestures at that time, the most rapid changes of expression, can take on an enormous significance. A fleeting light in the eyes betrays an advantage gained. An imperceptible alteration of the voice may be a confession.

Yes, an interrogation, a first interrogation most of all, is certainly a duel. At the beginning, the two adversaries feel each other out mentally. They estimate and evaluate. Questions and answers cross each other softly, with a sort of hesitation, like the swords of two adversaries who know nothing about their respective strengths. But the battle soon heats up. The combatants become animated by the clink of their swords and by their words. The attack becomes more pressing, the riposte more energetic. The feeling of danger disappears. And with equal chances, the advantage rests with the one who keeps his self-control best.

41

Monsieur Domini's self-control was becoming desperate.

"Come now," he continued after a pause. "Where did you spend the night, how did you get your money, why that address?"

"Eh!" Guespin cried out with the rage of impotence. "I would tell you, but you wouldn't believe me!'

The Investigating Magistrate was going to ask another question. Guespin cut him off.

"No, you wouldn't believe me," he continued, his eyes shining with anger. "Do men like you believe a man like me? I have a past. Right? Background as you call it. The Past. They have just this word to throw in your face, as if the future depends on the past. Well! Yes, it's true. I'm a debauchee, a gambler, a drunk, a good-for-nothing. But, so what? I've been picked up by the police and found guilty of disturbance of the peace at night and immoral behavior. What does that prove? I've destroyed my life, but who did I harm but myself? My past! Haven't I made hard enough amends for it?"

Guespin had regained full control of himself. And finding a kind of eloquence serving the sensations moving him, he expressed himself with a savage energy well chosen to impress his hearers.

"I haven't always worked for other people," he continued. "My father was well off, almost rich. He had rich gardens near Saumur and he was reputed to be one of the most knowledgeable horticulturist of Maine-et-Loire. I was taught and when I was sixteen-years-old, I started to work at the business of Messieurs Leroy, at Angers, to finish off my studies. At the end of four years, they considered me a boy who showed talent in the business. Unfortunately for me, my father, already a widow for several years, died. He left me at least 100,000 francs worth of excellent land. I sold them for 60,000 francs cash, and I went to Paris. I was like a crazy man in those days. I had a fever for pleasure that nothing could calm, a thirst for every type of enjoyment, iron health, and money. I found Paris too narrow for my vices. It seemed objects for my covetousness were lacking. I figured my 60,000 francs would last eternally."

Guespin stopped. A thousand memories of that time came back to his mind, and very low he murmured: "Those were good times."

"My 60,000 francs," he continued, "lasted eight years. I didn't have a *sou* and I wanted to continue my style of life. You understand, don't you? It was about that time that, one night, the city police picked me up. I was out of circulation for three months. Oh! You'll find my file at the Prefecture of Police. Do you know what it will tell you, that file? It will tell you that on leaving prison I fell into that shameful and abominable poverty of Paris. Into that poverty which doesn't eat, which gets drunk, which has no shoes, whose shoulders lean on the tables of public houses; into that poverty which hangs around at the doors of the dance halls in the slums, which swarms in disgusting furnished rooms and which plots robberies which won't succeed. It will tell you, my dossier, that I lived among pimps, crooks and prostitutes…and that's the truth."

The worthy Mayor of Orcival was astounded.

"*Justes Dieux!*" he was thinking. "What an audacious and cynical brigand. And to think that everyday people are exposed to bringing such miserable people into their house as servants."

The Investigating Magistrate was silent. He knew very well that Guespin was in one of those rare moments in which, governed by irresistible passion, a man abandons himself, lets the depth of his thoughts, right down to the deepest recesses of his heart be seen and surrenders himself entirely.

"But there is one thing," the unhappy man continued, "that my file won't tell you. It won't tell you that disgusted with that squalid existence, even to the temptation of suicide, he wanted to get out of it. It won't tell you anything of my efforts, of my desperate attempts, of my repentance, of my backsliding. A past like mine is a heavy burden. Finally, I was able to recover my situation. I'm clever. I was given work. I worked four places, one after the other, right up to the day when, through one of my former employers, I was able to enter service here. I settled in here well. I always used up my salary a month in advance, that's true. What do you expect? You can't make yourself over. But ask if there has ever been any complaint about me."

It is recognized that among the most intelligent criminals, those who have received a certain education, who have enjoyed a certain ease, are the most to be feared. In this category, Guespin was imminently dangerous.

That's what the listeners were telling themselves while, worn out by the effort he had just made, he wiped his forehead running with sweat.

Monsieur Domini hadn't lost sight of his plan of attack.

"All that's well and good," he said. "We'll come back to your confession at the time and place. For the moment it's a matter of stating how you spent your night and of explaining where the money found in your possession came from."

That insistence of the Judge seemed to exasperate Guespin.

"Eh!" he answered. "What do you want me to tell you? The truth? …You wouldn't believe it. I might as well be quiet. It's fate."

"In your own interest I'm warning you," the judge continued. "If you persist in not answering, the charges against you are such that I will be forced to have you arrested as a suspect in the murder of the Count and the Countess de Trémorel."

That threat seemed to have an extraordinary effect on Guespin. Two big tears filled his eyes, dry and shining until then, and rolled silently down his cheeks. His strength was at an end. He let himself fall to his knees, crying out:

"Have pity! I beg you, Monsieur, don't have me arrested. I swear to you that I'm innocent. I swear it to you!"

"Then speak."

"As you say," said Guespin, rising.

But suddenly changing tones:

"No!" he cried out in an access of rage. "No, I won't speak. I can't speak.

Only one man could save me. That's the Count and he's dead. I'm innocent and if you don't find those who're guilty, I'm doomed. Everything is against me; I know that very well. And now go ahead. Do whatever you want with me. I won't say another word."

Guespin's resolution, a determination his looks confirmed, didn't at all surprise the Investigating Magistrate.

He simply said, "You'll think better of it. However, when you've had time to think, I'll no longer have the confidence in your words I have at this moment. It could be"—and the Judge stressed his words so as to give them more weight and to make them appear in the eyes of the accused as a hope of pardon—"It could be that you had only an indirect part in this crime. In that case..."

"Neither indirect nor direct," Guespin interrupted. And he added with violence: "What bad luck! To be innocent and not be able to defend myself."

"If that's how it is," Monsieur Domini continued, "it should not matter to you to be put in the presence of Madame de Trémorel's body."

The accused received that threat without flinching. They took him to the room where they had placed the Countess. There he examined the Countess with a cold and calm eye. He only said:

"She's more fortunate than I am. She's dead. She doesn't suffer any more. And me, who's not guilty, I'm accused of killing her."

Monsieur Domini made another effort.

"Come now, Guespin," he said, "If you knew about this crime in any way I beg you, tell me so. If you know the murderers, name them to me. Try to merit some leniency by your frankness and your repentance."

Guespin made the resigned gesture of the unfortunate who have made their decision.

"By everything there is the most sacred in the world," he answered, "I'm innocent. And nevertheless, I certainly see that if the guilty are not found, I'm done for."

Monsieur Domini's convictions were coming together and being confirmed little by little. An investigation is not so difficult as might be imagined. The difficult thing, the major point, is to seize at the beginning, in the often tangled skein, the primary end of the thread, the one that has to lead to the truth through the maze of dodges, concealments, and lies of the guilty.

Monsieur Domini was certain to get hold of that thread. Having one of the murders, he knew very well that he would get the others. Our prisons in which they eat good soup, where the beds have a good mattress untie tongues just as well as did the racks and iron boots of the Middle Ages.

The Investigating Magistrate turned Guespin over to the Brigadier of the gendarmes, ordering him not to let him out of his sight. He then sent for old La Ripaille.

That good fellow wasn't one of those who could be shaken. He had so often been picked up by the law for petty theft that one more interrogation touched him only slightly. Père Plantat noticed that he seemed a great deal more annoyed than worried.

"That man has a very bad reputation in my commune," the Mayor said to the Investigating Magistrate.

La Ripaille heard that comment and smiled.

Interrogated by the Investigating Magistrate, he recounted the scene of the morning, his resistance, his son's insistence in a very plain and very clear way, very exact at the same time. He explained the prudent reasons for their lie. There again the chapter concerning past events recurred.

"I'm worth more than my reputation," Ripaille claimed. "And there are a lot of people who can't say as much. I know some men, I especially know some women—He looked at Monsieur Courtois—who, if I wanted to babble! ...You see a lot of things when you run around in the night... But, that's enough."

They tried to make him explain his allusions. In vain. When they asked him where and how he had spent the night, he answered that when he left the cabaret at 10:00 p.m., he had gone to place some snares in the Mauprévoir woods, and about 1:00 a.m. he had returned to go to bed.

"The proof," he said, "is that they must still be there and there might be some trapped game."

"Could you find a witness to confirm that you came in at 1:00 a.m.?" asked the Judge, who was thinking of the clock which had stopped at 3:20 a.m. "Well, I don't know anything about that," the old poacher answered, unconcerned. "It's possible my son didn't even wake up when I went to bed."

And as the judge was reflecting:

"I can certainly guess," he said to him, "that you're going to put me in prison until you find the guilty ones. If this were during the winter I wouldn't complain too much. You're all right in prison and it's warm there. But right at the time of the hunt, it's annoying. But this will be a good lesson for Philippe. This will teach him that it costs a lot to render a service to the bourgeois."

"That's enough!" Monsieur Domini interrupted severely. "Do you know Guespin?"

This name quickly extinguished LaRipaille's mocking eloquence. His little gray eyes showed unusual worry.

"Certainly," he answered in an embarrassed voice. "Several times we've played cards while sipping a Gloria."[1]

The fellow's worry impressed the four listeners. Père Plantat in particular showed profound surprise.

The old poacher was a great deal too sharp not to notice the effect produced.

"Well! Too bad!" he exclaimed. "I'm going to tell you everything. Every man for himself, right? If Guespin did the job, that won't make him any blacker than he is. And me, I won't have any worse reputation. I know this fellow because he gave me strawberries and grapes from the Count's greenhouse to sell. I suppose he stole them. And this is not perhaps very good; we shared the money I got for them."

Père Plantat couldn't hold back an "Ah!" of satisfaction which must have meant: "Finally! I knew that." When he had said they were going to put him in prison, LaRipaille wasn't wrong. The Investigating Magistrate ordered his arrest. It was Philippe's turn. The poor boy was in a pitiable state. He was weeping warm tears.

Reference to a drink made of coffee or sugared tea mixed with brandy.

"To accuse me of such a great crime," he kept repeating.

Questioned, he told purely and simply the truth, yet excusing himself for having dared to go into the park by jumping across the ditch.

When asked at what time his father had gotten in, he answered that he had no idea. He had gone to bed about 9:00 p.m. and had slept without waking right up to the morning. He knew Guespin by having seen him come to their house several times. He wasn't ignorant of the fact that his father was doing business with the Count's gardener, but he didn't know what business. Besides, he hadn't spoken to Guespin four times in all.

The Investigating Magistrate ordered Philippe released, not because he was absolutely convinced of his innocence, but counting on the fact that if a crime had been committed by several accomplices, it was good to leave one of them free. He would be watched and he would get the others arrested.

However, the body of the Count still had not been found. They had scoured the park with extreme care, searched the undergrowth, rummaged through the smallest clump of flowers in vain.

"They might have thrown him in the water," the Mayor suggested.

That was Monsieur Domini's opinion. Fishermen were recruited and ordered to drag the Seine, beginning their search a little above the spot where they had found the body of the Countess.

It was then about 3:00 p.m. Père Plantat remarked that very likely no one had eaten during the day. Wouldn't it be wise to eat something hastily if they wanted to continue the investigation right up to nightfall.

This reminder of the trivial requirements of our poor humanity displeased mightily the sensitive Mayor of Orcival and even humiliated him somewhat in his dignity as a man and as an administrator.

However, as everyone agreed with Père Plantat, Monsieur Courtois tried to follow the general example. God knows, however, that he hadn't the least appetite.

And then, around that table still moist with the wine spilled by the murderers, the Investigating Magistrate, Père Plantat, the Doctor and the Mayor sat down to eat an improvised snack quickly.

Chapter V

The stairwell had been closed off, but the vestibule was still open. Comings and goings, footsteps, stifled whispers came from there, then dominating this constant hum, the shouts and the oaths of the gendarmes trying to control the crowd.

From time to time a frightened head glided along the door of the dining room, that had remained ajar. Some curious person, more daring than the others, wanted to watch "the people from the law" eat and were trying to catch a few words to carry back and boast about it.

But "the people from the law"—speaking as they do at Orcival—were careful not to say anything serious with open doors and in the presence of a servant moving around the table to serve.

Very stirred up by this frightful crime, worried about the mystery which still covered that affair, they kept their own council and dissimulated their impressions. Each one studied the probability of his suspicions and kept his private thoughts to himself.

While eating, Monsieur Domini arranged his notes, numbering the sheets of paper, putting a cross by certain particularly significant answers of the accused which would be the basis of his report. Of the four guests at this gloomy meal, he was perhaps the least tormented. This crime didn't seem to him to be one of those that cause Investigating Magistrates to spend sleepless nights. He saw clearly the motive, which was enormous, and he had in custody La Ripaille and Guespin, the two guilty ones, or at least accomplices.

Seated next to each other, Père Plantat and Doctor Gendron were discussing the malady which had carried away Sauvresy.

As for Monsieur Courtois, he was lending an ear to the noises from outside. The news of the double murder had spread throughout the countryside. The crowd was growing by the minute. It filled the courtyard and was becoming more and more daring. The gendarmes were overwhelmed. It was now or never for the Mayor of Orcival to exert himself.

"I'm going to go make these people listen to reason," he said, "and urge them to withdraw."

And at that, he wiped his mouth, threw his rolled-up napkin on the table and left. It was time. The warnings of the Brigadier could no longer be heard. Some of the curious, more enraged than the others, had gotten the upper-hand and forced open the door leading into the garden.

The Mayor's presence didn't intimidate the crowd a great deal, perhaps, but it doubled the gendarme's energy. The vestibule was emptied. As a consequence, there were many grumblings against that act of authority.

What a superb opportunity to give a speech! Monsieur Courtois didn't miss it. He supposed that his eloquence, induced by the virtue of cold water showers, would calm the unusual unrest of his wisely administered citizens. Therefore, he mounted the steps, his left hand pass through the opening of his vest, gesticulating with his right, in that proud and impassive attitude that statuary lends to great orators. This was the way he posed in front of his council when, finding an unexpected resistance, he undertook to force his will and bring back the recalcitrant. This was how, in *L'Histoire de la Restauration*, at the moment of the famous "Grab that man there for me," he is represented.

His speech was arriving by snatches as far as the dining room. Depending on whether he turned to the right or the left, his voice was clear or distinct, or was lost in the void. He was saying:

"Gentlemen, and my dear constituents, a crime unheard of in the annals of Orcival, has just bloodied our peaceful and honest commune. I share your sorrow. I therefore understand and I can explain your feverish emotion, your legitimate indignation. As much as you, my friends, more than you, I cherished and respected that noble Count de Trémorel and his virtuous wife. They both have been the good angels of our region. We will weep for them together..."

Doctor Gendron was saying to Père Plantat: "I assure you that the symptoms that you tell me are not rare following pleurisy. You think you've conquered the malady; you stop using the lance; you're mistaken. From the acute state, the inflammation passes to the chronic stage and becomes complicated with pneumonia and tubercular phthisis."

The Mayor was continuing to speak: "But nothing justifies a curiosity which, by its inopportune and noisy manifestations hinders the action of the law and is, in any case, a punishable strike at the majesty of the law. Why this unwonted assembly, why this group shouting, why these rumors, these whispers, these premature suppositions?..."

Doctor Gendron was saying: "There were two or three consultations which didn't give favorable results. Sauvresy complained of pains completely strange and bizarre. He complained of sufferings so unlikely, so absurd, I can't find the right word, that he threw the conjectures of the most competent doctors off the track."

"Wasn't it R... from Paris who saw him?"

"Exactly. He came every day and often stayed at the chateau overnight. Many times I saw him, very worried, going down the main street of the village. He was going to oversee the preparation of his prescription by our pharmacist."

"...Therefore," Monsieur Courtois was shouting, "Learn to moderate your just anger; be calm; be dignified."

And Doctor Gendron was continuing: "Certainly your pharmacist is an intelligent man, but you have, in Orcival itself, a boy who can out-do him very well. He's a fellow who takes advantage of the simple and knows how to make money, a certain Robelot..."

"Robelot the bone-setter?"

"That's the one. I even suspect him of giving consultations and acting as a pharmacist behind closed doors. He's very intelligent. Besides, I was the one who instructed him. He was my laboratory assistant for more than five years and even now when I have some delicate experiment..."

The Doctor stopped, struck by the change in the expression of the impassive Père Plantat.

"Eh! Dear friend," he asked him "What's the matter with you? Are you ill?"

The Investigating Magistrate abandoned his papers to look.

"Really," he said, "Monsieur the Justice of the Peace is pale."

But Père Plantat had already regained his usual composure.

"It's nothing," he answered, "absolutely nothing. With my damned stomach, as soon as I change the time of my meals..."

Coming to the finale of his harangue, Monsieur Courtois inflated his voice and truly abused his capacity.

"Then go back to your peaceful dwellings," he said, "Go back to your occupations. Take up your work again. Be unafraid. The law protects you. Justice has already begun its work. Two of the authors of this heinous crime are in its power and we are on the trail of their accomplices."

"Of all the servants currently in the chateau," remarked Père Plantat, "there's not a single one who knew Sauvresy. Little by little the whole staff has been changed."

"It's a fact," answered the Doctor, "that the sight of former servants could only have been very disagreeable to Monsieur de Trémorel."

He was interrupted by the Mayor who was coming back in, his eyes shining, his expression animated, wiping the sweat from his forehead.

"I've made all those people understand the indecency of their curiosity," he said. "They've all gone away. The Brigadier told me they wanted to do something bad to Philippe Bertaud. Public opinion seldom misses the mark."

Hearing the door open, he turned around and found himself face to face with a man who was bowing so low, his hat pressed tightly against his stomach, his face could hardly be seen.

"What do you want?" Monsieur Courtois asked him rudely. "By what right do you come in here? Who are you?"

The man straightened up.

"I'm Monsieur Lecoq," he replied with the most gracious of smiles.

And seeing that this name meant nothing to anybody, he added:

"Monsieur Lecoq of the Sûreté, sent by the Prefecture of Police on the telegraphed request about the affair in question."

That declaration considerably surprised all the listeners, even the Investigating Magistrate.

It is understood in France that each occupation has its own exterior and insignia which identifies it on sight. Every profession has its conventional type.

And when his Majesty Opinion has adopted a stereotype, it doesn't want to admit that it's possible to stray from it. What's a doctor like? He's a serious man dressed all in black with a white tie. A man with a big stomach strung with gold chains can't be anything else but a banker. Everybody knows that the artist is a rake with a pointed hat, a velvet jacket, and big ruffles.

In virtue of all that, the employee of the Rue de Jérusalem[7] should have eyes full of treachery, something shady about his whole person, a grubby look and fake jewelry. The most obtuse of shop owners is persuaded that he can smell a policeman twenty feet away: a tall man with a mustache and a glossy soft felt hat, his neck imprisoned in a collar stiff as horsehair, dressed in a used frock coat, scrupulously buttoned up over the absence of underwear. Such is the stereotype.

Now, considering this, Monsieur Lecoq, coming into the dining room at Valfeuillu, certainly didn't have the look of a policeman. It's true that Monsieur Lecoq had whatever look it pleased him to have. His friends swear that he has his own countenance, which belongs to him, that he picks up again when he goes home and which he keeps so long as he is alone at his fireside, his feet in his house slippers. But that fact hasn't been proven. What is sure is that his mobile mask lends itself to strange metamorphoses; that he molds it, you might say, as he likes, just as the sculptor shapes the modeling clay. He changes everything about himself, even his expression that Gévrol, his supervisor and his rival, never managed to change.

"So," insisted the Investigating Magistrate, "You're the one that the Prefect of Police has sent me for the case where certain investigations will be necessary."

"Myself, Monsieur," answered Lecoq. "At your service."

No, he didn't have the right appearance, this man sent by the Prefect of Police, and Monsieur Domini's insistence was understandable. That day, Monsieur

---

[7] Location of the Sûreté, the French National Police. The Sûreté was founded in 1812 by a former criminal, Vidocq, with eight other former criminals. An interesting analogy to Vidocq has been made by Ernest Mandel in *Delightful Murder: A Social History of the Crime Story* when he says in Chapter 2, "From Villain to Hero": "The archetypal police figure of modern literature is modeled after history's first well-known policeman: Fouche's sidekick, Vidocq. Himself a former convicted bandit who pressed many criminals into the service of Napoleon's Ministry as informers, Vidocq forged his own legend, not only by his practical villainy, which was virtually unbounded, but also by his mendacious *Memoires*, published in 1828. Balzac's Bibi-Lupin and Victor Hugo's Inspector Javert were clearly patterned after this elusive and terrifying figure, whose actions and mentality alike bore the seeds that would one day germinate in such varied but equally unsavory characters as J. Edgar Hoover, Heinrich Himmler, and Beria."

Lecoq had given himself nice flat hair of that indecisive color called Parisian blond, with a pretentious, coquettish part on the side. Sideburns the shade of the hair framed a pale, fat, swollen face. His big eyes, not quite on the same level, seemed to be staring out of their red borders. A candid smile spread across his thick lips, which, on opening, showed a range of long, yellow teeth. In addition, his face had no precise expression. It was a mixture in almost equal doses of timidity, self-importance, and self-satisfaction. Impossible to attribute the least intelligence to the wearer of such a face. After having looked at him, one involuntarily searched for his goiter. Retail haberdashers who, after having stolen thirty years over their notions, threads and their needles, retire with 1,800 pounds of income, must have that inoffensive look.

His dress was as lifeless as his person. His frock coat resembled all frock coats, his trousers all trousers. A horsehair cord, the same color as his sideburns, held a big silver watch which bulged from the left pocket of his vest. While talking, he was handling a square transparent horn lozenge box full of little square licorice, jujube marshmallow lozenges, ornamented with the portrait of a very ugly and very proper woman, probably the portrait of his dead wife. And according to how the conversation went, whether he was satisfied or discontent, Monsieur Lecoq gobbled a square of lozenge or looked at the portrait poetically.

After having observed the man in great detail, the Investigating Magistrate shrugged.

"Finally," Monsieur Domini said,—and that "finally" was in answer to his own thoughts—"now that you're here, we're going to explain to you what it's about."

"Oh! Not necessary," answered Monsieur Lecoq with a little self-sufficient look, "perfectly unnecessary."

"However, it's indispensable that you know..."

"What? What the Investigating Magistrate knows?" interrupted the Sûreté agent. "I know it already. Let's say murder, having theft as a motive, and we'll start from there. We then have climbing the wall, breaking and entering, the apartments ransacked. The body of the Countess has been found, but the Count's body can't be found. What else? La Ripaille has been arrested. He's a cunning devil. In any case, he deserves a little prison time. Guespin returned drunk."

"Ah! There are serious charges against this Guespin,"

"His past actions are deplorable. It's not known where he spent the night. He refuses to talk. He's not furnishing an alibi. That's serious, very serious."

Père Plantat examined the mild-mannered agent with visible pleasure. The other listeners couldn't hide their surprise.

"Then who informed you?" demanded the Investigating Magistrate.

"Eh! Eh! Everybody a little bit," answered Monsieur Lecoq.

"But where?"

"Here. I arrived here more than two hours ago. I even heard the Mayor's speech."

And satisfied with the effect produced, Monsieur Lecoq swallowed a square lozenge.

"What," stated Monsieur Domini in a displeased tone, "then you didn't know I was waiting for you?"

"I'm sorry," answered the agent. "I hope, however, that the Investigating Magistrate will please hear me out. It's just that a study of the terrain is indispensable. You have to look around, prepare for the assault. I find it important to gather public rumors, public opinion, as they say, in order to distrust it."

"All of that," Monsieur Domini said severely, "doesn't justify being late."

Monsieur Lecoq looked tenderly at the portrait.

"The Investigating Magistrate has only to inform himself at the Rue de Jérusalem," he answered. "They will tell him I know my job. To do an investigation well, the important thing is not to be recognized. The police—that's as annoying as anything—have a bad reputation. Now that they know who I am and why I've come, they won't tell me anything. Or, if I interrogate, they will answer with a thousand lies. They will distrust me. There will be omissions."

"That's rather accurate," objected Monsieur Plantat, coming to the aid of the Sûreté agent.

"So," continued Monsieur Lecoq, "when people talked to me out there, it was in the country. I put on my country behavior. I arrived, and everybody, seeing me, said to himself, 'There's a very curious but not a bad fellow.' Then I slip in; I insinuate myself; I listen; I talk; I make people talk! I question. People answer me openly. I inform myself. I gather clues. People aren't uncomfortable with me. They're charming, these people of Orcival. I've already made several friends and I've been invited to dinner this evening."

Monsieur Domini didn't like the police and scarcely took any trouble to hide it. He submitted to his collaboration rather than accepted it, only because he couldn't do without it. In his moral uprightness, he condemned the methods it is sometimes forced to use, while at the same time recognizing the necessity for those same methods.

While listening to Monsieur Lecoq, he couldn't keep from approving him, and nevertheless looked at him with a less than friendly eye.

"Since you know so many things," he said to him dryly, "we're going to proceed to the scene of the crime."

"I'm at the service of the Investigating Magistrate," the agent of the Sûreté responded laconically.

As everyone was rising, he took advantage of the movement to approach Père Plantat and offer him his candy holder.

"The Justice of the Peace, does he use these?"

Père Plantat didn't think he should refuse. He swallowed a morsel of jujube and serenity reappeared on the face of the Sûreté agent. He needed, as do all great actors, a sympathetic audience, and he felt vaguely that he was going to work in front of an amateur.

Chapter VI

Monsieur Lecoq was the first to reach the stairway and the blood stains immediately jumped out at him.

"Oh!" he said with a revolted expression at each new stain. "Oh! Oh! The wretched people!"

Monsieur Courtois was very touched to encounter that sensitivity in a police agent. He thought that exclamation of commiseration applied to the victims. He was wrong, because Monsieur Lecoq, while climbing the stairs, continued:

"The wretched people. You don't get everything in a house dirty like this, or at least, you clean up. What the Devil! You take precautions!"

Coming to the second floor, at the door of the boudoir which led into the bedroom, the Sûreté agent stopped, looking at the layout of the apartment well before going in.

Having seen clearly what he wanted to see, he went in, saying:

"Well! I'm not dealing with some of my usual experienced criminals."

"But it seems to me," the Investigating Magistrate remarked, "that we already have the elements of investigation which should unusually facilitate your task. It's clear that Guespin, if he isn't an accomplice to the crime, at least knew about it."

Monsieur Lecoq glanced at the portrait on the lozenge box. It was more than a glance; it was a confidence. Evidently he was saying to his dearly departed one what he couldn't say aloud.

"I certainly know," he continued, "that Guespin is terribly compromised. Why won't he say where he spent the night? From another direction, he has public opinion against him, and then, as for me, naturally, I'm distrustful."

The Sûreté agent stood alone in the middle of the bedroom—on his request the other people remained on the threshold—and sweeping around him his lusterless glance, he looked for a meaning to the terrible disorder.

"Imbeciles!" he exclaimed in an irritated voice, "brutes two times over! No, really, you don't work this way. Just because you kill people to rob them, that's no reason to break everything in their house. What the devil! You don't smash the furniture. You bring some instrument with you to pick the locks, some nice lock picks that don't make any noise but do excellent work. Clumsy idiots! Wouldn't you say..."

He stopped, his mouth open.

"Eh!" he continued, maybe not so clumsy."

The witnesses of that scene stood immobile at the entryway, following with interest mingled with surprise, watching the movement—it's almost necessary to say the exercises of Monsieur Lecoq. Kneeling on the rug, he moved his flat hand over the thick carpet in the middle of the pieces of porcelain.

"It's moist, very moist. When they broke the porcelain all the tea hadn't been drunk. It should have been."

"A lot of the tea could have remained in the teapot," objected Père Plantat.

"I know that," answered Monsieur Lecoq, "and that's just what I was telling myself. Because of that, the dampness is not enough to tell us the exact time of the crime."

"But the clock gave it to us," exclaimed Monsieur Courtois. "And really very precisely."

"Actually," Monsieur Domini confirmed, "Monsieur Courtois explained very well in his testimony that in the fall the movement stopped."

"Well!" said Père Plantat, "It was actually the hour of that clock that struck me. It said 3:20 a.m. and we know that the Countess was completely dressed as for the middle of the day when she was struck down. Was she then still standing, drinking a cup of tea at 3:00 a.m. That's hardly likely."

"And I too was struck by that circumstance," the Sûreté agent continued. "And that's why a minute ago I said to myself: 'Not so stupid!' What's more, we're going to find out."

At that, with a thousand infinite precautions, he lifted the clock and placed it on the mantle of the fireplace, taking care to place it level. The hands were still stopped at 3:20 a.m.

"Three twenty," murmured Monsieur Lecoq, while sliding a small wedge under the pedestal. "What the devil! You don't drink tea at that hour! And still less, in the middle of July, at daybreak, do you murder people at that hour."

He opened, not without trouble, the casing of the face of the clock and pushed the big hand onto the half hour of three o'clock.

The clock struck eleven times.

"Well! What do you know! Finally the truth!" Monsieur Lecoq exclaimed, triumphant. And taking the candy box with a portrait out of his pocket, he swallowed a square of marshmallow lozenge.

"Jokers!"

The simplicity of this method of verification, which no one had thought about, caused the spectators no end of surprise.

Monsieur Courtois in particular was amazed.

"There is a man," he said to the Doctor, "who isn't without talent in his profession."

"Ergo," continued Monsieur Lecoq, who knew Latin, "we're not faced with brutes, as I almost believed at first, but with scoundrels who could see further than the end of their knife. They miscalculated their business. But you have to hand it to them, they did calculate. The clue is clear. They meant to lead the investigation astray by deceiving it about the time."

"I can't see their purpose clearly," insisted Monsieur Courtois.

"Nevertheless, it's very easy to see," responded Monsieur Domini. "Wasn't it in the murderers interest to have it believed that the crime was committed after the last train was on the way to Paris? By leaving his companions at the Lyon railroad station at 9:00 p.m., Guespin could be here by 10:00 p.m., murder his masters, grab the money that he knew was in the Count de Trémorel's possession and get back to Paris by the last train."

"These suppositions are very nice," objected Père Plantat. "But then, why did Guespin not go rejoin his comrades at Wepler's in the Batignolles? By doing that, he could create a kind of alibi up to a certain point."

From the beginning of the investigation, Doctor Gendron had been seated on the only unbroken chair in the bedroom, reflecting on the sudden indisposition that had caused Père Plantat to turn pale at the mention of Robelot, the bone setter. The Investigating Magistrate's explanations drew him out of his meditations. He rose.

"There is still another thing," he said. "That very useful advance of time for Guespin can become crushing for La Ripaille, his accomplice."

"But," answered Monsieur Domini, "it could very well be that LaRipaille wasn't consulted at all. As far as Guespin is concerned, he probably had good reasons for not going to the wedding. His confusion, after such a crime, would have hurt him even more than his absence."

Monsieur Lecoq himself didn't judge it the proper time yet to make a pronouncement. Like a doctor at the bed of a sick man, he wanted to be sure of his diagnosis. He had gone back to the fireplace and was again moving the hands of the clock. Successively, they struck the half hour of eleven o'clock, then midnight, then twelve thirty, then one o'clock.

While totally occupied doing that, he was grumbling.

"Amateurs! Second-hand brigands! You think you're clever, but you didn't think of everything. You gave the hands of the clock a little push but you didn't think about making the striking mechanism agree. Along comes a fellow from the Sûreté, an old monkey who knows the tricks, and the maneuver has been discovered."

Monsieur Domini and Père Plantat remained silent. Monsieur Lecoq came back toward them.

"Monsieur Domini," he said, "it may be certain now that the crime was committed before 10:30."

"Unless," observed Père Plantat, "the striking mechanism is off tract, which sometimes happens."

"That often happens," added Monsieur Courtois. "As proof of that, the clock in my drawing room has been like that I don't know how long."

Monsieur Lecoq was thinking.

"The Justice of the Peace could be right," he replied. "I have probability on my side but probability isn't enough at the beginning of a case. You have to have certainty. Fortunately, we still have a method of verification. We have the bed. I'll bet it hasn't been slept in."

And he spoke to the Mayor:

"I'll need a servant to give me a hand, Monsieur."

"That's not necessary," said Père Plantat. "I myself am going to help you. That will be quicker."

At that, the two of them lifted the canopy of the bed and put it on the floor, lifting the curtain hangings at the same time.

"*Hein!*" said Monsieur Lecoq. "Wasn't I right?"

"That's true," said Monsieur Domini. "The bed hasn't been slept in."

"Made ready for going to bed," responded the Sûreté agent, "but no one has slept in it."

Monsieur Courtois wanted, nevertheless, to object.

"I'm sure of what I'm suggesting," interrupted the man from the police. "Someone drew back the curtains of this bed, that's true, and they perhaps rolled on top of it, rumpled the pillowcases, pressed down the bed spread, creased the sheets, but, for an experienced eye, they weren't able to give it the appearance of a bed in which two people have slept. To unmake a bed is difficult, more difficult, perhaps, than to make it up again. To make it up again it isn't indispensable to turn back the sheets and bedspread, and turn over the mattress pad. To unmake it, it's absolutely necessary to sleep in it and leave body warmth. A bed is one of those terrible witnesses which is never wrong and which can't be falsified. Nobody slept in this one."

"I understand very well that the Countess was dressed, but the Count could have gone to bed first," Père Plantat remarked.

The Investigating Magistrate, the Doctor and the Mayor had come forward.

"No, Monsieur," answered Monsieur Lecoq," and I can prove it to you. Besides the explanation is easy, and after having heard it, a ten-year-old child wouldn't let himself be taken in by a fake break-in like this one."

He turned back the sheet and the covers on the middle of the bed while continuing.

"Both these pillows are very rumpled, aren't they? But check under the bolster. It hasn't been touched. You won't find any of those wrinkles that the weight of the head and the movement of the arms leave. That's not all. Look at the bed from the middle of the bed to the end of the bed. Since the bed covers have been well tucked in, the two sheets touch each other everywhere. Slide in your hand as I'm doing—and he slid in one of his arms—and you'll feel a resistance which wouldn't be there if the legs had been stretched out to this spot. Now, Monsieur de Trémorel was tall enough to occupy the whole length of the bed."

Monsieur Lecoq's demonstrations were so clear, so obvious were his proofs, that there was no way to doubt them.

"That's still nothing," he continued. "Let's go to the second mattress. You rarely think of the second mattress when, for whatever reason, you unmake a bed or when you try to spread it up again. Examine this one."

He lifted the top mattress and you could see that the fabric on the second mattress was perfectly taut. You could discern no sinking.

"Ah! The second mattress," Monsieur Lecoq murmured.

And you might say his nose twitched, probably at the memory of some good story.

"It appears proved to me that Monsieur de Trémorel had not gone to bed," the Investigating Magistrate murmured.

"What's more," added Doctor Gendron, "if they murdered him in his bed, his clothes would have remained on some piece of furniture."

"Without counting on the fact that at least one drop of blood would have been found on the sheets," Monsieur Lecoq said in an off-handed way. "Decidedly, these criminals weren't very good."

For a moment Père Plantat's eyes searched for those of the Investigating Magistrate. When their regards finally met each other;

"What appears surprising to me," said the old Justice of the Peace, giving by stress a particular importance to each word, "is how they were able to kill him in his own house anyway other than in his sleep, a man as young and vigorous as Count Hector was."

"And in a house full of guns," added Doctor Gendron, "because the Count's study is entirely covered with guns and hunting knives! It's a veritable arsenal."

"Alas!" sighed good Monsieur Courtois, "We know worse catastrophes. The audacity of criminals is growing because the lower classes in the great centers covet comfort, money to spend, luxury. There's not a week when the newspapers..."

He had to stop, not without great annoyance. No one was listening to him. They were listening to Père Plantat. He had never seen him so talkative. He was continuing:

"The ransacking of the house seems to you unexplainable. Well, I'm surprised it wasn't even worse still. I am, as much as to say, an old man. I no longer have the physical strength of a man of thirty-five. And, nevertheless, it seems to me that if murderers came into my house while I was still standing, they wouldn't get me without a fight. I don't know what I would do. I would probably be killed, but I would certainly manage to sound the alarm. I would defend myself. I would scream. I would open the windows. I would set fire to the house..."

What would you have said, those of you under the jurisdiction of the Justice of the Peace, if you could have seen the animation, the passion, of your emotionless Justice of the Peace!

"Let's add," the Doctor insisted, "that, if awake, it's difficult to be surprised. Some unusual sound always warns you. It's a door that screeches when turning on its hinges. It's one of the steps on the stairs that cracks. However clever a murderer may be, he can't strike his victim like lightning."

"It could be," Monsieur Courtois suggested, "that they used a gun. That's been known to happen. You're sitting very calmly in your bedroom. It's summer; your windows are open. You're chatting with your wife while drinking a cup of tea. Outside, the criminals are standing one on top of the other's shoulders. One of them comes abreast of the window. He takes aim at you at his pleasure. He pulls the trigger; the shot goes off..."

"And" the Doctor continued: "everybody in the neighborhood comes running."

"Let me go on, let me go on," retorted Monsieur Courtois. "In a town, in a large city, yes. Here, in the middle of a vast park, no. Think, Doctor, how isolated this house is. The closest of the houses lived in is that of Madame la Comtesse de Lanascol, and it's still more than five hundred meters away, and what's more, it's surrounded by big trees which shut off the sound and keep it from spreading. Let's try an experiment. If you'll allow it, I'm going to fire a pistol here, in this bedroom, and I'll bet you won't hear the detonation in the road."

"In the day time, maybe, but at night!"...

If Monsieur Courtois was talking such a long time, that was because the people listening to him were watching the Investigating Magistrate closely.

"Well," concluded Monsieur Domini, "if, against all hopes, Guespin doesn't decide to talk this evening or tomorrow, the Count's body will give us the key to the puzzle."

"Yes," responded Père Plantat, "yes, if it's found..."

During that rather long discussion, Monsieur Lecoq had continued his investigation, lifting furniture, studying breaks, investigating the smallest bit of debris, as if they were able to tell him the truth. Sometimes he took out from a kit holding a magnifying glass and various instruments with bizarre shapes, a steel shaft curved at the end which he inserted into and opened locks. He picked up several keys on the rug and on a clotheshorse he found a towel which must have shown him something unusual, because he laid it to one side. He came and went from the bedroom to the Count's study, sometimes not losing a word of what was being said, taking advantage of all the observations, gathering and taking down, in his head, less the sentences themselves than the stress of the various intonations.

In an investigation like that of the Orcival Crime, when several representatives of the law are together, they are reserved. They all know each other as being almost equally experienced, smart, perspicacious, similarly interested in discovering the truth, habitually very little satisfied with deceptive appearances, difficult to surprise, and the natural caution of each of them adds to the esteem he has for the wisdom and penetration of the others. It might be that each of them gives a different interpretation to the facts revealed by the investigation. It could even be that each of them has an opposite feeling about the basis of the affair. A casual observer would not be aware of these differences. While trying to hide his inmost thoughts, each tried to penetrate those of his neighbor and tried, if they were different from his, to bring his adversary around to his opinion, not by showing it to him frankly and without beating around the bush, but by calling his attention to the serious or inconsequential words that created it.

The enormous weight of a single word justified that hesitation. Men who have the liberty and the life of other men between their hands, who can with one pen stroke break an existence, feel the burden of their responsibility a great deal more strongly than is believed. To feel this burden shared brings an ineffable comfort.

It was for these reasons that no one dared take the initiative, nor explain himself clearly, why each waited for the positive expression of an opinion so as to adopt and approve it or to combat it. Therefore the interrogators exchanged many fewer positive statements than proposals. They moved forward by suggestions. From that fact came banal expressions, almost ridiculous suppositions, asides, which are almost like a provocation to an explanation. From that also results the almost impossibility of giving an exact and real characterization of a difficult investigation

So, in that affair, the Investigating Magistrate and Père Plantat were far from being of the same opinion. They knew that before having exchanged a word. But Monsieur Domini, whose opinion rested on material facts, on tangible circumstances, and for him beyond any discussion, was very little inclined to provoke any contradiction. What would be the use? On the other hand, Père Plantat, whose theory seemed to rest solely on his impressions, on a series of deductions more or less logical, wasn't able to explain himself clearly without a positive and pressing request. His last words, underlined by exaggeration, not having been picked up, he judged that he was far enough along, too far along, perhaps. So, to change the topic of conversation, he quickly spoke to the envoy of the Prefecture of Police.

"Well! Monsieur Lecoq, have you gathered some new clues," he asked him.

Monsieur Lecoq at that moment was regarding with fixed attention a large portrait of Monsieur le Comte Hector de Trémorel suspended in front of him. At Père Plantat's remark, he turned around.

"I haven't found anything decisive," he answered, "but neither have I found anything that changes what I expected. However..."

He didn't continue, he also stepping back from his part of responsibility.

"What?" Monsieur Domini questioned harshly.

"I wanted to say," Monsieur Lecoq continued, "that I don't have my business complete. I have my lantern in hand, and I even have a candle in my lantern. The only thing I lack is a match."

"Speak in ordinary language, please," the Investigating Magistrate said severely.

"Well," Monsieur Lecoq continued in a manner and in a tone too humble not to be feigned. "I'm still hesitating. I need some help. For example, if the

Doctor will be good enough to take the trouble to go ahead with the examination of the cadaver of Madame la Comtesse de Trémorel, he would do me a great favor."

"I was going to ask you to do precisely the same thing, my dear Doctor," Monsieur Domini said to Monsieur Gendron.

"Gladly," said the old doctor, who started toward the door,

Monsieur Lecoq held him by the arm, stopping him.

"I'll allow myself," he observed in a tone which didn't at all resemble the one he had used until then. "I'll allow myself to call the attention of Monsieur le docteur to the wounds made to the head of Madame de Trémorel by a blunt instrument that I take to be a cudgel. I've studied the wounds, me who am not a doctor, and they seem suspect to me."

"And to me also," Père Plantat said quickly. "It seems to me that there wasn't an outpouring of blood into the cutaneous vessels at the spot the blows were struck."

"The nature of those wounds," Monsieur Lecoq continued, "will be a precious clue which will decide me completely."

And as the Investigating Magistrate's harsh reply still rankled in his heart, he added with innocent vengeance:

"You're the one, Doctor, who holds the match."

Monsieur Gendron was getting ready to leave when the servant of the Mayor of Orcival, Baptiste, the man who isn't scolded, appeared on the threshold.

He bowed deeply and said:

"I've come to get Monsieur."

"Me! Why?" demanded Monsieur Courtois. "Can't they leave me in peace one minute? You can answer that I'm busy."

Placid Baptiste answered: "It's about Madame that we thought we should bother Monsieur. Madame, she's not well at all!

The excellent Mayor paled slightly.

Seriously disturbed, he exclaimed: "What do you mean? Explain yourself."

"Eh bien. Here's what happened," Baptiste continued the calmest way in the world. "The mailman arrived a while ago with the mail. All right! I carried the letters to Madame who was in the small drawing room. I had hardly turned on my heels when I heard a loud cry and a noise like somebody falling full length on the floor."

Baptiste was explaining himself slowly, putting, one felt, infinite art into adding to his master's worry.

"Then go on, keep talking," the Mayor said, exasperated. "Keep talking!"

"Naturally," the fellow continued without hurrying, "I opened the door to the little drawing room. What did I see? Madame stretched out full length on the floor. As was right, I called for help. The upstairs maid came, the cook, the others, and we carried Madame to her bed. It seems, Justine told me, that it was a letter from Mademoiselle Laurence that put Madame in that state."

The servant who was never scolded needed to be whipped. At each word he stopped and looked around. His eyes gave the lie to his contrite face, betraying the extreme satisfaction he felt about a misfortune experienced by his master.

That master, alas! was staggered. Just as happens to all of us, when we don't know exactly what misfortune awaits us, he was afraid to ask. He remained there, overwhelmed, not moving, lamenting instead of running.

Père Plantat took advantage of this pause to question the domestic and with such a look that the fellow didn't dare take any detours.

"What do you mean?" he asked him. "Mademoiselle Laurence, then she's not here?"

"No, Monsieur, she left yesterday night to go spend a month with one of the sisters of Madame."

"And how is Madame Courtois?"

"She's better, Monsieur, but she lets out pitiful cries."

The unfortunate Mayor had recovered from the blow. He seized his servant by the arm.

"But then, come on!" he shouted to him. "Come on!"

And they left running.

Père Plantat shook his head sadly.

"If that is all it is," he said sadly.

And he added:

"Remember, Monsieur, the allusions of LaRipaille."

Chapter VII

The Investigating Magistrate, Père Plantat, and the Doctor exchanged a look full of anxiety. What misfortune had struck Monsieur Courtois, that perfectly honorable, and despite his faults, so excellent a man? Was this then definitely a cursed day!

"If LaRipaille's allusions mean anything, I've been told, me who's been here only some hours, two very circumstantial stories. It seems that Laurence girl..."

Père Plantat quickly interrupted the Sûreté agent:

"Slanders," he exclaimed. "Odious slanders! The little people who're jealous of the rich wouldn't mind tearing them apart with their teeth, if they had nothing better. Didn't you know that? Hasn't it always been that way? The bourgeois, especially in little villages, lives, without knowing it, as if in a glass cage. Night and day, the eyes of the lynx envy is fixed on him, watches him, spies on him, finding out about his activities that he believes the most secret, to use them against him. He goes about his business, happy and trusting. His affairs prosper. He has the respect and the friendship of those like him, and all this time he is vilified by the lower classes, dragged through the mud, soiled by the most injurious suppositions!"

"If Mademoiselle Laurence has been slandered," Doctor Gendron said, smiling, "at least she has found a good lawyer to defend her case."

The old Justice of the Peace, the man of bronze, as Monsieur Courtois called him, blushed slightly, embarrassed at his heated defense.

"There are some cases," he said softly, "which defend themselves. Mademoiselle Courtois is one of those young ladies who merit every respect. But there are those abominations that no laws can reach and which revolt me. You have to think of the fact, Messieurs, that our reputation, the honor of our wives and our daughters are at the mercy of the first scoundrel gifted with enough imagination to invent an abominable slander. People would perhaps not believe it. That doesn't matter. People would repeat his slander. They would spread it. What's to be done about it? Can we know what's said against us, downstairs, in the shadows? Will we ever know?"

"Eh!" retorted Doctor Gendron. "What does that matter to us? For me, there is only one voice to be respected, that of conscience. As for what's called public opinion, since it's really the sum of the individual opinions of thousands of imbeciles and wicked people, I pay absolutely no attention to it."

The discussion would perhaps have been prolonged without the Investigating Magistrate who, taking out his watch, made a gesture of irritation.

"We're chatting," he said, "we're talking and time is passing. We must hurry. Let us, at least, divide the work remaining."

Monsieur Domini's commanding tone froze on Monsieur Lecoq's lips some thoughts he was waiting to get in.

It was then agreed that, while Dr. Gendron proceeded with the autopsy, the Investigating Magistrate would rework the report he intended to submit.

Père Plantat remained in charge of overseeing the next investigations of the man from the Prefecture of Police.

As soon as the Sûreté agent found himself alone with the old Justice of the Peace:

"Finally," he said, sighing deeply, as if he had been relieved of a heavy weight, "finally now we're going to be able to move forward."

And as Père Plantat smiled a little, he swallowed a square of lozenge and added:

"To come in when an investigation has begun is deplorable, Monsieur, completely deplorable. The people who've come before you have had time to develop a theory and if you don't adopt it right away, it's the devil!"

On the stairway they heard the voice of Monsieur Domini calling his stenographer who, arriving somewhat after him, had remained on the first floor.

"Well, Monsieur," the agent added, "here's Monsieur the Investigating Magistrate who thinks he's facing a very simple business, while I, me, Monsieur Lecoq, at least the equal of that fellow Gévrol, me, the cherished student of Père Tabaret"—he respectfully took off his hat—"I still can't see clearly."

He stopped, probably reviewing the result of his investigations and continued.

"No, it's true, I'm off the track. I'm almost lost. I'm guessing there is certainly something under all this, but what? What?"

Père Plantat's face remained emotionless, but his eyes were shining.

"Maybe you're right," he agreed in a detached tone, "perhaps in fact there is something."

The Sûreté agent looked at him. He didn't change expressions. He continued to offer the most indifferent expression in the world, while reading some comments in his notebook.

There was a rather long silence, and Monsieur Lecoq took advantage of it to confide to the portrait on the lozenge box the thoughts which were churning through his head.

Do you really see, dear little portrait, he thought, *this worthy Monsieur who looks to me like a sly old fox whose opinions and gestures you have to watch carefully. He doesn't share—he ought to—the opinions of the Investigating Magistrate. He has an idea he doesn't dare tell us. We'll find it out. He's a clever fellow, this country Justice of the Peace. He saw through us right off, despite our pretty blond hair. So long as he believed we were following in Monsieur Domini's footsteps, which were leading us astray, he followed us, supported us, showing us the way. Now that he feels we're on the right track, he crosses his arms and backs off. He wants to leave the honor of the discovery to us. Why?*

He's from around here. Is he afraid of making enemies? No. He's one of those men who's not afraid of much of anything. Then what is it? He recoils from what he thinks. He's found something so surprising he doesn't dare explain himself.

A sudden thought changed the course of Monsieur Lecoq's reflections.

Mille diables! he thought. *What if I'm mistaken. What if this good fellow isn't clever at all! What if he hasn't discovered anything, if he's only obeying chance impressions? More surprising things have been seen. I've known a lot of those people, whose eyes are like the circus sideshows which claim that the interior holds marvels. You go in and you don't see anything. You've been robbed. But no*—he smiled—*I'm going to find out what I'm dealing with.*

And assuming the silliest manner in his repertory, he said aloud. "On considering it, not very much remains to be done, Monsieur le juge de paix. They're holding indefinitely the two principally guilty persons, and when they decide to talk, which will happen sooner or later, we'll know everything, if the Investigating Magistrate wishes it."

A bucket of cold water poured on Père Plantat's head wouldn't have surprised him anymore, and, most of all, the surprise wouldn't have been more disagreeable.

"What," he stammered in an absolutely flabbergasted way, "it's you, the agent of the Sûreté a clever, experienced man, who..."

Delighted with the success of his ruse, Monsieur Lecoq couldn't stay serious, and Père Plantat, who perceived that he had fallen into a trap, began to laugh aloud.

Moreover, not a word was exchanged between these two men who were wise in the science of life, having equally subtle and active minds.

You, my good man, the Sûreté agent said to himself, *have something on your chest, but it is so enormous, so monstrous, that you wouldn't spit it out if it were a cannon ball. You want someone to force your hand. It will be forced.*

Père Plantat was thinking: *He's sly. He knows I have an idea. He'll look for it and he'll certainly find it.*

Monsieur Lecoq had put the lozenge box with a portrait back in his pocket, as he always did when he was working seriously. His ego as a student of Père Tabaret was agreeably excited. He was playing a role and he was an actor.

"So," he exclaimed, "let's get going and give me a hand. According to the verbal testimony of the Mayor of Orcival, the instrument with which everything was smashed was found here."

"In a bedroom on the third floor, facing the garden, we recovered a hatchet on the floor in front of a chest which had been struck lightly but not opened. I kept anyone from touching it," Père Plantat answered.

"Well, you did the right thing. Was it heavy, that hatchet?"

"It must have weighed a good kilo."

"That's prefect. Let's go up and look at it."

They went upstairs. And immediately Monsieur Lecoq, forgetting his role as a haberdasher careful of his clothes, stretched out on his stomach, alternately studying the hatchet, a terrible weapon, heavy, with an ash handle, and the shining and well-waxed floor.

The Justice of the Peace observed:

"I myself suppose that the criminals brought this hatchet upstairs and attacked this piece of furniture with the single objective of increasing the assumptions of the investigation, of complicating the problem. That hatchet wasn't necessary to break into that armoire, which doesn't have anything in it. I could break it with my fist. They gave it a single blow, one only, and calmly placed the hatchet on the floor."

The Sûreté agent had stood up and was brushing dust off himself.

"I believe, Monsieur," he said, "that you are mistaken. That hatchet wasn't placed calmly on the floor. It was thrown with a violence which betrayed great fright and violent anger. Look, see here, on the floor, these three marks following each other. When the criminal initially used the hatchet, it fell at first on the cutting edge, causing that gash. It then fell on the side, and the opposite side, which is a hammer, left that trace. See, here, under my thumb. Then it was thrown with such strength that it flipped over and again nicked the floor, there, at the spot where it is now."

"That's right!" said Père Plantat. "That's exactly right!"

And the agent's observations probably upsetting his theory, he added in an irritated way:

"I don't understand anything about it, nothing at all."

Monsieur Lecoq was continuing his observations.

"The windows that are open now," he demanded, "were they that way during the first investigations?"

"Yes."

"Then, that's how it was. The murderers heard some sort of noise in the garden and they went to look out the window. What did they see? I have no idea. What I do know is that whatever they saw terrified them and that they flung down the hatchet violently and left. Look at the position of the nicks. Look at them diagonally, of course. You'll see that the hatchet was hurled by a person who was standing, not near the armoire, but near the open window."

Père Plantat kneeled down in his turn, looking with extreme attention. What the agent said was true. He got up, a little disconcerted, and after a moment's reflection:

"That circumstance bothers me somewhat," he said, "but at the outside..."

He stopped, stood still, thinking, one of his hands pressed to his forehead.

"Everything can still be explained," he murmured, mentally rearranging the diverse pieces of his theory. "And in that case, the time indicated by the clock would be the true one."

Monsieur Lecoq didn't think of questioning the old Justice of the Peace. In the first place, he knew very well that he wouldn't answer. Next, his vanity was brought into play. How was it that he himself couldn't solve a puzzle someone else had solved?

"That circumstance of the hatchet threw me too off the track," he said in a loud and intelligible monologue. "I was supposing that the brigands were taking their time working, but not at all. I discover that they were surprised, that someone disturbed them, that they were afraid."

Père Plantat was all ears.

"It's true," Monsieur Lecoq continued, "that we must divide the clues into two categories. There are the clues left on purpose to deceive us, the unmade bed, for example; then there are the involuntary clues, such as the nicks by that hatchet. But here I'm hesitating. The hatchet clue, was it real or false, good or bad. I thought I was sure about the character of the murderers, and then the investigation was following its course, while now..."

He stopped. The wrinkles on his forehead, the contraction of his lips, betrayed how hard he was thinking.

"While now?"... Père Plantat asked.

At that question, Monsieur Lecoq had the astonished look of a man someone awakes.

"I beg your pardon, Monsieur," he said. "I forgot myself. That's a deplorable habit I have of reflecting and thinking out loud like that. That's why I'm almost always stubborn about working alone. My uncertainties, my hesitations, the vacillations of my suspicions, if somebody heard them, would make me lose my prestige as the soothsayer policeman, the agent for whom there is no mystery."

The old Justice of the Peace smiled indulgently.

"Ordinarily," the man from the Prefecture continued, "I don't open my mouth until I have everything ready to go, and then in a decisive tone I deliver my authoritative views. I say, 'It's this' or 'It's that.' But today I'm behaving without very much restraint, in front of a man who knows that you don't solve right away such a complicated problem as this one seems to me to be. I'm letting my fumbling be seen shamelessly. You don't reach the truth at one leap. You get there by a series of rather complicated calculations, thanks to a series of inductions and deductions which follow one another. Well, at this moment, my logic is lacking."

"How's that?" Père Plantat asked.

"Oh! It's very simple, Monsieur le juge de paix. I thought I had thoroughly understood the murders, got them down by heart. That was most important at the beginning and I was no longer seeing imaginary adversaries. Are they stupid? Are they extremely clever? I asked myself that. The ruse with the bed and the clock had, as I supposed, showed me exactly the measure and the extent of their intelligence and their capacity for invention. Deducting from the known to the unknown, I arrived by a series of consequences very simple to draw, to foresee all that they had been able to turn our attention aside and throw us off the track.

My point of departure taken, to arrive at the truth, I had only to take the opposite of the appearances. I said to myself:

"A hatchet was found on the third floor; therefore, the murders carried it there and forgot it on purpose. They left five glasses on the table in the dining room; therefore, they were more or fewer than five, but they were not five. There was something like left-overs of a supper on the table; therefore, they neither ate nor drank. The Countess' body was at the edge of the water; therefore, it was put there and nowhere else with premeditation. A piece of cloth was found in the hands of the victim; therefore, it was placed there by the murderers themselves. Madame Trémorel's body was pierced many times by a dagger and frightfully bruised; therefore she was killed with a single blow."

"Bravo! Yes! Bravo!" exclaimed Père Plantat, visibly delighted.

"Eh! No, not Bravo!" said Monsieur Lecoq, "because here my thread breaks off. I encounter a gap. If my deductions were true, that hatchet would have been placed harmlessly on the floor."

"Oh, no! Once again, Bravo!" continued Père Plantat, "because that circumstance is a peculiarity which doesn't weaken in any way our general theory. It's clear, it's certain, that the murderers intended to act as you said. An event they didn't foresee disturbed them."

"Maybe," the agent of the Sûreté agreed in a low voice. "Perhaps your observation is right. But the problem is that I still see something else."

"What?"

"Nothing...for the moment, at least. Before anything else, it's necessary that I see the dining room and the garden."

Monsieur Lecoq and the old Justice of the Peace went downstairs very quickly. Père Plantat showed the agent the glasses and the bottles that he had had put aside.

The man from the Prefecture took the glasses one by one, carried them up level with his eye, studied the damp spots that stained the crystal.

The exam terminated:

"No one has drunk from any of these glasses," he declared firmly.

"What? Not a single one?"

The Sûreté agent fixed on the old Justice of the Peace one of those looks which makes thought at the deepest recesses of the soul tremble and answered, putting a calculated interval between each one of his words.

"Not a single one."

Père Plantat answered only by a movement of his lips which clearly said: "You're perhaps making a lot of progress."

Monsieur Lecoq smiled, and going to open the door of the dining room, he called out:

"François!"

The valet of the late Monsieur le comte de Trémorel came running. The face of that good boy was distorted. An unheard of, a bizarre fact, this servant was sorry for his master; he was weeping for him.

"Listen to me well, my boy," the Sûreté agent said to him, using the familiar with him which characterized the employees of the Rue de Jérusalem. Listen to me well, and try to be exact, clear, and brief when answering me."

"I'm listening, Monsieur."

"In the chateau, do they usually bring up the wine from the wine cellar in advance?"

"No, Monsieur, I myself, before each meal, I go down to the cellar."

"Then there is never a certain quantity of full bottles in the dining room?"

"Never, Monsieur."

"But there must sometimes remain some not emptied."

"No, Monsieur. The late *Monsieur le comte* authorized me to carry the dessert wine to the servants' hall."

"And where do they put the empty bottles?"

"I place them, Monsieur, in the bottom of that corner cabinet and when there are a certain number, I take them to the wine cellar."

"When was the last time you took any down?"

"Oh!"—François seemed to be trying to remember—"It was a good five or six days ago."

"Good. Now, what liqueurs did your master like?"

"The dead Monsieur le comte,"—and the good boy shed a tear—"almost never drank liqueur. When by chance he wanted a little glass of brandy, he took it from the liqueur cabinet, there over the stove."

"Then there aren't any open bottles of rum or cognac in the armoires?"

"As for that, no, Monsieur."

"Thank you, my boy, you may go."

François was going to leave. Monsieur Lecoq called him back.

"Eh!" he said to him in a light tone, "while we're on the subject, look in the bottom of the corner cabinet if you want to get all your empty bottles."

"*Tiens!* There's not even one of them in it."

"Perfect," continued Monsieur Lecoq. "This time, my boy, you can show us your heels for good."

As soon as the valet had closed the door:

"*Eh bien!*" the agent of the Sûreté asked, "What does Monsieur le juge de paix think now?"

"You were right, Monsieur Lecoq."

Then the Sûreté agent smelled all the glasses and all the bottles one after the other.

"Well, good!" he exclaimed shrugging. "That's another new proof supporting my suppositions."

"What more?" asked the old Justice of the Peace.

"It isn't even wine, Monsieur, that's at the bottom of these glasses. Among all the empty bottles deposited in the bottom of that armoire, they found one of them, this one, containing vinegar. And it was from that bottle that the murderers poured out a few drops."

And grabbing the bottle, he put it under Père Plantat's nose, adding:

"Will Monsieur le juge de paix be good enough to smell."

There was nothing to disagree about. The vinegar was good, its odor the strongest. The criminals in their haste had left behind them that undeniable proof of their intention to mislead the investigation.

However, capable of the most complicated schemes, they didn't have the art to bring them to a successful conclusion. Their wickedness, as would have said the worthy Monsieur Courtois, the former colored cloth manufacturer, was sewn with white thread.

However, all their errors could be attributed to an enforced haste or to a problem they hadn't foreseen. The floor boards under your feet are on fire in a house where someone has committed a crime, a famous policeman has said.

Monsieur Lecoq seemed indignant, exasperated, as well a true artist might be, faced with the clumsy, pretentious and ridiculous piece of work of some affected schoolboy.

"That's going too far," he grumbled. "Riff-raff! Blackguards! Not just anyone can get it right. Clever riff-raff most of all. The qualities to bring it off are still needed, *Mille Diables!* and everybody, *Dieu merci!* doesn't have them."

"Monsieur Lecoq! Monsieur Lecoq!" the old Justice of the Peace exclaimed.

"Eh! Monsieur, I'm not telling anything but the truth. When you're candid to this point, you must certainly remain honest, purely and simply. It's so easy!"

Then, losing all sense of proportion, his anger seeming so great, he swallowed all at one time five or six assorted lozenge squares.

"Come now, come now," Père Plantat went on in that fatherly chiding tone used to calm a crying child. "Let's not lose our tempers. Those people lacked skill; that can't be contested. But think about the fact that in their calculations they couldn't have taken into account the cleverness of a man such as yourself."

Monsieur Lecoq, who had the vanity of all actors, was touched by the compliment and hid rather badly a grin of satisfaction.

"So let's be indulgent," continued Père Plantat. "Besides,"—He paused to give more weight to what he was going to say—"besides, you haven't seen everything yet."

One never knew when Monsieur Lecoq was acting. How could you know; he didn't always know himself. This great artist, passionate about his art, had practiced feigning all the manifestations of the soul, just as he had made a habit of wearing all sorts of costumes. And the conscientiousness of his studies had been such that, arrived at a perfection detrimental to reality, at that time he, perhaps, no longer had feelings as well as looks which were his own.

He fumed a great deal about the criminals. He made wild gestures, but he never stopped slyly observing Père Plantat and those last words made him prick up his ears.

"Then let's go see the rest," he said.

And while following the old Justice of the Peace to the garden, he spoke confidentially to the portrait on the lozenge box about his displeasure and his disappointment.

A plague on the secretive old man. We don't get anything out of that stubborn head by surprise. He'll give us the key to his puzzle when we've guessed it, not before. He's as strong as we are, my little dear. He's lacking absolutely nothing but a little practice. Nevertheless, you understand, for him to have found what escaped us, he must have had earlier clues which we don't know anything about.

Nothing had been touched in the garden.

"Look, Monsieur Lecoq," the old Justice of the Peace was saying as they followed one of the semi-circular paths which led to the Seine, "see, it's right over here, at this spot on the lawn that one of that poor Count's bedroom slippers was found. His scarf was over there, a little more to the right of that concert basket of geraniums."

They came to the edge of the river and lifted very carefully the planks the Mayor had caused to be placed there in order to keep the prints intact.

"We were conjecturing," said Père Plantat, "that the Countess, having managed to escape, was able to flee right to here and that they caught up with her and struck her a final blow here."

Was that the old judge's opinion, or was he just translating the morning's opinion? That was something Monsieur Lecoq couldn't guess.

"According to our calculations, Monsieur," the agent began again, "the Countess must not have fled. She must have been brought here dead, or logic isn't logic. What's more, let's make an examination."

He then kneeled as he had done before in the third floor bedroom, and even more carefully he studied the sand of the pathway, the stagnant water, and the tuffs of aquatic plants. Then, backing up a little, he took a stone and threw it, going forward immediately to see the effect produced in the silt. He then returned to the steps of the house and, going across the lawn, came back under the weeping willow trees, where there was still, very clear and very visible, the trail of a heavy object revealed that morning. Without the least regard for his trousers, he went across the lawn on all fours, investigating the smallest blade of grass, spreading apart the thick tuffs to see the soil better, observing very carefully the direction of the little broken stems.

That inspection terminated:

"Our deductions are confirmed," he said. "The Countess was carried here."

"Are you very certain?" asked Père Plantat.

There could be no mistake here this time, Evidently, on this point the old judge was uncertain and he was asking for an opinion other than his own, settling his hesitations.

"There is no possible error," the Sûreté agent answered.

And smiling slightly, he added:

"However, as two opinions are better than one, I'll ask you, Monsieur le juge, to hear me out. You can tell me what you think afterward."

In his investigations, Monsieur Lecoq had found a small, flexible stick and he used it while speaking to point out objects as do carnival barkers who point out the pictures on their tents which represent the marvels that can be seen on the inside.

"No, Monsieur le juge de paix, Madame de Trémorel didn't flee. If she had been struck down here, she would have fallen with some violence. As a consequence, her weight would have made the water splash out some distance and move not only the water but the silt also, and we would certainly find some washed out spots."

"But don't you think that since this morning, the sun..."

"The sun, Monsieur, would have dried up the water, but the patch of dried mud would still be there. I've looked in vain at all the pebbles on the riverbed, one at a time, and I didn't find anything. You might object that it was from the right to the left that the water and the silt gushed out. Me, I would then answer: 'Look at the clumps of gladiolas, these leaves of water lilies, these stalks of cane. On all these plants you find a layer of dust, very light, I know, but, even so, dust. Do you see a single drop of water? No. That's because there was no sudden gush of water, and therefore no violent drop. Consequently, the Countess wasn't killed here. It follows that someone carried her cadaver and they place it gently here where you found it."

Père Plantat didn't yet seem absolutely convinced.

"But those signs of a struggle, on the sand, over there," Monsieur Lecoq made a nice sign of protest.

"Monsieur le juge de paix must be joking," he said. "Those marks over there wouldn't deceive a secondary school student."

"It seems to me, however..."

"There is no way to make a mistake, Monsieur. That the sand has been moved about, burrowed into, that's positive. But all those trails which uncovered the soil covered by the sand were made by the same foot. Maybe you won't believe that. What's more they were made just with the end of the foot—and you can see that."

"Yes, in fact, I recognize that."

"Well! Monsieur, when there has been a fight on a terrain which allows investigation, as this one does, two very distinct kinds of footprints can be picked up, those of the assailant and those of the victim. The assailant, who rushes ahead, necessarily balances on the front part of his foot and leaves a print on the ground. The victim, on the contrary, who is defending himself, who is trying to avoid being fatally grabbed, puts his effort into going backward, bracing himself on his heels, and as a consequence leave the indentation of his heels in the dirt.

If the adversaries have the same strength, you find an almost equal number of prints from the end of the feet and the heels, according to how the fight proceeds. Here, what do we find?"

Père Plantat interrupted the Sûreté agent.

"Enough, Monsieur, enough," he told him. "The most incredulous man would now be convinced."

And after a moment's thought, answering his inmost thought, he added:

"No, there is no more, there can be no more objection here."

Monsieur Lecoq, on his side thought that his demonstration was well worth recompense and he swallowed a square of licorice.

"I haven't finished yet," he continued. "We're maintaining that the Countess couldn't have been finished off here. I'll add: She wasn't carried here, but dragged. The proof is easy. There are only two ways of dragging a cadaver. By the shoulders, and then the two feet drag the ground leaving two parallel furrows. By the legs, and then the head bearing down on the soil leaves a unique and rather large imprint."

Père Plantat nodded in agreement.

"In examining the lawn," the Sûreté agent continued, "I discovered the parallel furrows of the feet, but the grass was pressed down over a somewhat large space, Why?

"That was because it wasn't the cadaver of a man that had been dragged across the lawn, but that of a completely dressed woman whose petticoats were rather heavy, that of the Countess and not of the Count."

Monsieur Lecoq stopped, waiting for praise, a question, a word. But the old Justice of the Peace no longer seemed to be listening to him and appeared to be plunged into the most abstract calculations. Night was coming on. A fog, light as the smoke from a straw fire was settling over the Seine.

"We must go back in and see how the Doctor is coming along with the autopsy," Père Plantat suddenly said. And the police agent and he slowly returned to the house.

The Investigating Magistrate was standing on the steps getting ready to go meet them. Under his arm he was holding his big violet leather document case stamped with his initials, and had again put on his Orléans black overcoat.

He looked satisfied.

"I'm going to leave you in charge, Monsieur le juge de paix, he said to Père Plantat. If I want to see the Procureur Imperial [8] this evening, it's absolutely necessary that I leave this instant. This morning, when you sent for me, he had already left."

Père Plantat bowed.

"I would be very obliged to you," Monsieur Domini continued, "if you would oversee the end of the operation. Doctor Gendron has just told me he has

---

[8] Public prosecutor.

72

only a few minutes more work. I'll have his notes tomorrow morning. I'm counting on your cooperation to put on the seals everywhere they are needed and to instruct the guards. I plan to send an architect to draw up an exact plan of the house and the garden."

"Then," remarked the old Justice of the Peace, "some additional instruction will be needed probably?"

"I don't think so, "said the Investigating Magistrate in a firm tone.

Then, addressing Monsieur Lecoq:

"Well, Monsieur," he asked, "have you made some new discovery?"

"I've discovered several important facts," responded Monsieur Lecoq, "but I can't make a definite statement before having again looked upstairs in the daytime. Therefore, I'll ask you as the Investigating Magistrate not to give my report until tomorrow, in the afternoon. In addition, I believe I'll be able to answer, however confusing this affair may be..."

Monsieur Domini didn't let him finish.

"But," he interrupted. "I don't see anything confusing in this affair. On the contrary, everything seems very clear to me."

"However," Monsieur Lecoq objected, "I was thinking,..."

"I'm very sorry," the Investigating Magistrate continued, "that you were called too hastily and without great need. I now have, against the two men I had arrested, the most conclusive charges."

Père Plantat and Monsieur Lecoq exchanged a long look, betraying their great surprise. The old Justice of the Peace couldn't keep from saying, "What! Monsieur, you found some new clues!"

"Better than clues, I think," answered Monsieur Domini with a pucker of the lips which was a bad sign. "La Ripaille, that I interrogated a second time, began to get worried. He completely lost his arrogance. I was able to get him to contradict himself several times and he ended admitting to me that he had seen the murderers."

"The murderers!" exclaimed Père Plantat. "He said "the murderers?"

"He saw at least one of them. He persisted in swearing to me that he didn't recognize him. That's where we are. But the shadows of prison hold salutary terrors. Tomorrow, after a sleepless night, I'm persuaded it will be more explicit."

"But Guespin," questioned the old judge anxiously, "have your questioned Guespin again?"

"Oh!" said Monsieur Domini, "As far as that one's concerned, everything's been said."

"He confessed?" Monsieur Lecoq demanded, stupefied.

The Investigating Magistrate half turned toward the policeman as if he thought it wrong that he dared question him.

"Guespin didn't admit anything," he answered. "Nevertheless, that doesn't make his case any better. Our boatmen have returned. They haven't yet found the cadaver of Monsieur de Trémorel, that they think was swept away by the current. But they at first fished out, from the reeds at the end of the park, the other house shoe of the Count and then, in the middle of the Seine, under the bridge—pay close attention to this detail— a jacket of heavy cloth which still carries traces of blood."

"And that jacket belongs to Guespin?" the old Justice of the Peace and the Sûreté agent asked at the same time.

"Precisely. It was recognized by all the chateau servants, and Guespin admitted without any trouble that it belonged to him. But that isn't all." Monsieur Domini stopped as if to draw a breath, but really to keep Père Plantat in suspense. In the course of their differences of opinion, he thought he recognized in him a certain muted hostility, and—human frailty being what it is—it didn't make him unhappy to triumph a little.

"That's not all," he continued. "In the right pocket that jacket had a large tear and a piece of the material had been ripped off. That rag from Guespin's jacket, do you know what became of it?"

"Ah!" murmured Père Plantat, "that's the one we found in the hand of the Countess."

"It's as you said, Monsieur le juge de paix. What do you think, I ask you, of that proof of the accused's guilt?"

Père Plantat seemed dismayed. He slumped.

As for Monsieur Lecoq, who, in front of the Investigating Magistrate had again strictly assumed his attitude of retired haberdasher, he was so surprised that he almost strangled on a piece of lozenge.

"*Mille diables!*" he said, while coughing, "make a retraction; that's really too much."

He smiled in a silly way and added, in a lower voice and only for Père Plantat:

"Too much! Although just like our theory and foreseen by our calculations. The Countess held a scrap of cloth between her clenched fingers. Therefore, it must have been placed there intentionally by the murders."

Monsieur Domini hadn't picked up on the exclamation. He didn't hear Monsieur Lecoq's comment. He shook hands with Père Plantat and made an appointment with him for the next day, at the Law Courts. Then he left, taking his stenographer with him.

Guespin and the old La Ripaille, handcuffed, had been conducted by the Corbeil gendarmes some minutes earlier to the Corbeil prison.

Chapter VIII

In the billiard room of the Valfeuillu chateau, Dr. Gendron had just finished his gloomy task. He had taken off his big black suit with large sleeves, immense tails, and with the red ribbon boutonniere of the Legion of Honor, the true dress of a scientist, and he had rolled up, well above the shoulder, the sleeves of his heavy linen shirt.

Near him, on a little table used to serve refreshments, were spread out the instruments he had used, small, narrow surgical knives and several silver probes.

For his examination, he had had to undress the cadaver and following that he had recovered it with a large white sheet which vaguely showed the form of the body and on one side fell beyond the edge of the billiard table.

Night had fallen and a big lamp with a globe of unpolished crystal lit that sinister scene. Bending over a large basin of water, the Doctor was finishing washing his hands when the old Justice of the Peace and the Sûreté agent entered. At the sound of the door opening, Monsieur Gendron quickly looked up.

"Ah! It's you Plantat!" he said—in a voice in which the change was perfectly apparent. "Where is Monsieur Domini?"

"Gone."

The Doctor didn't try to hold back a movement of great impatience.

"Nevertheless, it's necessary that I speak to him," he said. "It's indispensable and the sooner the better. Because after all, I'm perhaps wrong; I could be wrong."

Monsieur Lecoq and Père Plantat had approached, closing the door the domestics of the chateau had crowded around. When they came into the circle of the lamp light, they could see how upset the usually calm expression of Monsieur Gendron was.

He was pale, paler than the dead woman stretched out under the large sheet.

The change in the Doctor's expression and voice could have been a result of the task he had just finished. Certainly, it was a painful one, but Monsieur Gendron was one of those old practitioners who have taken the pulse of all human miseries, whose loathing at the most hideous spectacles has been blunted; who, finally, have seen a great many more after all.

He must have discovered something extraordinary.

"I'm going to ask you, my dear Doctor, the question you asked me some hours ago," Père Plantat said to him. "You don't look well. Are you in pain?"

Monsieur Gendron shook his head sadly and answered with a calculated and perfectly concise meaning.

"I'll answer you, my friend, what you answered me: 'Thank you. It's nothing. I'm already better.'"

Then, these two observers, equally profound, turned away their head, as if, dreading to exchange their thoughts, they had betrayed themselves by the eloquence of their regards.

Monsieur Lecoq came forward.

"I think I know the reasons for the Doctor's emotion," he said. "He has just discovered that Madame de Trémorel was killed by just a single blow and that later the murderers furiously attacked a cadaver almost cold already."

The Doctor's eyes, halting on the Sûreté agent, had an expression of immense astonishment.

"How could you have guessed that?" he demanded.

"Oh! I didn't guess it all by myself," Monsieur Lecoq answered modestly. "I must share with the Justice of the Peace the honor of the theory that led us to foresee that fact."

Monsieur Gendron slapped his forehead.

"In fact, I now recall your recommendation," he exclaimed. "In my trouble, which was great, I really must confess, I totally forgot."

Monsieur Lecoq thought he should bow.

"Well," the Doctor continued, "what you foresaw is now fact. Between the first knife strike, which was deadly, and the others, there didn't pass, perhaps, the amount of time you might think. But I'm persuaded that Madame de Trémorel had been dead more than three hours when she was struck again."

Monsieur Gendrol had come to the billiard table and slowly lifted the mortuary sheet, uncovering the head and part of the bust of the cadaver.

"Bring us some light, Plantat," he asked.

The old Justice of the Peace obeyed. He took the lamp and went to the other side of the billiard table. His hand was trembling so much that the globe and the glass struck each other. The light vacillated, casting sinister shadows on the walls.

However, the Countess's face had been carefully cleaned. The blood stains and the mud had been removed. Thus the marks of the blows were more visible, but you could still see traces of her beauty on that livid face.

Monsieur Lecoq stood over the billiard table, bending over to examine more closely.

"Madame de Trémorel received more than eighteen knife wounds," Doctor Gendrol said. "Of all those stab wounds, only one was mortal. That's the one that's almost vertical. Look, over there, a little below the shoulder blade."

At the same time he exposed the gaping wound and with his left arm he lifted the cadaver, whose admirable blond hair spread over him.

The Countess' eyes had retained a terrified look. It seemed that from her partially open mouth this cry was going to come out: "Come to me! Help!" Père Plantat, the man with a heart of stone, turned his head away, and the Doctor, the first to master his emotion, continued in that rather emphatic voice of teachers in the surgical training room.

"The knife blade must be about three centimeters wide and about twenty-five meters long at least. All the other wounds, to the arms, to the chest, to the shoulders are relatively slight. You would have to suppose them made at least two hours after that which caused death."

"Good!" said Monsieur Lecoq.

"Note," the Doctor continued quickly, "that I'm not expressing certainty. I'm just pointing out a probability. The observed facts on which I'm basing my personal conviction, are too fleeting, by their nature too difficult to pin down, still too arguable, for me to say anything positive."

That explanation by the Doctor seemed to irritate Monsieur Lecoq considerably.

"Nevertheless," he said, "from the moment that..."

"What I can confirm, what I will confirm without reservations in front of a tribunal," Monsieur Gendron, quickly interrupted, "is that all the contusion wounds to the head, with the exception of one, were made much after death. No doubts, no arguments possible. See here, above the eye, the blow struck while she was alive. As you can see, the infiltration of blood into the openings in the tissues has been considerable. The tumor is enormous, very black in the center and filled. The other contusions have so little of this appearance that, even here, where the blow was violent enough to break the temporal bone, there is no trace of discoloration due to excess blood."

"It seems to me," Monsieur Lecoq suggested, "that from this observed and proven fact that the Countess was, after her death, struck by a blunt instrument, it can be concluded that it was equally when she had ceased to live that she was hacked by knife blows."

Monsieur Gendron thought a moment.

"It could be, Monsieur, that you're right," he finally said. "As for me, I'm persuaded of that. However, the conclusions in my report won't be the same as yours. Legal medicine must not make pronouncements except on proven facts, demonstrated, indisputable. If there is a doubt, the least one, the slightest, it must be silent. I'll say more than that: if there is uncertainty, my opinion is that the accused must receive the benefit of doubt and not the accusation."

That was certainly not the opinion of the Sûreté agent, but he was careful not to say anything. He had followed Doctor Gendron with passionate attention. The contraction of his facial expression showed the effort of his mental processes.

"It now seems to me possible to determine where and how the Countess was struck down," he said.

The Doctor had again covered the cadaver and Père Plantat had replaced the lamp on the little table. Both of them requested Monsieur Lecoq to explain himself.

"Well!" the man from the police took up again, "the direction of Madame de Trémorel's wound, proves to me that she was in her bedroom drinking tea, seated and her body leaning a little forward when she was murdered. The murderer came up from behind, his arm lifted. He had chosen his place well and struck with a terrible force. The violence to the body was such that the victim fell forward and that in the fall her forehead hit the corner of the table. She got the only wound showing an excess of blood in the tissues that we noticed on the head."

Monsieur Gendron looked from Monsieur Lecoq to Père Plantat who were exchanging looks which were at least unusual. Perhaps he suspected the game they were playing.

"Evidently," he said, "the crime must have taken place as the agent, Monsieur Lecoq, explains it."

There was another silence so embarrassing that Père Plantat judged it proper to interrupt it. Monsieur Lecoq's stubborn muteness worried him.

"Have you seen all you needed to see!" he asked him.

"For today, yes, Monsieur. For the few investigations which would still be useful for me, I need the light of day. Besides, it seems to me that, except for one detail which bothers me, I understand the affair completely."

"Then it will be necessary to get here tomorrow very early."

"I'll be here, Monsieur, at whatever time you please."

"When your investigations are finished, we'll go together to Corbeil, to the office of the Investigating Magistrate."

"I'm at the orders of Monsieur le juge de paix."

Again there was silence.

Père Plantat felt he had been found out. He understood nothing of the unusual caprice of the Sûreté agent, so talkative some hours earlier, to keep silent now.

Monsieur Lecoq himself, delighted to tease the Justice of the Peace a little, intended to astonish him prodigiously the next day by presenting him a report which would be a faithful exposé of all his ideas. While waiting, he took out his lozenge box and confided a thousand things to the portrait.

"If this is the situation," said the Doctor, "we have nothing more to do, it seems to me, but to leave."

"I was going to ask permission to do that," said Monsieur Lecoq. "I haven't eaten since this morning."

Père Plantat made a big decision.

"Are you going back to Paris this evening, Monsieur Lecoq?" he asked suddenly.

"No, Monsieur, I came here this morning with the intention of staying overnight. I even brought my overnight bag. Before coming to the chateau I dropped it at that little inn that's beside the road and that has a grenadier painted on its front. That's where I intend to eat supper and sleep."

"You'll be very uncomfortable at the Grenadier Fidèle," said the old Justice of the Peace. "You'd be better off coming to have dinner with me."

"Monsieur le juge de paix is really too kind."

"What's more, as we need to chat, and perhaps at some length, I'm offering you a bedroom. We can go pick up your overnight case as we pass by."

Monsieur Lecoq bowed, his heart in his mouth, both flattered and grateful for the invitation.

"And you, too, Doctor," continued Père Plantat. "Whether you like it or not, I'm going to take you along. Ah! Don't say no. If you absolutely insist on returning to Corbeil this evening, we'll take you there after supper."

The official seals still had to be placed. The job was quickly finished. The narrow bands of parchment, affixed by large wax stamps with the insignia of the Justice of the Peace, were placed on all the doors on the second floor, on the door of the bedroom of the hatchet, and also on the doors of the armoire where all the pieces of evidence gathered by the investigation and minutely taken down in the verbal testimony had been placed.

Chapter IX

In spite of all imaginable haste, it wasn't much before ten o'clock when Père Plantat and his invited guests could finally leave the Valfeuillu chateau.

Instead of taking the road followed in the morning, they started on a little uphill path which, skirting Madame de Lanascol's property, ran diagonally to the iron bridge. That was the shortest way to the inn where Monsieur Lecoq had left his light baggage.

While walking, the old Justice of the Peace, his mind somewhat distracted from the preoccupations of the investigation, was worrying about his friend, Monsieur Courtois.

"What misfortune has struck him?" he was saying to Doctor Gendron. "Thanks to the wicked silliness of that terrible fellow who works for him, we found out absolutely nothing. And it was on receiving the letter from his oldest daughter, Mademoiselle Laurence, that they sent for him."

They had arrived at the front of the Grenadier Fidèle.

At the door of the inn, his shoulders leaning against the door frame, his legs crossed, a big, red-faced, scurrilous fellow, built like Hercules, was smoking a long clay pipe while talking with a man just off the train, come especially from Evry to find out what had happened. He was the innkeeper.

As soon as he saw Père Plantat:

"Eh! Good! Monsieur le juge de paix," he shouted. "What a catastrophe! Come in, come in, there are several people in the room who saw the murderers. What a scoundrel that La Ripaille is! And that Guespin too! Ah! I'd be glad to make the trip to Corbeil the morning they start building their scaffold."

"Have a little charity, Master Lenfant. You're forgetting too quickly that Guespin and La Ripaille were your best customers."

The retort somewhat silenced Master Lenfant, but his impudence quickly regained the upper hand.

"Fine customers!" he answered. "That cheat Guespin got thirty-eight francs out of me that I'll never see again."

"Who knows!" The Justice of the Peace said ironically. "And, besides, this evening you're going to get more than that amount. You have as many customers as the Orcival festival has attendants."

During this short conversation, Monsieur Lecoq had gone into the inn to pick up his overnight bag.

His identity no longer a secret for anyone, he didn't receive the friendly greeting of the morning when he was taken to be a retired hosier.

Madame Lenfant, a stalwart woman who didn't need her husband to throw many drunkards out the door, scarcely deigned to speak to him. When he asked how much he owed, with a gesture of contempt she said: "Nothing."

80

As soon as he left the inn, holding his overnight bag:

"Now, let's go, quickly," said Père Plantat, because I want to pass by to get news of our poor Mayor."

The three men walked faster, and the old Justice of the Peace, agitated by gloomy forebodings, trying to fight off his worries, continued:

"If something serious has taken place at the Courtois' house, I would certainly have been told about it at this hour. Perhaps Laurence simply wrote that she was sick, or even a little indisposed. Madame Courtois, who is certainly the best woman in the world, gets upset over nothing. She would have wanted to send her husband to get their daughter immediately. This will be some false alert, you'll see."

No, some catastrophe had occurred.

In front of the iron gate of the Mayor's house were stationed some fifteen women of the neighborhood. In the middle of the group, Baptiste, the valet who did whatever he pleased, was holding forth, gesticulating.

But at the approach of the dreaded Justice of the Peace, the old gossips flew away like a flock of frightened seagulls. They had recognized him from a distance by the light of a street lamp.

Orcival possessed and proudly displayed twenty street lamps, a gift from Monsieur Courtois. They kept them lit until midnight during the evenings when there was no moon. The twenty oil street lamps were bought at an auction from a town, rich enough to pay for more dazzling light, which had just adopted gas. Orcival's street lamps didn't give off much light, perhaps, but during winter evenings, especially when there was fog, the oil let off an abominable odor.

The unexpected arrival of the old Justice of the Peace considerably irritated the tranquil Baptiste, interrupted by the flight of his audience right in the middle of a superb oratorical flourish. However, as he was very afraid of the good man, he hid his irritation under his habitual smile.

"Ah! Monsieur!" he exclaimed when Père Plantat was only three steps away, "Ah! Monsieur, what a story! I was running to get you..."

"Your master needs me?"

"You wouldn't believe it," Baptiste continued. "On leaving Valfeuillu this evening, Monsieur began to run so fast, really so fast that I could hardly keep up with him."

Baptiste interrupted himself to throw out a thought that had just come to him.

"Monsieur doesn't seem light on his feet, does he? Well! He is, you know, remarkably so, even though he's fat!"

Père Plantat tapped his foot impatiently.

"Well," the domestic continued, "we arrived here, good! Monsieur rushed like a hurricane into the drawing room where he found Madame weeping like a Mary Magdeleine. He was so out-of-breath that he could hardly speak. His eyes were bulging out of his head and he was saying like this: 'What is it? What is it?' Then Madame, who could no longer speak handed him Mademoiselle's letter that she was holding in her hand."

Baptiste's three listeners were as if on hot coals, and aware of that, the fellow spoke more slowly, drawing out his words more and more.

"Then that's how it was," he continued. "Monsieur took the letter and went to the window to see more clearly to read. Oh! He read everything in a glance. —You can really see some unusual things—He let out a hoarse cry, listen, like This, 'Oh!' Then he started to beat the air with both his hands, like a dog swimming. Then he turned around twice and he fell— *Pouf!*—like a sack, face down on the floor. That was the end."

"He's dead!" the three men cried out at the same time.

"Oh! No, Messieurs," Baptist answered with his friendly smile. "You'll see."

Monsieur Lecoq was certainly patient, but not so much as one might have thought. Irritated by the pace of the story, he put his overnight bag on the ground, and seizing Baptiste's arm with his right hand, while with his left he beat the air with a little very flexible cane, a silver-gilt weapon which he always carried.

"My boy," he said, "I urge you, right now, seriously, to hurry."

"That's all," he said. And the domestic that no one ever scolded had a terrible fear of this little blonde man with an unusual voice and a fist stronger than a vice.

This time he continued very quickly, his eye fixed on Monsieur Lecoq's cane.

"Monsieur had just had an attack. The whole house was up in the air. Everybody lost his head, except me. I thought about finding a doctor and I ran to look for someone, Monsieur Gendron, who I knew was at the chateau, or the local doctor, or the pharmacist, or just anyone. There was a bit of luck. Just at the corner of the street I met Robelot, the bonesetter.[1] 'You, I said to him, follow me.' He followed me. He pushed aside the others who were taking care of Monsieur and he bled him from both his arms. A short moment afterward, Monsieur came around; then he opened his eyes; finally he spoke. Now he's come round totally. He's stretched out on one of the drawing room couches weeping buckets of tears. He told me he wanted to see Monsieur the Justice of the Peace, and I immediately..."

"And...Mademoiselle Laurence?" Père Plantat asked, with tears in his voice.

Baptiste struck a tragic pose.

"Ah! Messieurs, don't ask me about that...It's heart-breaking!"

In rural areas a person illegally practicing medicine, setting bones, binding fractures, etc.

The Justice of the Peace and the Doctor didn't listen any further. They entered the house quickly.

Behind them came Monsieur Lecoq. He had given his overnight case to Baptiste, with: "Take that for me to the Justice of the Peace's house, and be quick about it," which made the domestic that nobody ever scolded tremble and gave his feet wings.

Misfortune, when it enters a house, seems to put its fatal mark on the threshold. Maybe that's not how it is in reality, but that's the feeling the people affected experience which cannot be overcome.

While the Doctor and Père Plantat were going across the courtyard, it seemed to them that that house, so hospitable, so gay, and so lively the evening before, had a gloomy appearance. On the upper floor, were seen lights coming and going. Someone was taking care of the younger of Monsieur Courtois' daughters, Mademoiselle Lucile, who had been overcome with a terrible attack of nerves. In the vestibule, a little fifteen-year-old girl who served as chamber maid to Mademoiselle Laurence was seated on the first step of the stairs. She had lifted her apron to cover her head, as do the country women in despair and was crying with heart-breaking sobs. Some servants were there, frightened, immobile, not knowing what to do, what would happen in this disarray.

The door to the salon, poorly lit by two candles, was wide open. In a huge armchair near the fireplace, Madame Courtois was reclining rather than sitting. At the back, near the windows looking out into the garden, Monsieur Courtois was stretched out on the couch.

They had taken off his coat and to act more quickly at the moment his life depended on being bled, they had torn and snatched off the sleeves of his shirt and his flannel cardigan. Bands of heavy cloth, as are put on after bleedings, were wrapped around his two naked arms.

Near the door a little man clothed like the comfortably situated artisans of the outskirts of Paris, seemed very embarrassed. That was Robelot, the bone-setter, who had been made to remain, fearing some new accident.

The entry of Père Plantat drew Monsieur Courtois out of the state of dismal stupor into which he had sunk. He got up and came staggering to throw himself, or rather to fall into the arms of the old Justice of the Peace.

In a harrowing voice he said:

"Ah! My friend, I'm very unfortunate! Yes, very unfortunate!"

He had changed so much the unfortunate Mayor was unrecognizable. No, he was no longer the happy man of the world with a smiling face, a look sure of himself, whose appearance, like a defiance thrown out to everyone, loudly proclaimed importance and prosperity. In a few hours he had aged twenty years. He was broken, crushed, and his distracted thoughts drifted in an ocean of bitterness. He could only repeat like meaningless words:

"Unfortunate man! Unfortunate man!"

The old Justice of the Peace, that man who had been so tested, was certainly the friend needed in those terrible crises. He had led Monsieur Courtois back to the couch, and seated near him there, he held his hands in his own. He forced himself to calm that limitless sorrow. He reminded this unfortunate father that he still had his wife, his life's companion, to mourn with him the poor dead girl. Didn't he have another daughter to love and to whom he must devote himself.

But that poor man was beyond hearing anything.

"Ah! My friend," he moaned, "You don't know everything. If she had died here, among us, surrounded by our attentions, warmed to her last breath by our tenderness, my despair would be infinite, but even so very weak in comparison to that which is killing me. If you knew! If you knew!"

Père Plantat had gotten up, as if horrified by what he was going to hear.

"But who could tell," the Mayor continued, "where and how she died! Oh! My Laurence, there was no one to hear the death rattle of your agony and to save you! What has become of you, you so young and so happy!"

He raised up, frightened by despair, and cried out:

"Let's go, Plantat. Let's go look in the Morgue." Then he fell back, murmuring the sinister word: "The Morgue."

All the witness of that heart-rending scene remained motionless and mute, frozen, holding their breath. Only the stifled groans of Madame Courtois and the sobs of the little servant girl broke the silence.

"You know that I'm your friend," murmured Père Plantat. "Yes, your best friend. Speak. Have confidence in me. Tell me everything."

"All right, then!" Monsieur Courtois began. "Know..."

But tears stifling him, he couldn't continue.

Then, holding out to Père Plantat a letter crumpled and stained with tears, he told him:

"Take it. Read it. It's her last letter."

Père Plantat approached the table where the candles were, and not without difficulty, because the writing was blotted out in several places, he read:

Forgive, Forgive, I beg you, your unfortunate daughter for the pain I'm going to cause you.

Alas! I am very guilty, but the punishment is terrible, Oh, Mon Dieu! In one misguided day, led astray by a fatal passion, I forgot everything: the example and the advice of my good and saintly mother, the most sacred duties, and your tenderness.

I didn't know how to, no, I couldn't resist the man weeping at my knees, swearing eternal love to me, and now who abandons me.

Now, it's finished. I am lost, dishonored. I am pregnant and it has become impossible for me to hide any longer the horrible sin.

Oh dear parents, do not condemn me. I am your daughter. I can't hide my face from contempt. I will not survive my honor.

When you get this letter, I will have ceased to exist. I will have left my aunt's house and I will have gone far, very far away, where no one will be able to recognize me. There I will end my misery and my despair.

Then, goodbye, oh! my beloved parents, goodbye! Let me one last time ask you on my knees to forgive me.

My dear mother, my good father, have pity on an unfortunate girl gone astray. Pardon me; forget me. May Lucile, my sister, never know...

Again, goodbye. I have courage. Duty commands.

For you, the last prayer and the supreme thought of your poor Laurence...

Big tears rolled silently down the cheeks of the old Justice of the Peace as he was deciphering that desperate letter. A rage, cold, mute, terrible, for those who knew him, tightened the muscles of his face. When he had finished he pronounced in a hoarse a single word: "Scoundrel!"

Monsieur Courtois heard that exclamation.

"Ah! Yes, scoundrel," he cried out. "Miserable man, this vile seducer who slid through the shadows to carry off my dearest treasure, my well beloved daughter. Alas! She knew nothing about life. He whispered in her ear words of love which make the heart of all young girls throb. She had faith in him, and now he has abandoned her. Oh! If I knew who he is, if I found out..."

He stopped abruptly.

The light of reason had just illuminated the abyss of despair into which he had fallen.

"No," he said. "You don't abandon in this way a beautiful and noble young girl. When she carries in her apron a dowry of a million francs, you don't abandon her, at least without being forced to. Love passes away. Cupidity remains. The infamous seducer isn't free; he was married. The scoundrel is and could only be the Count de Trémorel. He's the one who killed my daughter!..."

The silence which persisted, more doleful, proved to him that his thought was that of all those surrounding him.

"Then I was struck blind. Because I invited him to my house, that man; I held out the hand of friendship to him; I called him my friend. Oh! Don't I have a right to exact a terrible vengeance."

But he remembered the crime at Valfeuillu and it was with profound discouragement that he continued.

"And not even to be able to take revenge! I won't be able to kill him with my hands, see him suffer for hours, hear him ask for mercy! He's dead. He was felled by murderers less vile than he was."

The Doctor and Père Plantat vainly tried to calm the unhappy Mayor. He continued, exciting himself with the sound of his own words.

"Oh! Laurence, Oh, my dear one, why did you not have confidence in me. You were afraid of my anger, as if a father could ever stop loving his daughter. Lost, degraded, fallen to the level of the most vile creatures, I would still have loved you. Aren't you mine? Aren't you me? Alas! You didn't know what the heart of a father is. A father doesn't pardon; he forgets. See, you could have still been happy. Your child! Well! It would have been mine. It would have grown

85

up between us. And I would have carried over to him my tenderness for you. Your child, wouldn't that still be me. In the evening, at the fireside, I would have taken him on my knees as I took you when you were very little."

He was weeping. He had just felt tenderness. A thousand memories of the time when Laurence as a child played on the rug near him, came back to his thoughts. It seemed to him that it was yesterday.

He added: "Oh my daughter, is it society that frightens you, the wicked, hypocritical, and mocking world? But we would have gone away. I would have left Orcival, resigned as mayor. We would have gone to establish ourselves very far away, at the other end of France, in Germany, in Italy. With money everything is possible. Everything—No. I have millions and my daughter has committed suicide."

He hid his face in his hands. His sobs stifled him.

"And not to know what has become of her," he continued. "Isn't that terrible. What death has she chosen! Oh, my daughter, you so beautiful! Do you remember, you Doctor and you Plantat, her beautiful hair in curls around her very pure forehead, her big, trembling eyes, her long up-turned lashes. Her smile, you know, was the sunshine in my life. I loved her voice so much, and her mouth, her very fresh mouth which gave my cheeks wonderful, big resounding kisses. Dead! Lost! And not to know what has become of that lithesome and charming body. To think that it may lie abandoned in the slim of some river. Do you remember the Countess de Trémorel's cadaver of this morning? That's the thing that kills me. Oh *Mon Dieu!* my daughter, if I could see her again one hour, one minute, if I could place a last kiss on her cold lips.

Was this the same man who, just a short while ago from the top of the Valfeuillu steps uttered his banal remarks to the idle people of the commune? Yes. But all men are equal at the level of passion, which effaces all distinctions of the spirit and of the intellect. The despair of the man of genius doesn't express itself any differently than the despair of the imbecile.

For the last few moments, Monsieur Lecoq had been making the most sincere efforts to prevent a warm tear forming from dropping from his eyes. Monsieur Lecoq was stoic as a matter of principle and as a matter of profession. Faced with this prayer of a father in despair, he could no longer contain himself. Forgetting that they were going to see his emotion, he came out of the shadows where he had been standing, and spoke to Monsieur Courtois.

"Me," he said. "Me, Monsieur Lecoq of the Sûreté, I give you my word of honor to find the body of Mademoiselle Laurence."

The poor Mayor desperately grasped that promise as a drowning man does a blade of grass floating a hand's length away.

"Yes! We'll be able to find her, won't we. You'll help me. They say nothing's impossible for the police, that they see, that they know everything. We'll find out what became of my daughter."

"Thank you," he added. "You're a good man. I gave you a bad reception a while ago and judged you from the height of my stupid pride. Forgive me. There are stupid prejudices. I greeted you with disdain, me who didn't know how to do enough for this miserable Count de Trémorel! Thank you again; we will succeed; you'll see. We'll get help. We'll get all the police busy. We'll dig through all of France. That will take money; I have it; I have millions. Take them."

He was at the end of his strength. He trembled and fell back, exhausted, on the couch.

"He shouldn't stay here any longer," Doctor Gendron whispered in Père Plantat's ear. "He must go to bed. An inflammation of the brain wouldn't surprise me, after such shocks."

At that, the Justice of the Peace approached Madame Courtois, still collapsed in the armchair. Lost in her pain, she seemed not to have seen anything, heard anything.

"Madame," he called to her, "Madame!"

She trembled and rose in a distraught state.

"It was my fault," she said. "My very serious fault. A mother should be able to read the heart of her daughter like a book. I wasn't able to guess Laurence's secret. I'm a bad mother."

The Doctor in his turn had come forward.

"Madame," he pronounced in a commanding tone, "Your husband must be persuaded to lie down without delay. His condition is serious. And a little sleep is absolutely necessary. I'll have a potion prepared for you..."

"Ah! *Mon Dieu!*" the poor woman cried out, wringing her hands. Ah, *Mon Dieu!*"

And the fear of a new misfortune as appalling as the first, gave her back some presence of mind. She called to the servants, who helped Monsieur Courtois regain his bedroom.

She also went upstairs, followed by Doctor Gendron.

Only three people remained in the drawing room, the Justice of the Peace, Monsieur Lecoq, and, still near the door, Robelot, the bone setter.

"Poor Laurence," whispered the old Justice of the Peace. "Unfortunate young girl!..."

"It seems to me," remarked the Sûreté agent, "that it's her father most of all who's to be pitied. At his age, with such a blow, he may not get over it. Whatever happens, his life is ruined."

He also, the man from the police, he had been touched, and if he was hiding it as much as possible—everyone has his ego—he had formally admitted it to the portrait on the lozenge box.

The Justice of the Peace added: "I had something like a foreboding of what happened today. Me, I had guessed Laurence's secret. Unfortunately, I guessed it too late."

"And you didn't try..."

"What? In these delicate circumstances, when a respectable family's honor depends on a word, it's necessary to be extremely circumspect. What could I do? Warn Courtois? Evidently not. Besides, he would have refused to believe me. He's one of those men who won't listen to anything. Only the brutal fact will disabuse him."

"It could have been taken up with the Count de Trémorel."

"The Count would have denied everything. He would have asked me why I was meddling in his affairs. Such a course of action would simply have ended with a rupture with Courtois."

"But the young girl…?"

Père Plantat heaved a great sigh.

He answered: "Even though I detest getting mixed up in something which, after all, does not concern me, one day I tried to talk to her. Arming myself with infinite precautions, with a totally maternal delicacy, I may say, without letting her know that I knew everything, I tried to show her the abyss toward which she was running."

"And what did she answer?"

"Nothing. She laughed. She joked, as women who have a secret to hide laugh and joke. And after that, it was impossible for me to find myself alone with her fifteen minutes. And before that foolish action on my part, because speaking to her was foolish, I should have acted. I was her best friend. There wasn't a day that she didn't come to pillage my greenhouse. I let her devastate my rarest petunias, me, who wouldn't give the Pope a flower. She had taken on the authority to treat me like her local florist. It was for her that I brought together a collection of Cap heather. It was my job to take care of her window boxes."

His tenderness was at that point so unrestrained that Monsieur Lecoq, who was watching him out of the corner of his eye, couldn't hold back a mocking smile.

The Justice of the Peace was going to continue, when, having turned around at a sound coming from the vestibule, he was aware of the presence of Robelot, the bone setter. His expression immediately took on a look of the greatest annoyance.

"You, you're still here?" he asked.

The bonesetter smiled lowly and obsequiously.

"Yes, Monsieur le juge de paix, very much at your service."

"That is to say you were listening to us?"

"Oh!, as for that, no, Monsieur le juge de paix, I was waiting for Madame Courtois to find out if she has anything to ask me to do."

A sudden thought crossed Père Plantat's mind. The expression in his eyes changed. He made a sign to Monsieur Lecoq as if to call his attention, and speaking to the bonesetter in a gentler tone:

"Then come here, Master Robelot," he said.

With a glance Monsieur Lecoq had looked the man up and down and evaluated him. The Orcival bonesetter was a little man, puny in appearance, of Herculean strength in reality. His close-cropped hair revealed a wide and intelligent forehead. His pale eyes were of those in which burn all the fire of covetousness and which express, when he forgets to hide it, a cynical audacity. A vile smile always ran across his flat, thin lips. Not a single hair of a beard grew on his chin.

From a distance, with his diminutive stature and his beardless face, he resembled those odious Parisian street urchins who are almost the essence of all corruption. Their imagination is dirtier than the gutter where they look for lost *sous* among the paving stones.

At the invitation of the Justice of the Peace, the bonesetter, smiling and bowing, took several steps into the drawing room

"Does Monsieur le juge de paix, by chance and by my good fortune, need me?" he asked.

"Not at all, Master Robelot, in no way. I only want to congratulate you on your timely arrival to bleed Monsieur Courtois. Your lancing his wrist may have saved his life."

"As a matter of fact, that's very possible," the bonesetter answered.

"Monsieur Courtois is generous. He will recompense this very great service."

"Oh! I won't ask him for anything. I don't need, *Dieu Merci,* anyone. Let me be paid only what I'm due, and I'm happy."

"Yes, I know. I've been told that. Your business is doing very well. You must be content."

Monsieur Plantat's words had become friendly, almost fatherly. You could see that he was very interested in Master Roberlot's prosperity.

"Satisfied!" the bonesetter retorted, "not so much as Monsieur le juge de paix thinks. Life is very expensive for poor people. Then there are those taxes, those damned taxes that aren't paid."

"Nevertheless, it was you who bought the Morin meadow, at the bottom of the Evry hill."

"Yes, Monsieur."

"It's good property, that Morin meadow, even though it's a little wet. Fortunately you have some little gems in the pieces of land the widow Frapesle sold you."

The bonesetter had never seen the Justice of the Peace so talkative, so nice a fellow, and he couldn't help being a little surprised.

"Three really bad pieces of land," he said.

"Not so bad as you say. Then, didn't you also buy something at the Peyron miners liquidation at auction?"

"A patch of land worth nothing at all."

"That's true, but paid for in cash. You can see that the job of a doctor without a diploma isn't so bad."

Already charged several time for practicing medicine without a license,

Master Robelot thought he should protest.

"If I cure people," he maintained, "I don't make them pay."

Père Plantat continued: "Then there's your herb business which brings in money?"

Decidedly, the conversation was moving toward an interrogation. The bonesetter was becoming uneasy.

"I earn a little with the herbs," he answered.

"And, as you are a careful and economical man, you buy land."

"In addition, animals bring me in something," Robelot answered quickly. "People come to get me from three leagues away. I take care of horses, cows, and sheep."

"Still without a diploma?"

The bonesetter took on a disdainful expression.

"It's not a piece of parchment," he said, "that gives knowledge. Me, I'm not afraid of veterinarians trained in schools. It's in the fields and in the stables that I study animals. Without bragging, there's no one better than I am for treating swelling, dizziness, or the contagious diseases of sheep."

The Justice of the Peace's tone became friendlier and friendlier.

"I know," he continued, "that you are a clever man with a lot of experience. And let me tell you, Doctor Gendron, with whom you worked, praised your intelligence to me just a short time ago."

The bonesetter had a slight tremor, which, although very slight, did not at all escape Père Plantat, who continued:

"Yes, this dear doctor claimed never have met a laboratory assistant as capable as you. 'Robelot,' he said to me, 'has so much aptitude for chemistry, and likes it so much at the same time, that he understands as well as I do how to handle some extremely dangerous chemicals.'"

"*Dame!* I worked as well as I could, since I was well paid, and I've always liked to learn."

"And you were in a good school with Monsieur Gendron, Master Robelot. He's doing some very interesting research. His work and his experiments concerning poisons are especially very remarkable."

The uneasiness which, little by little, was coming over the bonesetter, was beginning to come apparent. His look became shifty.

"Yes," he said in order to have something to say, "I've seen some very curious experiments."

"Well," Père Plantat said, "You who like to learn, and who're curious, you have something to look forward to. The Doctor currently will have a nice subject to study. And he will certainly take you on as an assistant."

Master Robelot was a great deal too clever not to have already guessed for several minutes that that conversation, that interrogation, rather, had a purpose. But what? What was the Justice of the Peace getting at? He was asking himself, not without a kind of irrational terror. And going back over, with lightening rapidity of thought, how many questions, seemingly careless, he had answered and where these questions had led him, he trembled.

He thought he would be smart and dodge any other questions by saying:

"I'm always available to my old teacher whenever he needs me."

"He'll need you, I can guarantee you," pronounced Père Plantat.

And in a casual tone which belied the leaden look with which he menaced the bonesetter of Orcival, he added:

"The interest will be enormous and the task difficult. We are going, my good fellow, to exhume Monsieur Sauvresy's cadaver."

Robelot was assuredly prepared for something terrible and he was armed with all his audacity. Nevertheless, the name of Sauvresy fell on his head like a blow from a mallet. And it was in a strangled voice that he stammered:

"Sauvresy!"

Père Plantat, who didn't wish to look, had already turned away his head, and continued in the tone one takes in chatting about indifferent things, of one thing and another.

"Yes, we will exhume Sauvresy. It's suspected—the law always has suspicions—that he didn't die from a perfectly natural sickness."

The bonesetter leaned against the wall so as not to fall.

"Then," the Justice of the Peace continued: "Doctor Gendron has been called in. He has, as you know, found some reagents which can detect the presence of an alkaloid, whatever it may be, in material submitted for his analysis. He has told me about a certain treated paper."

Making a heroic appeal to all his strength, Robelot forced himself to recover under the blow and to compose his expression.

"I know about Dr. Gendron's work," he said, "but I don't see who the suspicions Monsieur le juge de paix is talking about could fall on."

Père Plantat from then on had made up his mind.

"I think they have something better than suspicions," he answered. "Madame de Trémorel was, as you know, murdered. Her papers had to be inventoried. They found letters, a most damning declaration, some receipts,… what else I don't know."

Robelot also knew what was coming up. Nevertheless, he still had the strength to say:

"*Baste!* You have to hope the law is making a mistake."

Then, such was that man's strength that despite the nervous trembling which shook his whole body as the wind moves about the leaves of the aspen tree, he added, forcing his thin lips to outline a smile:

"Madame Courtois is not coming down. I'm expected at home. I'll come back tomorrow. Good evening to you, Monsieur le juge de paix and the rest of the company."

He left and soon they could hear the sand in the court yard squeaking under his feet. He was going away, stumbling like a drunken man.

When the bonesetter had gone, taking off his hat, Monsieur Lecoq came to stand in front of Père Plantat.

"I surrender, Monsieur," he said, "and I bow to you. You are as clever as my teacher, the great Tabaret."

Decidedly, the Sûreté agent was intrigued. The artist in him came alive. He found himself faced with a beautiful crime, one of those crimes which triple the sales of the *Gazette des Tribunaux*.[9] Undoubtedly, many of the details escaped him. He didn't know the starting point, but he saw things as a whole.

Having penetrated the Justice of the Peace's theory, he had followed step by step the workings of that very nimble observer's thoughts. He was discovering the complications of an affair that had appeared so simple to Monsieur Domini. His subtle mind worked to take apart the entangled skein of deductions holding together all the circumstances revealed to him during the day, and he sincerely admired Père Plantat. While looking at the beloved portrait, he was thinking:

It's up to the two of us now, this cunning good fellow and me. We'll get to the bottom of everything.

However, it was a matter of not showing himself too inferior.

"Monsieur," he said, "while you were questioning this scoundrel who will be very useful to us, I haven't wasted my time. I've looked about a little everywhere, under the furniture, and I found this scrap of paper."

"Let's see."

"It's the envelope of Mademoiselle Laurence's letter. Do you know where the aunt she went to spend some days with lives?"

"At Fontainebleau, I believe."

"Well, this envelope bears a stamp from Paris, from the Rue Saint-Lazare office. I know this stamp doesn't prove anything..."

"It's still a clue."

"That's not all. I took the liberty of reading Mademoiselle Laurence's letter that is still on the table."

Involuntarily, Père Plantat frowned.

"Oh," Monsieur Lecoq continued, "that's perhaps not very delicate, but the end justifies the means! Well! Monsieur, you've read it, that letter. Have you thought it over, studied the hand writing, weighed the words, gone back over the closely related thoughts?"

"Ah!" exclaimed the Justice of the Peace, "then I wasn't wrong. You had the same idea as I did."

And in the enthusiasm of his hope, taking the hands of the man from the police, he pressed them between his own like those of an old friend. He was going to continue, but they heard footsteps on the stairs. Doctor Gendron appeared on the threshold.

---

[9] The most famous French legal periodical of the nineteenth century.

"Courtois is better," he said. "He's already half asleep. He'll pull out of it."

"Then we don't have anything more to do here," the Justice of the Peace said. "Let's leave. Monsieur Lecoq must be half dead with hunger."

He gave some orders to the servants who were still in the vestibule and rapidly took away his two guests.

The Sûreté agent had slid poor Laurence's letter and the envelope of that letter into his pocket.

Chapter X

The Justice of the Peace's house was narrow and small. It was the house of a wise man. There were three large rooms on the ground floor, four bedrooms on the second floor. An attic and some attic rooms under the eaves for servants made up all the rest of the dwelling.

There were signs everywhere of the carefree man who, shutting himself off from the free-for-all of the rest of the world, had withdrawn into himself many years ago. He was a man who had ceased attaching the least importance to the objects surrounding him. The furnishings, in the past very beautiful, had slowly deteriorated, had become worn out and had not been renewed. The moldings on the large pieces of furniture had peeled off. The clocks had stopped telling the hour. The horsehair stuffing in the armchairs could be seen through the upholstery in many places. The sun had eaten through the color of the drapes in spots.

Only the library showed the daily care given it. The volumes spread out their sad bindings and crinkled gold embossing on large shelves of sculpted oak. Near the fireplace, a movable shelf, marvelously constructed, held Père Plantat's favorite books, the discreet friends of his solitude.

The greenhouse, an immense, princely greenhouse marvelously laid out, furnished with all the improvements imaginable in these days, was the only luxury of the Justice of the Peace. There, in planters filled with sifted potting soil he planted his petunias in the springtime. There, the exotic plants Laurence liked to fill her window boxes were born and prospered. There, flourished 137 varieties of heather.

Two servants, Madame Petit, the widow, cook and housekeeper, and Louis, a gardener of genius, peopled that interior. If they didn't bring more cheerfulness to it, if they didn't fill it with noise, that was because Père Plantat, who seldom spoke, detested listening to people talk. In his house, silence was absolutely necessary.

Ah! That was hard for Madame Petit, especially at the beginning. She was a great talker, rattling away to the point that when she couldn't find anyone to chat with, in despair she went to confession. To confess, that was still to talk. Twenty times she almost quit her job. Twenty times the thought of an assured income, three-fourth honest and legal, stopped her. Then, days followed days, and in the long run she became accustomed to dominating her tongue's revolts. She became accustomed to that monastic silence.

But the devil takes his due. She took revenge outside for the deprivations of the inside, and among the neighbors she made up for the time lost in the house. It was certainly not without reason that she was reputed to be the worst gossip in Orcival. They said she could set the mountains to talking nonsense.

You could easily understand Madame Petit's anger the fatal day of the murder of the Count and the Countess de Trémorel. At eleven o'clock, after having gone for the news, she had prepared lunch. No Monsieur. She had waited an hour, two hours, five hours, keeping her water boiling for the *oeufs à la coque*. Still no Monsieur. She wanted to send Louis to look for him, but Louis, like all researchers, who talk very little and are very little curious, suggested to her that she go herself. And to top it all off, the house had been besieged by neighbors who, believing Madame Petit must be well informed, demanded news. No news to give them.

Nevertheless, about five o'clock, absolutely giving up on lunch, she started preparations for dinner.

What was the use! When eight o'clock struck on the handsome Orcival clock, Monsieur still hadn't returned. At nine o'clock the housekeeper was beside herself. And while eaten up with worry, as she put it strongly herself, she scolded the taciturn Louis who had just watered the garden and who, seated at the kitchen table was melancholically gulping down a bowl of soup.

A doorbell interrupted her.

"Ah! Finally," she said, "here's Monsieur."

No, it wasn't Monsieur. It was a little twelve-year-old boy that the Justice of the Peace had sent from Valfeuillu to tell Madame Petit that he was going to return bringing two guests who would dine and sleep at the house. Hearing that, the housekeeper almost fell backward. That was the first time in five years that Père Plantat had invited someone to dine. That invitation must hide some strange things.

So thought Madame Petit, and her anger redoubled with her curiosity.

"To tell me to fix a dinner at this hour!" she grumbled. "I ask you, is there any common sense to that?"

Then, reflecting that time was getting short:

"Let's go, Louis," she continued. "This isn't the time to stay planted in one spot. Get to work, my boy. The neck of three pullets have to be rung. Then go see if there are some ripe grapes in the greenhouse. Get me down some conserves. Go down in the cellar quickly!"

The dinner was well underway when the doorbell rang again. That time it was Baptiste, the servant of the Mayor of Orcival. He arrived in a very bad humor, carrying Monsieur Lecoq's overnight bag.

"Take this," he said to the housekeeper. "Here's what the individual who's with your master ordered me to bring."

"What individual?"

The servant that no one ever scolded still had a sore arm from Monsieur Lecoq's grasp. His resentment was great.

"How do I know! I was told he was a police spy sent from Paris for the business at Valfeuillu. He's probably not very good, has bad manners, is brutal...and a sloppy dresser."

"But he's not the only one with Monsieur?"

"No. Doctor Gendron is with him too."

Madame Petit was burning with impatience to obtain information from Baptiste, but Baptiste was in a hurry to return to what was happening at his master's house. He left without having said anything. More than one long hour still passed, and Madame Petit, furious, had just sworn to Louis that she was going to throw the dinner out the window, when the Justice of the Peace finally appeared, followed by his two guests.

Not a word had been exchanged between them since they left the Mayor's house. After the shocks of the evening, which had more or less thrown them out of their habitual frame of mind, they felt the need to think, to get back and resume their composure.

In vain Madame Petit, when they entered the dining room, searched her master's expression and that of his two guests. They told her nothing. But she didn't share Baptiste's opinion. She thought Monsieur Lecoq seemed meek and even a little stupid.

The dinner had necessarily to be less silent than the way home, but by a silent and understood agreement the Doctor, Monsieur Lecoq, and Père Plantat avoided even the slightest allusion to the day's events.

Seeing them so peaceful, so calm, conversing about unimportant things, you would never have thought that they had just been witnesses, almost actors in the drama at Valfeuillu. From time to time, it's true, a question remained without an answer. Sometimes a reply came late, but nothing appeared on the surface of the sensations or the thoughts the banal words exchanged hid.

Louis, who had gone to change into a clean jacket, came and went behind the guests, a white napkin draped over his arm, carving meat and serving drinks. Madame Petit brought in the various dishes, coming in three times when only one time was needed, eavesdropping, leaving the door open as often as she could.

Poor housekeeper! She had improvised an excellent dinner and no one took notice of it.

Certainly, Monsieur Lecoq didn't disdain good cuts of meat; fresh fruits and vegetables delighted him. Nevertheless, when Louis placed a basket of magnificent golden grapes on the table—from the 9th of July— there was no smile on his gourmand mouth.

Doctor Gendron himself would have been hard put to it to say what he had eaten.

The dinner coming to an end, Père Plantat began to suffer from the constraint the presence of the servants imposed. He called the housekeeper.

"You'll serve us coffee in the library. After that you'll be free to leave, as will Louis."

"But these gentlemen don't know where their bedrooms are," hinted Madame Petit. This advice, delivered in the tone of an order, threw off her projects of espionage. "These gentlemen may need something."

The Justice of the Peace said in a dry tone: "I will show these gentlemen their bedrooms. And if they need something, I'm here."

She had to obey. They passed into the library. There, Père Plantat reached for a box of Havana cigars from London. He offered it to his guests, saying:

"I think it would be healthy," he suggested, "to smoke a cigar before going to bed."

Monsieur Lecoq carefully took out the blondest and the best made of the London Havanas and when he had lit it:

"You can go to bed, gentlemen," he answered. "As for me, I see myself condemned to a sleepless night. Before beginning to write, I still need some information from Monsieur the Justice of the Peace."

Père Plantat nodded in sign of agreement.

"We must make a summary," the Sûreté agent continued, "and put our observations down in agreement. All our lights together aren't too much to throw a little daylight into this affair, one of the most shadowy that I've encountered in a long time. The situation is perilous and time is short. On our expertise depends the fate of several innocent beings that are overwhelmed with more than enough charges to snatch a 'YES!' from whatever jury. We have a theory, but Monsieur Domini has one of them too, and his is based on material facts, whereas ours is founded on only very debatable suspicions."

"We have better things than suspicions, Monsieur Lecoq," said the old Justice of the Peace.

"I think the same as you do, but we still have to prove them," seconded the Doctor.

"And, a thousand devils, I will prove it," Monsieur Lecoq quickly answered. "The business is complicated, difficult. So much the better! Eh! If it was simple, I would return immediately to Paris, and tomorrow I'd send you one of my men. I leave easy puzzles to children. Me, what I need is the unsolvable riddle to solve; the battle, to show my strength; the obstacle, to overcome."

Père Plantat and the Doctor couldn't believe their eyes when looking at the policeman. He was as if transfigured.

Yet he was the same man, yellow hair and sideburns, the frock coat of a bourgeois, and, nevertheless, his look, his voice, his expression, even his bearing had changed. His eyes glittered, his voice had a metallic and vibrant timber, his commanding gesture confirmed the audacity of his thoughts and the strength of his resolution.

"You've thinking, Messieurs," he continued, "that for the some thousand francs the Prefecture pays, you don't get a policeman like me. If you don't have the aptitude, you might as well set up shop as a grocer. Such as you see me, at twenty years old, after solid studies, I was employed as an arithmetician with an astronomer. It's a nice position. My employer gave me 70 francs a month and lunch. In consideration of which I should have been satisfied and cover I don't know how many square meters with ciphers every day.

Monsieur Lecoq suddenly took several puffs at his cigar, which was going out, while at the same time looking curiously at Père Plantat.

In a moment he continued.

"Well! You can imagine I didn't think myself the happiest of men. That's because I forgot to tell you. I had two small vices: I liked women and I liked gambling. Nobody's perfect. I thought the 70 francs from my astronomer not sufficient. And while lining up my columns of numbers, I was thinking about a way to make a fortune overnight. After all, there's only one way: appropriate someone else's wealth cleverly enough not to be caught. That's what I thought about from morning to night. My mind, active in drawing up schemes, presented me with a hundred projects, one more practical than the next. I would astonish you if I told you only the half of what I imagined at that time. You know, if there existed a lot of thieves as strong as I, it would be necessary to blot the word property from the dictionary. Precautions as well as safes would be useless. Fortunately for those who own anything, criminals are idiots. The swindlers of Paris— the capital city of intelligence—are still robbing in the American style and robbing like the petty thieves of the slums. That's shameful."

What's he getting at? wondered Doctor Gendron.

And he alternately examined Père Plantat, who seemed to be gathering his thoughts together, and the Sûreté agent, who was already continuing.

"As for me, one day I was afraid of my ideas. I had just invented a little operation by means of which you could lift 200,000 francs from just any banker without any more danger and as easily as I lift this cup. It was so good that I told myself: 'My boy, if this goes on, a moment will come when you will pass naturally from the idea to the execution.'

"That's why, being born honest—by chance—and absolutely insisting on using the aptitudes that were natural instincts, a week later I thanked my astronomer and I joined the Prefecture. Fearing to become a thief, I became a policeman."

"And are you happy with the change?" asked Doctor Gendron.

"*Ma foi!* Monsieur, I have yet to have my first regret. I'm happy because I'm exercising my abilities in calculation and deduction freely and usefully. Existence has an enormous attraction for me because I still have a passion which dominates all the others: curiosity. I'm curious."

The Sûreté agent smiled. He was thinking of the double meaning of that word: *curious.*

"There are some people," he continued, "who're passionate about the theater. That passion is somewhat mine. However, I don't understand how you can take pleasure in the miserable staging of fictions which are to life a little like the lamps of the footlights are to the sun. To be interested in feelings more or less well expressed, but fictitious, seems to me a monstrous custom. What! You can laugh at the jokes of an actor that you know to be the father of a needy family! What! You can pity the sad fate of a poor actress who poisons herself, when you know that on leaving the theater you're going to meet her on the boulevard! That's pathetic!"

"Let's close the theaters!" murmured Doctor Gendron.

"More demanding or more blasé than the public," Monsieur Lecoq continued, "me, I need real actors or real dramas. Society, that's my theater. My own actors have a natural smile and weep real tears.

"A crime is committed," he continued. "That's the prologue. I come in. The first act begins. At one glance I size up the least nuances of the stage setting. Then I try to get into the motives; I group my characters; I tie the episodes to the main plot; I put together all the situations. That's the exposition.

"Soon, the action becomes serious. The thread of my inductions leads me to the guilty person. I guess who he is; I arrest him; I deliver him to justice.

"Then, we come to the big scene. The accused person fights; he uses trickery; he wants to throw you off the track. But armed with the weapons I've forged, the Investigating Magistrate overwhelms him. He's troubled. He doesn't confess, but he's confused.

"And surrounding this principal character, how many secondary characters there are: the accomplices, the instigators of the crime, the friends, the enemies, the witnesses! Some of them are terrible, frightening, gloomy, others grotesque. And you don't know what the comic in the horrible is.

"The High Court, that's my last scene. The prosecution speaks, but I'm the one who furnished the ideas. The sentences are the embroidery thrown on the canvas of my report. The Judge puts the questions to the jury members. What emotion! The fate of my drama will be decided. If the jury answers NO, it's all over. My play was bad. I was booed off the stage. On the contrary, if it's YES, my play was a good one. They applaud me. I triumph.

"Without adding the fact that the next day I can go see my principal actor and slap him on the back, saying to him: 'You lost, old boy; I'm stronger than you are!"

Monsieur Lecoq, at this very moment, was he in good faith, or was he playing a role! What was the purpose of that autobiography?

Without seeming to notice the surprise of his listeners, he took a new London cigar that he lit from the top of the glass globe of the lamp. Then, on purpose or by accident, instead of putting the lamp back on the table, he placed it on the corner of the fireplace mantle. In that way, thanks to the large lampshade, Père Plantat's face was fully illuminated, whereas that of the Sûreté agent, who remained standing, was in the shadows.

"I must admit without false modesty," he continued, that I've rarely been booed off the stage. And nevertheless I'm not as much of a fop as people like to say. Like every man I have my Achilles' heel. I have conquered the demon of gambling. I haven't triumphed over that of women."

He let out a big sigh which he accompanied by that sad, resigned gesture of men who have accepted their shortcomings.

"That's how it is. There's a certain woman for whom I'm nothing but an imbecile. Yes, me, a Sûreté agent, the terror or robbers and murderers, me, who has flattened all the plots of all the swindlers in every level of society, who for ten years has swum in the middle of vice, in the middle of crime, who has washed the dirty linen of all types of corruptions, who has measured the depth of all human infamy, me, who knows everything, who has seen everything, who has heard everything, me, Lecoq, at the end, for her I'm simpler and more naïve than a child. She deceives me. I see it, and she proves to me that I'm mistaken. She lies. I know it; I prove it to her... and I believe her."

He added lower and sadly, "That's because it's one of those passions that age, far from extinguishing, only fans and to which a feeling of shame and powerlessness gives a terrible bitterness. You love and the certainty of not being able to be loved is one of those pains that has to be experienced to understand its immensity. In rational hours, you look at yourself and judge yourself. You say to yourself: 'No, that's impossible; she's almost a child and I'm almost an old man.' You tell yourself that, but, always, at the bottom of your heart, stronger than reason, stronger than the will, than experience, a light of hope persists. And you say to yourself: 'Who knows? Perhaps! You wait for, what? A miracle? There's no longer any. That doesn't matter. You hope."

Monsieur Lecoq stopped, as if emotion kept him from continuing.

Père Plantat had continued methodically smoking his cigar, blowing out smoke at regular intervals, but his face had an indefinable look of suffering, his moist expression wandered, his hands trembled. He stood up, took the lamp from the mantle, put it back on the table and sat down.

The meaning of that scene finally burst through the mind of Monsieur Gendron.

In reality, without going too far from the truth, the Sûreté agent had just attempted one of the most perfidious experiments in his repertory. He thought it useless to push it any further. Henceforth he knew what he needed to know.

After a moment of silence, Monsieur Lecoq shook as if waking from a dream. Taking out his watch, he said:

"*Mille diables!*" he said, "Here I am babbling away, and it's getting late."

"And Guespin is in prison," said the Doctor.

"No, we'll get him out, Monsieur," answered the Sûreté agent, "if he's innocent after all. Because this time I have my business in hand, my novel, if you like, and without the slightest gap. However, there's one fact of capital importance that I can't explain by myself."

"Which one is that?" questioned Père Plantat.

"Is it possible that Monsieur de Trémorel had an immense interest in finding something, a legal document, a letter, a paper, just some object in a thin volume hidden in his own house?"

"Yes," answered the Justice of the Peace. "That's possible."

"What I need is certainty," said Lecoq.

Père Plantat thought a moment.

"Well, then! I'm sure, perfectly sure, that if Madame Trémorel died suddenly, the Count would have torn down the house to find a certain paper he knew to be in the possession of his wife, and that I myself have had in my own hands."

"Then," continued Monsieur Lecoq, "that's the drama. Coming into Valfeuillu, I was, as were you, Messieurs, struck with the terrible disorder in the apartment. Like you, I at first thought that this disorder was simply artificial. I was wrong. A closer examination convinced me of that. The murderer, it's true, had torn up everything, broken the furniture, hacked up the armchairs, to make it appear a band of furious men had come through. But in the middle of these acts of premeditated vandalism, I was able to follow the involuntary traces of an exact, minute, and I would add, patient, search.

"Everything seemed pillaged haphazardly, didn't it? A hatchet was used to break into furniture that could be opened by hand. They had broken apart drawers that were not locked, or to which the key was in the lock. Was this stupidity? No. Because in reality there wasn't a single place that could conceal a letter which was not looked into. The drawers of various pieces of small furniture had been thrown about here and there, but the narrow spaces between the grooves and the body of the pieces of furniture had been examined. And I had the proof of that when I made out finger prints in the dust that had accumulated in those places. The books were laying on the floor pell-mell, but all of them had been shaken, and some with such violence that the bindings had been ripped off. We had found all the planks of the mantel piece in place, but some had been lifted up The chairs hadn't had a sword stuck through them just for the pleasure of tearing up the stuffing. The seats were being probed.

"The quickly acquired certainty of an intense search, at first threw off my suspicions. I told myself: *The criminals were searching for hidden money; therefore, they were not members of the household.*"

"But," objected the Doctor, "they could be members of the household and not know where the valuables were hidden. This brings in Guespin..."

"Pardon," interrupted Monsieur Lecoq. "I'll explain myself another way. I found some clues such that the murderer could only be a person unusually tied to Madame de Trémorel, such as her lover or her husband. Those were my ideas at the time."

"And now?"

"Right now," answered the agent, "and with the certainty that they were looking for something other than money, I'm not very far from believing that the guilty person is the man whose cadaver they're now searching for, Count Hector de Trémorel."

Doctor Gendron and Père Plantat had guessed this name, but no one had yet dared to formulate these suspicions. They were expecting this name, de Trémorel, and nevertheless, thrown out thus in the middle of the night in that big dark room, by this person, who was at best bizarre, made them tremble with an unspeakable fright.

"Notice," Monsieur Lecoq continued, "that I said, 'I believe.' For me, at the moment, the Count's crime is only extremely probable. Let's see if the three of us can arrive at certainty.

"Because, you see, Messieurs, the investigation of a crime is nothing more than the solution to a problem. Given the crime, obvious, clear, you begin by looking into all the serious or useless circumstances, the details, the particulars. When circumstances and particulars have been carefully collected, you classify them by order and by date. In this way you understand the victim, the crime and the situation. The thing remaining to be found is the third term, the X, the unknown. That is to say, the guilty person.

"The task is difficult, but not so great as is thought. It's a question of looking for a man whose guilt explains all the circumstances, all the revealed particulars—all, understand me well. Encountering that man is probable—and nine times out of ten the probability becomes reality—you get the guilty person.

"This is the way, Messieurs, Tabaret, my master, the master of all of us, went about it, and in his whole life he never made a mistake but three times."

Monsieur Lecoq's explanation had been so clear and his demonstration so logical that the old judge and the doctor couldn't hold back an exclamation of admiration:

"Very well done!"

After taking a bow, the Sûreté agent said: "Then let's examine together if the hypothetical guilt of the Count de Trémorel explains all the circumstances of the crime at Valfeuillu."

He was going to continue, but Doctor Gendron, seated near the window, suddenly stood up.

"Someone is walking in the garden!" he exclaimed.

They all came to the window. The weather was superb. The night was clear. A large open space spread out in front of the library windows. They looked out. They saw no one. Monsieur Lecoq continued.

"Then let us suppose, Messieurs, that—guided by certain events that we'll look into later—Monsieur de Trémorel was led to resolve to get rid of his wife. The crime decided on, it's clear that the Count must have thought about and looked for the means to commit it without getting caught, weighing the consequences and evaluating the dangers of the enterprise.

"We must admit then that the events which led him to that extremity must have been such that he feared being concerned about and dreading later searches even in case his wife died of natural causes."

"That's the truth," approved the Justice of the Peace.

"So Monsieur de Trémorel came at last to the plan of killing his wife brutally, striking her with a hatchet, with the idea of arranging things in such a way as to have it believed that he also had been murdered, letting suspicions hover

over someone innocent, or at least on an accomplice infinitely less guilty than he.

"He resigned himself in advance, in adopting this system, to disappearing, to fleeing, to hiding, to changing personalities, to getting rid of, in a word, Count Hector de Trémorel, in order to reappear under another name, a new official identity.

"These premises, very admissible, are enough to explain a whole series of circumstances, irreconcilable at first view. First of all, it explains to us how, precisely the night of the crime, he had a whole fortune at Valfeuillu.

"And that circumstance seems decisive to me. Usually, when you receive important valuables to keep at your house, you ordinarily hide it as much as possible. Monsieur de Trémorel didn't take that elementary precaution. He showed everybody the stacks of bank bills. He handled them; he spread them out; the servants saw them, almost touched them. He wanted everyone to be sure to know and repeat that he had considerable sums at his home, easy to take, to carry away, to hide.

"And what moment did he choose for staging this, imprudent at any time? Just at the moment he knew, when everyone in the neighborhood knew, that he would spend the night alone with Madame de Trémorel in the chateau.

"Because he wasn't ignorant of the fact that all the servants were invited in the evening of the 8th of July to the marriage of the former cook, Madame Denis. He was so little ignorant of that fact that he was the one who paid for the marriage and set the date himself when Madame Denis came to introduce her future husband to her former employers.

"You may tell me, perhaps, that it was by chance that sum—which one of the chambermaids described as immense—was sent to Valfeuillu precisely the day before the crime. As a last resort, it could be admitted.

"However, believe me, this was not by chance and I'll prove it. Tomorrow we'll go to Monsieur de Trémorel's banker and we'll ask him if the Count didn't ask him, verbally or in writing, to send him the funds exactly on the day of the 8th of July.

"Now, Messieurs, if the banker answers us affirmatively, if he shows us a letter, if he gives us his word of honor that the money was asked of him aloud, I will have, admit it, more than a probability in favor of my theory."

Père Plantat and the Doctor nodded in a sign of agreement.

"So," the man from the Prefecture asked, "up to this point there's no objection?"

"Not the least," answered the Justice of the Peace.

"My preliminary assumptions have the advantage of clearing up Guespin's situation. Let's admit it frankly. His attitude is suspicious and fully justifies his arrest. Is he mixed up in the crime? Is he totally innocent? That's what we can't decide, because I don't see any clue to guide us. What's sure is that he fell into a cleverly laid trap.

"In choosing him for victim, the Count took very good steps to have all the doubts of a superficial investigation fall on him. I would bet that Monsieur de Trémorel, knowing the life of this unfortunate man, thought, not without a motive, that the past events would add verisimilitude to the accusation and add terrible weight to the scales of justice.

"Perhaps he also told himself that Guespin would without fail get out of it, and he only wanted to gain time and avoid immediate searches, by rerouting the investigation.

"Investigators careful of details, we couldn't be deceived. We know the Countess was killed with one blow, the first one, as if struck by lightning. Therefore, she didn't put up a struggle; therefore she couldn't have been able to grab a scrap of material from the clothing of the murderer.

"To admit Guespin's guilt would be to admit that he was foolish enough to place a piece of his jacket in his victim's hands. It would be to admit that he was simple enough to go throw that torn and bloody jacket in the Seine, from the top of the bridge in a place which he must certainly have thought they would search. And it would be to admit that he did that without even taking the common precaution to tie a stone to it to keep it at the bottom of the water.

"That would be absurd."

"Therefore, for me, that scrap of cloth, that bloody jacket affirms both the innocence of Guespin and the villainy of the Count de Trémorel."

"However," Monsieur Gendron objected, "if Guespin is innocent, why doesn't he talk? Why doesn't he bring up an alibi? Where did he spend the night? Why did he have his billfold full of money?"

"Note, Monsieur," answered the Sûreté agent, "I didn't say that he is innocent. We are still dealing with probabilities. Couldn't it be supposed that the Count de Trémorel, perfidious enough to lay a trap for his servant, was clever enough to take away from him any means of furnishing an alibi?"

"But you yourself," insisted the Doctor, "you deny the Count's cleverness."

"Pardon, Monsieur, let's understand each other. Monsieur de Trémorel's plan was excellent. Only the execution was defective. That's because the plan was conceived and came to fruition in security. Once the crime was committed, the murderer, upset, terrified of the danger, lost his head and only half completed what he had planned.

"But there are other suppositions.

"One can wonder if, while the Countess was being murdered, Guespin wasn't committing another crime somewhere else."

That hypothesis seemed to Doctor Gendron so unlikely that he couldn't keep from protesting.

"Oh!" he burst out.

"Don't forget, Messieurs," Lecoq answered, "that the field of conjectures has no limits. Imagine whatever complication of events you like, I'm ready to maintain that that conjecture has been presented or will be presented. Didn't Lieuben, a German maniac, bet that he would be able to turn up a stack of cards in the order dictated by the spoken bet? For twenty years, ten hours a day, he shuffled, turned over, reshuffled, and turned over again his cards. By his own admission, he had repeated that operation 4,246,028 times when he won."

Monsieur Lecoq was perhaps going to continue his citations when Père Plantat interrupted him with a gesture.

"I admit," he said, "your preliminary theories. I hold them for more than probable, for true."

Monsieur Lecoq was then speaking while walking up and down from the window to the library shelves, halting at decisive words, like a general dictating to his aides de camp the battle plan for the following day.

And his listeners were amazed to see him and to hear him. For the third time since that morning he showed himself to them under an absolutely different aspect. This was neither the retired haberdasher of the investigation nor the cynical and sentimental policeman of the biography.

It was a new Lecoq with a dignified look, an eye shining with intelligence, with clear and concise language, to sum it up, the Lecoq who knew the magistrates who utilized the investigative genius of this remarkable agent.

He had long since put away the lozenge box with a portrait. It was no longer a question of lozenge paté squares, which, to use one of his vocabulary expressions, made up one of the accessories of his country look.

"Now," the Sûreté agent was saying, "listen to me."

"It's ten o'clock in the evening. There is not a sound outside, the road way is deserted, the Orcival lights have gone out, the chateau servants are in Paris, Monsieur and Madame de Trémorel are alone at Valfeuillu. They have retired to their bedroom to go to bed. The Countess is seated at the table on which tea has been placed. The Count, while chatting with her, walks up and down in the bedroom.

"Madame de Trémorel has no misapprehension. Hasn't her husband been more affectionate for several days, more than he has ever been! She has no distrust and thus the Count can approach her from behind without her thinking to turn her head. If she hears him approaching in this fashion, softly, she imagines he wants to surprise her with a kiss.

"He, however, armed with a long sword, is standing near his wife. He knows where to strike for the wound to be mortal. He looks for and chooses the spot. He found it. He strikes a terrible blow, so terrible that the hilt of the sword left an imprint on the two sides of the wound.

"The Countess falls without letting a cry, striking her forehead on the corner of the table, which turns over.

"Doesn't that explain the location of the terrible wound under the left shoulder, an almost vertical wound, going from right to left?..."

The Doctor made a sign of agreement.

"And what other man, other than the lover or husband of a woman, can come and go in her bedroom, approaching her when she's seated, without her turning around?"

"That's obvious," murmured Père Plantat, "that's obvious."

"Then that's how it was," continued Monsieur Lecoq. "There's the Countess dead.

"The murderer's first feeling was a feeling of triumph. Finally! There he was, rid of that wife of his, that he hated enough to decide to commit a crime, to decide to change his happy, splendid, envied existence for the terrible life of the scoundrel, henceforth without a country, without a friend, without asylum, outlawed by every civilization, tracked by all police forces, punished by the laws of the whole world.

"His second thought was for that letter, that paper, that legal document, that title, that object in a thin volume that he knew to be in his wife's possession, that he had asked for a hundred times, that she didn't want to give to him, and that he had to have."

"Add that this document was one of the reasons for the crime," Père Plantat interrupted.

"That very important act, the Count imagined he knew where it was. He believed he was going to put his hand on it right off. He was mistaken. He looked in all the pieces of furniture his wife used. He found nothing. He rummaged through the drawers. He lifted up the marble tops. He turned over everything in the room. Nothing.

"Then he had an idea. Couldn't that letter be under the fireplace mantle top? Lifting it up with his arm, he threw down the bric-a-brac. The clock fell and stopped. It wasn't yet 10:30 p.m."

"Yes," Doctor Gendron said in a low voice, "the clock told us that."

"Under the mantle top," the Sûreté agent continued, "he still found nothing but the dust which kept the traces of his fingers.

"Then the murderer began to be worried.

"This very precious paper, for which he had risked his life, where could it be? He became angry. How could he get into the locked drawers? The keys were on the rug where I found them among the debris of the tea service. He didn't see them.

"He needed a weapon, a tool to break everything open. He went downstairs to look for a hatchet.

"On the stairway, the drunkenness of having spilt blood, of vengeance, dissipated. His terror began. All the dark corners were peopled with those specters which follow assassins. He was afraid. He hurried.

"He wasn't long in coming back up, and, armed with an enormous hatchet, the hatchet found on the third floor, he made everything around him fly about in splinters. He went about like a madman. He ripped open the furniture haphazardly. But among the debris he continued his desperate search whose traces I found.

"Nothing, still nothing.

"Everything was upside down in the bedroom. He went into the study and the destruction continued. The hatchet rose and fell without stopping. He broke up his own office, not that he wasn't familiar with his own drawers, but because he might find there some hiding place he didn't know about. That desk, he wasn't the one who bought it. It belonged to the first husband, to Sauvresy. He took down all the books in the library, one by one, shook them furiously and threw them around the room.

"The damned letter couldn't be found.

"From this point his agitation was too great for him to bring the least method to his investigations. His dimmed reason no longer guided him. He wandered about without any fixed purpose, without thinking, from one piece of furniture to another, rummaging through the same drawers ten times, while there were some very near that he totally forgot about.

"That was when he thought that document which would damn him could be hidden among the stuffing of some chair. He took out a sword and, to probe more accurately, he hacked into the velvet of the armchairs and the couches in the drawing room and the other rooms."

Monsieur Lecoq's voice, his accent, his gestures, gave a thrilling character to his story. He seemed to be living the crime, taking part in the terrible scenes he was describing. His listeners held their breath, even avoiding an approving gesture which might distract his attention.

"At this moment," the Sûreté agent continued, "the Count de Trémorel's rage and fright were at their height. He had told himself, when he premeditated the crime, that he would kill his wife, that he would get hold of the letter, that he would quickly complete his very perfidious plan and that he would flee.

"And here all his projects had gone awry.

"How much time had been lost, when each minute flown away carried with it a chance of salvation.

"Then the probability of a thousand dangers he hadn't thought about came to mind. Why might not a friend drop in on him to ask hospitality, as had happened twenty times? What would a passer-by stopped on the road think of that light moving from room to room? Might not one of the servants come back?

"Once in the drawing room, he thought he heard someone ringing at the gate. Such was his terror that he dropped the candle he was holding. I found the mark of that fallen candle on the rug.

"He heard strange noises, such as had never before struck his ears. The floor squeaking, it seemed to him that someone was walking in the neighboring room. Was his wife really dead? Did he really kill her? Wasn't she suddenly going to get up, run to the window, and call for help?

"It was with these terrifying thoughts that he went back to the bedroom, that he took up his sword again and that he again struck the cadaver of the Countess.

"But his hand was so little accurate that he only made superficial wounds.

"You noticed it, Doctor, and put it down in your report, all the wounds go in the same direction. They form a right angle with the body which proves that the body was lying down when she was hacked in this way.

"Then, carried away by his frenzy, the miserable man stomped on the body of that woman he murdered. The heels of his boots made those contusions which had no ecchymose revealed by the autopsy."

Monsieur Lecoq stopped to catch his breath.

He not only told the drama, he mimicked it, he acted it, adding the movement of gestures to the sway of the words. Each one of his sentences reconstituted a scene, explained a fact or dissipated a doubt. As all artistic geniuses, who truly become incarnated in the character they represent, the Sûreté agent actually felt something of the sensations he was translating. His changing mask had then a frightening expression.

"There you have it," he continued, "the first part of the drama.

"The Count's light-headed delirium was followed by an irresistible prostration. The various circumstances I'm describing to you happen in almost all major crimes. After the murder, the murderer is always seized with a terrible and inexplicable hatred against his victim, and he often furiously attacks the cadaver. Then comes a period of weakness, of torpor so invincible that these miserable creatures have been seen to literally go to sleep in the blood. When someone surprises them asleep, they have all the trouble in the world to wake them.

"After he had frightfully mutilated his wife's corpse, Monsieur de Trémorel must have fallen into one of the armchairs in the bedroom. And, in fact, the shred of the fabric of one of the seats kept certain wrinkles which indicate that someone sat on it.

"What then were the thoughts of the Count? He thought about the long hours flown away, of the short hours remaining to him. He had found nothing. The thought that he would hardly have time before daylight to take the measures, the total of which must throw off the investigation and make sure he wouldn't be suspected by making it thought he was dead. And he had to flee, quickly, flee without that damned paper.

"He gathered his strength; he got up, and do you know what he did?

"He seized a pair of scissors and he cut off his carefully tended beard."

"Ah!" interrupted Père Plantat, "that's why you were looking at the portrait so much."

Monsieur Lecoq was paying too much attention to following the line of his deductions to acknowledge the interruption.

"There are," he continued, "some of those common details which precisely, just the triviality, render terrible when they're surrounded by certain circumstances.

"Can you imagine the Count de Trémorel, pale, covered with his wife's blood, standing in front of the mirror shaving, putting shaving soap on his face in that wrecked bedroom, when on the floor three feet from him the warm, still throbbing cadaver was stretch out.

"To look at himself, to see himself in a mirror after a murder, is, believe me, an act of extraordinary strength which few criminals are capable of.

"What's more, the Count's hands were trembling so much that he could hardly hold the razor, and his face must be streaked with cuts."

"What!" Doctor Gendron exclaimed, "you're supposing the Count wasted time in shaving himself?"

"I'm positively sure of it," responded Monsieur Lecoq, "Pos-i-tive-ly," he added, stressing all the syllables.

"I recognized on a towel one of those marks—just one—that a razor leaves when it's wiped. That put me on the trail of this detail.

"I looked around and I found a box of razors. One of them had been used a short time ago, because it was still damp.

"I carefully locked away the towel and the box.

"And if these proofs aren't enough to support my claim, I'll have two of my men come from Paris. They'll be able to find somewhere in the chateau or in the garden Monsieur de Trémorel's beard and the linen on which he wiped his razor. I examined carefully the remaining soap on the bathroom cabinet and everything leads me to believe that the Count didn't use a shaving brush.

"As for the idea that surprises you, Monsieur le docteur, to me it seems natural. I would add, it was the necessary consequence of the plan adopted.

"Monsieur de Trémorel has always worn a full beard. He cuts it and his face in this way is so changed that if he meets someone in his flight, they won't recognize him."

Doctor Gendron must have been convinced, because he made a gesture of agreement and murmured:

"That's clear, that's evident!"

"Once he had changed his looks," the Sûreté agent continued, "the Count started to hastily bring together all the elements of his plan, to put in place the appearances designed to throw you off, to make you believe he had been murdered by a band of thieves at the same time as his wife. He went to find Guespin's clothes. He tore the pocket and placed a fragment in the Countess' hand. Picking up the cadaver, crosswise, he took it downstairs. The wounds bled terribly; that was the cause of all the stains found on the steps.

"When he had reached the bottom of the stairs, he had to put the cadaver on the floor to go open the door to the garden. That action perfectly explains the very large blood stain in the vestibule.

"The door opened, the Count came back to pick up the cadaver and he carried it in his arms to the edge of the lawn. There, he stopped carrying it. Walking backwards, he dragged it, holding it by the shoulders. He thought he could in this way prepare prints which would make it believed that his own body was dragged and thrown in the Seine.

"However, the miserable man forgot two things that found him out. He didn't think about the fact that the Countess' skirts, dragging across the grass, would unmask the trick. He didn't think about the fact that his elegant and arched foot, wearing fine boots with very high heels, would make prints in the wet ground of the lawn, leaving proof against him clearer than day."

Père Plantat suddenly stood up.

"Ah!" he interrupted. "You didn't mention that circumstance to me."

Monsieur Lecoq made a nice gesture of self-importance.

"Nor several others, but at that time, I didn't know—his glance tried to meet that of Père Plantat—I absolutely didn't know a lot of things that I know now. And as I had some reason to believe Monsieur le juge de paix better informed than I, I wasn't bothered about taking a little revenge for discretion incomprehensible for me."

"And you've gotten your revenge," Doctor Gendron said, smiling.

"On the other side of the lawn," Monsieur Lecoq continued, "the Count again lifted the cadaver. But, then, forgetting the effects of water when something is thrown in it, or perhaps, who knows, fearing to get wet, instead of throwing the body violently in the water, he put it there gently, with a thousand precautions.

"That wasn't all. He wanted it to be believed that a terrible fight had taken place between the Countess and the murderers. What did he do? He dug up and made ridges in the sand of the pathway with the end of his foot. And he thought that would deceive the police."

"Yes," murmured Père Plantat, "that's exact; that's true. I saw it."

"When he'd gotten rid of the cadaver, the Count went back to the house. Time was getting short, but he still wanted to search for the damned document. So he hurried to take the last measures which, he thought, would assure the success of his projects.

"He took his house shoes and a scarf that he stained with blood. He threw one of his house shoes and the scarf on the lawn. He threw the other in the Seine.

"His haste explains to us the defects and the lack of success of his actions. He was in a hurry. He committed blunder after blunder.

"The bottles he placed on the table were empty bottles. He didn't believe what the valet told us. He thought he was pouring wine in the five glasses. He poured vinegar in them, which proved that nobody drank from them.

"He went back upstairs. He put the hand of the clock forward, but he advanced it too much. In addition, he forgot to make the striking mechanism and the hands agree.

"He unmade the bed, but he unmade it poorly, and he still didn't see that it's absolutely impossible to reconcile the three things: the unmade bed, the clock showing 3:20 a.m., and the Countess dressed for the middle of the day.

"He increased the disorder as much as he could. He snatched down the bed's canopy. He dipped a piece of linen in the blood and he stained the drapes and the furniture. Finally, he marked the entry door with the imprint of a bloody hand. The imprint is too clear, too distinct, too well placed, not to be put there on purpose.

"To this point, Messieurs, is there a circumstance, a detail, something particular to the crime, that doesn't explain Monsieur de Trémorel's guilt?"

"There's the hatchet," Père Plantat answered, "the hatchet found on the third floor. Its position seemed to you very extraordinary."

"I'm coming to that, Monsieur le juge de paix," answered Monsieur Lecoq. "There is one point in this dark affair that, thanks to you, we have completely settled.

"We know that Madame de Trémorel possessed and hid, unknown to her husband, a paper, a document, a letter, which he coveted and she absolutely refused, despite his prayers, to give to him.

"You've made clear to us that the desire—perhaps the necessity—of getting hold of that paper contributed powerfully to arming the Count's hand.

"We wouldn't be rash in supposing this document had an importance not only extraordinary, but even completely exceptional.

"We have to believe, with very strong reason, that it is by its nature extremely compromising. But who does it compromise? Both the Count and the Countess, or only the Count? Regarding that, I'm reduced to making conjectures.

"What we do know is that this document is a menace—executable on the spot—suspended over the head of the one or the ones it concerns.

"What's certain is that Madame de Trémorel considered that piece of writing either as a guarantee or as a terrible weapon putting her husband at her discretion.

"What's a fact is that in order to get rid of that perpetual menace which troubled his life, Monsieur de Trémorel killed his wife."

The deduction was so logical, its last terms made the evidence stand out so well, that the Doctor and Père Plantat couldn't hold back an exclamation of agreement.

They both exclaimed at the same time:

"Well done!"

Monsieur Lecoq began again: "Now it must be concluded, from the diverse elements that formed our convictions, that the content of that letter is such that, found again, it would take away our last hesitations. It should explain the crime and render the murderer's precautions useless. The Count must then do everything in the world, attempt the impossible, not to leave that danger behind him.

"That's why, the preparations finished that should, according to him, throw off the law, despite the feeling of imminent danger, despite the passing time, despite the approaching daylight, Monsieur de Trémorel, instead of fleeing began again more frenzied than ever his futile search. He went back over the furniture his wife used, the drawers, the books, the papers. In vain. Then he decided to explore the third floor, and still armed with his hatchet, he went upstairs.

"He had already struck one piece of furniture when a cry in the garden stopped him. He ran to the window. What did he see? Philippe and Old La Ripaille were standing at the edge of the water near the cadaver, under the weeping willow trees in the park.

"Just imagine the terrible fright of the murderer!

"From this point there wasn't a minute to lose. He had already waited too long. The danger was pressing, terrible. It was daylight. The crime was discovered. People were going to come. He saw himself lost without any option. He had to flee, flee immediately, at the risk of being seen, of been encountered, of being arrested.

"He violently threw away his hatched which nicked the floor. He went downstairs. He slid the packets of bank bills into his pockets. He grabbed Guespin's torn and bloody jacket that he threw in the river from the top of the bridge and he dashed away through the garden.

"Forgetting all caution, lost, beside himself, covered with blood, he ran, he jumped the ditch. He was the one La Ripaille saw reaching the Mauprévoir woods, where he hoped to repair the disorder of his clothes.

"He was saved for the moment. But he left behind him that letter which is, you can believe, a formidable accusation which will enlighten the law, which will proclaim very loudly the villainy and the treachery of his actions.

"Because he didn't find that letter, but we will find it. We need it to shake Monsieur Domini. We need it to change our doubts into certainty."

Chapter XI

A long silence followed the statement of the Sûreté agent. His listeners may have been looking for objections.

Finally, Doctor Gendron spoke.

"In all of that, I don't see Guespin's role."

"I don't see it either, Monsieur," answered Monsieur Lecoq. "And here I must confess the strength and weakness of my system of investigation. With this method, which consists of reconstructing the crime before investigating the criminal, I can neither make a mistake nor be half right. Either all my deductions are correct, or not one of them is. It's all or nothing. If I am right, Guespin isn't mixed up in the crime—at least directly—since there isn't one circumstance leading to a suspicion of outside help. If on the other hand, I'm making a mistake..."

Monsieur Lecoq stopped. He seemed to be listening to some unusual noise coming from the garden.

"But I'm not wrong," he continued. "I have still another charge against the Count that I haven't talked to you about and which seems to me conclusive."

"Oh!" said the Doctor. "What more is needed?'

"Two sure things are worth more than one, Monsieur, and I always have doubts. So, left alone a moment, just a while ago, by the Justice of the Peace, I asked François, the valet, if he knew the exact number of his master's shoes. He told me he did and took me to the cabinet where they stow away shoes. A pair of boots with Russian leather tops, put on that same morning by the Count de Trémorel—François is sure of it—were missing. These boots, I looked for them with minute care. I didn't find them.

"Finally, the tie the Count wore on the day of the 8th, which was blue with white stripes, has also disappeared."

"There you have it," exclaimed Père Plantat. "There's the undeniable proof of your suppositions as to the house shoes and scarf."

"It appears to me, in fact," the Sûreté agent answered, "that the facts are established enough to allow ourselves to go forward. Now let's look for the events which must determine..."

While speaking, Monsieur Lecoq had for a moment been slyly observing the outside.

Suddenly, without a word, with that lightening daring and accurate spring of the cat which bounds onto the mouse he's watching, he threw himself though the sill of the open window, and from there into the garden.

Almost simultaneously they heard the noise of a fall, a stifled cry, an oath, then the sounds of a fight.

The Doctor and Père Plantat ran to the window. Day was beginning to break, the trees trembled in the fresh morning breeze, objects were beginning to appear somewhat distinct, without set shapes, through the white fog which hovers in summer nights over the Seine valley.

In the middle of the lawn in front of the library windows the Doctor and the Justice of the Peace caught a glimpse of two men, two shadows rather, struggling with each other, furiously striking each other. At some moments, at intervals very close together, they heard the soft, slapping noise of a firm fist brought down squarely against living flesh. Soon the two shadows formed only one; then they separated to come together again. One of the two fell, got up immediately, and fell down again.

"Don't trouble yourselves, Messieurs," cried out the voice of Monsieur Lecoq. "I've got the scoundrel."

The shadow still standing, which must be that of the Sûreté agent, bowed, and the combat, which had seemed ended, began again. The shadow stretched out on the ground defended himself with the very dangerous energy of despair. His torso in the middle of the lawn formed something like a big, brown stain, and his kicking legs moved up and out convulsively.

There was a confused moment so that Monsieur Gendron and Père Plantat were no longer able to distinguish which of the two shadows was that of the Sûreté agent. They had gotten up and were fighting. Suddenly an exclamation of pain rang out, accompanied by an oath:

"Ah! You rascal!"

And almost immediately a loud cry, a piercing cry, crossed the space and the mocking voice of the man from the Prefecture said:

"Here he is! I've made him decide to come present you his compliments. Give us a little light."

Both the Doctor and the Justice of the Peace rushed toward the lamp. Their hurry resulted in a delay and at the moment Doctor Gendron took hold of the light, lifting it to his height, the door of the drawing room, roughly pushed, opened.

The Sûreté agent said: "I present to you, Messieurs, Master Robelot, the Orcival bonesetter, a herbalist by caution and a poisoner by vocation."

The stupefaction of Père Plantat and Doctor Gendron was such that neither one nor the other could answer.

It certainly was the bonesetter, in fact, moving his dislocated jaw up and down. His adversary had thrown him down with that terrible knee kick which is the supreme defense and the ultimate ratio of the worst prowlers of the Parisian barrios.

But it wasn't the presence of Robelot, although almost inexplicable, which so much surprised the Doctor and his friend. Their stupor came from the appearance of that other man who, with steel fists as rigid as handcuffs grasped the Doctor's former laboratory boy and shoved him forward.

His voice was incontestably that of Monsieur Lecoq. He had on his suit, his pretentiously tied cravat, his watch chain of yellow horsehair, and nevertheless he was not—no, he was no longer Monsieur Lecoq. He had gone out of the window blond, with carefully combed sideburns. He came back in the door a clean-shaven brunet.

The man who had gone out was a mature man, with a changeable expression, taking at will an idiotic or intelligent look. The one who reentered was a handsome thirty-five-year-old young man with a confident look, a quivering lip, and with magnificent dark curly hair setting off his light olive complexion and the firm outline of his strong head.

There was a bleeding wound on his neck a little below his chin.

"Monsieur Lecoq!" finally recovering his voice, the Justice of the Peace exclaimed.

"Himself," replied the Sûreté agent, "and just for this time the real one."

And addressing the bonesetter, while at the same time shoving him by the shoulder.

"March, you!" he said.

The bonesetter fell backward onto a chair, but the policeman continued his hold.

"Yes," he continued, "this scoundrel snatched off my blond decoration. It's thanks to him, and very much against my will, that I appear to you in my natural state, with the head the Creator gave me, which is really mine."

He made a casual gesture and added, half angry, half smiling.

"I am the real Lecoq, and without lying I can say there are no more than three people after you who know it, Messieurs: two trustworthy friends and a lover who is infinitely less so, the one I told you about a while ago."

Père Plantat and Monsieur Gendron's eyes were questioning with so much insistence that the Sûreté agent went on:

"What do you expect! Everything isn't rosy in this business. To clean up society you run risks which must earn you the esteem of your contemporaries if not their affection. The way you see me now, I'm under a death sentence by seven criminals, the most dangerous in France. I had them caught and they swore—and these are men who keep their word—that I wouldn't die except by their hand. Where are they, these miserable men? Four are in prison in Cayenne; one is in prison in Brest. I have news of them. But the two others? I've lost their trail. Who knows but what one of the two has followed me here. Who can tell but what tomorrow at the bend in an empty road I'll get six ounces of steel in the stomach."

He smiled sadly.

"And there's no reward for the dangers we face," he continued. "If I fell tomorrow, they would pick up my cadaver. They would take it to one of the official buildings where they know me and that would be all."

The policeman's tone had become bitter. The dull irritation in his voice clearly betrayed his resentment.

"Fortunately, I have taken my precautions," he continued. "So long as I'm on duty, I'm wary; I trust no one. And when I'm on my guard, I'm not afraid of anyone. But there are days when you're tired of being afraid, when you want to turn a street corner without fearing being stabbed. On those days, I become myself again. I wash my face; I take off my disguise. My personality gets rid of the thousand disguises I put on one after the other. I have been at the Prefecture fifteen years. Nobody there knows my real face, nor the color of my hair."

Master Robelot, uncomfortable in his chair, tried to move.

"Ah! Don't lose your temper," Monsieur Lecoq said to him, suddenly changing tone. "You'll be sorry if you do. Instead, get up and tell us what you were doing in the garden."

"But you're hurt," exclaimed the Justice of the Peace, noticing the stream of blood flowing down the length of the Sûreté agent's shirt.

"Oh! That's nothing, Monsieur, a scratch. This funny fellow had a big kitchen knife with a sharp point he wanted to play with..."

The Justice of the Peace absolutely insisted on examining that wound and it was only when the Doctor had made certain that it was completely harmless that he paid attention to the bonesetter.

"Let's see, Master Robelot, what did you come to my house to do?"

The miserable man didn't answer.

"Be careful," insisted Père Plantat. "Your silence will make us believe that you came with the worst intentions."

But Père Plantat used his persuasive eloquence in vain. The bonesetter withdrew into a dogged and silent immobility.

Then Monsieur Gendron decided to take over, hoping, not without reason, that he had some influence over his former servant.

"Answer," he questioned him, "what do you want?"

The bonesetter made an effort and his eyes showed great suffering. With his dislocated jaw, it was painful to talk.

"I came to rob you," he answered. "I admit it."

"To rob me! Of what?"

"I don't know."

"You don't scale a wall; you don't risk prison without a plan well established in advance."

"Well, then, I wanted..."

He stopped.

"What? Speak."

"To take some rare flowers from the greenhouse."

"With your kitchen knife, right?" Monsieur Lecoq asked, sniggering.

The bonesetter, throwing him a terrible look, Lecoq continued.

"Don't look at me like that. I'm not afraid of you. But you're clever. Don't say silly things to us. If you think we're a lot stupider than you are, you're mistaken. I warn you."

116

"I wanted to get the pots," Master Robelot, stammered, "to resell them."

"Come now!" the Sûreté agent said, shrugging. "Don't repeat your totally idiotic remarks. You, a man who buys and pays cash for excellent pieces of land, steal pots of heather! Think of something else. This evening, my boy, you've been turned inside out like an old glove. Very much in spite of yourself, you've let out a secret which is tormenting you devilishly. You've come here to try to get it back. And thinking about it, you said to yourself, you a crafty man, that Monsieur Plantat had probably not yet spoken to whoever it might be and you came with the ingenious project of keeping him from speaking to any living soul from now on."

The bonesetter tried to protest.

"So shut up," Monsieur Lecoq said to him. "And what about your kitchen knife?"

During this rough interrogation of the bonesetter, Père Plantat was thinking:

"Perhaps," he murmured, "perhaps I spoke too soon."

"Then why is that?" the Sûreté agent questioned. "I was looking for a tangible proof to give Monsieur Domini. We'll serve him up this pretty boy. And if that doesn't make him happy, he's really very hard to please. There must be some place in the house to lock him up. If it's necessary, I'll tie him up."

"I have a small storage closet over there," the Justice of the Peace said.

"Is it secure?"

"Three of the sides are thick walls. The fourth, which opens on to here, is closed by a double door, no openings, no windows, nothing."

"That's what we need."

Père Plantat then opened the storage closet which served to hold the overflow from his library, a sort of black hole, damp because of lack of air, narrow, and completely stuffed with discarded books, stacks of newspapers, and old papers.

"You'll be like a little king in there," the agent said to the bonesetter.

And after having searched him, he pushed him into the cubbyhole. Robelot didn't resist, but he asked for a drink and a light. They passed him a carafe full of water and a glass.

"As for the light," Monsieur Lecoq said to him, "you can do without it. All we need is for you to pull some sort of trick."

The door to the storage unit closed, Père Plantat held out his hand to the Sûreté agent.

"Monsieur Lecoq," he said to him in an emotional voice, "you have probably just saved my life at the risk of your own. I won't thank you. A day will come, I hope, where it will be possible for me to do so."

The man from the Prefecture interrupted him with a gesture.

"You know, Monsieur," he said, "how much my life is at risk. To risk it one more time isn't to my credit. And, then, saving a man's life, that's not always to do him a service."

He remained thoughtful for some seconds and then said:

"You can thank me later, Monsieur, when I have acquired other rights to your gratitude."

Monsieur Gendron, he also, had given a cordial handshake to the Sûreté agent.

"Let me," he said, "express to you all my admiration. I had no idea what the investigations of a man of your caliber could be. Arrived this morning, without any details, without any information, you have managed just by examining the theater of the crime, just by the strength of reasoning and of logic, to find the guilty man. And more than that, to demonstrate to us that the guilty man can be no one other than the one you say."

Monsieur Lecoq bowed modestly. In reality, the praise of this very competent judge tickled his vanity delightfully.

"Nevertheless," he said, "I'm not completely satisfied. Certainly Monsieur de Trémorel's guilt is superabundantly proven to me. But what motives pushed him to it? How was he led to that terrible determination to kill his wife and to try to make it be believed that he himself had been murdered?"

"Can't it be supposed," objected the Doctor, "that, disgusted with Madame de Trémorel, he got rid of her to rejoin another beloved woman, adored even to madness?"

Monsieur Lecoq shook his head.

"You don't kill your wife," he said, "just for the single reason that you don't love her anymore and you adore another. You leave your wife; you go live with your mistress, and that's the end of it. You see that every day and neither the law nor public opinion condemns very severely the man who acts that way. "

"But," the Doctor objected, "when it's the wife who has the fortune!..."

"That's not the case here," said the Sûreté agent. "I got information. Monsieur de Trémorel possesses in his own name 100,000 *écus*, the debris of a colossal fortune saved by his friend Sauvresy. And his wife, by their marriage contract, gave him in addition to that 500,000. With 800,000 francs you can live comfortably anywhere. Besides, the Count was in complete control of all the community property. He could sell, buy, trade stock, borrow, place and move funds about at his fantasy."

The Doctor had nothing to reply. Monsieur Lecoq continued, speaking with some hesitation, while his eyes questioned Père Plantat.

"It's in the past, I feel it, that we have to look for the reasons for today's murder and for the motives for the terrible resolution of the murderer. A crime links the Count and the Countess so indissolubly that only the death of one of them could restore liberty to the other. This crime, I suspected it from the first. I caught a glimpse of it every moment since this morning. And the man we've just locked up there, Robelot the bonesetter, who wanted to murder *Monsieur le juge de paix*, was the agent or the accomplice."

Doctor Gendron hadn't been present at the various scenes which, the day at Valfeuillu, the evening at the house of the Mayor of Orcival, had set up a tacit understanding between Père Plantat and the man from the Prefecture. He needed all the insight with which he was gifted to fill in the gaps and to guess the implications of the conversation he had been listening to for the last two hours. The last words of the Sûreté agent were a ray of light for him. He exclaimed:

"Sauvresy..."

"Yes," Monsieur Lecoq answered, "yes, Sauvresy! And the paper the murderer was looking for with so much desperation, that letter for which he neglected taking care of his own safety, must contain the indisputable proof of the crime."

And despite the most significant looks, the most direct attempts to provoke an explanation, the old Justice of the Peace was silent. He seemed to be a hundred leagues from the present explanation. His regard, lost in the past, seemed to follow forgotten events in the fog of the past.

Monsieur Lecoq, after a deliberation inside his own mind, decided to strike a major blow.

"What past was this one, the burden of which was so crushing, that, to get out from under it, a young man, rich, happy, comes to coldly put together a crime, resigned in advance to disappearing afterwards, to cease existing legally, to lose, all at the same time, his personality, his situation, his honor and his name! What a past that must be, the weight of which can make a young twenty-year-old girl decide to commit suicide!"

Père Plantat had stood up, pale, more emotional than he had been perhaps during the day.

"Ah!" he cried out in a changed voice, "You don't know what you're saying. Laurence never knew anything."

Monsieur Gendron, who was studying the real Lecoq, thought he saw a slight smile light up the very intelligent policeman's face. The old Justice of the Peace, however, continued from that point calm and dignified, in a tone which wasn't without a certain haughtiness.

"Neither tricks nor subterfuges are needed, Monsieur Lecoq, to determine me to say what I know. I have shown enough esteem and confidence in you for you not to have the right to arm yourself against me with the sad secret—ridiculous, if you like—that you surprised."

However great his confidence, the Sûreté agent was somewhat disconcerted and tried to protest.

"Yes, your supreme investigative genius led you to the truth. But you don't know everything. And even now I would still be silent if the reasons that commanded my silence hadn't ceased to exist."

He opened the secret drawer of an old oak desk placed near the fireplace, and took out a rather voluminous file that he placed on the table.

"Here are four years," he continued, "that day by day, I might say hour by hour, I followed the various phases of the terrible drama which, last night at Valfeuillu ended in blood. At first, it was pure curiosity of a bored former lawyer. Later, I hoped to save the existence and the honor of a person very dear to me.

"Why didn't I say anything about my discoveries? That, Messieurs, is my conscience's secret. It doesn't at all reproach me. And besides, yesterday I still closed my eyes to the evidence. It took the brutal testimony of the fact..."

It was daylight. The cheeky blackbirds ran around chirping on the garden paths. The pavement of the Evry road echoed under the hoofs of the morning teams going to the fields. No sound broke the gloomy silence of the library, none, except for the rustle of the leaves of paper the old Justice of the Peace was turning and from time to time a complaint from the bonesetter who was shut up in the cubbyhole suffering and moaning.

"Before beginning," said Père Plantat, "I must, Messieurs, ask how tired you are. We've now been up twenty-four hours."

But the Doctor and the Sûreté agent protested that they had no need of rest. The fever of curiosity had chased away weariness. Finally, they were going to have the key to that bloody enigma.

"So be it," the Justice of the Peace continued. "Then hear me out."

Chapter XII

At twenty-six-years-old, Count Hector de Trémorel was the supreme model, the perfect ideal of the pleasure-seeking gentleman, such as can exist in our time. Useless to himself and to others, even detrimental, he was seemingly put on earth just to amuse himself at the expense of everything and everybody.

Young, very noble, elegant, a millionaire, gifted with a constitution of iron, this last descendant of a great race squandered in the most foolish way, some say in the most disgraceful way in the world, both his youth and his patrimony.

It is true that by these excesses of every type he had acquired a magnificent and hardly enviable celebrity. People cited his stables, his carriages, his servants, his furnishings, his dogs, his mistresses.

His horses ready to be put out to pasture were considered still prime, and a hussy that caught his attention, immediately acquired a greater value than a commercial note bearing the signature of Monsieur de Rothschild.

But please don't think this young man was born wicked. He had heart and even generous ideas, in the past, when he was twenty. Six years of unhealthy pleasures had spoiled him right down to his marrow bones. Vain even to madness, he was ready to do anything to protect his notoriety. He had the fierce and terrible egotism of someone who has never had to think of anyone else and has never suffered. Drunk to the point of vomiting with the fawning of his so-called friends his money brought him, he admired himself in good conscience. He took his brutal cynicism for wit and for character his superb disdain of all morality, his absolute lack of principle, and his idiotic skepticism.

And added to that, he was weak, having caprices, never willpower, weak as a child, as a woman, as a girl. His biography can be found in all the minor newspapers of the moment which spread as gossip to be envied the words he said, or that he might have said in his hours of leisure. His least doings and gestures were talked about. One night, having supper at the Café de Paris, he threw all the dishes out the window. That cost him 1,000 *louis*. The next day, after drinking, he caused a scandal with a hussy in a first row theatre box and the police had to be called. It couldn't have been more like the Regency. One morning, Paris gossipers learned with amazement that he had flown away to Italy with the wife of Banker X, the nineteen-year-old mother of a family.

He fights a duel and wounds his adversary. What courage! The following week he receives a saber thrust. He's a hero!

Once he went to Baden and broke the bank. Another time after a sixty-hour gaming session, he managed to lose 120,000 francs against a Russian prince. He had one of those spirits that success exalts, which covets applause, but that never worries about the nature of those it receives. Count Hector was a little more than delighted with the figure he cut in society. To have his name, his initials, constantly in the *Monde Parisien* seemed to him the height of honor and glory. However, he never let anything of that appear and after each new adventure even said with a charming offhanded manner:

"Will they never stop paying attention to me?"

Then, on important occasions, borrowing a phrase from Louis XV, he said: *"Après moi le déluge!"* [10]

The deluge came in his own lifetime.

One morning in the month of April, his valet, who was an immoral bastard of some Parisian porter, taught how to behave, dressed, and styled by him, woke him at 9:00 a.m. saying:

"Monsieur, downstairs in the antechamber there's a bailiff who claims he's come to take possession of Monsieur's goods."

Hector turned over on his side, yawned, stretched, and answered:

"All right, tell him to start with the stables and the carriage houses and come back upstairs and get me dressed."

He didn't show any other emotion and the servant was surprised and amazed at his master's composure.

That was because the Count had at least the merit of knowing exactly what his financial situation was. He had foreseen that invasion by the bailiff; I would say he was expecting it.

Three years before, following a fall from a horse which put him in bed for six weeks, the Count had measured the depth of the gulf toward which he was hastening. At that time he could still have saved himself. But what! He would have had to change his life style, revise his living arrangements, learn that it takes 20 franc coins to make a *louis*. Fi! Never!

It seemed to him that to give one *louis* less a month to his current mistress would be to eat away a centimeter from the pedestal on which his contemporaries had placed him. He'd rather die! And after mature thought, he told himself he would go on right to the end. His ancestors, didn't they all die out the way they had lived? When the critical time came, he would run away to the other end of France, take the identification marks off his linen and blow his brains out in the corner of some woods.

The due date had come.

By contracting debts, by signing *lettres de change*, by renewing bank notes, by paying interest, and interest on the interest, by paying commissions and bribes, by always borrowing and never paying back, Hector had eaten up the princely patrimony, nearly four million in lands—received on the death of his father.

The winter just past had cost him 50,000 *écus*. A week before, he had at-

---

[10] French expression first attributed to Marquise de Pompadour, Louis XV's mistress, meaning "I don't care what happens after I'm gone" in reference to the biblical account of the Great Deluge that destroyed the world.

tempted to borrow 100,000 francs and had failed. They had refused him not because his property wasn't worth more than he owed, but the lenders were cautious and understood the unbelievable depreciation of goods sold at auction.

That's why the Count de Trémorel's valet entering and saying: "Monsieur le bailiff," seemed in reality some specter of a commander saying "Use the pistol now."

He took the warning gallantly and rose up saying: "Let's go. It's over."

He was very calm and full of fine self-possession, although a little dizzy. But vertigo is somewhat excusable when you go from everything to nothing. Convinced that he was getting dressed for the last time, he didn't want it to be inferior to the way he dressed every day. *Parbleu!* French nobility went into battle in full court dress.

In less than an hour he was ready. As usual he passed his watch chain studded with diamonds through the buttonhole of his vest. Then he slid into the side pocket of his light overcoat a charming pair of little two-shot pistols with ivory butts, a masterpiece by Brigt, the English arms artist.

He then sent away his servant and opening his secretary he inventoried his ultimate resources. He had left ten thousand and some hundred francs.

With that sum he could take a trip, prolong his existence by three or four months, but he pushed that thought away with horror—unworthy of his beautiful character—of a miserable subterfuge, a disguised delay, a recourse to mercy.

On the contrary, he thought that these ten thousand franc bills were going to allow him a sumptuous generosity which society would talk about. He told himself it would be chivalrous to go have lunch with his mistress and then make her a present of that money at dessert. During lunch he would be stunning with eloquence, with gaiety, with mocking skepticism, then, at the end, he would announce his suicide.

That girl would be sure to go everywhere recounting the scene. She would repeat his last conversation—his political will—and in the evening they would talk about it in all the cafes; it would appear in all the newspapers. That idea, the prospect of drama unusually cheered him up and comforted him completely. He was leaving when his glance fell on the mass of documents his secretary contained. Perhaps something forgotten in writing capable of soiling the steel purity of his memory might be there. He quickly emptied the drawers into the fireplace without looking, without choosing, and he set fire to that mass of papers. It was with a feeling of very legitimate pride that he saw all those pieces of paper, love letters or business letters, mortgaged bonds, titles of nobility or to property, go up in flames. Wasn't that his dazzling past burning in the fireplace?

The last scrap of paper consumed, he thought about the bailiff and went downstairs.

This ministerial official exercising his duties was none other than Monsieur Z…the highest rated bailiff, the best and the politest of bailiffs, a man of taste and intellect, a friend of artists, himself a poet in his free time. In the stables, he had already taken possession of eight horses with their harnesses, saddles, bridles, bits, blankets, and in the carriage house, five carriages with their apparatus: double padding, convertible tops, spare shafts, when he noticed Count Hector in the courtyard.

After greeting him, he said:

"I'm going forward very slowly, Monsieur le Comte. Perhaps you would like to stop the proceedings. The sum is important, that's true, but in your position..."

"Please understand, Monsieur," Monsieur de Trémorel answered haughtily, "that if you are here, that's because it is convenient for me. My townhouse no longer pleases me. I'll never set foot in it again. So, you are in control. Go ahead."

He turned on his heels and left.

And Monsieur Z…,very disillusioned, went back to work. He went from room to room, admiring and taking possession. He inventoried the silver-plated cups won at the racecourse, the collection of pipes, the weapon trophies. He seized the bookcase, a splendid piece of furniture and all the volumes it contained: A *Manuel d'hippiatrique, La Chasse et la pêche, Les Mémoires de Casanova, Le Duel et les duellistes, Thérèse, La Chasse au chien d'arrêt.*

During this time, the Count, more than ever resolved on suicide, went up the boulevard to the house of his mistress, who occupied a little apartment renting for 6,000 francs. Hector had launched that mistress into the demimonde eight or ten months earlier under the name of Miss Jenny Fancy. The truth was that her name was Pélagie Taponnet, and she was, unknown to the Count, the child born of adultery to the sister of his valet. Protected by the Count de Trémorel, Miss Fancy had had a real and resounding success in costume and beauty in the Parisian demimonde.

She was, however, far from being beautiful in the classical acceptance of the word. But she was a perfect example of the "pretty" Parisian, a type which, by common agreement, didn't have fewer passionate admirers. She had perfectly formed delicate hands, a tiny foot, superb brown hair, white, cat-like teeth, and above all, big dark eyes, eyes brazen or languorous, caressing, provocative, eyes to make stone saints descent from their niches. Miss Fancy was not extremely intelligent, but she quickly picked up the easy glibness of those frequenting opening nights; in sum, she did credit to her eccentric get-ups.

The Count had picked her up one evening in a lower class public dance hall where, by the greatest of chances he had entered when she was dancing some risqué steps in open-toed little ankle boots. In fewer than twelve hours, without any transition, she went from the most frightful poverty to luxury that she obviously couldn't even imagine. She woke up one morning on the dirty pallet of a furnished cubbyhole rented for twelve franc a month; she went to sleep that evening under the satin canopy curtains of a rosewood bed.

This dazzling change didn't surprise her as much as you might suppose.

There isn't in Paris any somewhat pretty little girl, who, full of confidence, doesn't expect even more surprising adventures. It takes a workman who has taken fifteen years to become rich to become accustomed to wearing a dark suit. The little Parisian girl takes off her ten *sou* dress to put on velvet and moiré, and you would swear that she had never worn anything else.

Forty-eight hours after she was installed, Miss Fancy had gotten the servants off on the right foot. They obeyed her when she beckoned and when she glanced at them. She made her dressmakers and her milliners obey her bidding.

However, the first dizziness of an absolutely new pleasure wears off quickly. Soon, Jenny, alone for part of the day in her beautiful apartment, didn't know how to amuse herself. Her outfits, which at first had transported her, no longer meant anything to her. A woman's enjoyment isn't complete unless doubled by the jealousy of rivals. Now, Jenny's rivals lived in the Temple neighborhood, at the top, near the barrio. They couldn't envy her splendor if they didn't know about it. And she had been absolutely forbidden to go show herself to them, to crush them with her new wealth. So what! Then call a carriage!

As for Trémorel, Jenny was tolerating him, not being able to do any better. He seemed to her the most boring of men. She considered his friends deadly dull. Perhaps she sensed an enormous contempt under the ironically polite manners, and understood how little she mattered to all those rich people, those pleasure lovers, those gamblers, those blasé people, those who needed nothing. Her pleasures, and she still tasted them in moderation, were an evening in the company of some woman like herself, a night of baccarat where she won, a supper where she had too much of everything.

The rest of the time she was bored. She was bored to death. She was nostalgic for the muddy little street of her neighborhood, for her revolting furnished room. A hundred times she had wanted to walk out on Trémorel, to give up her luxury, her money, her servants and to take up her former existence. Ten times she packed her bags. Her ego always held her back at the last moment.

Such was, as exactly as possible, the morning of the bailiff's seizure, the woman to whom Count Hector presented himself at 11:00 a.m. Certainly, she hardly expected him so early in the morning. And she was very much surprised when he told her he had come to have lunch, asking her to have the cook hurry because he was short of time.

Miss Fancy had never seen her lover so amiable. Above all, she had never seen him so gay. During lunch he was, as he had promised himself, sparkling with eloquence.

When coffee was served, Hector judged the moment opportune to speak.

"All this, my child," he said, "is only a preface to prepare you for rather surprising news. So, you will find out that I'm ruined."

She looked at him dumbfounded, seeming not to understand.

"I said ruined," he repeated, laughing very loudly, "the most completely ruined, ruined, beaten flat."

"Ah! You're making fun of me; you're joking!

"I've never spoken more seriously," Hector continued. "That seems to you very unlikely, doesn't it? Well! Nevertheless, it's true."

Jenny's big eyes were still questioning.

"What do you expect," he continued with a superb lack of concern, "life is a bunch of grapes that you eat slowly, one grape at a time, or that you squeeze out into a glass to drink it down all in one gulp. My own bunch of grapes was made up of four million francs. They've been drunk. I don't regret them. I've had my money's worth out of life. But at present I can flatter myself to be as much a beggar as just any French beggar. At this hour everything at my house has been seized. I don't have a dwelling; I no longer have a *sou*."

He went on talking, talking, becoming excited by the shock of the various thoughts that came tumbling into his head, exciting himself with the rattling of the words. And he wasn't acting. His good faith was complete, intact, whole. He wasn't even thinking about how well he was doing.

"But...then..." Miss Fancy ventured.

"What? You think you're free? That goes without saying"

She didn't know whether she should pity herself or rejoice.

"Yes," he declared, "I give you your freedom."

Jenny made a gesture that Hector misunderstood.

"Oh! But don't worry," he added quickly. "I'm not leaving you like this. I don't want you to find yourself in need tomorrow. The lease here is in your name; the furnishings belong to you, and what's more, I have taken care of you. I have here in my pocket 500 *louis*. That's my whole fortune. I'm bringing it to you."

At the same time he presented her on a plate, imitating the café waiters who bring back change, his ten last thousand franc bills.

She pushed them away with horror.

"Well!" he said, again assuming his tone of a superior man, "that's a nice gesture my child. That's good, very good. I've always thought, and always said, you know, that you were a good girl, even too good. You need correcting."

Yes, she was a good girl, Miss Jenny Fancy, formerly called Pélagie Taponnet, because instead of grabbing the bank bills and throwing Hector out the door, as was incontestably her right, believing him very unhappy, she tried to console him, to comfort him. Since Hector had confessed to her that he was without a *sou*, she almost didn't hate him anymore. And, with a turnaround frequent in women of that type, she even began to love him.

Hector, his goods seized, nowhere to go, was no longer the terrible man, paying to be the master, a millionaire whose caprice could throw back in the gutter the woman he had taken out of it by a whim. He was no longer the tyrant, the detested being. Ruined, he had descended from his pedestal. He came back to everyday life. He became a man like any other, preferable to others, being really remarkably handsome. Then, taking the last trick of a sick vanity for a generous heart-felt gesture, Fancy was extremely touched by this gift of 10,000 francs.

"You're not as poor as you say," she continued, "since you still have that amount of money."

"Ah! Dear child, that's hardly what you cost me each month. I've given you two or three times that much for some little diamonds you wore one evening."

She thought a moment, and very astonished, as if having discovered something:

"Well!" she said, "Maybe it's true."

Hector hadn't been as amused in a long time.

'But," Miss Fancy continued gravely, "I can spend less, oh! a great deal less and be just as happy, I assure you. In the past—before I knew you— when I was young (She was nineteen.) 10,000 francs seemed to me one of those fabulous sums that are talked about, but that few man have seen put into one stack, that very few have held between their hands."

She was trying to put the 10,000 francs into the pockets of the Count, who was trying to prevent it.

"So, here, take it back."

"What do you want me to do with it?"

"I don't know, but it seems to me that money can bring in more. Can't you play the stock market, bet at the racetrack, win gambling at Baden, then try to do something? I've heard about people who're now rich as kings, who began with nothing, and who didn't have your background. You've seen everything; you know everything. Why don't you do what they did?"

She was speaking quickly, with that energy of the woman who is trying to make her idea triumph. And he, looking at her, stupefied at finding in her that sensitivity, that disinterested interest in his person, more astonished than a teacher who, getting ready dissections for a course in anatomy, finds, when preparing his lesson, his subject's heart on the right rather than on the left.

"You'll do it, won't you? she insisted. "You'll do it?"

He shook off the sort of charming stupor into which his mistress' affectionate expression had plunged him.

"Yes," he said, "you're a good girl, but take these 500 *louis* because I'm giving them to you and don't worry about anything."

"But you, do you still have some money? How much do you have left?"

He stopped, inspected his pockets, counting the gold in his money holder, something that had never before happened to him.

"Ma foi! I still have 340 francs. That's more than I'll need. Before I leave, I want to give ten *louis* to your servants. They served me very well."

"And what happens to you afterwards? *Mon Dieu!"*

He sat back down on his chair, carelessly caressing his beautiful beard.

"I'm going to blow out my brains," he said.

"Oh!" she cried out, alarmed.

Hector supposed that the young woman doubted it. He took out of his pocket his little pistols with the ivory butts, and showing them to her, said:

"You see these little playthings?" he said. "Well, when I leave you, I'm going to go somewhere; it doesn't matter where. I'll place the barrels like this, on my temples—he showed her how—I'll press the trigger and all will be over."

She looked at him, her eyes dilated by fear, pale, breathing hard.

But at the same time she admired him. She was amazed at so much courage, at that calmness, at that carefree joking. What superb disdain for life! To eat up his fortune and kill himself afterwards without crying out, without tears, without regrets, seemed to her an unheard of act of heroism, unexampled, unparalleled. And in her ecstasy, it seemed to her that a new man stood before her, unknown, handsome, radiant, dazzling. She felt herself feeling infinite tenderness for him. She loved him as she had never loved before. Unknown ardor stirred in her.

"No!" she cried out, "No! That can't happen."

And she got up suddenly; she dashed to Hector. She was hanging on to the neck of her lover, her head thrown backwards to see him better, to plunge her eyes into his. She was continuing:

"You won't kill yourself, will you? Promise me. Swear it to me. No, that's not possible. You don't want to do it. Because I love you, you see. I love you—me who couldn't stand you in the past. Ah! I didn't understand you, while now... Come now! We'll be happy. You who've always lived in grandeur, you don't know what 10,000 francs are, but me, I know. "You can live a long time, a very long time, and very well with that. Without counting on the fact that if we want to sell everything here that's useless, the horses, the carriage, my diamonds, my green cashmere, we'll clear a good triple, even quadruple that sum. Thirty thousand francs! That's a fortune. Think how many happy days that sum represents!"

The Count de Trémorel shook his head negatively, smiling delightedly. Yes, he was delighted. His vanity, deliciously tickled, expanded in the warmth of that passion which shone in Miss Fancy's very beautiful eyes. That's how he was loved, him. How he would be missed. What a hero the world was going to lose.

"Because we won't stay here," Jenny continued. "We'll go hide in a little lodging at the other end of Paris. You don't realize that on the side of Belleville, in the hills, for a thousand francs a year you can find delightful little accommodations surrounded by gardens. How good we'll be there, close together, squeezed one against the other. You'll never leave me. Because I'll be jealous, you see. Oh! How jealous! We won't have any servants and you'll see that I know very well how to take care of our little household..."

Hector still didn't answer.

"As long as the money lasts, we'll have a good time. When there isn't any more, if you still want to kill yourself, you'll kill yourself; that is to say, we'll kill ourselves together. But not with a little pistol. That would make too much of a mess. We'll build a big coal fire in a stove. We'll go to sleep in each other's' arms. And all will be over. It seems that you don't suffer at all. One of my girl-friends, who had already lost consciousness when they broke down the door, told me she hadn't felt anything, just a slight headache."

That suggestion tore Hector out of his voluptuous drossiness in which the looks and the embrace of his mistress had kept him. She aroused a memory in him which wounded all his vanity as a gentleman and as a person with a reckless life style. Three or four months earlier he had read in a newspaper an account of the suicide of a chef's assistant at Vachettes. In a fit of amorous desperation he had stolen a large portable chafing dish from his employer and had gone bravely to asphyxiate himself in his miserable hovel. Before dying, he had even written a very touching letter to his unfaithful lover. That idea of ending up like the cook made him shiver. He could foresee the possibility of a horrible comparison. What ridicule! And the Count de Trémorel, who had spent his life professing to be afraid of nothing, had a mad fear of ridicule. To go do himself in by charcoal at Belleville with a common working girl. Horror!

He almost brutally untwined Miss Jenny's arms and pushed her away.

"Enough of sentiments like that," he said in his former tone. "All you're saying, my dear child, is very pretty, but completely absurd. A man with my name doesn't demean himself. He dies. And taking out the bills Miss Fancy had slid into his pocket, he threw them on the table.

"So, goodbye!"

He wanted to leave, but disheveled, her eyes flaming with resolution, Jenny ran to place herself in front of the door.

"You won't leave here," she cried out. "I don't want you to. You're mine, do you understand, because I love you. If you take a step, I'll scream."

The Count de Trémorel shrugged.

"Nevertheless, we have to get it over with," he said.

"You won't get out."

"Very well! Then I'll blow out my brains here."

"And taking out one of his little pistols, he placed it against his temples, saying:

"If you scream, if you don't open the door for me, I'll fire."

If Miss Fancy had called out, the Count de Trémorel very certainly would have pulled the trigger.

But she didn't call out. She couldn't. She let out a loud cry and fell in a faint.

"Finally," said Hector, putting his firearm in his pocket.

At that, without taking the trouble to pick up his mistress stretched out on the floor, closing and double locking the door, he left.

Then, in the antechamber, having called the servants, he gave them ten *louis* to share and walked rapidly away.

Chapter XIII

As he came to the street, Count de Trémorel was starting to go up the boulevard, when the thought of his friends came to mind. The story of his goods being seized, spread by his servants, must already be making its way rapidly around the city.

"No, not that way," he said to himself.

In fact, in that direction he would infallibly meet some one of his "very dear" friends. And it seemed to him he could hear the compliments of condolences and the ridiculous offers of help. He saw the contrite grimaces badly hiding a personal and delicious satisfaction. In his lifetime he had wounded so many vanities, crushed so many egos, that he must expect terrible reprisals.

And why not tell it all? All the friends of a man favored by unusual prosperity resemble more or less—voluntarily or without suspecting it— that eccentric Englishman who followed about a wild beast trainer with the gentle hope of seeing him eaten alive. Fortune also sometimes devours those who tame it.

Hector, then, crossed the sidewalk, took the Rue Duphot, and reached the Quay. Where was he going? He had no idea. He didn't even ask himself that. He walked haphazardly, along the parapets, drawing deep breaths of pure and refreshing air, savoring that physical well-being that follows a good meal. He was happy to feel himself alive in the warm rays of the April sun. The weather was splendid and all Paris was outside. The city seemed to have a festival air. Strollers filled the streets. The busy crowd slowed its pace; all the women were pretty. At the corners of the bridges, women tended their trays of violets spreading perfume.

Near the Pont Neuf, the Count bought one of those bouquets that they hawk for ten centimes and he put a flower in his boutonniere. He threw twenty *sous* to the merchant, and without waiting for her to give him the change, he continued on his way. When he came to that big square at the end of the Boulevard Bourbon, which in the open air is always full of trapeze artists and merchants showing off curiosities for sale, the crowd, the noise, the heartbreaking music, snatched him out of his lethargy, bringing him suddenly back to the present situation.

"It's a question of leaving Paris," he told himself.

And walking quickly, he made his way toward the Orléans Railway Station. He saw the buildings across from him, on the other side of the Seine. At the ticket window, he asked when a train for Etampes left. Why did he choose Etampes?

He was told that a train had just left only five minutes before, and that there wouldn't be another one until 2:00 p.m. He was very annoyed and as he couldn't wait there until 2:00 p.m., he left. To kill time he went into the *Jardin des Plantes.*[11] It was certainly ten or twelve years since he had set foot there. He hadn't come there since the time he was in the lycée and they took students there on outings to visit the menagerie or play on the bars. Nothing had changed. There were the same chestnut trees, the same worm-eaten trellises, the same little walkways cutting through the squares full of plants bearing their name on a placard fixed to an iron rod.

The wide pathways on that side were almost deserted. He sat down on a bench in front of the mineralogy museum. Who knows! Perhaps when he was in the lycée ten years earlier, tired of running and playing, he came here to rest on this same bench. Between that time and today, what a difference! Life to him seemed then like a long avenue, so long you couldn't see the end, sanded with golden sand, shady, delightful, holding a surprise, a new exquisite pleasure with each step, Well, he had just gone down that pathway. He had come to the end. What had he found? Nothing.

No, nothing. Because at that hour when he went back over the years that had elapsed, he couldn't find for himself, among so many days, a single day that had left him one of those delightful memories which ravish and console. Millions had slid through his prodigal hands, and he couldn't remember one useful, truly generous, expenditure of twenty francs. He, who had had so many friends, so many mistresses, he searched his memory in vain for the name of a friend, a name of a woman to murmur. The past appeared to him like a faithful mirror. He was surprised, dismayed with the pointlessness of his pleasures, which had been the goal and the purpose of his existence. And for whom had he actually lived? For others. He had thought he was posing on a pedestal. He had been walking back and forth on a trestle.

"Ah! I was a fool," he said to himself, *"I was a fool!"* not seeing that after having lived for others, he was going to kill himself for others.

He began to feel sorry for himself. In a week, who would think about him. Nobody. Oh, yes, one person, Miss Jenny, a prostitute. And still, no. In a week she would have been consoled and she'd be laughing about him with a new lover. But he really cared about Fancy, really!

However, the garden was getting ready to close. Night had fallen and with night a thick and cold fog had risen. The Count de Trémorel left his bench. He was chilled right to the bone.

"Let's go back to the railroad station," he said to himself.

Alas! At this moment, the idea of blowing out his brains in the corner of some woods, as he was saying so joyously that morning, filled him with horror. He could see his disfigured, bloody cadaver lying at the bottom of some ditch. What would happen to him? Some beggars or some marauders would pass by and strip him. And after that? The law would come. They would take up the

---

[11] Botanical Gardens located in the 5ème arrondissement of Paris, on the left bank of the Seine; it covers 28 hectares.

unidentified body, and waiting for it to be identified, they would probably take it to the morgue.

He shivered. He saw himself stretched out on one of those large marble slabs that are sprayed by a constant jet of cold water. He could hear the shuddering of the crowd that an unhealthy curiosity drew to that sinister place. Then how could he die? He thought about it and settled on the idea of killing himself in some furnished hotel on the left bank.

So that's decided, he thought.

And leaving the garden with the last group of walkers, he reached the Latin Quarter. His carefree attitude of the morning had given way to a gloomy resignation. He was suffering; he had a headache; he was cold.

If I'm not going to die tonight, he thought, *I'm going to have a very bad cold tomorrow.*

That clever point made mentally didn't make him smile, but it made him aware that he was a very strong man. He turned into the Rue Dauphine and looked about for a hotel. Then he thought that, since it wasn't yet seven o'clock, to go to check into a room might raise certain suspicions. He reflected that he still had 140 francs in his pockets and he decided to go have dinner. That would be his last meal. So, he went into a restaurant on the Rue Counterscarp and ordered.

But he tried in vain to shake off the more and more anxious sadness which overcame him. He began to drink. He emptied three bottles without being able to change the direction of his ideas. Attributing to the wine the bitterness of his own thoughts, it seemed detestable to him, although it was excellent and the most expensive of the establishment, costing twenty-five francs ordered from the menu.

The waiters looked with surprise at this gloomy diner who hardly touched what he ordered and, the more he drank, the gloomier he became. The bill for his dinner came to ninety francs. He threw his last one hundred franc bill on the table and left. It still wasn't late. He went into a café-bar full of students who were drinking. He went to sit down at an empty table, at the very back of the room, behind the billiard tables. They brought him a carafe of coffee. He emptied it all into his cup, then a second carafe, then a third.

He didn't want to acknowledge it, to admit it to himself; he was trying to heighten his sensibilities, to built himself up to the level of courage he was going to need. He wasn't succeeding. During the dinner and while he had been in the café, he had drunk an enormous amount. At any other time he would have been drunk. But the alcohol, far from giving him temporary madness, turned his stomach and upset it. He was there at his table, his forehead between his hands, when a waiter crossing the room held out to him a newspaper. He mechanically took it, opened it, and read:

Just as we were going to press we learned about the disappearance of a very well-known person, who had, we add, announced his formal intention of committing suicide. The facts recounted to us are so strange, that, not having time to verify them, we will hold off the details until tomorrow.

These few words burst like a bombshell into the Count de Trémorel's head. This was his death warrant, without a suspended sentence, signed by that tyrant for whom for years he had been the assiduous courtesan: public opinion.

They will never tire of being interested in me! he murmured in a muffled voice of rage—and sincerely for the first time in his life.

Then, resolutely, he added:

All right. It has to be finished.

Five minutes later, in fact, provided with a book and some cigars, he knocked at the door of the Hotel Luxembourg.

Taken by the servant to the best room in the house, he had a fire lit and asked for some sugar water and writing materials. His resolution was at this moment as unshakeable as it had been that morning.

There's no more hesitating, he mumbled. *There's no more turning back.*

He sat down at the table, in front of the fireplace, and with a firm hand wrote the statement destined to the Commissioner of Police. He began and ended it with the recommendation that the owner of the hotel be indemnified. The clock showed 10:55 p.m. He placed his little pistols on the mantle, murmuring;

At midnight I will blow out my brains. I still have an hour to live.

The Count de Trémorel had fallen back into his armchair, his head resting on the back, his feet on the fireplace guard. Why didn't he kill himself immediately? Why give himself, impose on himself, that hour of waiting, of agony, of torture. He wouldn't have been able to say. He was trying to look back over the different circumstances of his life. He was struck by the dizzying rapidity of events that had led him to this miserable bedroom of a furnished hotel. How time passes! It seemed to him yesterday that he had gone for the first time to borrow 100,000 francs. But what good does it do the man who has rolled to the bottom of the abyss to know the cause of his fall!

The big hand of the clock had passed 11:30.

He again thought about that newspaper article that had just fallen under his eyes. Who was responsible for communicating the news? Miss Fancy, without a doubt. The door of the dining room open, she had gotten on her feet, half dressed, frenzied, weeping. When she didn't see him on the boulevard, where did she go? To his house, first of all, then to the club, then to the house of one of his friends. She had spread the news so well that at this evening, even at this moment, among his acquaintances they were talking of nothing else but him. All those who had known him, and they were numerous, came up to each other saying:

"Have you heard the news?'

"Ah! Yes. Poor Trémorel, what a fall! He was a fine fellow. Only..."

It seemed to him he could hear the litany of the "only" greeted by sniggering and jokes in bad taste. Then, his suicide verified or not, they would share what he'd left behind. One would take his mistress, another would buy his horses, a third would go through his moveable property. Time was passing. The strident vibration which announced the stroke of the pendulum was heard. It was time.

The Count got up, seized his pistols and went to stand near the bed, placing himself so that he wouldn't roll to the floor. This is a useless precaution, incomprehensible in a cool moment, and a precautions which all those who commit suicide take.

The first stroke of midnight struck. He didn't fire. Hector was brave and his reputation for courage wasn't something he had to prove. He had fought a duel at least ten times and on the dueling field people had always admired his carefree mockery. One day he had killed his man and that evening he had slept very peacefully. His reckless betting was cited as signs of rash madness. Yes, but he still didn't fire.

That was because there are two types of courage. The first, the false, shines from far off, like the sequined cloak of the strolling player. But it has to have full sunlight, the excitement of the fight, the transport of anger, the uncertainty of the outcome, and above all, the audience which applauds or boos. That's the common courage of the duelist, of the cross-country steeplechase rider. The other one, the real one, doesn't wrap himself in anything. He despises public opinion. He obeys his conscience and not passion. He doesn't worry at all about success. He does his work without public acclaim. That's the courage of the strong man, who, having coldly measured the danger, says: "I'll do this!" and does it.

Midnight had struck two minutes before, and Hector was still there, the pistol pressing his temple.

Could I be afraid? he asked himself.

He was, in fact, afraid and didn't want to admit it. He put his weapons down on the table and went to sit again by the fire. All his limbs were trembling.

It's nerves, he told himself. *That will pass.*

He gave himself until 1:00 a.m. He made unbelievable efforts to prove to himself, to demonstrate the necessity of suicide. What would become of him if he didn't commit suicide? How would he live? Would he therefore have to resign himself to working! Besides, how could he reappear, since through the mouth of his mistress he had announced his suicide to all of Paris? What boos if he showed himself, what jibes! He had a movement of fury which he took for a flash of courage and he jumped to pick up his pistols. The cold steel on his flesh caused him such a feeling that he almost fainted, dropping his weapon, which fell on the bed.

Ah! Why didn't he choose a gentler death! Why hadn't he chosen poison or even asphyxiation, like the little cook at Vachettes. But ridicule from the other side of the tomb no longer frightened him. He was afraid of only one thing:

not having the courage to kill himself. He put it off from half hour to half hour. It was a horrible night, an agony which must be like that of those in their cells condemned to death. He wept with sadness and rage. He wrung his hands; he asked for mercy; he prayed.

Finally, in the morning, broken, devastated, he fell asleep in his chair. Three or four knocks on the door brought him out of a sleep peopled with phantoms. He went to open the door. It was the bellboy who had come to find out if he wanted anything. The boy remained petrified on the threshold at the sight of that man with his clothes in disorder, his tie undone, livid, with swollen eyes, his hair stuck to his temples with sweat.

"I don't need anything," Hector answered. "I'm coming down."

He went downstairs. He had just enough money, barely, to pay his bill. He couldn't give the bellboy but six *sous* as a tip.

It was without a goal, without any ideas, that he left the hotel where he had suffered so much. More than ever he was determined to die. He hoped just for some days to delay, a week, to pull himself together, to get back to his old self. But how could he live a week? He no longer had a centime on him.

An idea of salvation came to him: the Mont-de-Piété pawn shop.

He knew that heaven-sent, 12% remedy only by reputation, just enough to know that they would lend a certain sum on his jewelry. But where could he find one of their offices? Not daring to ask directions to one, he looked about haphazardly throughout the Latin Quarter, that he scarcely knew. He raised his head; he walked with a firm step. He was looking for something; he had a goal.

On the Rue de Condé he saw a sign at the top of a big dark house: *MONT-DE-PIÉTÉ.*[12] He went in. The room was small, humid, dirty and full of people. It was true that if the place was sad, the borrowers seemed to wear their poverty gaily. These were students or women from the neighborhood of the schools, chatting and talking while waiting their turn. The Count de Trémorel went forward, holding in his hand his watch, his watch chain and a very beautiful diamond that he had taken off his finger. The timidity of poverty got hold of him. He didn't know whom to address. A young woman took pity on his embarrassment.

"Look," she told him, "put your things over there on that little shelf in front of the wire netting with green drapes."

At the end of a minute, a voice which seemed to come from a neighboring room, shouted:

"Twelve hundred francs for the watch and the ring."

The enormous amount of the sum produced such a sensation that all conversations stopped. All eyes looked for the millionaire who was going to pocket such a sum. Hector didn't react. Fortunately, the same woman who had already

---

[12] Institutional pawnbroker run as a charity in Europe from the later Middle Ages times till today.

advised Hector, pushed his arm.

"That's for you, the 1,200 francs," she told him. "Answer if you accept or not."

"I accept," Hector exclaimed.

A profound, immense joy made him forget even his torture of the preceding night. Twelve hundred francs! How many days did that sum represent? Hadn't he heard it said that there are some workers who didn't earn that much a year. The other borrowers were making fun of him. They seemed at home there. They had a certain way of answering: "Yes," which got a lot of laughs. Some of them were chatting in a friendly way with the employees or made comments. Hector had been waiting for quite a long time when another employee who was writing behind another grill work cried out:

"Whose are the 1,200 francs?"

The Count went forward. He understood the system.

"They're mine," he answered.

"Your name?"

Hector hesitated. Pronounce his noble name aloud in such a place, never. He chose a name at random:

"Durand."

"Where are your papers?"

"What papers?"

"A passport, a rental receipt, a hunting license."

"I don't have any of that."

"Go get it or bring back two authorized witnesses."

"But, Monsieur..."

"Don't Monsieur me! Next..."

As stunned with the set-back as Hector was, the employees tone made him indignant.

"Then," he said, "give me back my jewelry."

The employee gave him a quietly ironic look.

"Impossible. No registered loan can be returned without proof of legitimate possession."

And without listening to anything else, he continued his work.

"A French shawl, thirty-five francs, whose is it?"

Hector left the Mont-de-Piété surrounded by jibes. The Count de Trémorel had never suffered so much. He had never even had an idea of such agony. After that glimmer of hope, quickly extinguished, the shadows seemed to him deeper and more inexorable. He remained more naked, more robbed of everything than the shipwrecked man from whom the sea has snatched away the last piece of wreckage. The Mont-de-Piété had taken his last resources.

All the poetic fanfare with which he had been pleased to decorate his suicide, vanished, letting him see the saddest, the most ignoble reality. He was going to make an end, not like the handsome gambler who voluntarily leaves the

136

green cloth of the gaming table where he's leaving his fortune, but like the Greek, surprised and turned away, knowing every door will be closed to him. His death would have nothing voluntary about it. He could neither hesitate nor choose his time. He was going to kill himself because he couldn't live another single day. And existence had never seemed to him such a good thing. He had never before felt that exuberance of strength and youth. He suddenly discovered around him, as if in an unexplored country, a host of pleasures, one more enviable than the next, and that he had never tasted. He who prided himself with having wrung pleasure out of life, he had never lived. He had had everything that's sold and bought, nothing that is given or conquered. He had had nothing.

He wasn't yet at the point of reproaching himself for the 10,000 francs offered to Jenny. He regretted lesser things. He regretted the 200 francs divided among the servants, the tip left the evening before for the restaurant waiter, even lesser things: the twenty *sous* thrown to the violet merchant. He had placed that wilted bouquet in his boutonnière, the faded past. What good had it done him? Whereas those twenty *sous!* He no longer thought of the millions wasted. He couldn't chase away the thought of that miserable franc.

Because the roué, the happy man of the world, the man who the evening before had his town house, his ten servants, eight horses in his stables, the credit which comes from a colossal fortune wasted, the Count de Trémorel wanted to smoke and he didn't have anything to buy a cigar with. He was hungry and he didn't have anything to pay for a mean meal in the smallest of greasy spoons.

Of course, if he had wanted to, he could still have procured a lot of money. He had only to go tranquilly back home, stand up to the bailiffs, fight in the middle of the ruins. But what! Then he would confront his social class. Then he would confess his invincible terrors at the last moment. He would be subjected to looks more terrible than a pistol ball. You don't have the right to deceive your public in this way. When you've announced your suicide, you kill yourself. So Hector was going to die because he had said he would, because the newspaper had announced the event. That at least he admitted to himself, and while walking along, he addressed the bitterest reproaches to himself. He remember a pretty place where he had once fought a duel, in the Viroflay Woods. He told himself he would kill himself there. And he went there, following that charming route from the Point-du-Jour. Just as the evening before, the weather was superb. And at every moment groups of women and young men went past him. Those were going to somewhere in the country. When they were already far away, their bursts of laughter still could be heard. In the little restaurants on the edge of the water, under the arbors the honeysuckles were budding out, the workers drinking, clinking their glasses.

All those people seemed happy and content. That gaiety seemed to Hector to insult his present misery. Was he the only unhappy person in the world? He was thirsty, however, intensely, unendurably thirsty. So, when he came to the Pont de Sèvres, he left the road and went down the bank, rather steep at that point. He reached the edge of the Seine. He bent down, dipped some water into the palm of his hand and drank. A fatigue he couldn't resist came over him. There was grass there. He sat down, or rather fell down. The fever of despair came and death now seemed to him a refuge. He thought almost with joy that his ability to think was going to be blotted out and he would suffer no more.

Above him, some meters away were the open windows of one of the Sèvres restaurants. He could be seen there, as well as from the bridge, but he didn't worry about it. He no longer worried about anything.

Just as well here as anywhere else, he told himself.

He was already putting bullets into his pistol when he heard someone calling him:

"Hector! Hector!"

In a bound he was standing, hiding his weapon, looking to see who was shouting his name. On the bank, five feet away, a man was running toward him, his arms outstretched. It was a man his age, a little stout, perhaps, but well made, with a good expansive expression, lit by big dark eyes from which shone frankness and goodness. It was one of those men, likeable at first sight, whom you love when you've known them a week. Hector recognized him. It was his oldest friend, a comrade from secondary school. They had been as close as possible in the past, but the Count, not finding him strong enough to keep up with him, had stopped seeing him little by little. And he hadn't seen him for two years.

"Sauvresy!" he exclaimed, stunned.

"Myself," answered the young man, who arrived out of breath and very red. "I've been following your movements for two minutes. What are you doing here?"

"But...nothing," Hector, embarrassed, answered.

"Mad man," Sauvresy continued, "is it really true what they told me at your house, because I went to your house..."

"What did they tell you?"

"That they didn't know what had happened to you, that the evening before you had left your mistress, telling her you were going to blow your brains out. A newspaper has already announced your death with a lot of details."

That news seemed to make a terrible impression on the Count.

"Then you can see very well, " he answered in a tragic tone, "that I have to kill myself."

"Why? To keep the newspaper from having to make a retraction?"

"People will say I couldn't do it."

"Very nice! Then, according to you, you are forced to commit a folly just because they said you would! That's absurd. Why do you want to kill yourself?"

Hector thought a moment. He could foresee the possibility of living.

"I'm ruined," he answered sadly.

"Then if that's the reason... Look, my friend, let me tell you, you're crazy. Ruined! That's a misfortune, but when you're our age, you remake your fortune.

Without counting on the fact that you're not as ruined as you say, since I have, myself, a hundred thousand pounds of income.

"A hundred thousand pounds..."

"At the last accounting. All my fortune is in land, which doesn't bring in 4%."

Trémorel, knew his friend to be rich, but not so much as that. It might have been an irrational movement of envy that made him say:

"Well! I who had more than that, I haven't eaten this morning."

"Unfortunate man! And you didn't say anything to me about it! But it's true; you're in a pitiable state. Then come on, come on quickly."

And he led him toward the restaurant. Trémorel followed with bad grace that friend who had just saved his life. He was aware of having been surprised in a frightfully ridiculous situation. A man very determined to blow out his brains, if someone shouts to him, presses the trigger and doesn't hide his weapon. Among all his friends, only one loved him enough not to see the ridiculousness. Only one had enough generosity not to make fun of him outrageously. That man was Sauvresy.

But, seated in a booth, in front of a well-supplied table, Hector didn't have the strength to keep up his rigidity. He had that hour of mad sensitivity, of abandoned expansion which follows salvation after immense danger. He was himself. He was alive. He was real. He told Sauvresy everything, absolutely everything, his boasting in the past, his terror at the last moment, his agony at the hotel, his rages, his regrets, his anguish at the Mont-de-Piété.

"Ah!" he said, "You've saved me; you are my friend, my only friend, my brother!"

They stayed there talking more than two hours.

"Let's see," Sauvresy said. "Let's draw up our plans. You want to disappear for a few days; I understand that. But this very evening you're going to address four lines to the newspapers. Tomorrow I'm going to take charge of your affairs. I know how to do it. Without knowing what state they're in, I'll take it on myself to still save a nice living for you. We have money. Your creditors will be accommodating."

"But what will become of me, "asked Hector, frightened by just the thought of being alone.

"What do you mean! I'm taking you with me, *parbleu!* To my house, to Valfeuillu! Didn't you know I was married? Ah! My friend, there's no man happier than I am. I married, for love, the most beautiful and the best of women. You'll be like a brother to us. But come, my carriage is there, in front of the gate."

139

Chapter XIV

Père Plantat stopped. His listeners had allowed themselves neither a gesture nor a word while he was speaking. While listening, Monsieur Lecoq was reflecting. He was wondering where all these details, precise right down to minutia came from. Who had set down Trémorel's terrible biography? And his look moving to the file, he saw very well that all the pages were not written with the same handwriting.

But the old Justice of the Peace was already continuing.

Become Madame Sauvresy thanks to an unexpected twist of fate, Berthe Lechaillu did not love her husband. That daughter of a poor country school teacher, whose wildest visions of ambition in the past didn't go beyond the job of an assistant mistress in one of the Versailles boarding schools, wasn't satisfied with her situation. Absolute queen of the most beautiful domain in the country, surrounded by all the satisfactions of luxury, disposing as she liked of a considerable fortune, loved, adored, she thought herself to be pitied.

That so well-ordered life, so constantly happy, without upheavals, seemed to her heartbreakingly insipid. Weren't they always the same dull pleasures, coming in a certain monotonous order according to the season! You gave receptions or you went out in society; you took horseback rides; you went hunting; you took carriage rides. And it would always be the same way! Ah! That wasn't the kind of life she had dreamed of. She was born for stronger and sharper pleasures. She thirsted for unknown emotions and sensations, looking forward to the uncertainty of the future, the unexpected, changes, passions, adventures, and even many other things.

And then, Sauvresy had displeased her from the first day, and to the extent that she was sure of her hold over him, her secret aversion grew. She found him common, vulgar, ridiculous. He never pretended and she took the perfect simplicity of his behavior for stupidity. She examined him and she could see nothing that stood out on which to hang any admiration. If he was speaking, she didn't listen to him, having in her wisdom decided that he couldn't say anything that wasn't dull and commonplace. She held it against him that he hadn't had one of those stormy youths that appall families. She reproached him for not having lived.

Nevertheless, he had done like everybody else, as much as possible. He had gone to Paris in the past and had tried his friend Trémorel's kind of life. At the end of six months, he had opened his eyes and gone back very quickly to Valfeuillu, taking a rest from the hard work of pleasure. That experience had cost him 100,000 francs, and he didn't regret, he said, having learned at that price what "a life of pleasure" really was.

Berthe was even more infuriated with Sauvresy's perpetual and unlimited adoration. She had only to wish for something to be instantly obeyed and that blind submission to everything she wanted seemed to her servility in a man. A man, she told herself, was born to command and not to obey, to be the master and not the slave. To sum it up, she would have preferred one of those husbands you stand at the window watching for, who come back home in the middle of the night, still warm from an orgy, having lost at cards, and who, if you complain, strike you. Tyrants, but men.

Some months after her marriage, she suddenly began to have the most absurd fantasies, the most extravagant caprices. It was a test. She wanted to see just how far his long-suffering indulgence would go. She thought she could wear him out. She was the one who wore herself out, furious with not having encountered either resistance or objection. To be sure of her husband, absolutely sure, to know that you fill his heart so completely that there is no place for anyone else, to have nothing to fear, not even a seduction, or a whim of a day, seemed to her depressing, intolerable. Then what was the good of being beautiful, witty, young, coquettish enough to turn everyone's head!

"Perhaps Berthe's aversion went further back. She understood herself and admitted to herself that if Sauvresy had just wanted to, he could have made her his mistress and not his wife. He had only to wish it, the honest man, the imbecile! She was so bored in her father's house, morally scraping all her vanities on the thorns of poverty until the blood ran, that just for the promise of a nice apartment and a carriage in Paris, she would have left without turning her head to say a last goodbye to the paternal roof. A carriage! She would have run off for a lot less. Her instincts only lacked the opportunity. And she scorned her husband because he didn't feel enough contempt for her!

Nevertheless, people constantly told her she was the happiest of women. Happy! And there were days when she wept thinking of her marriage. Happy! But there were moments when she had a mad desire to flee, to leave in quest of emotions, adventures, pleasures, of everything she wanted and didn't have, and would never have. The fear of poverty—she knew what it was—held her back. That fear was somewhat due to a wise precaution of her father, recently deceased. She ostentatiously wore mourning for him. She wept warm tears for him, but she damned his memory. At the time of his marriage, Sauvresy wanted to provide 500,000 francs for his wife in the marriage contract. The good man Lechaillu, was formally opposed to that act of generosity.

"My daughter is not bringing you anything," he declared. "You can say she brought 40,000 francs of dowry, if you like, but not a *sou* goes to her. If otherwise, there's no marriage.[13]

And when Sauvresy insisted:

---

[13] Under French contractual marital law, if she was said to have brought 40,000 francs in dowry, this amount would be returned to her upon the dissolution of the marriage for whatever cause.

"Let me hear no more about it," he answered. "My daughter will be, I hope, a good and worthy spouse, and in that case your fortune is hers. If, on the contrary, she should behave badly, 40,000 francs would still be too much. After that, if you fear you may die first, you're free to make a will."

"Obedience was forced. Perhaps Père Lechaillu, the worthy school master, understood his daughter. In this case, he was the only one who did. Never was more complete hypocrisy put in the service of perversity so profound that it could have been thought exaggerated, of inconceivable depravity in a young woman who had seen so little of the world. If, at the bottom of her heart she felt herself the most unfortunate of creatures, nothing of that appeared; it was a well-guarded secret. All of her actions were so well characterized by a calculating political standpoint that her admirable play-acting created an illusion, even to the piercing eye of jealousy. She had learned how to show her husband, instead of love which she did not feel, the appearances of a passion both ardent and discreet, certain surreptitious looks thrown out furtively—and surprised—a word, her expression in the drawing room when he entered. She did it so well that everybody said:

"Beautiful Berthe is mad about her husband."

That was Sauvresy's conviction. He was the first to say, not hiding the joy it gave him:

"My wife adores me."

Such was exactly the situation at Valfeuillu when Sauvresy met at Sèvres, on the edge of the Seine, his friend Trémorel, his pistol in his hand. That evening, for the first time since his marriage, Sauvresy missed dinner after having promised to return on time, and they were waiting for him. His being late was so incomprehensible that Berthe should have been worried. She was only indignant at what she called an absolute lack of consideration. She was even wondering what punishment she should give the guilty man, when at 10:00 p.m. the Valfeuillu drawing room door opened suddenly. Sauvresy was on the threshold, gay, smiling:

"Berthe," he said, "I'm bringing you a ghost."

She hardly deigned to raise her head and went on with the newspaper paragraph she was reading. Sauvresy continued:

"Here's a man come back from the dead that you know, whom I've often spoken to you about. You'll love him, since I love him. He's my oldest comrade, my best friend."

And standing aside, he pushed Hector into the drawing room, saying:

"Madame Sauvresy, allow me to introduce you to Monsieur le Comte Hector de Trémorel."

Berthe suddenly stood up, embarrassed, nervous, agitated by an inexpressible emotion as if confronted by a frightening apparition. For the first time in her life she was confused, intimidated, not daring to lift her big clear blue eyes with glints of steel grey.

"Monsieur," she stammered, "Monsieur, please believe…from the moment my husband... Please feel welcome."

She was very familiar with that name of de Trémorel, which suddenly burst out in her drawing room. In addition to the fact that Sauvresy had told it to her, she had seen it in the newspapers. All her neighbors from the neighboring chateaux had said it.

In her mind, according to what she had read or heard, the man who bore it must be a huge personality, almost superhuman. He was, she had been told, a hero from another age, a mad man, pleasure-seeking to an excess.

He was one of those men whose life horrifies common people, whom the idiotic bourgeois think has no faith or law, whose inordinate passions explode the narrow framework of prejudices. He was one of those men who dominate others, who's feared, who kills anyone who gives him a filthy look. He was a man who threw out gold with a prodigal hand, whose iron health resisted terrible excesses. He was a man who ruled with the same whip his mistresses and his horses, his mistresses the most beautiful and the most extravagant in Paris, his horses the most noble beasts from England.

Often, in her desperate dreams, she had tried to imagine what this fearful Count de Trémorel might be like. She attributed to him qualities she supposed he had, those of the heroes on whose arms she fled toward the land of adventures, very far from her husband. And there he had suddenly appeared.

"So, shake hands with Hector," Sauvresy said.

She held out her hand. Hector squeezed it lightly and at that contact it seemed to her that she received an electric shock.

Sauvresy had thrown himself into an armchair.

"So you see, Berthe," he said. "Our friend Hector is worn out by the life he leads. At least anyone would be. He's been told he should rest. And he's come to look for that rest here, near us."

"But, my love," Berthe answered, "Aren't you afraid that *Monsieur le comte* will be a little bored here?"

"He, why?"

"Valfeuillu is very quiet; we're poor country people."

Berthe was speaking just to be speaking, to break the silence weighing heavily on her, to force Trémorel to answer and to hear his voice. While talking she was watching him and observing the effect she had on him. Usually, her radiant beauty struck those who saw her for the first time clearly with astonishment. He remained impassive.

Ah! How well she recognized that coldness, that superb indifference of the blasé *grand seigneur*, the man of the world who has tried everything, experienced everything, worn out everything. And the fact that he didn't admire her made her admire him more.

She was thinking: *What a difference from this commonplace Sauvresy, that just anything astonishes, who is astounded with everything, whose expression shows everything he's thinking, whose eyes announce everything he's going to say well before he opens his mouth.*

Berthe was mistaken. Hector was neither so cold nor so impassive as she supposed. Hector was simply worn out with sheer fatigue. His nerves, overextended during forty-eight hours were relaxing. He could hardly remain upright. He soon asked permission to retire.

Alone with his wife, Sauvresy recounted the deplorable circumstances—that was his word—which brought the Count to Valfeuillu. A true friend, he avoided all the details capable of making his friend look ridiculous.

"He's a big child," he said, "a madman, his head is sick, but we'll take care of him; we'll cure him."

Berthe had never listened to her husband with that much attention. She seemed to agree with him, but in reality she admired Trémorel. Yes! Like Miss Fancy she was struck by that heroism: to waste his fortune and then kill himself.

Ah! she sighed, *Sauvresy isn't the one who would do that much.*

No, Sauvresy wasn't the man to behave himself like the Count de Trémorel. The day after the arrival of the Count at Valfeuillu, he announced his intention of taking care of his friend's affairs without delay; that was when getting up from lunch in the pretty greenhouse arranged as a living room off the billiard room.

Well-rested after a good and long night in an excellent bed, without pressing worries for the moment, his dress restored to order, Hector showed nothing of the shipwreck of the evening before. He had one of those personalities that events do not affect, that forty-eight hours console for the worst catastrophes, who forget the most severe lessons of life. Turned out by Sauvresy, he wouldn't have known where to go, and nevertheless he had already again assumed that carefree haughty attitude of the millionaire man of the world, habituated to bending men and circumstances at his pleasure. He had again become impassive, coldly joking, as if years had gone by since his night in the furnished room, as if the disasters to his fortune had been repaired.

And Berthe was astonished by this calm after such surprising reversals, considering as strength of soul what was only childish lack of forethought in Trémorel.

"All right," Sauvresy said, "since I'm becoming your business agent, give me some instructions and some indispensable ideas. What is, or were, whichever you like, the amount of your fortune?"

"I have absolutely no idea."

Sauvresy, who had armed himself with a pencil and a big sheet of white paper, ready to set the figures in battle array, seemed a little surprised.

"All right," he answered, "let's put an X on what you borrowed and go on to what you owe. What do you owe?"

Hector made a gesture beyond disdainful.

"*Ma foi!*" he answered, "I don't know anything about that."

"What! Not even vaguely?"

"Oh! Yes, I do, in fact. I owe between 500,000 and 600,000 francs to the Clair bank; to Dervoy, 500,000 francs; about the same amount to Dubois d'Orléans."

"And in addition to that?"

"My exact recollections stop there."

"But you at least probably have somewhere a notebook in which you wrote the amount of the different sums you borrowed?"

"No."

"At least you kept the titles, the terms of the amounts you borrowed, the main points of your various obligations?"

"Nothing. Yesterday morning I made a bonfire of all my pieces of paper."

The master of Valfeuillu was startled. Such behavior seemed to him monstrous. He couldn't suppose that Hector was acting. Nevertheless, he was acting. That pretense of ignorance was the ultimate conceit of the fashionable man of the world. To bankrupt himself without knowing how it happened, was very noble, very distinguished, very *Ancien Régime.*

"But, then, unfortunate man," Sauvresy exclaimed. "How do I go about cleaning up your affairs?"

"Don't clean them up. Do as I do; let my creditors go ahead. They'll know how to sort it all out. Take it easy. Let them auction off my estate."

"Never! If it comes to an auction, you're absolutely ruined."

"Baste! A little or a little less!"

What sublime disinterest, Berthe was thinking. *What a carefree attitude, what an admirable contempt for money, what noble disdain for the petty little details which occupy common men!*

Was Sauvresy capable of such detachment? She certainly couldn't accuse him of avarice. For her he had become as prodigal as a thief. He never refused her anything. He anticipated her most costly fantasies. But at the end he had the greed for gain of a peasant's son. And despite his great fortune, he kept something of the paternal veneration for money. When he had some business to do with one of his farmers, he wasn't afraid to rise very early in the morning, get on a horse, even in the middle of the winter, to ride three or four leagues in the rain to collect a few *écus.* She was convinced he would have bankrupted himself for her, if she had wanted him to. But he would have ruined himself as cheaply as possible, in an orderly way, like the dull bourgeois who opens a bank account for his vices.

Sauvresy was thinking.

"You're right," he told Hector. "You creditors must know your situation exactly. Who knows but what they didn't collaborate on it? The way they refused you a loan of 100,000 francs with the most touching togetherness, makes me suppose they did. I'm going to go find them."

"The Clair Bank, where I made my first loans, should be the best informed."

"All right, I'll go see Monsieur Clair. But, listen, if you were reasonable, do you know what you would do?"

"Tell me."

"You'd go with me to Paris, and together we'd..."

At that suggestion, Hector stood up, very pale, his eyes shining.

"Never!" he violently interrupted. "Never!"

His "very dear friends" at the club still terrified him. What! Out of favor, fallen, ridiculed because of his failed suicide, he should dare reappear in the theater of his glory! Sauvresy had opened his arms to him. Sauvresy was a brave heart who loved him enough not to dwell on the falseness of his situation, not to judge him a coward for having drawn back, but the others...!

"Don't talk to me anymore about Paris," he added in a calmer tone. "I swear to you, I'll never set foot there again in my lifetime."

"All right, so much the better. Stay here with us. I'll not be the one to complain about that, nor will my wife. And one fine day, we'll find an heiress for you in the neighborhood."

Berthe nodded agreement without lifting her eyes.

"All right," Sauvresy continued. "It's time for me to leave if I don't want to miss the train."

"I'll go with you to the train," Trémorel said quickly.

That wasn't a purely friendly consideration on his part. He wanted to ask his friend to inquire about the objects left at the Mont-de-Piété pawnshop on the Rue de Condé and also to ask him to go by to see Miss Fancy.

From bedroom window, Berthe followed the two friends who, arm in arm, were going up the Orléans road. *What a difference between these two men,* she was thinking.

A little while ago my husband said he would like to be his friend's steward. In fact, he looks only too much like his steward.

What a truly noble bearing he Count has, what easy grace, what outstanding distinction. And my husband, I'm sure, disdains him because he bankrupted himself doing foolish things. Ah! Why isn't he himself capable of doing the same thing. I thought I saw he had put on certain protective airs. Poor boy!

But doesn't everything about Monsieur de Trémorel show an innate or acquired superiority, everything, right down to his first name: Hector! How nice it sounds, that name! And she took pleasure in repeating it: *Hector! Hector! My husband's first name is Clément!*

Monsieur de Trémorel came back alone from the railway station, happy as a convalescent on his first outing. As soon as Berthe saw him, she quickly left the window. She wanted to be alone, to think about that event suddenly fallen into her life, to analyze her feelings, to listen to her premonitions, to study her impressions, to make herself mistress of herself. And lay out, if she could, a plan of behavior. She reappeared only to come to the dinner table when her husband,

146

whom they had waited for, came back at 11:00 p.m.

Sauvresy was dying of hunger and thirst. He appeared exhausted with fatigue, but his excellent face was shining.

"Victory! friend Hector," he was saying while swallowing his too hot soup. "We'll snatch you from the hands of the Philistines. *Dame!* The most brilliant plumes of your wings will stay there, but you'll be saved enough down to make a nice nest with."

Berthe gave her husband a look of thanks.

"And how can you do that?" she asked.

"It's very simple. First of all, I guessed the game of our friend's creditors. They counted on getting permission to auction off your estate as a whole. They bought them as a unit, at a vile price. As always in situations like these, they resell individual pieces at a very high price and share the profits."

"And you can prevent that?" Trémorel asked in a disbelieving tone.

"Perfectly, and I threw these Messieurs plans off track. I succeeded, which was taking a chance, but I had the good fortune to get them all together the same evening. I told them: 'You're going to let us voluntarily sell by mutual agreement; if not, I'll join the game and mix up the cards.' They gave me an ironic look. But my notary, that I had taken with me, added: 'This gentleman is Monsieur Sauvresy, and if he asks, the Crédit Foncier[14] tomorrow will advance him 2,000,000 francs.'

"Our men opened their eyes wide and agreed to whatever I wanted."

Whatever he might have said, Hector knew enough about his affairs to know that transaction would save him a fortune, small in comparison to what he had possessed, but a fortune after all. That certainty delighted him and with a movement of true gratitude, squeezing Sauvresy's hand between his own hands:

"Ah! my friend," he exclaimed, "you're restoring my honor after having saved my life. For what you're giving me, how can I ever thank you!"

"By committing only reasonable follies in the future. See, like me," he added, leaning over to embrace his wife, while adding:

"And nothing more to fear!"

"Nothing! Because I would have borrowed the two million, yes, and they saw that I would. But that's not all. The proceedings are stopped. I went to your town house and I took it on myself to dismiss all your servants with the exception of your valet and a groom. If you'll take my advice, as of tomorrow we'll send all your horses to Tattersal, where they'll sell very well. As for the horse you usually ride, he'll be here tomorrow. "

These details shocked Berthe. She thought her husband was being too obliging, descending right down to servility.

Decidedly, she thought, *he was born to be a steward.*

Sauvresy was continuing:

---

[14] National mortgage bank created in 1852.

"And last of all, do you know what I did? Thinking that you arrived here like a little St. John, I ordered them to fill three or four trunks with your personal items. They took them to the train station and when I arrived I sent a servant to get them.

Hector himself was beginning to find Sauvresy's kindness excessive and that he was treating him a great deal too much like a child who couldn't take care of anything. The circumstances of his destitution recounted in front of a woman wounded him. He was forgetting that that same morning he had found it very simple to send to borrow linen from his friend.

He was looking for one of his clever jokes which saved a situation, when he heard a loud noise in the vestibule. The trunks had probably arrived. Berthe left to give orders.

"Quickly, while we're alone," said Sauvresy, "here is your jewelry. Ah! I had a lot of trouble getting them. They're mistrustful at the Mont-de-Piété. I really think they at first took me for a member of a band of thieves."

"At least you didn't say my name!"

'That would have been useless. Fortunately, my notary was with me. No, you never know all a notary can do to be of service. Don't you think society is unjust toward notaries?"

Trémorel thought his friend was speaking very lightly about serious things, sad even, and that light tone irritated him.

"Finally," Sauvresy continued, "I paid Miss Jenny a visit. She had been in bed since the evening before. She had been taken there after your departure, and her maid told me that since the evening before she hadn't stopped crying so much it would break your heart."

"And she had let no one come to see her?"

"Absolutely no one. She believed you were really dead. And when I swore to her that you were with me, very much alive and in very good health, I thought she would go mad with joy. Don't you know she is really pretty?"

"Yes, she's not bad."

"And what's more, I believe she's really a good person. She told me extremely touching things. I would almost bet, my dear friend, that she has sincere affection for you."

Hector showed a beautiful smile of self-satisfaction. Affection! The word was pale...

"In brief," Sauvresy added, "she wanted to follow me, to see you, to speak to you. For her to let me leave, I had to swear to her with terrible oaths that she would see you tomorrow, not in Paris, since you had declared to me that you never want to set foot there again, but in Corbeil."

"Ah! If you put it like that..."

"Tomorrow, then. At noon she'll be at the station. We'll leave here together. While I take the train to Paris, you yourself will get on the one to Corbeil. Arrange it so that you seem to be going to eat out and you can, over there, have lunch with Miss Fancy at the Belle Image hotel."

"Would there be anyone there to see us?"

"Not the least. The Belle Image is a large inn. Its location at the entry into the village puts it absolutely away from the curious and indiscreet. From here, by following the edge of the water and by taking the street which goes around the Darblay mill, you can go and come without being seen by anyone."

Hector was preparing an objection. Sauvresy with a gesture made him be silent.

"Here's my wife," he said. "Not a word."

Chapter XV

Going upstairs to bed that evening, the Count de Trémorel was a great deal less enthusiastic about his friend Sauvresy's devotion. There's no diamond in which a flaw isn't found if it's examined with a magnifying glass.

There he is, he said to himself, *ready to take advantage of his role as savior. He passes himself off as a mentor and makes speeches. Don't people know how to help you without making you feel it? Doesn't it seem that because he stopped me from blowing out my brains, I become something that belongs to him? If he had gone a little further this evening he was going to reproach me for Fancy's exorbitant cost! Where will his zeal stop?*

That didn't prevent him at breakfast the next day from pretending not to feel well in order not to eat and he pointed out to Sauvresy that he was going to miss the train.

As the evening before, Berthe, resting her elbows on her window sill, watched them leaving. She had been so upset for forty-eight hours that she no longer recognized herself. She was already at the point of not daring to reflect or to descend into the depths of her heart. So what mysterious power did he possess, that man, to have entered her life so violently! She was hoping that he would go away and never come back. At the same time she admitted that in leaving he would carry all her thoughts with him. And, under his spell, she debated with herself, not knowing if she ought to rejoice or curse herself for the unexplainable emotions that stirred in her, irritated for submitting to domination stronger than her will.

She decided that she would go down to the drawing room that day. He couldn't—if only through politeness—not come down, and then, she thought seeing him closer, making him talk, getting to know him better, his prestige would vanish He was certainly going to come back, and she watched for his return, ready to go downstairs as soon as she saw him coming from the Orcival road. She waited for him with feverish quivering, as anxious as at the moment of a battle, feeling certain that this first têteà-tête without her husband's presence would be decisive.

But time passed. He had left with Sauvresy more than two hours before and he had not come back. Where could he be?

At that same moment, Hector was walking up and down the Corbeil railway waiting room, anticipating Miss Fancy's arrival. Finally, he heard a great commotion. The employees were running about; the baggage men rolling carts were going across the tracks; doors were opening and closing noisily. The train was arriving.

Soon Miss Fancy appeared.

Her sadness, her joy, her emotions hadn't kept her from thinking about her outfit and she had never been more flashily elegant and pretty. She was wearing a pea-green dress with a train a half-meter long, a velvet coat which seemed to have no end, and one of those hats called an "accident hat" because it caused the horses pulling boulevard carriages to rear up.

As soon as she saw Hector, who had remained standing near the exit door, she let out a cry, roughly pushing aside the people who found themselves in her path and ran to throw her arms around his neck, laughing and crying at the same time. She spoke in a very loud voice with gestures that her outfit made seem more untidy, and everyone could hear her.

"Then you didn't kill yourself," she was saying. "How I suffered, but how happy I am today!"

Trémorel himself struggled as well as he could, trying to calm Fancy's loud demonstrations, pushing her away gently, both delighted and irritated. As a Parisian accustomed to passing though crowds unnoticed, he was exasperated by all those big eyes fixed on him.

But none of the travelers left. They all remained there, mouths agape, looking, waiting. They were staring at them; they made a circle around them; they were all over them.

"All right! Come on!" Hector, at the end of his patience, said.

And he dragged her away, hoping to escape that naïve and imprudent curiosity of idle people for whom everything is a distraction. But they didn't escape it. They were followed at a distance. Some Corbeil citizens, mounted on the top seats of the bus which went ran between the railway station and the train, asked the conductor to go slowly so that they might not lose sight of those unusual strangers. And it was only when they had disappeared under the portico of the hotel that the vehicle picked up a trot.

Sauvresy's plans were thus upset, Jenny's too triumphal entry made a sensation. The citizens were uneasy; they went to get information; the hostess was cleverly questioned, and soon they knew that the gentleman who waited for such eccentric ladies at the railroad station was the intimate friend of the owner of Valfeuillu.

Neither Hector nor Jenny suspected then that they were the subject of every conversation. They lunched gaily in the prettiest bedroom of the *Belle Image*. It was an immense room decorated with well-varnished and framed pictures of gentlemen on horseback. It had two beds and a single window looking out over the square.

To double his mistress's admiration, Trémorel, to explain his resurrection, had fabricated a somewhat probable novel where he played a heroic role. Then, in her turn, Miss Fancy unfolded her plans for the future which were, you have to give her credit, most reasonable. Even so and more than ever resolved to remain faithful to her ruined Hector, she was going to give up her six thousand franc apartment, sell its contents, and begin an honest business. She had just run into one of her old friends, a very talented worker in women's fashions, and who asked nothing better than to become associated with a friend who would supply the money while she contributed her know-how. They would buy a milliner's shop in the Bréda neighborhood. In their hands it couldn't fail to prosper and to bring in a nice profit.

Jenny was speaking with a little knowledgeable air, exhausting her repertory of technical terms and Hector was laughing. These business projects seemed to him comic in the extreme, but he was very touched by that self-denial of a young and pretty woman willing to work, to do something, and to do that to please him.

Unfortunately, they had to separate. Jenny had come to Corbeil intending to stay there a week, but the count told her that was absolutely impossible. At first she wept a great deal, got angry, then finally was consoled with the idea of returning the following Tuesday.

"All right, then, good-bye," she said, embracing Hector. "Think about me."

And smiling, with a mischievous gesture, she added:

"However, I should be worried. There were some gentlemen on the train who know your friend and who said that his wife is perhaps the most beautiful woman in France. Is that true?

"I couldn't tell you! I forgot to look at her."

Hector wasn't lying. Without its being apparent, he was still dominated by the distress of his failed suicide. He was undergoing that dizziness which, like violent shocks to the head, follows great moral crises and prevents attention being directed to exterior things. But those words, "the most beautiful woman in France," caught his attention and he could that very evening repair his forgetfulness.

When he got back to Valfeuillu, his friend had not yet returned. Madame Sauvresy was alone, reading, in the very well-lit drawing room. Seated facing her, but a little to one side, Hector could observe her at his ease, while throwing out some banal sentences.

His first impression was unfavorable to Berthe. He found her beauty too statuesque and also far too perfect. He looked for imperfections in her and, not finding any, he became almost afraid of that beautiful immobile face, of those very clear eyes whose look struck you like the point of a sword. Perhaps just his instinct made him, the weak, vacillating, irresolute man, fear an energetic, determined personality of implacable daring. Little by little, however, he became use to spending a great part of the afternoon with Berthe while Sauvresy ran about taking care of liquidating his affairs, selling, bargaining, using his days lowering interest rates, talking with lawyers and business men.

He became quickly aware of the pleasure she took in listening to him, and because of that, he judged her a very witty woman and well above her husband. He had no wit himself, but only a store, inexhaustible for years, of anecdotes and adventures. He had seen so many things; he had brushed up against so many people, that he was interesting to leaf through like a newspaper. He still had a certain sparkling verve which wasn't lacking in brilliance and a polite cynicism which was at first surprising.

Less under his spell, Berthe would have judged him at his true worth, but she had lost her free will. She listened to him, plunged into a sort of mindless ecstasy, as you listen to a traveler returned from those foreign lands, who has visited peoples whose very existence you were ignorant of, and lived in the middle of customs and civilizations incomprehensible for us.

However, days passed, weeks, months, and the Count de Trémorel wasn't as bored at Valfeuillu as it was supposed he would be. He slid, without knowing it, down that gentle slope of material well-being which leads straight to brutishness. His fever of the first days had been followed by a physical and moral dullness, without disagreeable sensations, if it was lacking in anything exciting.

He ate and drank a great deal and got his twelve hours sleep. The rest of the time, when he wasn't talking with Berthe, he wandered around the grounds, rocked in an American rocking chair, or went horseback riding. He even went so far as going fishing at the end of the garden under the weeping willow trees. He gained weight.

His best days were those he spent in Corbeil with Miss Fancy. In her he found something of his past and she always had some quarrel with which to wake him up. Besides, she brought him some whiffs of Paris air in the folds of her dress, and in her little boots the mud of the boulevards.

Jenny came exactly on time every week, and her love for Hector, far from growing weaker, seemed to grow with each meeting. Perhaps she wasn't explaining perfectly all her feelings. The poor girl's affairs were going rather badly. She had bought her stock a great deal too high priced and her associate, at the end of a month had decamped, carrying with her three thousand francs. She understood nothing about the business she had undertaken and she was shamelessly robbed on all sides. She wasn't telling Hector anything about her worries, but she was certainly counting on him to come to her aid. That was the least he could do after the great sacrifice to which she had resigned herself for him.

At the beginning, the regular visitors to Valfeuillu were somewhat astonished at the continued presence of the tall young man who dragged around his idleness like a cannon ball. Then, they grew use to him. Hector had ended up putting on an expression suitable for a being tested by unbelievable misfortunes and to whom life had lied about its promises. He seemed harmless. They adopted him. They said:

The Count de Trémorel has charming simplicity.

But he had, at certain moments, when he was alone, sudden and terrible reversals. *Life can't go on like this,* he thought, and he was carried away by childish rages when he compared the past with the present. How could he shake off this gloomy existence, how could he get rid of all these people, straight as morality, flatter than reality, who surrounded him, who were Sauvresy's friends? But where could he flee, where take refuge? The temptation to reappear in Paris never occurred to him. And, besides, what would he do there? His former town-house had been sold to a former patent leather merchant. He had no money except what he borrowed from Sauvresy. And this Sauvresy was, in Hector's thoughts, a terrible, intruding, implacable friend, hard as the surgeon who takes very little thought about making the patient he's trying to save cry out under the scalpel.

"Your boat is sinking," he had said to Hector. "Let's throw overboard all that's superfluous first of all. Let's keep nothing from the past. It's dead; let's bury it and let nothing remind us of it. Your situation turned into cash, we'll see."

That liquidation was very laborious. Creditors popped up from the ground, from every direction, and the list was never finished. They even came from abroad, from England. Several of them had certainly been paid, but they couldn't be presented a receipt and they grew angry. Some, whose claims were far too exorbitant, were turned down and threatened a lawsuit, hoping that they would pay to avoid a scandal.

And Sauvresy tired out his friend with his constant activity. Every two or three days he went to Paris and he made several trips at the time of the sale to the property in Bourgogne and Orléanais. After at first having taken him to be a clown, the Count de Trémorel frankly detested him. He hated him. Sauvresy's constantly happy appearance, made him despair. Jealousy poisoned him. Just one thought, one detestable thought, consoled him a little.

Sauvresy's happiness, he told himself, *comes most of all from the fact that he's an imbecile. He believes his wife is crazy about him, and the truth is that she can't stand him.*

In fact, Berthe had come to the point of letting Hector guess her aversion for her husband. She was no longer studying her heart's reactions, she loved Hector and she admitted it to herself. In her preconceived ideas, he absolutely filled the ideal of her feverish dreams. But she was at the same time exasperated by not seeing in him any love for her. Her beauty was not then irresistible, as she has heard it said so many times. Toward her he was attentive, even gallant, but nothing more. She thought, not without anger:

If he was in love with me, daring as he is with women, fearing nothing or nobody, he would tell me so.

And she began to detest that woman—that rival—that he went to meet every week in Corbeil. She wanted to know about her, see her. What could she be like? Was she very beautiful?

Hector had been impenetrable on the subject of Miss Fancy. Cleverly questioned, he had responded only vaguely, not being sorry to let Berthe's imagination stray into suppositions which could only be very flattering for him.

Finally there came a day when she could no longer resist the obsession of her curiosity. She put on the simplest of her black dresses, put on a very thick veil over her hat, and ran to the Corbeil station at the hour she guessed the unknown woman was to leave.

She installed herself in the courtyard on a bench hidden by two trucks. She didn't have long to wait. Soon, at the end of the avenue, that she could watch from her position, she saw the Count and his mistress approaching. They were arm in arm and seemed the happiest of lovers in the world. They passed within three feet of her, and as they were walking very slowly, she could examine Miss Fancy; at her leisure. She found her pretty and without the least distinction.

Having seen what she wanted to see, reassured by that certainty, proving her inexperience, that Miss Jenny, being a woman of nothing, being nothing to fear, Berthe was no longer thinking of anything but leaving very quickly. But she chose her time badly! Just as she was going past the vehicles hiding her, Hector came out of the station. They crossed each other at the grillwork fence and their eyes met.

Did he recognize her? His face expressed the greatest surprise. Nevertheless, he didn't greet her in any way.

Yes, he recognized me, Berthe was thinking as she regained Valfeuillu by the road running along the edge of the water. And surprised, somewhat frightened by her audacity, she asked herself if she ought to be mortified or rejoice because of that encounter. What would come of it?

Ten minutes behind her, Hector was following her on that road that hugged the Seine. He was, himself, unusually astonished. Already for some time, his vanity, always on the lookout, had told him what was going on in Berthe's mind. But even though modesty was not one of his flaws, he was far from believing in a feeling strong enough to bring about such a step.

She loves me, he kept repeating to himself while walking. *She's in love with me!*

He didn't yet know what to decide to do. Should he take flight? Should he behave the same way as usual with her, pretending not to have seen her? However, there shouldn't be any hesitation. He must leave quickly, that same evening, without hesitating, without looking back; flee as if the house was about to crumble over his head. That was his first thought. It was promptly stifled by the explosion of base and vile passions fermenting inside him.

Ah! Sauvresy himself had held out his hand to him when he was drowning! Sauvresy had taken him in after having saved him. He opened his heart, his house and his purse to him. At this very moment he was wearing himself out in efforts to restore his fortune. Men of the stamp of the Count de Trémorel could receive so many and such great services only as outrages. Wasn't his stay at Valfeuillu a continual suffering? Wasn't his ego tortured from morning to night? He could count the days by the humiliations. What! He must submit to, if not recognize, the superiority of a man he had treated as an inferior!

Besides, he was thinking, judging his friend's heart by his own, *Isn't it only through pride, through ostentation, that he seems to conduct himself so well toward me? What am I in his chateau if not the living testimony of his bounty, of his generosity, and of his devotion? He seems no longer to live except for me: Trémorel here! Trémorel there! He triumphs by my defeat. He makes my ruin his decoration. He makes it a glory and a title to public admiration.*

Decidedly, he couldn't pardon his friend for being so rich, so happy, so respected, for having known how to conduct his life while he, at thirty had wasted his. And he shouldn't seize the opportunity that was presenting itself to avenge himself for so many kind deeds that were overwhelming him? Oh! Yes he would!

After all is said and done, he told himself, trying to silence the dull murmurs of his conscience. *Did I go after his wife? She's coming to me of her own free will, without the least attempt at seduction. To push her away would be trickery.*

Envy has irresistible arguments. Hector's determination was irrevocable. When he entered Valfeuillu, he didn't leave. And nevertheless he had neither the excuse of passion nor the excuse of seduction. He was not in love. He never loved his friend's wife and his infamy was thought out, reasoned, coldly premeditated. But between her and him, a chain was forged, more solid that the fragile chains of adultery: their mutual hatred of Sauvresy. They both owed him too much. His hand had held them back at the edge of the cesspit toward which they were going to roll. Because Hector would not have blown out his brains, because Berthe would not have found a husband. They would have met their fate, he to drag along a great dishonored name behind the knights of industry; she to show off a faded beauty on the chairs of the boulevard.

The hours of their first rendezvous were spent in angry words rather than in words of love. They felt too deeply, too cruelly the ignominy of their conduct not to try to reassure themselves there was no need for remorse. They forced themselves to prove to each other that Sauvresy was ridiculous and odious. As if, by supposing he was ridiculous, they were forgiven.

If our society is horrible to the point that confidence is considered stupidity, then, he was a fool, that man of courage they were deceiving under his eyes, in his house. He was a fool because he had faith in his wife and in his friend. He didn't suspect anything and every day he congratulated himself for having saved Trémorel, for having given him stability. He repeated his famous sentence to everyone he met: "I am too happy!"

Berthe, it's true, expended treasures of duplicity to maintain his happy illusions. So often capricious, nervous, self-willed in the past, she became little by little submissive even to acting selflessly and with angelic sweetness. The future of her liaison depended on her husband. It was worth anything to avoid the slightest suspicion from touching his naïve security. She was paying the horrible price of adulterous women, brought down by fear, by worry every moment, to the most shameful and the most dishonorable tricks of passion. Besides, their caution was such that no one around them ever suspected anything, a rare occurrence.

And nevertheless, Berthe wasn't happy. That love gave her none of the celestial joy she had anticipated. She had hoped to be wafted into the clouds, and she remained on earth, coming up against all the vulgar miseries of a life of lies and fear of approaching catastrophe. Perhaps she realized that for Hector she was mainly a vengeance, that in her he loved, above all, the wife taken away from a friend that he cowardly envied. And to top it all off, she was jealous! After several months, she hadn't been able to get Trémorel to break off his affair with Miss Fancy. Each time she resigned herself to bringing up that question, so humiliating for her, he gave the same answer, cautious and sensible, but certainly injurious and irritating:

"Please, Berthe, I ask you," he answered, "think about the fact that Miss Fancy is our security."

The fact was, however, that he was thinking about ways to get rid of Jenny. The enterprise presented difficulties. Fallen into relative poverty, the poor girl had become more clinging than ivy and was desperately holding on to Hector. She often made scenes in front of him, claiming he was no longer the same, that he had changed. And she was sad; she wept; she had red eyes.

One evening, in an excess of anger after having waited for her lover for a part of the day, she made some unusual threats.

"You have another mistress," she told him. "I know it. I have proof. Be careful! If you ever leave me, my anger will fall on her. And you can be sure I'll hold nothing back."

The Count de Trémorel made the mistake of attaching no importance to Miss Fancy's words. However, they hastened the separation.

She's becoming insupportable, he thought, *and if I didn't show up one day, she would be capable of following me back right to Valfeuillu and making a terrible scandal there.*

That was why, with the help of Berthe's complaints and tears, he armed himself with courage and left for Corbeil, ready to break it off at any cost. To announce his intentions, he took all imaginable precautions, looking for good reasons, for plausible pretexts.

"You have to be sensible, you know, Jenny," he said, "and for once stop thinking about us. I'm ruined. You know that. Only a marriage can save me."

Hector had prepared himself for a terrible explosion of anger, for high-pitched screams, for an attack of nerves, for fainting. Nothing. To his amazement, Miss Jenny didn't say a single word. She only became whiter than her ruffles. Her lips, usually so red, turned white. Her big eyes filled not with blood, but with bile. Her teeth, clenched by her controlled anger.

"So," she said, "you're going to be married!"

"It has to be, alas!" he answered with a hypocritical sigh. "Remember that lately I haven't been able to help you except by borrowing money from my friend. His purse won't be eternally available to me."

Miss Fancy took Hector's hands and drew him into the light near the window. There, staring at him, as if her obstinate look could shake the truth out of him, she said to him slowly, emphasizing each word:

"Is it really true, if you are leaving me, it's to marry?"

Hector freed one of his hands to place it over his heart.

"I swear it to you, on my honor," he maintained.

"Then I have to believe you."

Jenny had returned to the middle of the bedroom. Standing in front of the mirror, she put back on her hat, dangling the straps gracefully, quietly, as if nothing had happened. When she was ready to leave, she came back to Trémorel:

"One last time," she asked in a tone she forced to remain steady and which belied her eyes shining with a tear ready to fall, "a last time, Hector, it's really over?"

"It has to be."

Fancy made a gesture Trémorel didn't see. Her face took on a menacing look. Her lips half opened for an ironic answer, but she changed her mind almost immediately.

"I'm leaving, Hector," she said after thinking a moment. "If you are really leaving me to be married, you will never hear any more from me." "Eh! My child, I really hope I will stay your friend." "All right! All right! If, on the other hand, as I think, you're leaving me for another mistress, remember what I'm telling you. You're a dead man, and she's a lost woman." She opened the door. He tried to take her hand. She pushed him away. "Adieu!" Hector ran to the window to be sure she had left. Yes, she was resigned.

She was going up the avenue leading to the station.

Well, he said to himself, *that was hard, but not as hard as I thought it would be. Truly, Jenny is a good girl.*

Chapter XVI

When he spoke to Miss Fancy about a marriage settled on, Count de Trémorel was only half-way lying. It was in fact a question of a marriage for him. And if things weren't as far along as it pleased him to say, at least the preliminaries seemed to indicate a prompt and favorable outcome.

The idea came from Sauvresy, who more than ever desired to complete his work of salvation and restoration. One evening, about a month after that, he drew Trémorel into his study.

"Pay attention to me for a quarter of an hour," he said to him, "and above all don't answer me without thinking. The propositions I'm going to make to you deserve the most serious attention."

"Oh! Come now, I know how to be serious when it's necessary."

"Then let's begin with the liquidation. It's not yet finished, but it's far enough along to predict the results. As of today, I'm certain that you will retain 300,000 or 400,000 francs."

Never in his most optimistic dreams had Hector dared hope for such success.

"I'm going to be rich!" he exclaimed joyously.

"Rich, no, but well beyond being needy. And there is, I believe, a way to get back the position you lost."

"A way! What is it! *Bon Dieu!*"

Sauvresy took a moment to answer. He searched his friend's eyes to be very certain of the impression his proposition was going to produce.

He finally said: "You must get married."

The opening seemed to surprise Trémorel, but not disagreeably so.

"Get married! That advice is easier to give than to follow."

"Pardon. You must know that I never speak lightly. What would you say to a girl from an honorable family, young, pretty, well brought up, so charming that after my wife I don't know any one more charming. And she would bring you 1,000,000 in dowry."

"Ah! My friend, I would say that I adore her. And you know that angel?"

"Yes, and so do you, because that angel is Mademoiselle Courtois."

At that name, Hector's radiant face turned gloomy and he made a gesture of discouragement.

"Never!" he answered him. "Never would Monsieur Courtois, that former businessman, as little likely to be misunderstood than is a number, that man created by his works—to use his language—consent to give his daughter to a man silly enough to have wasted his fortune."

The owner of Valfeuillu shrugged.

"There you have a man who has eyes and can't see," he answered him.

159

"You should know that this Courtois, that you say is so down to earth, is actually the most romantic of men, the ambitious man that he is. To give his daughter to the Comte Hector de Trémorel, the cousin of the Duc de Samblemeuse, related by marriage to the Commarin-d'Arlange, would seem to him a superb business deal, even if you didn't have a *sou*. What wouldn't he do to get that rare and delicate pleasure to be able to say loudly: 'The Count my son-in-law!' or, 'My daughter, Madame la Comtesse Hector!' And you're no longer ruined. You have, or you're going to have, a 20,000 franc income which, added to the two pounds of titles of nobility that you possess, are well worth a million."

Hector was silent. He had thought his life was over. And suddenly here there were magnificent perspectives unfolding before him. He was going to be able to throw off the humiliating tutelage of his friend! He would be free, rich. He would have a wife superior—in his opinion—to Berthe. His lifestyle would eclipse that of Sauvresy. The image of Berthe crossed his mind and he thought that in this way he would escape that very beautiful, very loving mistress, but who was also haughty, who was intrusive, whose demands and domination were beginning to weigh heavily on him.

"I can assure you," he answered his friend seriously, "that I have always considered Monsieur Courtois an excellent and most honorable man, and Mademoiselle Laurence seems to me one of those accomplished young ladies that anyone would be happy to marry without a dowry."

"So much the better, my dear Hector, so much the better. Because there is a condition with this marriage which I, in addition, believe you very capable of fulfilling. Most of all, Laurence must be pleased. Her father adores her, and he wouldn't give her, I'm sure, to a man she wouldn't have chosen.

"Don't worry," Hector answered with a triumphant gesture. "She will love me."

And the very next day, in fact, he took steps to run into Monsieur Courtois, who took him to visit some colts he had just bought and who, at the end of the visit, invited him to diner.

For Laurence, the Count de Trémorel deployed all his seductions, superficial it's true and tasteless, but so brilliant, so clever that they must have surprised, dazzled and charmed a young girl. Soon in the Mayor of Orcival's household they no longer swore by anyone but that dear Count de Trémorel.

There was still nothing official. There had been neither an overture, nor an approach, nor even an allusion. Nevertheless, Monsieur Courtois was certainly counting on Hector, one of those days, asking him for the hand of his daughter. And he was so much more delighted to answer "yes," because he really thought Laurence would not say "no."

And Berthe didn't suspect anything. When such a great danger was threatening what she called "her happiness," Berthe was still worrying about Miss Jenny Fancy.

It was after an evening at Monsieur Courtois, an evening in which the prudent Hector had not left a table of whist, that Sauvresy decided to speak to his wife about this marriage. He thought to give her a pleasant surprise. She turned pale at the first words. So great was her emotion that, fearing she was going to betray herself, she had just time to dash into her dressing room. Calmly sitting in one of the chairs in the bedroom, Sauvresy continued to lay out the considerable advantages of this marriage, raising his voice so that his wife in the next room could hear him.

"Can you see now," he was saying, "our friend controlling 60,000 pounds of income? We will track down some property near our door, and we'll see him, as well as his wife, everyday. That will be very pleasant and precious society for us during our autumn evenings. Hector is over all a good and worthy boy, and Laurence, you've told me a thousand times, is charming."

Berthe didn't answer. This unexpected blow was so terrible that, in the terrible confusion of her thoughts, she couldn't think clearly.

"You aren't saying anything," Sauvresy continued. "Don't you approve of my project? I thought that you would be delighted."

She understood that if she stayed silent any longer her husband would come in. He would see her collapsed on a chair. He would guess everything! Therefore she made an effort. In a strangled voice, without attaching any sense to the words she was saying, she answered:

"Yes! Yes! That's an excellent idea."

"How you said that!" Sauvresy answered. "Can you see any objections?"

That was precisely what she was looking for, objections, and she couldn't find any reasonable ones that she could put forward.

"I tremble a little for Laurence's future," she finally said.

"Bah! And why?"

"I'm just repeating what you said. Monsieur de Trémorel, you told me, has been a libertine, a gambler, a spendthrift..."

"One more reason to have confidence in him. His past follies guarantee his future good behavior. He got a lesson he will never forget. Besides, he will love his wife."

"What do you know about that?"

"*Dame!* He's already in love with her."

"Who told you that?"

"He himself."

And Sauvresy began to joke about Hector's fine passion which would turn into, he was sure, a pastoral love affair."

"Would you believe," he said, laughing, "that he's at the point where he finds that good Courtois amusing and witty! Ah! lovers wear blinders! He spends two or three hours with him every day at the Mayor's office. But what the devil are you doing in that dressing room? Can you hear me?"

With superhuman efforts, Berthe had succeeded in dominating her awful trouble. She reappeared with an almost smiling expression. She moved about, calm in appearance, torn by the worst agony a woman can endure. And not to be able to run to Hector to know, from his own mouth, the truth! Because Sauvresy must be lying. He was deceiving her. Why? She didn't know. That didn't matter. And she felt her aversion for him redouble, even to disgust. For she excused her lover. She forgave him. And it was only her husband she held it against. Who had thought about this marriage? He did. Who had raised Hector's hopes? Who encouraged them? Him, always him.

Ah! So long as he had remained inoffensive, she had been able to pardon him for having married her. She forced herself to endure him. She resigned herself to feign a love far from her heart. But here he was becoming dangerous. Would she be able to endure that stupidly, by a caprice, would he break a liaison that was her life? After having dragged him about like a cannon ball, was she going to find him standing in the way of her happiness!

She didn't close her eyes. She had one of those horrible nights in which crimes are conceived. It was only after lunch the following day that she could find herself alone with Hector in the billiard room.

"Is it true?" she asked.

The expression on her face was so atrocious that he was afraid. He stammered:

"True...what?"

"Your marriage?"

He was silent at first, wondering if he should accept the explanation or dodge it. Finally, hurt by Berthe's commanding tone, he answered:

"Yes!"

That answer struck her like a lightning bolt. Until that time she had had a glimmer of hope. She had thought that in any case he would try to reassure her, to deceive her. There are circumstances in which the lie is a supreme tribute. But no; he was admitting it. She was crushed; she had no words to express her sensations.

Then Trémorel began very quickly to explain to her the reasons for his behavior.

Could he live forever at Valfeuillu! With his tastes and his habits what would he do with 15,000 pounds of income. At thirty, it was now or never to think of the future. Monsieur Courtois was giving 1,000,000 to his daughter. And, at his death, they would receive an even more considerable sum. Should he let this unique opportunity pass by? He certainly cared very little about Laurence. Only the dowry made him decide. Slandering himself he made himself ignoble and low to please, swearing that marriage was only business, an arrangement, that he was simply exchanging his name and titles for money.

Berthe stopped him with a crushing look of disdain.

"Spare yourself any more cowardly behavior," she said. "You love Laurence."

He tried to protest. He rebelled.

"That's enough," Berthe continued. "Any other woman would have re-proached you. Me, I simply tell you this marriage won't take place. I don't want it to. Believe me, give it up openly. Don't force me to act."

She left, slamming the door violently, leaving Hector furious.

How she's treating me, he said to himself. *A queen wouldn't have spoken any differently to a peasant that she had raised to her level. Ah! She doesn't want me to marry Laurence!...*

But with coolness, the most disturbing thoughts came to him. If he stubbornly went forward with this marriage, wouldn't Berthe put her threats into execution? Yes, evidently she would. He felt only too well that she was one of those women who never retreat, that nothing touches, that no human considera-tion is capable of stopping. As to what she would do, he could guess, or rather he knew from what she had told him once during a big quarrel about Miss Fan-cy.

I'll go admit everything to Sauvresy and we'll be more bound by shame than by all the formalities of the Church and the Mayor's office.

That was certainly the method she intended to use to break up that mar-riage that she found insupportable. And the Count de Trémorel trembled at the thought that his friend would know everything.

What would he do if Berthe told him everything, Hector thought. *He would try to kill me on the spot. That's how I would react in his place. Suppose he missed me. Then I would be obliged to fight a duel with him. And if I got out of it alive, I'd be forced to leave the country. And whatever happened, my marriage would be irrevocably broken off and Berthe would fall back into my arms forev-er."*

I must wait, he told himself.

And he was waiting, going to Monsieur Courtois' house in secret, because he truly loved Laurence. He waited, eaten up with anxiety, struggling between Sauvresy's serious requests and Berthe's threats. How he detested that woman who held him, whose will bent him like wicker! Nothing could shake her fero-cious stubbornness. She could feel nothing but her *idée fixe.* He had thought to please her by sending away Jenny. Error! When he told her, the evening of the rupture:

"Berthe, I will never again in my life see Miss Fancy," she answered him ironically:

"Mademoiselle Courtois will be very grateful to you for that."

That same evening, Sauvresy, crossing the courtyard, saw a beggar in front of the gate motioning to him. He approached him:

"What do you want, my good man?"

The beggar glanced around him to be sure no one was watching.

He answered rapidly in a low voice: "I've been charged with giving you a note that I have here. I've been told to give it only to you, and, what's more, asking you to read it without being seen."

And he mysteriously slid a carefully sealed note into Sauvresy's hand. He added, winking: "That comes from a pretty lady. You know about that."

Sauvresy, his shoulder turned to the house was reading:

Monsieur,
*   You will render an immense service to a poor, very unhappy girl, by taking the trouble to come, tomorrow, to Corbeil, to the Hotel Belle Image. I'll wait for you there all day.*
*   Your very humble servant,*

*   Jenny Fancy.*

There was a post script:

*   Please, Monsieur, I beg of you, not a word of what I'm asking to Monsieur le comte de Trémorel.*

Sauvresy thought:
*   Eh! Eh! There's discord in the illegitimate household of this dear Hector. That's a good sign for the marriage.*

"Monsieur," the beggar insisted, "I was told there should be an answer." Throwing him a forty *sou* coin, Sauvresy answered: "Say that I will go."

164

Chapter XVII

The next day the weather was cold and wet. There was a fog so thick you couldn't see objects ten feet in front of you. Nevertheless, after lunch, Sauvresy picked up his gun and whistled for his dogs.

"I'm going to take a turn through the Mauprévoir Woods," he said.

"Strange idea!" Hector remarked. "Once in the woods, you won't even be able to see the end of your gun barrel."

"What does that matter, provided I can see some pheasants."

That was only a pretext, because on leaving Valfeuillu, he took the road to Corbeil on the right and a half hour later, faithful to his promise, he entered the Hotel Belle Image.

Miss Fancy was waiting for him in that big bedroom with two beds that they always reserved for her, since she was one of the hotel's good clients. Her eyes were red from recent tears. She was very pale and her blotchy face showed very well that she hadn't slept. Her lunch, that she hadn't touched, was still on the table near the fireplace where there was a big fire burning,

When Sauvresy came in, she rose to go meet him, holding out her hand in a friendly way.

"Thank you," she said. "Thank you for coming. You, you're good."

Jenny was nothing but a prostitute and Sauvresy detested prostitutes. However, her sadness was so evident and seemed so deep that he was sincerely moved.

"You're in pain, Madame?" he asked.

"Oh! yes, Monsieur, yes. I'm suffering cruelly." Tears choked her. She hid her face in her handkerchief. *I guessed it,* Sauvresy thought. *Hector has told her it's over. It's up to me now to delicately dress the wound while at the same time saying reconciliation is impossible.*

And as Fancy was still weeping, he took her hands and, gently, in spite of her, uncovered her face.

"Have courage," he said to her. "Have courage."

She lifted her big watering eyes, to which sadness gave a ravishing expression.

"Then you know?" she asked.

"I don't know anything, since at your request I didn't ask Trémorel anything, but I can guess."

"He never wants to see me again," Miss Fancy said sadly. "He's chasing me away."

Sauvresy called up all his eloquence. The moment had come to be both persuasive and banal, paternal but firm.

He drew up a chair near Miss Fancy and sat down.

"Come now, my child," he continued. "Be strong, learn how to resign yourself. Alas! your liaison was wrong, like all similar liaisons that caprice binds together and necessity breaks apart. You can't always be eternally young. In life, a time comes when, whether you like it or not, you have to listen to the voice of reason. Hector is not chasing you away. You know that very well. But he understands the necessity of taking care of his future, of establishing his existence on the more solid bases of the family. He feels the need of a family life."

Miss Fancy was no longer crying. Her ordinary behavior came to the forefront, and her tears were dried by the fire of anger which returned. She stood up, turning over the chair. She walked up and down the bedroom, incapable of staying in one place.

"Do you believe that, Monsieur?" she asked. "You believe that Hector is worried about the future? You can certainly see that you know nothing about his character. He, think about a married life, a family! He has never thought and will never think of anyone but himself. If he had had any courage, would he have gone to hang on to you as he did? Didn't he have two arms to earn his bread and mine. I was ashamed, me who's talking to

you, to ask him for money, knowing that what he gave me came from you."

"But he's my friend, my dear child."

"Would you have behaved as he did?"

Sauvresy truly didn't know what to answer, embarrassed by the logic of that girl of the common people, judging her lover as they judge among the lower classes, brutally, without caring for the imaginary conventions of good society.

"Ah! Me, I understand him." Jenny continued, getting excited as memories came back to her. "He deceived me only one time, the morning that he came to tell me he was going to kill himself. I was stupid enough to believe him dead and to weep for him. Him, kill himself! Don't believe it. He's too much afraid to hurt himself. He's much too cowardly. Yes, I love him, yes. It's stronger than I am, but I don't respect him. That's our fate, some of us women, not be able to love any men but those we scorn."

Jenny could be heard in all the neighboring rooms, because she was shouting, gesticulating, and sometimes striking the table with her fist, shaking the bottles and glasses.

And Sauvresy was somewhat worried about the people of the hotel who knew him and had seen him enter might think. He was beginning to regret having come and did his best to calm down Miss Fancy.

"Hector isn't abandoning you," he repeated. "Hector will see that you have a little settlement."

"Eh! I couldn't care less for his settlement! Do I need him? So long as I have ten fingers and good eyes, I will never be at the mercy of a man. He made me change my name. He wanted me to get use to high living. *La Belle Affaire!* Today there's no more Miss Fancy and no more wealth. But there's still Pélagie who'll take charge of earning her fifty *sous* a day without any trouble."

"No," Sauvresy tried to say, "you'll no longer have to..."

"What? To work? But that pleases me. Me, I'm not a do-nothing. Well! I'll go back to my old life. Do you think I was very unhappy? I dined on one *sou* of bread and one *sou* of fried potatoes, and I wasn't any the less full of energy. On Sunday somebody took me to dine at the Turk, for thirty *sous*.

That's where you have a good time! I laughed more there in one evening than in the years I've known Trémorel."

She was no longer crying. She was no longer angry. She was laughing. She was thinking about the cornet of fried potatoes and the dinners at the Turk restaurant.

Sauvresy was astounded. He had no idea of the Parisian character, detestable and excellent, changeable to an excess, nervous, always changing, that weeps and laughs, caresses and slaps in the same minute, which a fleeting idea passing through can lead present sensations a hundred leagues away.

"So," Jenny, become calmer, concluded, "I don't care anything at all about Hector—" She had just said precisely the opposite and had forgotten that. "I don't care anything more about him but I won't endure his abandoning me like this. No, it won't be said that he left me for another mistress. I don't wish it."

Miss Fancy was one of those women who don't think things out, who feel. It is folly to reason with them because despite the most victorious arguments their *idée fixe* always comes to the forefront as a cork fallen into and stuck in a bottle, always comes back up as soon as you pour out wine, no matter what you do.

While wondering why she had asked him to come, Sauvresy told himself that the role he had first proposed for himself would be difficult to fill. But he was patient.

"I see, my dear child," he began again, "that you have neither understood, nor even listened. I told you, Hector has a marriage in view."

"Him!" Jenny shouted, with one of those ironic street gestures, which are the equivalent of slang. "He get married!"

She thought a moment and then added:

"However, if it were true...?"

"I swear to you," Sauvresy pronounced.

"No," Jenny shouted, "no, a thousand times no. That's not possible. He has a mistress. I know it. I'm sure of it. I have proof."

Sauvresy's smile was triumphant because a hesitation had halted her.

"Then what about that letter," she continued with violence, "that I found in his pocket, more than six months ago? It's not signed, that's true, but it could only have come from a woman."

"A letter?"

"Yes, and that doesn't leave any doubts. You're wondering why I didn't speak to him about it. Ah! That's something I didn't dare do. I love him. I've been cowardly. I told myself: 'If I speak, and if he really loves someone else, it's over. I'm doomed.' Between sharing him and being abandoned, I chose a shameful sharing. And I killed myself. I resigned myself to humiliation. I hid my weeping. I embraced him smiling while I looked for the place on his forehead where someone else had kissed him. I told myself: 'He'll come back to me.' Poor fool! And I didn't argue about sharing him with that woman who had made me suffer so much."

"Eh! My child, what do you want to do?"

"Me? I have no idea—everything. I haven't said anything about that letter, but I kept it. It's my own weapon. I'll use it. When I really want to, I'll know who she is and then..."

"You will force Trémorel, who thinks so well of you, to use violent methods?"

"Him! What can he do to me? I'll stick to him. I'll follow him like his shadow. I'll go everywhere shouting the name of the other woman. He'll have me thrown in St. Lazare. (French Prison) You can get out from there. I'll make up the most horrible slanders against him. I won't be believed on the spot. There'll still be something else for later. I have nothing to fear. Me, I have neither relatives, nor friends, nor anyone in the world who cares about me. That's what comes of picking up a mistress in the streets. I've fallen so low that I defy him to push me any lower. So, you see, Monsieur, you're his friend. Believe me. Advise him to come back to me."

Sauvresy couldn't keep from being frightened. He strongly felt how real all Jenny's threats were. There are persecutions against which the law is absolutely powerless. And even so! When you jump into mud, you always splatter some mud on yourself more or less.

But he hid his fear under the most paternal appearance he could assume.

"Listen, my dear child," he continued. "If I give you my word, will you really believe me? On my word of honor, I'm telling you the truth. Do you believe me?"

She hesitated a moment and then said:

"Yes! You're honorable, you are. I'll believe you."

"Then I swear to you that Trémorel hopes to marry a young girl, immensely rich, whose dowry will assure his future."

"He told you that. He made you believe it."

"To what purpose? I swear to you that since he's been at Valfeuillu, he hasn't had, he couldn't have had any other mistress than you. He lives in my house like my brother, between my wife and myself. I could tell you how he spends every hour of every day as well as I could my own."

Miss Fancy opened her mouth to answer, but one of those sudden thoughts that change the most fixed determinations, froze the words on her lips. She was silent and became very red, and looked at Sauvresy with an expression difficult to define.

He didn't observe it. He was motivated by one of those childish curiosities, without a precise purpose, that can't be explained, but are nevertheless compelling. The proof that Jenny spoke of intrigued him.

"However, if you would show me that famous letter..."

She reacted to those words as if receiving an electric shock.

"You," she said, shaking, "You, Monsieur! Never!"

You're asleep. Thunder rumbles. The storm breaks out without slumber being troubled. Then suddenly, at a certain moment, the imperceptible wing of a passing insect wakes you.

Miss Fancy's trembling was for Sauvresy that hardly perceptible vibration. The sinister light of doubt lit up his soul. That was the end of his security, of his happiness, of his repose, of his life.

He stood up, his eyes shining, his lips trembling.

"Give me that letter," he said, in a commanding tone.

Jenny was so frightened that she recoiled three steps. She hid her impressions as well as she could. She even tried to smile, to turn the situation into a joke.

"Not today," she answered. "You're too curious. Some other day."

But Sauvresy's anger grew, terrible, horrifying. He had become as purple as if on the point of having a stroke. And he repeated in a hardly audible voice:

"That letter. I want that letter."

"Impossible," Fancy stammered, "Impossible."

And falling back on a clever idea, she added:

"Besides, I don't have it here."

"Where is it?"

"At my place, in Paris."

"Let's go then. Come on."

She felt herself trapped. And she so clever, she so cunning, as she herself liked to say, could find neither a trick nor a clever way out. It would, however, have been easy for her to follow Sauvresy, to quiet his suspicions, to pretend gaiety, then, once in Paris streets to lose him, to dodge him.

No, she didn't think about that. She thought only about fleeing quickly, on the spot. She thought she had time to reach the door, open it, dash down the stairs. She hurried. With one leap, Sauvresy was on her, closing the already half-opened door, kicking it with his foot, making a noise that shook the room's partitions.

"Miserable woman!" he said in a hoarse and dull voice, "miserable creature, do you want me to kill you!"

With a terrible movement, pushing her away, he threw her into an armchair. Then giving a double turn to the door's lock, he put the key in his pocket.

"Now," he continued, coming back to Fancy, "the letter."

Never in her life had the poor girl experienced such terror. That man's anger overwhelmed her. She understood that he was beside himself, that she was in his hands, at his mercy, that she could be broken apart. Nevertheless, she still fought.

"You've hurt me," she whispered, trying the power of her tears, "very much, but I haven't done anything to you."

He took her wrists, and leaning over her so that he grazed her face:

"One last time," he said, "that letter, give it to me or I'll take it from you by force."

It was foolish to resist any longer. Fortunately, she didn't think about screaming. Someone would have come and it would all have been over for her.

"Turn me loose," she said. "You're going to get it."

He turned her loose, remained standing over her, while she rummaged through all her pockets. Her hair had come undone during the fight, her ruffles were torn, her face was drained of color, her teeth were chattering, but her eyes were shining with audacity and a virile resolution.

While seeming to search, she was whispering:

"Wait…there it is…no, that's odd, but I was sure I had it. I was holding it just a while ago."

And suddenly, with a gesture quicker than a bolt of lightning, she carried to her mouth the letter she had rolled up into a ball, trying to swallow it.

She couldn't do it. Sauvresy gripped her throat, choking her. She groaned, then let out a stifled cry:

"Ah!"

Finally he was in control of that letter.

His hands were shaking so much it took him more than a minute to open it. Nevertheless, he got it open.

Ah! His suspicions were right. He hadn't made a mistake. It really was Berthe's handwriting. He had a horrible, indescribable sensation, vertigo, a cerebral concussion, the sensation of a man who has fallen from a dizzying height to earth and is aware of the fall and the shock. He could no longer see clearly. He seemed to have a red cloud before his eyes. His legs gave way under him. He shook and his hands flailed in the air looking for some support.

Having somewhat come to herself, Jenny watched him out of the corner of her eyes. She thought he was going to fall down and she jumped forward to support him. But the contact of that woman horrified him. He pushed her away.

What had happened? He wouldn't have been able to say. Then he approached the table. He poured and drank two big glasses of water, one after the other. With the feeling of cold, the blood which had rushed to his head returned to its normal course. He could see.

It was a five-line letter. He read:

Don't go tomorrow to Petit-Bourg, or rather, come back from there before lunch. He has just now told me that he has to go to Melun and he will return late. A whole day!

He... that was himself. Hector's other mistress, that was his wife. That was Berthe.

For the moment he couldn't see anything beyond that. All ability to think was dead in him. His temples were pulsating out of control. His ears head an unendurable buzzing. It seemed to him the universe was crumbling under him.

He had let himself fall into a chair. He had turned from purple to livid. Great scalding tears rolled down his cheeks. On seeing that immense pain, that silent despair, on seeing that courageous man thunderstruck, Jenny understood the infamy of her behavior. Wasn't she the cause of all this? She had guessed the name of Hector's mistress. When asking to see Sauvresy, she had intended to tell him everything, taking vengeance in this way on both Hector and the other woman. Then, seeing that honorable man refusing to understand her allusions, not having the shadow of a suspicion, she had been seized with pity. She had realized that he would be the one most cruelly punished. And then she had drawn back, but too late, too clumsily, and he had torn her secret from her.

She went up to Sauvresy, trying to take his hands but he pushed her away again.

"Let me alone," he said.

"Monsieur, forgive me. I'm so unhappy. I'm horrified with what I've done."

He stood up straight, little by little returning to the feeling of terrible reality.

"What do you want with me?"

"That letter...I had guessed..."

He burst out with a sinister, distressing laugh, the loud laughter of a mad man.

"God forgive me! My dear," he said, "you've dared suspect my wife!"

And while Jenny was stammering unintelligible excuses, he took out his money holder and took out everything it contained, seven or eight bills of a hundred francs, that he placed on the table.

"Take that from Hector," he said. "We won't let you be in need of anything. But believe me, let him get married."

Then, with the same mechanical movement that had horrified Miss Jenny, he took his gun, that he had placed in a corner, opened the door and left.

His dogs, that had stayed outside, jumped up to caress him. He kicked them away with his foot.

Where was he going? What was he going to do?

171

Chapter XVIII

A fine, penetrating, freezing, little rain had followed the morning's fog. But Sauvresy didn't notice it. Bare-headed, he went into the countryside, through cross-roads, haphazardly, without direction. While walking, he was talking aloud to himself, stopping suddenly, then starting to walk again, and strange expressions escaped him. The peasants in the vicinity that he met, and all knew him, turned around flabbergasted after they had greeted him. Gazing after him, they wondered if the master of Valfeuillu had not gone mad.

Unfortunately, he wasn't mad. Thunderstruck by an unexpected catastrophe, which hit him when he was completely happy, his head had for a moment been paralyzed. But, one by one, he gathered together his scattered thoughts. And with the faculty of thought, came the faculty to suffer.

There are moral crises as there are physical crises. Immediately after a terrible shock which fractures the head or which breaks a limb, there is terrible pain, it's true. But it's vague, and in no particular location. And there follows a more or less prolonged numbness. The real pain comes later. It will grow, doubling in intensity from minute to minute, poignant, intolerable, right up to the moment it reaches its highest pitch. Just so, each of the thoughts of this very unhappy man added to his mortal agony. What! It was Berthe and Hector who were deceiving him, who were dishonoring him. She a woman loved even to idolatry; he, his best, his oldest friend, an unfortunate man he had snatched from poverty, who owed him everything, a ruined gentleman that he had picked up when he had a pistol to his head and that he had then re-established. And it was in his own house, under his own roof, that infamy without a name had been hatched. Hadn't they played enough on his noble confidence! Hadn't he been enough taken for their dupe!

The horrible discovery poisoned not only the future, but even the past. He would like to have been able to erase from his life, destroy the past years spent near Berthe, that just the evening before he had called the only years he had been happy. The memory of his former happiness filled his soul with disgust, just as the thought of certain food turns the stomach.

But how did that happen? When? How was it he didn't notice anything?

A thousand details came back to his memory which should have enlightened him if he had not been blind. He recalled certain of Berthe's looks, certain inflexions of the voice that were an admission. And in all that story about Trémorel's marriage with Mademoiselle Courtois, how they had mocked his credulity. He thought Hector's hesitations, his sudden enthusiasms, his shifts in position could be explained in this way. This project, which had been drawn out such a long time, was a thicker blindfold put over his eyes. Some moments, he tried to doubt. There are some misfortunes so great that take more than evidence for them to be absolutely believed.

"This is not possible," he whispered. "This is not possible."

Seated on a fallen tree trunk in the middle of the Mauprévoir, he studied for the tenth time in four hours, that fatal letter.

It tells everything, he told himself, *and it tells nothing.*

And he read it yet another time: *Don't go to Petit Bourg tomorrow...*

Well, in his imbecilic confidence, hadn't he said many times to the Count de Trémorel: "I'll be gone tomorrow, so stay here and keep Berthe company."

That sentence, then, had no positive meaning. But then, why add: *Or rather come back from there before lunch.*

That's what revealed the fear, or, that is to say, the sin. To leave, to come back soon, that was to take precautions, to ward off suspicions.

Then why "He," and not "Clément?" The use of this word is revealing. "He" is the beloved being, the one adored, or the master one hates. There's no middle ground: It's the husband or the lover. "He" is never an indifferent person. A husband is lost the day his wife starts speaking of him as "He."

And when did Berthe write these five lines? One evening after they had retired in the conjugal bedroom, probably. He had told her: "I'm going to Melun tomorrow," and immediately she had scribbled this note and had sent it folded in a book to her lover.

"Her lover!" He pronounced this word aloud, as if to learn it, as to convince himself of the horrible reality. He said:

"My wife, my Berthe, has a lover!"

The structure of his happiness which had seemed to him so solid it could defy all the storms of life was crumbling, and he remained there, lost, in the middle of its rubble.

No more happiness, joy, hope, nothing. All his projects for the future, rested on Berthe alone. Her name was mingled with all his dreams, or, rather, she was the future and the dream at the same time. He had loved her so much that she had become part of himself and he couldn't think of himself without her. Berthe lost, he could see no goal to direct himself toward. He no longer had a reason to live. He felt so strongly that everything in himself had been broken that he had the thought of ending it. He had his gun, his ammunition. His death would be blamed on a hunting accident, and that would be all.

Yes, but them!

Ah! Probably they would continue their revolting comedy. They would pretend to weep for him, while in reality their heart was overflowing with joy. No more husband, no more constraints, no more ruses, no more scares. His will would give all his fortune to Berthe. They would be rich. They would sell everything. And they would go happily away to love each other in freedom very far away, in Italy, in Venice, in Florence. As for his own memory, the poor too trusting husband, he would remain for them the memory of a ridiculous being that they deceived, that they scorned, and that they despised.

"Never!" he shouted, drunk with fury, "never! I want to kill myself, but before I do that, I have to get revenge."

But he looked in vain. He could find no punishment, cruel enough, terrible enough. What agony could atone for the terrible tortures he was enduring? He told himself that to make his vengeance more certain, he had to wait. And he swore to himself that he would wait. He swore to himself that he would know how to fake an inalterable security, that he would resign himself to see everything, to hear everything.

My treachery will equal theirs, he thought.

A wise duplicity was indispensable. Berthe was cleverness itself, and she was a woman, who, at the first suspicion that her husband suspected anything, would flee with her lover. Thanks to him, didn't Hector now possess almost 400,000 francs?

The thought that they might escape his vengeance gave him back all his energy and his lucidity of thought. Only then did he think about the time that had passed, the rain which was falling in torrents, and the state of his clothes.

"*Bast!*" he said. "I'll make up a story according to what they say to me."

He was scarcely a league from his house, but it took him, him, an excellent walker, more than an hour and a half to do that league. He was broken, wiped out. He felt frozen right down to his bone marrow. But when he got back to Valfeuillu, he had managed to resume his usual expression, his gaiety which expressed his perfect security so well. They had waited dinner for him, but in spite of his oaths, he couldn't make himself sit down at the table between that man and that woman, his most cruel enemies. He declared that he had taken a cold and didn't feel well and was going to go to bed.

Berthe insisted in vain that he take some very hot bouillon and a glass of Bordeaux.

"Seriously," he said, "I don't feel well."

When Sauvresy had left:

"Did you notice, Hector?" she asked.

"What?"

"There's something extraordinary wrong with my husband."

"That's very possible, after having stayed out in the rain all day."

"No, his eyes had an expression that I don't recognize in him."

"He seemed to me in a very good mood, as always."

"Hector! My husband suspects something."

"Him! Ah! The poor dear friend has a great deal too much confidence in us to think about being jealous."

"You're wrong, Hector. He didn't kiss me when he came in, and that's the first time since our marriage."

So, at his beginning, he had made an error. He knew that very well, but to kiss Berthe at that moment was well above his strength. However, he was a lot sicker than he had said, and, most of all, what he had thought.

When his wife and friend went up to the bedroom after dinner, they found him shivering under his covers, his forehead burning up with fever, his throat dry, his eyes shining with a disturbing light. Soon a terrible fever took hold of him, accompanied by awful delirium. They sent for a doctor, who said at first that he couldn't determine his state and that he couldn't give an answer. The next day he was worse.

From that moment, the Count de Trémorel and Madame Sauvresy showed the most admirable devotion. Were they thinking that in this way they could atone for their crime? That was doubtful. More probably they were trying to make a show for public opinion. Everybody was interested in Sauvresy's health. In any case, they didn't leave him for one minute, taking turns at night at his bedside. And certainly that watch was painful. Delirium, terrible delirium never left him. Two or three times force had to be used to keep him in his bed. He wanted to jump out the window. The third day, he had an unusual fantasy. He absolutely didn't want to stay in his bedroom. He screamed like a mad man:

"Take me away from here; take me away from here!"

On the doctor's advice, they did as he asked. They set up a bed for him on the first floor in the little drawing room which looked out on the garden. But the fever didn't draw a word from him which related to his suspicions. Perhaps a strong will was in control even in delirium. Finally, in the afternoon of the ninth day, the fever broke. His labored breathing became calmer. He went to sleep. He had all his faculties when he woke up.

That was a terrible moment. It was if he had to again assume his unhappiness. He at first thought that it was the memory of a horrible nightmare coming back to him. But no, he hadn't dreamed. He recalled the Hotel Belle Image, Miss Fancy, the Mauprévoir Woods, and the letter. What had happened to that letter? Then, as he had the vague certainty of a serious illness, of an access of delirium, he wondered if he hadn't said something.

That certainty kept him from making the slightest movement. And, with infinite precautions, gently, he risked opening his eyes.

It was 11:00 p.m. All the servants had gone to bed. Hector and Berthe were sitting up with him. He was reading a newspaper; she was working on a piece of crochet. From their calm expressions, Sauvresy knew he hadn't said anything. But why was he in that room?

He moved slightly and immediately. Berthe got up and came over to him.

"How do you feel, my good Clément," she asked, kissing him on the forehead.

"I'm in no pain."

"You see, however, what happens after careless behavior."

"How many days have I been sick?"

"For eight days."

"Why was I brought down here?"

"That's what you asked."

Trémorel, in his turn, had come to the bedside.

"You even strongly insisted," he maintained. "You refused to remain upstairs. You even struggled like mad."

"Ah!"

"But don't tire yourself," Hector continued. "Go back to sleep and tomorrow you'll be well. And good night. I'm going to bed very quickly so I can come relieve your wife tomorrow at 4:00 a.m."

He left, and Berthe, after having given a drink of water to her husband, went back to her seat.

"What an incomparable friend Monsieur de Trémorel is," she whispered.

Sauvresy didn't answer that terribly ironic exclamation. He had again closed his eyes. He pretended to sleep and thought about the letter. What had he done with it? He distinctly recalled having carefully folded it and tucked it tightly into the side pocket of his vest. He needed that letter. Fallen into the hands of his wife, she would understand he was getting even, and she might come across it from one moment to the next. It was a miracle his valet had not placed it on the mantle as he did with all the objects he found in his pockets. He thought about ways to get it back, of the possibility of going up to his bedroom where his vest must be, when Berthe softly rose. She came to the bedside and whispered very gently:

"Clément! Clément!"

He didn't open his eyes, and persuaded that he was asleep, lightly, on tiptoes, holding her breath, she left.

Oh! The miserable woman! Sauvresy thought. *She's going to go meet her lover.*

At the same time, with idea of getting revenge, the necessity of regaining possession of the letter, came to his mind more poignantly, more urgently.

I can, he thought, *get back to my bedroom without being seen by way of the garden and the service stairs. She believes I'm asleep. I can be back in bed before she returns.*

Immediately, without asking if he was not too weak to make the climb, without worrying about the danger he was running by exposing himself to the cold, he stood up at the foot of his bed, put on a robe placed over a chair, and his naked feet in house shoes, he started toward the door, telling himself:

If somebody comes in, if I meet someone, I'll blame everything on the delirium.

The vestibule lamp had gone out. He had some trouble opening the door. He succeeded, however, and went down into the garden. The cold was intense and he fell down in the snow. The wind mournfully shook the tree branches frozen stiff by the cold. The façade of the house was dark. Only one window was lit up, that of the Count de Trémorel. It was made very bright by a lamp without a shade and by a great blazing fire. The shadow of a man, the shadow of Hector, was outlined with the most precise contours on the curtains of fine muslin.. He was standing in front of the casement, his forehead leaning against a glass pane.

Sauvresy instinctively stopped to look at that friend. He was in his house as if in his own, and in exchange for the most brotherly hospitality, brought dishonor, despair, death. What thoughts nailed him to that window, his look lost in the shadows? Was he thinking of his dastardly conduct? But he moved suddenly. He turned around as if surprised by some unusual noise. What was it? Sauvresy knew only too well. A second shadow appeared on the thin curtain, the shadow of a woman, the shadow of Berthe.

And he, who had really forced himself to doubt! New proofs came to him without his having to look for them. What reason had brought her into that bedroom at that hour? She was speaking with some animation. He seemed to hear that full and sonorous voice, sometimes with a metallic sound, sometimes soft and caressing, which made all the cords of passion vibrate in him. He saw again her very beautiful eyes, which had reigned despotically over his heart and which he thought he knew all their expressions so well.

But what was she doing?

She had probably come to ask Hector something. He seemed to be refusing her and she was begging him. Yes, she was begging him and Sauvresy could make that out very well by Berthe's gestures. They clearly reproduced themselves on the muslin, like the black specter of Chinese shadows on oil paper. He knew that ravishing gesture of supplication very well when she wanted something! She had her two hands joined at the height of her forehead, bowing her head, half-closing her eyes to double their brightness. What languid voluptuous her voice had when she said:

"Say so, my good Clément, you'll do it, won't you? You will do it!"

And it was for another man that she was making this charming gesture, this look, these intonation. Sauvresy had to lean against a tree in order not to fall. Evidently, Hector was refusing what she wanted. Now she wagged the lifted index finger of her right hand, not saying anything, shaking her head with a pouting expression. She must be saying to him:

"You don't want to, you see. You don't want to."

Ah! Sauvresy thought, *he knows how to resist a prayer she utters. Me, I never had that courage. He can keep his reason, his cool head, his will power. I never told her no, or, rather, I never waited until she asked me for anything. I spent my life lying in wait for her least fantasies to provide them in advance. Maybe that's what condemned me.*

Hector was being stubborn and little by little Berthe became animated. She must have been getting angry. She stepped back, extended her arm, her bust forward. She was threatening him.

Finally, he gave in. He nodded: "Yes."

Then she ran to him. She threw herself on him with open arms, and the two shadows mingled in one long embrace. Sauvresy couldn't hold back a terrible cry, lost in the howling of the wind. He had asked for confirmation: he had it.

The truth broke forth, indisputable, evident. He had nothing more to look for now, nothing but the method to punish surely, terribly.

Berthe and Hector were having a friendly chat. She was leaning against his chest. He was bending his head from time to time to kiss her beautiful hair.

Sauvresy knew that she was going to come downstairs. He couldn't think of going to look for the letter. He quickly went back in. He was so afraid of being surprised that he forgot to lock the doors to the garden. It was only when he had gotten to his bedroom that he saw he had stayed a long time in the snow. He had even kept some big flakes on his shoes and they were completely wet. He quickly threw them under the bed at the very back. He went back to bed, pretending to be asleep.

It was just in time. Berthe came back in. She came over to her husband, and thinking that he had not awakened, she went over to work on her embroidery near the fire. She hadn't done six stitches when Trémorel reappeared. He hadn't remembered to take his newspaper upstairs and had come downstairs to look for it. He seemed upset.

"Have you gone out this evening, Madame?" he asked her in that whispering voice one involuntarily takes in the bedroom of a sick person.

"No."

"Have all the servants actually gone to bed?'

"At least I suppose so. But why these questions?"

"That's because since I went upstairs, that is to say less than half an hour ago, someone has gone in the garden and come back in."

Berthe looked at him with an unusually disturbed expression.

"Are you sure of what you're saying?"

"Perfectly. There's snow out there, and the person who went out brought some back in on his shoes. That snow, when it fell on the vestibule tiles, melted..."

Interrupting Hector, Madame Sauvresy suddenly took the lamp.

"Come," she said.

Trémorel wasn't mistaken. Some very obvious little flakes of snow could be seen here and there on the black tiles.

"Maybe that water has been there for some time," Berthe suggested.

"No, there was nothing there a while ago, I'd swear to it. And besides, look, there. See, there's a little..."

"It was very likely a servant."

Hector had gone to examine the door.

"I don't think so. A servant would have put back on the locks. And you see they've been taken off. I'm the one, however, who locked the doors this evening and I perfectly recall having put them on."

"That's extraordinary."

"And what's more, notice this. The traces of water don't go any further than the door to the drawing room."

They remained silent, quivering, exchanging looks full of anxiety. The same terrifying thought came to both of them.

What if he was the one? But why would he have gone into the garden? It wouldn't be to spy on them. They didn't think about the window.

"That couldn't be Clément," Berthe finally said. "He was sleeping when I left and he's till sleeping now with the calmest and deepest sleep."

Sitting up in his bed, Sauvresy listened to those who had become his most hated enemies. He damned his carelessness, understanding quite well that he wasn't made for perfidious machinations.

Provided, he was thinking, *they don't get the idea of picking up my bedroom robe and looking for my house shoes.*

Fortunately, that very simple idea never came to them. They separated after having done everything to mutually reassure each other. But each one, at the bottom of his soul, carried away a poignant doubt.

That very night Sauvresy underwent a terrible crisis. After that light of reason, delirium, that terrible guest, again filled his head with its phantoms. The next morning, Doctor R. declared him to be more in danger than ever. So much so that at this point he sent a telegram to Paris to alert them to his absence. He announced that he was going to stay two or three days at Valfeuillu.

The sickness redoubled in violence, but its course became more and more certain. The most contradictory symptoms occurred. Every day there was a new phenomenon, upsetting everything the doctors had expected. As soon as Sauvresy had one hour of remission, he saw again that abominable scene at the window and his recovery flew away.

Besides, he hadn't been mistaken. Berthe that evening had had a favor to ask Hector.

The Mayor of Orcival was supposed to go to Fontainebleau the next day with his whole family and he had suggested that the Count de Trémorel accompany them. Hector had eagerly accepted the invitation. They had hooked up a big hunting carriage with large reins that he would drive. Monsieur Courtois had—with good reason—the greatest confidence in his ability.

Now Berthe, who couldn't endure the idea that he would be able to spend a whole day with Laurence, had come to beg him to get out of the commitment. She proved to him that he didn't lack excellent reasons. Was it proper that he go on a pleasure outing while his friend's existence was in peril! At first, he absolutely refused. But through the use of prayers and, most of all, threats, she convinced him. She didn't go downstairs until he had sworn that he would write a letter of excuses to Monsieur Courtois that same evening.

He kept his word, but at the end he was exasperated by that tyranny. He was tired of constantly sacrificing his willpower, of sacrificing his freedom to the point that he could plan nothing, say nothing, promise nothing, without consulting the blue eyes of that jealous woman who wouldn't allow him to be away from her coat tails. The chain was becoming more and more heavy and murderous. He was beginning to understand that in the long run she alone would never release herself, but sooner or later he would have to break it.

He had never loved Berthe, nor Fancy, nor anyone, probably, and he loved the daughter of the Mayor of Orcival. The million that would make up her marriage crown had at first dazzled him. But, little by little, he had come under the influence of the deep charm of Laurence's personality. He had been seduced, he, the blasé man about town, by so many graces, so much naïve innocence, by so much candor and beauty. He was so much in love that he would have married Laurence if she were poor, just as Sauvresy had married Berthe. But that Berthe! He was too much afraid of her to suddenly stand up to her. He resigned himself to still waiting, to finding a way to outsmart her.

Following the day of the scene on the subject of Fontainebleau, he said he wasn't feeling well, attributing his discomfort to a lack of exercise and every day he rode horseback for two or three hours. He didn't go very far. He went only as far as Monsieur Courtois' house.

At first Berthe hadn't seen anything suspicious in these rides of the Count de Trémorel. He left on horseback and that reassured her, as certain husbands think themselves sheltered from all misfortune because their wife only goes out in a carriage. But after a few days, examining the matter further, she thought she saw a certain personal satisfaction in him that he forced himself to hide by looking tired. He wasn't successful. His whole being radiated happiness. She had doubts and they grew with each new outing. The saddest conjectures agitated her so long as Hector was absent. Where had he gone? Probably to pay a visit to that Laurence she feared and detested.

Her foreboding of a jealous mistress didn't deceive her. She saw that very well.

One evening Hector reappeared wearing in his boutonniere a sprig of heather that Laurence herself had put there and that he had forgotten to take out. Berthe gently took out that flower, examined it, smelled it, and forced herself to smile while she endured the cruelest heartbreaks of jealousy.

"That's a charming variety of heather," she said.

"That's how it seemed to me," Hector answered in an off-handed way, "although I don't know much about it."

"Would I be indiscreet to ask you who gave it to you?"

"Not at all. It was a gift of our dear Justice of the Peace, Père Plantat."

All Orcival knew perfectly well that never in his life had the Justice of the Peace, that maniacal horticulturist, given a flower to whomever it might be, except to Mademoiselle Courtois. The slip was unfortunate and Berthe wasn't fooled by it.

"You promised me, Hector," she began, "to stop seeing Mademoiselle Courtois and to give up this marriage."

He tried to answer.

"Let me speak," she said, "and you can answer afterward. You broke your word. You took advantage of my confidence. I'm foolish to be surprised at that. However, after having thought about it seriously today, I've come to tell you that you will not marry Mademoiselle Courtois."

Thereupon, without waiting for his answer, she let out the eternal litany of seduced women, or of those who pretended to have been. Why had he come there? She was happy in her household before she knew him. She didn't love Sauvresy, that's true, but she respected him. He was good to her. Since she didn't know anything about the divine happiness of true passion, she didn't desire it. But he showed up and she hadn't been able to resist his fascination. Why had he taken advantage of that fact, so that she felt irritably attracted to him. And now, after having caused her fall, he claimed he wanted to leave, to marry someone else, leaving her shame and remorse for an abominable sin as a souvenir of his passing through.

Trémorel listened to her, dumbfounded with her daring. It was unbelievable! What! She dared to claim that he was the one who took advantage of her inexperience, when, on the contrary, on knowing her better, he had sometimes been astounded at her perversity. The depth of the corruption he found in her was such that he wondered if he was her first lover or the twentieth.

But she had pushed him so much to the end, she had made him so strongly aware of her implacable will, that he had decided to risk everything rather than endure any longer this despotism. He had promised himself that at the first opportunity he would resist. He resisted.

"Well, yes," he declared definitely, "I deceived you. I have no future. This marriage assures me one. I'm getting married."

And he repeated all the past reasons, swearing that he loved Laurence less than ever, but that he coveted the money more and more.

"The proof is," he continued, "that if you tomorrow found me a woman having 1,200,000.00 francs instead of 1,000.000.00, I would prefer to marry her rather than Mademoiselle Courtois."

She would never have believed he would have so much courage. She had molded him like soft wax for such a long time that unexpected resistance disconcerted her. She was indignant, but at the same time she experienced that sick satisfaction that delights certain women when they encounter a master who beats them. Her love for Trémorel, which had been weakening, gathered new strength. And then this time he had found arguments that would convince her. She had enough scorn for him to suppose him very capable of marrying only for money.

When he had finished:

"Then it's really true," she asked him, "you're only interested in the million?"

"I've sworn it to you a hundred times."

"You really don't love Laurence?"

"Berthe, my beloved, I have never loved, and I will never love anyone but you."

He thought that by lulling Berthe with words of love, he would manage to keep her asleep right up to the day of his marriage. And once married, he was really very little worried of what would come after that. What did Sauvresy matter to him! The life of a strong man is only a series of broken friendships. What is a friend, after all? A person who can and must serve you. Cleverness consists precisely in breaking off with people the day they cease being useful to you.

Berthe, on her side, was thinking:

"Listen," she finally told Hector, "I'm not at the point of coldly resigning myself to the sacrifice that you ask. Please, give me a few more days to get used to the terrible blow. Listen...you owe me at least that. Let Clément get well."

He didn't expect to find her so easy and so gentle. Who would have expected to obtain concessions so easily? He never thought about a trap. In his delight, he was carried away by an enthusiasm which should have enlightened Berthe, but it went by unnoticed. He took her hand and kissed it, beside himself with joy, saying:

"Ah! You're good. I truly love you."

Chapter XIX

Hector didn't think the delay Berthe asked for could be of very long duration. For a week, Sauvresy seemed to be better. He was now getting out of bed, he walked about in the house, and he even received the visit of numerous friends in the neighborhood without too much fatigue.

But, alas! The master of Valfeuillu was no longer anything but a shadow of himself. To see him pale as wax, ashen, trembling, his cheeks sunken, his eyes shining with a dark fire, you would never have recognized that robust young man with red lips, a beaming face, who, beside the restaurant in Sèvres, had halted Trémorel's hand. He had suffered so much! The sickness had almost destroyed him twenty times. Twenty times the strength of his unbeatable will had gotten the upper hand. He didn't want to die, no, he wouldn't die before being avenged on those dastards who had taken away his happiness and his life.

But what punishment could he inflict on them? He searched for one and that was the constant idea which burned in his head, lighting up the flame in his eyes. Three options present themselves to serve the anger and hatred of a deceived husband in the ordinary circumstances of life. He has the right, almost the duty, to turn his wife and her accomplice over to the law courts. The law is on his side. He can cleverly spy on the guilty ones, surprise them, and kill them. There is an article in the Penal Code that doesn't *absolve* him, but which *excuses* him. Finally, nothing prevents him from pretending a philosophical indifference, to laugh the first and the hardest at his misfortune, to purely and simply turn out his wife and leave her destitute.

But what poor, what miserable examples of revenge!

To give his wife over to the law? Wouldn't that be to go out gaily looking for public disgrace, to offer up his name, his honor, his life to public laughter? Wouldn't it be to put him at the mercy of a lawyer who would drag him through the mud? You don't defend the adulterous woman, you attack her husband. That's easier. And what satisfaction would he have? Berthe and Trémorel would be condemned to a year in prison, to eighteen months, to two years at the most.

To kill the guilty ones seemed simpler to him and more! He would enter, shoot them with a revolver. They wouldn't have the time to recognize him. Their agony would last only a minute. And afterwards? He would have to be taken prisoner, submit to a trial, defend himself, ask for the indulgence of the court, risk being condemned.

As for turning out his wife, that would be voluntarily turning her over to Hector. He had to assume that they adored each other, and he saw them leaving Valfeuillu hand in hand, happy, laughing, mocking him, poor fool!

It's so true that the keen spikes of ego add more pain to the most painful wounds that at that thought an excess of cold rage came over him. None of these common types of revenge could satisfy him. He wanted something undreamed of, bizarre, excessive, something like the offense and like its tortures. And he again started to think of all the sinister stories he had read, looking for a torture fitting the present circumstances. He had the right to be demanding. He was determined to wait and he had sacrificed his life in advance.

Only one thing could reverse his plans, the letter torn from Jenny Fancy. What had happened to it? Had he then lost it in the Mauprévoir Woods? He had looked everywhere and he had not found it. Besides, he was growing accustomed to faking, finding a cruel pleasure in the constraint he imposed on himself. He had been able to put on an expression which allowed nothing to be guessed of the thoughts that haunted him. It was without obvious trembling that he submitted to the corrupt caresses of that woman so loved in the past. He had never held out to his friend Hector a more generously open hand. In the evening when they were all three united around the lamp, he took it on himself to be gay. He built a thousand happy castles in the air for when he would be allowed to go out, when he would be completely well.

The Count de Trémorel rejoiced.

"Clément's on his feet for good this time," he said to Berthe one evening.

She understood only too well what that sentence meant.

"Then you're still thinking about Mademoiselle Courtois?" she asked.

"Haven't you allowed me to hope?"

"I asked you to wait, Hector, and you've done well not to be too hasty. I know a woman who would bring you not one but three million in dowry."

He was painfully surprised. In truth, he was thinking only of Laurence, and here was a new obstacle popping up!

"And who is that woman?"

She leaned over to whisper in his ear, and in a trembling voice:

"I'm Clément's only heir," she said. "He may die. I could be a widow tomorrow."

Hector was petrified.

"But Sauvresy is doing well," he said "Thank God! He's doing marvelously."

Berthe fixed her big blue eyes on him and said with frightening calm:

"What do you know about it?"

Trémorel didn't want to, didn't dare to, ask what these strange words meant. He was one of those weak men who flee from explanations, who, rather than take precautions while there is still time, let themselves be foolishly forced into a corner. These soft and spineless beings, with cowardly premeditation blindfold themselves in order not to see the danger which menaces them. To a situation precise and definite that they don't have the courage to face, they prefer the suspense of doubt and the compromise of uncertainty. Besides, although he feared Berthe and detested her a little, considering his anxieties, he experienced a childish satisfaction. Seeing the determination and the persistence she was using to fight for and to keep him, he conceived a greater esteem for his value and his merit.

Poor woman, he was thinking, *in her sadness to lose me, to see me belong to someone else, she has come to hope for her husband's death.*

And his lack of a sense of morality was such that he didn't at all understand what there was vile, repugnant, odious in the ideas he assumed Madame Sauvresy had and in his own thoughts. However, Sauvresy's condition, alternately better and worse, proved the Count de Trémorel's assurance wrong. That same day, when they really believed that finally Sauvresy's convalescence was going to go forward rapidly, he was obliged to return to bed. That relapse took place after he drank a glass of wine flavored with cinchona bark that for a week he'd had the habit of taking before his evening meal. Only, this time the symptoms changed completely, as if a different malady had followed the one that had almost carried him away.

He complained of his skin tingling, vertigo, convulsions which contracted and twisted all his limbs, particularly his arms. Intolerable attacks of facial neurology sometimes made him scream. A terrible pepper taste, persistent, tenacious, that nothing could lessen, made him constantly open and close his mouth. He felt a worrying agitation which resulted in insomnia that high doses of morphine couldn't overcome. Finally, he experienced mortal weakness and more and more intense cold, coming not from the exterior, but from the inside, as if his body temperature had gradually diminished.

As for the delirium, it had completely disappeared. He kept the perfect clarity of his intelligence during the sickness. Sauvresy showed the most unconquerable courage throughout such trials, reacting as much as he could against the pain.

He had never attached such great importance to the administration of his immense fortune. He was constantly conferring with business people. He summonsed notaries and lawyers about everything and shut himself up with them for entire days.

Then, claiming he needed distraction, he received all the people of Orcival who came to see him. And when, by chance, there was no one, he sent for someone to be found, saying he was certain that if he was alone he couldn't keep from thinking about his illness, which would cause him to suffer even more. There was not a word about what he was doing, about what he was plotting, and Berthe, reduced to guessing, was eaten up with worry. Often when a business man had stayed several hours with her husband, she lay in wait for him as he left. Making herself as friendly, as seductive as possible, she brought forth all her cleverness to obtain some information to enlighten her. But none of those she talked to could, or didn't want to, satisfy her curiosity. They all gave only vague answers. It could have been that Sauvresy had told them to be discreet, or they had nothing to tell.

In addition, no one heard Sauvresy complain. His conversation usually centered around Berthe and Hector. He wanted to tell everyone about their devotion. He never called them anything but his "guardian angels," blessing heaven for having given him such a wife and such a friend.

Amid all that, his situation was so serious that Trémorel's optimism began to be desperate. He was seriously alarmed. What would be his situation after the death of his friend? Berthe, as a widow, would be implacable. She would be free to dare anything, and what couldn't she dare?

He promised himself that at the first opportunity he would force himself to untangle Madame Sauvresy's exact feelings. She came by herself, before he could do as he intended. It was in the afternoon. Père Plantat was with the sick man. They were certain not to be overheard nor interrupted.

"I need advice, Hector," Berthe began, "and you're the only one who can give it to me. How would it be possible to find out if, during these last days, Clément hasn't changed his arrangements in my regard?"

"His arrangements?"

"Yes, I told you that, according to the will I have a copy of, Sauvresy wills me his entire fortune. I tremble that he has revoked it."

"What an idea!"

"Ah! I have reasons to be afraid. Doesn't the presence of all those lawyers at Valfeuillu betray some deceitful scheme? Don't you understand that man can, with one stroke of a pen, ruin me? Don't you understand that he can take away his millions and leave me with only the fifty thousand (Her father recommended forty.) of my dowry!"

"But he won't do that," he answered, trying stupidly to reassure her." He loves you."

"Who guarantees you that?" she quickly interrupted." I told you 3,000,000.00, Hector. It's 3,000,000.00 I need. Not for me, Hector, but for you. I want them. I will have them. But how to find out? How to find out?"

Trémorel was greatly indignant. That was where his procrastination, his making a display of his coveting money had led him. Now she thought she had the right to do whatever she liked with him without worrying about what he wanted, buying him, in a way. And not to be able, not to dare to say anything!

"You have to be patient," he advised, "wait."

"Wait for what?" she answered with violence, "until he's dead?"

"Don't talk like that," he said.

"Then how should I talk?" she said.

Berthe came up to him and in a low voice whispered:

"He has only eight more days to live, and look..."

She took out of her pocket and showed him a little blue glass bottle with an emery stopper.

"This is what makes me sure I'm not mistaken."

Hector turned white and couldn't hold back a cry of horror. Now he understood everything. He could explain to himself Berthe's unexplainable ease in no longer talking about Laurence, her bizarre words, her assurance.

"Poison," he stammered, staggered by so much villainy, "poison!"

"Yes, poison."

"You didn't use any of it?"

She looked at him with unendurable fixity, that look which broke his will, under which he usually fought in vain, and with a calm look, stressing each word, she answered:

"I used it."

The Count de Trémorel was certainly a dangerous man, without thought of the future, without scruples, not holding back from any infamy when it was a question of satisfying his passions, capable of anything. But this horrible crime brought forth in him all that remained in him of honest strength.

"Well!" he exclaimed. "You won't use any more of it."

He started toward the door, shaking, disoriented. She stopped him.

"Before going ahead," she said coldly, "think a moment. You're my lover. I can furnish proof. Who could ever make believe that being my lover you weren't also my accomplice?"

He felt all the implications of that terrifying threat in Berthe's mouth.

"Go on," she continued in an ironic tone, "talk. Ask to bring things out in the open. Whatever happens, in happiness or in shame, we'll never again be separated. Our destinies run parallel."

Hector had let himself fall heavily into an armchair, more stunned than if hit on the head by a mallet. In his clenched hands he put his forehead, which seemed to him about to break, apart. He saw himself, he felt himself, enclosed in a hellish circle without a way out.

"But I'm ruined," he stammered, without knowing what he was saying. "I'm ruined!"

He was pitiable. His face was terribly distorted; great beads of sweat stood out at the root of his hair; his eyes had the wildness of madness.

Berthe shook him roughly by the arm. His miserable cowardice made her indignant.

"You're afraid," she told him, "you're trembling! Ruined! You wouldn't say this word if you loved me as much as I love you. Will you be ruined because I will be your wife, because we can finally love each other freely, in front of all the world. Ruined! But then do you have any idea of what I've endured? Then you don't understand that I'm tired of suffering, of being afraid, of pretending!"

"Such a great crime!"

She burst out with laughter which made him shiver.

She continued with a crushing look of scorn:

"You should start thinking about the day you took me away from Sauvresy, the day you stole the wife of that friend who saved your life. Do you think that crime was less great, less terrible? You knew as well as I did all about the love for me at the bottom of my husband's heart. You knew that between dying and losing me in that way, he would not have hesitated."

"But he doesn't know anything. He doesn't suspect anything." Hector stammered.

"You're wrong. Sauvresy knows everything."

"That's impossible."

"Everything, I tell you, and he's known that since the day he came back so late from hunting. Do you remember that when I saw how he looked at me I told you: 'Hector, my husband suspects something!' You shrugged. Do you remember the steps in the vestibule the evening I went to meet you in your bedroom? He spied on us. And last of all, do you want stronger, more decisive proof? Look at this damp letter I found crumpled up in the pocket of one of his coats."

And while saying this, she put the letter snatched from Miss Jenny under his eyes. He recognized it immediately.

"It's disaster," he repeated, visibly devastated, defeated. "But we can break it off, Berthe. I can go away."

"It's too late. Believe me, Hector, it's our life we're fighting for today. Ah! You don't know Clément. You have no idea what the fury of such as man as he can be when he finds out that someone has odiously abused his confidence, that he has been unworthily betrayed. If he hasn't said anything to me, if he hasn't let us see anything of his merciless resentment, that's because he's thinking of some horrible plan of revenge."

All that Berthe was saying was only too probable and Hector understood that very well.

"What's to be done," he asked. "What are we to do?" he asked, without any idea, almost without a voice.

"Find out what arrangements he might have made."

"But how?"

"I don't know yet. I've come to ask your advice and I find you more cowardly than a woman. Let me see what I can do. Don't you do anything more, because I'm taking everything on myself."

He tried to object.

"That's enough," she said. "He must not be able to ruin us. I will see. I will think."

She was called downstairs. She went down, leaving Hector lost in mortal agony.

That evening, after some hours, during which Berthe appeared happy and smiling, his own face bore so well the signs of his harrowing emotions that Sauvresy affectionately asked him if he didn't feel indisposed.

"You're wearing yourself out sitting up with me, my good Hector. How can I ever repay your fatherly devotion?"

Trémorel didn't have the strength to answer.

And that man there could know everything, he thought. *What strength! What courage! Then what fate does he have in store for us?*

Nevertheless the spectacle he witness horrified him.

Every time Berthe gave her husband a drink, she took out a long black hair pin, plunged it into the blue glass bottle and drew out in this way some whitish granules that she dissolved in the medicines ordered by the doctor.

You must assumed that, controlled by atrocious circumstances, harrowed by growing terrors, the Count de Trémorel had completely given up Monsieur Courtois' daughter. You would be wrong. As much and more than ever he was thinking about Laurence. Berthe's threats, the obstacles that had become insurmountable, the worry, the crime had only increased, not of his love but of his passion for her, and fueled his coveting her body.

A light, small, puny, trembling, which lit up the shadows of his despair, consoled him, gave him new life, made the present for him more endurable. He told himself that Berthe couldn't consider marrying just after the death of her husband. Months would pass, a year, and afterward he would know how to gain time. Finally, one day he would let his wishes be known. What could she say? Would she talk about the crime? Would she compromise him as an accomplice? Who would believe her? How would she be able to prove that he, loving and marrying another woman, had any interest in Sauvresy's death? You don't kill a man, your friend, for your pleasure. Would she ask for an exhumation?

He was supposing that she was at present finding herself in one of those crises which suppress both free will and reason. Later she would reflect and then she would be stopped by just the probability of dangers, the certainty of which, at this moment, didn't at all frighten her.

He didn't want her for a wife at any price, ever. He would have detested her rich, with millions. He hated her poor, ruined, reduced to living on her own means. And she could be ruined, she must be, if you granted that Sauvresy had known everything. Waiting didn't bother him. He knew that Laurence loved him enough to be sure that Laurence would wait for him a year, three years if necessary. He had already established control over her that was so much more absolute because she sought neither to fight nor to push away that thought of Hector, who had softly invaded, penetrated her whole being, filling her heart and her mind.

In giving the greatest thought to the matter, Hector told himself that perhaps in the interest of his passion, it was just as well that Berthe had acted as she did. He forced himself to conquer the revolt of his conscience by proving to himself that after all he wasn't guilty. Whose idea was it? Hers. Who carried it out? Only she. He couldn't be reproached for a moral and involuntary complicity, forced, imposed in some way by the need for his legitimate defense.

Nevertheless, sometimes bitter repugnance stuck in his throat. He could have understood a sudden, violent, rapid murder. He could have explained to himself a blow with a knife or a sword. But this slow death, poured out drop by drop, sweetened by tenderness, hidden under kisses, seemed to him particularly hideous.

He was afraid and horrified by Berthe, as of a reptile, as of a monster. If they sometimes found themselves alone and she kissed him, he shivered from his head to his toes. She was so calm, so pleasant, so natural. Her voice still had the same soft and caressing inflections that he couldn't believe it. It was without interrupting a chat that she slid her hat pin into the blue bottle. And he couldn't find in her, he who studied her, neither wincing, nor trembling, nor even a batting of the eyelashes. She must have been made of bronze. However, he found that she didn't take enough precautions. She could be discovered, surprised. He told her about his fears and how she made him shudder every moment.

"Have confidence in me," she answered. "I want to succeed. I'm careful."

"People could get suspicious."

"Who?"

"Eh! How do I know? Everybody, the servants, the doctor."

"There's no danger. And even if there were!"

"They'll investigate, Berthe. Had you thought about that? They would do the most minute investigations."

Her smile manifest the most magnificent certainty.

"They can look, examine, experiment," she said. "They won't find anything. Do you think I would be silly enough to use arsenic?"

"Please, be quiet!"

"I was able to procure one of those still unknown poisons, which defy all analysis. It's one of those poisons that right now many doctors, and I'm talking about real ones, wouldn't even be able to tell the symptoms."

"But where did you get...?"

He stopped short before saying the word "poison." He didn't dare pronounce it.

"Who gave you *that?*" he continued.

"What does that matter to you? I've been able to take such precautions that the one who gave it to me runs the same dangers as I do. And he knows it. So, there's nothing to fear from that side. I've paid him dearly enough for him never to have the shadow of a regret."

An abominable objections rose to his lips. He wanted to say: "It's very slow!" He didn't have the courage, but she read his thought in his eyes.

"It's very slow because it suits me this way," she said. "Most of all, I have to know what to expect in the matter of the will. I'm working on it."

In fact, she was busy with nothing but that. During the long hours she spend near Sauvresy's bed, little by little, delicately, without obvious nuances, with the most infinite precautions, she led the sick man's defiant thoughts to his last wishes. She did it so well that he himself brought up the subject of such poignant interest to Berthe.

He didn't understand, he said, why people didn't always have their affairs in order and their last wishes written down in case of misfortune. What did it matter if one was healthy or sick? At the first words, Berthe tried to stop him. In a whining voice she said that such ideas would cause him too much pain. She even wept very real tears, which slid, brilliant as diamonds down her cheeks and made them more beautiful and more irresistible, real tears which dampened her handkerchief of fine batiste.

"Silly," Sauvresy said to her, "dear foolish woman. Do you think that could cause death?"

"No, but I don't want you to."

"Let's leave that. Have we been less happy because the day after my marriage I made a will that gives you all my fortune? And, look, you should have a copy. If you wanted to please me, you would go find it."

She became very red, then very pale. Why did he want that copy? Did he want to tear it up? A quick thought reassured her. You don't tear up a piece of paper that a word on another piece of paper can annul.

Nevertheless, she protested a little.

"I don't know where that copy is."

"I myself know. It's in the left-hand drawer of the armoire with a mirror. Go on. That would please me very much."

And while she was gone:

"Poor woman," Sauvresy said to Hector. "Poor adored Berthe. If I died, she wouldn't survive me."

Trémorel couldn't find anything to respond, his anxiety was so inexpressible and so visible.

And does that man there suspect anything? he was thinking. *No, that's impossible.*

Berthe came back in.

"I found it," she said.

"Give it to me."

He took the copy of his will and read it with evident satisfaction, shaking his head at certain passages where he recalled his love for his wife.

When he had finished reading:

"Now," he said, "give me a pen with some ink."

Hector and Berthe pointed out to him that writing would tire him, but they had to please him.

Placed at the foot of the bed, out of the range of Sauvresy's vision, the guilty couple exchanged the most worried looks. What could he be writing in that way? But he had just finished.

"Take it," he said to Trémorel, "read aloud what I've just added."

Hector did as his friend desired, although feeling that emotion must make his voice quaver. He read:

"Today (the day and the date), sound of mind, although suffering, I declare I do not have a line to change in this testament. I have never loved my wife more. I have never so much wanted to make her my heir, if I die before she does, of all that I possess." Clément Sauvresy

Berthe was so strong, so perfectly and always mistress of her impressions, that she managed to repress the immense satisfaction that came over her. All her wishes had reached their summit, and nevertheless she managed to replace with sadness the gleam in her beautiful eyes.

"What good does that do?" she said with a sigh. She said that, but a half hour later, alone with Trémorel, she gave way to the most childish expressions of the most insane joy.

"There's nothing more to fear," she said, "nothing more. It's all ours now: liberty, wealth, the drunkenness of our love, pleasure, life, all of life! Three million, Hector. We have at least three million! I've got it, then, that will! From now on no business man will come in here again. Now's when I must hurry."

Without a doubt the Count was glad to know she was free, because you can get rid of a millionaire widow easier than a poor woman without a *sou*. Sauvresy's action calmed his sharpest anxieties. Nevertheless, that show of gaiety which seemed like a burst of laughter, that unchanging feeling of security, seemed monstrous to him. He would have wished for more solemnity in the crime, something serious and reverential. He judged that he should at least calm that delirium.

"You'll think more than once about Sauvresy," he said in a somber voice.

She did a musical trill: *prrr,* and answered quickly:

"About him? When and why should I do that? Ah! his memory won't be hard to bear. I certainly hope we won't stop living at Valfeuillu, which I like. Only, we will have a townhouse in Paris, yours that we'll buy back. What happiness, my Hector, what felicity!"

Just the prospect of such envisioned happiness terrified him to the point of inspiring him with a good impulse. He hoped to reach Berthe.

"One last time, I beg of you," he said to her, "give up this terrible, this dangerous project. You see very well that you're deceiving yourself, that Sauvresy doesn't suspect anything, that he still loves you."

The expression on the face of the young woman changed suddenly. She became pensive.

"Let's don't talk about that anymore," she finally said. "It's possible that I'm mistaken. It's possible that he has only doubts. It's possible that, even having discovered something, he hopes to get me back by using goodness.

Because you see..."

She stopped talking. Perhaps she didn't want to frighten him.

He was already only too much so. The next day, not able to endure the sight of that agony, fearing constantly to betray himself, he left for Melun without saying anything. But he had left his address behind and on a note from her, he cowardly returned. Sauvresy was screaming for him again.

She had written him a letter with an inconceivable lack of caution which made the hair on his head stand up. He had planned to reproach her on his return. She was the one who reproached him.

"Why that flight?"

"I'm unable to stay here. I suffer; I tremble. I'm dying."

"How cowardly you are," she said.

He wanted to answer, but she put her finger on her lips, and pointing to the door of the adjacent room with the other hand:

"Chut! There are three doctors there who have been in consultation for three hours and I haven't been able to overhear a single one of their words. Who knows what they're saying? I won't rest easy until after they leave."

Berthe's concern wasn't without some foundation. After Sauvresy's last relapse, when he complained of very painful neuralgia in his face, and of an obnoxious taste of pepper, Doctor R had moved his lips in an unusual way. This movement was nothing, but Berthe had accidentally seen it. She thought she could guess in it an involuntary expression of a rapid suspicion. It remained present in her mind as a warning and a menace.

Nevertheless, the suspicion, if there ever was one, must have vanished very quickly. Twelve hours later the phenomena had completely changed, and the next day the sick man experienced something else completely different. That variety of signs, that inconsistency of symptoms must not have been a small contribution to leading the doctor's conjectures astray.

For some days, Sauvresy was almost no longer suffering, he claimed, and he slept rather well at night. But he threw off what covered him in bizarre, disconcerting and sometimes wild ways. Evidently, he was growing weaker and weaker from hour to hour. He was fading, and everybody saw it. Things were in that state when Doctor R had asked for a consultation and when Trémorel reappeared. Berthe, deeply upset, was waiting for its result. Finally the door of the little drawing room opened and the calm faces of the men of art must have reassured the poisoner.

The conclusion of that consultation was distressing. Everything had been attempted, exhausted. Not one of the human resources had been neglected. Only the strong constitution of the sick man could any longer be relied on.

Colder than marble, motionless, her eyes full of tears, Berthe, on hearing that cruel death sentence, demonstrated so well the perfect image of sadness here below, that all the old doctors were touched. Doctor R hardly dared to reassure her somewhat. He answered her with some of those vague banal comments which mean everything and say nothing and which are the commonplace consolations that one knows to be useless.

"It's not necessary to despair," he said. "With sick men Sauvresy's age, nature often does miracles when it's least expected."

But, having taken Hector aside, he urged him to prepare that unhappy young woman, so devoted, so concerned, who loved her husband so much, for the terrible blow.

"Because, you see," he added, "I don't believe that Monsieur Sauvresy can live any longer than two days."

Her ears pricked up, Berthe had overheard the fatal ultimatum of the Medical Faculty. When Trémorel returned from conducting the consulting doctors to the door, he found her beaming. She threw herself around his neck.

"Now's when the future really belongs to us," she said. "There's just one hardly noticeable dark spot blurring our horizon and it's gone away. Now it's up to me to bring about Doctor R's prediction."

They ate dinner together as usual in the dining room while one of the chambermaids remained near the sick man. Berthe was unrestrained in her gaiety, which she had trouble hiding. The certainty of success and impunity, the assurance of reaching the end, made her cast off her very clever dissimulation. In spite of the presence of the servants, she spoke enthusiastically about her coming deliverance in veiled words. The word *deliverance* was pronounced.

She was carelessness itself that evening. A doubt in just one of the servants, less than that, one of them in a bad mood, and she could be compromised, lost. Hector, who felt the hair on his head bristle, kicked her under the table from time to time, rolling wide open eyes to make her be silent. In vain. There are those times when the armor of hypocrisy becomes so heavy to bear that it must be taken off, if only for an instant to relax, to unburden oneself, whatever the cost. Fortunately, coffee was brought in and the servants retired.

While Hector was smoking his cigar, Berthe, less constrained, followed up on her dream. She intended to spend the period of her mourning at Valfeuillu. And Hector, to keep up appearances, would rent a pretty little house in the neighborhood where she would drop in on him in the mornings. The boring thing was that it would be necessary to weep for Sauvresy dead as she had pretended to love him when he was alive. Would she never be done with that man! Finally a day would come when she could take off her black garments. What a celebration! Then they would get married. Where? In Paris or in Orcival.

Then she worried about the length of time required before a widow had the right to choose a new husband, because there was a law regarding that subject. And she said she wanted to finish her mourning period the same evening of that required period. That would be a day gained. Hector had to take a long time proving to her that waiting was indispensable: one could run up against real dangers. Nevertheless, he also wanted to see his friend under the ground in order to be finished with his terrors, in order to throw off Berthe's appalling obsession.

Chapter XX

It was getting late. Hector and Berthe had to go back to Sauvresy's bedroom. He was sleeping. They noiselessly sat down, one on each side of the fireplace as they did every evening. The chambermaid left. So that the lamp light did not bother the sick man, they had arranged the curtains at the head of the bed in such a way that when he was in bed he couldn't see the fireplace. To see it, he had to raise himself off his pillows and lean over, supporting himself on his right arm.

But he was sleeping, a painful, feverish sleep troubled by convulsive shudders. His heavy, whistling breathing raised the covers at equal intervals. Berthe and Trémorel were no longer exchanging a word. The gloomy, sinister silence was disturbed only by the *tic-tac* of the clock's pendulum or the sound of the pages being turned in the book Hector was reading.

Ten o'clock struck.

Shortly afterward, Sauvresy moved about. He turned over; he woke up. Nimble and attentive like a devoted spouse, with one movement, Berthe was near the bed. Her husband had his eyes open.

"Do you feel a little better, my dear Clément?" she asked.

"Neither better nor worse."

"Do you want something?"

"I'm thirsty."

Hector, who had raised his eyes at his friend's first words, went back to his reading.

Standing in front of the mantle, Berthe prepared with minute care the last potion prescribed by Doctor R which required certain precautions.

The potion ready, she took the blue glass vial out of her pocket and, like every evening, dipped one of her hat pins in it. She didn't have time to take it out before she was touched lightly on the shoulder. A shudder shook her right down to her heels. She turned around quickly and uttered a terrible cry, a cry of fear and horror.

"Oh!"

The hand that had touched her was that of her husband. Yes, while she was standing in front of the mantle, putting in the poison, Sauvresy had softly gotten up. He had then gently pushed aside the bed curtains, it was his emaciated arm stretched out toward her, and it was his terrifying eyes filled with hatred and anger flaming into hers.

At Berthe's cry another muffled cry, a rattle rather, had answered. Trémorel had seen everything, understood everything. He was shattered.

"Everything is discovered!"

These words burst into their minds like bombshells. They stood out everywhere around them, written in letters of fire. There was a moment of unspeakable stupor, a minute of silence so profound that the beating of Hector's temples could be heard.

Sauvresy had gone back to bed and was under the covers. He was laughing a loud and lugubrious laugh, as would a skeleton when its jaws and teeth chatter, hitting each other. But Berthe wasn't one of those creatures that a single strike, however terrible it might be, can beat down. She was trembling more than a leaf. Her knees were buckling, but her thoughts were already moving toward possible subterfuges. What had Sauvresy seen? Had he even seen anything? What did he know? And even if he had seen the blue glass flacon, those things could be explained. That could have been, that must have been by simple luck that her husband had touched her shoulder just at the moment of the crime. All these thoughts went through her mind at the same time and in one second, as rapidly as a flash of lightning brightens up shadows. And then she dared, she had the strength to dare, to approach the bed and to say with an affectionate smile, constrained but still a smile:

"How you just frightened me!"

He looked at her for a second which seemed to her a century and simply answered:

"I know!"

There was no more uncertainty possible. In her husband's eyes, Berthe read only too clearly that he knew. But what? And about what? She managed to make herself continue:

"Are you in more pain?"

"No."

"Then why did you get up?"

"Why?"

He succeeded in pulling himself up on his pillows and with a strength of which he would not have been thought capable, in about a minute, he continued:

"I got up to tell you that's enough of this kind of torture. I've come to the limits of human endurance. I won't be able to endure one day more this unbelievable torture, to see myself, to feel myself having death measured out to me slowly, drop by drop, by the hands of my wife and my best friend."

He stopped. Hector and Berthe were thunderstruck.

"I would like to tell you something else. Enough being careful, enough refinements. I'm suffering. Ah! Don't you see how horribly I'm suffering? Hurry up! Shorten my agony. Kill me, but kill me all at one time, poisoners!"

At this last word, "poisoners," the Count de Trémorel stood up straight as if pushed by a spring, his eyes haggard, his arms extended in front of him.

Sauvresy himself, at this movement, quickly slid his hands under the pillows and took out a revolver. He aimed the barrel toward Hector, shouting:

"Don't come near!"

He believed that Hector was going to jump on him and, because the poison had been discovered, strangle him, suffocate him. He was wrong. Hector felt that he had gone mad. He fell back in a heap. Berthe, stronger, tried to defend herself, forcing herself to shake off the torpor of the fright coming over her.

"You are sicker, my Clément," she said. "It's still that terrible fever that frightened me so much which has come back. The delirium..."

"Am I really delirious?" he interrupted with a surprised air.

"Alas! Yes, my beloved. That's what's haunting you. It fills your poor, sick head with horrible visions."

He looked at her curiously. He was really stupefied by that audacity which grew with the circumstances.

"What! Would we who're so dear to you, your friends, me, your..."

Her husband's unwavering look forced her, yes, forced her to stop. The words died on her lips.

"Come now, Berthe," he continued, "enough lies. They're useless. No, I didn't dream. No, I wasn't delirious. The poison is only too real and I could tell you its name without taking it out of your pocket.

She drew back, terrified, as if she had seen her husband's had extended to grab the crystal vial.

"I guessed it and recognized it from the first moment, because you chose one of those poisons which hardly leave any traces, it's true, but their signs can't be mistaken. Do you remember the day I complained of a pepper taste? The next day I was certain and I was almost not the only one. Doctor R had a doubt.

Berthe wanted to stammer some words. Sauvresy interrupted her. He continued in a frighteningly ironic voice:

"You should try out poison before you use it. Didn't you know about yours? Didn't you know its effects? Clumsy! What! Your poison causes intolerable neuralgia, insomnia which nothing can stop, and you stupidly watched me, without any surprise, sleep entire nights. What! I complained of a devouring fire inside me, while your poison brings about ice in the veins and in the entrails. And you weren't astonished! You saw all the symptoms disappear and change and you weren't enlightened! You are indeed fools! Do you know what I had to do to mislead Doctor R's suspicions? I had to be quiet about the real pain caused by your poison and complain about imaginary, ridiculous, absurd pains. I showed exactly the opposite of what I was experiencing. You were lost. I saved you."

Under so many repeated blows, Berthe's criminal strength wavered. She wondered if she wasn't going mad. Was she hearing right? Was it really true that her husband had known that they were poisoning him and had said nothing, that he had even deceived and mislead the doctor? Why? For what purpose?

Sauvresy had paused for several minutes. Soon he started again.

"If I didn't say anything, if I saved you, it was because the sacrifice of my life was already complete. Yes, I was struck to the heart, never to recover, the day I learned that you were taking advantage of my confidence, that you were unfaithful to me."

He was speaking without any apparent emotion about his death, about the poison they were giving him. But at the words, *You were unfaithful to me,* his voice changed and trembled.

"I didn't want to believe it; I couldn't believe it at first. I doubted the testimony of my senses rather than you. I had to give in to the evidence. I was no longer in my own house but in one belonging to grotesque tyrants that mock and make outrageous fun of me. However, I was still in your way. You needed more space and more freedom for your love-making. You were tired of constraints, exasperated with tricks. And it was then that, thinking that death would make you free and rich, you tried poison to get rid of me."

Berthe at least had heroism in crime. Everything had been discovered. She threw off the mask. She tried to defend her accomplice who remained totally collapsed in a chair.

"I'm the one who did everything," she exclaimed. "He's innocent."

A movement of rage turned Sauvresy's pale face red.

"Ah! "Really," he said. "My friend Hector is innocent! Then he wasn't the one who, to pay me, not for his life—he was too cowardly to kill him-self—but the honor he owes me, took my wife? Miserable man! I held out my hand to him when he was drowning. I took him in like an older brother and as payment for my services, he brought adultery into my household, not that glaring adultery which has passion as an excuse and the poetry of grave danger, but the middle-class, low, ignoble, adultery of common life.

"And you knew what you were doing, my friend Hector; you knew. I had told you a hundred times that my wife was everything on this earth to me, the present and the future, reality, the dream, hope, life itself. You knew that, for me, to lose her was to die.

"If you had even loved her! But, no, it wasn't her that you loved. It was me you hated. Envy was eating you alive. And you really couldn't say to me, face to face: 'You're too happy; tell me the reason for it.'

"Then, cowardly, in the shadows, you dishonored me. Berthe was only the instrument of your resentment. And today she's a burden to you. You scorn her and you fear her. My friend Hector, you've behaved in my house like the vile lackey who wants to take revenge for his low position by soiling with his spit the dishes he brings to the master's table!"

The Count de Trémorel answered only by a whimper. The terrible words of that dying man fell on his conscience more cruel than slaps on his cheeks.

"There, Berthe," Sauvresy continued. "There's the man you preferred to me, for whom you betrayed me. You never loved me. I recognize that now. Your heart never belonged to me. And me, I loved you so much!

"From the day I saw you, you became my only thought, or, rather, my thought itself, as if your own heart was beating where mine should be.

"Everything about you was dear and precious to me. I adored your caprices, your fantasies. I even adored your faults. There was nothing I wouldn't have done for one of your smiles, to make me say 'thank you,' between two kisses. You don't know that for many years after our marriage it was still happiness, a celebration, to wake up first to look at you sleeping like a child, to admire, to touch your beautiful blonde hair spread out on the batiste pillows. Berthe!"

He became tender at the memory of his past happiness, at pleasures which were not tangible because they were deep and which would never come back. He forgot their presence, their infamous betrayal, the poison. He forgot that he was going to die, assassinated by that woman he had loved so much. His eyes filled with tears. His voice choked in his throat. He stopped.

More motionless and whiter than marble, Berthe listened, trying to penetrate the sense of that scene.

"It's indeed true that those beautiful, limpid blue eyes light up a soul of mud!" the sick man continued. "Ah! Who wouldn't have been deceived as I was! Ah! Berthe, what were you thinking of when you were sleeping cradled in my arms? What wild dreams did you madness caress?

"Trémorel arrived and you thought you saw in him the ideal of all your dreams. You admired the early wrinkles of the worldly man, which resembles the stamp that marks the forehead of the fallen arch-angel. You took for purple ribbons the glittering rags of his past that he shook under your eyes.

"Your love, with no care about mine, threw itself at him, who wasn't even dreaming of you. You went toward evil as toward your own essence. And me, who thought your thoughts purer than the Alpine snow. And you didn't even put up a fight. You didn't give in; you offered yourself. No worry showed me your first sin. You offered me without blushing your forehead with your lover's kisses hardly wiped off."

Weakness conquered his strength. Little by little, his voice had a catch in it and became weaker.

"You were holding your happiness, Berthe, in your hands and you carelessly broke it apart as a child breaks a toy whose value he doesn't know. What did you expect from this miserable man for whom you had the horrible courage to kill me, a kiss on your lips, gently slowly, hour by hour? You believed you loved him, but disgust must have come in the long run. Look at him and judge us. See what this man is, me, stretched out on this bed where he's going to give up his last breath in a few hours, and him, dying of fear in his corner. You have the strength for crime. He has only the baseness. Ah! If I called myself Hector de Trémorel and a man dared to speak to me as I have just done, that man would no longer exist, even if he had ten revolvers like the one I'm holding."

Kicked into the mud, Hector tried to get up, to answer. His legs no longer supported him. His throat uttered only harsh and inarticulate sounds. And in fact, examining the two men, Berthe realized her error with rage. At this moment her husband seemed to her sublime. His eyes had unbelievable depth. His face was shining, whereas the other one. The other one! Just looking at him made her nauseous. So, all the deceptive wild dreams she had run after, love, passion, poetry, she had had them in her hands. She had held them and hadn't been able to see it. But what was Sauvresy coming to? What idea was he pursuing?

He continued painfully.

"So, then, here's our situation. You've killed me. You're going to be free, but you'll hate each other. You'll despise each other."

He had to interrupt himself. He was choking. He tried to raise himself on his pillows, to sit on the side of the bed. He was too weak. Then, he addressed his wife.

"Berthe, help me sit up."

She leaned over the bed, and leaning against the back of the bed, taking her husband under the arms, she managed to situate him as he wanted. He appeared more comfortable in that new position and he took two or three deep breaths.

"Now," he said, "I'd like something to drink. The doctor has allowed me a little old wine, if I took a notion for some. Give me three fingers deep of old wine."

She quickly brought him a glass. He emptied it and gave it back to her.

"There wasn't any poison in it, was there?" he asked.

That frightening question, the smile which accompanied it, broke Berthe's resistance.

For a moment, with her disgust for Trémorel, the remorse in her had awakened and she was already horrified at herself.

"Poison!" she answered violently. "Never!"

"Nevertheless, you're going to have to give me some in a little while to help me die."

"You! Die, Clément! No, I want you to live so that I may atone for the past. I'm a despicable person. I've committed an abominable crime, but you're good. You'll live. I don't ask to be your wife, but your servant. I'll love you. I'll humiliate myself. I'll serve you on my knees. I'll serve your mistresses if you have any. I'll do so much that after ten years, after twenty years, of expiation, you'll forgive me."

In his mortal trouble, Hector had scarcely been able to follow that scene. But from Berthe's gestures and tone, above all from her last words, he had something like a glimmer of hope. He believed that perhaps everything was going to end well, be forgotten, that Sauvresy was going to forgive. He half rose. He stammered:

"Yes, have mercy, have mercy!"

Sauvresy's eyes threw out lightning. Anger gave his voice powerful vibrations.

"Mercy! Pardon!" he shouted. "Did you have any mercy for me during the year you made a plaything of my happiness, in the week that you've mixed poison in all my tea. Mercy? Are you mad? Then why do you think I didn't say anything when I discovered your infamy, that I let myself be quietly poisoned, that I was careful to throw the doctors off the track? Do you think I acted this way just to prepare a heart-rending goodbye scene and at the end of it give you my blessings? Ah! Understand me better!"

Berthe was sobbing. She tried to take her husband's hand. He pushed her away roughly.

"Enough lies," he said. "Enough treachery! I hate you! You cannot understand that there's nothing alive in me anymore but hatred!"

At this moment Sauvresy's expression was atrocious.

"It will soon be two months," he continued, "that I have known the truth. Everything in me is broken, soul and body. Ah! It has cost me to remain silent. I almost died because of it. But one thought sustained me: I wanted revenge. In the hours I wasn't suffering I thought only of that. I looked for a punishment which would fit the offense. I didn't find any. No, I couldn't find any. Then you decided to poison me. The day I guessed about the poison, I trembled with joy. I had my revenge.

An ever increasing terror overcame and stupefied Berthe as well as Trémorel.

"Why do you want my death?" Sauvresy continued. "To be free? To be married? Well! That's what I want also. The Count de Trémorel will be the widow Sauvresy's second husband."

"Never!" Berthe exclaimed, "no, never!"

"Never!" Hector repeated like an echo.

"Nevertheless that will be, because I myself wish it. Oh! My precautions have been well taken. And you won't be able to escape me. So listen to me. As soon as I was certain of the poison, I began writing a very detailed history of all three of us. What's more, I kept day by day, you might say hour by hour, a very exact journal of my poisoning. Finally I kept some of the poison you gave me..."

Berthe made a gesture that Sauvresy took for a denial, because he insisted:

"Oh! I certainly did collect some, and I can even tell you how. Every time that Berthe gave me a suspicious potion, I kept back a mouthful and very carefully spit that mouthful into a bottle hidden under my bolster.

"Ah! You're wondering how I've been able to do all these things without your suspecting it, without any servant noticing it? You should know that hatred is even stronger than love and that adultery will never have the treachery of revenge. You can be sure I've left nothing to chance, forgotten nothing."

Hector and Berthe looked at Sauvresy with that kind of fixed attention bordering on stupidity. They were trying to understand. They didn't yet understand.

"Let's be finished with it," the dying man said. "My strength is giving out. So, this morning that bottle, containing about a liter of potion, our biographies, and the story of how I was poisoned, have been placed in the hands of a trustworthy and devoted man that you couldn't manage to corrupt if you knew him. Be reassured. He doesn't know the contents of what's been entrusted to him.

The day you're married, he'll give you everything. If, on the contrary, you are not married a year from today, he has orders to put everything entrusted to his honor in the hands of the National Prosecutor."

Two cries of horror and torture told Sauvresy that he had chosen his revenge well.

"And consider this well," he added. "Once the package is put in the hands of the law, it's prison, if not the scaffold, for you."

Sauvresy had exhausted his strength. He fell back on his bed panting, his mouth half open, his eyes dim, his sunken features so decomposed that it would have been thought he was about to die. But neither Berthe nor Trémorel was thinking about helping him. They stayed there, facing each other, their pupils dilated, numb, as if their thoughts had met each other in that merciless future imposed on them by that man they had outraged. They were now united forever, joined in a parallel destiny, with nothing able to separate them but death. A chain bound them with narrower and stronger links than those of galley slaves, the chain of infamy and crime. The first link of the chain was a kiss and the last poisoning.

At this point, Sauvresy could die, his revenge hovering over their heads, casting a shadow across their sun. Seeming to be free, they were going to go through life crushed by the burden of the past, more slaves than the Blacks in the mosquito-infested swamps of the American South. Separated by hatred and scorn, they saw themselves riveted by the common terror of punishment, condemned to an eternal embrace.

But it would be to misunderstand Berthe to believe that she held it against her husband. It was at this moment, when he was grinding her underfoot, that she admired him.

In agony, he took on super-human proportions in her mind. She had no idea that so much determination or so much courage could be combined with so much dissimulation and genius. How he had guessed about them! How he had been able to outwit them! To be the strongest, the master, he had only to will it. Up to a certain point she was enjoying the strange atrocity of that scene, too extreme to be one of those that find their way into human expectations. She was feeling something like bitter pride in seeing herself participating and playing a role in it. At the same time, she was carried away by rage and regrets when thinking that that man she had had for herself, in her power, that he had been at her knees. She was very near to being in love with him. Among all the men whose destinies she could have been mistress of, it was he she would have chosen. And he was going to escape her.

However, it has to be admitted, Berthe's character was not unusual. Similar personalities are very often encountered. However, hers was pushed to an extreme. According to circumstances, the imagination is the hearth which gives life to the household or the fire that destroys it. Berthe's imagination, lacking nourishment for its flame, brought to life all her bad instincts. Women gifted with this terrible strength are not mediocre, neither in crime nor in virtue. They are sublime heroines or monsters. They can be angels of devotion, the Sophie Gloires or Jane Lebons. In that case, they would share the martyrdom of some obscure inventor or give their life for an idea. In other cases, they horrify society by their cynicism. They poison their husband while writing letters in beautiful style and end up in institutions for the insane. But all in all, a passionate personality like that of Berthe is preferable to a flabby and soft temperament like that of Trémorel.

Passion, at least, follows its own terrible course like that of a bullet. Weakness is like a mass of lead suspended at the end of a cord. It goes hurtling and wounding right and left, according to the direction the first passer-by gives it. While the most violent feelings were boiling in Berthe's soul, Trémorel began to come to himself. As always, the crisis past, he revived, like those reeds the wind pushes down into the mud, which rise up again muddier after each gust of wind. He began to comprehend that henceforth Laurence was lost to him and his despair was boundless. So the silence lasted at least a quarter of an hour.

Finally Sauvresy conquered the spasm that had brought him down. He could breathe; he could talk.

"I haven't yet said everything," he said.

His voice was almost a whisper, and nevertheless it carried to the ears of the poisoners like a strong howl.

"You're going to see whether I've calculated everything, foreseen everything. Once I'm dead, the idea of flight may perhaps come to you, perhaps to go abroad. That's something I won't permit. You must stay in Orcival, at Valfeuillu. A friend—not the one who received the package—another one, is charged with watching you, without knowing the reason. If one of you—mark my words well—disappears for eight days, the ninth day the man who has the package will receive a letter which would make him decide to go immediately to alert the National Prosecutor.

Yes, he had foreseen everything, and Trémorel, who had already had the idea of flight, was overwhelmed.

"Besides, I have arranged for that temptation to flee not to be too strong for you," Sauvresy continued. "I'm leaving, it's true, all my fortune to Berthe, but I leave it only for her lifetime. The raw land will belong to her only the day after your marriage.

Berthe made a gesture of repugnance, which her husband wrongly interpreted. He thought she was thinking about that copy of the will to which he had added several lines.

"You're thinking about that copy of the will you had in your hands," he told her. "That's a useless copy. If I added some words without any value, it was because I was afraid of your covetousness and I had to lull your suspicions to sleep. My will, the real one"—and he stressed the word *real*—"the one that I entrusted to the Orcival notary and which will be communicated to you, postdated two days. I can read the rough draft to you."

He took out a piece of paper from the billfold, hidden like the revolver at the head of the bed.

"Struck by a malady which does not pardon and which I know to be incurable, I express here, with the full use of all my faculties, my last wishes.

"My dearest wish is that my beloved widow, Berthe, marry, as soon as the legal delays have expired, my dear friend, Count Hector de Trémorel. Having been able to estimate the grandeur of soul and the nobility of soul of my wife and of my friend, I know that they are worthy of each other, and one with the other they will be happy. I die more peacefully knowing that I leave my Berthe a protector of whom I have approved..."

It was impossible for Berthe to listen to any more.

"Mercy!" she cried out. "Enough!"

"Enough, so be it," Sauvresy answered. "I read this rough draft to show you that, if on the one hand I have made sure my wishes will be carried out, on the other, I have done everything to maintain society's opinion of you. Yes, I want you to be esteemed and honored. I'm counting just on you for my revenge. I have tied a cable around you that you won't be able to break. You're triumphing. My tombstone will be what you hoped: your marriage altar. If not, prison."

Under so much humiliation, so many whip lashes straight in his face, at the end Trémorel's pride revolted.

"You have forgotten one thing, friend Sauvresy," he shouted. "It is possible to die."

"Pardon," the sick man continued coldly, "I foresaw that situation and I was going to warn you about it. If one of you dies suddenly before the marriage, the Procurer Imperial will be notified."

"You misunderstand. I meant to say: suicide is possible."

Sauvresy threw Hector an offensive look.

"You, kill yourself! Come now! Jenny Fancy, who despises you almost as much as I do, brought me up to date about your threats of suicide. Kill yourself! All right, here's my revolver. Blow your brains out and I'll forgive my wife."

Hector gestured with rage, but he didn't take the revolver his friend was holding out to him.

"You can certainly see I understand very well. You're afraid," Sauvresy said.

And speaking to Berthe:

"There's your lover," he said.

Extreme situations are bizarre in this way: The actors behave naturally in the exceptional situation. So, Berthe, Hector, and Sauvresy accepted, without being aware of it, the abnormal conditions in which they found themselves. And they spoke almost in a matter of fact way, as if it were a question of everyday things and not of monstrous facts.

But time was flying and Sauvresy felt life leaving him.

"There is only one act left to play," he said. "Hector go call the servants. Get those up who've gone to bed. I want to see them before I die."

Trémorel hesitated.

"Go ahead. Do you want me to ring. Do you want me to fire a shot to draw the attention of the whole house?"

Hector left.

Berthe was alone with her husband: alone! She had hoped that perhaps she might succeed in making him reverse his resolutions, that she might obtain her pardon. She remembered the time when she was all powerful, the time when a look from her could melt the resolutions of that man who adored her. She kneeled beside the bed. She had never been so beautiful, so seductive, so irresistible. Her harrowing emotions of the evening had brought her whole soul to her face. Her beautiful eyes, wet with tears were begging, her throat was palpitating, her mouth was half-opened as if for kisses. That passion for Sauvresy, born in frenzy, burst into delirium.

"Clément," she stammered, in an overexcited, lustful voice full of caresses, "my husband, Clément!...

He looked down at her with a look of hatred.

"What do you want?"

She didn't know how to begin. She was hesitating. She was trembling. She was worried. She was in love.

"Hector didn't know how to die, but I..."

"Well, what do you mean? Speak up."

"Miserable woman that I am, I'm killing you. I won't survive you."

An inexpressible agony contracted Sauvresy's features. She, commit suicide! But then there was no more revenge for him. Her own death would be no more than an absurd, ridiculous, grotesque suicide. And he knew that Berthe wouldn't lack courage at the last moment. She was waiting. He was thinking.

"You're free to do so," he finally answered. "That will be a last sacrifice for your lover. Once you're dead, Trémorel will marry Laurence Courtois and in a year he will have forgotten even the memory of your name."

In one bound, Berthe was on her feet, terrible. She could see Trémorel married, happy!...

A smile of triumph, like a ray of sunshine, lit up Sauvresy's pale face. He had hit the right spot. He could go peacefully to sleep in his revenge. Berthe would live. He knew what enemies he left facing each other.

But the servants were already arriving one by one. Most of them had been in Sauvresy's service for many years already and they loved him. He was a good master. Seeing him lying in his bed, gaunt, disheveled, already wearing the imprint of death on his face, they were moved. They were weeping. Then, Sauvresy, whose strength really was at an end, began to talk to them in a hardly audible voice broken by sinister coughs. It was important to him, he said, to thank them for their attachment to his person and to let them know that in his wishes he had left each of them a small fortune.

Then, coming to Berthe and Hector, he continued.

"You have witnessed, my friends, the cares I have been the object of on the part of that incomparable friend and my adored Berthe. You have seen their devotion. Alas! I know what regrets they will have. But if they wish to soften my last moments and let me have a happy death, they will agree to the pray I have continually addressed to them. They will swear to marry each other after my death. Oh! My beloved friends, that seems cruel to you at this moment. But don't you know that all human sadness becomes dulled. You are young. Life still has happiness for you. I beg of you, give in to the wishes of a dying man."

They had to give in. They came forward to the bed and Sauvresy put Berthe's hand in that of Hector.

"Do you swear to obey me?" he asked.

They shuddered to be in that position. They seemed about to faint. Nevertheless they answered loud enough to be heard.

"We swear."

The servants left, distressed by that heart-breaking scene and Berthe whispered:

"Oh! It's revolting. It's horrible!"

"Revolting, yes," Sauvresy whispered, "but not more revolting than your caresses, Berthe, than your handshakes, Hector…nor more horrible than your projects, than your covetousness…than your hopes…"

His voice was stifled by a death rattle.

Soon his death agony began. Horrible convulsions twisted his limbs in his bed like vine tendrils. Two or three times he cried out: "I'm cold. I'm cold."

His body was in fact freezing and nothing could give it warmth.

The household was in despair. No one had believed the end would be so quick. The servants came and went, frightened. They said to each other: "He's going to pass. That poor gentleman; that poor lady!"

But the convulsions soon stopped. He remained stretched out on his shoulder, his breathing so faint that they twice believed that it was all over. Finally, a little before two o'clock, his cheeks suddenly took on color. A shiver shook him. He sat up in his bed, his eyes dilated, his stiff arm pointing in the direction of the window. He cried out;

"There, behind the curtain, I see them."

A last convulsion threw him back on his pillow. Clément Sauvresy was dead.

Chapter XXI

The old Justice of the Peace had finished reading his voluminous file more than five minutes before, and his listeners, the Sûreté agent and the Doctor, still felt the effects of this distressing story. It's true that Père Plantat had an unusual way of speaking well-suited to impress those who heard him. He became passionate while speaking as if his personality were in play, as if he had been, in some way, a part of that dark affair and if his own interests were engaged in it.

Monsieur Lecoq was the first to come back to the sentiment of the moment.

"A gallant man, that Sauvresy!" he exclaimed.

The envoy of the Prefecture put all of himself in that exclamation. What struck him in that affair was the extraordinary plan of Sauvresy. What he admired was "his playing the game," in a game where he knew he must lose his life.

"I don't know many people," he added, "capable of such awful firmness. To let himself be poisoned very gently by his wife...brrr...that makes the blood run cold just to think about it."

"He knew how to get revenge," Doctor Gendron said softly.

"Yes," Père Plantat answered, "yes, Doctor, he knew how to avenge himself and more terribly still than he thought and you can imagine."

The Sûreté agent had gotten up a moment before. For more than three hours, nailed to his seat by the interest of the story, he had stayed motionless and he felt his legs going to sleep.

"Monsieur le juge de paix must excuse me," he said. "So far as I'm concerned, I can conceive very well the idea of the infernal existence of the poisoners the day after their victim's death. What characters! And you, Monsieur, have sketched them for us with the hand of a master. From your analysis, one knows them as if one had studied them with a magnifying glass for ten years."

He was speaking very deliberately, but at the same time he was looking at Père Plantat's face to see the effect of his compliment.

Where the devil did this good man get these details? Is he the one who drew up this memoir? And if he isn't the one, who could it be? If he possessed such information, why didn't he say anything?

Monsieur Plantat didn't react to Monsieur Lecoq mute interrogation.

"I know," he said, "that Sauvresy's body had not grown cold when his assassins were already exchanging death threats."

"Unfortunately for them," Doctor Gendron observed, "Sauvresy had already foreseen the situation where his widow would have wanted to use the remainder of the blue glass vial."

"Ah! He was smart," Lecoq said, in a convinced tone, "very smart."

"Berthe," continued Père Plantat, "couldn't forgive Hector for not having taken the revolver held out to him and for not having blown his brains out. Sauvresy had foreseen that also. Berthe imagined that if her lover were dead her husband would have forgotten everything. And you can't say whether or not she was wrong."

"And the public never knew anything about the terrible war inside the household."

"The public never suspected anything."

"That's marvelous!"

"You say, Monsieur Lecoq, that's hardly believable. Never was dissimulation so clever nor, most of all, so marvelously kept up. As the first one of Orcival's inhabitants you meet. They'll answer you as good Monsieur Courtois answered the Investigating Judge. He would say that the Count and the countess were model spouses and that they adored each other. Eh! Listen, I was taken in by it myself, me who knew what had happened. Who suspected it, I meant to say."

As fast as Père Plantat had been to reverse himself, the mistake did not escape Monsieur Lecoq.

Was that really only a mistake, only a lapse? he wondered.

But the old Justice of the Peace was continuing.

"Vile criminals had been atrociously punished. You couldn't feel sorry for them. All would have been for the best if Sauvresy, carried away by hatred, having only one obsessive idea, revenge, hadn't himself done something foolish that I consider almost like a crime."

"A crime!" the Doctor exclaimed, stupefied. "A crime, Sauvresy!"

Monsieur Lecoq smiled slightly and whispered. "Oh!" very low: "Laurence."

As softly as he had spoken, Père Plantat still heard him.

"Yes, Monsieur Lecoq," he answered, "yes, Sauvresy committed a detestable action the day he thought to make that unfortunate child the accomplice, I mean, the instrument, of his anger. He was the one who threw her between two loathsome beings, without pity, without wondering if she would be broken apart there. It was the name of Laurence that made Berthe decide to live. And nevertheless he knew Trémorel's passion. He knew about the love of that unfortunate girl, and he knew her lover capable of anything. He didn't even deign to foresee that Laurence might be seduced and dishonored. And he left her defenseless before the seduction of the most cowardly and the most infamous of men."

The Sûreté agent was thinking;

"There's one circumstance I can't explain to myself," he objected. "Why didn't these two accomplices, who loathed each other, whom the unforgiving will of their victim chained together against all their instincts, separate by mutual agreement the day after their marriage, the day following the day they came into possession of the document which set forth their crime?"

The old Justice of the Peace shook his head.

"I can truly see that I haven't managed to make you understand Berthe's horrifying character. Hector would have been overjoyed with a separation. His wife couldn't consent to it. Ah! Sauvresy really understood her. She felt her life was lost. Horrible regrets tore her apart. She needed a victim, a creature she could use to expiate her own mistakes and crimes.

Hector was that victim. Attached to her prey, she wouldn't have released him for anything in the world."

"Ah! *ma foi.*" Doctor Gendron remarked, "Your Trémorel was also too cowardly. What did he have to fear, once Sauvresy's manuscript was done away with?"

"Who told you it had been?" interrupted the old Justice of the Peace.

On that response, Monsieur Lecoq stopped walking up and down the library and came to sit down across from Père Plantat.

"The proofs—have they or have they not, been done away with? For me, for the investigation, everything hangs on that."

Père Plantat didn't judge it the right time to answer directly.

"Do you know who the person Sauvresy chose as the depository of the documents?"

"Ah!" shouted the agent from the Sûreté, slapping himself on the forehead as if struck with a sudden idea. "The person holding the documents, that was you, Monsieur le juge de paix."

And to himself he added: *Now, my good fellow, I'm beginning to understand where your information comes from.*

"Yes, I was the one," Père Plantat continued. "The day after the marriage of Madame, the widow of Sauvresy, and the Count de Trémorel, following the last wishes of my dying friend, I went to Valfeuillu and I asked for Monsieur and Madame de Trémorel."

Although they had many people waiting to see them, although very busy, they received me immediately in the little drawing room on the first floor where Sauvresy had been murdered. They were both very pale and very upset. They certainly guessed the reason for my visit. They had guessed it when they heard my name announced and they then gave me an interview.

"After greeting them both, I spoke to Berthe, as was prescribed in the minute instructions which had been given to me in writing, and which Sauvresy's diabolical foresight had made shockingly clear.

"Madame," I said to her, "I have been charged by your departed first husband to give you, the day after your second marriage, what he entrusted to me."

"She took the package holding the bottle and the manuscript with a very happy look, even joyous, thanking me many times and immediately left.

"The Count's face immediately changed. He seemed to me very upset, very nervous. It was as if on hot coals. I could certainly see that he was burning to rush after his wife's steps and didn't dare. I was going to leave, but he held me there. What's more, he suddenly said to me:

'Pardon! You'll excuse me, won't you? I'll be with you in an instant.'

"And he dashed out. When I saw him as well as his wife some minutes later, they were both very red. Their eyes had an extraordinary gleam, and their voice was still shaking when, with polite formalities, they saw me to the door. They had certainly just had an altercation of the greatest violence."

"And it's possible to guess the rest," Monsieur Lecoq interrupted. "The dear lady had left to put the manuscript of her dead husband in a safe place. And when her new husband asked her for it, she answered him: 'Look for it.'"

"Sauvresy had told me to put the packet in her hands only."

"Oh! He knew how to set up revenge. To keep Trémorel under her feet, he gave his widow a terrible weapon always ready to strike. That was the magic whip she used if, by chance, he revolted. Ah! He was a miserable creature, that man, but she must have made him suffer terribly."

"Yes," Doctor Gendron broke in, "right up to the day he murdered her."

The Sûreté agent had again taken up his walk up and down the library.

"There remains," he said, "the question of the poison, a simple question to solve, since we hold there in the closet, the man who sold it."

"Besides," the Doctor replied, "as far as the poison is concerned, I make that my business. It was from my laboratory that scoundrel Robelet stole it. I know only too well what it is, that poison, as well as the symptoms so well described by Père Plantat, even if I wasn't told its name. I was doing research concerning monkshood at the time of Monsieur Sauvresy's death. He was poisoned with aconitum."[15]

"Ah!" Monsieur Lecoq exclaimed. "Aconitum. This is the first time in my career that I'm encountered that poison. Is it new?"

"Not exactly," Monsieur Gendron said, smiling. "They say Medea [16] extracted her most terrible toxins from Monkshood. Rome and Greece employed it the same time as hemlock as an agent for judicial executions."

"And I didn't know about it! I have so little time to work, it's true. That poison of Medea is perhaps lost, as are those of the Borgias. So many things are lost![17]

"No, it hasn't been lost, you can be sure. However, we today hardly know anything about it except from the experiments of Mathiole, on those condemned to death in the 16th century; by the work of Hers, who, in 1833, isolated the principal active ingredient, the alkaloid, and finally by some essays of Bouchardat, who claims…"

When by some misfortune Doctor Gendron got started on his poisons, it

---

[15] Monkshood, also called Wolfsbane, a plant that can be used for medicinal purposes, but also has poisonous properties.

[16] A famous sorceress from the Greek legends.

[17] Italian family reputed to have poisoned their enemies.

was difficult to stop him. But on the other hand, Monsieur Lecoq never lost sight of his purpose.

"Pardon me if I interrupt you, Doctor," he said. "Would traces of aconitum still be found in a corpse buried more than two years? Because, after all, Monsieur Domini will require the body be exhumed."

"The reactives of aconitum, Monsieur, are not well enough know to permit their isolation in cadavers. Bouchardat actually suggested introducing potassium iodine which would give an orange precipitate, but that experiment didn't succeed for me."

"The Devil! That's annoying," said Monsieur Lecoq.

The Doctor smiled with triumph.

"Don't worry," he said. "The procedure didn't exist. I invented it."

"Ah!" exclaimed Père Plantat. "Your litmus paper treated to detect the smallest differences!"

"Precisely."

"And you would be able to isolate aconitum in Sauvresy's body?"

"Monsieur l'agent, I could find a milligram of aconitum in a cart of manure."

Monsieur Lecoq seemed radiant, like a man who has acquired the certainty of bringing to a good conclusion a task which had seemed somewhat difficult.

"So!" he exclaimed. "It's finished here. Our investigation is complete. The victim's backgrounds set forth by Monsieur le juge de paix gives us the key to all the events that followed the death of that unfortunate Sauvresy. So, that explains the hatred of the spouses seemingly so well united. So, that explains why Count Hector made a charming young girl, who had a million in dowry, his mistress and not his wife. There's no longer anything surprising in the fact that Monsieur de Trémorel resigned himself to throwing his name and his personality in the Seine, to recreate a civil status for himself. If he killed his wife, it was because he was constrained to do so by the logic of the events. If she were alive, he couldn't flee. Nevertheless, he couldn't continue living at Valfeuillu. Finally, that paper he was searching for with such determination, when each minute could cost him his life, the proof of his first crime, was Sauvresy's manuscript."

Monsieur Lecoq was speaking with extraordinary animation, as if he had some personal motives for animosity against Count de Trémorel. He was so constituted, and he willingly admitted, laughing, that he couldn't keep from having it in for criminals it was his duty to track down. There was an account to settle between him and them. The disinterested ardor of his investigations resulted from that fact. Perhaps in his case it was simply a matter of instinct, similar that which drives the hunting dog to follow the traces of game.

"It's now clear that it was Mademoiselle Courtois who put an end to Trémorel's eternal irresolution," he continued. "His passion for her, irritated by obstacles, must have touched on delirium. Learning about his mistress' pregnancy—because I would bet she really is pregnant—that miserable man, losing his head, forgot all caution and all moderation. He must have been so tired of a torture which for him began again every morning. He saw himself lost. He saw his terrible wife turning him over to justice just for the pleasure of doing so. Terrified, he took the initiative and decided on the murder. That was the whip lash that made him, like the hesitating horse, jump the ditch."

Many of the circumstances which established the certainty of the Sûreté agent had of necessity escaped Doctor Gendron.

"What!" He exclaimed, stupefied. "You believe in the complicity of Mademoiselle Laurence?"

The man from the Préfecture made a gesture of strong protestation.

"No, Monsieur le docteur, no, certainly not. Heaven preserve me from such an idea. Mademoiselle Courtois did not know, and still does not know, about the crime. But she knows that Trémorel is leaving his wife for her. That flight had been discussed between them, agreed on, settled. They had given each other a rendezvous for a certain day, for a predetermined place."

"But that letter," exclaimed the Doctor, "that letter!"

Since it was now a question of Laurence, Père Plantat was badly disguising his agony and his emotions.

"That letter," he cried out, "that's plunging a whole family in the most terrible sadness, which may kill my poor Courtois, is only one scene in the infamous comedy created by the Count."

"Oh!" exclaimed the Doctor. "Is that possible?"

"I'm absolutely of the opinion of Monsieur le juge de paix," affirmed the Sûreté agent. "Yesterday evening, at the Mayor's house, we had the same suspicion at the same time. I read and reread Mademoiselle Laurence's letter and I would wager it's not from her. The Count de Trémorel placed a draft in front of her that she copied. Let's not fool ourselves, Messieurs, that letter was meditated, thought out, composed at leisure. No, those aren't, those couldn't be the words of an unhappy, young girl twenty years old who's going to kill herself to escape dishonor."

"Perhaps you're right," the Doctor, evidently shaken, said. "But how do you imagine Monsieur de Trémorel succeeded in making Mademoiselle agree to that abominable expedient?"

"What! Look, Doctor, I'm not an authority in such matters, having rarely had the opportunity to study on the spot the feelings of well-brought-up young ladies. Nevertheless, the thing seems to me very simple. A young girl, in the situation Mademoiselle Courtois finds herself in, who sees the fatal moment approaching when her shame will become public, must be ready for anything, agree to anything, even to die."

Père Plantat seemed to shiver. A conversation he had with Laurence came to mind. She had asked him—he remembered it—information about certain poisonous plants that he cultivated, concerned a great deal about the methods used to extract deadly juices.

"Yes," he said. "She was thinking about suicide."

"Well!" The Sûreté agent continued, "It was at the moment these gloomy thoughts were occupying the poor child's mind that the Count de Trémorel was easily able to complete his work of perdition. She probably told him she preferred death to shame. He proved to her that, being pregnant, she didn't have the right to kill herself. He told her he was very unhappy, that not being free he couldn't repair the horrible fault, but at the same time he offered to sacrifice his life for her.

"What must she do to save everything? Leave her family, make everyone believe she had committed suicide, while he, on his side, would desert his house and abandon his wife. She must have tried to ward off that prospect, resist. But must he not have been able to get everything he wanted from her—to snatch the most unlikely agreements from her—by speaking of that child moving in her womb, that they would bring up between them, and who would thus have a father!

"And she consented to everything. She ran away. She recopied and threw that infamous letter prepared by her lover in the mail."

The Doctor was convinced.

"Yes," he murmured," those are really the means of seduction he must have used."

"But how clumsy he was," the Sûreté agent continued, "what stupidity, not to think that bizarre coincidence between the disappearance of his corpse and Mademoiselle Courtois' suicide wouldn't, infallibly, be noted. What the Devil! Cadavers don't get lost just like that! But no! Monsieur told himself: 'People will believe I've been once and for all murdered just like my wife, and the law, having its guilty man, that is to say, Guespin, won't ask anything more.'"

Père Plantat made a desperate gesture of impotent rage.

"Ah!" he exclaimed, "not to know where the miserable man is hiding so we can take Laurence from him!"

The Sûreté agent took the arm of the old Justice of the Peace and gripped it tightly.

"Rest easy, Monsieur," he said in a cold tone. "We'll find him, or my name won't be Lecoq. And to be frank, I must admit to you that the task doesn't seem to me very difficult."

Three or four discreet knocks at the door interrupted Monsieur Lecoq. It was getting late and those in the household were already awake and moving about. Ten times at least, Madame Petit, eaten up with worry, sick, and almost weeping with disappointed curiosity, had come to stick her ear to the keyhole. Alas! In vain.

"What can they be plotting in there?" she asked Louis, her calm table mate. "They've been shut up in there for twelve hours without eating or drinking. Is that sensible! Well! I'm still going to prepare lunch."

Nevertheless, it wasn't Madame Petit who put herself at risk by knocking.

It was Louis, the gardener, who came to report to his employer concerning some extraordinary damages done to the garden. The lawn had been wrecked, stomped down, vandalized. At the same time he brought in some unusual objects he had picked up left by those who had damaged the lawn. Monsieur Lecoq recognized those objects at first glance.

"Heavens!" he exclaimed, "I forgot myself. Here I am calmly chatting with an uncovered face, as if we weren't in full daylight, as if some indiscreet person might not come in at any moment!"

And speaking to Louis, who was very surprised to find this young dark-haired man there he hadn't seen come in the evening before:

"Give me, my boy," he said to him, "these toilette articles that belong to me."

Then, in no time, while the master of the house went to give some directions, he readjusted his facial make-up of the previous evening. He did it so well that, Père Plantat, when he returned, couldn't believe his eyes. Near the fireplace, he saw his Lecoq with the silly look he had at the Investigation. He really had the same flat hair, fawn-colored side-burns, that idiotic smile. He was playing with the same lozenge box with the portrait.

The old Justice of the Peace had just told his guests lunch was ready. As silent as the dinner of the evening before, the meal didn't last long. The guests knew what minutes were costing. Monsieur Domini was waiting for them at Corbeil and he very likely was becoming impatient with their lateness.

Louis had just placed a magnificent basket of fruits on the table when Monsieur Lecoq thought about the bonesetter.

"The miserable man probably needs something," he said.

Père Plantat wanted to send his servant to get Master Robelot. The Sûreté agent opposed that idea.

"He's a dangerous fellow," he said. "I'll go myself."

He left and ten seconds hadn't gone by when they could hear him shouting:

"Messieurs!" he cried out, "Messieurs!!!"

The Doctor and the Justice of the Peace went running to him. The lifeless body of Robelot was stretched across the door to the closet. The scoundrel had committed suicide.

Chapter XXII

The Orcival bonesetter had needed unusual presence of mind and rare courage to kill himself in that dark closet without drawing the attention of the guests in the library by any suspicious noise. A piece of cord, found by groping around in the darkness among the old books and the bundles of newspapers, had been the instrument of his suicide. He had tied it tightly around his neck and using a bit of pencil as a tourniquet, he had strangled himself. However, he didn't show anything of that hideous aspect popular belief attributes to individuals who perish by strangulation. He had a pale face, half-opened eyes, a gaping mouth and the stupid look of the man who, as a result of a stroke, little by little, loses consciousness.

"Maybe it might still be possible to bring him back to life," said Doctor Gendron.

And taking out his medical kit quickly, he knelt beside the cadaver. That suicide seemed to greatly upset and even distress Monsieur Lecoq. Just when everything was rolling along smoothly, here was his principal witness, the man he had arrested at the peril of his life, escaping him. Père Plantat, on the contrary, seemed almost happy, as if that death served certain plans he had not yet spoken of and answered some secret hopes. That was of no importance, however, if it was only a matter of combating Monsieur Domini's opinions and furnishing him with the elements for a new conviction. This cadaver spoke more eloquently than the most explicit confession.

The Doctor had just stood up. He recognized his cares were useless. He had gone through all the actions that experience in the matter of strangulation recommends. He had opened the jugular vein without success.

"He's really dead," he said. "The compression was particularly heavy between the hyoid bone and the thyroid cartilage. Asphyxiation must have been complete in a very short time."

The bonesetter's corpse was then stretched out the library rug.

"There's nothing more to do but to have him carried back to his house. We'll accompany him there to put seals on all his furniture, which might contain some important papers."

And turning toward his servant:

"Run to the Mayor. Ask for a stretcher and two willing men."

Doctor Gendron's presence was no longer necessary. He promised Père Plantat that he would rejoin him and he left to go inform himself about Monsieur Courtois's state.

However, Louis wasn't slow in reappearing, followed, not by two willing men, but by ten. They placed Robelot's corpse on the stretcher and the funeral cortege got on its way. The Orcival bonesetter lived at the bottom of the hill, to the right of the iron cable bridge. He lived alone in a little three-room house, one of which he used as a shop encumbered with packets of plants, dried herbs, seeds and a hundred other things in his business as a herbalist. He slept in the room at the back, better furnished than country bedrooms usually are.

The porters deposited their sad burden on the bed. They would have probably been at a loss as to what to do if the village drummer, who was also the Orcival grave digger, had not been one of them. That man, who was an expert in everything that concerned funerals, gave directions for the corpse's last toilette. He himself, with a skillful and swift hand, arranged the mattress as the rite required, folded and tucked in the sheets as it was usually done. During this time Père Plantat went through all the furniture. He had the keys they had taken from the dead man's pockets.

The wealth found in that man's possession who, two or three years earlier lived from hand to mouth and didn't possess as much as a *sou,* must have been an overwhelming witness against him and added one more proof to the others, morally indisputable, but not evidence of his complicity, however.

But the old Justice of the Peace searched in vain. He didn't find anything that he didn't already know. There were titles to the Morin meadows property, to the Frapesle fields and the Peyron pieces of land. To the titles were joined two mortgages, one for a hundred and fifty francs, and the other for eight hundred and twenty francs, payable to Master Robelet by two inhabitants of the commune. Père Plantat hid his disappointment badly.

"No cash," he whispered in Monsieur Lecoq's ear. "Can you understand that?"

"Very well," answered the Sûreté agent. "He was a cunning fellow, that Robelot, careful enough to hide his sudden fortune, patient enough to appear to have spent years becoming rich. You won't find anything in his secretary, Monsieur, except the money he could admit having without danger. How much does he have there?"

The Justice of the Peace rapidly added up the different sums and answered:

"Fourteen thousand, five hundred francs."

"Madame Sauvresy gave him more," the man from the Préfecture declared positively. "Having only 14,000 francs, he wouldn't have been foolish enough to invest it in land. He must have a pile of money somewhere."

"Very likely. I'm of that opinion, but where?"

"Ah! I'm going to look around."

He did look around, in fact, without appearing to do so. He wandered around the bedroom, moving the furniture, sounding the floor in certain cases with the heel of his boot, putting his ear to the wall in certain places. Finally, he came back to the fireplace, where he had already stopped several times.

"This is the month of July," he said, "and nevertheless there are a lot of ashes in this fireplace."

"People don't always take them out at the end of winter," the Justice of the

Peace objected.

"That's true, Monsieur, but don't these here seem very clean and neat to you? I don't see that light coat of dust and soot that should cover them, since no fire has been lit here in several months."

He went back to the second room. He had had the stretcher-bearers leave when their job was finished. He said:

"Try to find me a pick."

All the men rushed out. He came back near the Justice of the Peace. As if an aside, he whispered, "These ashes have certainly been moved about recently, and if they've been moved about..."

He had already bent down, and, brushing aside the ashes, he had uncovered the hearthstone. Then taking a thin piece of wood, he easily inserted it into the joints of the stone.

"You see, Monsieur le juge de paix, not an atom of cement and the stone is moveable. The money must be stashed here."

They brought him a pick. He struck only one blow. The hearth stone tipped up, leaving a rather deep gaping hole.

"Ah!" he exclaimed, with an air of triumph. "I was right about that."

The hole was filled with rolls of twenty-franc coins. They counted and they found 19,500 francs.

At this moment the face of the old Justice of the Peace showed profound sadness.

Alas! he was thinking, *Here's the price of my poor Sauvresy's life.*

The Sûreté agent had taken from the hiding place at the same time as the gold a little piece of paper covered with numbers. It was the bonesetter's master record book. On one side, the left, he had inscribed the sum of forty thousand francs. On the other side, the right, he had put down different sums, the total of which came to twenty-one thousand five hundred francs. These different sums added up to the price of his acquisitions. It was only too clear. Madame Sauvresy had paid Robelot forty thousand francs for her blue crystal bottle.

Père Plantat and the Sûreté agent had nothing more to learn at the bonesetter's house. They locked the gold from the cache in the secretary and affixed everywhere the seals that had to stay guarded by two of the men present. But Monsieur Lecoq was still not completely satisfied. What really was that old manuscript the old Justice of the Peace had read? For a while he had thought that it was just a copy of the denunciation Sauvresy had put in his care. But, no, it couldn't be that. Sauvresy wouldn't have been able to describe the last, very terrible scenes of his agony.

This point, which remained obscure, bothered the man from the Préfecture of Police prodigiously and poisoned the joy he experienced from having brought such a difficult investigation to a good conclusion. He wanted to try again to force the truth out of Père Plantat. Taking him not too carefully by the collar of his frock coat, he drew him to the window, and in his most innocent air:

"Pardon," he said to him in a low tone, "aren't we going to go back to your house?"

"Why do that, when Doctor Gendron, when he leaves the Mayor's house, is supposed to meet us here."

"Because, Monsieur, I believe we will need the file you read to us last night to bring it to the attention of the Investigating Magistrate."

The Sûreté agent was expecting to see the man questioning him start at that proposition. His expectations were wrong.

Père Plantat smiled sadly and looked him straight in the eyes.

"You're very clever, dear Monsieur Lecoq," he said, "but I'm clever enough to keep the last word for myself. You've guessed a good part of it."

Monsieur Lecoq almost blushed under his faun-colored side-burns.

"Believe me, Monsieur...," he stammered.

Père Plantat interrupted him:

"I believe you would be very pleased to know the source of my information. Your memory is too good not to have remembered that when I began, yesterday evening, I warned you that story was for you only and that I had only one goal in telling it to you: to help our investigation. What do you expect the Investigating Magistrate to do with totally personal notes having no recommendation of authenticity?"

He thought a few seconds, as if he was looking for a sentence to add to his thoughts. He added:

"I have too much confidence in you regarding this matter, Monsieur Lecoq, and I have too much esteem for you, not to be certain in advance that you won't speak in any way about absolutely confidential documents. What you will say is worth all I have written, now that you have Robelet's body and the considerable sum found in his possession to support your assertions. If Monsieur Domini still hesitates to believe you, you know Dr. Gendron is expert enough to recover the poison that killed Sauvresy."

Père Plantat stopped. He hesitated.

"Finally," he continued. "I believe you will be able to keep quiet what you have guessed."

Proof that Monsieur Lecoq was really a strong man was that finding a partner as competent as he was didn't displease him. Certainly, in matters of police work, he was very superior to Père Plantat. But he had to acknowledge that this old Justice of the Peace lacked only a little more practice and less personal involvement. Several times since the evening before he had already bowed before his superior insight. This time he took his hand and shook it in a telling way.

"You can rely on me, Monsieur," he said.

At that moment, Doctor Gendron appeared on the threshold.

"Courtois is better," he declared. "He's crying like a baby. He'll come out of it."

"Thank Heavens!" answered the old Justice of the Peace. "But, now that you're here, let's go; let's hurry. Monsieur Domini, who's expecting us this morning, must be mad with impatience."

Chapter XXIII

When Père Plantat spoke of the Investigating Magistrate's impatience, he was certainly very far from reality. Monsieur Domini was furious. He understood nothing concerning the prolonged absence of his collaborators of the evening before: the Justice of the Peace, the Doctor and the Sûreté agent.

He had come to settle in at his office very early in the morning, wearing his justice's robe and counting the minutes. The reflections of the night, far from shaking and troubling his theories, had only confirmed them. The further he got away from the hour of the crime, the simpler, the more natural, the easier to explain he found it.

But his present conviction that his opinion was not that of the other agents of the investigation, bothered him, no matter what he might tell himself, and made him wait for their report in a state of nervous irritation. His stenographer was only too aware of that. Fearing he wouldn't be there the moment Monsieur Lecoq arrived, dreading remaining one moment more in uncertainty, he had even had his breakfast brought to him in his office. That was a useless precaution. The hands of the clock with blue designs on its face which ornamented the Law Court's wall were moving forward and no one was arriving. To kill time, he had thoroughly questioned Guespin and La Ripaille. These new interrogations didn't tell him anything. One of the accused men swore by all the great gods that he didn't know anything more than he had already said. The other remained locked in a bitter silence—that couldn't be more irritating— saying only: "I know that I'm condemned. Do with me whatever you like." Monsieur Domini was going to have a mounted policeman sent to Orcival to ask the reasons for that unexplained delay, when the bailiff on duty announced those he was expecting.

He quickly gave the order to have them shown in, and his curiosity was so extreme that, despite what he called his dignity, he himself rose to go meet them.

"How late you are!" he exclaimed.

"Even so," the Justice of the Peace said, "we haven't wasted a minute and we haven't slept."

"Is there something new?" he asked them. "Have they found the Count de Trémorel's body?"

"There's something new, Monsieur," Monsieur Lecoq answered, "and a great deal of it. But the body of the Count hasn't been found, and I can even confirm that it won't be found. There's a very simple reason for that: because he wasn't killed. He wasn't one of the victims as he was for a while thought to be, because he is the murderer."

At that claim, very clearly stated by the man from the police, the Investigating Magistrate jumped out of his chair.

"But that's madness," he exclaimed.

Monsieur Lecoq never allowed himself to smile when in front of an Investigating Magistrate.

"I think not," he answered coolly. "I'm even persuaded that if the Investigating Magistrate would be willing to give me a half-hour of his attention, I would have the honor of bringing him to share my convictions."

Monsieur Domini's barely noticeable shrug didn't escape the man from the Rue de Jérusalem. So, he believed he should insist.

"What's more, I'm certain that Investigating Magistrate won't let me leave his office without having issued me an arrest warrant for the Count de Trémorel, that he presently believes dead."

"So be it," Monsieur Domini said. "Go on."

Monsieur Lecoq then began rapidly to lay out the facts gathered by himself as well as by the Justice of the Pease since the beginning of the Investigation. He set them forth, not as he had learned them or guessed them, but in their chronological order and in such a way that each new fact that he brought up flowed naturally from the preceding one.

More than ever, he had taken on his personality of a kindly tradesman, speaking in a little piping voice, using obsequious formulas excessively: "I'll have the honor of," or "If Monsieur the Judge will deign to allow me…" He had again taken out the lozenge box with the portrait. And, as he had done at Valfeuillu the evening before, at exciting or decisive passages, he swallowed a piece of liquorice.

As he went on with his story, Monsieur Domini's surprise became more evident. At times he let out an exclamation.

"Is that possible! That's not believable!"

Monsieur Lecoq had finished. He calmly swallowed a square of marshmallow and added:

"What does the Investigating Magistrate think now?"

Monsieur Domini, it has to be admitted, was only partially satisfied. It's never without secret irritation that one sees an inferior with one brutal finger wreck a theory you've taken the trouble to put together and layout. But no matter how firm his opinions were, how little disposed he was to allow himself to share someone else's wishes, this time he really had to bow before the blinding evidence.

"I'm convinced," he answered, "that a crime was committed against the person of Monsieur Clément Sauvresy with the assistance, dearly paid for, by that Robelot. This is so true that tomorrow Dr. Gendron will receive an order to go ahead without delay to the exhumation and autopsy of the cadaver."

"And I will recover the poison," the Doctor affirmed. "You can be sure of that."

"Very good," Monsieur Domini continued. "But, because Monsieur de

Trémorel poisoned his friend in order to marry his widow, does it necessarily, strictly follow that yesterday he murdered his wife and then took flight? I don't believe so."

Père Plantat was so afraid he would lose his temper that he didn't dare say anything. He was tapping his foot in rage. Monsieur Domini was digressing.

"Pardon, Monsieur," Monsieur Lecoq gently objected, "it seems to me that Mademoiselle Courtois' suicide—everything leads us to believe her supposed suicide—proves at least something."

"That's a fact that must be cleared up. The coincidence you cite may be only a pure result of chance."

"But, Monsieur," the Sûreté agent insisted, visibly annoyed, "I'm sure Monsieur de Trémorel shaved himself. I can prove it. We didn't find the boots that, according to the valet, he wore in the morning..."

"Gently, Monsieur," the Judge interrupted. "More softly, please. I don't claim that you're absolutely wrong. It's just that I must tell you my objections. Let's admit, I'm in agreement there, that Monsieur de Trémorel killed his wife. He's alive; he has fled. I agree to that. Does that prove Guespin's innocence or that he took no part in the murder?"

Evidently that was the weak side of Monsieur Lecoq's argument. But, convinced, sure of Hector's guilt, he was very little worried about the poor gardener. He told himself that his innocence must necessarily be clear of itself when they laid their hands on the guilty man. Nevertheless, he was going to answer when the sound of footsteps was heard in the corridor, then whispering voices.

"Well," said Monsieur Domini, "we're probably going to learn some interesting details of great interest about Guespin."

"Were you expecting some new witness," Monsieur Lecoq asked.

"No, but I'm expecting an employee of our Corbeil police force. I sent him on an important mission."

"About Guespin?"

"Precisely. This morning very early a female worker in the city that Guespin was courting brought me a photograph that she claimed looked very much like him. I gave this photograph to my agent with the address of the *Forges de Vulcain,* that was found in the possession of the accused man yesterday. I commissioned him to find out if Guespin had been seen in that store and if he had bought anything there in the evening before yesterday."

If there was ever a jealous hunter, not liking to see anyone poaching on his territory, it was assuredly Monsieur Lecoq. The action of the Investigating Magistrate hurt his pride so much that he couldn't hide a terrible forced smile.

"I am truly sorry," he said in a dry tone, "to have inspired so little confidence in the Investigating Magistrate that he thinks he must give me help."

That susceptibility amused Monsieur Domini very much.

"Eh! Monsieur Lecoq," he said, "you can't be everywhere at the same time. I believe you are very capable, but I didn't have you near at hand, and I was in a hurry."

"A false approach is often irreparable."

"Don't worry. I sent an intelligent man."

The office door opened at the same moment. The emissary the Investigating Magistrate spoke of appeared at the door.

He was a vigorous man about forty-years-old, with a soldierly rather than a military bearing. He wore a coarse bristly mustache. He had gleaming eyes shaded by bushy eyebrows which came together in a formidable bouquet in the middle above his nose. He appeared crafty rather than clever, and more underhanded than clever. This was so apparent that just his appearance must raise all sorts of mistrust and put people instinctively on guard.

"Good news," he said in a thick voice, hoarse and broken by alcohol. "I didn't make the trip to Paris for no results. We're well on the trail of this scoundrel Guespin."

Monsieur Domini interrupted him with a kindly, almost friendly, gesture.

"Look, Goulard"—his name was Goulard—"let's proceed in an orderly and methodical way, if possible. Following my orders, you went to the *Forges de Vulcain* store?"

"Immediately on leaving the train, yes, Judge."

"Had they seen the accused?"

"Yes, Monsieur, Wednesday the 8th of July in the evening."

"At what time?"

"About ten o'clock, a few minutes before the store closed. That fact made him noticed and very well observed."

The Justice of the Peace moved his lips, probably to present an objection. A gesture from Monsieur Lecoq, who was watching him, his index finger placed on his lips, stopped him.

"And who recognized the photograph?" Monsieur Domini continued.

"Three employees, neither more nor less. I have to tell you that Guespin's behavior immediately drew their attention. He had an extraordinary appearance, they told me, to the point that they thought they were dealing with a drunken man, or at least with someone who was tipsy. Then, what made them remember him was that he talked a lot. He claimed he would buy a lot of garden tools for a company that had confidence in him, the *Gentil Jardinier*. He even went so far as to say he would guarantee them not to tell if they guaranteed him a kick back."

Monsieur Domini stopped the interrogation to consult the already voluminous file placed in front of him on his desk. It really was, in fact—if the witnesses are to be believed—through the *Gentil Jardinier* that Guespin was placed with the Count de Trémorel's household.

The Investigating Magistrate noted that aloud, and added:

"The identification, at least, can't be contested. It's established by the prosecution that Guespin was, Wednesday evening, at the Forges de Vulcain."

"So much the better for him," Monsieur Lecoq couldn't keep from saying.

The Magistrate heard that exclamation very well, but in spite of the fact that it seemed unusual to him, he didn't note it down and continued to question his confidential man.

"That being so," he continued, "they must have been able to tell you what objects the accused had come to buy."

"The employees actually remember that. He first bought a hammer, a cold chisel, and a file."

"I was right!" the Investigating Magistrate exclaimed. "And after that?"

"After that, Monsieur..."

At this point, the man with the bristly mustache, jealous to strike his listeners' imagination, thought he should roll his eyes in a terrible way and take on a sinister voice.

"Then he bought a short sword."

The Investigating Magistrate couldn't hold still. He had beaten Monsieur Lecoq on his own territory. He had triumphed.

"Well!" he asked the Sûreté agent in his most ironic tone, "What do you think of your client now? What do you say of that honest and worthy boy who, the evening of the crime itself, gave up going to a wedding where he would have had a good time, in order to go buy a hammer, a chisel, a short sword, all the instruments, in a word, indispensable for breaking and entering and for the murder?"

Doctor Gendron seemed somewhat disconcerted by these revelations suddenly produced, but Père Plantat's lips had a slight smile. As for Monsieur Lecoq, he had the priceless expression of a superior man lacerated by objections that he knew he must with a word reduce to nothing. He looked resigned to seeing time he could put usefully to profit wasted in pointless parley;

"I think, Monsieur," he replied humbly, "that the murders at Valfeuillu used neither a hammer nor a cold chisel, nor a file, that they didn't bring tools from outside, because they used a hatchet."

"They didn't have a short sword either?" the Judge demanded, more and more quietly ironic to the extent he felt surer of being on the right path.

"That is another question," the Sûreté agent said, "but one it's not hard to solve."

He was beginning to lose patience. He turned toward the Corbeil agent and rather brusquely asked him:

"Is that all you know?"

The man with the bushy eyebrows looked that harmless little bourgeois with a cheap turn of phrase up and down who dared to question him in this way. He hesitated so long in honoring Monsieur Lecoq with an answer that Monsieur Lecoq had to repeat his question, brutally this time.

"Yes, that's all," he finally said, "and I find that's enough because it's the opinion of the Investigating Magistrate, the only one who can give me orders and whose approval I need."

Monsieur Lecoq shrugged his shoulders as high as he could while examining Monsieur Domini's messenger.

"Let's see," he asked, "did you even ask what exactly was the shape of the sword Guespin bought was? Was it big, little, wide, narrow? Did it have a fixed blade?"

"*Ma foi,* no. Why should I have?"

"Simply, my man, to put that weapon into the victim's wounds to see if its guard corresponds to the one which left a clear and visible imprint between the victim's shoulders.

"That was an oversight, but it's easy to repair it."

Had Monsieur Lecoq not had, to over excite his insight, the stings of his wounded vanity, he would have made prodigious efforts to answer the looks that Père Plantat was giving him.

"A misadventure is understandable," he said, "but at least you're going to tell us what money Guespin paid for his purchases with?"

The poor Corbeil detective, so humiliated, so annoyed, seemed so embarrassed with the figure he cut that the Investigating Magistrate thought he should come to his aid.

"The nature of the money matters very little, it seems to me," he objected.

"I beg Investigating Magistrate to excuse me. I'm not of his opinion," Monsieur Lecoq answered. "That circumstance may be one of the most important. What was the most serious charge brought against Guespin by the investigation? It was the money found in his pocket. Now, let's suppose for a moment that yesterday at ten o'clock he changed a thousand franc bill in Paris. Could this bill have come from the Valfeuillu crime? No, because at that time the crime had not yet been committed. Where did it come from? That's something I haven't yet researched. But if my hypothesis is correct the law will be forced to agree that the some hundred francs with which the accused was provided, could and must be the remainder of the bill."

"That's still only a hypothesis," stressed Monsieur Domini in a more and more bad-tempered tone.

"That's true, but one that can be changed into a certainty. I still must ask Monsieur—he pointed to the man with the mustache—how Guespin brought back the things he bought. Did he simply slip them in his pocket? Or did he put them in a package? And where is that package?"

The Sûreté agent was speaking in a cutting, hard, glacial tone, underlined with bitter mockery. This was done so well that the poor devil's expression had lost all its assurance and was no longer twirling his mustache as he had been.

"I don't know," he stammered, "I wasn't told; I believed..."

Monsieur Lecoq raised both his hands as if to call Heaven as a witness. Actually, he was delighted with that superb opportunity which presented itself to avenge himself for Monsieur Domini's disdain. To the Investigating Magistrate he couldn't, he didn't dare, he didn't want to say anything, but he had the right to scorn the unfortunate agent, to dump his anger on him.

"Ah! Well, my boy," he said to him, "then what did you go to Paris to do? To show Guespin's photographs and tell the story of the Orcival Crime to the gentlemen at the Forges de Vulcain? They must have appreciated your attention. But Madame Petit, the Justice of the Peace's housekeeper, could have done as much."

Ah! That did it! At that attack, the man with the bristly moustache was almost on the point of getting angry. He frowned with his thick eyebrows and in his roughest voice:

"That does it, Monsieur," he began.

"Ta, ta, ta!" the Sûreté agent interrupted, using the familiar "tu" for the first time.[18]

"Leave me alone and try to understand who's talking to you. I'm Monsieur Lecoq."

The effect the name of the celebrated policeman produced on a fellow employed for several months as an auxiliary in the mobile units of the Rue de Jérusalem was magical. He dropped his defenses and his attitude immediately became respectful, like that of a common foot soldier who finds his general under the frock coat of a grocer.

To be called "my boy," spoken to in the familiar, even ill-treated by that illustrious person, far from offending him, almost flattered him. He was one of those toadies that fall apart when hit with certain cudgels. With an astonished look full of admiration, he murmured:

"What! Is it possible! Monsieur Lecoq, you! A man like this!"

"Yes, it's me, my boy. But don't worry. I don't hold it against you. You don't know your job, but you've done me a service. You had the good sense to bring me conclusive proof of the innocence of my client."

Monsieur Domini didn't witness that scene without secret displeasure. His man had gone over to the enemy, recognizing without contest an established first class superiority. Monsieur Lecoq's assurance when speaking of an accused man's innocence, whose guilt seemed to him indisputable, exasperated him.

"And what is that famous proof, if you please?" he asked.

"It's simple and enlightening, Monsieur," Monsieur Lecoq answered, amusing himself by exaggerating his stupid air to the extent that his deductions narrowed the field of possibilities. "You probably remember that during our investigations at the Valfeuillu chateau, we found the hands of the bedroom clock stopped at 3:20 p.m. Being suspicious that a traitorous thumb had moved it, I put the striking mechanism of that clock in movement. Do you remember? What happened then? It struck eleven times. From that moment, it was patently

---

[18] French has two forms of the pronoun you. The familiar form, " tu," is used for familiars, family members, animals and inferiors.

clear to us that the crime had been committed before eleven o'clock. Now if Guespin was in the Forges de Vulcain, he couldn't be a Valfeuillu before midnight. Therefore he wasn't the one who committed the crime."

And with that conclusion, the Sûreté agent took out his lozenge box, treating himself to a square of marshmallow. He threw the Investigating Magistrate a nice smile which clearly signified: "Get yourself out of that."

That meant, if Monsieur Lecoq's deductions were rigorously correct, the Investigating Magistrate's entire theory fell apart.

But Monsieur Domini couldn't admit that he had been so wrong. He could not, while putting the discovery of the truth well above petty personal considerations, give up a conviction confirmed by mature thought.

"I don't claim," he said, "that Guespin was the only guilty person. He may be only an accomplice, but an accomplice he is."

"An accomplice! No, Monsieur, but a victim. Ah! That Trémorel is a very wicked man! Do you now understand why he pushed the hands forward? Me, at first, I didn't see the use of that advance of five hours. Now the reason is clear. It was necessary, for Guespin to be seriously harassed and compromised, that the crime be committed well after midnight. It was necessary..."

But suddenly, he stopped. His mouth gaping, his eyes staring, as much as to say on alert. An idea had just passed through his head.

The Investigating Magistrate, entirely immersed in his dossier, looking for arguments in favor of his theory, didn't notice this movement.

"But then, how do you explain Guespin's obstinately refusing to say anything, to refuse to say what he did that night?"

Monsieur Lecoq had very quickly gotten control of his emotion. But Doctor Gendron and Père Plantat, who were watching him with the most ardent attention, watching every move, the slightest contractions of his facial muscles, saw the light of triumph come into his eyes. He undoubtedly had found a solution to the problem posed to him. Eh! And what a problem! It was a question of a man's liberty, the life of an innocent man.

"I understand, sir; I can explain to myself the obstinately mute behavior of Guespin. I would be extremely surprised if, right now, he wasn't deciding to talk."

Monsieur Domini misunderstood the meaning of that explanation. He even thought he could detect a carefully veiled attempt at mockery.

"Nevertheless, he had the night in which to reflect," he answered. "Twelve hours, isn't that enough to construct a method of defense?"

The Sûreté agent shook his head with a look of doubt.

"That's certainly more than is necessary," he said, "but our accused isn't very worried about a method. I would put my hand in the fire about that."

"If he remains silent, that's because he hasn't found anything plausible."

"No, Monsieur, no. You can be certain he isn't looking for anything. In my opinion, Guespin is a victim. I must tell you that I suspect Trémorel laid an infamous trap for him and he fell into it. He feels himself so trapped there that any struggle seems to him meaningless. This unfortunate man is convinced that the more he struggles, the more he tightens the mesh of the net holding him."

"That's also my opinion," Père Plantat confirmed.

"The real guilty man," the agent of the Sûreté continued, "Count Hector, went mad at the last moment and caused all the precautions he had thought about to pull the wool over everyone's eyes to be fruitless. But don't let us forget, he's an intelligent man, wicked enough to bring to completion the most odious plots. He is far enough removed from scruples to execute them. He knows that justice needs a certain number of accused persons: one for each crime. He's not ignorant of the fact that so long as the police don't have their guilty person, they're still on alert, eyes and ears on the lookout. He threw us Guespin, just as the hunter, followed too closely, throws his glove to the bear pursuing him. He might not have counted on the error causing an innocent man's head, but he certainly hoped to gain time in this way. While the bear smells the glove, turns it over and over, the clever hunter gains ground, slips away and gets to safety. That's what Trémorel proposed to do."

Of all Monsieur Lecoq's listeners, henceforth the most enthusiastic, without a contest, was the Corbeil agent, who, just a while ago looked at him so fiercely. Goulard literally drank in the words of his chief. He had never heard a colleague express himself with that verve, that authority. He had no idea of such eloquence. And he recovered his confidence, as if something of the admiration he saw on all the faces had reflected on him. At the idea that he was a soldier commanded by such generals, he grew in his own esteem. He no longer had an opinion of his own. He had the opinion of his superior.

Unfortunately, it was more difficult to seduce, to conquer and convince the Investigating Magistrate.

"Nevertheless," he objected, "you saw Guespin's expression."

"Eh! Monsieur, what does the facial expression prove and what does it matter? How do we know, you and I, how we would appear, if tomorrow we were arrested, accused of a terrible crime?"

Monsieur Domini didn't take the trouble to hide a most significant surprise. The supposition seemed to him one of the most unseemly.

"However, you and I are familiar with the make-up of the law. The day I arrested Lanscot, that poor servant in the Rue de Marignan, his first words were: 'Well! that's it for me!'"

"The morning Père Tabaret and I seized the Viscount Commarin, accused of having murdered the Widow Lerouge, he exclaimed: "I'm lost." However, neither of them was guilty. But both of them, the noble Viscount and the insignificant valet, made equal when faced with a possible judicial error, evaluating with one glance the charges which were going to overwhelm them, had a moment of horrible discouragement."

"But that discouragement didn't last two days," Monsieur Domini said.

Monsieur Lecoq didn't answer. He continued, becoming more animated as more striking examples came to his mind.

"We have seen, Monsieur, you as a judge and me as a humble policeman, enough accused men to know how much appearances can be deceptive, how little they can be trusted. It would be folly to base a judgment on the attitude of an accused man. The man who's the first to speak about 'a cry of innocence,' just as the man who claims to point out the 'pale stupor' of an accused man, is a fool. Unfortunately, neither crime nor virtue has a particular countenance. The Simon daughter, accused of having killed her father, stubbornly refused to answer for twenty-two days. The twenty-third the murderer was discovered. As for the Sylvain business..."

The Investigating Magistrate interrupted the Sûreté agent with two light taps on his desk.

As a man, Monsieur Domini held much too strongly to his opinions. As a magistrate he was equally stubborn, but ready to sacrifice the last of his ego, if he heard the voice of duty.

Monsieur Lecoq's arguments hadn't cut into the granite of his convictions, but he had an obligation to become clear in his own mind now, to oppose the man from the Prefecture or to admit himself vanquished.

"You seem to be pleading a case, Monsieur," he told the policeman from the Sûreté. "In the Investigating Magistrate's office it isn't necessary to plead. There is no lawyer or judge here. The same generous and honorable intentions animate both of us. Each of us, in the sphere of his functions, searches for the truth. You see it shining forth where I discover only shadows, but you as well as I could be mistaken."

And with rather stiff condescension, a veritable act of heroism, but spoiled by a slight ironic point, he added:

"According to you, Monsieur, what should I do?"

The Judge was at least recompensed for the effort he made by an approving look from Père Plantat and Doctor Gendron.

But Monsieur Lecoq wasn't in any hurry to answer. He had a large number of weighty reasons to offer. He felt that wasn't what was necessary. He must present facts there, on the spot. In that situation, he must make one of those proofs you can put your finger on stand out. How to go about it? His mind, so fertile in resources, was unduly tense.

"Well!" insisted Monsieur Domini.

"Ah! exclaimed the Sûreté agent, "Why can't I myself ask this unfortunate Guespin three questions?"

The Investigating Magistrate frowned. The suggestion seemed to him hasty. Legal procedure says that the interrogation of the accused must be done secretly by the judge assisted only by his stenographer. On the other hand, after having been interrogated a first time, the accused may be confronted by witnesses. Then there are exceptions as regards the representatives of the public forces.

Monsieur Domini reviewed his texts in his mind, looking for precedents.

He finally answered: "I don't know just how far the regulations authorize me to allow you to do what you ask. Nevertheless, since I am in good conscience persuaded that the interest of the truth takes precedence over all the regulations, I'm going to take it on myself to let you question your client."

He rang. A bailiff appeared.

"Have they taken Guespin back to the prison?" he asked him.

"Not yet, Monsieur."

"That's good! Tell them to bring him to me."

Monsieur Lecoq was beside himself with joy. He hadn't dared to count on his eloquence to that extent. Above all, he hadn't hoped for such prompt and surprising success, given Monsieur Domini's character.

"He'll talk," he said, so full of confidence that his lusterless eyes brightened and he forgot the lozenge box portrait. "He'll talk. I have three ways to loosen his tongue. At least one of them will succeed. But before he arrives, please, Justice of the Peace, some information? Do you know if, after Sauvresy's death, Trémorel saw his former mistress again?"

"Jenny Fancy?" Père Plantat asked, somewhat surprised.

"Yes, Miss Fancy."

"Certainly. He saw her again."

"Several times?"

"Rather often. Following the scene at the Belle Image, she threw herself into the most frightful debauchery. Did she have remorse for the denunciation? Did she understand that she had killed Sauvresy? Did she suspect the crime? I don't know. In any case, from that moment she began to have bouts of drinking, sinking more deeply into the mire week by week."

"And the Count could agree to continue to see her?"

"He had to. She harassed him. He was afraid of her. As soon as her money ran out, she sent sinister looking fellows to demand some, and he gave it. Once he refused. She arrived that same evening, drunk, and he had all the trouble in the world getting rid of her. In essence, she knew he had been Madame Sauvresy's lover. She threatened him. It was organized blackmail. I had the story from him about how she hounded him. He told me he hadn't been able to get rid of her except by having her arrested, but he found the method repugnant."

"Was the last meeting very long ago?"

"*Ma foi!*" Doctor Gendron answered. "I had a consultation in Melun not three weeks ago, and I saw the Count and his flibbertigibbet at the window of a hotel. But when they saw me they quickly stepped back."

"Then," the Sûreté agent murmured, "there's no longer any doubt."

He stopped talking. Guespin had come in between two gendarmes.

In twenty-four hours, the unfortunate Valfeuillu gardener had aged twenty years. His eyes were haggard and his clenched lips were bordered with foam. From time to time the contractions in his throat betrayed the difficulty he had swallowing his saliva.

"Come now," the Investigating Magistrate asked him, "Have you changed your mind?"

The accused man didn't answer.

"Have you decided to talk?"

A convulsion of rage shook Guespin from head to foot. His eyes shot out flames.

"Talk," he said in a hoarse voice, "talk! Why!"

And after one of those desperate gestures of the man who gives in, who renounces any kind of fight as well as all hope, he exclaimed:

"What have I done to you, *mon Dieu!* for you to torture me this way? What do you want me to tell you? That I was the one who did the job? Is that what you want? All right then, yes, it was me! That should satisfy you. Now cut off my head, but do it quickly. I don't want to suffer."

A gloomy stupor greeted that declaration of Guespin. He was confessing...!

Monsieur Domini had at least the good taste not to act triumphant. He remained impassive. However, that confession surprised him more than he could show.

Only Monsieur Lecoq, although surprised, was not absolutely disconcerted. He approached Guespin, and tapping him on the shoulder:

"Now, my comrade," he said in a paternal tone, "what you're telling us is absurd. Do you think the Investigating Magistrate has some secret reason for having it in for you? No, he doesn't, does he? Do you suppose I have some reason to want you dead? It's not that either. A crime has been committed. We're looking for the guilty man. If you're innocent, help us find the one who isn't. What did you do between Wednesday and Thursday mornings?"

But Guespin persisted in his fierce stubborn, stupid refusal, the stubbornness of the idiot or the brutish beast.

"I've said what I have to say," he answered.

Then Monsieur Lecoq changed tones, moving from the friendly tone he had used to become severe, moving backward in order better to judge the effect he was going to produce on Guespin.

"You don't have the right to be silent, do you understand me?" he continued. "And even if you won't talk, imbecile, don't the police know everything? Your master gave you an errand Wednesday evening, didn't he? What did he give you, a thousand franc bill?"

The accused man gave Monsieur Lecoq an absolutely stupid look.

"No," he stammered. "It was a five hundred franc bill."

Like all great artists, at the moment of their great scene, the Sûreté agent was truly nervous. His surprising investigative genius had just inspired him with that daring strategy, which, if it succeeded, would mean he had won the game.

"Now," he said, "tell me the name of that woman."

"I don't know it, Monsieur."

"Then are you an idiot? She's petite, isn't she! Rather pretty, brunette and pale, with very big eyes."

"Then you know her?" Guespin said, in a voice trembling with emotion.

"Yes, my comrade, and if you want to know it, in order to say it in your prayers, her name is Jenny Fancy."

Truly superior men, in whatever specialty it may be, never meanly abuse their superiority. The self-satisfaction they feel in seeing it recognized is sufficient recompense for them.

Monsieur Lecoq gently enjoyed his victory while his listeners marveled at his insight. It was in fact a series of rapid calculations that revealed to him not only Trémorel's thoughts, but also the means he had to use to arrive at his ends.

In Guespin, anger gave way to immense astonishment. He was wondering, and you could see the effort of his thought on his brow, how that man had found out about actions that he had every reason to believe secret. But the Sûreté agent had already come back to his accused man.

"Since I told you the name of the brunette woman, then explain to me how and why the Count de Trémorel gave you a five-hundred franc bill," he asked him.

"Just at the moment I was going to leave, the Count didn't have any change. He didn't want me to get the five hundred francs changed in Orcival. I was supposed to bring back the remainder."

"And why didn't you rejoin your comrades at Wepler's in the Batignolles?"

No answer.

"What errand were you supposed to do for the Count?"

Guespin hesitated. His eyes went from one to the other of his listeners, from the Investigating Magistrate to Père Plantat, to the Doctor, to the Corbeil agent. It seemed to him he could detect an ironic expression on all the faces.

It occurred to him that all these people were making fun of him, that they had laid a trap for him, and that he had fallen in it. He believed his answers had just made his situation worse. He was immediately gripped with terrible despair.

"Ah!" he exclaimed, "You've tricked me. You didn't know anything, You set out the false to find out the true. I was silly enough to answer you and you're going to turn all my words against me."

"What! Are you going to be unreasonable again?"

"No, but I see what you're up to and you won't catch me again. Now, Monsieur, I would rather die than say another word."

The Sûreté agent was going to try to reassure him. Guespin answered with idiotic stubbornness:

"Besides, I'm as clever as you are. You see, I told you nothing but lies."

The accused man's sudden reversal surprised no one. If some of the accused, once locked into a method of defense, never leave it any more than a tortoise does his shell, there are others who, at each new interrogation, are changeable, denying today what they admitted yesterday, inventing the next day some absurd episode which they will later deny.

Monsieur Lecoq tried in vain to get Guespin to break his stubborn silence. Monsieur Domini, in his turn, vainly tried to get some words out of him. To all these questions, he had a set answer:

"I don't know."

The Sûreté agent finally became impatient.

"Look here," he said to the accused man, "I took you for an intelligent boy and you're nothing but a fool. Do you think we know nothing? Listen to me. The evening of Madame Denis' wedding, just as you got ready to leave with your comrades, when you had just borrowed twenty francs from the valet, your master called you. After having told you to be absolutely discreet about a secret, a secret that you've kept, you have to be given credit for that, he told you to leave the other servants at the Lyon station and go to the Forges de Vulcain, to buy him a hammer, a file, a cold chisel, and a short sword. You were supposed to take these objects to a woman. That's when your master gave you that famous five-hundred franc bill, saying that you could return the rest to him on your return the next day. Is that right?"

Yes, that was right. You could see it in the eyes of the accused. Nevertheless, he still answered:

"I don't remember."

"Then," Monsieur Lecoq continued, "I'm going to tell you what happened next. You started drinking. You got drunk, so drunk that you squandered a part of the bill given to you. That's what caused your fright when you were taken into custody yesterday morning before anyone had said a word to you. You thought you were being arrested for misappropriation of funds. Then, when you found out the Count had been murdered during the night, you remembered you had bought all sorts of tools for theft and murder. Remembering that you had neither the name nor the address of the woman you gave the package to, you thought no one would believe you if you explained the origin of the money found in your pocket. Instead of thinking about way to prove your innocence, you became afraid. You thought you could save yourself by keeping silent."

It's certain that the accused man's expression changed in the blink of an eye. His nerves relaxed; his lips, a moment ago clenched, loosened. His mind began to hope. But he resisted.

"Do whatever you like with me," he said.

"Eh! What do you want us to do with an idiot like you?" Monsieur Lecoq burst out, definitely angry. "I'm beginning to believe that you're a bad guy. A nice fellow would understand that we're trying to get him out of a bad situation and would tell us the truth. You're voluntarily prolonging your stay in jail. This way you'll learn that the cleverest way is to tell that happened. One last time, will you answer?"

Guespin shook his head "no."

"Then go back to jail and to solitary confinement, since that's what it pleases you to do," the Sûreté agent concluded.

And having glanced at the Investigating Magistrate for his approval:

"Gendarmes," he said, "take the accused back to prison."

The Investigating Magistrate's last doubts faded away like fog before the sun. To tell the truth, he felt somewhat pained at having treated the Sûreté agent so badly. He at least tried to make up for his past harshness as much as he could.

"You're a clever man," he told Monsieur Lecoq. "Your interrogation of a moment ago is a masterpiece of its kind, not to mention your surprising insight, which could pass for the gift of second sight. You therefore have my congratulations without reservations. I intend to ask your chiefs to give you a reward."

At this compliment, the Sûreté agent lowered his eyes with the modesty of a virgin. He looked at the ugly woman on the lozenge box tenderly, and he was probably saying to her:

"Finally, my dear, we've won him over. That stern magistrate who so strongly detests the institution, of which we're the shining light, is making honorable restitution. He recognizes and praises our valuable services."

And aloud, he answered:

"I can accept only half of your praise, Monsieur. Allow me to give the other half to the Justice of the Peace. "

Père Plantat tried to protest.

"Oh! For some information!" he said. "Even so, you would have arrived at the truth without me."

The Investigating Magistrate had risen. Nobly, but not without a certain effort, he held out his hand to Monsieur Lecoq, who shook it with respect.

"You have spared me great remorse," Monsieur Domini told him. "Certainly, Guespin's innocence would have been recognized sooner or later. But the idea of having kept an innocence man in prison, of having harried him with my interrogations, would have tormented my conscience and troubled my sleep for a long time."

"God knows, however, this poor Guespin is scarcely helpful. I would hold it against him cruelly if I wasn't certain that he is more than half crazy."

Monsieur Domini winced.

"I'm going to have him removed from solitary confinement, today, right this instant," he said.

"That would certainly be a charitable act," Monsieur Lecoq said. "But, plague takes the stubborn man. It would be so easy for him to simplify my job. I have, in fact, luck helping me, been very able to put together the main facts, to find out about the errand, to suspect the intervention of a woman. Not being a sorcerer, I can't guess the details. How is Miss Fancy mixed up in this business? Was she an accomplice? Did she only play a role in a plot whose aim she didn't know? Where did she meet Guespin? Where did she take him? It's evident that she's the one who got the poor devil drunk to keep him from going to the

Batignolles. Trémorel must have told her some story. What story?"

The Justice of the Peace interrupted, saying: "Me, I think Trémorel wouldn't have gone to the trouble to dream up something for such a little thing. He would have given Guespin and Fancy an errand without giving them the least explanation."

Monsieur Lecoq thought a minute.

"You may be right, Monsieur," he finally said. "However, it would have been necessary for Fancy to have precise orders in order to keep Guespin from having an alibi to furnish."

"But that Fancy will explain everything to us," said Monsieur Domini.

"I'm certainly counting on that, Monsieur, and I really hope that within forty-eight hours I will have found her and sent her along to Corbeil with a good escort."

With these words, he stood up and went to pick up his cane and his hat that, on entering, he had put in a corner. "Before I leave..." he said to the Investigating Magistrate. "Yes, I know," Monsieur Domini interrupted him, "you're waiting for the arrest warrant for Count Hector de Trémorel." "I am, in fact," Monsieur Lecoq answered, "since you now think as I do that he is alive." "I don't think that. I'm sure of it." And drawing his chair up to his desk, Monsieur Domini began to draw up that terrible document called an arrest warrant.

On behalf of the law

We, the investigating magistrate, sitting at the major tribunal of the administrative division, etc., by virtue of articles 91 and 94 of the investigative criminal code:

Alert and order all agents of the public forces to arrest in conformance with the law, the named Hector de Trémorel, etc., etc.

When he had finished, giving the arrest warrant to Monsieur Lecoq, he said: "Take this, and may you soon succeed in finding this very guilty man."

"Oh! He'll find him!" the Corbeil agent exclaimed.

"At least I hope so. As to saying how I'll go about it, I don't yet know. I'll draw up my battle plan tonight."

The Sûreté agent then took leave of Monsieur Domini, and left, followed by Père Plantat. Doctor Gendron stayed with the Judge to confer with him on the subject of Sauvresy's exhumation.

Monsieur Lecoq was about to leave the Law Courts when he felt someone pulling him by his sleeve. He turned around. It was the Corbeil agent, who had come to ask his help, begging him to take him with him, persuaded that after having served under such a great captain, he also would be very capable. Monsieur Lecoq had a great deal of trouble getting rid of him.

Finally, he found himself alone in the street with the old Justice of the Peace.

"It's getting late," Père Plantat said to him. "Would you again agree to share my modest dinner and accept my cordial hospitality?"

"I'm very sorry to have to refuse you, Monsieur," Monsieur Lecoq answered, "but I must be in Paris this evening."

"But," the old Justice of the Peace continued—and he hesitated—it's just that I would greatly like to speak to you, interview you..."

"About Mademoiselle Courtois, right?"

"Yes, I have a plan. If you would be willing to help me..."

Monsieur Lecoq shook the old Justice of the Peace's hands with affection.

"I've known you only a very few hours, Monsieur," he said, "and nevertheless I'm as devoted to you as I would be to an old friend. Everything that is humanly possible that I can do for you that is helpful or useful, I will do."

"But where can I meet you, because today I'm expected at Orcival."

"Well! Tomorrow morning, at nine o'clock, be at my house, Rue Montmartre, Number..."

"Thank you! Thank you a thousand times. I'll be there."

And, having come abreast the Hotel Belle Image, they separated.

Chapter XXIV

It had just rung nine o'clock on the Saint-Eustache church clock, and you could still hear the great clock of the Halles,[19] when Père Plantat arrived at the Rue Montmartre and started up the obscure little path that led to the house with the Number __.

"Monsieur Lecoq," he questioned an old woman busy preparing to give breakfast to three enormous tomcats meowing around her.

The woman porter looked him up and down in a manner both surprised and ironic.

That was because Père Plantat, when he was dressed up, looked more like an old gentleman than a former lawyer of a small city. Now, although the Sûreté had many visitors from many different levels of society, it wasn't exactly old men from the Saint-Germain neighborhood[20] who rang his doorbell.

"Monsieur Lecoq," the old woman finally answered, "is on the fourth floor, the door facing the stairs."

The Justice of the Peace climbed the stairs slowly. Those stairs were narrow, badly lit, slippery, made almost dangerous by their dark corners and slimy ramp.

He thought about how unusual the action he was going to attempt was. An idea had come to him. He didn't know if it would work. And in any case, he needed the advice and help of the man from the Prefecture. He was going to be forced to give up his most secret thoughts, to go to confession, so to speak. His heart was beating.

The door "facing" the stairway on the fourth floor didn't resemble the other doors. It was of solid oak, thick, without any moldings, and made even more solid by iron cross pieces, neither more nor less like the cover to a safe. A Judas peephole was placed in the middle fitted with interlaced bars through which you could scarcely pass your finger. You would swear it was the door of a prison, if its sadness were not brightened by one of those engravings that in the past were printed in the Rue St. Jacques stuck above the peephole. That engraving with bright colors represented a crowing cock, with this legend: *Toujours vigilans.*

Was it the agent who stuck his meaningful arms there? Wouldn't it be one of his men instead?

You could see the doors to the right and left were sealed off.

After an examination that lasted more than a minute, and hesitations resembling those of a secondary school student at his girl friend's door, Père Plantat finally decided to press the copper door bell.

---

[19] Historic Paris market near the Seine, renovated in the 20th century.

[20] Elegant district of Paris located on the left bank in the 6th arrondissement..

A grinding of locks answered his ring. The peephole opened and through the narrow grill work he could make out the mustached face of a strong masculine woman.

"Who do you want?" that woman asked in a beautiful low voice.

"Monsieur Lecoq."

"What do you want with him?"

"He gave me an appointment for this morning."

"Your name? Your profession?"

"Monsieur Plantat, Justice of the Peace at Orcival."

"All right. Wait."

The Judas peephole closed and the old judge waited.

"Peste!" he grumbled. "It seems not just anybody who wants to can enter this worthy Monsieur Lecoq's house."

He had scarcely finished that reflection than the door opened, not without some fracas of chains, bolts, and locks.

He went in, and the masculine-looking woman, after having taken him across a dining room having as its only furniture a table and six chairs, introduced him into a vast room with a high ceiling, half dressing room, half study, lit by two windows fitted with strong bars very close together looking out on the courtyard.

"If Monsieur will please sit down," the servant said. "Monsieur won't be long in coming. He's giving instructions to one of his men."

But the old Justice of the Peace didn't sit down. He preferred to examine the curious place in which he found himself.

All one side of the wall was taken up with a coat rack where the strangest and the most ill-assorted cast off clothes were hanging. Costumes belonging to all classes of society were hung up there, from the morning coat with turned up cuffs, in the latest fashion, decorated with a red rosette, to the black wool shirt of the barrio tyrant. On a shelf above the coat rack were spread out, on wooden heads, a dozen wigs of all shades. On the floor were assorted shoes for the various costumes. Finally, in a corner, there was a rather complete assortment of canes, varied enough to set a collector to dreaming.

Between the fireplace and the window was a marble make-up table cluttered with make-up brushes and little jars holding paste and colors, a dressing table to make a lady from Swan Lake turn pale with envy. The other section of the wall was taken up by a library full of scientific works. Books on physics and chemistry dominated. The middle of the room was filled by a vast desk on which were piled, probably for months, newspapers and papers of all kinds.

But the piece of furniture, that is to say, the utensil, the most apparent and the most unusual in that room was a large ball of black velvet shaped like a diamond hung beside the mirror. A large number of pins with big bright heads were stuck in that ball so as to represent letters, the whole of which formed these two names: HECTOR, FANCY. These names which were shining in silver on the black velvet background struck the eyes at the door and could be seen from all parts of the room. That must be Monsieur Lecoq's reminder. That ball's function was to remind him every hour of the day of the accused persons he was following. A great number of names had probably shone in their turn on this velvet, because it was much frayed.

An unfinished letter remained open on the desk. Père Plantat leaned over to read it, but he got nothing for his pains of indiscretion. It was in code.

However the old Justice of the Peace had finished his inspection when the noise of a door opening made him turn around. He found himself facing a man almost his own age, with a respectable face, distinguished manners, a little bald, wearing spectacles with gold legs and wearing a bedroom robe of light weight, colorless flannel.

Père Plantat bowed.

"I'm expecting Monsieur Lecoq here," he began.

The man wearing the gold spectacles, burst out laughing, joyously, frankly, striking his hands together.

"What! Dear Monsieur, don't you recognize me? So, look at me. It's me; it's really me, Monsieur Lecoq."

And to convince the Justice of the Peace, he took off his glasses.

In a pinch, those could be Monsieur Lecoq's eyes. That could also be his voice. Père Plantat was dumbfounded.

"I would not have recognized you," he said.

"It's true I'm a little changed...office dress! Alas! What can you say... job requirements!"

And bringing forward an armchair for his visitor:

"I must apologize to you a thousand times for the formalities at the entrance of my house," he continued. "That's a necessity I don't like very much. I've told you about the dangers I'm exposed to. Those dangers follow me right up to my official domicile. Take, for instance, last week. A railroad employee came bringing a package to my address. Janouille— she's my maid—she picked up a remarkable face at Fontevrault[21] didn't suspect anything and let him come in. He gave me the package. I stuck out my hand to take it. *Pif! Pif!* Two pistol shots rang out. The package was a revolver wrapped in oil cloth. The employee was an escapee from Cayenne that I had locked up the year before. Ah! I owe my boss a lot for that business."

He talked about that terrible adventure in an off-handed way, as if it were the most natural thing in the world.

"But," he said, "letting yourself die of hunger while waiting for a successful attempt would be silly."

He rang and the masculine woman immediately appeared.

"Janouille," he said to her, "lunch, quickly, two places and especially some

---

[21] French prison.

239

good wine."

The Justice of the Peace was having some trouble recovering.

"You're looking at my Janouille," he went on. "A pearl, dear Monsieur, who treats me like a baby and who would go through fire for me. And strong, too. I had a lot of trouble the other morning keeping her from strangling the disguised employee. I have to say I took the trouble to select her for my service from among three or four thousand convicts. She had been condemned for infanticide and arson. Right now she's the most honest of creatures. I would bet that in the three years she's been in my service she hasn't even thought of stealing a centime from me."

But Père Plantat was only half listening. He was looking for some way to cut short Janouille's praises, well merited perhaps, but in his opinion, out of place. He wanted to bring the interview back to the facts of the evening before.

"Am I perhaps disturbing you a little this morning, Monsieur Lecoq?" he began.

"Me! Then you didn't see my sign? Always vigilant! As you see me right now, I've already done ten pieces of minor business this morning and sent three of my men out on jobs. Ah! People like us don't have a slow season! But I even went to the Forges de Vulcain to pick up information about that poor Guespin."

"And did you get any?"

"Just about what I guessed. It was Wednesday evening at a quarter to ten that he changed the five hundred franc bill."

"That means he's off the hook?"

"Or just about. He will be completely when we find Miss Jenny."

The old Judge couldn't hide a movement of irritation.

"That could perhaps be a long time, very difficult?" he said.

"*Baste!* Why should that be? She's on my ball. We'll pick her up, unless we run into bad luck, before the end of the day."

"Do you really think so?"

"To anyone other than you, Monsieur, I'd answer: 'I'm sure of it.' Remember, that creature has been the mistress of the Count de Trémorel, a man in the public eye, a prince of fashion. When a prostitute falls back in the gutter after having, as they say, dazzled all of Paris by her wealth for six months, she doesn't disappear completely, like a stone in the sludge. When she no longer has any friends, there are creatures who hang onto her, who watch her, keeping an eye out for the day when fortune will again smile on her. She doesn't worry about them. She thinks they've forgotten about her. Error! There is a certain woman who deals in female fashion whose head holds both the Vapereau and the Bottin[22] of the fashionable world. She's often helped me out, that worthy woman. If you want to, we're going to see her after lunch, and in two hours she

---

[22] French directory of commercial and industrial addresses launched by Sébastien Bottin in 1797.

240

will have given us the address of that Miss Fancy. Ah! If I were as sure of nabbing Trémorel..."

Père Plantat smiled with satisfaction. The conversation was finally turning in the direction he wanted.

"Then you're thinking about him?" he asked.

"Am I thinking about him!" exclaimed Monsieur Lecoq. This doubt made him jump up from his chair. "Just look at my ball! I have thought absolutely, exactly, only about this miserable man since yesterday. He's the reason I didn't close my eyes last night. I need him. I want him. I will get him."

"I have no doubt about that," the Justice of the Peace said, "but when?"

"Ah! That's just it. Maybe tomorrow, maybe only in a month. That depends on the accuracy of my calculations, the correctness of my plan."

"What! Your plan is complete?"

"And put into operation, yes, Monsieur."

Père Plantat had become attention itself.

"I take as a starting point," the Sûreté agent continued, "that it's impossible for a man accompanied by a woman, to hide from police investigations. In this case, the woman is young; she's pretty; and she's pregnant; three additional possibilities.

"This principle admitted, let's study the Count de Trémorel. Is he a man with superior insight? No, since we have discovered his tricks. Is he an imbecile? No, since his maneuvers have almost taken in people who are not idiots. Therefore he is a man with an average mind whose upbringing, reading, acquaintances have given a sum of knowledge which he will make use of.

"That's enough for his mind. We know his character; soft, weak, changeable, acting only at the last extremity. We've seen him being horrified by definite determinations, always looking for dodges, compromises. He's led to create illusions about himself, to consider his wishes as accomplished facts. Finally, he's a coward.

"And what's his situation now? He has killed his wife. He hopes he has made people believe that he's dead. He's run away with a young girl. He has in his pockets a sum of money which approaches, and perhaps even surpasses, a million francs.

"Now, given the situation, the character and the mind of the man, by making the effort to think about it, reasoning about his known actions, can we perhaps discover what he has done in such and such a circumstance? I think we can, and I hope to prove it to you."

Monsieur Lecoq had gotten up and was walking up and down his study, as he was accustomed to doing every time he laid out and discussed his police theories.

"Let's see, then," he continued, "what I must do to be able to discover the probable behavior of a man whose background, character, and mind are known to me? To begin with, I get rid of my own personality and take on his. I substitute his intelligence for mine. I cease being an agent of the Sûreté to become that man, whoever he might be.

"In our case, for example, staying myself, I know very well what I would do. I would take such measures that I would throw all the detectives in the universe off the track. But I'm forgetting Monsieur Lecoq to guess what Hector de Trémorel would do.

"Then let's look into what must have been the reasons a man scoundrel enough to steal his friend's wife and then let that friend be poisoned right under his eyes. We already know that Trémorel hesitated a long time before deciding on the crime. The logic of events, that imbeciles call fate, pushed him to it. It's certain that he looked at the murder from all angles, that he studies its consequences, that he looked for all the ways to avoid the action of justice. All his actions had been put together and planned a long time in advance and neither immediate necessity nor the unexpected entered his mind.

"From the moment the crime had been decided on in his mind, he told himself: 'Once Berthe is murdered, thanks to the steps I've taken, I'll be thought dead also. Laurence, that I'm running away with, will write a letter announcing her suicide. I have money, what needs to be done?' The problem was really posed this way, at least I think so."

"Yes, exactly," Père Plantat approved.

"Naturally, Trémorel must have chosen, from among all the methods of flight that he had heard talked about, or he could imagine, the one that seemed to him the safest and the fastest. Did he think of going abroad? That's more than probable. Only, as he's not completely devoid of sense, he understood that it's most of all in a strange land that it's difficult to cover your tracks. Leaving France to avoid punishment for a crime, there's nothing easier. To cross the frontier with a crime posted on all the extradition coalitions, is simply an enormous absurdity.

"And can you imagine a man and a woman wandering about in a country where they don't speak the language? They soon attract attention, are observed, noticed, followed. They don't make one purchase which isn't noticed. There isn't one of their movements that escape the attentions of those who have nothing better to do.

"The further they go, the more the danger of being caught increases. Do they want to cross the Ocean and reach that free America, where lawyers rob their clients? You have to take a boat, and the day you set foot on the deck of an ocean-going vessel, you can consider yourself lost. There are nineteen chances out of twenty that at the port of entry you'd find a policeman armed with an arrest warrant.

"Note that I'm speaking only by memory about the police of the country where people take refuge, which, even so, always keeps an eye open for strangers.

"In London itself it takes me only a week of hard work to find a Frenchman, unless sometimes he speaks fluent enough English to call himself a citizen of the United Kingdom. Such were probably Trémorel's thoughts. He remembered a thousand failed attempts, a hundred surprising adventures published by the newspapers, and he most certainly gave up thoughts of going abroad."

"That's obvious," exclaimed Père Plantat. "That's clear; that's exactly right. We must look for the fugitives in France."

"Yes, Monsieur, yes," Monsieur Lecoq answered. "You've said it. Then let's examine where and how you can hide in France. Would it be in a province? No, evidently not. In Bordeaux, one of our largest cities, people look at the passing man who isn't from Bordeaux. The keepers of the little shops who stroll up and down on the steps of their store, ask each other 'Eh! Do you know that Monsieur over there?'

"There are two cities, however, where you can walk about unknown: Marseille and Lyon. But they are very far away. You have to risk a long trip. And nothing is more dangerous than the railway since the establishment of the electric telegraph. You can run away, that's true. You can ago fast, that's positive. But when you get into a railway car where they close off every exit, just as you get out, you fall into the hands of the police. Trémorel knows all this as well as we do. Then let's leave aside all provincial cities. Let's also leave aside Lyon and Marseille.

"Impossible then to hide in the provinces."

"Pardon, there is one way. It's simply a question of buying some modest property far from every village, far from the railroad, and getting established there under a false name. But this excellent method is far out of our man's reach. Carrying out his plan requires advance preparation that he couldn't risk, watched as closely as he was by his wife.

"Then the field of useful investigations are unusually narrowed. We leave to one side foreign lands, the provinces, the big cities, the country. There remains Paris. It's in Paris, Monsieur, that we must look for Trémorel."

Monsieur Lecoq expressed himself with the confidence and certainty of a mathematics professor from the Ecole Normale,[23] who, standing in front of the blackboard, a piece of chalk in his hand, victoriously demonstrates to his students that two parallel lines, indefinitely prolonged, would never meet.

The old Justice of the Peace was listening. He was listening as students don't listen. But he was already accustomed to the surprising lucidity of the Sûreté agent and he was no longer astonished. During the twenty-four hours he had witnessed the calculations and the tentative research of Monsieur Lecoq, he had picked up the mechanism of his investigations and almost appropriated the procedure. He found reasoning in this way very straightforward. Now he could

---

[23] The École Normale was conceived during the French Revolution to provide the Republic with a new body of professors, trained in the critical spirit and secular values of the Enlightenment.

explain to himself certain exploits of the active police that until then had seemed to border on the remarkable.

But what Monsieur Lecoq was calling a restricted field of investigation, still seemed to him immense.

"Paris is big," he observed.

The Sûreté agent gave a huge smile.

"You say immense," he said, "but it's mine. All of Paris is under the microscope of the Rue de Jérusalem, just like the ant hill is under the microscope of the naturalist.

"That being so, you ask me, why are there still professional criminals in Paris?

"Ah! Monsieur, that's because legality makes us hush things up. We aren't the masters, unfortunately. The law condemns us to use only polite weapons against adversaries for whom all means are good. The Prosecution ties our hands. The crooks are clever, but you can believe that our skill is a thousand times superior."

"But," Père Plantat interrupted, "from now on Trémorel is outside the law. We have a warrant to bring him in."

"What does that matter? Does the warrant give me the right to search on the spot the houses where I have reason to suppose he has taken refuge! No. If I presented myself at the house of one of Count Hector's former friends, he would slam the door in my face. In France, Monsieur, the police have not only the scoundrels against them, but also honest people."

Every time that Monsieur Lecoq by chance brought up that subject he got carried away and came to strange conclusions. His resentment was as profound as injustice. Being aware of the immense services rendered, he felt a kind of disapproval that exasperated him. Fortunately, just at the moment he was the most animated, a sudden movement brought him in front of the ball. He stopped short.

"The Devil!" he said. "I was forgetting Hector."

Père Plantat, himself, while submitting to the man from the Préfecture's excesses of indignation, because he couldn't do anything else, couldn't stop thinking about the murderer, Laurence's seducer.

"You were saying," he said," that we must search for Trémorel in Paris."

"And I was telling the truth," Monsieur Lecoq answered in a calmer tone. I have come to that conclusion, that it's here, perhaps two streets from us, perhaps in the next house, that our fugitives are hiding. But let's go back to our calculation of probabilities.

"Hector knows his Paris too well to hope to hide himself even a week in a hotel or even in a furnished house. He knows the furnished rooms—the Hotel Meurice as well as the Limace Inn—are the object of a very special surveillance and are in the hands of the Prefecture. Having some time in front of him, he certainly thought about renting an apartment in some house to his liking."

"About a month or a month and a half ago, he made three or four trips to Paris."

"Then there's no more doubt. He rented an apartment under a false name. He paid the rental period in advance, and today he's right at home."

At that assertion of the Sûreté agent, Père Plantat's expression expressed terrible discouragement.

"I feel only too much that you are right, Monsieur," he said sadly. "But is the scoundrel out of our reach? Will we have to wait until chance gives him to us? Will you go through all the houses in Paris one by one!"

The Sûreté agent's nose twitched under his gold glasses, and the Justice of the Peace, who had observed that twinkle was a good sign, felt all his hopes reborn in himself.

"It's just that I've dug into my head in vain..."

"Pardon," Monsieur Lecoq interrupted, "Trémorel having rented an apartment, he must, isn't it true, been busy getting it furnished."

"Obviously."

"And what's more, to furnish it sumptuously. First of all because he loves luxury and he has money. Next, because by running away with a young girl he can't make her pass from her father's rich house into a hovel. I would gladly wager that they have a drawing room as elegant as that of Valfeuillu."

"Alas! What does that matter to us!"

"*Peste!* Dear Monsieur, that makes a lot of difference to us, as you'll see. Wanting a great deal of furniture, and beautiful furniture, Hector didn't go to a second-hand dealer. He didn't have time to buy at the Rue Drouot, nor to run around the Faubourg Saint-Antoine. Therefore he simply went to look for a decorator."

"Some fashionable decorator..."

"No, he would risk being recognized, and it's clear he introduced himself under a false name, under the one he used to rent the apartment. He chose some competent and modest decorator. He placed the order, made sure everything would be delivered at a fixed date, and paid."

The old Justice of the Peace Judge couldn't hold back an exclamation of joy. He was beginning to understand.

"This merchant," Monsieur Lecoq continued, "must remember that rich client who didn't bargain and who paid cash. If he saw him again, he would recognize him."

"What an idea!" exclaimed Père Plantat, beside himself. Quickly, very quickly, let's get some pictures of Trémorel. Let's send a man to Orcival."

Monsieur Lecoq showed the slight smile that came to his lips every time he gave a new proof of how clever he was.

"Calm down, Monsieur," he said. "I've done everything that's necessary. Yesterday, during the investigation, I slid three of the Count's cards into my pocket. This morning I took the name and address of all the decorators in Paris from the Bottin and I made three lists. Right now three of my men each have a list and a photograph and are going from decorator to decorator asking: 'Are you this Monsieur's decorator?' If one of them answers 'yes,' we have the man."

"And we have him!" Père Plantat, pale with emotion, exclaimed.

"We can't sing victory, not yet. It's possible that Hector was cautious enough not to go in person to the decorator. In that case, we're left behind. But no! He wouldn't have been that prudent."

Monsieur Lecoq interrupted himself. For the third time, Janouille, half opening the study door, proclaimed in her beautiful bass voice:

"Lunch is served!"

At the first taste, Père Plantat was aware that Janouille, the former convict, was a formidable *cordon bleu* cook. But he wasn't hungry and he couldn't force himself to eat. It was impossible for him to think of anything else but the project he wanted to submit to Monsieur Lecoq. He felt the sad oppression which precedes putting into execution an act resolved on only with regret.

In vain the Sûreté agent, who was a big eater, like all men who have an all-consuming activity, tried to cheer up his guest. In vain he filled his glass with an exquisite Bordeaux wine, a present from a banker whose teller had gone to take the air in Brussels and Lecoq had brought him back.

The old Justice of the Peace remained silent and sad, answering only with monosyllables. He tried to talk and inside himself was fighting the childish ego that held him back at the last moment. When coming, he didn't think he would have this hesitation he called absurd. He had told himself: 'I'll go in and I'll explain myself.' But here he was overcome by that irrational sense of propriety which embarrass an old man obliged to confess his weakness to a young man and which make him blush.

Then was he fearing ridicule? No. Besides, his passion was well above sarcasm or an ironic smile. And what did he risk? Nothing. And this policeman, to whom he hadn't dared to confess his secret thoughts, hadn't he guessed them? Hadn't he been able to read into his soul from the first moments? And later, hadn't he snatched an admission from him? These were his thoughts when the doorbell rang.

"Monsieur," Janouille came to say, "a Corbeil agent named Goulard asks to speak to you. Shall I let him in?"

"Yes, and have him come in here."

They could hear the noise of the locks and the chains of the door. Goulard immediately appeared in the dining room.

That agent, dear to Monsieur Domini, had put on his most beautiful suit, a white shirt and wore his highest horsehair collar. He was respectful and stiff, as befits a former military man who learned in the regiment that respect is measured by how straight you stand.

"Why the devil did you come to find me here," Monsieur Lecoq asked him roughly. "And who allowed himself to give you my address?"

"Monsieur," Goulard answered, visibly intimidated by that reception, "I was sent by Dr. Gendron to give this letter to the Orcival Justice of the Peace."

"In fact," said Père Plantat, "Yesterday evening I asked Gendron to let me know the results of the autopsy, and not knowing what hotel I would stay at, I permitted myself to ask him to address it to me here."

Monsieur Lecoq immediately wanted to give his guest the letter Goulard has just handed him. "Oh! Open it," said the Justice of the Peace. "There's no indiscretion in that..."

"All right," the Sûreté agent answered. "We'll go into my office." And calling to Janouille: "Give some lunch to that fellow over there," he told her. "Have you eaten this morning?"

"I had a bite, Monsieur, that's all."

"Then bite into something while you're waiting for me. And drink a bottle to my health."

Shutting himself up again in his office with Père Plantat:

"Let's see what the Doctor tells us," the Sûreté agent said.

He broke the seal and read:

My dear Plantat. You asked me to send you a telegram. Instead, I'm going to scribble some twenty lines in all haste. I'll have them brought to you at the house of our sorcerer...

"Oh!" murmured Monsieur Lecoq, interrupting, "Monsieur Gendron is too good, too indulgent, really..." "That doesn't matter. The compliment comes from the heart." He continued:

This morning at 3:00 a.m., we proceeded to the exhumation of poor Sauvresy's corpse. Certainly, I more than anyone deplore the terrible circumstances of the death of this worthy and excellent man. But, on the other hand, I can't keep myself from being glad for this unique and admirable opportunity offered me to experiment seriously and to demonstrate the infallibility of my litmus papers.

"Damned scientists!" Père Plantat exclaimed. "They're all the same."

"Why? I can easily understand that involuntary feeling of the Doctor. May I not be delighted when I encounter a lovely crime?" And without waiting for the Justice of the Peace's reply, he continued reading the letter:

The experiment promises to be so much more conclusive since aconitum is one of the alkaloids which stubbornly resist investigation and analysis.

Do you know how I proceeded? After having heated at a very high temperature the suspect materials in twice their weight in alcohol, I gently poured the liquid into a container with slightly elevated edges. The bottom of this container held papers on which I had managed to fix my reactors. Would my paper keep its color? If it did, there was no poison. Would it change color? If it did, the poison was identified.

Here, my paper, a light yellow, was covered with brown spots, or even became completely brown, if we aren't mistaken. I had explained the experiment to the Investigating Magistrate and to the experts with me.

Ah! My friend, what success! At the first drops of alcohol, the paper became the most beautiful dark brown. That means your story was exact to the last degree.

The material submitted for my experiment was literally saturated with aconitum. In my laboratory, working at my leisure, I never obtained more decisive results.

I expect to see the accuracy of my experiments contested by my audience, but I have methods of verification and counter-expertise such that I will certainly stagger all the chemists brought to oppose me.

I think, my dear friend, that you won't be indifferent to my legitimate satisfaction...

Père Plantat's patience was at an end.

"This is unheard of," he exclaimed furiously. "Yes, on my word, this is unbelievable. To think the poison that killed pour Sauvresy was stolen from his laboratory and he was searching for it in Sauvresy's cadaver! What can I say? That cadaver was no more for him but the "suspect material." And he already sees himself in the Court d'Assises discussing the merits of his litmus paper."

"It's a fact that he's right to acknowledge there will those who contradict him."

"And while he's waiting, he practices his skill, he experiments, he analyses in the most cold-blooded way. He continues his abominable cooking. He boils; he filters; he prepares his arguments!"

Monsieur Lecoq was far from sharing the Justice of the Peace's anger. That perspective of fierce debates pleased him well enough. In advance, he could imagine some terrible scientific battle between the provincial chemists and the Parisian chemists, recalling the famous dispute between Orfila and de Raspail.

"It's certain," he pronounced, "that if this cowardly scoundrel de Trémorel has enough character to deny Sauvresy's poisoning, which would be in his interest, we'll witness a superb trial."

Just that word, "trial" put an end to Père Plantat's irresolution.

"There can't be," he cried out, "no, there must not be a trial."

The incredible violence of that very calm, very cold, usually very in control of himself, man seemed to puzzle Monsieur Lecoq.

Eh! eh! he thought, *I'm going to find out everything.*

Then aloud he added:

"What, no trial!"

Père Plantat had become whiter than his shirt. A nervous trembling shook him; his voice was hoarse; and seemed broken by sobs.

"I would give my fortune," he continued, "to avoid any debates. Yes, my fortune and my life in the bargain, although it's not worth very much, but how can this miserable Trémorel be kept from the legal process? What subterfuge can be dreamed up? Only you, Monsieur Lecoq, only you can advise me in this terrible extremity you see me reduced to. Only you can help me; give me your hand. If there exists any way in the world, you'll find it. You'll save me."

"But, Monsieur..." the Sûreté agent began.

"Please, listen to me and you'll understand me. I'm going to be frank, as sincere as I would be with myself. And you'll understand my irresolution, my reluctance, in a word, all my behavior since yesterday."

"I'm listening to you, Monsieur."

"It's a sad story. I had come to that age when a man's fate is, they say, settled, when suddenly death took my wife and my two sons, all my joy, all my hopes in this world. I found myself alone in this life, more lost than a shipwrecked man in the middle of the sea without any wreckage to hold onto. I was nothing but a body without a soul when by chance I came to live at Orcival.

"At Orcival I saw Laurence. She had just turned fifteen. There was never one of God's creatures who united so much intelligence, grace, innocence, and beauty.

"Courtois was my friend. She soon became like my daughter. I probably was in love with her at that time, but I didn't admit it to myself. I didn't see clearly into myself. She was so young and me, I had white hair. It pleased me to persuade myself that my affection was that of a father and she treated me like a father. Ah! What can I say about the delightful hours spent listening to her sweet babble and her naïve confidences? When I saw her running about in the paths pillaging the roses I raised for her, devastating my greenhouses, I was happy. I told myself that existence is a beautiful present from God. My dream then was to follow her life. I loved to think of her married to a good man who would make her happy. And I would remain the friend of the woman after having been the confident of the girl. If I took care of my fortune, which is considerable, it was because I was thinking of her children. It was for them that I accumulated money. Poor, poor Laurence."

Monsieur Lecoq seemed ill at ease in his armchair. He shifted about a good deal. He coughed. He wiped his face with his handkerchief, at the risk of removing his makeup. The truth was that he was much more touched than he wanted it to appear.

"One day," Père Plantat continued, "my friend Courtois spoke to me about the marriage of his daughter and the Count de Trémorel. That day I measured the depth of my love. I felt some of those atrocious pains that it's impossible to describe. It was like a fire that had been smoldering a long time, and suddenly, if you open a window, roars into life and destroys everything. To be an old man and in love with a child! I thought I was going to go mad. I tried to reason with myself, to mock myself. What can sarcasm or logic do against passion? *'Old Celadon,* [24] I told myself, *'Aren't you ashamed of yourself? Why don't you keep quiet!'* I held my tongue and I suffered. Laurence chose me to confide in. What torture! She came to see me to talk about Hector. She admired everything about him and he seemed to her superior to other men, to the point that no one could even be compared to him. She was ecstatic about how well he sat a horse; she found his least words sublime. I was an old fool, that's true, but she was a young fool."

"Did you know, Monsieur, what a scoundrel this Trémorel was?"

"Alas! I didn't know it then. What did that man who lived at Valfeuillu matter to me? But from the day I found out he was going to snatch my most precious treasure from me, that they were going to give him my Laurence, I wanted to study him. I would have found a sort of consolation in knowing he was worthy of her. So I attached myself to him, Monsieur Lecoq, as you attach yourself to the suspect that you're following. How many trips I made to Paris at that period. I wanted to get into his life! I did your job. I went to question all those who had known him, and the more I came to know him, the more I learned to despise him. That's how I discovered the rendezvous with Miss Fancy, how I discovered his relations with Berthe."

"Why didn't you say something?"

"Honor demanded my silence. Did I have the right to dishonor a friend, to ruin his happiness, to destroy his life to benefit a grotesque, hopeless love? I kept silent, limiting myself to speaking about Fancy to Courtois, who only laughed at what he called a passing infatuation. For the ten words I had dared to say against Hector, Laurence almost stopped coming to see me."

"Ah!" the Sûreté agent exclaimed, "I wouldn't have had either your patience or your generosity, Monsieur."

"That's because you're not my age, Monsieur! Ah! I hated that Trémorel cruelly. Seeing three women so different smitten with him, I asked myself: 'What does he have to be so loved?'"

"Yes!" Monsieur Lecoq murmured, answering a secret thought, "women often deceive themselves. They don't judge men as we judge them."

"How many times," the old Justice of the Peace continued, "how many times I thought about challenging that miserable man to a duel, to fight with him, to kill him! But Laurence would not have wanted ever to see me again. Nevertheless, I would have spoken up, perhaps, if Sauvresy hadn't fallen ill and hadn't died. I knew he had made his wife and his friend swear to marry. I knew that a terrible reason forced them to keep their word. I believed Laurence was saved. Alas! On the contrary she was lost. One evening as I was walking along beside the Mayor's house, I saw a man getting into the garden by climbing over

---

[24] Character in *L'Astrée* by H. d'Urfe (1508–1625).

the wall. That man was Trémorel. I recognized him perfectly. I felt terrible rage. I swore to myself that I was going to wait for him and kill him. And I waited. He didn't come back out that night."

Père Plantat had hidden his face in his hands. His heart broke at the memory of that night of agony, spent just to wait for a man in order to kill him.

Monsieur Lecoq himself trembled with indignation.

"But this Trémorel is the worst of scoundrels!" he exclaimed. "There could be no excuse for his infamies and his crimes. And you would wish, Monsieur, to snatch him from the Cour d'Assises, to save him from prison or the scaffold that's waiting for him!"

The old Justice of the Peace didn't answer for a moment.

As happens in great crises, among all the tumultuous ideas forcing themselves into his head, he didn't know which one to take up first. Words seemed to him powerless to express his feelings. He would have wished to translate all he was feeling, as he was feeling it, into one sentence.

"What's Trémorel to me?" he finally asked. "What do I care about him? If he lives or if he dies, if he manages to escape or if he ends up one morning at the Place de la Roquette, what does that matter to me!"[25]

"Then why this horror of the legal process?"

"Because..."

"Are you a friend of the family; do you care about the great name he's going to cover with mud and doom to infamy?"

"No, but I worry about Laurence, Monsieur. Her dear thought never leaves me."

"But she's not an accomplice. She doesn't know anything. Everything tells us and confirms that she doesn't know her lover killed his wife."

"In reality Laurence is innocent," Père Plantat continued. "Laurence is only the victim of an odious scoundrel. It's none the less true that she will be more cruelly punished than he will be. If Trémorel appears before the Court d'Assises, she will appear at his side as a witness, if not as an accused. And who knows whether they wouldn't go so far as to question her testimony. They would ask themselves if she really had no knowledge of the murder plan, if she hadn't encouraged him. Berthe was her rival. She must have hated her. If I were an Investigating Magistrate, I would include Laurence in my accusation."

"With your help and mine, Monsieur, she would victoriously demonstrate that she was ignorant of everything, that she was abominably deceived."

"Right! And would she be any less dishonored, lost forever! Even so, wouldn't she have to appear before the Court, answer questions of the President, tell the public about her shame and her misfortune. Wouldn't she have to tell where, when and how she lost her virtue; wouldn't she have to repeat the words of her seducer? Do you understand that she resigned herself to announcing her

---

[25]Place of public executions in Paris.

suicide at the risk of making all her family die of shame. No, isn't that true? She would have to explain what threats or what promises were able to make her accept that horrible idea, which, certainly, didn't come from her. Finally, worse than all that, she would be forced to confess her love for Trémorel."

"No," the Sûreté agent answered, "Let's not exaggerate anything. You know as well as I do that the law has infinite consideration for the innocent whose name has been compromised in affairs of this type."

"Consideration! Eh! Could the law deal gently with her, even if it wanted to, with that absurd publicity that's now given to trials. You could touch the hearts of the magistrates, I'm sure. What do you expect from fifty journalists who have been sharpening their pens and preparing their paper ever since the Valfeuillu crime became known? Aren't the newspapers there, always on the look out for whatever can pique and arouse the unhealthy curiosity of the crowd? Do you think that, just to please us, they're going to leave in the dark these scandalous debates that I fear and which the great name of the guilty man will draw immense crowds? Doesn't this trial bring together all the conditions which assure the success of judicial dramas? Oh! Nothing is missing there, neither adultery, nor poison, nor vengeance, nor murder. Laurence will represent the romantic and sentimental. She will become, she, my daughter, the heroine of the Law Courts. She will be the center of attention, as the readers of the *Gazette des Tribunaux* say. The stenographers will tell if she blushed or how many tears she shed. Whoever wants to can go into the most accurate detail about her person, describe what she's wearing and her behavior. The newspapers will make her more public than a prostitute. Every reader will have some part of her. Isn't that odious enough? And after the horror, the irony, the photographers will besiege her door and if she refuses to be photographed, they will sell a photograph of some hussy as if it were hers. She would want to go into hiding. But where? What iron gates, what locks can protect her from greedy impure curiosity? She'll be famous. The ambitious café owners will write to her to suggest she sit at their counter. And the Englishmen who're bored with life will offer her their hand. What shame and what misery! For her to be saved, Monsieur Lecoq, not even her name must be pronounced. I ask you: Is it possible? Answer me."

The old Justice of the Peace was speaking with extreme violence, but simply, without the pompous phrases of passion, which are always overdone, no matter what is claimed. Anger made his eyes glitter. He was young. He was twenty years old. He was in love and he was defending the woman he loved.

Since the Sûreté agent didn't say anything, he insisted:

"Give me an answer."

"Who knows?" Monsieur Lecoq answered.

"Why try to delude me?" Père Plantat continued. "Don't I have as much experience as you do in matters of the law? If Trémorel comes to trial, everything is over for Laurence. And I love her! Yes, I've dared to admit that to you. I've let you see the depth of my despair. I love her as I have never before loved her. She's dishonored, doomed to contempt. She may perhaps adore the miserable man whose child she's going to bear. What does that matter? Look, I love her a thousand times more than before her sin, but then I loved her hopelessly, whereas now..."

He stopped, appalled by what he was going to say. Under the look in the Sûreté's eyes, he looked down, blushing with that shameful hope, and nevertheless very human in what he had let come out.

"You know everything now," he continued in a calmer tone. "Will you agree to help me? Ah! If you would help me, I wouldn't think I had repaid you by giving you half of my fortune, and I'm rich."

Monsieur Lecoq stopped him with a commanding gesture.

"Enough, Monsieur, " he said in a bitter tone. "I can render a service to a man I esteem, that I love, that I pity with all my soul, but this service I could never sell him."

"Do you think," Père Plantat stammered, "that I meant to..."

"Oh, yes, Monsieur, yes, you wanted to give me money. Oh, don't defend yourself, don't deny it. I know only too well that there are fatal professions where the man and honesty seem to be of no consequence. What reason do you have to offer me money? What reasons do you have to judge me so vile to the point that my complacency can be bought? Then you are like the others, who have no idea what a man in my position is! If I wanted to be rich, richer than you, I could be so in two weeks. Then you aren't aware of the fact that I hold the lives of fifty people in my hands? Do you think I tell everything I know? I have here"—and he tapped his forehead— "ten secrets that I could sell tomorrow if I wanted to, a hundred thousand francs each. And I would get it."

He was indignant. You could see that, but under his anger a certain sad resignation could be detected. Many times he had had to refuse similar offers.

He continued: "So try to fight a centuries-old prejudice. Say that an agent of the Sûreté is honest and he has to be. Say; that he is ten times more honest than just any businessman or lawyer, because he has ten times as many temptations without having the benefits of his honesty. Say that and people will laugh in your face. By sending a wire, tomorrow, I can collect at least a million, without fear of being caught. Who can suspect it and who can trace it to me? I'm bound by conscience, that's true, but a little respect wouldn't displease me. When it would be so easy for me to take advantage of what I know, of what people have been forced to confide to me or what I found out accidentally, there might be some merit in not taking advantage of it. And nevertheless, tomorrow, the first one that comes along—a shady banker, a businessman convicted of fraudulent bankruptcy, a captain of industry—if he found himself forced to walk up the boulevard with me, he would find himself compromised. A policeman, *Fi donc!* 'Don't worry," Père Tabaret, my teacher and my friend, told me, the disdain of these people is only a type of fear."

Père Plantat was dismayed. How could he, a sensitive old Judge, prudent and clever, how could he have been guilty of such extraordinary clumsiness? He just wounded, and wounded cruelly, that man who was so well disposed toward him and from whom he had everything to expect.

"Far be from me, Monsieur," he began, "that offensive intention you think I have. You misunderstood the meaning of something I said that was not clear, that I thoughtlessly said and which was of no importance."

Monsieur Lecoq calmed down.

"All right. Being more than others open to offenses, you'll pardon me for being more sensitive. Let's leave this subject, which is painful to me, and go back to the Count de Trémorel."

The Justice of the Peace wondered if he should talk about his plans again. The delicacy of Monsieur Lecoq, who put him back on the path, touched him unusually.

"I have only to wait for your decision," he said.

The Sûreté agent continued:

"I won't hide from you the fact that what you're asking me is very difficult, and what's more is contrary to my duty. My duty commands me to look for Monsieur de Trémorel, arrest him, and deliver him to the law. You, you're asking me to shield him from the effects if the law."

"It's in the name of an innocent girl you know is innocent."

"Only once in my life, Monsieur, did I go against my duty. I wasn't able to resist the tears of an old mother who embraced my knees, asking pardon for her son. I saved the son and he became an honest man. For the second time, I'm going today to go beyond my duty, risk something that my conscience may perhaps reproach me for. I will do as you ask."

"Oh! Monsieur," Père Plantat exclaimed, transported with joy. "How grateful I am!"

But the Sûreté agent remained grave, almost sad. He was thinking.

"Let's not lull ourselves with a hope that may be deceptive. I don't have two ways to keep a criminal like Trémorel from appearing before the Cour d'Assises. I have only one. Will it succeed?"

"Yes, yes, if you want it to."

Monsieur Lecoq couldn't keep from smiling at the old Justice of the Peace's faith.

"I'm certainly a very competent agent," he answered, "but I'm only a man and I can't answer for what other men will do. Everything depends on Hector. If he reacts like every other guilty man, I would tell you: 'I'm sure.' With him, I must tell you, I'm doubtful. We must count on Mademoiselle Courtois' strength, above all. She's strong, you've told me?"

"She's strength itself."

"Then there's hope. What will happen when they find Sauvresy's denunciation, which Trémorel wasn't able to find and which must be hidden somewhere at Valfeuillu?"

"They won't find it," Père Plantat answered quickly.

"Do you think so?"

"I'm sure of it."

Monsieur Lecoq gave the old Justice of the Peace one of those looks which make the truth apparent on the face of those questioned.

"Ah!"

And he was thinking: *Finally I'm going to know where the dossier read to us the other night comes from and why the two different handwriting styles.*

After a moment of hesitation, Père Plantat said:

"I have placed my existence in your hands, Monsieur Lecoq. I can certainly trust my honor to you. I know you. I know that whatever happens..."

"I won't speak. You have my word."

"Well! The day I surprised Trémorel with Laurence, I wanted to change the suspicions I had into certainty. I broke open the envelope Sauvresy had left with me."

"And you didn't use it!"

"I was astounded at my abuse of confidence. Then, did I have the right to take away his revenge from this man who had let himself die to avenge himself?"

"But gave that denunciation back to Madame de Trémorel."

"That's true, but Berthe had a vague premonition of the fate awaiting her. About two weeks before the crime, she came to entrust me with her husband's manuscript, that she had taken care to complete. I was to break the seals and read it if she were to die a violent death."

"Why then didn't you speak up? Why did you let me search, hesitate, grope about..."

"I love Laurence, Monsieur, and to turn in Trémorel would have been to open up an abyss between her and me."

The Sûreté agent bowed.

The devil! he was thinking: *He's clever, this Orcival Justice of the Peace, as clever as I am. Well! I like him. I'm going to give him some support he doesn't expect.*

Père Plantat was longing to question Monsieur Lecoq, to find out from him what was the only method which would result in relatively sure success that he had discovered to prevent the trial and to save Laurence. He didn't dare.

The Sûreté agent was then leaning on his elbows at his desk, his look lost in the void. He was holding a pencil and mechanically tracing on a piece of white paper fantastic designs. Suddenly, he seemed to leave his reverie. He had just solved a last difficulty. His plan was now entire, complete. He looked at the clock.

"Two o'clock!" he exclaimed. "And I made an appointment between three and four with Madame Charman for Jenny Fancy."

"I will follow your orders," the Justice of the Peace said.

"Very good. However, since we have to get busy with de Trémorel after Miss Jenny, let's try to finish everything today."

"What! You hope to bring everything to a good conclusion today..."

"Certainly. Speed above all is indispensable in our job. It sometimes takes months to make up for a lost hour. We're lucky to reach Hector quickly right now and surprise him. Tomorrow it will be too late. We'll have him in twenty-four hours, or we must start again. Each of my three men has a good horse hitched up to a carriage. They should finish their rounds of the decorators in an hour. If my reasoning is accurate, in an hour, two hours at the most, we'll have the address and then we'll move."

While he was talking, he took out from a box a piece of paper stamped with his motto—a crowing rooster with the words *Toujours vigilans*—and rapidly wrote some lines on it.

"Look," he said to Père Plantat, "here's what I wrote to one of my lieutenants:

Monsieur Job,
Get together immediately six or eight of our men and take them to await my instructions at the wine merchant's at the corner of the Rue des Martyrs and the Rue Lamartine.

"Why down there and not here at your place?"

"Because, dear Monsieur, we want to avoid useless running around. Down there we're two steps from Madame Charman's and very near Trémorel hiding place, because the scoundrel rented his apartment in the Notre Dame-de-Lorette neighborhood."

The old Justice of the Peace seemed surprised.

"What makes you think that?" he asked.

The Sûreté agent smiled, as if the question seemed to him naïve.

"Don't you remember, Monsieur, that the envelope of the letter addressed by Mademoiselle Courtois to her family to announce her suicide bore a Paris postmark, the office on the Rue St. Lazare? Now, listen to this carefully. When she left her aunt's house, Mademoiselle Laurence must have gone directly to the apartment rented and furnished by Trémorel. Therefore he had given her the address and promised to join her there Thursday morning. She wrote from that apartment. Can we take into consideration that he had the idea to mail her letter in a neighborhood other than her own? That's not very probable since she didn't know what reasons her lover had to fear pursuit and prosecution. Was Hector careful enough, having enough foresight to point out that ruse to her? No, because if he weren't an idiot, he would have advised her to mail that letter somewhere other than Paris. Therefore, it's impossible that letter was not carried to a post office in the neighborhood of the apartment."

These thoughts were so simple that Père Plantat was astonished that he had not had them. But you don't see very clearly in an affair in which you have a powerful interest. Passion blurs the eyes as a hot apartment does the glasses. He had lost part of his insight when he lost his cool head. It seemed to him that Monsieur Lecoq was using unusual methods to keep his promise.

He couldn't prevent himself from saying: "It seems to me that if you want keep Hector from going to trial, the men you've brought together will be more a hindrance than help to you."

In the looks as well as in the tone of the Justice of the Peace, Monsieur Lecoq thought he could detect a certain doubt that shocked him.

"You don't trust me, Monsieur?" he asked.

Père Plantat wanted to protest.

"Believe me, Monsieur..."

"You have my word," Monsieur Lecoq continued, "and if you knew me better, you would know I never go back on it once I've given it. I swore to you that I would do everything I could to save Mademoiselle Laurence. I will do so. But don't forget that I promised you my help and not success. Let me take the steps I think are needed."

Saying that, without paying any attention to the Justice of the Peace's abashed looks, he rang for Janouille.

"All right," he said to her, "here's a letter that needs to be taken immediately to Job."

"I'm going to carry it myself."

"Not at all. You're going to do what I like by staying here without budging to wait for the men I sent to make the rounds this morning. As they come in, you'll send them to report at the wine merchant's shop on the Rue des Martyrs. You know the one, across from the church. They'll find a lot of good company there."

He was giving his orders at the same time that he was putting on a long black frock coat and adjusting his wig solidly.

"Monsieur will be back this evening?" Janouille asked.

"I don't know."

"And if somebody comes from down there?"

"Down there," for a man in the profession, always meant the Prefecture.

"You'll say I'm out taking care of the Corbeil affair."

Monsieur Lecoq was ready. He truly had the look, the get-up, the physiognomy, and the manners of a respectable fifty-year-old bureau chief: gold-rimmed glasses, an umbrella, everything about him let off a perfume that couldn't be more bureaucratic.

"Now," he said to Père Plantat, "let's hurry."

In the dining room, Goulard, who had finished having lunch, waited at attention for his great man to pass by.

"Well! My boy," Monsieur Lecoq asked him, "Do you have anything to say about my wine?"

"Delicious, Monsieur," the Corbeil agent answered. "Perfect, that is to say, a true nectar."

"Did it at least cheer you up?"

"Oh! Yes, Monsieur."

"Then you can follow us fifteen feet behind us and you'll mount guard in front on the house you see us enter. I'll probably put you in charge of a pretty girl that you'll take to Monsieur Domini. And keep your eyes open. She's a clever thing, very capable of taking you in and slipping through your fingers."

They left and Janouille barricaded the door solidly after them.

Chapter XXV

Do you need money? Do you want living quarters completely furnished in the latest fashion, a barouche with an eight spring mechanism, or a pair of ankle-boots? Do you need Indian cashmere, a porcelain service or a good picture cheap? Is it furniture you're looking for, walnut or rosewood, or diamonds, or sheets, or lace, or a country house, or your firewood supply for the winter?

Go see Madame Charman, 136, Rue Notre Dame-de-Lorette, on the second floor above the mezzanine because she has all that and even more things that it's forbidden to consider as merchandise. If you're a man and have some security to show her, even if it's only a an attractive demeanor, if you're a woman, and you're young, pretty and not at all antisocial, Madame Charman would be happy to help you out at two hundred percent interest.

At this interest rate, she has a great number of customers and nevertheless she hasn't yet made a fortune. That because she's forced to take a lot of risks, and there are enormous losses even if there are prodigious profits. And often what's brought in by the flute goes out with the drum. And, then, as she likes to say, she is too honest. And it's at least true that she's honest. She would sell her last embroidered chemise rather than let someone default on her note. In addition, nobody resembles less than Madame Charman that horrible fat woman with a husky voice, with cynical gestures, loaded down with rings and gold chains, who is typical of the female merchant of toilet accessories. She's blond, thin, sweet, not lacking a certain distinction and invariably wears, summer and winter a black silk dress. You're assured that she has a husband, but no one has ever seen him. But that doesn't keep her conduct from being above suspicion, according to her concierge.

However honorable Madame Charman's profession may be, she more than once had dealt with Monsieur Lecoq. She needed him and was as afraid of him as she was of fire.

And so she greeted the Sûreté agent and his companion—that she took to be a colleague, of course—a little like an assistant greets his director who's come to see him.

She was expecting them. When they rang her doorbell, she met them at the entry hall, gracious, respectful, a smile on her lips. She insisted that she, rather than her maid, have the honor of showing them into her drawing room. She drew up the best armchairs and even offered them some refreshments.

"I see, dear Madame," Monsieur Lecoq began, "that you received my little note."

"*Oui*, Monsieur, this morning, very early. I was still in bed."

"Very good. And have you been kind enough take care of my little errand?"

"Heavens! Monsieur Lecoq, how can you ask me that, when you know I would be delighted to go through fire for you. I took care of it immediately. I got out of bed just for that."

"Then you have found the address of Pélagie Taponnet, called Jenny Fancy?"

Madame Charman thought she should make the most gracious of her bows.

"*Oui*, Monsieur, *oui*," she answered. You can be sure. If I were a woman to overestimate my value, I could tell you I had infinite trouble getting that address, that I ran all over Paris, that I spent ten francs on carriages. I would lie."

"Get to the facts. Get to the facts," Monsieur Lecoq insisted.

"The truth is that I had the pleasure of seeing Miss Jenny Fancy day before yesterday."

"You're joking."

"Not the least in the world. And speaking about that, let me even tell you she's a very nice and honest person."

"Really!"

"That's how it is. Can you imagine? She's owed me four hundred eighty francs for more than two years. Naturally, as you can understand, I put a P on that debt and I scarcely thought any more about it. But here you are, day before yesterday, my Fancy came to me, all spruced up. She said to me: 'I got an inheritance, Madame Charman. I have money and I'm bringing you some.' And she wasn't joking. She had a purse full of bank bills. I was paid the entire bill."

And as the Sûreté agent didn't say anything, she added with profound and affectionate conviction:

"Really a good girl! A worthy creature!"

At that statement of the merchant, Monsieur Lecoq and Père Plantat exchanged glances. They had had the same idea at the same time.

That inheritance Miss Fancy claimed, all those bank bills, could only be the payment for a great service she had rendered Trémorel. However, the Sûreté agent wanted to have more positive information.

"What was that prostitute's situation before the inheritance?" he asked.

"Ah! Monsieur, she was in a terrible situation, you know. Since her Count left her and her venture into ladies' fashions ate up, kit and caboodle, all her savings, she's fallen lower and lower. A woman I saw fashionably dressed in the past... After all that, you know, when a woman has troubles with a love affair! She took everything she possessed to the pawnshop or sold piece by piece. Lately, she's hung out with the worst crowd; she drinks absinthe, I'm told. And she didn't even have any decent clothes. When she received money from her Count, because he still sent her some, she spent it on parties with no account women instead of buying something to wear."

"And where does she live?"

"Very near here, in a furnished house in the Rue Vintimille."

"That being so," Monsieur Lecoq said severely, "I'm surprised she's not here."

"That's not my fault, you know, dear Monsieur. If I know where the nest is, I don't know where the bird is. She flew the nest this morning, when my first girl went to her house."

"*Diable!* That's very annoying. I'll have to have her looked for very quickly."

"Don't worry. Fancy is supposed to come back before four o'clock and my first girl is waiting for her at the concierge's apartment. She has orders to bring her back to me without even letting her go up to her bedroom."

"Then let's wait for her."

Monsieur Lecoq and Père Plantat had been waiting about a quarter of an hour when suddenly Madame Charman, who had a very keen ear, became alert.

"I recognize my first girl's footsteps on the stairs," she said.

"Listen," Monsieur Lecoq said, "since that's the case, set it up in a way that Fancy believes you're the one who had her sent for. My friend and I'll act as if we found ourselves here by the greatest of luck."

Madame Charman motioned in agreement.

"Understood," she said.

She was already making her way toward the door, when the Sûreté agent held her back by her arm.

"One more word," he added, "when you see the girl and me start to talk with each other, please go supervise your workers in your workshop. What I have to talk about won't interest you at all."

"I understand, Monsieur,"

"But no tricks, you understand. I know about the little closet in your bedroom where not a word that's said here is lost, because I've used it."

The first girl opened the drawing room door. There was a loud swishing sound of a silk dress gliding along the door frame and Miss Jenny Fancy appeared in all her glory.

Alas, she was no longer that fresh and pretty Fancy Hector had loved, that provocative Parisian girl with big eyes, alternately languorous or passionate, with a pretty face, with an alert expression. A single year had caused her to fade just as a too hot summer makes roses wither. Her fragile beauty was destroyed forever, that Parisian beauty, that devilish beauty.

She wasn't twenty years old and it would have taken the eyes of a connoisseur to see that she had been charming in the past, when she was young.

Because she had grown old as vice, her tired expression, and her flabby cheeks revealed the disorder of her life. Her eyes with dark circles under them had lost their long lashes and they were already turning red and squinting. Her mouth had a pathetic expression of stupidity. Absinthe and obscene songs had broken the very clear notes of her voice.

She was dressed in great style, with a new dress, bright and outrageous, an immense lace shawl, and an unbelievable hat. Nevertheless, she seemed miserable. And to top it all off, she was wearing outrageous make-up, all smeared with red, white, blue, carmine and off white.

She seemed very angry.

"What are you thinking of?" she burst out as she entered the door, without greeting anyone. "Does it make any sense to send to get me this way, almost by force, and by a working girl? That's the last insult."

But Madame Charman had rushed up to her former client, hugged her anyway and pressed her to her heart.

"What! Dear little girl," she said, "you're angry? I was counting on your being delighted and thank me nicely."

"Me! Why!"

"Because, beautiful sweet thing, I wanted to surprise you. Ah! I'm not ungrateful. You're going to be able to take advantage of a magnificent sale. I have right now a large quantity of velvet..."

"Was that worth the trouble to disturb me?"

"All silk, my dear, at thirty francs a meter. *Hein!* This seldom happens; it's somewhat unbelievable; somewhat..."

"Eh! What do I care about your sales! Velvet in the middle of July. Are you kidding me?"

"Let me show it to you."

"Never. They're waiting for me now to go dine at Asnières."

She was going to leave, despite the very sincere efforts of Madame Charman, who was, perhaps, trying to kill two birds with one stone. Monsieur Lecoq thought it was time for him to step in.

"But if I'm not mistaken," he exclaimed with the expression of a flirtatious old codger, "It's really Miss Jenny that I have the pleasure of seeing again."

She looked him up and down with an expression half angry, half surprised, saying:

"Yes, it's me! So!"

"What! Have you now forgotten? You don't recognize me?"

"No, not at all."

"I used to be, however, one of your admirers, my beautiful child. I had the pleasure of having lunch at your apartment when you lived near the Madeleine: It was during the time of the Count."

He took off his glasses, as if to wipe off the lenses, but in reality to glance furiously at Madame Charman, who, not daring to resist, beat a discreet retreat.

"I was in rather good standing with the Count at that time," Monsieur Lecoq continued. "And speaking of the Count, has it been a long time since you've heard from him?"

"I say him a week ago."

"Well! Well! Well! Then you know about that horrible concerning him."

"No, so what is it?"

"Really, you don't know? You don't read the newspapers? But it's an abominable story, my dear child. There's been no talk of anything but that for the last forty-eight hours."

"Tell me quickly."

"You know that after his bankruptcy he married the widow of one of his friends. People thought he was very happy in his marriage. Then suddenly he murdered his wife by stabbing her."

Miss Fancy turned pale under her thick layer of make-up.

"Is that possible?" she stammered.

She said: "Is that possible?" but if she was very upset, it was certain that she wasn't very surprised. Monsieur Lecoq picked up on that extremely well.

"It's so possible," he answered, "that right now he's in prison, that he'll come to trial, and very certainly he'll be condemned."

Père Plantat was watching Jenny with curiosity. He was expecting an explosion of despair, an outcry, tears, a slight attack of nerves at least. Error.

Fancy had come to detest Trémorel. She, in the past sometimes very impatient with contempt directed toward her, she felt the weight of her shame. And it was Hector she very unjustly accused for her present ignoble situation. She hated him meanly, as prostitutes hate, smiling at him when she saw him, getting as much money as possible from him, and wishing all sorts of misfortunes on him.

Far from dissolving in tears, Jenny burst out in idiotic laughter.

"Trémorel's done for," she said. "Why did he leave me? She got what was coming to her also..."

"What do you mean, she also?"

"Of course. Why did she deceive her husband, a charming fellow? She's the one who took Hector away from me. A married woman and rich! Hector's nothing but a scoundrel. I always said so."

"Frankly, that's my opinion also. You see, when a man behaves like Hector did toward you, people judge him."

"Yes, don't they?"

"Parbleu! So I'm not surprised about his conduct. Because, you know, murdering his wife isn't the least of his crimes. Now it seems he trying to blame the murder on someone else."

"That wouldn't surprise me."

"He's accusing a poor devil, as innocent as you and me, and who, nevertheless, may be condemned to death for not being able to say where he spent the evening and the night from Wednesday to Thursday."

Monsieur Lecoq had pronounced that sentence in a light tone, but with calculated slowness, in order to judge accurately the impression it produced on Jenny. The effect was so terrible that she trembled.

"Do you know who that man is?" she asked in a trembling voice.

"The newspapers say he's Trémorel's poor gardener."

"A short man, isn't that right? Thin, very dark with black straight hair?"

"Exactly."

263

"And whose name is…wait a minute…whose name is…Guespin."

"Ah, so you know him then?"

Miss Fancy hesitated. She was trembling greatly. You could see she regretted having gone so far.

"Bah!" she finally said. "I don't see why I shouldn't tell what I know. Me, I'm an honest girl, even if Trémorel's a scoundrel. I don't want a poor devil that's innocent to get his head cut off."

"Then you know something?"

"You can say I know everything. And it's very simple, you see. About a week ago, Hector, who supposedly didn't want to see me anymore, wrote me to set up an appointment with me at Melun. I went there; I met him; and we had lunch together. So he suddenly tells me he's worried, that his cook is getting married, but that one of his servants is so in love with her that he is capable of making a scene at the wedding, of breaking up the dance, and even attempting something bad."

"Ah! He told you about the wedding!"

"So, wait. My Hector seemed very embarrassed, not knowing how to avoid the trouble he could foresee. It was then that I advised him to keep the servant away during that day. He thought a moment and told me I had a good idea.

"'I've found a way,' he added. 'I won't tell this fellow anything about it before hand, but I'll give him an errand to do with you, letting him suppose that it's a matter of some business I want to hide from my wife. You, you'll go disguise yourself as an upstairs maid and you'll wait for him in a cafe on the Place du Chatelet, between 9:30 and 10:30 in the evening. So that he'll recognize you, you'll sit at the table closest to the entry on the right. You'll have next to you a big bouquet. He'll give you a package, and you'll invite him to have something to drink. You'll get him drunk, if possible, and you'll wander around Paris until the next day.'"

Miss Fancy was expressing herself with difficulty, hesitating, drawing out her words. You could see she was trying to recall Trémorel's exact words.

"And you," Monsieur Lecoq interrupted, "an intelligent woman, you believed that story of domestic jealousy?"

"Not exactly. But I imagined that he had some mistress in play, and it didn't bother me to help him deceive his wife I detested and who had done me wrong."

"So you obeyed."

"As exactly as it was set up, and everything happened as Hector had foreseen. At exactly 10:00 my gardener servant arrived. He took me for a maid and gave me the package. Naturally, I offered him a beer. He accepted and offered me another one that I also accepted. He was all right, this gardener, friendly and polite. I can assure you I spent an excellent evening with him. He knows a lot of stories, one funnier than the next..."

"Go on, go on. What did you do next?"

"After the beer, we drank some small glasses of wine—He had his pockets full of money, that gardener—and after the little glasses of wine, some more beer, then some punch, then some warm wine. At 11:00 he was already very drunk and was talking about taking me to the Batignolles to dance a quadrille. Me, I refused and I told him that to be gallant, he had to take me back to the house of my mistress, who lived up the Champs Elysées. So then we left the cafe and went from wine merchant to wine merchant the length of the Rue de Rivoli, In short, about 2:00 in the morning, that poor devil was so drunk that he fell in a heap on a bench near the Arc-de-Triomphe, where he fell asleep and where I left him."

"And you, what did you do?"

"Me, I went back to my place."

"What happened to the package?"

"Ma foi! I was supposed to throw it in the Seine, but I forgot to. You understand. I had drunk almost as much as the gardener, especially at the beginning. So much that I took it back to my place, where it still is."

"But did you open it?"

"You can certainly believe I did."

"What was in it?"

"A hammer, two other big tools and a big knife."

Guespin's innocence was from that point evident. Everything the Sûreté agent had foreseen had come about.

"So," Père Plantat said, "there's our client out of the business. There remains to find out..."

But Monsieur Lecoq interrupted him. He now knew everything he needed to know. Jenny no longer had anything to enlighten him. He suddenly changed tones, breaking off the honeyed tones of the old codger for the dry and brutal tone of the man from the Prefecture.

"My pretty child," he said to Miss Fancy, "you have in fact just saved an innocent man. But what you've just told me you must repeat to the Investigating Magistrate in Corbeil. However, as you could get lost on the way, I'm going to give you a guide."

He went to the window, opened it and seeing on the opposite sidewalk Monsieur Domini's agent, caring very little about compromising Madame Charman, he shouted as loud as he could:

"Goulard, hey! Goulard, come up here."

Coming back then to Miss Fancy, who was so troubled, so overwhelmed, that she didn't dare either question or get angry.

"Tell me," he asked her, "how much did Trémorel pay you for the service you rendered him?"

"Ten thousand francs, Monsieur, but they really belong to me, I swear to you. He's been promising them to me for a long time, to put myself back afloat. He owes them to me."

"That's all right, that's all right. We won't take them away from you." And pointing out to her Goulard, who was entering:

"You're going to take this Monsieur to your place when you leave here," he told her. "You'll pick up the package Guespin gave you and you'll leave immediately for Corbeil. Above all," he added in a terrible voice, "no childish behavior, or watch out for me!"

Hearing the noise coming from the drawing room, Madame Charman came in just in time to see Fancy leave, escorted by Goulard.

"What's happening, *Grand Dieu!*" she, all in tears, asked Monsieur Lecoq.

"Nothing, dear lady, nothing at all that regards you in the least. And now, good-bye and thanks. We're very much in a hurry."

Chapter XXVI

When Monsieur Lecoq was in a hurry, he walked fast. He almost ran going down the Rue Notre Dame-de-Lorette, which is the street in Paris they pave the most often. He was running so fast that Père Plantat had all the trouble in the world keeping up with him. Hastening his steps, preoccupied with the measures he was going to take to assure the success of his plans, he was carrying on a monologue which the Justice of the Peace caught some snatches of here and there.

"Everything is going well," he was muttering, "and we'll succeed. It's rare that a campaign begins so well and doesn't end happily. If Job is at the Wine Merchant's, if one of my men was successful in his rounds, the Valfeuillu crime is settled, solved, wound up in the evening and in a week no one will talk about it anymore."

Having come to the end of the street, across from the church, the Sûreté agent stopped short.

"I must ask your pardon," he said to the Justice of the Peace, "for having dragged you along after me and having condemned you to do my job. But in addition to the fact that your assistance was very useful to me at Madame Charman's, it has become absolutely indispensable now that we get seriously busy with Trémorel."

He immediately crossed the intersection and went into the wine merchant's shop at the corner of the Rue des Martyrs. Standing behind his pewter counter, busy pouring into liter bottles the contents of an enormous jug, the owner seemed only moderately surprised to see venture into his shop two men who appeared to belong to the highest class of society. But Monsieur Lecoq, like Alcibiades, was at home in and spoke the language of every milieu in which he found himself.

He asked the wine merchant: "Isn't there a group of eight or ten men in your shop who're waiting for others?"

"Yes, Monsieur, these Messieurs arrived about an hour ago."

"They're in the big private room at the back, aren't they?"

"Precisely, Monsieur," the retailer, suddenly become obsequious, answered.

He didn't know exactly what person was interrogating him, but he smelled some high ranking agent from the Prefecture. Because of that he wasn't at all surprised to see this very distinguished gentleman knew, as he did, those in his house, and opened with no hesitation the door to the room pointed out. In this area in the back, separated only by a simple frosted glass partition, ten men in various dress were drinking and playing cards.

They rose respectfully at the entrance of Monsieur Lecoq and Père Plantat, and those who still wore their hat or cap removed it.

"Good, Monsieur Job," the Sûreté agent said to the man who appeared to be the leader of the group. "You're on time. I'm glad. Your six men will be enough for me, since I see here my three agents from this morning."

Monsieur Job bowed, glad to have satisfied a master who wasn't lavish in testifying approval.

"You're going to wait for me here a minute," Monsieur Lecoq continued. "My instructions will depend on the report I hear."

Addressing then the men he had sent out earlier.

"Which of you was successful," he asked.

"Me, Monsieur," answered a tall boy with a pale face, a little puny moustache, a true Parisian.

"You again, Pâlot. You're decidedly a lucky boy. Follow me into the next room, but before that, tell the owner to bring us a bottle and watch to see we aren't disturbed."

The orders were soon carried out and after having made Père Plantat sit down, Monsieur Lecoq himself turned the lock in the door.

"Speak, now," he said to his man, "and be brief."

"All right, Monsieur. I had showed my photograph to a dozen business people without any result, when one of the decorators on the Rue des Saints Pères, in the Saint-Germain neighborhood, recognized it."

"Report to me what he said, word for word, if possible."

"That portrait," he told me, "is that of one of my clients. This client came to me about a month ago to buy a complete household of furniture— drawing room, dining room, bedroom, and everything else—that was to go to a little townhouse he had just rented. He didn't bargain about anything. He put only one condition on the transaction. Everything had to be ready, delivered, and in place, the drapes put up, the rugs put down, three weeks from that date. That would be a week from last Monday.

"And how much did everything he bought cost?"

"Eighteen thousand francs, half in advance, half the day of the delivery."

"Who paid the funds the second time?"

"A servant."

"What name did this Monsieur give to the decorator?"

"He said his name was Mr. James Wilson, but Monsieur Rech told me he didn't look like an Englishman."

"Where does he live?"

"The furniture was delivered to a little townhouse on the Rue Saint-Lazare, No.—, near the Havre railway station." [26]

Monsieur Lecoq's face, rather worried up until then, expressed the greatest joy. He felt the very legitimate pride so natural to the captain who sees the strat-

---

[26] Today's Gare Saint-Lazare.

egies succeed which must destroy the enemy. He allowed himself to give a friendly tap on the shoulder of the old Justice of the Peace, saying just one word:

"Got him!"

But Pâlot shook his head.

"That's not certain," he said.

"Why?"

"You can be sure, Monsieur, that, knowing the address and having some time left, I went to check out the place, that is to say, the little townhouse."

"And then?"

"The renter was named Wilson, but he wasn't the man in the portrait, I'm sure of it."

The Justice of the Peace made a gesture of disappointment, but Monsieur Lecoq didn't disappoint so easily.

"How did you get this information?"

"I spoke to a servant."

"That's unfortunate!" Père Plantat exclaimed. "You may have aroused suspicions!"

"As for that, no." Monsieur Lecoq said. "Pâlot is my student. I'll answer for him. Explain yourself, my boy."

"Then, Monsieur, the townhouse recognized, a rich dwelling, *ma foi!* I said to myself, 'Here's the cage, let's find out if the bird's inside. But how can that be done? Fortunately, by the greatest luck. I had a *louis* on me. I slipped it into the duct that took the household water of the townhouse to the gutter."

"Then you rang the bell?"

"That's right. The concierge—because there is a concierge—came to open the door and I, putting on my most annoyed look, told him that when I took my handkerchief out of my pocket I had dropped twenty francs. I asked him to lend me something to use to try to recover them. He lent me a piece of steel and took another for himself and in less than no time we had recovered the coin. I immediately began to jump up and down as if I were the happiest of men. I asked him to let me buy him a glass of whatever by way of thanks."

"Not bad!"

"Oh! Monsieur Lecoq, that's one of your tricks. But you're going to hear the rest, which is mine. My concierge accepted and there we were, the best friends in the world, drinking a glass of bitters in a shop that's across from the townhouse. We were chatting happily, when I suddenly stooped down, as if I had seen something on the floor, something surprising. So I picked up what? The photograph that I had dropped and crushed a little with my foot. 'Well! I said. 'A photograph!' My new friend looked at it and didn't seem to recognize it. Then, to be sure, I insisted and I said: 'He's nice looking, this Monsieur. Your master must look like this, because all well-off men look alike.' But his answer was negative, saying the man in the photograph had a full beard, whereas his master was shaved as close as a monk. 'Besides,' he added, 'My master is an

American. He gives us orders in French, that's true, but Madame and he always speak in English.'"

As Pâlot continued talking, Monsieur Lecoq's eyes again were shining.

"Trémorel speaks English, doesn't he," he asked Père Plantat.

"Very acceptably, and Laurence also. That being so, your trail is the right one, because we know Trémorel shaved his beard the evening of the crime. We can start the..."

However, Pâlot, who was expecting some praise, looked disappointed.

"My boy," the Sûreté agent said to him, "I find your investigation very nice. A good bonus will prove that to you. Not knowing what we know, your deductions were right. Now let's get back to the townhouse. You probably have the lay-out of the first floor?"

"Certainly, Monsieur, and of the second also. The porter, who isn't a deaf-mute, gave me a lot of information about the masters, although he hasn't been employed but two days. The lady is terribly sad and does nothing but cry."

"We know that. The lay-out, the lay-out."

"Down below, outside, there's a large and high arch. It's paved for the passage of carriages. On the other side of the arch there's a rather large courtyard. The stables and the storage area are at the back of the courtyard. To the left of the arch is the concierge's lodging. To the right is a glassed door opening onto a stairway with six steps which leads to the vestibule. The drawing room, the dining room and two more small rooms open off the vestibule. On the second floor are the bedrooms of Monsieur and Madame, the study, a..."

"That's enough!" Monsieur Lecoq interrupted. "I have my plan of attack." And rising quickly, he opened the door of his secret room and went out into the larger room, followed by Monsieur Plantat and Pâlot. As they had the first time, all the agents stood up.

"Monsieur Job," the Sûreté agent then said to his lieutenant, "listen to this order carefully. As soon as I leave, you'll go pay what you owe here. Then, because I need you close at hand, you will all go settle in at the first wine shop you find on the right, going up the Rue d'Amsterdam. Eat, you have time, but stay sober, you understand."

He took two *louis* out of his money holder that he placed on the table, saying:

"Here's money for diner."

Then he left, after having ordered Pâlot to follow him closely. Before everything else, Monsieur Lecoq was in a hurry to see for himself the townhouse where Trémorel lived. With one glance he verified that the interior plan was exactly as Pâlot had described.

"This is good," he said to Père Plantat. "We have the right position. Our chances at this time are ninety per cent."

"What are you going to do?" asked the old Justice of the Peace, who was getting more excited as the decisive moment approached.

270

"For the moment, nothing. I don't want to make a move until night fall. So," he answered almost gaily, "since we have two hours before us, let's do what our men are doing. I actually know a restaurant in this neighborhood, two steps from here, where the food is very good. Let's go have dinner."

Just as Monsieur Lecoq had claimed, the food was very good at the Havre restaurant. It was unfortunate that Père Plantat couldn't judge for himself. Even more than in the morning, he had a heavy heart. To swallow even a mouthful would have been impossible for him. If only he had understood something of his guide's plans! But the Sûreté agent had remained impenetrable. Answering every question with:

"Let me do my job. Have confidence in me."

Certainly, Monsieur Plantat's confidence was great, but the more he thought about it, the more the attempt to keep Trémorel from going to trial, seemed dangerous to him, fraught with difficulties, almost insane. The most poignant doubts besieged his mind and tortured him. In essence it was his life that was at stake, because he had sworn that he wouldn't survive the downfall of Laurence, reduced to making a confession in open court of both her dishonor and her love for Hector.

Monsieur Lecoq tried in vain to cheer up his guest. He tried to get him to at least eat some soup and drink a glass of old Bordeaux. He soon recognized that he was wasting his time and started to dine as if alone. He was very worried, but not knowing the outcome of a case had never made him lose his appetite. He ate for a long time and well, slowly emptying his bottle of Léoville. However, night came on, and the waiters were already beginning to light the chandeliers. Little by little the room had emptied, and Père Plantat and Monsieur Lecoq found themselves almost alone.

"Isn't it finally time to make a move?" the old Justice of the Peace asked timidly.

The Sûreté agent took out his watch.

"We still have almost an hour before us," he answered. "However, I'm going to prepare everything."

He called the waiter and ordered a cup of coffee, and at the same time, something to write with.

"You see, Monsieur," he continued, "even though we're in a hurry to get it done, the important thing for us is to get to Mademoiselle Laurence without Trémorel knowing it. We need a ten minute interview with her and at her lodgings. That is the indispensable condition for our success."

The old Justice of the Peace was probably expecting some immediate, dramatic and decisive turn of events, because Monsieur Lecoq's statement seemed to bother him.

"If that's how it is," he said with a sad gesture, "we might as well give up our project."

"Why?"

"Because obviously Trémorel must not leave Laurence alone for a minute."

"So, I have thought about bringing him outside."

"And you, Monsieur, ordinarily so perceptive, you can suppose that he would venture out into the street! You're not taking into account his situation at this moment. Think about the fact that he must be in prey to unlimited terrors. We ourselves know that Sauvresy's denunciation won't be found, but he himself doesn't know it. He's telling himself that this manuscript may be found, that people are suspicious, and without doubt he's being look for, followed, tracked by the police."

Monsieur Lecoq smiled triumphantly.

"I told myself all that," he responded, "and many other things besides. Ah! To find a way to flush out Trémorel isn't easy. I've looked for one a long time, but I've finally found it, just as we entered here. In an hour Count de Trémorel will be in the Saint-Germain neighborhood. It's going to cost me a forgery, but you'll grant there are extenuating circumstances. Besides, the ends justify the means."

He took the pen, and without taking his cigar out of his mouth, he wrote rapidly:

Monsieur,

Four of the thousand franc bills you gave me are counterfeit. I just found that out when I took them to my banker. If you're not at my place of business before ten o'clock to explain how this happened, I will regretfully have to file a complaint this same evening with the police.

Rech

"There, Monsieur," Monsieur Lecoq said, passing the letter to Père Plantat. "Do you understand?"

The old Justice of the Peace read it at a glance. He couldn't hold back an exclamation of joy that made all the waiters turn round.

"Yes," he said, "yes, in fact on receiving that letter he would be struck with terror that would master all his other terrors. He would tell himself that among the bills he paid with he might have slid some in some counterfeit ones without noticing it. He told himself that a complaint filed before the bench would cause an investigation. That he would have to prove that he really was Monsieur Wilson, and then he would be lost."

"Then you understand why he'll come out?"

"I'm sure of it, unless he's gone mad."

"Then we'll succeed, I repeat to you, because I've just overcome the only serious obstacle."

He suddenly interrupted himself. The restaurant door had been pushed ajar, and a man had passed his head though the opening, and immediately withdrawn it.

"There's my man," said Monsieur Lecoq, calling the waiter to add up the bill. "Let's go. He must be waiting for us in the passageway."

There was in fact a young man, dressed like the decorator workers, waiting, while seeming to be killing time, looking in the shops of the covered passageway. He had long brown hair and moustache. His eyebrows were the most beautiful black. Père Plantat certainly did not recognize Pâlot. Monsieur Lecoq, who had more experienced eyes recognized him very well and he seemed displeased.

"Bad," he grumbled, when the decorator worker greeted him."Do you think, my boy, that it's enough to change the color of your beard to disguise yourself. Look at yourself a little in that shop window and tell me if your face isn't exactly the same as it was before. Your eyes and your smile, aren't they the same? Then, look, your cap is too much to one side. That's not natural. And your hand isn't rammed down brazenly enough in your pocket."

"I'll try to do better next time," Pâlot said modestly.

"I certainly hope so, but then, for this evening, the concierge from an earlier time won't recognize you, and that's all that's necessary."

"And now what should I do?"

"Here are your instructions," Lecoq said, answering Pâlot. "And above all, don't make a mistake. First of all, you're going to get a carriage with a good horse. Then you'll go to the wine merchant's to pick up one of our men, who will go with you as far as Monsieur Wilson's townhouse. When you get there, you'll go in alone and give the concierge this letter here, saying that it's of the highest importance and most urgent. When you've finished what you came to do, you with your agent will set up an ambush in front of the hotel. If Monsieur Wilson comes out, and he will come out, or I'm not Monsieur Lecoq, your companion will come tell me immediately. As for you, you'll stick to Monsieur Wilson, and you won't let him out of your sight. He will certainly take a carriage. You'll follow him in yours. Be sure to sit on the seat beside the driver. And keep your eyes open. He's a fellow very capable of slipping out one of the doors during the chase and leaving you chasing an empty carriage."

"All right, from the moment I know..."

"Silence when I'm talking. He'll probably go to the shop of the decorator in the Rue des Saints-Pères. However, I could be wrong. It's possible that he may have himself driven to some railway station and take the first train that comes in. In that case, you'll get into the same car as he does and you'll follow him wherever he goes. Be sure, however, to send me a telegram as soon as you can."

"Yes, Monsieur, very good. However. if I must take a train..."

"What? You don't have any money?"

"Right."

"Then,"—Monsieur Lecoq took out his money holder, "take this five hundred franc bill. That's more than necessary to go around the world. Have you understood everything completely?"

"Pardon…what if Monsieur Wilson purely and simply goes back to his townhouse. What should I do?"

"Let me finish. If he goes back, you'll go back with him. The moment his carriage stops in front of the townhouse, you'll give two loud whistles. Then you'll wait for me in the street. Be careful to keep the carriage that you'll lend to Monsieur, if he needs it."

"Understood!" said Pâlot, who left running.

Now alone, Père Plantat and Monsieur Lecoq began to walk up and down under the covered archway. They were serious, silent, as you always are at the decisive moment of a game. Nobody talks around gaming tables.

Suddenly Monsieur Lecoq came alive. He had just seen his agent at the other end of the gallery. He was so impatient that he ran to him.

"Well?"

"Monsieur, the game has been flushed out and Pâlot is following him."

"On foot or in a carriage?"

"In a carriage."

"That's enough. Go back to your companions and tell them to stay ready."

Everything was going the way Monsieur wished, and he turned around triumphantly to the old Justice of the Peace. He was struck by the change in his expression.

"Are you ill, Monsieur? he asked, very upset.

"No, but I'm fifty-five years old, Monsieur Lecoq, and at my age there are some emotions that can kill. Look. At the moment of seeing my wishes come true, I'm trembling. I sense that a disappointment would mean my death. I'm afraid. Yes, I'm afraid... Ah! Why can't you do without me and let me stay here?"

"But your presence is indispensable, Monsieur. Without you, without your help, I can do nothing."

"What good would I be to you?"

"To save Mademoiselle Laurence, Monsieur."

That name, said in that way, gave the Justice of the Peace of Orcival back a part of his strength.

"If that's the way it is!" he said.

He was already going with determination toward the street. Monsieur Lecoq held him back.

"Not yet," he said. "Not yet. Winning the battle depends on the precision of our movements, Monsieur. A single mistake and all my plans fail miserably and I'll be forced to arrest and deliver the accused man over to the law. We need a ten-minute interview with Mademoiselle Laurence, but not a great deal more. And it's absolutely essential that that interview be interrupted by the return of Trémorel. Let's review our calculations. It will take this scoundrel thirty minutes to go to the Rue des Saint-Pères, where he won't find anyone; the same amount of time to return. Let's add fifteen minutes wasted. In all an hour and a quarter. We still have forty minutes to wait."

Père Plantat didn't answer, but Lecoq understood that it would be impossible for him to remain standing such a long time, after the day's fatigues, emotional as he was and not having eaten anything since the evening before. He then led him into a neighboring cafe and forced him to eat a piece of bread dipped in a glass of wine. Then, understanding that all conversation would be troublesome to that very unhappy man, he picked up an evening newspaper and soon appeared to be absorbed by news from Germany.

His head leaning back against the velvet of the wall seat, his eyes lost in the void, the old Justice of the Peace let his mind run back over the events of those four years which had just passed. It seemed to him that it was just yesterday that Laurence was still a child, coming to run across the grass on his lawn and pick his roses. How pretty she was already and what a divine expression her big eyes had. Then from one evening to the next morning, you might say, like a rose that blossoms one June night, she became the radiant young lady. But timid and reserved with everyone, she wasn't so with him. Hadn't he been her old friend, the confident of her little problems and her innocent hopes. How candid and pure she was! What divine ignorance of evil!…"

Nine o'clock struck. Monsieur Lecoq put his newspaper on the table. "Let's go," he said.

"Père Plantat followed him with firmer footsteps and soon, accompanied by Monsieur Job's men, they arrived in front of the townhouse occupied by Mr. Wilson.

"All of you agents," Monsieur Lecoq said to his agents, "wait to enter until I call. I'm going to leave the door ajar."

At the first ring of the doorbell, Père Plantat and the Sûreté agent were under the canopy. The concierge was on the threshold of his apartment.

"Mr. Wilson," Monsieur Lecoq asked.

"He's out."

"Then I'll speak to Madame."

"She's out also."

"Very well! However, since I absolutely must speak to Mrs. Wilson, I'll go upstairs."

The concierge was getting ready to put up a stiff resistance, but Monsieur Lecoq having called his men, he understand who he was dealing with. Full of caution, he said nothing. The Sûreté agent then posted six of his men in the courtyard, in such a position that they could easily be seen from the second floor windows. He commanded the others to go place themselves on the opposite sidewalk, ordering them to openly watch the house.

These measures taken, he came back to the concierge.

"You, fellow," he commanded, "pay attention. When your master, who's out, starts to come back in, be careful not to tell him the house is surrounded and that we are upstairs. A single word will compromise you terribly."

Monsieur Lecoq's expression and tone were so menacing that the concierge trembled. He saw himself at the bottom of the dampest cells.

"I'm blind," he said, "I'm deaf."

"How many servants are there in the house?"

"Three, but they're all out."

The Sûreté agent then took Père Plantat's arm and holding it tightly:

"You see, Monsieur, "everything is going our way. Come on, in the name of Mademoiselle Laurence, have courage!"

Chapter XXVII

All the things Monsieur Lecoq had foreseen came about. Laurence was not dead. Her letter to her family was nothing but an odious deception. It really was she who, under the name of Mrs. Wilson, lived in the townhouse which Père Plantat and Monsieur Lecoq had just entered.

How had the beautiful and noble young girl so beloved of the Judge of Orcival come to this terrible extremity? That's because the logic of life, alas! links all our choices fatally one to the next. That's because often an action of no consequence, very little reprehensible in itself, can be the starting point of a crime. Each of our new resolutions depends on the ones preceding it and is the mathematical consequence of it. In many ways it is the same as the total of a list of numbers is the product of the numbers put down.

Woe to the man who, giving in to the first vertigo at the edge of an abyss, doesn't flee as fast as possible without looking back. If he looks back, he's done for. Soon, giving into an irresistible attraction, he bravely approaches the danger, his foot slides. He's lost. He vainly returns to reality and makes unbelievable efforts to hold himself upright. He can't do so. He hardly manages to slow down his ultimate fall. Whatever he tries and whatever he does, he will roll lower, always lower, to the bottom of the gulf.

But Trémorel had nothing of the implacable character of murderers. He was only weak and cowardly, and nevertheless he had committed abominable crimes. All his misdeeds went back to the first feeling of envy he had toward Sauvresy that he hadn't tried to surmount. God told the sea: "You will go no further." But there is no man who, breaking the dike of his passions, knows how to stop them.

Thus, the day that Laurence, the poor child, in love with Trémorel, let him squeeze her hand, hiding from her mother, she was a lost girl. That hand squeeze had led her to feign suicide, to run away with her lover. It could very well have led her to infanticide.

Alone after Hector's departure to the Saint-Germain neighborhood as a result of Monsieur Lecoq's letter, the unhappy Laurence forced herself to go back over the events of the last year. How unexpected and rapid they had been! It seemed to her that, carried away by a whirlwind, she hadn't had a second to get her bearings, to return to her free will. She wondered if she were not the plaything of a hideous nightmare and that she would not wake up at Orcival in her young girl's white bedroom.

Was this really she in a strange house, dead to everyone, leaving a tarnished memory, reduced to living under a borrowed name, henceforth without a family, without friends, without anyone in the world to lean on in her weakness. She was at the mercy of a man, a fugitive as was she. He was free to break tomorrow the fragile ties of the fantasy which bound him today.

Finally, was this really she, who, feeling a child moving in her womb, was going to be a mother and who found herself reduced by that excess of misery to be ashamed of that motherhood that is the pride of young women. A thousand memories of that past existence came back to her mind and cruel remorse deepened her despair. Her heart broke when thinking about her friendships in the past, about her mother, about her sister, about pride in her innocence, about the pure joys of her father's household.

Semi-reclined on a couch in Hector's study, she freely wept warm tears. She wept for her life broken at twenty-years-old, her lost youth, her vanished radiant hopes, society's respect, her own respect for herself that she would never recover.

Suddenly the study door opened noisily. Laurence thought it was Hector returning and got up quickly, passing her handkerchief over her eyes to try to hide her tears.

On the threshold a man she didn't know—Monsieur Lecoq—bowed respectfully.

She was afraid. Many times the last two days Hector had repeated to her: "We're being followed. Let's be sure we're well hidden." But then, even when she thought she had nothing more to fear, she was trembling without knowing why.

"Who are you?" she asked in a haughty tone. "Who let you come in here? Who are you?"

Monsieur Lecoq was one of those men who never leave anything they've set up to chance, who foresee everything, who organize the actions of life like scenes in the theater. He was expecting that legitimate anger, those questions, and he had staged his reactions.

As the only response, he stepped aside, thus revealing Père Plantat behind him.

Laurence was so shocked at seeing her old friend that despite her strength she was almost ill.

"You," she stammered, "You."

The old Justice of the Peace was, if possible, even more emotional than she was. Was that really his Laurence standing there before him? Sorrow had done its work so well that she seemed old. Risking dying, she had stopped trying to gird herself in. Her pregnancy was very apparent.

"Why have you looked for me?" she continued. "Why add one more sorrow to my life? Ah! I was right when I told Hector that no one would believe the letter he dictated to me. There are some misfortunes for which only death is a refuge."

Père Plantat was going to answer, but Monsieur Lecoq had promised himself that he would direct the interview.

"It's not you we're looking for Madame, but actually Monsieur de Trémorel."

"Hector! And why, if you please.?"

At the moment of striking down that unfortunate child, guilty only of having believed what a scoundrel swore to her, Monsieur Lecoq hesitated. Nevertheless, he was one of those who believe that the brutal truth is less frightening than cruel tact.

"Monsieur de Trémorel has committed a great crime," he continued.

"He! You're lying, Monsieur."

The Sûreté agent sadly shook his head.

"I'm telling the truth, unfortunately," he insisted. "Monsieur de Trémorel murdered his wife in the night between Wednesday and Thursday. I'm a policeman and I have orders to arrest him."

He thought that terrible accusation was going to stun Laurence and cause her to faint. He was wrong. She was stunned, but she remained standing. The crime horrified her, but it didn't seem to her absolutely unlikely. She knew the hatred Berthe inspired in Hector.

"All right! So be it," she exclaimed, made sublime by strength and despair. "So be it. I'm his accomplice. Arrest me."

That cry, which seemed to come from the deepest mad passion, floored Père Plantat, but didn't at all surprise Monsieur Lecoq.

"No, Madame, no," he continued. "You're not that man's accomplice. Besides his wife's murder is the least of his crimes. Do you know why he didn't marry you? Because with the complicity of Madame Berthe, who was his mistress, he poisoned Sauvresy, who saved him, his best friend. We have proof of that."

But she didn't doubt it. That terrible revelation stripped away the veil which had until then covered the past for her. Yes, Sauvresy's poisoning explained all Hector's conduct to her, his position, his fears, his lies, his hatred, his abandon, his marriage, his flight, finally, everything.

Nevertheless, she still tried, not to defend him, but to accept half of his crimes.

"I knew that," she stammered, with a voice broken by sobs. "I knew everything."

The old Justice of the Peace was in despair. "How you loved him, poor child," he exclaimed. "How you loved him!"

That sad exclamation gave back Laurence all her strength. She made an effort and straightened up, her eyes shining with indignation.

"I love him!" she cried out, "I! Then I can explain to you, my only friend, my conduct, because you are worthy to understand me. Yes, I loved him, that's true. Loved him to the point of forgetting duty, to the point of abandoning myself. But one day he revealed himself to me as he is. I judged him, and my love didn't resist the contempt. I didn't know about the terrible murder of Sauvresy, but Hector told me that his life was in Berthe's hands..., and that she was in love with him. I gave him leave to abandon me, to get married, sacrificing in this way more than my life to what I thought was his happiness. And nevertheless, I have no more illusions. By running away with him, I'm sacrificing myself again. When I saw that hiding my shame was becoming impossible, I wanted to die. If I'm alive, if I wrote an infamous letter to my unhappy mother, if, in a word, I gave in to Hector's prayers, that's because he begged me in the name of my child…our child.

Monsieur Lecoq, who felt time was growing short, tried to make an observation. Laurence didn't hear him.

"But what does that matter!" she continued. "I loved him; I followed him; I belong to him. Fidelity, that's the only excuse for a sin like mine. I will do my duty. I can't claim to be innocent when my lover has committed a crime. I want half of the punishment."

She was speaking with such extraordinary animation that the Sûreté agent was despairing of calming her down, when they could hear two whistles coming from the street. Trémorel was coming back in. There was no longer time to hesitate. Lecoq, almost roughly, seized Laurence's arm.

"All that, Madame," he said in a harsh tone, "you can tell to the judges. My orders concern only Master Trémorel. What's more, here's the arrest warrant."

At these words, he took out the warrant issued by Monsieur Domini and placed it on the table.

By exercising willpower, Laurence had become almost calm again.

"Will you please allow me a five minute interview with *Monsieur le comte de Trémorel?*" she asked.

Monsieur Lecoq trembled with joy. That question, he had foreseen it; he was waiting for it.

"Five minutes, all right," he responded. "But give up any hope of helping the accused escape. The house is surrounded. Look down in the courtyard and in the street. You will see my men lying in wait. Moreover, I'm going to stay over there, in the next room."

They could hear the Count's steps on the stairway.

"There's Hector," Laurence said. "Quickly, very quickly, hide."

And as they were disappearing, she added, so low that the Sûreté agent didn't hear it: "Don't worry. We won't escape." She closed the door; it was just in time. Hector came in. He was paler than death. His eyes had a terrible expression of distraction.

"We're lost," he said. "They're following us. See, this letter I've just received. It wasn't written by the man whose signature's on it. He told me so. Come, let's leave, let's get out of this house…"

Laurence crushed him with a look filled with hatred and contempt, and said:

"It's too late."

Her expression, her voice, were so extraordinary that Trémorel, despite his worry, was struck by it and asked:

"That's that?"

"They know everything. They know that you murdered your wife."

"That's a lie."

She shrugged.

"Eh, all right then, yes, it's true, yes, because I loved you so much."

"Really! Was it also because you loved me that you poisoned Sauvresy?"

He understood that he had actually been found out, that he had fallen into a trap, that someone had come, during his absence, and told Laurence everything. He didn't try to deny it.

"What can we do?" he exclaimed. "What's to be done?"

Laurence drew him toward her and in a trembling voice she murmured:

"Save the name of de Trémorel. There are guns here."

He drew back as if he had seen death itself.

"No," he said. "I can still get away, I can leave alone to go into hiding. You will come join me."

"I've already told you. It's too late. The police have surrounded the house. And you know it's prison or the scaffold."

"We can escape through the courtyard."

"It's guarded. Go look."

He ran to the window, saw Monsieur Lecoq's men and came back made hideous with terror, half mad.

"We can always try," he said, "wearing a disguise."

"Mad man! There's a policeman here. He's the one who left that arrest warrant on that table."

He saw that he was lost, with no way out.

"Then, do I have to die?"

"Yes, you have to, but before that, write an omission of your crimes. They may suspect innocent people."

He sat down mechanically, took the pen Laurence handed him, and wrote:

Near to appearing before God, I swear that I alone, and without accomplices, poisoned Sauvresy and killed the Countess de Trémorel, my wife.

When he had signed and dated it, Laurence opened one of the drawers of a bureau where there were pistols. Hector seized one; she took the other.

But, just as in the hotel in the past, just as in the bedroom of dying Sauvresy, Trémorel, at the moment of putting the weapon against his forehead, felt he lacked the courage. He was livid; his teeth were clacking. He was trembling to the point that he almost dropped the pistol.

"Laurence, my beloved," he stammered, "what will become of you?"

"Me! I've sworn that I would follow you everywhere and forever. Do you understand?"

"Ah! This is horrible," he still said. "I wasn't the one who poisoned Sauvresy. She did. There's proof. Maybe with a good lawyer..."

Monsieur Lecoq lost neither a word nor a gesture of that poignant scene. Willingly or unwillingly, who knows? He pushed the door, making noise.

Laurence believed the door was opening, that the policeman was coming back in, that Hector was going to fall into the hands of the police alive.

"Miserable coward!" she cried, putting the pistol back against his forehead, "fire, if not..."

He hesitated. There was again noise from the door. She fired. Trémorel fell dead. With a rapid movement, Laurence picked up the other pistol and had already turned it against herself, when Monsieur Lecoq dashed to her, snatching the weapon from her hands.

"Unhappy girl!" he exclaimed. "What do you mean to do?"

"To die. Can I live now?"

"Yes, you can live," the Sûreté agent answered. "And I can add more. You must live."

"I'm a lost woman."

"No, you're a poor child seduced by a scoundrel. You tell yourself you are very guilty. So be it. Live to make amends. Great sadness like yours has its mission in this life, a mission of devotion and of charity. Live, and the good that you do will make you again a part of life. You gave in to the deceptive promises of a scoundrel. Remember when you're rich that there are poor honest girls forced to sell themselves for a morsel of bread. Go to these unfortunate women. Take them out of debauchery and their honor will be yours also."

Monsieur Lecoq was watching Laurence while he was talking, and he saw he had reached her. Nevertheless, her eyes remained dry and had a disturbing luster.

"Besides," he said. "Your life isn't your own. You're a mother."

"Eh! It's for my child that I must now die, if I don't want to die of shame when he asks me who is his father."

"You will answer him, Madame, by showing him an honest man, by showing him an old friend, Monsieur Plantat, who is ready to give him his name."

The old Justice of the Peace was dying of anxiety. Nevertheless, he still had strength to say:

"Laurence, my beloved daughter. I beg you, accept..."

These simple words, spoken with infinite gentleness, finally softened the unhappy young girl and decided her. She burst into tears. She was saved.

Monsieur Lecoq immediately hurried to throw a shawl he had seen on a piece of furniture over Laurence's shoulders. Passing the young girl's arm under that of Père Plantat:

"Leave," he said to the old Justice of the Peace. "Take her away. My men have orders to let you pass. And Pâlot will give you his carriage."

"But where will we go?"

"To Orcival. Monsieur Courtois has been informed by my letter that his daughter is alive and he's expecting her."

Alone, having heard the carriage carrying Laurence and Père Plantat rolling away, the Sûreté agent went to stand over Trémorel's cadaver.

There, he said to himself, *is a scoundrel that I killed instead of arresting him and delivering him over to justice. Did I have the right to do that? No, but my conscience doesn't reproach me for anything. Therefore, I did the right thing.*

Chapter XXVIII

The same day as the death of Trémorel, La Ripaille and Guespin were released from prison. One received four thousand francs to buy a boat and a net with regulation mesh. The other received ten thousand francs, with the promise of a similar sum at the end of a year if he would return to establish himself in his own area. Two weeks later, to the great surprise of the Orcival gossips, who never knew the details of the story, Père Plantat married Mademoiselle Laurence Courtois and the same evening the newlyweds left for Italy, announcing they would stay there for at least a year.

As for Père Courtois, he has just put his beautiful domain at Orcival up for sale. He intends to get himself established in the south of France and is looking for a commune needing a good mayor.

Like everyone Monsieur Lecoq would have forgotten that affair at Valfeuillu, which remained very obscure for the public, if it hadn't happened that the other morning a notary came personally to bring him a very gracious letter from Laurence, and a big volume with stamps on it.

The papers in the big volume were none other than the titles to Père Plantat's beautiful house in Orcival "in its present state and contents, with its furniture, stable, sheds, garden, various things therein, and several acres of prairie around it."

"Oh! Marvels!" Monsieur Lecoq exclaimed. "I didn't help out ungrateful people! As this so seldom happens, I agree to become a land owner."

FILE 113

Chapter I

In the February 28, 186* evening newspapers, people read the following news item:

A very important robbery committed against an honorable banker of the capital, Monsieur André Fauvel, has excited the entire Rue de Provence neighborhood.

The police, as soon as notified, displayed its usual zeal and its investigations were crowned with success. Already, it is said, an employee of the establishment, the honorable P. B., has been arrested; everything seems to indicate that his accomplices will soon be in the hands of the police.

For four whole days, all of Paris could talk of nothing but this robbery. Then serious events took place: a circus acrobat broke his leg, a young lady made her debut in a minor theater, and the news item of February 28 was forgotten. But this time the newspapers had been badly, or at least inaccurately, informed—perhaps on purpose. It's true that a sum of 350,000 francs had been taken from Monsieur André Fauvel's establishment, but not in the way stated. An employee had, in fact, been at first arrested; but they hadn't lodged any definite charge against him. This theft of unusual importance remained, if not unexplainable, at least unexplained.

In addition, here are the facts, such as they are found with meticulous exactness in the verbal testimony of the investigation.

Chapter II

The André Fauvel Bank, Number 87, Rue de Provence, is very important, and thanks to its numerous personnel, almost has the appearance of a ministry. The offices are situated on the first floor, and the windows, which look out onto the street, are fitted with bars big enough and close enough together to discourage all attempts at a break-in. A large glassed door gives access into an immense vestibule, where three or four guards are stationed from morning until night. On the right are the rooms where the public is admitted and a corridor which leads to the principal cashier's counter. The offices of correspondence, debt registry, and general accounting are on the left. There can be seen a little glassed court at the back, off of which open seven or eight cashier counters. Unused in ordinary business, they are indispensable at certain repayment dates.

Monsieur André Fauvel's office is on the second floor, at the back of his beautiful living quarters. This office communicates directly with the bank offices by way of a little narrow and very steep black stairway, which leads to the room occupied by the head cashier. That bank room, called 'the vault,' is safe from forceful entry, almost from a veritable siege. Shut off as it is, it is neither more nor less vulnerable than the underwater monitor, the *Ironclad*, used during the American Civil War. Thick sheets of steel cover the doors and the partition where the cashier's work is done, and a strong grill obstructs the opening to the fireplace. There, sealed into the wall by enormous iron clamps, is located the main safe. It is one of those fantastic and formidable furnishings which sets to dreaming the poor devil whose entire fortune is easily held in a wallet.

This masterpiece of the Becquet Company, this safe is two meters high and one-and-a-half meters wide. Made entirely of forged iron, it is triple plated, and the interior has separate compartments in case of fire. A small and pretty key opens this storage unit. But to open it, the key is the least of things. Five discs of movable steel, engraved with all the letters of the alphabet, make up, most importantly, the ingenious and strong closing apparatus. Before thinking about putting the key into the lock, it's necessary to place the letters on the discs in the same order as when it was closed. Thus, at Monsieur Fauvel's bank, as everywhere else, the safe is closed with a word which is changed from time to time. Only the head of the bank and the main cashier know this word. In addition, they each have a key. With such a safe you must sleep peacefully, even if you possess more diamonds than the Duke of Brunswick. It seems you could run only one danger, that of forgetting the word that is the 'Open Sesame' of the iron door.

On the morning of February 28, the employees of the Fauvel Bank arrived at their jobs as usual. At 9:00 a.m. when everyone was at work, a middle-aged man, very tanned, with a military air, and in full mourning, presented himself at the office in front of the safe where five or six employees were working. He asked to speak to the head cashier. He was answered that the head cashier hadn't yet arrived, and besides the safe didn't open until 10:00 a.m., as was announced in large letters placed in the vestibule. This answer seemed to disconcert and annoy the newly arrived man to the greatest degree.

"I thought," he said in a dry tone bordering on impertinence, "that I would find someone to speak to, having agreed yesterday with Monsieur Fauvel. I am Marquis Louis de Clameran, owner of the Oloron Ironworks. I have come to withdraw 300,000 francs deposited in the bank by my brother. I'm his heir. It's surprising that orders haven't been given…"

Neither the title of the owner of the ironworks nor his reasons seemed to touch the employees.

"The cashier hasn't come in yet," they repeated. "We can't do anything."

"Then let me see Monsieur Fauvel."

There was a certain hesitation, but a young employee named Cavaillon, who was working near the window, spoke up.

"The boss is always out at this hour," he answered.

"Then I'll come back," said Monsieur de Clameran.

And he left as he had entered, without saying goodbye, or even touching the border of his hat.

"Not polite, that client," said the young Cavaillon fellow, "but he's not lucky, because there's Prosper now."

The head cashier of the Fauvel Bank, Prosper Bertomy, was a tall, handsome, thirty-year-old fellow, blond, blue-eyed, and dressed with studied elegance in the latest fashion. He would have been really very attractive if he hadn't overdone the English affectation, (making himself cold and formal whenever he liked), and if a certain self-satisfied air hadn't spoiled his naturally pleasant face.

"Ah, here you are," exclaimed Cavaillon, "Somebody has already come in asking for you."

"Who? An ironworks owner, wasn't it?"

"Exactly."

"Well! He'll come back. Since I knew I would come in late this morning, I set up things yesterday."

Prosper had opened his office while talking and he went in, closing the door after him.

"He's got it made," exclaimed one of the employees. "The boss has made a scene to him twenty times because he comes in late. He doesn't let that bother him. He acts as if he has some special advantage."

"He is perfectly right, because he gets everything he wants from the boss!"

"Besides, how could he arrive early in the morning, a fellow who leads a hellish life, who's out all night? Have you noticed? This morning he looks like some dead man who's been dug up."

"He's been gambling again, like last month. I know through Couturier that in a single night he lost 1,500 francs."

"Has he done his work any less well?" interrupted Cavaillon. "If you were in his place…"

He stopped short. The door to the vault had just opened and the cashier came out staggering

"Robbed!" he stammered. "I've been robbed!"

Prosper's face, his hoarse voice, and the trembling which shook him, showed such terrible agony that all the employees rose at one time and ran to him. He let himself almost fall into their arms. He could no longer stand; he was sick. He had to sit down. Nevertheless, his colleagues surrounded him. They questioned him all at once, pressed him to explain himself.

"Robbed?" they were saying, "Where? How? Who?"

Little by little Prosper came to himself.

"They took everything I had in the vault," he answered. "Everything?" "Yes. Three bundles of 1,000 francs in 100 franc bills, and one of 50. The four packages were wrapped in a piece of paper and tied together."

As fast as a bolt of lightning, the news of a robbery spread throughout the bank. The curious ran from every direction. The office was full.

"Tell us," young Cavaillon asked Prosper, "did they force the vault?"

"No, it's intact."

"Well, then…"

"Then it's no less a fact that yesterday evening I had 350,000 francs and I can no longer find them this morning."

Everyone was silent. Only one old employee did not join in the general consternation.

"Don't lose your head this way, Monsieur Bertomy," he said. "Think about the fact that the boss must have done something with the cash."

The unhappy cashier suddenly straightened up. He clung to that idea. "Yes!" he exclaimed. "That's it. You're right. It must've been the boss."

Then, reflecting, "No," he said in a tone of deep discouragement. "No, that's not possible. Never! In the five years I've been at the cashier's job, never has Monsieur Fauvel opened it without me. The two or three times he's needed cash, he waited for me or had me sent for rather than touch it in my absence."

"That doesn't matter," objected young Cavaillon, "Before giving up hope, he must be told."

But Monsieur André Fauvel had already been alerted. An office boy had gone up to his office and told him what had happened. At the moment when Cavaillon was suggesting that they go look for him, he appeared. Monsieur André Fauvel was a man of about fifty, of medium height, with graying hair. He was rather large, somewhat stooped like all intense workers, and he had a habit of waddling when he walked. Not one of his actions ever belied the expression of goodness on his face. He had a candid air, lively and frank eyes, red and very wide lips. Born in the Aix region, whenever he was excited he fell back into a slight Provençal accent, which gave a particular flavor to his wit—because he was witty.

The news the boy brought had excited him. Ordinarily very red, he had become completely pale.

"What have I been told?" he asked the employees who stepped aside respectfully before him. "What's happened?"

Monsieur Fauvel's voice gave the cashier the artificial energy of great crises. The decisive and dreadful moment had come. He rose and stepped forward toward his employer.

"Sir," he began, "since I needed the disbursement you know about for this morning, yesterday evening I sent to the Bank to get 350,000 francs."

"Why yesterday, Monsieur?" interrupted the banker. "It seems to me I've warned you a hundred times to wait until the exact day."

"I know that, Monsieur. I was wrong, but the damage is done. Yesterday, I locked up this cash. It's disappeared, and nevertheless, the safe has not been forced open."

"But you're crazy!" exclaimed Monsieur Fauvel. "You're dreaming!"

These few words crushed all hope. Just the horror of the situation gave Prosper not the logic of a thought-out resolution, but that sort of stupid indifference that follows unexpected catastrophes. It was almost without any apparent worry that he answered.

"I'm not crazy, unfortunately; I'm not dreaming. I'm telling what has happened."

And that lack of emotion in such a moment seemed to exasperate Monsieur Fauvel. He seized Prosper by the arm and shook him violently.

"Speak!" he shouted. "Speak! Who do you think opened the safe?"

"I can't say."

"You and I are the only ones who know the word! Only you and I have a key!"

That was a formal accusation. At least all the listeners understood it to be such. However, the cashier's frightful calm didn't contradict it. He gently released himself from his employer's grasp, and, very slowly he said:

"In fact, Monsieur, I'm the only one who could've taken that money."

"Wretched man!"

Prosper stepped back, and with his eyes stubbornly fixed on Monsieur Fauvel's eyes, he added:

"Or you!"

The banker made a threatening gesture, and one doesn't know what might have happened if there wasn't suddenly heard the noise of a discussion at the door opening onto the vestibule. A client was absolutely insisting on entering in spite of the protestations of the guards, and in fact he entered. It was Monsieur de Clameran.

All the employees who were gathered in the office stood immobile, frozen. The solemn silence was profound. It was easy to see that some terrible question was being debated among all the men, a question of life or death.

The ironworks owner didn't stop to observe anything. He came forward, his hat on his head, and in the same impertinent tone he had used earlier, he said, "It's after ten o'clock, Messieurs."

Nobody answered. Monsieur de Clameran was going to continue, when he noticed the banker, whom he had not seen. He walked straight to him.

"Finally! Monsieur!" he exclaimed. "I find you, and that's really very fortunate. I have already presented myself once this morning. The safe wasn't open. The cashier hadn't arrived. You weren't here."

"You're wrong, Monsieur. I was in my office."

"I was assured to the contrary, however, and over there, that's the gentleman who confirmed it to me."And with his finger, the ironworks owner pointed to Cavaillon. "Not only was the safe closed, but they refused to let me enter the offices. I had to push past the guards. Are you going to tell me, yes or no, if I can withdraw my cash...?"

Monsieur Fauvel listened, trembling with rage. From being pale, he had become crimson. However, he maintained his self-control.

"I would be obliged, Monsieur," he said in a dull voice, "If you would allow me a delay."

"It seems to me that you told me..."

"Yes, yesterday. But this morning, just now, I've learned that I'm the victim of a robbery of 350,000 francs."

Monsieur de Clameran bowed ironically.

"And will it be necessary to wait a long time?"

"The time to go to the Bank."[27]

Then turning his shoulder to the ironworks owner, he went back to his head cashier.

"Prepare a note," he told him. "Send it quickly. Take a carriage in order to withdraw the available funds from the Bank."

Prosper didn't move.

---

[27] Monsieur Fauvel's bank is a small, privately-owned merchant bank, as were all the XIX century French banks, called "Maisons de Haute Banque." Isaac Mallet, a French banker who had emigrated to Switzerland, returned to France and with his son, Guillaume Mallet and other Swiss bankers, founded the Banque de France in 1799 to fund Napoleon. Representatives of the private mercantile banks, the Maisons de Haute Banque, such as Monsieur Fauvel's bank, sat on the Board of Directors. The central bank, or Banque de France, was nationalized in 1936. A member of the Mallet family sat on the Board of Directors throughout all that time. This is the Bank to which Monsieur André Fauvel is to send for a replacement for the missing 350,000 francs.

"Did you hear me?" repeated the banker, almost ready to explode.

The head cashier trembled. You would have said that he was waking from a dream.

"It's useless to send," he replied coldly. "Monsieur's credit is for 300,000 francs and we have only a 100,000 francs remaining in the Bank."

You would have sworn that Monsieur de Clameran expected that answer, because he murmured, "Naturally."

He said only this. But his voice, his gesture, and the expression on his face all clearly indicated: "The comedy is well carried out, but it's an act, and I'm not fooled."

Alas! While the ironworks owner thus brutally revealed his opinion, the employees, after Prosper's answer, didn't know what to think. That was because Paris, at this time, had just experienced startling financial crises. The uncertainty brought about by speculation had shaken old and solid banks. Some of the proudest honorable men had been seen going from door to door begging for aid and assistance. Credit, that rare bird of calm and peaceful times, hesitated to light, and was ready to open its wings and fly away at the least suspicious noise. Because of this, the idea of an act agreed on in advance by the banker and his head cashier could very well present itself to the minds of people. If not already accusing, they were at least very ready to be aware of all the contrivances, which, helping to gain time, might bring about rescue.

Monsieur Fauvel had too much experience not to guess the impression produced by Prosper's words. He read the most mortifying doubt in all eyes.

"Oh! Be calm, Monsieur," he said quickly to Monsieur de Clameran. "My bank has other resources. Please be patient. I'll be back."

He left, went up to his office, and at the end of five minutes, he reappeared, holding in his hand a letter and a stack of stock certificates.

"Quickly, Couturier," he said to one of his employees, "Take my carriage that they're harnessing up now, and go with Monsieur to Monsieur de Rothschild's bank. Give him this letter and these certificates here, and in exchange, they will count out 300,000 francs that you will give to Monsieur."

The owner of the ironworks was visibly disappointed. He seemed to want to excuse his impertinence.

"Please believe me, Monsieur, that I had no intention of giving offense to you. We have done business together for years, and never..."

"That's enough, Monsieur," interrupted the banker. "There's no need for your excuses. In business, there are neither acquaintances nor friends. I owe you. I'm not able to pay. You're...pressing. That's as it should be. You're within your rights. Go with my clerk. He'll give you your cash."

Then, turning toward the employees drawn by curiosity, the banker spoke, "As for you, Messieurs, please go back to your duties."

In a moment, the room in front of the cashier's office was empty. Only the clerks who worked there remained. Seated in front of their desks, their noses in their paper work, they seemed absorbed by their jobs. While still under the pressure of the rapid events which had followed one after the other, Monsieur André Fauvel was walking up and down, agitated, feverish, and letting out some low exclamations at intervals. Prosper himself had remained standing, leaning against the partition. Pale and crushed, his eyes fixed, he seemed to have lost even the ability to think. Then, after a long silence, the banker stopped in front of Prosper. He had made up his mind and taken a position.

"We must have a talk," he said. "Let's go into your office."

The head cashier obeyed without saying a word, almost mechanically, and his employer followed him, taking care to close the door. Nothing in this office indicated that criminals not familiar with the bank had been there. Everything was in place. Not a paper had been moved. The strong box was open, and on the upper level there were a certain number of gold rolls, forgotten or disdained by the robbers. Not troubling to examine anything, Monsieur Fauvel took a chair and told his head cashier to sit down. He had regained complete control of himself and his face had resumed his usual expression.

"Now that we're alone, Prosper," he began, "do you have anything to tell me?"

The head cashier trembled, as if that question astonished him.

"Nothing that I haven't told you, Monsieur."

"What! Nothing? You persist in sticking to a ridiculous, absurd fairytale that nobody will believe. That's madness. Confess to me; there's your salvation. I'm your employer, that's true. But I'm also and above all your friend, your best friend. I can't forget that fifteen years ago your father entrusted you to me, and since that time I've done nothing but pride myself on your good and loyal services. Yes, you've been in my house fifteen years. I was beginning then to build up my fortune, and you've seen it grow stone by stone, layer by layer. And to the extent that I became richer, I was careful to raise your own position. Still very young, you are nonetheless the oldest of my employees. I added to your salary as we took stock at each stage.

Prosper had never heard his employer express himself in such a gentle, such a paternal voice. His features showed profound surprise.

"Answer me," Monsieur Fauvel went on. "Haven't I always been like a father to you? From the first day that you came to me, my house has been open to you. I wished my family to be yours. For a long time you've lived like my son with my two sons and my niece Madeleine. But you got tired of this happy life. One day, about a year ago, you began to turn from us, and since…"

Memories of this past brought up by the banker came crowding into the mind of the unfortunate head cashier. Little by little he was moved. Finally, he broke into tears, hiding his face in his hands.

"You can tell your father everything."

Monsieur André Fauvel, touched by Prosper's emotion, began again. "Don't be afraid. A father doesn't offer to pardon, but to forget. Don't I know the terrible temptations that can overwhelm a young man in a city like Paris? There are some covetous desires which break down the most solid honesty. There are times of bewilderment and vertigo when one is no longer himself, when one acts like a fool, like a madman, without being, you might say, conscious of his actions. Speak, Prosper, speak."

"Ah! And what do you want me to say?"

"The truth. A really honest man can fall, but he can get up and atone for his fault. Say to me: 'Yes, I was lead astray, dazzled. The sight of those masses of gold that I move about troubled my mind. I am young. I have passions!'"

"Me!" murmured Prosper. "Me!"

"Poor child!" the banker said sadly. "Do you really think I don't know about your life, during the year since you deserted my household? Then you don't understand that all your colleagues are jealous of you, that they don't forgive you for earning 12,000 francs a year. You've never committed a folly that I haven't been alerted to by an anonymous letter. I can tell you the number of nights you spent gambling and the amounts you lost. Oh! Envy has good eyes and keen ears. I know how much stock should be put in cowardly denunciations, but I had to inform myself. It's only right that I should know how the man lives to whom I entrust my fortune and my honor."

Prosper tried to make a gesture of protestation.

"Yes, my honor," Monsieur Fauvel insisted in a voice that the resentment of an endured humiliation made more vibrant. "Yes, my credit, which might have been compromised today by that man. Do you know what the funds that they're going to give to Monsieur de Clameran are going to cost me? And the stock certificates that I'm sacrificing? I might not have had them. You didn't know about them."

The banker stopped, as if he expected an admission. It didn't come.

"Come now, Prosper, have courage. Straighten up! I'm going to leave and you're going to look into the safe again. I'll wager that in your trouble you didn't look around very well. This evening I'll come back, and I'm sure that during the day you will have found, if not the 350,000 francs, then at least the major part of that sum…and tomorrow neither you nor I will remember this false alarm."

Monsieur Fauvel had already risen and was advancing toward the door. Prosper held him back by the arm.

"Your generosity is useless, Monsieur," he said in a bitter tone. "Having taken nothing, I can't give anything back. I have searched carefully. The bank notes have been stolen."

"But by whom, poor fool! By whom?"

"By everything that's sacred in the world, I swear it wasn't me."

A rush of blood turned the banker's forehead purple.

"Wretched man!" he exclaimed, "What do you mean to say? Therefore it was I?"

Prosper lowered his head and didn't reply.

"Ah! That's how it is," continued Monsieur Fauvel, unable to contain himself. "You dare...then between the two of us, Monsieur Prosper Bertomy, the law will decide! God is my witness that I've done everything to save you. What's going to happen to you is only up to you. I've asked the Commissioner of Police to please come here. He's to wait for me in my office. Must I have him brought in?"

Prosper made the gesture of frightful resignation as of a man who gives up, and in a stifled voice he answered, "Do it!"

The banker was near the door. He opened it. After throwing a last look at his head cashier, he shouted to an office boy, "Anselme, ask Monsieur the Police Commissioner to be good enough to come down."

Chapter III

If there is any man in the world that no event can excite or surprise, always on guard against lies and appearances, capable of admitting everything and of explaining everything, it is certainly a Paris Police Commissioner. While the judge, from the height of his tribunal bench adjusts which articles of the Law Code dictate to the acts, the Commissioner of Police observes and looks over all the odious facts that the law wouldn't be able to touch. He is the obligated confidant of details of infamy, of domestic crimes, of ignominies tolerated. Perhaps when he was first put in charge, he still had some illusions. After a year though, he no longer had any. If he didn't absolutely despise humankind, it was because often, besides abominations certain not to be punished, he discovered sublime generosities which remained without recompense. It was because of this, therefore, that if he saw impudent scoundrels steal public respect, he consoled himself by thinking about the modest and obscure heroes he knew.

What he had thought should happen had been thwarted so many times that he'd come to the most complete skepticism. He believed in nothing, no more in evil than in absolute good, no more in virtue than in vice. He had necessarily arrived at the heart-breaking conclusion that there are not men, only events.

Informed by the office boy, the police commissioner called by Monsieur Fauvel was not long in appearing. It was in the calmest way, it must be said, in the most indifferent way, that he came into the office. A short man, dressed completely in black with a string tie around a dubious false collar, followed him. The banker hardly took the trouble to greet him.

"Without a doubt, Monsieur," he began, "you have been informed about the painful circumstances which forced me to call you in."

"They told me it's a matter of a robbery."

"Yes, Monsieur, an odious, inexplicable theft committed in the office where we are, from that safe you see there, opened, and to which only my head cashier—" and he pointed out Prosper, "has the code word and the key."

That statement seemed to draw the unfortunate head cashier out of his gloomy stupor.

"Pardon me, Monsieur Commissioner," he said in a low voice, "my employer, he also has the key and the code word."

"Of course, that goes without saying."

So from the first words, the Commissioner had the picture. Obviously these two men were accusing each other. By their own admission, one of them must be the guilty man. And one was the head of a very important bank, the other a simple cashier. One was the employer, the other the employee. But the Commissioner of Police was much too accustomed to hiding his impressions for anything on the outside to betray what he was thinking. Not a muscle of his face budged. Only becoming more serious, he alternately observed the cashier and Monsieur Fauvel, as if from their expressions, or from their attitudes, he could draw some useful induction. Prosper, still very pale and as beaten down as possible, was seated in his chair. His arms hung down, inert the length of his body. The banker, on the contrary, was standing, red and excited with his eyes shining, expressing himself with an extraordinary violence.

"And the importance of the amount taken is enormous," continued Monsieur Fauvel. "A fortune has been stolen from me, 350,000 francs! This theft can have disastrous consequences for me. In a moment like this, lacking that sum, the credit of the richest bank may be compromised."

"I certainly understand it. The date a payment is due…"

"Well! Monsieur, it was precisely today that I had a considerable withdrawal due."

"Ah! Really!"

It was impossible to misunderstand the Police Commissioner's tone. A suspicion, the first, passed through his mind. The banker understood that. He trembled and continued very quickly.

"I have met my commitments, but at a disagreeable sacrifice. I must add that if my orders had been carried out, those 350,000 francs wouldn't have been found in the safe."

"How's that?"

"I don't like to have large sums in my bank overnight. My head cashier had instructions always to wait until the last hour to send for the funds deposited with the Bank of France. I had distinctly forbidden him to keep anything in the safe overnight."

"Do you hear that?" the Commissioner asked Prosper.

"Yes, Monsieur," answered the cashier. "What Monsieur Fauvel says is perfectly true."

Following that explanation, the Police Commissioner's suspicion, far from being confirmed, dissipated.

"So," he began again. "A theft was committed. By whom? Did the thief come from the outside?"

The banker hesitated a moment.

"I don't believe so," he finally answered.

"And I," declared Prosper, "am sure that's not the case."

The Commissioner of Police was ready for these answers. He expected them. But he was not ready at that exact moment to follow up all the consequences.

"However," he objected, "we must take everything into account." And speaking to the man accompanying him, "Look and see, Monsieur Fanferlot," he said, "if you can't discover some clue that escaped the attention of these Messieurs."

Monsieur Fanferlot, called 'the Squirrel,' owed the nickname he was proud of to a tremendous agility. Thin and puny in appearance despite his muscles of steel, seeing him buttoned up to his chin in his straight black frock coat, you could've taken him for a bailiff's sixth level clerk. His facial features were disturbing. He had an odiously turned-up nose, thin lips, and little round eyes of annoying mobility. Employed for five years with the Sûreté Police, Fanferlot had a burning desire to distinguish himself, to make a name for himself. He was ambitious. Alas! Occasions to show his expertise were always lacking. Already, before the Commissioner had spoken, he had pried about everywhere, studied the doors, knocked on the partitions, examined the counter, and stirred up the cinders in the fireplace.

"It seems to me very difficult," he answered, "for an outsider to have gotten in here."

He took a turn around the office.

"That door," he demanded, "is it closed in the evening?"

"Always, with a key."

"And who keeps that key?"

"The office guard, to whom I give it every evening as I leave," Prosper answered.

"That guard," added Monsieur Fauvel, "sleeps in the entry hall on a fold-up portable camp bed that he puts down every evening and takes up every morning."

"And is he here?"

"Yes, Monsieur," answered the banker. On that, he opened the door and called out, "Anselme!"

A completely trusted man, that guard had been In Monsieur Fauvel's service for ten years. Certainly, he could not be suspected. He knew that; but the thought of a robbery is terrible, and he was trembling like a leaf when he came forward.

"Did you sleep last night in the adjoining room?" the Commissioner of Police asked him.

"Yes, Monsieur, as usual."

"What time did you go to bed?"

"Toward 10:30 p.m. I spent the evening in the café next door, with Monsieur's valet."

"And you didn't hear any noise last night?"

"None! And nevertheless I sleep so lightly that if Monsieur sometimes comes down to the safe when I'm asleep, the sound of his footsteps wakes me."

"Monsieur Fauvel often comes down to the vault at night?"

"No, Monsieur, on the contrary, very rarely."

"Did he come down last night?"

"No, Monsieur. I am perfectly certain, having hardly closed my eyes because of the coffee I drank with the chamber valet."

"That's fine, my friend," said the Commissioner of Police. "You may leave."

Anselme left. Monsieur Fanferlot started looking around again. He had opened the door to the banker's little staircase. "Where does that stairway lead?"

"To my office," Monsieur Fauvel answered.

"Isn't that where they took me when I arrived?" asked the Commissioner.

"Exactly."

"I'll need to see it," declared Monsieur Fanferlot. "I'd like to study that exit."

"Nothing is easier," Monsieur Fauvel said eagerly. "Come Messieurs; come too, Prosper."

Monsieur Fauvel's private office had two rooms. The first room was a sumptuously furnished waiting room. Then there was a working office, having as its total furnishings an immense desk, three or four leather armchairs, and on each side of the fireplace a secretary and a file cabinet. Those two rooms had only three doors: one to the hidden staircase, the other opening into the banker's bedroom, the third opening on to the landing of the main staircase. Clients and visitors entered and left through the last one.

With a glance, Monsieur Fanferlot inventoried the room where the desk was located. He seemed disappointed, like a man who had flattered himself with the hopes of seizing some clue and finds nothing.

"Let's see the other side," he said.

On that, he went into the waiting room, followed by the banker and the Commissioner of Police. Prosper remained alone in the office. The confusion of his thoughts was so great he couldn't even understand that from minute to minute his situation was becoming more serious. He had asked for, and he had accepted, the battle with his employer. That battle was in progress, and henceforth it no longer depended on his will to stop it or stop the consequences. Without a truce or mercy they were now going to fight, using every weapon until one of the two succumbed, paying for his defeat with his honor. In the eyes of the law, who would be the innocent one?

Alas! The unfortunate employee felt only too well how little the chances were equal, and the feeling of his inferiority overwhelmed him. Never, no never, did he believe his employer would follow through on his threats. Because after all, in a criminal proceeding like the one which was beginning, Monsieur Fauvel had as much to risk, and more to lose, than his employee. Seated in an armchair near the fireplace, he was sunk in the gloomiest of thoughts, when the door to the banker's bedroom opened. A remarkably beautiful young girl appeared on the threshold.

She was rather tall, svelte, and her morning dress, held together above the hips by a silk cord, showed all the beauties of her shape. Brunette, with large, deep, gentle eyes, her complexion had the pale, uniform olive of the white camellia. Her beautiful dark hair, still in disorder and escaping from the light tortoise shell comb holding it, was falling in a profusion in bunches of curls over her shoulders in the most exquisite design. That was Monsieur Fauvel's niece, Madeleine, of whom he had spoken earlier.

Seeing Prosper in this office where she probably believed she would meet only her uncle, she couldn't hold back an expression of surprise.

"Oh!"

Prosper himself had risen as if he had received an electric shock. His completely dull eyes shone suddenly, as if he had encountered a messenger of hope.

"Madeleine!" he exclaimed. "Madeleine!"

The young girl had become redder than a peony. She seemed at first about to leave; she had even stepped backward. But as Prosper moved toward her, a feeling stronger than her will came over her and she extended her hand, which he took and clasped respectfully. They remained facing each other in this way, immobile, breathless, and so full of emotion that they both lowered their heads, fearing to encounter each other's looks. They had so much to say to each other that, and not knowing where to begin, they were silent. Finally, Madeleine murmured in a hardly audible voice:

"You, Prosper, you!"

Just these words broke the charm. The cashier dropped the very white hand he was holding, and in the bitterest tone he answered.

"Yes, it's really Prosper, your childhood companion, accused today of the most cowardly and the most shameful theft. Prosper, that your uncle has just delivered over to the law. Before the end of the day he'll be arrested and thrown in prison."

Madeleine made a gesture of the most sincere fright. Her eyes expressed the deepest compassion.

"*Grand Dieu!*" she exclaimed. "What do you mean?"

"What? Mademoiselle, don't you know about it? Mademoiselle, your aunt and your cousins have said nothing to you?"

"Nothing. I have hardly seen my cousins this morning and my aunt is so ill that I'm very concerned. I've come to find my uncle. But please, speak, talk to me, tell me what's happened to you."

The cashier hesitated. Perhaps he thought about opening his heart to Madeleine, letting her know his most secret thoughts. A memory from the past crossed his heart, freezing his confidence. He sadly shook his head and said:

"Thank you, Mademoiselle, for this proof of interest, the last, probably, that I'll have from you. But allow me by being silent, to spare you sorrow, to spare me the pain of blushing before you."

Madeleine interrupted him with a commanding gesture.

"I want to know," she stated.

"Alas! Mademoiselle," answered the cashier. "You'll know my misfortune and my shame only too soon, and then, yes, then, you'll applaud what you did."

She wanted to insist. Instead of commanding, she begged, but Prosper's decision was made.

"Your uncle is over there, Mademoiselle," he continued, "with the Commissioner and a policeman. They're going to return. Please, leave, so they don't see you."

While speaking, he gently pushed her away. Although she resisted a little, he managed to close the door. It was just in time. The Commissioner of Police and Monsieur Fauvel came back in. They had visited the waiting room, examined the main staircase, and they hadn't been able to find out anything about what had happened in the office. But Fanferlot had listened on their behalf. That excellent bloodhound hadn't let the cashier out of his sight. He had said to himself: "He's going to think he's alone. His expression will speak. I'll surprise a smile, or see a blink of his eyes, which will enlighten me."

Leaving Monsieur Fauvel and the Commissioner to their investigations, he stationed himself on the lookout. He'd seen the door open and Madeleine enter. He'd lost neither a gesture nor a word of the rapid scene which had just taken place between Prosper and the young girl. That scene wasn't anything, that's true, each word leaving concealed something to be guessed. But Monsieur Fanferlot was clever enough to complete all the things implied. He had yet only a suspicion; but a suspicion was something, a hypothesis, or a point of departure. He was so prompt to build a whole plan on the smallest incident. It even seemed to him that, in the past of these people he didn't know, he could see a complete drama. This was because, if the Commissioner of Police was a skeptic, the policeman had faith. He believed in wickedness.

He was thinking: "Here's how it is. The young man loves that young girl. She is, I must say, very pretty; and he is, on his side, very handsome. He is loved in return. Their love affair displeased the banker. I can understand that. And not knowing how to get rid of that unwelcome lover honestly, he made up this accusation. He's rather ingenious."

So, in Monsieur Fanferlot's thoughts, the banker had simply robbed himself; and the cashier, innocent, was a victim of the most odious plot. But that Sûreté policeman's conviction could hardly, for the moment at least, help Prosper. Fanferlot, the ambitious man who wants to succeed and who is thirsty for a reputation, decided to keep his conjectures totally to himself:

"I'm going to let others set things in motion," he said to himself, "and I'll work alone from my side. Later, when thanks to unceasing espionage and by means of patient investigation I've put together all the elements of a beautiful and perfect condemnation, I'll unmask the criminal."

Moreover, he was beaming. He had finally found the crime he had so looked for which must make him famous. There was nothing missing here, not the odious circumstances, not the mystery, nor the romantic and sentimental element represented by Prosper and Madeleine. To succeed seemed difficult, almost impossible; but Fanferlot 'the Squirrel' was confident of his genius as an investigator. However, the visit to the upper floor had finished and they were coming back down to Prosper's office.

The Commissioner of Police, so calm when he came in, was becoming more and more concerned. The time to take a position was approaching, and he was still hesitating. You could see that.

"You can see, Messieurs," he began, "our search has only confirmed our first impressions."

Monsieur Fauvel and the cashier made the same sign of agreement.

"And you, Monsieur Fanferlot," continued the Commissioner, "what do you think?"

The Sûreté agent didn't answer. Busy studying the lock of the safe with a magnifying glass, he gave signs of the greatest surprise. He'd probably just discovered something of the greatest importance. Apparently struck with a similar emotion, Monsieur Fauvel, Prosper, and the Commissioner of Police rose quickly and surrounded the Sûreté agent.

"You've found something?" asked the banker.

Fanferlot turned around as if annoyed. He reproached himself for not having hidden his impressions better.

"Oh!" he threw out carelessly, "What I've found isn't very important."

"Still, may we know…" insisted Prosper.

"I've just simply acquired the proof that this safe has very recently been opened or closed, I don't know which, with some violence and great haste."

"How's that?" asked the Police Commissioner, who'd become very attentive.

"Here, Monsieur, look, on the lock. Do you see that scratch which comes away from the lock?"

The Commissioner took the magnifying glass which the Sûreté agent had just used, bent over and in his turn, examined the safe carefully for a long time. It was very easy to see a slight scratch which had lifted a layer of varnish the length of twelve or fifteen centimeters from top to bottom.

"I see," said the Commissioner, "but what does that prove?"

"Oh! Nothing at all," answered Fanferlot. "That's exactly what I was saying."

Yes, in fact, Fanferlot was saying that; but he wasn't thinking that. That scratch—recent, it couldn't be denied—had significance for him which escaped the others. He found in it a confirmation of his suspicions. He was telling himself that the cashier, if he had taken millions, had no reason to be in a hurry. On the other hand, the banker coming down to empty his own safe at night, on tiptoe for fear of arousing the guard sleeping nearby, had a thousand reasons to tremble, to hurry, and to remove the key hastily. Sliding the key out of the lock had scratched the varnish.

Resolved to untangle by himself the tangled skein of that affair, the Sûreté agent had to keep his conjectures to himself, just as he had kept silent about the interview between Madeleine and Prosper. What's more, he was in a hurry, as much as he could be, to cause that incident to be forgotten.

"To sum it all up," he continued, speaking to the Commissioner of Police, "I declare that no one from the outside was able to come in here. Besides which, that vault is perfectly intact. No suspect pressure was exerted on the moveable discs. I can confirm that no one tried to use any tool to break the lock. Nobody tried to pick the lock. Those who broke in knew the word and had the key."

Such a formal confirmation from a man he knew to be clever put an end to the Commissioner of Police's hesitations.

"This being said," he stated, "I have nothing more to do but to ask Monsieur Fauvel for a moment's interview."

"I'm at your service, Monsieur," answered the banker.

Prosper understood. He deliberately placed his hat in full view on a table, as if to show he didn't intend to leave, and passed into the neighboring office. Fanferlot also left, but the Police Commissioner had had time to give him a signal that the others hadn't seen, and to which he responded. The signal meant, 'You'll watch that man for me.'

The Sûreté agent had no need for that encouragement for close surveillance. His suspicions were too vague and his desire to succeed too strong for him to let Prosper out of his sight, and to cease to study him. That's why, when entering the office following the footsteps of the cashier, he went to stand watch at the back in the shadows. On a bench, seemingly trying to find a comfortable position, he turned and turned, yawned so as to almost dislocate his jaw, and finally closed his eyes.

Prosper himself had gone to sit down in front of a desk in the place of one of the employees who was absent for the moment. The others were burning to know the result of the short investigation. The most ardent curiosity shone in their eyes; however, they didn't dare question him. Not being able to hold back any longer, little Cavaillon, the cashier's defender, risked asking:

"Well?" he hesitatingly asked.

Prosper shrugged.

"They don't know."

Was this a consciousness of his innocence, a certainty of avoiding punishment, and no concern for the result? The employees noticed, not without profound astonishment, that the cashier had again resumed his habitual attitude, that sort of cold haughtiness which kept people at a distance and which had made him so many enemies in the bank. Of his earlier emotion which was so great that it was pitiful to see, he had kept no trace; but he had a greater pallor, a darker circle around his red eyes, and disordered hair still humid from the cold sweat of fear. A stranger entering would never have supposed that this young man, seated there mechanically playing with a pencil, had been struck with an accusation of theft and was going to be arrested. Soon, however, he stopped moving about the pencil he was holding. He reached for a piece of paper and hastily scribbled some lines on it.

Fanferlot 'the Squirrel,' whose hearing and sight functioned miraculously despite his sound sleep, thought, *"Ah! Ah! These little confidences are being put down on paper. We're finally going to have something positive."*

His short letter written, Prosper folded it carefully, reducing it to the smallest possible extent. After a furtive look at the Sûreté agent still motionless in his corner, he threw it to little Cavaillon with this word, 'Gypsy!'

All those actions were carried out with such self-control, so quickly, and with such rare skill. An amateur! Fanferlot was amazed at it, confused, and even a little worried.

He said to himself, *"Diable!* For someone who's innocent, my young man has more stomach and more nerve than a lot of my old hands. It may be the result of education."

Yes, innocent or guilty, Prosper had to be endowed with robust strength to affect such untroubled calm showing proof of that presence of mind, since, on the other side, in this exact moment, his fate, his future, his honor, and his life were being decided. And he was thirty years old!

Before taking action, either because of very natural deference or hoping through a private conversation to make a breakthrough, the Police Commissioner was anxious to forewarn the banker.

"Doubt is no longer possible, Monsieur," he said as soon as they were alone. "It's this young man who robbed you. I would be remiss in my duty if I didn't take him into temporary custody; the grounds will then get broader or will continue to his arrest."

That declaration seemed to unusually touch the banker.

"Poor Prosper!" he murmured. And seeing the astonishment of his questioner, he added, "Until today, Monsieur, I had the most absolute faith in his honesty. I would have, without hesitation, put my fortune in his care. I almost put myself on my knees to get an admission of a misguided moment, promising him to pardon and to forget. I wasn't able to get to him. I loved him, and even now, in spite of the sorrow and the humiliation that I foresee, I can't hate him."

The Commissioner seemed not to understand.

"What do you mean, humiliation," he asked.

"What! Monsieur," Monsieur Fauvel said sharply, "must not justice be, and isn't it, the same for everyone. Does it follow that since I'm head of a bank while he's only an employee, I must be believed on my word? Why would I not have robbed myself? There have been such cases. I'll be asked for facts. I'll be obliged to show a judge the exact situation of my bank, explain my business to him, while revealing the secret and the mechanics of my operation."

"It could be, Monsieur, that in fact you'll be asked some explanations; but your well-known honorable reputation…"

"Alas! He too was honest. Who would have been suspected, if this morning I hadn't been able to find on the spot, 100,000 *écus*? Who would be suspected if I couldn't prove that my available assets exceeded my pending outlay by more than 300,000?"

For a sensitive man, the thought, the possibility, or even the appearance of a suspicion is cruel pain. The Commissioner could see the banker was suffering.

"Rest easy, Monsieur," he said. "Before a week is out, the law will have gathered enough evidence to establish the guilt of this unfortunate man that we can now have come back in."

Called back in, Prosper came with Monsieur Fanferlot, whom they'd had great trouble waking. He was without a tremor; everything about him showed the most complete lack of emotion, as he heard it announced that he was arrested. He simply answered, without the least emphasis, "I'm innocent!"

Monsieur Fauvel, a great deal more troubled than his cashier, made a last effort.

"There's still time my child," he said. "In the name of Heaven, think..."

Prosper didn't seem to hear him. He took out of his pocket a little key that he placed on the mantle.

"Here, Monsieur," he said, "is the key to your safe. I hope, for my sake, that you'll recognize one day that I haven't stolen anything from you. I hope, for your sake, that you don't recognize it too late."

Then as no one said anything, he continued.

"Before leaving, here are the books, the papers, and the information necessary for the one who replaces me. In addition, I must tell you that, not counting the 350,000 francs stolen, I'm leaving a deficit in the safe."

A deficit! This sinister word in the mouth of a cashier exploded like a shell in the ears of those listening to Prosper. However, his declaration could be very differently interpreted.

"A deficit!" thought the Commissioner of Police. *"How, after that, could this young man's guilt be doubted? Before robbing the safe of the large amounts, he tried his hand at cheating with small amounts."*

"A deficit," the Sûreté agent said to himself. "Now, to doubt the innocence of this poor devil, you'd have to suppose he had an inadmissible perversity of premeditation. Guilty, he would obviously have put back the money he'd taken out."

The explanation Prosper gave greatly diminished both the significance and the seriousness of the fact.

He continued, "My cash box is missing 3,500 francs which was expended in this way: 2,000 francs were taken by me as an advance on my salary, 1,500 francs were advanced to several of my colleagues. Today is the last day of the month; as a consequence, salaries are paid tomorrow."

The Police Commissioner interrupted him.

"Are you authorized" he asked severely, "to dip into the safe for your needs and to make advances?"

"No, but it's evident that Monsieur Fauvel would not have refused permission to help out comrades. What I did is done everywhere. I simply followed the example of my predecessor."

304

The banker replied by a gesture of approval.

"As for me, personally," continued the cashier, "I have in some way the right that I took on myself, having all my savings in the bank, that is to say 15,000 francs."

"That's true," seconded Monsieur Fauvel. "Monsieur Bertomy has at least that sum in my bank."

That last incident cleared up, the Commissioner of Police's mission was finished. His preliminary verbal investigation was closed. He announced that he was going to leave and he ordered the cashier to prepare to follow him.

Ordinarily this moment is terrible—when brutal reality bursts through, when one feels he no longer belongs to himself and when he is losing his liberty. At that fatal injunction of 'Follow me!' which you might say opens the doors of prison, you see the most unconcerned and the most hardened weaken and begin crying and asking for pardon. Prosper himself lost nothing of the studied coolness that he affected. The Commissioner of Police, to himself, attributed that to extraordinary impudence. Slowly, with as much calmness and ease as if it were just a matter of going to have dinner in town, Prosper picked up his overcoat, repaired the disorder of his hair, took his gloves and said:

"I'm ready to accompany you, Monsieur."

The Commissioner of Police had already closed his notebook and said goodbye to Monsieur Fauvel.

"Let's go!" he said.

They left; it was with deep sadness that the banker watched them leave, his eyes wet with the tears that he held back with great difficulty.

"*Mon Dieu!*" he murmured. "Would that someone had stolen twice as much and would that I could still have confidence in my poor Prosper and keep him near to me as in the past."

It was Fanferlot, the man with an always listening ear, who picked up and took down that sentence. Prompt to be suspicious, and too disposed to attribute to others a depth of craftiness equal to his own, he wasn't too far from believing that it had been said for his benefit.

He had remained the last person in the office, with the pretext of looking for an umbrella that he'd never had. He went out with a calculated slowness, not without having repeated several times that he would come back to see if someone hadn't found it.

Usually, he was the one who would have been given the job of guarding and taking Prosper away. However at the moment of departure, he approached the Commissioner of Police, and in the interest of the affair, he asked for and received permission to act on his own recognizance.

The note that Prosper wrote, that note that he felt was in little Cavaillon's pocket, ran through his head. Indeed, once he had gone back into the cashier's office, he took great care to leave the door ajar, watching from the corner of his eye, ready to go into action at the young employee's least motion. To get a hold of that written clue, which must be important, would appear to be the easiest thing in the world. How to do it? He could arrest Cavaillon, scare him, demand he give up the note, and if need be, take it from him by force. For a moment the Sûreté agent entertained that idea. But what would that disturbance lead to? It would lead to nothing, or at least to an incomplete and equivocal result. Fanferlot was convinced that the note was destined to a third person, not to the young employee. If constrained, would Cavaillon tell who that person was, which very well might not be the name pronounced by the cashier, Gypsy? And putting everything in the best light, if he talked, wouldn't he lie?

After serious consideration, the Sûreté agent decided, in his wisdom as a policeman, that it was childish to demand a secret when you could get it by surprise. To spy on Cavaillon, to follow him and to seize him when he was so obviously guilty that he couldn't deny anything, was clearly child's play. Besides, this method of operation was a great deal more in the character of the employee of the Rue de Jérusalem. Such an employee is naturally gentle and silent, and professionally has a horror of publicity or of everything which resembles violence. Fanferlot's plan was irrevocably fixed when he arrived in the vestibule. There he cleverly made an office boy talk. After four or five questions, casual in appearance, he acquired the certainty that the Fauvel bank didn't have an exit on the Rue de la Victoire and that the employees could only enter and leave by the main door on the Rue de Provence. From this moment, the task he taken on himself didn't pose the shadow of a difficulty. He walked rapidly across the street, and went to settle himself facing the bank, under a coach entry. His observation post was admirably chosen. Not only could he watch those coming in and going out of the bank from his location, but he even had a view of all the windows. By standing on his tiptoes, he could distinguish, through the panes, Cavaillon leaning over his desk.

Fanferlot remained a long time under the coach entry door. He was patient. He had, many times in a lesser case, remained on lookout entire days and nights. In addition, he didn't have the leisure to be bored. He studied the value of his discoveries, weighed his chances, and, like Perrette thinking of the sale of her jar of milk, he built the edifice of his fortune on his success.[28]

Then, about 1 p.m., the Sûreté agent saw Cavaillon get up, take off his office jacket to put on his street clothes, and pick up his hat.

"Good! The fine fellow is leaving. Let's keep an eye out," he said to himself.

The instant afterward, in fact, Cavaillon appeared at the door of the bank. But before stepping out onto the sidewalk, he looked to the right and left. He hesitated.

---

[28] Allusion to the La Fontaine fable of the milk maid who, walking to market with a jar of milk to sell, daydreams about what purchases the sale can lead to, and not being careful, stumbles and breaks the jar of milk.

"Does he suspect something?" Fanferlot wondered.

No, the young employee wasn't suspicious of anything. Only, having an errand to run and fearing that his absence would be noticed, he was wondering which way would be shortest. Soon, he decided. He went toward the Faubourg Montmartre, went up it and took the Rue Notre-Dame-de-Lorette. He was walking very quickly, paying very little attention to the complaints of the passers-by that he jostled, and the Sûreté agent almost had trouble following him. When he arrived at the Rue Chaptal, Cavaillon stopped short and went into the house bearing the number 39. He had hardly made three steps inside the rather narrow corridor when, feeling himself struck on the shoulder, he brusquely turned around and found himself face to face with Fanferlot. He recognized him very well, so well that he became very pale and stepped backward, looking around for an exit through which to flee. But the Sûreté agent had foreseen this temptation. He barred the passageway completely. Cavaillon felt himself trapped.

"What do you want with me?" he asked in a voice strangled by fear.

What distinguished Monsieur Fanferlot 'the Squirrel' from his colleagues, more than anything, were his exquisite gentleness and his unequaled sophistication. He was perfect even in his way of going about his business. And it was with the greatest respect, the most obsequious expressions of civility, that he nabbed and sent people to prison.

"Please, dear Monsieur," he answered, "excuse my great liberty, but I must ask you to oblige me with a little information."

"Information, from me?"

"From you yes, dear Monsieur, from Eugène Cavaillon."

"But I don't know you."

"Oh! Yes, you do. You saw me very well this morning. Nevertheless, it's just a question of something of no great importance. If you'll do me the honor of accepting my arm and go out with me for an instant, you would do me the greatest honor."

What could he do? Cavaillon took Monsieur Fanferlot's arm and went out with him.

The Rue Chaptal isn't one of those busy and crowded thoroughfares where carriages constitute a perpetual danger for pedestrians. There are only two or three small shops there. From the corner of the Rue Fontaine occupied by a pharmacist, right across from the Rue Léonie, extends a large sad wall, pierced here and there by little windows which provide light to cabinet makers' workshops. It's one of those streets where you can chat at your ease without having to get off the sidewalk every moment, and Monsieur Fanferlot and Cavaillon didn't need to fear being troubled by passers-by.

"Here's the fact, dear Monsieur," began the Sûreté agent. "This morning Monsieur Bertomy very skillfully threw you a little note."

Cavaillon vaguely sensed that he was going to be questioned about that note. He was doing his utmost to prepare himself, to be on his guard.

"You're mistaken," he answered, turning red right up to his ears.

"Pardon me! Please believe me, I would regretfully contradict you. But I'm certain of what I maintain."

"I assure you that Prosper didn't give me anything."

"Please, dear Monsieur, don't deny it." insisted Fanferlot. "You'd force me to prove to you that four employees saw him throw you a note written in pencil and folded very small."

The young employee understood that to persist in his story in the presence of a man so well informed would be madness. Therefore he changed his story.

"All right," he said. "That's true. I did get a note from Prosper. But, as it was for me alone, after reading it I tore it up, and threw the pieces in the fire."

That very well could be the truth. Fanferlot was afraid of that. But how could he be sure? He remembered that the most unsophisticated ruses are those that work best, and confident in his guess, he said, at random, "I'll permit myself, dear Monsieur, to call your attention to the fact that this is not at all true. The note was given to you to be transmitted to Gypsy."

A desperate gesture from Cavaillon told the agent that he was not mistaken. He breathed easy.

"I swear to you, Monsieur," began the young messenger.

"Don't swear, dear Monsieur," Fanferlot interrupted. "All the oaths in the world are useless. Not only did you not tear up this note, but you've entered this house to give it to the one it's meant for, and you have it in your pocket."

"No, Monsieur, no!"

Monsieur Fanferlot didn't pay attention to that denial. He continued in his sweetest voice:

"And I'm sure you're going to be nice enough to let me have this note. Understand, that without absolute necessity…"

"Never!" answered Cavaillon.

And thinking the moment favorable, he tried with a violent shake to pull away his arm held under Fanferlot's arm and to flee. But his attempt was useless. The Sûreté agent was as strong as he was gentle.

"Be careful not to hurt yourself, my young Monsieur," said the man from the Prefecture, "and believe me, you're going to give me that note."

"I don't have it!"

"All right, fine! Then you're going to make me resort to painful extremes. Do you know what's going to happen if you persist in being stubborn? I will call two municipal policemen, who will each take one of your arms and take you to the Police Commissioner. Once there, I will sadly be obliged to search you whether you like it or not. Look, frankly, you distress me."

Certainly, Cavaillon was devoted to Prosper, but it was clear as day to him that resisting wouldn't lead to anything; he wouldn't even have time to get rid of the evidence. To give up the note under these conditions, wasn't a betrayal. He resigned himself, cursing his powerlessness, almost weeping with rage.

"You are stronger than I am," he said. "I'll do as I am told."

At the same time, he took out of his wallet the unfortunate note and gave it to the Sûreté agent. Fanferlot's hands trembled with pleasure in unfolding the paper. Nevertheless, faithful to his habit of meticulous politeness, once the letter was opened he bowed to Cavaillon, murmuring:

"You'll allow me, will you not, dear Monsieur? I'm upset, really, about the indiscretion." Finally, he read:

Dear Nina,

If you love me, quickly, without hesitating a moment, without thinking, obey me. When you get this note, take everything in the house that belongs to you—absolutely everything—and go get yourself established in some furnished house at the other end of Paris. Don't show yourself. Disappear as much as you can. My life may depend on your obedience. I have been accused of a considerable theft and I'm going to be arrested. There should be 500 francs in the secretary. Take them. Leave your address with Cavaillon, who will explain what I can't tell you. Wish for the best, even so, and see you soon,

Prosper.

If he had been less upset, Cavaillon would have been able to surmise on the Sûreté agent's face all the signs of immense disappointment. Fanferlot had deluded himself that he was going to get a hold of a very important document. And, who knows? Maybe it would be the undeniable proof of Prosper's innocence or guilt. Instead of that, he had gotten his hands on a love letter, from a man less worried about himself than about the beloved one. He wracked his brain in vain. He didn't discover in that letter any precise meaning, no actual message. It proved nothing, neither for nor against the person who had written it. These two words, "absolutely everything," were, it's true, underlined; but they could be interpreted in so many ways! However, the Sûreté agent believed he should continue.

"That Madame Nina Gypsy," he asked Cavaillon, "is probably Monsieur Prosper Bertomy's friend?"

"She's his mistress."

"And she lives here, in number 39?"

"You know that very well, since you saw me come in."

"In fact I thought so, dear Monsieur. And tell me, is the apartment she occupies rented in her name?"

"No, she lives with Prosper."

"Perfect, and on what floor, please?"

"On the second."

Monsieur Fanferlot had carefully refolded the note as it had been folded. He slid it into his pocket.

"A thousand thanks, dear Monsieur," he said, "for your information. In exchange, if you don't mind, I'll save you the errand you were going to run."

"Monsieur!"

"Yes, with your permission, I'll deliver this letter myself to Madame Nina Gypsy."

Cavaillon put up some resistance. He tried to argue, but Monsieur Fanferlot was in a hurry. He cut short his protests.

"I'm going to dare to give you some advice I think good, dear Monsieur," he told him. "If I were you, I'd go back to my office peacefully, and I wouldn't get mixed up in this business. Oh! Not at all."

"But, Monsieur, Prosper has been my protector. He got me out of poverty. He's my friend."

"That's another reason for you to keep quiet. Can you be of service to him? No, correct? Well, I myself will tell you that you can destroy him. People know that you are devoted to him. Won't they notice your absence? If you get involved, if you try things which come to nothing, won't people interpret them badly?"

"Prosper is innocent, Monsieur. I'm sure of it."

That was positively Fanferlot's opinion. But it wasn't to his advantage to let his private thoughts be guessed. Furthermore, in the interest of his following investigations, it was important that he make sure the young employee was prudent and discreet. He would have preferred to ask him to be quiet about what had just happened between them, but he didn't dare.

"What you say is very possible," he answered, "and I hope so for Monsieur Bertomy's sake. I hope so for you more than anything. If he's guilty, you will inevitably be implicated, given your well-known friendship, and maybe even suspected of complicity."

Cavaillon ducked his head. He was dumbfounded.

"So believe me, my young Monsieur," Fanferlot went on, "go back to your job and...I hope to see you again."

The poor boy obeyed. Slowly, with a very heavy heart, he went back to the Rue Notre-Dame-de-Lorette. He wondered how he could help Prosper, how to warn Madame Gypsy, and above all how to get revenge on that odious policeman who had just so grossly humiliated him. As soon as he had disappeared at the corner of the street, Fanferlot went into the house, gave the porter Prosper Bertomy's name, mounted the stairs and rang the bell at the door on the second floor. A servant about fifteen-years-old, wearing coquettish livery, came to the door.

"Madame Nina Gypsy?" he asked.

The little groom hesitated.

"See this." Monsieur Fanferlot showed his letter. "I'm sent," he insisted, "by Monsieur Prosper to give this letter to Madame and to wait for an answer."

"Come in then. I'll tell Madame."

Prosper's name had produced its effect. Fanferlot was shown into a little sitting room decked with buttercup yellow silk damask, contrasted with very blue trimmings and ornaments. There were triple drapes on the windows, curtains on all the doors. A splendid rug covered the floor.

"Peste!" murmured the Sûreté agent. "He has nice lodgings, our cashier."

But he didn't have time to follow-up his inventory. One of the door curtains was lifted. Madame Nina Gypsy appeared. Madame Gypsy is, or to speak more accurately, was then a very young woman, frail, delicate, and petite, with the feet and hands of a child. Her hair was brown, with gold tones like a Havana quadroon. Long eyelashes, silky and turned up, subdued the too direct brilliance of her great black eyes. Her lips, though somewhat wide, smiled showing teeth whiter than those of a cat. They were small, brilliant, mother-of-pearl teeth, sharp enough to crunch ten inheritances.

She hadn't yet dressed to go out, and feeling cold, was enveloped in an ample velvet dressing gown. Through its openings, waves of lace on her nightgown escaped. But she had already been in the hands of a hair dresser or of a skillful maid. Her hair was crimped and curled on the front all around the forehead, held back by little bands of red velvet, and lifted into an enormous, very high chignon on her neck. She was ravishing in this fashion, of a beauty so insolent and so striking that Fanferlot was dazzled by it and was immediately speechless.

"Saperlotte!" he said, thinking of the noble and stern beauty of Madeleine, seen some hours earlier. "He has good taste, our cashier, very good taste...too good taste."

While he was thinking this very sheepishly, wondering how to begin the interview, Madame Gypsy coughed in a most disdainful manner. She was astounded to see in her drawing room this skinny and shabby personage, wearing a greasy hat refurbished with a crepe band. Since she had creditors, she was trying to remember which one might have that underling countenance, or at least which one would allow himself to send this ill-mannered man to wipe his worn out boots on the high wool pile of her carpet.

Her examination finished:

"What do you want?" she asked finally, making her eyelids blink in a most impertinent way. Anyone other than Fanferlot would have been revolted by these looks and this tone. He paid no more attention to them except to get some idea about the character of the young woman.

"She's not at all moral, no! And not the least well-bred."

He was slow to answer. Madame Gypsy tapped her foot in impatience.

"Will you speak up?" Madame Gypsy repeated. "What do you want?"

"I'm sent, dear Madame," the Sûreté agent said in his sweetest and most humble voice, "to give you a little note from Monsieur Bertomy."

"From Prosper? Then you know him?"

"I have that honor and if I dare express myself in this way, I'm even among his friends."

"Monsieur!" said Madame Gypsy, her pride wounded.

Monsieur Fanferlot didn't deign to pay any attention to that insulting exclamation. He was ambitious. Scorn rolled off him like water off a duck's back.

"I said, 'one of his friends'," he insisted, "and I'm sure there are very few people now who would have the courage to openly admit their friendship with him."

The Sûreté agent expressed himself with a seriousness so convincing that Madame Gypsy was struck by it.

"I never knew how to guess riddles," she said dryly. "What do you mean to insinuate, please?"

The man from the Prefecture of Police slowly took from his pocket the letter he had taken from Cavaillon and presented it to Madame Gypsy.

"Read it," he said.

She certainly wasn't expecting anything announcing misfortune. Although she had the best eyes in the world, before unfolding the letter, she settled on her nose a charming pair of glasses. She read its entirety in a glance. At first she became very pale, then very red. A nervous tremble shook her from head to foot. Her knees buckled. She shivered. Fanferlot, thinking she was going to fall, held out his arm to support her. A useless precaution! Madame Gypsy was one of those women whose carefree idleness masks a wild energy, fragile creatures whose strength of resistance has no limits, cats by their grace and delicateness, cats also by their nerves and muscles of steel. The vertigo from the bludgeon she had just received lasted no longer than a flash of lightening would. She tottered, but she didn't fall. She straightened up stronger, seized the wrists of the Prefecture agent, and with her little hands gripped them hard enough to make him cry out.

"Explain yourself," she said. "What does this mean? Do you know what this letter has told me?"

As brave as he was, he who everyday confronted the most dangerous criminals, Fanferlot was almost afraid of Madame Gypsy's anger.

"Alas!" he murmured.

"They want to arrest Prosper. They accuse him of theft!"

"Yes. They claim that he took 350,000 francs from his safe."

"That's not true!" the young woman cried out. "That's despicable and absurd."

She had released Fanferlot's wrists, and her fury, a real rage of a spoiled child, vented itself in uncoordinated gestures. She carelessly tore pitilessly at her beautiful dressing gown and lace.

"Prosper, steal" she said, "that would be too stupid. Steal! Why? Doesn't he have a great fortune?"

"That's precisely the point, dear lady," insinuated the Sûreté agent. "They claim that Monsieur Bertomy is not rich, that he has nothing to live on but his salary."

That answer seemed to confuse all Madame Gypsy's ideas.

"Nevertheless," she insisted, "I've always seem him with a lot of money. Not rich...but then..."

She didn't dare finish; but as her eyes met those of Fanferlot they understood each other. Madame Nina's look meant, *"Then it was for me, for my luxury, for my fantasies that he would have stolen."*

"Perhaps!" the Sûreté agent's look answered.

It took maybe ten seconds of thought to give the young woman back her first assurance. The doubt, which had brushed through her mind, fled away.

"No!" she exclaimed. "Never, unfortunately, would Prosper have stolen a sou for me. A cashier might take out by the handfuls from a safe given to him to guard on his honor, for a woman that he loves. That's understandable and can be explained, but Prosper doesn't love me; he's never loved me."

"Oh! Beautiful lady," protested the gallant and polite Fanferlot, "You can't believe what you're saying."

She shook her head sadly. A tear, held back with great trouble, veiled the brilliance of her beautiful eyes.

"I think so, and it's true," she said. "He's ready to satisfy all my fantasies, you'll say. What does that prove? When I say he doesn't love me, I'm only too persuaded of it, you see, and I know what I'm talking about. Once in my life I was loved by a man of passion, and because I've been suffering for a year, I understand how unhappy I made him. I'm nothing in Prosper's life, hardly an accident."

"But then, why..."

"Ah, yes..." interrupted Madame Gypsy, "Why? You yourself would be very clever if you could tell me why. For a year I've been vainly looking for an answer to that question, terrible for me, and I'm a woman! But you try to find out the thoughts of a man so master of himself that nothing that happens in his heart reaches his eyes. I've observed him as a woman knows how to observe the man her destiny depends on. Wasted effort! He's good, he's gentle, but he can't be reached. People think he's weak. They're wrong. He's a steel bar who looks like a broken reed, that blond-haired man."

Carried away by the violence of her emotions, Madame Nina opened up, right to the bottom of her soul. She was without distrust, not doubting the quality of that man listening to her, unknown to her, but in whom she saw Prosper's friend. As for Fanferlot, he applauded inwardly his good fortune and his skill. Only a woman can draw a true portrait. In an emotional moment, she had just given him the most precious information. From now on, he knew what sort of man he was dealing with, which in an investigation is the most important point.

"From what they say," he threw out, "Monsieur Bertomy is a gambler, and gambling leads far afield."

Madame Gypsy shrugged.

"Yes, that's true," she answered. "He gambles. I've seen him, without moving a muscle, win and lose considerable sums. He gambles, but he's not a gambler. He gambles as he eats dinner, as he gets drunk, and as he amuses himself, without passion, without feeling, and without pleasure. Sometimes he frightens me. It seems to me he drags about a body where there's no longer a soul. Ah! I'm not happy, you can see. I've never found anything in him but a profound indifference, so immense that it has often seemed like despair to me. And that man could have stolen! Just think about it! Look, you can't keep me from thinking that there's something terrible in his life, some secret, or some great misfortune; I don't know what, but something."

"And he's never talked to you about his past?"

"Him? Haven't you understood what I've been saying? I've told you. He doesn't love me."

Madame Gypsy had little by little become emotional. She was weeping, and big tears rolled silently down her cheeks. It was only a moment of despair. She soon got a hold of herself. Her eyes shone with the most generous resolutions.

"But me, I love him!" she burst out. "And it's up to me to save him. Ah! I know how to talk to his employer, this miserable man who's accused him, and to the judges, and to everybody. He's been arrested. I'll prove he's innocent. Come, Monsieur, let's go. And I promise you, before the end of the day he'll be free or I'll be in prison with him."

Madame Gypsy's project was laudable, assuredly, and dictated by the noblest sentiments. Unfortunately, it wasn't practical. In addition, it had the mistake of going against the Sûreté agent's intentions. As decided as he was to keep to himself the difficulties as well as the benefits of this investigation, Monsieur Fanferlot knew very well he couldn't hide Madame Nina from the Investigating Magistrate. One day or another, she would necessarily come into the action and be looked for. Above all, because of that he didn't want her to show herself on her own. He himself intended, shamelessly and no matter what, to make her appear when and how he judged it appropriate, in order to claim credit himself for having discovered her. That meant that he immediately made a conscientious effort to calm the young woman's emotion. He thought it would be easy to show her that the least movement in favor of Prosper would be rank folly.

"What would you gain, dear Madame?" he asked her. "Nothing. And you don't have, I swear to you, the least chance of success. And think of the fact that you're going to compromise yourself seriously. Who knows if the law would see in you an accomplice of Monsieur Bertomy?"

But these disturbing possibilities, which had stopped Cavaillon and had made him stupidly give up a letter that he could very well have defended, only stimulated Madame Gypsy's enthusiasm. That was because men reason, while women follow the inspirations of their hearts. In situations where the most devoted friend hesitates and holds back, the woman marches on with her head bowed, not thinking of the outcome.

314

"What does the danger matter!" she cried out. "I don't believe there is any, but if it exists, so much the better. It will give some merit to a completely natural attempt. I'm sure Prosper is innocent, but if by some impossibility he is guilty, all right! I want to share the punishment that awaits him."

Madame Gypsy's insistence was becoming disturbing. She had hastily thrown a large cashmere shawl over her shoulders, put on her hat and, dressed like this in a dressing gown and house shoes, she pronounced herself ready to leave, ready to go find all the Investigating Magistrates in Paris.

"Are you coming, Monsieur?" she asked with a feverish impatience. "Are you coming?"

Fanferlot was far from decided. Fortunately, he always had several strings to his bow. Personal considerations had no part in that energetic personality. He resolved to bring up Prosper's personal interests.

"I'm ready to go with you, beautiful lady," he answered. "Only, let me tell you while there's still time, that very probably we're going to do Monsieur Bertomy the worst service."

"By doing what, if you please?"

"By going to surprise him, by attempting to do something he can't expect, according to what he wrote to you."

The young woman made a gesture of reckless pride. She had no second thoughts.

"There are some people, Monsieur," she answered, "that you must save without telling them and in spite of them. I understand Prosper. He's a man who would let himself be killed without fighting, without saying a word, giving him-self up by indifference and by despair."

"Pardon, dear Madame, pardon!" interrupted the Sûreté agent. "Monsieur doesn't precisely appear to be a man who gives up, as you say. I would be will-ing to believe, on the contrary, that he's already built his plan of defense. How do you know, but what by appearing, when he's advised you to go into hiding, that you aren't going to upset his surest means of justification?"

Madame Gypsy was slow to answer. She was examining the validity of Fanferlot's objections.

"Nevertheless, I can't stay here doing nothing, without trying to contribute something toward saving him," she continued. "Don't you understand that the floor here is burning my feet?"

Evidently, if she wasn't absolutely convinced, her resolution was shaken. The man from the Prefecture of Police felt that he had persuaded her, and that certainty gave him more freedom, gave more authority to his eloquence.

"You have, dear lady," he continued, "a very simple way to help the man you love."

"What, Monsieur, what!"

"Obey him, my child," Monsieur Fanferlot stated in a fatherly way.

Madame Gypsy was expecting different advice.

315

"Obey!" she murmured. "Obey…"

"That's your duty," continued Fanferlot, having become serious and dignified. "Your sacred duty."

She still hesitated. He took Prosper's letter from the table where she had put it, and he continued:

"Well! Monsieur Bertomy, in a terrible moment when he was going to be arrested, wrote you to lay out what you should do, and you want to undo that wise precaution! What did he tell you? Look, let's read together this letter, which is like the testament of his freedom. He says to you, *If you love me, I beg you, obey…* And you're hesitating to obey. He tells you more, *It's a question of my life.* Then don't you love him? What! Don't you understand, unhappy child, that in begging you to flee and to hide, Monsieur Bertomy has his over-riding, terrible reasons?"

These reasons Monsieur Fanferlot had understood in setting foot in the Rue Chaptal apartment; and if he hadn't yet laid them out, it was because he was keeping them like a good general keeps his reserve troops, to win the victory. Madame Gypsy was intelligent enough to guess them.

"Reasons!" she began. "Then Prosper doesn't want people to know about our affair."

She remained thoughtful an instant and then light dawned in her mind, and she exclaimed:

"Yes! I understand now. Fool that I am not to have seen that right off! In fact, my presence here, where I've been a year, would be a damning charge against him. They would make an inventory of all I possess—my dresses, my laces, and my jewels, and they would make my luxury a crime. They would ask him where he got enough money to shower me with gifts to the point that I have nothing left to desire."

The Sûreté agent nodded in sign of agreement.

"That's how it would be," he answered.

"But then I must leave, Monsieur, and leave very quickly! Who knows but what the police are already alerted, if they aren't going to arrive."

"Oh!" said Monsieur Fanferlot, in the most casual way, "You have time. The police are neither so clever nor so prompt."

"That doesn't matter!"

And leaving the Sûreté agent alone, Madame Nina dashed into her bedroom, yelling out to her maid, her cook, and the little groom himself, commanding them to empty the drawers and the armoires, to throw everything which belonged to her pell-mell into baggage, and, above all, to be quick, to hurry. She herself gave the example as fast as she could, when suddenly a thought brought her back near Fanferlot.

"Everything will be ready in a minute," she said, "and I'll leave, but where will I go?

"Didn't Monsieur Bertomy tell you, dear lady? Go to the other end of Paris, in a furnished house, in a town house."

"But I don't know any."

The man from the Prefecture, pretended to think. He had a thousand pains hiding a conspicuous joy which flashed into his little round eyes, no matter what he did.

"I myself know a hotel very well," he finally said. "But it may not suit you, Madame! It's not as luxurious as here!"

"Will I be all right there?"

"With my recommendation, you will be treated like a little queen, and above all, hidden."

"Where is it?"

"On the other side of the river on the Quai Saint-Michel, the Grand-Archange Hotel, kept by Madame Alexandre…"

Madame Nina was never long in making a decision.

"Here's something to write with. Write out your letter of recommendation."

In a minute he had finished.

"With these three lines, beautiful lady, you may have whatever you like from Madame Alexandre."

"That's good! Now, how can I let Cavaillon know my address? He was the one who was supposed to deliver Prosper's letter to me."

"He couldn't come, dear Madame," broke in the Sûreté agent, "but I'm going to see him in a little while and I'll tell him where to find you."

Madame Gypsy was going to send someone to find a carriage. Fanferlot, who said he was in a hurry, said that he would take care of it. It was a good pretext to slip away. In addition, he was lucky that day. A carriage was passing in front of the house. He stopped it. He said to the coachman, after having showed his identification,

"You will wait here for a little brunette lady who will come down with her baggage. If she tells you to take her to the Quai Saint-Michel, you'll whip up your horses. If she gives you a different address, get down from your seat before leaving as if you're going to fix a carriage harness. I'll be close enough to see and to hear."

At that, he went to stand watch on the other side of the street, in a wine merchant's shop. He was completely dazed by what he had just learned, and not knowing exactly what to think, he needed to put his thoughts in order. He scarcely had time to do so. The loud noise of a whip being cracked broke the silence of the street. Madame Nina was headed for the Grand-Archange.

"Well!" he exclaimed gaily, "at least I've got that one."

Chapter IV

At the exact time that Madame Nina Gypsy was going to seek refuge at the Grand-Archange Hotel, which had been pointed out to her by Monsieur Fanferlot, Prosper Bertomy was being booked into the Prefecture of Police holding cells. Since the moment when he was again in control of his feelings and had managed to resume his habitual demeanor, his coolness was no longer in doubt. The people who surrounded him, clever observers, had searched in vain for a flinching in his look or a doubtful facial expression. They had found him like marble. You could even have thought him unaware of his frightful situation, if it hadn't been for a sad oppression which made his breathing heavier, and for the drops of sweat which were like pearls along his temples, betraying horrible anxiety. In the office of the Police Commissioner, where he had stayed more than two hours while they went to pick up orders, he had chatted with the two city police officers who were guarding him. Toward noon and not having eaten, according to what he said, he felt the need to eat something. They had lunch brought to him from the restaurant next door and he ate with a rather good appetite and drank almost an entire bottle of wine.

While he was there, at least ten agents and various Prefecture employees, who have business every morning at the office of the Commissioner of Police, came to look curiously at his countenance. Everybody was of the same opinion, and expressed it in almost exactly the same terms. They said:

"He's a hardened crook!"

Or else, "This fellow is too quiet not to be planning something."

When they told him a carriage was waiting for him downstairs, he got up quickly. But before going down, he asked permission to light a cigar, permission which was granted him. A flower merchant usually had a stand at the entry to the Commissioner's building. He bought a small bouquet of violets from her. That woman, knowing he'd been arrested, said to him in way of thanks:

"Good luck, my poor gentleman!"

He appeared touched by that ordinary mark of interest and answered:

"Thank you my good woman, but I haven't had any for a long time."

It was magnificent weather, a glorious springtime day. All along the Rue Montmartre on which the carriage was driving, Prosper put his head out of the window several times, complaining or smiling about being put in prison away from that beautiful sun, when it would be so nice to be outside.

"The unusual thing," he said, "is that I've never wanted so much to take a walk."

One of his guards, who was a big fellow, cheerful and stout, greeted that thought with an enormous laugh, and said:

"I understand that."

At the booking office, while they were filling out the necessary paperwork for the prison entry, Prosper answered the questions he was asked with haughtiness mingled with disdain. But when ordered to empty his pockets on the table and someone approached him to search him, a light of indignation shot from his eyes; then a big, warm tear quickly dried on the warmth of his cheeks. This was only a flash. He let himself be searched, lifting his arms, while from head to toe, rough hands patted him to be sure he wasn't hiding some suspicious object under his clothes. The investigation would have been carried further and would have been a great deal more ignominious, if it hadn't been for the intervention of a middle-aged man. He was of distinguished appearance, wearing a white tie and glasses with gold frames. He was warming himself near the stove, and seemed to be at home in that place.

Seeing Prosper, who came in followed by policemen, he made a gesture of surprise and seemed extremely affected. He even came forward as if to speak to him, but changed his mind. As upset as the cashier was, he couldn't help but notice that that man's eyes remained doggedly staring at him. Then, did he know him? He searched his memory without success. He couldn't remember ever having seen him before.

That man, who appeared to be the head of the bureau, was none other than the illustrious employee of the Prefecture, Monsieur Lecoq. Just as the agents who had searched Prosper were getting ready to make him take his boots off—a file or a gun take up so little room— Monsieur Lecoq motioned to them and said:

"That's enough."

The others obeyed. All the formal registry papers were filled out, and finally they led the unfortunate cashier to a narrow cell. The big reinforced door with bolts and locks closed on him. He breathed. He was alone. Yes, he thought himself alone, totally alone! He didn't understand that prison is made of glass, that the man shut up there is like a miserable insect under the microscope of the entomologist. He didn't know that the walls have ears, always listening. The openings to cell doors have eyes that never close. He was so sure of being alone that all his pride dissolved in a torrent of tears, his impassive mask fell away. His anger so long contained, broke out violently and terribly like a fire which, covered for a long time, dries out all the inflammable material.

He let himself go wild. He shouted, he used curses and blasphemies. He bruised his fists on the wall in an excess of mad, impotent rage, like a caged wild beast after the first moment of stupor. It seemed that Prosper Bertomy wasn't what he appeared to be. This haughty and correct gentleman, a sort of frozen dandy, had hot passions and a fiery temperament.

One day, when he was about twenty-four years old, ambition had eaten into his heart. While all his desires had been thwarted, imprisoned in mediocrity like a schoolboy in a tunic too tight for him, he saw around him all those rich people that money serves as the magic wand to the *Thousand and One Nights*, and he envied their situation. He researched the origins and the starting point of all the wealthy heads of great financial enterprises, and he saw that when they began that most of them had possessed less than he. Then how did they raise themselves? It was through strength of energy, intelligence, and audacity. For them, a productive mind had been like the magic lantern in Aladdin's hands. He swore then to imitate them and to get ahead like them. From that day onward, with strength of character, a great deal less rare than it's thought to be, he silenced his instincts; he reformed, not his character, but the exterior of his character. And his efforts were not wasted. People believed in his character and in his methods. Those who knew him said: "He'll get ahead!" But there he was in prison, accused of theft: that is to say, lost. But he didn't deceive himself. He knew that innocent or guilty, the man under suspicion is marked with a stigma which couldn't be erased any more than could the letters burned with a red-hot iron into the shoulders of criminals in the past. Because of that, what was the good of fighting? What would be the use of a triumph which didn't wash away the stain!

When the guard on evening duty brought him his meal, he found him stretched out on his bed, his head dug into his pillow, weeping warm tears. Ah! He was no longer hungry. Now that he was alone, he was filled with an insurmountable numbness. His lost will-power floated in an opaque fog. The night came, long and terrible; for the first time, to measure the hours, he had only the cadenced footsteps of the sentinels making their rounds. He suffered. In the morning, however, sleep came with the daylight and he was still sleeping when the jailer's voice reverberated in the cell.

"Let's go, Monsieur," he said, "to the Investigating Magistrate."

With a bound, he was standing. So, he was to be interrogated.

"Let's go," he said, without thinking about adjusting his clothing. During the trip, his guard said to him:

"You're in luck. You're going to be assigned to a very good man."

The guard was right a thousand times over. Gifted with remarkable penetration, firm and incapable of taking sides and equally far from false pity and excessive harshness, Monsieur Patrigent possessed to an outstanding degree all the qualities required for the delicate and difficult mission of the Investigating Magistrate. Perhaps he lacked some of the feverish activity necessary to strike quickly and accurately; but he possessed one of those robust, patient characters which nothing tires out nor discourages. In addition, he was very capable of following an investigation for years. He had, for example with the Belgian bills affair, tied up the ends after only four years of investigation. Because of this, it was in his office that unsolved or incomplete cases, investigations dropped midway, or unfinished procedures wound up. As exacting as possible, such was the man to whom they conducted Prosper, but they led him by a very circuitous path. They made him follow a long corridor, go across a room full of Paris gendarmes, go down a stairway, traverse a sort of basement, and then climb a narrow and straight staircase which seemed unending. Finally, he came to a long and narrow gallery, with a low ceiling, off of which a large quantity of numbered doors opened. The guard of the unfortunate cashier halted him in front of one of the doors.

"We're here," he told him. "Here's where your fate will be decided."

At this comment of the guard, said in a tone of deep commiseration, Prosper couldn't help shivering. It was true, however. There, behind that door, was the man who was going to interrogate him; and depending on how he answered, he would be released, or the temporary warrant they had held him on the night before would be converted into a warrant to put him into a holding cell at the Depot. Nevertheless, calling up all his courage, he had already placed his hand on the doorbell, when his guard stopped him.

"Oh! Not yet," he told him. "You don't go in like that. Sit down. They'll call you when your turn comes."

The unfortunate man obeyed, and the guard sat down next to him. There is nothing more frightening, and nothing gloomier, than a seat outside in that dark hallway of the Investigating Magistrates. From one end to the other, great oak benches blackened by daily use are placed against the wall. One involuntarily thinks about the fact that one by one, for ten years, all the accused, all the thieves, and all the murderers of the Department of the Seine have come to sit down on these benches. The fact is that sooner or later, inevitably, just as filth goes into the sewer, crime comes to this terrible hallway. It has one door leading to prison, and the other to the scaffold platform. There, according to the blunt but firm expression of the First President, is the great laundry of all of the dirty linen of Paris. At the hour Prosper arrived, the hallway was very busy. The bench was almost completely occupied. Beside him, so close that he almost rubbed shoulders with him, they had placed a man in rags with a sinister face. In front of each Investigating Magistrate's door, groups of witnesses stood around or talked in low voices. Meanwhile, Paris gendarmes, with heavy boots resounding on the tiles, came and went while bringing in or taking away prisoners. Sometimes penetrating the dull murmur, you could hear a sob, as a woman, either the mother or the sister of an accused man, passed a handkerchief over her eyes. At short intervals, a door opened and closed, and a bailiff called out a name or a number.

In this spectacle, with these corrupting contacts in the middle of that warm atmosphere filled with strange smells, the cashier was feeling faint. At that time, a little old man, dressed in black with the insignia of his office and a steel chain across his shoulders, cried out:

"Prosper Bertomy!"

The poor man stood upright, and without knowing how, found himself pushed into the Investigating Magistrate's office. At first, he was blinded; he had left a very dark area. The window of the room he had entered, situated across from the door, threw daylight out in dazzling and glaring waves. Like all those in the hallway, this office had nothing particularly noticeable about it. It was just like that of any businessman. It was hung with cheap deep green wallpaper and the floor was covered with a poor rug with common black designs. Across from the door was a big desk, loaded with files. Behind this sat the Magistrate, facing those who entered in such a way that his face remained in the shadows, while that of the accused or the witnesses that he interrogated was in full sunlight. At the right was a little table where the secretary, that indispensable aide to the Magistrate, wrote.

But Prosper didn't take notice of these details. All his attention was concentrated on the Magistrate; and as he was able to examine him better, he told himself that his guard hadn't misled him. It was true that Monsieur Patrigent's irregular face, framed by short red sideburns, and animated by lively and intelligent eyes, exuded goodness, and was one of those which reassures and attracts at first sight.

"Take a chair," he said to Prosper.

This courtesy was even more appreciated by the accused, since he was expecting to be treated with the greatest contempt. It seemed to him a good sign and set him somewhat at ease. However, Monsieur Patrigent had motioned to his stenographer:

"We're ready, Sigault," he said to him. "Pay attention."

And, turning back to Prosper, he spoke:

"What's your name?" he asked him.

"Auguste-Prosper Bertomy, Monsieur."

"How old are you?"

"I'll be thirty years old next May 5th."

"What is your profession?"

"I am, that is to say, I was, the cashier of the André Fauvel banking house."

The Magistrate interrupted him in order to consult a small note-pad placed near him. Prosper, who was following all his movements, began to take hope, telling himself that a man seeming so little biased against him could never keep him in prison. Finding the information he was looking for, Monsieur Patrigent returned to the interrogation.

"Where do you live?" he asked him.

"39 Rue Chaptal the last four years. Before that I lived at 7 Boulevard des Batignolles."

"Where were you born?"

"In Beaucaire, in the Gard Department."

"Are your parents still living?"

"I lost my mother two years ago, Monsieur, but I still have my father."

"Does he live in Paris?"

"No, Monsieur, he lives in Beaucaire with my sister, who's married to one of the Midi Canal engineers."

Prosper was answering these last questions in a terribly troubled voice. That was because there are times in life when the memory of family encourages and consoles, and there are those horrible moments when one would like to be alone in the world and be brought up in an orphanage. Monsieur Patrigent was aware of and noted down the emotion of his accused when he had talked about his parents.

"And what is your father's profession?" he continued.

"He was, Monsieur, head of the bridges and highways, employed by the Midi Canal like my brother-in-law. He is now retired."

There was a moment of silence. The investigating Magistrate had placed his chair in such a way, that, seeming to have his head turned, his ploy lost absolutely nothing of Prosper's expression.

"Well!" he suddenly said, "You are accused of having stolen 350,000 francs from your employer."

For twenty-four hours the unhappy young man had had time to become familiar with the terrible idea of that accusation; nevertheless, thus summed up and stated, it stunned him, and he was unable to get out a word.

"What do you have to say?" insisted the Investigating Magistrate.

"I'm innocent, Monsieur. I swear to you, I'm innocent!"

"I hope so, for your sake," said Monsieur Patrigent, "and you can count on me to help you prove your innocence with all my power. Have you, at least, some facts to set forth in your defense, some proofs to give?"

"Ah! Monsieur, what can I say, since I myself don't understand what could have happened. I can only put forth my entire life…"

The Magistrate interrupted Prosper with a gesture.

"Let's be precise," he said. "The theft was committed in such circumstances that suspicion, it seems, could only fall on Monsieur Fauvel and on you. Can any other person be suspected?"

"No, Monsieur."

"You claim you are innocent. Then the guilty man is Monsieur Fauvel?"

Prosper didn't answer.

"Have you," insisted Monsieur Patrigent, "any reason to believe that your employer robbed himself? However slight it may be, tell it to me."

And as the accused still kept silent:

"Well," continued the judge, "I can see that you still need time to think. Listen to the statement of your interrogation that my stenographer is going to read to you. Then you'll sign it and they'll take you back to prison."

The unfortunate man was stunned. The last glimmer which had lit up his despair had faded. He understood nothing that Sigault read to him, and he signed it blindly. He was shaking so on leaving the Magistrate's chambers that his guard suggested he lean on him.

"Then it didn't go well?" that man asked him. "Come now, Monsieur, you must have courage."

Courage! Prosper had none left when he found himself again in his cell. But with anger, hatred entered his heart. He promised himself that he would speak to the Investigating Magistrate, that he would defend himself, and that he would establish his innocence. They hadn't given him time. He bitterly reproached himself for having believed in the appearance of good will.

"What a joke!" he said. "Is that what an interrogation is?"

No, that was not an interrogation, in fact, just a simple formality. In having Prosper appear, Monsieur Patrigent was obeying Article 93 of the Code of Criminal Justice Procedure, which says: *'Every accused person named in an arrest warrant will be interrogated within twenty-four hours at the latest.'* But it wasn't done in twenty-four hours, especially in an affair like this one, in the absence of any body of evidence, of any material proof, even of any clue that an Investigating Magistrate could put together or form the elements for an investigation. To conquer the stubborn defense of an accused man who shuts himself inside absolute denial as in a fortress, you needed weapons. Monsieur Patrigent was busy preparing those weapons. If Prosper had stayed one hour longer in the gallery, he would have seen the same bailiff who had called him in, leave the chambers of the Investigating Magistrate and shout: "Number 3!" The witness who had the number three was seated on the wooden bench, waiting his turn. He was Monsieur André Fauvel. The banker was no longer the same man. As much as in his offices he had seemed animated by good intentions, similarly did he seem irritated with his young cashier when he entered the Magistrate's chambers. Reflection, which usually brings calmness and the need to pardon, had brought him only anger and the desire for vengeance.

The inevitable questions which begin every interrogation had scarcely been put to him, when he was carried away by his naturally fiery disposition. He poured out recriminations, and even invectives against Prosper. Monsieur Patrigent had to ask him to be silent, reminding him of what he owed to himself, whatever might be the wrongs of his employee. As before with the accused, the investigating judge became attentive and meticulous. That was because Prosper's interrogation had been only a formality, the setting forth of a brutal fact. Now it was a question of researching additional facts and particulars, to put together most seemingly insignificant circumstances, and to draw a conviction from them.

"Let's take things in order," he said to Monsieur Fauvel. "And for the moment, limit yourself, please, to answering my questions. Did you doubt your cashier's honesty?"

"Certainly I did not! And nevertheless a thousand reasons should have bothered me."

"What reasons, may I ask?"

"Monsieur Bertomy, my cashier, gambled. He spent nights playing the card game, baccarat. Several times I knew he had lost large sums. He had bad acquaintances. Once with one of the clients of my bank, Monsieur de Clameran, he got mixed up in a scandalous gambling affair, which had started at a woman's house and ended in a police station."

And for more than a minute, the banker accused Prosper terribly. When he finally stopped:

"Admit, Monsieur," said the judge, "that you were very imprudent, not to say very guilty, for having trusted your safe to such a man."

"Oh! Monsieur," answered Monsieur Fauvel. "Prosper hasn't always been like that. Right up until last year, he was a model for men of his age. Admitted into my home, he was almost a part of the family. He spent all his evenings with us. He was the close friend of my elder son, Lucien. Then suddenly, brusquely, from one day to the next, he stopped coming and we haven't seen him return. However, I have every reason to believe him to be in love with my niece, Madeleine."

Monsieur Patrigent frowned a certain way, which was his custom when he thought he had snatched some clue.

"Couldn't it have been precisely that inclination," he asked, "which might have caused Monsieur Bertomy to stay away?"

"Why?" the banker in the most surprised way asked. "I would have given him Madeleine's hand the most willingly in the world, and to be frank, I supposed that he was going to ask me for it. My niece would have been a good catch, an unexpected catch for him. She's very pretty and she'll have a half million as a dowry."

"Then you don't see any motive for your cashier's behavior?"

The banker seemed to be looking for one.

"Absolutely none," he answered. "I've always supposed that Prosper was led astray by a young man he met at my house during that time, Monsieur Raoul de Lagors."

"And who is this young man?"

"He's a relative of my wife, a charming boy, intelligent and well brought up, a little scatterbrained, but rich enough to pay for his flightiness."

The investigating Magistrate no longer seemed to be listening. He was writing the name Lagors in his notebook, at the bottom of an already long list of names.

"Now," he continued. "Let's get to the facts. You're sure that the theft wasn't committed by anyone in your household?"

"Yes, I'm absolutely sure, Monsieur."

"Your key never left you?"

"Seldom, at least. And when I don't carry it on me, I put it in one of the drawers of the secretary in my bedroom."

"Where was it the evening of the theft?"

"In my secretary."

"But then..."

"Pardon, Monsieur," interrupted Monsieur Fauvel, "let me point out to you, that for a strong safe like mine, a key doesn't mean anything. More than anything you must know the word with which the five moveable discs turn. With this word, you can, with great difficulty, open it without a key. But without the word…"

"And, you didn't tell this word to anyone?"

"No, to no one in the world, Monsieur. And you see, I have sometimes been very embarrassed, unsure with what word the safe was closed. Prosper changed it whenever it seemed right to him. He told me about it and I sometimes forgot it."

"Had you forgotten it the day of the theft?"

"No, the word had been changed the day before and it struck me by its unusualness."

"What was it?"

"Gypsy. G Y P S Y," said the banker, writing the letters.

Monsieur Patrigent also wrote down that word.

"One more question, Monsieur," he said. "Were you at home the evening of the theft?"

"No, Monsieur, I was having dinner at the home of one of my friend's, and I spent the evening there. When I returned to my house, about 1:00 a.m., my wife was in bed and I myself went immediately to bed."

"And you didn't know the amount of money in that safe?"

"Absolutely not. According to my formal orders, I had to suppose that there was only an insignificant sum there. I stated that to the Police Commissioner and Monsieur Bertomy confirmed it."

"That's true. The verbal testimony backs it up."

Monsieur Patrigent was silent. For him, everything was in this fact: the banker didn't know there were 350,000 francs in the safe and Prosper was remiss in his duty by having them withdrawn from the bank, therefore…the conclusion was easy to draw.

Seeing that he was no longer being questioned, the banker thought he could finally say everything he had on his mind.

"I believe it myself, Monsieur," he began. "And nevertheless I won't sleep easy until the guilt of my cashier has been completely established. Slander prefers to attack the man who has succeeded in business. I can be slandered. Three hundred and fifty thousand francs are a fortune capable of tempting the richest. I would be grateful to you if you would examine the situation of my bank. That examination will prove the prosperity of my business and that I have nothing to gain by robbing myself."

"That will be all, Monsieur."

It was enough, in fact. Monsieur Patrigent was already informed and knew as well as the banker what to make of his situation. He asked him to sign his interrogation and conducted him as far the door of his chambers, a rare favor on his part.

Monsieur Fauvel left. Sigault, the stenographer, allowed himself an observation.

"This is a devilishly obscure business," he said. "If the cashier is clever and stands firm, it seems to me it would be very difficult to convict him."

"Maybe," said the judge, "but let's see the other witnesses."

The man who had the number four was none other than Lucien, the elder son of Monsieur Fauvel. This young man, a tall and handsome fellow, twenty-two years old, answered that he liked Prosper very much. He said that he had been very close to him, and that he had always considered him an honest man, incapable of even an indelicacy. He declared that even at the present time, he couldn't explain to himself how and by what set of fatal circumstances Prosper had come to commit a crime. He was aware that Prosper gambled, but not as much as people claimed. He had never observed that he lived above his means. On the subject of his cousin Madeleine, he answered:

"I've always thought that Prosper was in love with Madeleine. Until yesterday I was convinced that he would marry her, knowing that my father didn't oppose the marriage. I have always attributed Prosper's leaving to a quarrel with my cousin, but I was persuaded that they would at last make up."

This information, even better than that of Monsieur Fauvel, threw light on the cashier's past; but apparently it didn't reveal any clue on which one could make a determination in the present circumstances.

Lucien signed his deposition and left. It was the young Cavaillon's turn to be interrogated. When he came before the judge, the poor boy was in a pitiable state. The evening before, having recounted his adventure with the Sûreté agent in great secret to one of his friends, a lawyer's clerk, the clerk had outrageously teased him about his cowardice. He had experienced extreme remorse and had spent the night reproaching himself for having betrayed Prosper. Unfortunately, moreover, not having any proof to furnish to back up what he said, his expression of passionate friendship for Prosper took away much of the value of his declarations.

After Cavaillon, six or eight employees of the Fauvel bank successively filed into the Magistrate's chambers, but their depositions were almost all insignificant. One of them, however, gave a detail the Magistrate noted. He claimed to know that Prosper had speculated on the French Stock Exchange, the Bourse, through Monsieur Raoul de Lagors as an intermediary, and had earned important sums. It was

5:00 p.m. when the list of witnesses for that day was exhausted. But Monsieur Patrigent's task still wasn't finished. He rang for his stenographer, who appeared almost immediately, and said:

"Go, as quickly as you can, and find me Fanferlot."

The Sûreté agent was a long time coming in response to the Magistrate's orders. Having run into one of his colleagues in the hallway, he felt himself obligated, out of politeness, to have a drink with him. The stenographer had been obliged to go chase him out of a small café/ brasserie on the corner.

"How long did you expect me to wait?" the Magistrate asked severely when he entered.

Fanferlot came in bowing to the ground, and then if it were possible, bowed more deeply still. That was because, despite his smiling face, a thousand worries were tormenting him. In order to follow the Bertomy affair by himself, he had to play a double game, which might be discovered. To manipulate the justice system like a goat hoping to get a bite of cabbage, here meaning his ambition, he was running great risks, the least of which was losing his job.

"I had a lot to do," he answered to excuse himself, "and I didn't waste my time."

And at that, he began to give an account of his actions. Not without inconvenience, of course, because he didn't speak without all sorts of restrictions, sorting out what he had to say and what he could keep quiet. So he gave up the story of Cavaillon's letter, and even gave that letter which he had stolen from Gypsy to the judge; but he didn't breathe a word about Madeleine. In return, he gave a mass of biographical details picked up a little everywhere about Prosper and Madame Gypsy. The further he went into his report, the more Monsieur Patrigent's convictions were confirmed.

"Obviously," he said, "this young man is guilty." Fanferlot didn't disabuse him of that thought. That opinion wasn't his, but he was delighted with the idea that the Magistrate was on the wrong track, telling himself that he would have even more glory in seizing the truly guilty one. The annoying thing was that he didn't yet know how to arrive at that beautiful result.

When he had gathered all of his information, the Magistrate dismissed his agent, giving him various missions and assigning to him a rendezvous for the next day.

"Above all," he told him in summing up, "don't lose sight of the Gypsy girl. She must know where the money is and can lead us to it."

Fanferlot had a malicious smile.

"Monsieur, the Magistrate can rest easy," he said. "The woman is in good hands."

Alone again, and even though the evening was late, Monsieur Patrigent still took up a good number of measures which would bring depositions into his chambers. That affair had taken absolute hold of his mind and irritated and attracted him at the same time. He seemed to discover certain obscure and mysterious sides which he swore to himself to look into.

The next day, well before his usual hour, he entered his chambers. He expected to interview Madame Gypsy that day, to have Cavaillon recalled, and to send for Monsieur Fauvel. And he expected to spend the following days on that work. However, two witnesses called didn't appear. The first was the office boy Prosper had sent to the bank. He was seriously hurt in a fall. The second was Monsieur Raoul de Lagors. But their absence didn't keep Prosper's file from getting larger. And the following Monday, that is six days after the theft, Monsieur Patrigent believed he had in his hands enough moral proofs to crush his accused.

Chapter V

While his whole life was under the minutest investigation, Prosper was in prison in solitary confinement. The first two days hadn't seemed too long to him. They had brought him, when he insisted, some numbered sheets of paper which he must answer for; he wrote down with a sort of rage some plans for defense and some justifying memories. The third day, he began to worry about not seeing anybody except the condemned men employed in the solitary confinement area, and the jailer in charge of bringing him his meals.

"Are they going to question me again?" he asked each time.

"Your turn will come, you can be sure." the jailer invariably answered.

Time passed. Tortured by the agony of solitary confinement which breaks the strongest natures, the unfortunate man fell into the deepest despair.

"Then am I here forever?" he cried out.

No, he hadn't been forgotten, because on the following Monday at 1:00 p.m., a time jailers never come, he heard the grating of the cell locks. With one leap, he stood up and ran toward the door. But seeing a man with gray hair standing on the threshold, he was totally dumbfounded.

"Father," he stammered, "Father!"

"Yes, your father."

Now, however he comes, a father is a friend to be counted on. In terrible times when all support is gone, one remembers that man one leaned on as a child. Even if he couldn't do anything, his presence was reassuring, like that of an all-powerful protector.

Without thinking, and carried away by a rush of outpouring tenderness, Prosper opened his arms as if to throw himself around his father's neck. Monsieur Bertomy pushed him away roughly.

"Get back," he ordered him.

The two men faced each other, Prosper broken and stunned, Monsieur Bertomy irritated and almost menacing. Repulsed by this last friend, a father, the cashier seemed to stiffen under an atrocious pain.

"You too!" he cried out. "You!...You think I'm guilty."

"Spare yourself a shameful comedy," interrupted Monsieur Bertomy. "I know everything."

"But Father, I'm innocent. I swear to you on the sacred memory of my mother..."

"Miserable man," exclaimed Monsieur Bertomy, "don't blaspheme."

An irresistible softness came over him, and it was with a weak, almost unintelligible voice that he said:

"Your mother is dead, Prosper, and I didn't know that a day would come when I would bless God for having taken her from me. Your crime would have killed her!"

There was a long silence. Finally, Prosper spoke again.

"You're crushing me, Father, and that is just when I need all my courage, at the time when I'm the victim of the most odious plot."

"Victim!" Monsieur Bertomy burst out. "Victim!…You mean that with your insinuations you're trying to brand the honorable and good man who took care of you, who showered you with benefits, who assured you of a brilliant position, and who prepared you for an un-hoped for future. It's enough to have stolen from him. Don't slander him."

"Have pity! Father, let me tell you…"

"What! Are you, perhaps, going to deny the goodness of your employer? You were so sure of his affection. One day you even wrote to me, telling me to be prepared to make the trip to Paris to ask Monsieur Fauvel for the hand of his niece. Then, was that a lie?"

"No," answered Prosper in a stifled voice. "No."

"That was a year ago. You were in love with Mademoiselle Madeleine then. At least you wrote to me that you were."

"But I love her, Father, more than ever. I've never stopped loving her."

Monsieur Bertomy made a gesture of pitying scorn.

"Really!" he cried out. "And the thought of the chaste and pure young woman that you loved didn't halt you on the threshold of debauchery. You loved her! How dare you present yourself then, without blushing, before her when leaving your corrupt companions?"

"Oh! In the name of Heaven! Let me explain to you by what fatality Madeleine…"

"Enough, Monsieur, I know everything. I've told you so. I saw your employer yesterday. This morning I saw your Investigating Magistrate, and it was through his kindness I was able to come here to see you. Do you know that I had to let myself be searched, me, almost undressed, to get in here? They thought I was bringing you a weapon."

Prosper didn't try to fight any longer. Hopeless, he let himself fall back on his prison bench.

"I saw your apartment and I understood your crime. I saw the silk hangings on all the doors, and the paintings with gold frames along all the walls. In my father's house the walls were whitewashed and there was only one armchair in the house, and that was for my mother. Our honesty: that was our luxury. You are the first one in the family to have Aubusson rugs. It's equally true that you're the first thief found in our family."

At that last insult, the blood rushed to Prosper's cheeks, but he didn't move.

"Now luxury is necessary," Monsieur Bertomy went on, becoming more animated and excited by the sound of his own voice. "You must have luxury at any price. People want the extraordinary and showy opulence of the newly successful man, without being newly successful. They keep mistresses who wear satin slippers embroidered with peacock feathers, like those I saw at the foot of your bed; and they have servants wearing livery. And they steal! And bankers have been reduced to no longer daring to trust anyone with the key to their safe. And every morning, some unexpected theft covers honorable families with mud."

Monsieur Bertomy stopped suddenly. He had just noticed that his son seemed to be beyond the ability to hear him.

"Let's leave it there," he continued. "I didn't come here to reproach you. I came here to save something of our honor, if it can be done, and to keep them from printing our name in the legal notices among the names of thieves and murderers. Get up and listen to me."

At the commanding tone of his father, Prosper stood up straight. All the successive blows had reduced him to that state of grim insensibility of the miserable man who no longer has anything to lose.

"First of all," Monsieur Bertomy began, "how much do you still have of the 350,000 francs that you stole?"

"One more time, Father," answered the unfortunate man with a tone of terrible resignation. "One more time, I'm innocent."

"So be it. I expected that answer. Then it's our family who'll repair the damage you caused to your employer."

"What's that? What do you mean?"

"The day he told us about your crime, your brother-in-law came to bring me back your sister's dowry, 70,000 francs. On my side I was able to get together 140,000 francs. That makes in all 210,000 francs that I have on me. And I'm going to take them to Monsieur Fauvel."

That threat brought Prosper out of his stupor.

"You won't do that!" he cried out with barely contained violence.

"I will do that before the end of the day. Monsieur Fauvel will give me time to repay the rest of the amount. My retirement pension is 1,500 francs. I can live on 500. I'm still strong enough to take a job. For his part, your brother-in-law…"

Monsieur Bertomy stopped short, startled by the expression on his son's face. An anger so furious that it seemed near madness contracted his face. His eyes, dull just a moment ago, flashed lightening.

"You don't have the right, Father!" he screamed. "No, you don't have the right to do this! You're free to refuse to believe me. You cannot begin an action which will be an admission of guilt and therefore doom me. What makes you so sure that I'm guilty? What? While the law hesitates, you my father, you don't hesitate; and more pitiless than the law, you condemn me without listening to me."

"I'll do my duty!"

"That means that I'm at the edge of a precipice, and that you're going to push me over! Is that what you call your duty? What! Between strangers who accuse me and me who cries out to you that I'm innocent, you don't hesitate to choose? Why? Is it because I'm your son? Our honor is in danger, that's true; that's more reason to support me, to help me to defend it and to save it."

Prosper had found the right words and tone to penetrate the doubt of the most profound consciences and shake the most solid convictions. Monsieur Bertomy was moved.

"However," he murmured, "everything accuses you."

"Ah! Father, that's because you don't know that one day I had to flee Madeleine. It had to be. I was desperate. I wanted to forget—I looked for forget-fulness. I found disgust and shame. Oh, Madeleine!"

His manner became gentle, but soon he continued with increasing violence.

"Everything is against me; that doesn't matter. I'll be able to clear myself or perish in the attempt. Human justice is subject to error. Even though innocent, I can be condemned. So be it. I can endure my pain. But people do get out of jail..."

"Unfortunate man, what are you saying?"

"I'm saying, Father, that I'm now a different man. My life has a purpose from now on—vengeance. I'm the victim of an infamous plot. So long as I have a drop of blood in my veins, I will pursue its author. And I'll find him. He'll have to pay for my torture and my agony. It began in the Fauvel bank and that's where search must begin."

"Be careful!' said Monsieur Bertomy. "Anger is leading you astray!"

"Yes, I understand. You're going to throw Monsieur André Fauvel's hon-esty in my face. You're going to tell me that all virtue finds a resting place in the bosom of that family. What do you know about it? Would this be the first time that beautiful appearances of honesty hid the most shameful secrets? Why did Madeleine one day suddenly forbid me to think about her? Why did she send me away when she still loves me, since she suffered as much as I did from our sepa-ration? Understand me well. She loves me. I'm sure of it. I have the proof."

The hour that was allowed to Monsieur Bertomy for an interview with his son had expired. The jailor came to tell him so. A thousand different sentiments tore apart this unfortunate father's heart, and deprived him of all freedom to think. What if Prosper was telling the truth! What would his remorse be later for having added to his misfortune, which was already so great! And what proof was there that he wasn't telling the truth! The voice of his son, whom he had been proud of for such a long time, brought out in him all the violently sup-pressed paternal tenderness. Ah! If he was guilty, and guilty of an even worse crime, was he any less his son? His expression had lost all its severity; his eyes were shining with tears ready to fall. He wanted to leave as serious and as irri-tated as he had entered. He didn't have that cruel courage. His heart was break-ing. He opened his arms and pressed Prosper to his heart.

"Oh! My son!" he murmured on leaving. "May it be that you have told the truth!"

Prosper had gotten his agreement. He had almost convinced his father of his innocence. But he didn't have time to rejoice over that victory. The door of the cell opened almost as soon as it was closed after his father, and the voice of the jailor, like the first time cried out:

"Let's go to the interrogation, Monsieur…"

So, it was necessary to obey. He obeyed. But his attitude wasn't that of the first days. A complete change had just taken place in him. He walked with his head high and with a confident step, the fire of resolution shining in his eyes. He knew the way now and he walked a little ahead of the Paris guard who accompanied him. As he was going across the little low room where the agents and the guards were on duty, he was approached by that man with the gold-rimmed spectacles, the one who in the booking room had stared at him for such a long time.

"Have courage! Monsieur Prosper Bertomy," this person said to him. "If you are innocent, we'll help you."

Prosper stopped in surprise. He was trying to find a response, but the man had already passed on.

"Who is that gentleman?" he asked the guard following him.

"What! You don't know him?" answered the guard with great surprise. "That's Monsieur Lecoq of the Sûreté."

"Lecoq. Who's that?"

"You could certainly say 'Monsieur.' That wouldn't scorch your tongue," said the offended Paris guard. "Monsieur Lecoq is a man you don't lie to and who knows everything he wants to know. If you'd had him instead of that imbecile Fanferlot, your affair would have been finished a long time ago. With him you don't wait around. But he seems to be one of your acquaintances."

"I never saw him before the day that they brought me here."

"You don't need to swear to it because, you see, nobody can brag about knowing the real face of Monsieur Lecoq. He looks one way today and another tomorrow—sometimes brunette, sometimes blond, sometimes very young, at other times so old you'd think he was a hundred years old. Look, I'm telling you. He throws me off the track whenever he likes. I'm talking with someone I don't know. Poof! It's him. Just anybody could be him. If someone told me you were he, I'd say: "That's very possible." Ah! That man, he can brag about doing whatever he likes with his body."

The Paris guard would have gone on a long time setting forth the legend of Monsieur Lecoq, but he arrived with his accused at the corridor of the Investigating Magistrates. This time Prosper didn't have to wait on the humble wooden bench. On the contrary, the Magistrate was expecting him. Having observed in depth the movements of the human soul, it was, in fact, Monsieur Patrigent who had arranged the interview of Monsieur Bertomy with his son. He was sure that between the father, a man of upright honesty, and the son accused of theft, a

334

heart-rending sorrowful scene would take place. He was counting on that scene to break Prosper. He told himself that if he then ordered the accused to be brought before him, he would come with his nerves vibrating, terribly emotional, and he could snatch the truth by way of his trouble and his despair. Therefore he was somewhat surprised by the cashier's attitude. It was an attitude of resolution without coldness, proud and assured, without impertinence or defiance.

"Well!" he asked him immediately, "Have you thought it over?"

"Not being guilty, Monsieur, I don't have anything to think over."

"Ah!" said the judge, "Prison hasn't been a good advisor for you. You've forgotten that sincerity and repentance, above all, are necessary to those who wish to merit the indulgence of judges."

"I don't need either indulgence or grace, Monsieur."

Monsieur Patrigent couldn't hold back a movement of irritation. He was silent a moment, then suddenly said:

"What would you say to me," he asked, "if I told you what became of the 350,000 francs?"

Prosper shook his head sadly.

"If you knew," he simply answered, "I would be free and not here."

The commonplace method used by the Investigating Magistrate very often succeeds. But here with an accused with such self-control, he had hardly any chance of success. However, he had tried it completely at random.

"So," he began again, "You stick to your first claim. You continue to accuse your employer."

"Him or someone else."

"Pardon me...Only him, since he was the only one with the word. Did he have any reason to rob himself?"

"I've thought about it, Monsieur. I can't see that he had one."

"Well!" the Magistrate pronounced severely. "I'm going to tell you what reason you yourself had to steal it."

Monsieur Patrigent spoke like a man sure of his facts, but his assurance was only a pose. He had been prepared to strike a last bludgeoning blow to an accused who'd come before him panting. He was thrown off track to see him so calm and so determined in his resistance.

"Will you tell me?" he began in a tone which showed his irritation, "Can you tell me, how much you spent the last year?"

Prosper didn't need to think nor to calculate.

"Yes, Monsieur," he answered without hesitating. "The circumstances were such that I brought the greatest order to my disorder. I spent about 50,000 francs."

"And where did you get them?"

"First of all, Monsieur, I had 12,000 francs bequeathed to me by my mother. I earned 14,000 francs at Monsieur Fauvel's by my salary, and my stock market shares earned about 8,000 francs. I borrowed the rest. I owe it, but I can repay it, since I have 15,000 francs of my own in Monsieur Fauvel's bank."

The summary was clear, precise, and easy to verify. It had to be correct.

"Who then lent you money?"

"Monsieur Raoul de Lagors."

This witness, who had left on a trip the very day of the theft, hadn't been able to be questioned. Monsieur Patrigent could do nothing else, at least for the moment, but agree with Prosper's declaration.

"So be it," he said. "I won't insist on this point. Let me know why, despite the explicit orders of your employer, you had money brought from the Bank of Paris on the evening before and not on the same day as the disbursement?"

"That was because Monsieur de Clameran had let me know that it would be agreeable for him, Monsieur, even useful to have the cash early in the morning. He will testify to that, if you have him called. On the other hand, I thought that perhaps I'd arrive late to my office."

"Then is this Monsieur de Clameran one of your friends?"

"Not at all. I even felt a sort of repugnance for him which, I admit, nothing justified. But he is very close to my friend Monsieur de Lagors."

During the rather long time required by the stenographer Sigault to write down the accused's answers, Monsieur Patrigent was racking his brains. He was wondering what kind of scene had taken place between Monsieur Bertomy and his son to thus transform Prosper.

"Another thing," the Investigating Magistrate took up again, "how did you spend your evening, the evening of the crime?"

"Leaving my office at 5:00 p.m., I took the Saint Germain train and I went to Vésinet, to the country house of Monsieur Raoul de Lagors. I carried to him the 1,500 francs that he had asked me for. Since he was absent, I left it with his servant."

"Did anyone tell you that Monsieur Lagors was supposed to leave on a trip?"

"No, Monsieur. I don't even know if he's away from Paris."

"Very well. And on leaving your friend's, what did you do?"

"I returned to Paris and I had dinner on the boulevard with one of my friends."

"And then?"

Prosper hesitated.

"You're silent," continued Monsieur Patrigent. "So, I'm going to tell you how you spent your time. You went to your house, on the Rue Chaptal. You got dressed and you went to an evening party given by one of those women who call themselves dramatic actresses, who dishonor the theaters where they appear, who cost 100 écus for an appointment, and who have horses and carriages. To the Wilson woman's."

"That's true, Monsieur."

"Do they play for high stakes at the Wilson woman's?

"Sometimes."

"What's more, you make a habit of these sorts of gatherings. Didn't you find yourself mixed up in a scandalous affair that took place at the residence of a woman of this sort, a woman named Crescenzi?"

"The fact is, I was called to give a deposition, having witnessed a theft."

"In fact, the gambling led to the theft. And at the Wilson woman's, didn't you play the card game, baccarat, and didn't you lose 1,800 francs?"

"Pardon, Monsieur, only 1,100."

"All right. You paid in the morning with a 1,000 franc bill?"

"Yes, Monsieur."

"What's more, there remained 500 francs in your secretary; and when you were arrested, you had 400 francs in your billfold. That means that in all, in twenty-four hours, a sum of 4,500 francs."

Prosper's self-possession was not only shaken, but he was astounded. He hadn't realized what powerful methods of investigation the public Magistrates had available. He wondered how in so short a time the Magistrate could be so exact in his information.

"Your information is correct, Monsieur," he finally said.

"Then where did that money come from, when just the evening before you were so short of cash that you had put off paying a bill of so little importance?"

"Monsieur, on the day you're talking about, I sold some stocks I had through a stock broker, for something like 3,000 francs. In addition, I had taken a 2,000 franc advance on my salary from my cashbox. I have nothing to hide."

Obviously, the accused had answered everything. Monsieur Patrigent had to find another point of attack.

"If you have nothing to hide," he said, "why is there this note, thrown mysteriously to one of your colleagues?"

The blow, that time, carried home. Prosper's eyes shifted under the gaze of the Investigating Magistrate.

"I thought," he stammered, "I wanted…"

"You wanted to hide your mistress."

"All right! Yes, Monsieur, that's true. I knew that when a man is accused of a crime, as I am, all the weaknesses and all the failings of his life become terrible accusations."

"This means that you understood that the presence of a woman in your apartment gave enormous weight to the accusation. Because it's true that you were living with a woman."

"I am young, Monsieur."

"That's enough! The law can pardon certain temporary misguided behavior. It can't excuse the scandal of these unions, which are a permanent defiance of public morality. The man, who so little respects himself as to live with a fallen woman, doesn't raise that woman to his level. He falls down to hers."

"Monsieur!"

"I imagine you know who that woman is to whom you give the honorable name worn by your mother?"

"Madame Gypsy, Monsieur, was an elementary school teacher when I met her. She was born at Porto and came to France as a part of a Portuguese family."

The Investigating Magistrate shrugged.

"Her name is not Gypsy," he said. "She was never an elementary school teacher. She is not Portuguese."

Prosper wanted to protest, but Monsieur Patrigent motioned him to be silent. He was looking through the documents contained in an enormous file placed in front of him.

"Ah! Here it is," he said. "Listen. Palmyre Chocareille; born in Paris 1840; daughter of Chocareille, Jacques, an employee of a funeral home and Caroline Piedlent, his wife."

The accused gestured with impatience. He didn't know that at this moment the Magistrate wanted to above all prove that nothing escaped the police.

"Palmyre Chocareille," he continued, "at twelve-years-old was placed as an apprentice to a shoe maker, and she stayed there until she was sixteen. Information is missing for the next year. At seventeen, she was employed as a servant with a Dombas couple, owners of a grocery store, and stayed there three months. That year—1857—she had eight or ten jobs. In 1857, tired of domestic service, she took a job as a shop girl with a merchant of fans in the Passage Choiseul."

While he was reading, the Investigating Magistrate was observing Prosper's face to see what effect these revelations produced.

"At the end of 1858, the Chocareille girl entered the service of a Lady Nunes, and left with her for Lisbon. How long did she stay in Portugal? What did she do there? My reports are silent in this regard. What is certain is that in 1861 she was back in Paris and was sentenced there by the Paris law courts to three months in prison for assault. Ah! She brought the name Nina Gypsy back from Portugal."

"But, Monsieur, I assure you…"

"Yes, I understand. That history is less romantic than the one she told you. It has the merit of being true. We lose sight of Palmyre Chocareille when she leaves prison. But we find her again six months later, having met a traveling salesman named Caldas, who, taken with her beauty, had set her up in an apartment near the Bastille. She was living with him and wore his name, when she left him to follow you. Have you ever heard of this Caldas?"

"Never, Monsieur."

"That unfortunate man loved that creature so much that, when he found that she had left him, became almost insane with sadness. It seems that he was a strong man, and that he had sworn publicly that he'd kill the man who'd taken his mistress. There is reason to believe that since then he has committed suicide. What can be proved is that a little while after the departure of the Chocareille girl, he sold the apartment furniture and disappeared. All efforts to find out what happened to him were in vain."

The investigating judge stopped a moment as if to give Prosper time to think and, stressing all his words, he added:

"There is the woman whom you made your companion, the woman for whom you stole!"

Once again, badly served by Fanferlot's incomplete information, Monsieur Patrigent took the wrong direction. He had hoped to snatch a passionate cry from Prosper, wounded to the quick. Not at all. He remained emotionless. From everything the Magistrate had said, he retained only the name of this poor traveling salesman, Caldas.

"At least admit that the girl caused your fall," Monsieur Patrigent insisted.

"I can't admit that, Monsieur, because that didn't happen."

"She was, however, the reason for your greatest expenditures. And look here…" and the Magistrate drew a bill from the dossier, "in just the month of last December, you paid the dressmaker Van-Klopen on her behalf, 900 francs for two city dresses, 700 francs for an evening dress, and 400 francs for a masked ball costume decorated with lace."

"I spent all that money freely, with a clear head, expecting nothing in return."

Monsieur Patrigent shrugged.

"You're denying the evidence," he said. "Do you also claim that it wasn't because of that woman that you gave up the habit of several years and stopped spending your evenings at your employer's house?"

"It wasn't because of her, Monsieur, I can assure you."

"Then why, suddenly, do you no longer appear in a house where you seemed to be courting a young girl, one whose hand in marriage, Monsieur Fauvel tells me, you wrote to your father had been given to you."

"I have reasons I can't say," answered Prosper, whose voice trembled.

The Magistrate breathed a sigh of relief. He had finally found a chink in the armor of the accused.

"Could it have been that Mademoiselle Madeleine sent you away?" he asked.

"Speak up," Monsieur Patrigent, insisted. "I must warn you that such a circumstance is most serious in the eyes of the prosecution."

"Whatever the dangers of silence may be, I must be silent."

"Be careful," said the Magistrate. "The law can't be satisfied with scruples of conscience."

Monsieur Patrigent stopped talking. He was expecting an answer. It didn't come.

"You still won't talk," he started again. "All right! Let's continue. In a year you have spent, you say, 50,000 francs. The prosecution says 70,000, but let's take your figure. Your resources are at an end. Your credit is exhausted. It is impossible to continue your style of life. What do you expect to do?"

"I have no plans, Monsieur. I told myself that what would happen would happen, and after that…"

"And after that, 'I would dip into the safe,' right?"

"Ah! Monsieur," Prosper cried out. "If I were guilty, I wouldn't be here. I wouldn't be so stupid as to return to my office. I would have fled…"

Monsieur Patrigent couldn't hide a smile of satisfaction.

"Finally," he said. "That was the argument I was waiting for. It's precisely in not running away, in staying to wait out the storm, that you proved your intelligence. Several recent trials have taught untrustworthy cashiers that fleeing to a foreign land is a pitiful method of evasion. The train travels fast, but the electric telegraph goes even faster. Belgium is two steps away. In London, by advertising, a French thief was picked up in forty-eight hours. Even America is no longer a safe haven. Prudent and wise, you stayed, telling yourself, 'I can get out of it; and if worse comes to worst and I'm convicted, after three to five years of prison I'll get back a fortune.' Many people would sacrifice five years of their life for 350,000 francs."

"But, Monsieur, if I had calculated the way you say, I wouldn't have been satisfied with 350,000 francs, I would have waited for an opportunity and stolen 1,000,000."

"Oh!" said Monsieur Patrigent. "You can't always wait."

Prosper was reflecting, and the contraction of his facial muscles showed the effort of his concentration.

"Monsieur," he finally said. "In my trouble there is a detail that I forgot, which now I remember and can help in my justification."

"Explain what you mean."

"The office boy who went to get the cash at the Bank brought it to me as I was waiting only for him to return to leave. I'm sure, yes, I'm certain that I tied up the bank bills in front of him. Oh! If he only noticed it! In any case, I left my office before he did."

"All right," said Monsieur Patrigent. "The boy will be talked to. Now they're going to take you back to your cell, and take my advice, think about it."

If Monsieur Patrigent was dismissing his accused so brusquely, it was because this new fact suddenly revealed to him bothered him. The office boy's deposition was going to have enormous importance. What if that man came to swear that he'd had seen the cashier shut up the bills and leave? Would it have been impossible for Prosper to have bought him off?

"Tell me, Sigault," he asked his stenographer when the accused had left, "This office boy the accused was talking about, this Antonin; isn't he the one who didn't come to give a deposition, and who was excused with a certification from his doctor verifying his medical condition?"

"Exactly, Monsieur."

"Where does he live?"

"Monsieur," Sigault answered. "Fanferlot told me he's no longer at his house. His situation was serious. Having to stay in bed a long time, he had himself transported to the Dubois Hospital."

"Well! I'm going to question him today, right this instant. Take everything you need and go find a carriage."

From the Palais de Justice Law Courts to the Dubois Hospital is a long way. But Monsieur Patrigent's coachman, spurred on by the promise of a magnificent tip, was able to give his skinny nags the speed of thoroughbreds. Would Antonin be in any condition to answer? That was the question. But the hospital director promptly reassured the Investigating Magistrate in that regard. The unfortunate office boy had fallen and broken his knee. He was suffering terribly, but his mind was clear.

"Since that's the situation, Monsieur," said the Magistrate, "please take me to this man that I must question. But it's necessary that no one be close enough to listen to his deposition, if it's possible."

"Oh! Nobody will hear," the Director answered. "He's in a room with four beds, that's true, but he's alone."

"Very good! Then let's go."

On seeing the Investigating Magistrate, followed by a tall thin young man carrying a lawyer's briefcase, Antonin, who knew the business world, guessed what it was about.

"Ah!" he said, "Monsieur is coming about the Monsieur Bertomy business."

"Exactly."

Monsieur Patrigent remained standing near the sick man's bed, while the stenographer Sigault got himself settled with his papers at a little table. The office boy answered all the usual questions, swearing that his name was Antonin Poche, forty years old, born in Cadajac, in Gironde Province, a bachelor.

"Let's see, my friend, do you feel well enough to answer me?"

"Perfectly, Monsieur."

"Were you the one who went on the 27th of February, to bring back from the Bank the 350,000 francs which were stolen?"

"Yes, Monsieur."

"What time did you return?"

"Rather late. I had some business at the Credit Mobilier on leaving the Bank. It must have been 5:00 p.m. when I got back."

"Do you recall what Monsieur Bertomy did when you gave him the cash? Don't be in a hurry to answer. Get your recollections together."

"Let's see. First of all, he counted the bills and he put them in four stacks that he placed in the safe, and then... Yes, I'm not mistaken, yes! He left."

He pronounced these last words with such energy that, forgetting his knee, he made a movement that caused him to cry out.

"You're very sure of what you've just said?" the Investigating Magistrate asked.

Monsieur Patrigent's solemn tone seemed to frighten Antonin.

"Sure!" he answered with visible hesitation. "I would bet my life; of more I cannot be sure."

It was impossible to lead him to state his deposition more clearly. He was afraid. He saw himself already involved. For something insignificant, he would have retracted his statement. The effect had been produced, nevertheless; and in leaving, Monsieur Patrigent said to his stenographer:

"This is serious! Very serious!"

Chapter VI

The Grand-Archange, Madame Gypsy's refuge, was the most magnificent hotel on the Quai Saint-Michel. When you pay in advance and pay on time every two weeks, you're treated very well there. This Madame Alexandre was in the past a beautiful woman, and was now a powerful woman. Terrible, girded into her corsets, and always wearing too much make-up, she loved golden chains rolling in cascades down the slopes of her robust breast. She still had sparkling eyes and white teeth, but alas, a red nose. That was because of all her tastes, and God knows she'd had some of all sorts during her life, only one had survived. She loved good food, washed down with a lot of wine. Pardon me! She also adored her husband, and just as Monsieur Patrigent was returning from the hospital to his office, she was very impatient because she hadn't seen her 'little man' come back for dinner. She was just going to sit down at the table, when a boy who worked in the hotel exclaimed:

"There comes Monsieur."

And Fanferlot in person appeared on the threshold. Three years before that time, Fanferlot had had a little clandestine detective agency. Madame Alexandre, a toiletry merchant without a license, needed some suspicious creditors followed; and from there came their first relationship. And if they married each other both in the city hall and in church, that was because it seemed to them that a holy sacrament would be like a baptism which would wash away their past. From that day onward, Fanferlot gave up his detective bureau to work only for the Prefecture, where he was already employed, and Madame Alexandre gave up business altogether. Making a single lump of their savings, they rented and outfitted the Grand-Archange Hotel. They prospered and were respected, or almost so, by the neighbors of the area who didn't know anything about Fanferlot's ties to the Prefecture of Police.

"How late you are coming back, my little man!" she exclaimed, dropping her soup spoon to run and hug him.

But he was distracted as he received her caresses.

"I'm tired out," he said. "I played billiards all day with Evariste, Monsieur Fauvel's valet. I let him beat me as often as he liked, a boy who doesn't even know what a '*masse*' is![29] I met him the day before yesterday and I'm now his best friend. If I want to get a job as an office boy in Antonin's place, I'm sure of Monsieur Evariste's protection."

"What! You'd work as an office boy, you?"

"Damn! I would if it was absolutely necessary to get a good view into the Fauvel bank and to study my characters up close."

---

[29] The large end of a billiard cue.

"Then the valet didn't tell you anything?"

"At least nothing I could use, and even so, I played him like a fiddle. This banker is like a man you seldom see. Evariste tells me he has no vices, not even a poor little fault for which a valet could earn ten écus. He doesn't smoke, he doesn't drink, he doesn't gamble, and he doesn't have a mistress. He's a real saint! He's a millionaire. He lives economically, stingily like a grocer. He's mad about his wife. He adores his children. He entertains frequently, but goes out seldom."

"Then his wife is young?"

"She must be about fifty."

Madame Alexandre thought a moment.

"Did you get any information about the other people in the family?"

"Certainly. One of the sons is an officer in the military; I don't know where. Let's not talk about him. He's the youngest. The elder, Lucien, lives with his parents, and it seems he's a real little lady as far as his behavior is concerned."

"And the wife, and the niece you told me about?"

"Evariste didn't have anything to say about them."

Madame Alexandre shrugged.

"If you didn't find out anything," she said, "there isn't anything. And, listen, if I were in your place, do you know what I'd do?"

"Go on."

"I'd go consult Monsieur Lecoq."

At that name, Fanferlot jumped as if someone had shot a pistol near his ears.

"Good advice!" he said. "Do you want me to lose my job? If Monsieur Lecoq even suspected what I want to do!"

"Who's saying anything about telling him your secret. You ask him his opinion in an off-handed way. You keep what he can come up with that's good, and later you do whatever you like."

The Sûreté agent seemed to weigh his wife's reasoning.

"You may be right," he said. "However, he's terribly clever, Monsieur Lecoq, and very capable of seeing through me."

"Clever!" Madame Alexandre, stung, countered. "Clever! All of you at the Prefecture have made his reputation by continuing to repeat that."

"Well," concluded Fanferlot, "I'll see about it. I'll think about it. But in the meantime, what does the little girl say?"

The little girl was Nina Gypsy. By coming to settle-in at the Grand-Archange, the poor girl thought she was following good advice. And even now, when Fanferlot hadn't showed up, she remained convinced that she was obeying Prosper's friend. When she received the citation from Monsieur Patrigent, she admired the cleverness of the police who'd been able, in so short a time, to discover her hiding place. She had registered at the hotel under a false name, that is, under her real name, Palmyre Chocareille. Cleverly questioned by the former merchant of toilette articles, she hadn't suspected anything and had told her whole history. And that was how, with so little cost, Fanferlot had been able to pose in front of the Magistrate as having superior ability.

"The little girl stays upstairs—always, and she doesn't suspect anything. But to keep her is becoming more and more difficult. I don't know what the Magistrate said to her, but she came back to me beside herself. She wanted to go create an uproar at Monsieur Fauvel's bank. A little later, after a fit of anger, she wrote a letter and gave it to Jean to mail; but I got a hold of it to show you."

"What!" interrupted Fanferlot. "You have a letter and you haven't told me, and it may hold the key to the puzzle! Quick! Give it to me."

At the command of her husband, the former merchant of toiletries opened a little chest and took out Madame Gypsy's letter, which she gave to him.

"Here," she said to him. "Are you satisfied?"

In fact to tell the truth, for a former ladies' maid, Palmyre Chocareille become Gypsy, didn't have bad handwriting. The letter's address, written in beautiful French, was stated thus:

Monsieur
L. de Clameran, Foundry Owner At the Hotel du Louvre To be given to M. Raoul de Lagors. Urgent.

"Oh! Oh!" exclaimed Fanferlot, accompanying his exclamation with a little whistle, customary with him when he had made some discovery, "Oh! Oh!"

"Are you going to open it?" asked Madame Alexandre.

"Just slightly," answered Fanferlot, breaking open the seal with marvelous dexterity.

He read it, and Madame Alexandre, leaning over the shoulder of her 'little man,' read also.:

Monsieur Raoul, Prosper is in prison, accused of a theft he didn't commit. I'm sure of it. I have already written you three days ago, about this matter...

"Why! What!" Fanferlot interrupted himself. "That little person wrote and I haven't seen her letter!"

"But, my good little man, that unhappy girl might have put her letter in the mail herself when she went out to go to the Palais de Justice."

"Actually, that's possible," said Fanferlot, a little calmer. He continued reading:

...I have already written you three days ago, about this matter, and I have no news. Then who will come to Prosper's aid if his best friends abandon him?

If you leave this letter without an answer, I will believe myself released from a certain promise, which you are aware of. Without any scruples, I will tell Prosper about the conversation I happened upon between you and Monsieur de Clameran. But I can rely on you, can't I? I will wait for you at the Hotel Grand-Archange the day after tomorrow, from noon until four o'clock.

Nina Gypsy.

Having read that letter, Fanferlot, without saying a word, began to copy it. "Well!" asked Madame Alexandre, "What do you have to say about that?"

Fanferlot was delicately putting the copied letter back into its envelope when the door of the hotel office suddenly opened, and the porter whistled twice: "Pssst! Pssst!"

Fanferlot, with marvelous speed, disappeared into a closet which opened into the dining room. He didn't even have time to close the door; Madame Gypsy was coming in.

Alas! She had changed cruelly, the poor girl. She had become pale. She had sunken cheeks. Her lips had lost their provocative allure. And her eyes, burning with fever and red from crying, had large brown circles around them. Seeing her, Madame Alexandre couldn't hold back a cry of surprise.

"Dear child, are you going out?"

"I must, Madame. And I've come downstairs to ask you that if someone comes for me in my absence, you would please ask them to wait."

"But where are you going? *Bon Dieu!* At this hour, as sick as you are?"

Madame Gypsy hesitated for an instant.

"Oh! All right," she finally said. "You've been so good to me, I can tell you. Read this note a messenger just brought me a moment ago."

"What," said Madame Alexandre, stunned, "A messenger? Who went up to your room?"

"Why is that so surprising?"

"Oh! Nothing, nothing," answered the ex-retail merchant. And very loudly, so as to be better heard in the closet, she read:

A friend of Prosper, who can neither invite you to his place, nor come to you, absolutely needs to talk to you. This evening, Monday, at exactly 9:00 p.m., come to the omnibus office which is across from the Saint-Jacques tower. The one writing to you will approach you and tell you what he has to tell you. I'm giving you this rendezvous place so you will not be afraid.

"And you're going to go to this rendezvous?" exclaimed Madame Alexandre.

"Certainly."

"But that is terribly unwise, madness. It's a trap someone's setting for you."

346

"Ah! What does that matter, Madame?" Gypsy interrupted. "I am unhappy enough to have nothing to fear from now on."

And without waiting to hear another word, she left. Madame Gypsy hadn't reached the street when Fanferlot had leaped out of his hiding place. The 'gentle' agent was pale with fury and swore like a man possessed.

"A hundred thousand thunderations!" he cried out. "So what is this Grand-Archange, where people come and go like they were in a public place?"

The former toiletry merchant, abashed and trembling, didn't know what to do.

"Have you ever seen such a thing!" the agent went on. "A messenger came, and nobody saw him. How did he manage to get in so slyly? Ah! I smell some scoundrel in this! And you, Madame Alexandre, you an intelligent woman: you were as simple as to try to keep that little viper away from the rendezvous..."

"But, my love..."

"What! Didn't you already know I would be going to follow her and so find out what someone's hiding from us? Come on quickly, help me. She must not be able to recognize me."

In a flash, Fanferlot no longer resembled himself, dressed up in a wig and a thick beard. He had put on a workman's shirt and had all the appearances of one of those not very honest workers who look for work, while praying to God not to find any. Then he was ready.

"Do you have your identity card and your little pocket pistol?" asked Madame Alexandre, who was always full of solicitude.

"Yes, yes! Have someone throw that unhappy girl's letter to Monsieur de Clameran in the mail...and be on the look-out."

And without hearing his wife, who was shouting "Good-luck!" at him, Fanferlot dashed outside.

Madame Gypsy was eight or ten minutes ahead of him, but he slowly caught up with her. In following her, he had taken the route the young woman must have followed, and he joined her about the middle of the Pont-au-Change. She was walking along as if she couldn't make up her mind. Sometimes very fast, sometimes taking little steps, she was like a person who, impatient to get to a rendezvous, had left too soon and was trying to kill time. She walked two or three times around the Place du Chatelet, went up to some theater billboard advertisements, sat down for a moment on a bench, and finally, at just about 8:45 p.m., she went to sit down on one of the little benches of the omnibus office. Fanferlot came one minute after her. But despite his thick beard, he thought Madame Gypsy still might recognize him, and he went to place himself in the shadows on the other side of the office.

"A strange place for an encounter!" he thought, while studying the young woman. *"But who could have made this appointment with her?"*

From the curiosity I read in her eyes and her obvious uneasiness, I'd judge she doesn't know the person she's waiting for."

The office, however, was crowded. Every minute, employees called out the destination of an in-coming bus. A number of people who asked for tickets or changed their transfer tickets came in and went out. At each new arrival, Gypsy trembled and Fanferlot wondered: *"Is he the one?"*

Finally, as 9:00 p.m. rang out on the city clock, a person came in. Without asking for a ticket at the office window, he went straight up to Madame Gypsy, greeted her, and sat down near her. He was a man of middle height, rather fat, wearing thick sideburns, with deep blond hair and a reddish face. His dress was like that of all well-off businessmen, showing nothing remarkable, nor did his person.

Fanferlot stared at him.

"You, my good man," he thought, *"Wherever I meet you now, I'll recognize you. And by following you this very evening, I'll know who you are."*

Unfortunately, he listened in vain. He could hear absolutely nothing of what the newly arrived man and Madame Gypsy were saying. All he could do was to try to guess the subject of their conversation by their gestures and the expressions on their faces.

At first, when the fat man had greeted her, the young woman had looked so surprised that it was clear she was seeing him for the first time. When he said some words to her after being seated, she half rose with a frightened gesture, as if she wanted to run away. A single glance was enough to make her sit back down. Then, as the fat man continued speaking, Gypsy's attitude showed a certain apprehension. She made a negative gesture, but she seemed to give in to a very good reason given to her. At one moment, she seemed near to tears; but almost immediately a smile lit up her beautiful face. Finally, she held out her hand, as if she had sworn an oath. But what could that mean? Fanferlot, on his little bench, was biting his nails...

"I was an idiot to take a position so far off," he told himself.

He was thinking about how to execute some clever maneuver so as to get closer without arousing suspicion, when the fat man got up, gave his arm to Madame Gypsy, who just accepted it, and they walked together toward the door. They seemed so preoccupied with each other that Fanferlot didn't see any reason not to follow them rather closely, a wise precaution, because the boulevard was crowded. When they got to the door, he saw the fat man and Gypsy cross the sidewalk and approach a carriage not far from the omnibus office and get into the carriage.

"Perfect!" grumbled Fanferlot. "I've got them. There's no reason now to be in a hurry."

While the coachman was gathering up his reins, the Sûreté agent was limbering up his legs. When the carriage started off, in three strides he was behind it, determined to follow it to the ends of the world. The carriage went up the Boulevard de Sebastopol. It was making good time, but it wasn't for nothing that Fanferlot had been nicknamed 'the Squirrel.' His elbows glued to his body and controlling his breathing, he kept up. However, arriving at the Boulevard Saint-Denis, he began to be out of breath. He felt a slight pain in his side when the carriage, after having gone across the causeway, turned into the Rue Faubourg-Saint-Martin. But Fanferlot who, when he was eight years old, ran freely across the paving stones of Paris, was a resourceful man. He got a hold of the carriage springs, pulling himself up to the carriage hand over hand, and held himself suspended there, his legs braced against the axle of the back wheels. He certainly wasn't comfortable, but he no longer ran the risk of being outdistanced.

"Now," he said to himself, laughing in his false beard, "Use your whip, coachman!"

The coachman did use his whip, and he went up the rather steep incline of the Faubourg-Saint-Martin at a full trot. Finally, at the Square of the former Paris Gate, the carriage stopped at a wine merchant's shop. The coachman got down from his seat and went in to order a glass for himself. The Sûreté agent himself had left his uncomfortable post and had gone to hide in the corner of a door. He was waiting for the fat gentleman and Gypsy to get out, ready to dash forward on their trail. But at the end of five minutes, they hadn't gotten out yet.

"Then what are they doing?" the agent wondered.

He approached with some precaution.

Oh! What a disappointment! The carriage was empty! This was like a dash of cold water falling on Fanferlot's head. He stayed there, rooted to the spot, more crystallized than Lot's wife. When at the end of several seconds he recovered, it was to throw out a dozen curses which shook the windows of the neighborhood.

"Robbed!" He screamed. "I've been made a fool of, had, stuck, cheated! Ah! They'll pay for this."

In a moment, his agile mind ran through the gamut of probable and improbable eventualities.

"Evidently," he murmured, "that individual and Gypsy got in one of the carriage doors and left by the other. That trick is elementary. But if they used it, that was because they were afraid of being followed. If they were afraid if being followed, that means they don't have a clear conscience, so…"

He interrupted his monologue, because the idea had just come to him to question the coachman, who could very well know something. Unfortunately this coachman, who had a very bad disposition, refused to say anything, and even flicked his whip in a way so disturbing that Fanferlot decided to beat a retreat.

"Ah! Well, is the coachman in on it too?" he asked himself.

What could be done, however, at this hour? He had no idea. Again, he sadly picked up the Quai Saint-Michel road, and it was at least

11:30 p.m. when he rang at his door. "Has the little girl come back?" he asked immediately. "No, but two large packages came for her." Slowly, with great care, Fanferlot untied the packages. The pack ages contained three Indian dresses, heavy shoes, very simple skirts, and some linen bonnets.

The agent couldn't hold back a movement of irritation.

"Well, what do you know," he said. "Now it looks like she's going to disguise herself. On my word! I don't understand it!"

When he was coming down from the heights of the Faubourg Saint-Martin, Fanferlot had sworn to himself that he certainly wouldn't tell his wife anything about how he'd been thrown off the track. But once back home, faced with a new fact of a type to throw off all his conjectures, his consideration for his ego vanished. The Sûreté agent admitted everything: his hopes so little realized, his unbelievable misadventure, his suspicions! The husband and wife remained a long time discussing and studying the affair from all sides, looking for a plausible explanation. That was why they had definitely decided not to go to bed before the return of Madame Gypsy, from whom Madame Alexandre intended to get some explanations. But would she come back? That was the question.

She came back about an hour later, when the couple had already given up and begun to tell each other: "We won't see her anymore."

At the sound of the door bell, Fanferlot slid into the black cabinet and Madame Alexandre remained alone in the hotel office.

"Finally you're here, dear child!" she cried out to her. "Did anything happen to you? Ah! I was terribly upset."

"Thank you for your concern, Madame," Gypsy answered, "but did anyone bring anything for me?"

She had returned very different than when she had left, that poor Gypsy. She was very sad, but was no longer beaten down. Her desperation of the preceding days was replaced by a firm and generous resolution, which showed itself in her bearing and in the light in her eyes.

"Someone brought the packages over here," answered Madame Alexandre. "So, you saw Monsieur Bertomy's friend?"

"Yes, Madame, and his advice has even changed my plans so much that tomorrow I'll regretfully have to say good-bye. I'm leaving."

"Tomorrow!" said the former toiletry merchant. "Then something has happened?"

"Oh! Nothing which could interest you…"

And having lit her candle from the gas light, she went to bed after a most significant, "Good evening. Have a good night."

"What do you think about that reentry, Madame Alexandre?" asked Fanferlot, coming out of his closet.

"I can't believe it! That little girl wrote to Monsieur de Clameran to give him an appointment here, and she's not going to wait for him."

"Obviously, she distrusts us. She knows who I am."

"Then it was that friend of the cashier's who informed her."

"Who knows? Well, I'm beginning to believe that I'm dealing with very strong thieves. They've guessed that I'm on their trail, and they want to throw me off the track. If someone told me tomorrow that that hussy had the loot and was running away with it, I wouldn't be surprised."

"That's not my opinion," said Madame Alexandre. "But listen, I'm coming back again to my idea. You must see Monsieur Lecoq."

Fanferlot remained a moment, thinking.

"All right! So be it!" he exclaimed. "I'll go see him, but just to have a clear conscience; because where I didn't see anything, he won't see anything. It doesn't matter if he's fierce, he doesn't scare me. If he takes it into his head to mistreat me or to be insolent, I'll know how to put him in his place."

Despite that, the Sûreté agent did not sleep well that night; or, to be more specific, he didn't sleep at all, more occupied with the Bertomy affair than a dramatist with a play germinating in his head. At 6:30

a.m. he was up—you have to get up early if you want to catch Monsieur Lecoq—and his stomach fortified with a café-au-lait, he made his way toward the famous policeman's dwelling.

Certainly Fanferlot 'the Squirrel' was not afraid of the boss, as he called him; and the proof was that he left the Grand-Archange with his head held high, his hat tilted to one side. However, when he got to the Rue Montmartre where Monsieur Lecoq lived, his jauntiness had considerably diminished. His heart was palpitating somewhat when he turned into the passageway leading into the house, and he stopped several times as he went up the stairs. When he came to the fourth floor, in front of the door decorated with the arms of the famous agent—a rooster, the symbol of vigilance—he almost lost his courage, and he had trouble deciding to ring the bell.

Monsieur Lecoq's servant Janouille, a former prisoner in solitary confinement and more devoted to her master than a shepherd's dog to his master, came to the door dressed like an Italian policeman.

"Ah!" she said when she saw him. "You're right on time, Monsieur Squirrel. The boss is expecting you."

Hearing that statement, Fanferlot was seized with a violent desire to beat a retreat. Why, how, and by what fate, was he expected? But while he was hesitating, Janouille grabbed him by the arm and, pulling him after her, made him come into the apartment, saying:

"Do you want to grow roots there? Come on, let's go; the boss is working in his office."

In the middle of a vast strangely furnished room, one-half the library of a well-read man and one-half the dressing room of an actor, sitting behind a desk writing, was the same person with the gold-framed eyeglasses, who had said to Prosper Bertomy: "Have courage!" It was Monsieur Lecoq with his official appearance. At the entrance of Fanferlot, who came forward bowing almost to make his spine a circle, he lifted his head slightly, put down his pen and said:

"Ah! Finally you are here, my boy. Well! It's not going well, that Bertomy business?"

"What?" stammered Fanferlot, "you know…?"

"I know that you've so mixed up things that you can't see any further, that you've given up."

"But, Boss, it wasn't me…"

Monsieur Lecoq had gotten up and was walking up and down his office. Suddenly he came back in front of Fanferlot. He asked in a hard and ironic tone:

"What do you think, Master Squirrel, of a man who abuses the confidence of those who employ him, who reveals just enough of what he's discovered to lead the prosecution astray, who, to profit his stupid vanity, betrays both the cause of justice and that of an unfortunate accused man?"

Fanferlot, frightened, had stepped a foot backward.

"I'd say," he began, "I'd say…"

"You think that that man should be punished and dismissed, and you're right. The less a profession is honorable, the more those who follow it should be honorable. It's you, however, who has betrayed! Ah! Master Squirrel, we're ambitious, and we try to act out an imaginary police. We let the law wander about in one direction and we search in another. It would take a better bloodhound than you are, my boy, to go hunting without a huntsman and on his own."

"But, Boss, I swear to you…"

"Be quiet. Would you be able to prove to me that you told everything to the Investigating Magistrate, as was your duty? Come now! While they were gathering evidence against the cashier, you yourself were gathering evidence against the banker. You spied on him. You made friends with his valet."

Was Monsieur Lecoq really angry? Fanferlot, who knew him well, somewhat doubted it; but with this devil of a man you never knew how to take him.

"If you were even clever…but no. You want to be a master and you're not even a good workman," he continued.

"You're right, Boss," Fanferlot, who no longer thought about denying, said piteously. "But how do you move forward in an affair like this one, where there's not one trace, not one piece of evidence, not one clue, nothing at all!"

Monsieur Lecoq shrugged.

"Poor boy!" he said, "You must understand that the day that you were sent with the Commissioner of Police to investigate the robbery—I don't say certainly, but very probably—you held between your two big stupid hands, the means of knowing which of the keys, the banker's or the cashier's, was used to commit the theft."

"What do you mean?"

"You want proof? All right. Do you remember that scratch that you discovered on the side of the safe? It struck you as important because you couldn't hold back an exclamation when you saw it. You examined it carefully with a magnifying glass, and you convinced yourself it was still fresh, very recent. You told yourself, and rightly so, that the scratch dated from the time of the theft.

But, what was it made with? With a key, obviously. That being so, you should have asked for the banker's and the cashier's keys, and studied them carefully. One of the two should have kept on its end at least some traces of the green paint with which they coat the steel of safes."

Fanferlot listened to that explanation with his mouth hanging open. At the last words, he struck his forehead violently and exclaimed:

"Imbecile!"

"You said it," Monsieur Lecoq continued. "Imbecile! What! These clues jumped out at you and you didn't pay any attention to them. You didn't draw any conclusion from them! In that, however, is the real fact, the point of departure for the affair. If you find the guilty person, it will be thanks to that scratch. And I'll find him! I will do it."

At a distance, Fanferlot 'the Squirrel' willingly cursed Monsieur Lecoq and stood up to him courageously; but up close he inevitably succumbed to the influence that extraordinary man exercised over all who approached him. Such precise information, the minute details he had just been given, reversed all his ideas. Where and how had Monsieur Lecoq gotten them?

"Then, you've been working on this affair, Boss?" he asked.

"Most certainly. But I'm not infallible. I could've let some precious clue slip by. Take a chair and tell me all you know."

You don't equivocate with Monsieur Lecoq; you don't use cunning. Fanferlot told the complete truth, which he rarely did. However, toward the end of his story and gripped by the remorse of vanity, he didn't tell how he had let himself be tricked by Madame Gypsy and the fat gentleman the evening before. The problem was that Monsieur Lecoq was never just half informed.

"It seems to me, Master Squirrel," he said, "that you're forgetting something. How far did you follow the empty carriage?"

Fanferlot, despite his self-possession, blushed right up to his ears and looked down, neither more nor less than like a schoolboy caught in a misdeed.

"What! Boss," he stammered, "You know about that also? How did you..."

But a thought suddenly crossed his mind. He stopped short, jumped out of his chair and exclaimed:

"Oh! I've got it...that fat gentleman with the red sideburns, that was you."

Fanferlot's surprise gave his face such an unusual expression that Monsieur Lecoq couldn't help smiling.

"So, it was you," the astounded agent continued. "You were that fat gentleman I stared at, and I didn't recognize you! Ah! Boss, what an actor you would be, if you wanted to be one! Me, too, I disguised myself!"

"And very badly, my poor boy, to tell you the truth. And do you think, then, that it's enough to wear a thick beard and a workman's shirt to be unrecognizable? But the eyes, unfortunate man, the eyes! It's the eyes you have to change. That's the secret."

That theory, about the importance of the look in the eyes in the matter of disguise, explains why the official Lecoq, who thought of the smallest details, had never been met in the Prefecture of Police's corridors without his golden eyeglasses.

"But, then, Boss," said Fanferlot, following his own idea, "you've gotten the truth out of that little girl that Madame Alexandre wasn't able to? You know why she left the Archange, why she didn't wait for Monsieur de Clameran, why she bought herself Indian clothes?"

"She was only acting as I advised her to."

"In that case," the agent said, deeply discouraged, "there's nothing left for me to do but to admit that I'm nothing but a fool."

"No, Squirrel," Monsieur Lecoq continued with kindness, "you're not a fool. You were simply wrong in attempting a task beyond your ability. Have you made any headway in the affair since you've been following it? No. That's because, you see, incomparable as a lieutenant, you don't have the clear-headedness of a general. I'm going to make you a gift of an aphorism. Remember it and it will become the rule for your behavior. 'Some can stand out in second place who'd be overshadowed in first place.'"

Never, no, never had Fanferlot seen the boss so talkative and such a nice fellow. Seeing that he'd been found out, he'd expected a storm which would floor him, but not at all. He'd gotten off with a rain shower which had hardly wet his head. Monsieur Lecoq's anger dissipated like those black clouds on the horizon which sometimes threaten, and which a slight wind sweeps away. However, Madame Alexandre's husband was nervous. He was wondering if that surprising affability didn't hide some second thoughts.

"Knowing all that, Boss," he asked, "do you know who the guilty man is?"

"No more than you do, my boy; and I don't even know what to think, while you already have a set opinion. You swear to me that the cashier is innocent and that the banker is guilty, and I don't know if you're right or wrong. Since I got there after you, I'm still at the beginning of my investigation. I'm sure of only one thing: there's a scratch on the safe door. That's where I'll start."

While he was talking, Monsieur Lecoq had unrolled and spread out an immense sheet of drawing paper taken from his desk. The door of Monsieur Fauvel's safe was photographed on that sheet. All the information was shown in the greatest detail. You could easily see the five moveable brass discs with engraved letters, and the narrow copper lock standing out clearly. The scratch showed up with admirable clarity.

"There, then," Monsieur Lecoq began, "is our scratch. It goes from top to bottom, from the keyhole of the lock, diagonally, and please note, from left to right. That is to say, it stops on the side of the door to the hidden staircase leading to the banker's apartments. Very deep near the lock, it ends as hardly noticeable."

"Yes, Boss, that's how it is; I see it."

"Naturally, you thought that scratch must have been made by the one who removed the money? Let's see if you were right. I have here a little steel strong box, painted green like Monsieur Fauvel's safe. Here it is. Take a key and try to scratch it."

Without understanding too much about the end result that his superior was suggesting, the Sûreté agent did as he was ordered, rubbing the strong box vigorously with the end of a key.

"Diable!" He said, after two or three tries. "That paint is hard to cut into."

"In fact, very hard my boy. And nevertheless, that of the safe is even more solid, I'm sure. Therefore the scratch that you found couldn't have been made by the trembling hand of a thief letting the key slide!"

"Sapristi!" exclaimed Fanferlot, stunned. "I wouldn't have found that out. But it's true; to scratch the safe, you'd have to apply great force. "

"Yes, but why. As you see me now, I scratched my head for three days, and it was only yesterday that I found out. Let's examine together to see if my conjectures present enough chance of probability to become the point of departure for my investigation."

Monsieur Lecoq had left the photograph to go towards the door leading from his office to the bedroom; he'd removed the key, and had kept it in his hand.

"Come here," he said to Fanferlot. "Place yourself there, beside me. Very good. Let's suppose that I want to open this door and you don't want it opened. When you see me start to put the key in the lock, what's your instinctive reaction?"

"I put both my hands around your arm, which I pull toward me with such a force that you can't put the key in the lock."

"Exactly. Then let's repeat this action. March."

Fanferlot obeyed, and the key Monsieur Lecoq held, kept from entering the lock, slid the length of the door and traced a perfectly clear scratch, from top to bottom, diagonally, in an exact reproduction of the one shown in the photograph.

"Oh!" said Madame Alexandre's husband in three different tones, "Oh! Oh!"

And he stayed in front of the door, thinking.

"Are you beginning to understand?" asked Monsieur Lecoq.

"Do I understand! Boss, even a child could work it out now. Ah! What a man you are! I can see the scene just as if I were there. At the time of the theft, there were two people near the safe: one of them wanted to grab the bills; the other one didn't want them to be touched. It's clear; it's obvious; it's sure."

Accustomed to a great number of other triumphs, the famous policeman was much amused at the stupor and the enthusiasm of the agent.

"You're getting carried away again," he told him gently. "You're taking a circumstance for a certainty and as proven, which might be an accident or, at

355

most, probable."

"No, Boss, no!" Fanferlot exclaimed. "A man like you can't be mistaken. No doubt is possible."

"Then it's up to you to work out the consequences of our discovery."

"First of all, this proves that I wasn't mistaken in my hunch. The cashier is innocent."

"Why?"

"Because, free to open and close the safe whenever he wanted to, he wouldn't have gone looking for a witness just at the time of the robbery."

"Good reasoning. Only if that's true, the banker is also innocent. Think a moment."

Fanferlot reflected and all his enthusiasm vanished.

"That's true!" he said, as if desperate. "That's true! Then, what else can be done?"

"Look for the third thief—that is to say, the one who opened the safe and took the bills, and who is sleeping peacefully while others are being suspected."

"Impossible! Boss, impossible! Didn't they tell you that Monsieur Fauvel and his employee each had a key which never left them?"

"Pardon me. The evening of the robbery, the banker had left his key in his secretary."

"Ah! The key alone was not enough. The word was still needed."

Monsieur Lecoq impatiently shrugged.

"What was the word?"

"Gypsy."

"That is the name of the cashier's mistress. Well, my boy, start looking. The day you find a man closely enough linked to Prosper to suspect how the name was chosen, as familiar with Monsieur Fauvel's household so as to be able to go so far as the bedroom, and that day you'll have the real guilty person. The problem will be resolved."

An egoist, like all great artists, Monsieur Lecoq had never sought to have a student and was not looking for one. He worked alone. He hated collaborators, wanting neither to share the joys of triumph nor the bitterness of defeat. So Fanferlot, who knew his boss like the back of his hand, was startled to hear him, who never gave anything but orders, give advice. He was even so much intrigued that, despite more important preoccupations, he couldn't help showing his surprise.

"Boss, you must have a strong personal interest in this affair, to have studied it in this way," he hesitatingly said.

Monsieur Lecoq had a nervous tremor which his agent didn't notice; then his brows knitted, and he answered in a harsh tone:

"It's your business to be curious, Master Squirrel; however, you shouldn't be too curious. Do you understand?"

Fanferlot tried to apologize.

"Well! Well!" Monsieur Lecoq interrupted. "If I give you a hand, it's because that suits me. It pleases me to be the head, while you'll be the arm. Alone with your preconceived ideas, you'd never have found the guilty person. The two of us together will find him, or I'm no longer Monsieur Lecoq."

"We'll succeed, because you're taking part in it."

"Yes, I'm getting mixed up in it, and for the last four days I've learned a lot of things. Only keep this in mind. I have reasons for not coming out in the open at all in this business. Whatever happens, I forbid you to utter my name. If we succeed, we must attribute the success just to you alone. And, most of all, never try to find out more than this. Be satisfied with the explanations which I'll be pleased to give you."

These conditions don't seem at all to displease the Sûreté agent.

"I'll be discreet, Boss," he declared.

"I'm counting on it, my boy. To begin with, you're going to take this photograph of the safe and go to the Investigating Magistrate. Monsieur Patrigent, I know, is as puzzled as possible in what concerns the accused. You'll explain to him, as if it's coming from you, what I've just pointed out to you. You'll go through my demonstrations again, and I'm convinced those clues will make him determined to have the cashier released. In order for me to begin my operations, Prosper must be free."

"I understand, Boss, but should I also let him see I suspect there is someone guilty other than the banker or the cashier?"

"Absolutely! The legal officials must not ignore the fact that you are following this affair. Monsieur Patrigent will order you to follow Prosper. Answer him that you won't lose sight of him. I myself can assure you that he's in good hands."

"And if he asks me for news of Gypsy?"

Monsieur Lecoq hesitated a moment.

"You'll tell him," he finally said, "that you persuaded her, in Prosper's best interest, to establish herself in a house where she can watch someone you are suspicious of."

Completely happy, Fanferlot had rolled up the photograph, picked up his hat, and was getting ready to leave. Monsieur Lecoq held him back with a gesture.

"I haven't finished," he said. "Do you know how to drive a carriage and take care of a horse?"

"What! Boss! You're asking me that, me a former horseman in the Bouthor Circus!"

"That's right. Since that's how it is, as soon as the Magistrate has sent you away, you'll go back to your place quickly. You'll put on a facial disguise and the clothes of a valet from a respectable house. You'll go, with this letter, to the employment bureau at the corner of the Passage Delorme."

"But Boss…"

"There's no but, my boy. This employment bureau will send you to Monsieur Clameran, who's looking for a valet. His left him yesterday evening."

"Excuse me if I take the liberty of telling you you're mistaken. This Clameran doesn't have the necessary requirements. He's not the cashier's friend."

"There you go, interrupting me already," Monsieur Lecoq said in his most commanding tone. "Just do what I tell you and don't worry about the rest. Monsieur de Clameran isn't Prosper's friend, that's true; but he is the friend and he's the protector of Raoul de Lagors. Why? How did this intimate relationship between two men of such different ages come about? We have to know. We have to know also who this foundry owner is, who lives in Paris and doesn't take any interest in his blast furnaces. He's a fellow who has decided to take up lodgings at the Hotel du Louvre, in the middle of constantly changing crowds, and he's difficult to follow. Through you, I can keep an eye on him. He has a carriage; you'll drive it. In next to no time you'll know who he sees and you can give me an accounting of his least movement."

"You'll be obeyed, Boss."

"Just one more word. Monsieur de Clameran is a very touchy man and even more suspicious. You'll be introduced to him under the name of Joseph Dubois. He'll ask you for letters of recommendation. Here are three that attest to the fact that you have worked for the Marquis de Sairmeuse, the Comte de Commarin, and that your last employment was in the house of the Baron de Wortschen, who's gone to Germany. Keep your eyes open. Be careful of your bearing. Watch how you behave. Be well behaved, but not excessively so. And, above all, don't be too honest. You'll raise suspicions."

"Don't worry, Boss. But where shall I go to report?"

"I'll see you every day. Until I tell you differently, you're forbidden to set foot here—you could be followed. If an unexpected circumstance arises, send a telegram to your wife; she'll warn me. Go...and be careful."

The door closed on Fanferlot and Monsieur Lecoq passed quickly into his bedroom. In the wink of an eye, he had divested himself of his bureaucratic appearance, the stiff tie and the gold-rimmed spectacles, and shaken loose his thick black hair. The official Lecoq disappeared and gave way to the real Lecoq that nobody knew, a handsome boy with clear eyes and a resolute air. But he stayed himself only for an instant. Seated in front of a dressing table more cluttered with creams, perfumes, colors and artifices for make-up than the dressing table of a young woman in the acting profession, he began to re-create God's creation and to re-compose features for himself. He worked slowly, manipulating his little brushes with great care. But at the end of an hour, he had finished one of his daily masterpieces. When he had finished, he was no longer Lecoq: he was the fat monsieur with red sideburns that Fanferlot hadn't recognized.

"All right," he said, throwing a last look at his mirror. "I haven't forgotten anything. I've left almost nothing to chance. All my nets are cast. I can leave.

Time to go. Let's hope Fanferlot doesn't waste any time."

But Fanferlot was too full of joy to waste a minute. He didn't run— he flew to the Palais de Justice. Finally! He was going to be able, in his turn, to show superior insight. As for telling himself that he was going to triumph with someone else's ideas, he didn't think about that at all. With the best faith in the world, it's almost always that the jay bird struts about as if he had the plumes of the peacock. In addition, the situation didn't disappoint his hopes. If the Magistrate was not fully and absolutely convinced, he at least admired the ingeniousness of the procedure.

"This decides it for me," he said, dismissing Fanferlot. "I'm going to present a favorable report to the Council Chamber, and very probably tomorrow the cashier will be released."

In fact, he began to draw up one of those terrible orders of "NO BILL," which returns the accused man his liberty, but not his honor, and which says he's not guilty, but doesn't say that he's innocent.

Considering that there does not exist sufficient evidence against the accused Prosper Bertomy, according to Article 128 of the Criminal Code, we declare there are no grounds to continue action, at the present time, against the above mentioned; we order that he be removed from the place where he is detained, and that he be set free by the authorities, etc.

When he had finished, he said to his stenographer, Sigault, "All right. This is another of those crimes that the law can never solve, one more file to deposit in the stenographic archives." And with his hand he set down on the cover the number of the case: *FILE 113.*

Chapter VII

Prosper Bertomy had been in prison for nine days, in solitary confinement, when one Thursday morning the jailor came to show him the "NO BILL" order. They took him to the booking office. They returned to him several small objects that had been taken from him when they searched him on his arrival: his watch, a knife, and some jewelry; and they made him sign a big sheet of paper. Then they pushed him out into a dark, very narrow corridor. A door opened, and then closed after him with a sinister noise. He found himself on the quay. He was alone. He was free. Free! That was to say, that the law declared itself powerless to convict him of the crime of which he had been accused. Free! He could walk about and breathe pure air, but he was going to find all doors closed to him at his approach. To be acquitted after a trial, that's restoration. Stopping prosecution with a "NO BILL" leaves eternal suspicion hovering over a man who has been arrested. Public opinion can be punishment more formidable than solitary confinement.

At this moment when freedom had been returned to him, Prosper felt the horror of his situation so cruelly that he couldn't hold back a cry of rage and hate.

"But I'm innocent!" he cried out. "I'm innocent."

What was the use? Two passers-by going along the quay stopped to look at him. They thought he was a crazy man. The Seine was there, at his feet. The thought of suicide passed through his mind.

"No!" he said. "I don't even have the right to kill myself. No, I don't want to die before I establish my innocence!"

Many times in the Prefecture holding cell, Prosper Bertomy had repeated the word "restoration." Having in his heart that cold, logical hate which gives the strength or the patience to break through or to overcome all obstacles, he had said to himself: "Ah! If I were free!"

He was free, and only at that hour did he become aware of the immense difficulties of his task. The law requires a criminal for each crime. From this point on, he couldn't establish his innocence except by delivering up a guilty person. How could that person be found and be brought to justice?

In despair, but not discouraged, he started back to his lodgings. A thousand worries were bothering him. What had happened during the nine days that he had been as if erased from the number of the living? Nothing had reached him. The silence of the solitary confinement cells is as terrible as that of the tomb.

He walked slowly along the streets, his head lowered, not meeting the eyes of the people he met. He, so proud, was then going to learn first hand about scorn. He was going to see faces become cold at his approach, conversations stop. Every hand would be withdrawn when he held out his.

Only if he still had a friend! But what friend would believe him when his father, that last friend in supreme crises, had refused to believe him. At the height of his torture, the most heartrending that could be imagined, Nina Gypsy's name came to his lips. He had never loved her, the poor girl. At times he had hated her; but at this moment the memory of her had infinite sweetness for him. That was because he felt she loved him, because he was sure she would not doubt him when he talked to her. It was also because he knew that a woman remains firm in her beliefs, even faithful in misfortune, she who hadn't always been so in prosperity.

When he came in front of his house on the Rue Chaptal, he hesitated to cross the threshold. He was suffering from the timidity of a suspected honest man. He would have liked to never again see a face he knew. Nevertheless, he couldn't stay there on the sidewalk. He went in.

Seeing him, the concierge exclaimed in joy.

"Finally, you're here, Monsieur!" he cried out. "Me, I was saying that you'd get out white as snow. When I read in the newspapers that they'd accused you of theft, I told all those who wanted to listen to it, "My fourth floor renter, a thief, who says so?""

That man's congratulations, perhaps clumsy but certainly sincere, affected Prosper painfully. He wanted to cut short any explanation.

"Madame has probably left. Do you know where she's gone?" he asked.

"*Ma foi!* No, Monsieur. The day you were arrested, she sent for a carriage. They loaded all her things on top, and since then we've neither seen nor caught sight of her. We haven't heard anything more about her."

For the unhappy cashier, this was a sorrow added to his other sorrows.

"And what happened to my servants?"

"Gone also. Your father paid them and sent them away."

"Then, do you have my key?"

"No, Monsieur. When your father left this morning at 8:00 a.m., he told me he was leaving one of his greatest friends in your apartment, that I should consider him as the master until you returned. You probably know him: a big man, about your height, with red sideburns."

Prosper was as astonished as he could be. A friend of his father's, in his apartment. What did that mean? However, he didn't let anything of his astonishment show.

"Yes, I know," he answered. "I know."

And rapidly climbing the stairs, he rang at his door. His father's friend came to open the door. He was just as the concierge had described him: rather fat and red-faced, with sensual lips and with extraordinarily lively eyes, seemingly a nice ordinary looking fellow. The cashier had never seen him before.

"Charmed to meet you, Monsieur," he said.

He was in Prosper's apartment as if he was in his own place. On the table in the drawing room, there was a book he'd picked up in the library. Before long, he would have shown Prosper around the apartment.

"I must admit, Monsieur," the cashier began...

"That you are surprised to see me here, right? I understand that. Your father intended to introduce me to you, but he was forced to leave this morning for Beaucaire. I will add that he left convinced, as I am, that you didn't take a penny from Monsieur Fauvel."

With this news as a happy sign, Prosper couldn't hold back an exclamation of joy.

"So," continued the fat man, "I hope that this letter of your father's, that I'm supposed to give to you, will replace an introduction."

The cashier took the letter held out to him and opened it. As he read it, his face lit up and blood came back into his pale cheeks.

When he had finished reading, he held out his hand to the fat man.

"Monsieur," he said, "my father tells me that you are his best friend. He advises me to have the most absolute confidence in you and to follow your advice."

"That's right. This morning, your good father said to me: 'Verduret—that's my name—Verduret, my son's in a mess. You have to get him out of it.' I answered, 'Present,' and here I am. The ice is broken, isn't it? Then, let's get at the thing. What do you intend to do?"

That question rekindled all of the cashier's anger. His eyes flashed lightening.

"What do I intend to do?" he answered in a trembling voice. "I want to find the miserable man who sold me out, who turned me over to the law, and in a word, to avenge myself."

"Naturally. And do you have some means to get to this end?"

"None at all. Nevertheless, I'll succeed; because a man who gives his entire life to a task, who gets up each morning wanting what he wanted the evening before, is sure of success."

"Well said, Monsieur Prosper; and frankly you see, I was expecting to find you in this frame of mind. And the proof is that I have thought and looked around on your behalf. I have a plan. To begin with, you're going to sell your furnishings, leave this house, and disappear."

"Disappear!" the cashier cried out, revolted. "Disappear! Do you think so, Monsieur? That would be to admit guilt—that would be to authorize everybody to say I'm hiding out to enjoy in peace the 350,000 stolen francs."

"Well! So what!" the man with the red sideburns said coldly. "Haven't you just sworn to me that you've sacrificed your life? The skillful swimmer that criminals throw into the water is careful not to come to the surface immediately. On the contrary, he dives. He swims underwater as long as he can hold his breath. He reappears as far away as possible. He comes to land out of sight, and it's when they think he's lost, drowned, that he suddenly surfaces and takes revenge. You have an enemy? Only a mistake on his part could give him away.

362

But so long as he can see you out in the open, he'll be afraid."

It was with a sort of stunned submission that Prosper listened to that man, who, while a friend of his father, was unknown to him. Without being aware of it, he submitted to the dominance of a nature stronger than his own. He lacked everything. He was glad to find support.

After thinking some moments, Prosper answered, "I'll follow your advice."

"I was sure of it, my dear friend. Then, we'll clear things out today. And note that what the sale produces will be devilishly useful. Do you have any money? No. We need some, however. I was so sure of convincing you that I had a furniture merchant come. He'll take the whole thing here for 12,000 francs, except for the paintings."

In spite of himself, the cashier jumped. Monsieur Verduret noticed.

"Yes, it's hard, I know, but it's necessary. Listen," he added, in a tone that cut through the rest of the conversation. "You're the sick man; I'm the doctor in charge of curing you. If I cut into the quick, cry out, but let me cut. Salvation is in that."

"Cut, Monsieur," Prosper answered, submitting more and more to his dominance.

"Perfect. And let's get started, because time is short. You're the friend of Monsieur de Lagors?"

"Of Raoul? Yes, Monsieur, a close friend."

"Well then, who is this individual?"

Qualifying him as "an individual" seemed to wound Prosper.

"Monsieur de Lagors, Monsieur," he answered in an irritated tone, "is Monsieur Fauvel's nephew. He's a very young man, rich, distinguished and witty, and the best and most loyal friend I know."

"Hmm!" said Monsieur Verduret, "There's a mortal endowed with many qualities, and I'm delighted at the thought that I'm going to meet him. Because, I'll have to admit to you, I wrote him a little note in your name to ask him to come here, and he answered that he'd come."

"What!" Prosper exclaimed, dumbfounded. "Are you supposing…?"

"Oh! I don't suppose anything. Only, I must see this young man. I've even composed a little conversation plan in my head, and I'm going to submit it to you."

A doorbell ring interrupted Monsieur Verduret's words.

"Sacrebleu!" he said. "Here he is. Goodbye my plan! Where can I hide that I can hear and see?"

"There in my bedroom, by leaving the door open and the door curtains lowered."

There was a second ringing of the doorbell.

"I'm coming! I'm coming!" the cashier shouted.

"On the pain of your life, Prosper," said Monsieur Verduret, in a tone which would carry conviction into the most rebellious man, "On your life, not a word about your plans or about me. For him, show yourself discouraged, weak, hesitating…"

And he disappeared while Prosper ran to open the door. The portrait of Monsieur de Lagors by his friend hadn't been just flattery. Never was a more attractive countenance joined to a noble character. Raoul hardly appeared to have twenty of the twenty-four years he claimed. Of middle height, he was admirably proportioned. Thick, light chestnut brown hair curled naturally around his intelligent forehead. His big blue eyes shone with frankness and pride.

The first thing he did was to throw his arms around the cashier's shoulders.

"Poor dear friend," he said, gripping Prosper's hands. "Poor dear Prosper!"

Underneath these affectionate demonstrations however, a certain constraint broke through and which, if it escaped the cashier, had to be noticed by Monsieur Verduret.

Once seated in the drawing room, Raoul continued. "Your letter, my friend, gave me a terrible scare. I was terrified. I asked myself, 'Has he gone crazy?' So, I dropped everything and dashed here."

Prosper, preoccupied with that letter he hadn't written, seemed scarcely to hear. "What had been said to him? Who was this man whose help he had accepted?"

"Would you lack courage?" continued Monsieur de Lagors. "Why despair? At our age there's still time to start life over. Even so, you have friends. If I came, it was because I wanted to say to you, 'Count on me. I'm rich. Half of my fortune is at your disposal.'"

That generous offer, made at this moment with the noblest simplicity, touched Prosper profoundly.

"Thank you, Raoul," he answered in an emotional voice. "Thank you! Unfortunately, all the money in the world wouldn't help me right now."

"How's that? What are your plans? Do you intend to stay in Paris?"

"I don't know, my friend. I don't have any plans. I can't think straight."

"I've told you," Raoul continued warmly, "you have to start life over. Excuse my frankness. It's said in friendship. So long as this mysterious theft hasn't been explained, staying in Paris is impossible."

"And what if it's never explained?"

"That's one more reason to make people forget about you. Look. I was talking about you one hour ago with Clameran. You're unjust toward him, because he actually likes you. 'In Prosper's place,' he said to me, 'I would turn everything into cash, I would go to America, I would make a fortune, and I would come back to crush with my millions those who suspected me.'"

That advice revolted Prosper and his pride. He made no objection, however. He remembered the words of that unknown man listening at this moment.

"Well?" Raoul insisted.

"I'll think about it," murmured the cashier. "I'll see. I'd like know what Monsieur Fauvel says."

"My uncle! You know that since I turned down the proposition he made me to enter his offices, we've almost broken off. It's been a month at least since I've set foot in his house, but I've had news of him."

"By whom?"

"By your protégé, young Cavaillon. It appears that since the affair, my uncle is more upset than you. He seldom goes to his offices. You'd think he'd just recovered from some terrible sickness."

"And Madame Fauvel, and…" The cashier hesitated. "And Mademoiselle Madeleine?"

"Oh!" said Raoul, in a light tone. "My aunt is still very religious. She has masses said for the guilty person. As for my beautiful and icy cousin, she can't be bothered with vulgar details, as taken up as she is with the preparations for the costume ball that the Messieurs Jandidier are giving. One of her friends told me she had ferreted out an unknown dressmaker genius, who has made her a lady-in-waiting to Catherine-de-Medici costume which is a marvel."

It's true that an excess of suffering, dulling thought, brings a sort of insensibility. Prosper had suffered terribly. This last blow overwhelmed him.

"Madeleine!" he murmured. "Madeleine!"

Monsieur de Lagors thought he shouldn't notice the exclamation. He rose.

"I must leave you, my dear Prosper," he said. "I'll see these ladies at the ball on Saturday, and I'll give you their news. Until then have courage, and remember, whatever happens, you can count on me."

Raoul shook Prosper's hand once again before leaving. He must have been already in the street, while the unhappy cashier was still standing in the same spot, immobile, crushed. To bring him out of these gloomy thoughts, it took the mocking voice of the man with the red sideburns, who had come to stand in front of him.

"Now there are friends!" Monsieur Verduret said.

"Yes!" Prosper answered bitterly. "And, nevertheless, you heard him. He offered me half his fortune."

Monsieur Verduret shrugged with an air of compassion.

"That was stingy of him," he said. "Why didn't he offer his whole fortune while he was at it? These kinds of offers aren't binding. Nevertheless, I'm persuaded this handsome boy would give ten nice 1,000 franc bills to know there was an ocean between you and him."

"Him? Monsieur…but why?"

"Who knows? Maybe for the same reason he was careful to have you note that he hadn't set foot in your uncle's house for a month."

"But that's the truth, Monsieur. I'm sure of it."

"Naturally!" answered Monsieur Verduret, sneeringly. "But, look," he continued seriously, "this is enough about this pretty boy. I've seen what he is. That's all I wanted. Now, please change clothes, and together we're going to pay a visit to Monsieur Fauvel."

That suggestion seemed to revolt Prosper.

"Never!" he cried out with unusual violence. "No, never! I couldn't agree to see that miserable man."

That resistance didn't surprise Monsieur Verduret.

"I understand you," he said. "And I excuse you, but I hope you'll think twice about it. Just as I had wanted to see Monsieur de Lagors, I want to see Monsieur Fauvel. I have to, do you understand? Are you so weak to the point that you can't control yourself for five minutes? I will introduce myself as one of your relatives. You won't have to say a word."

"If it's absolutely necessary," Prosper said. "If you wish it."

"Yes, I wish it. Let's go, *Morbleu!* So, have a little trust and some confidence. Quickly, go straighten up your clothes a little. It's late and I'm hungry. We'll have lunch on the way while we talk."

The cashier had hardly gone into his bedroom, when doorbell rang again. Monsieur Verduret went to open it. It was the concierge. He held a rather voluminous envelope in his hand.

He said, "Here's a letter someone brought for Monsieur Bertomy this morning. When I saw him, I was so excited that I didn't think to give it to him. Even so, it's a strange letter, isn't it Monsieur?"

An unusual letter indeed! The address wasn't handwritten. The words forming it were made of printed letters, carefully cut from a book or a magazine, and glued onto the envelope.

"Oh! What's this?" exclaimed Monsieur Verduret.

And speaking to the concierge, "Sit down an instant, old fellow. I'll be back."

He left the concierge in the dining room and passed into the sitting room, where he was careful to close the door. Prosper found him there. He had heard the doorbell first of all and then the sound of voices. He had come to find out what was going on.

"Here's something that was brought for you," said Monsieur Verduret. And without asking permission, he opened the envelope. Some bank bills fell out. He counted them. There were ten.

Prosper had turned purple.

"What does this mean?" he asked.

"We're going to find out," answered Monsieur Verduret. "There's a note attached to the envelope."

This letter, like the address, was made up of printed letters and words, cut out and glued on. It was short, but explicit.

My dear Prosper, a friend who knows the horror of your situation has passed on this help to you. Understand that he has a heart which has shared all your agony. Go away. Leave France. You are young. The future belongs to you. Leave. I hope this money brings you luck.

366

Prosper's anger increased as the man with the red sideburns continued reading. It was an insane anger, because he didn't know how to explain the events following one after the other, and he felt he was losing his sanity.

"Then everyone wants me to leave!" he cried out. "Then it's a conspiracy!"

Monsieur Verduret hid a smile of satisfaction.

"Finally!" he said. "You're opening your eyes; you're beginning to understand. Yes, my child, there are people who hate you for all the evil they've done to you. Yes, there are people for whom your presence in Paris would be a constant threat and who want to send you away at any cost."

"But who are these people, Monsieur? Tell me. Tell me who would permit himself to send me this money?"

Monsieur Bertomy Senior's friend sadly shook his head.

"If I knew, my dear Prosper," he answered, "my job would be finished, because I'd then know who committed the robbery you've been accused of. But we're going to look for them. I finally hold one of those clues which become, sooner or later, an incontrovertible accusation. I now have a fact that proves to me that I wasn't wrong. I was operating in the dark. Now I have a light to guide me."

Monsieur Verduret, that insignificant-looking man with the easy enthusiasm of the traveling salesman, could find, when he wanted to, commanding tones which imposed on and dominated sick spirits.

Listening to him, Prosper had some reassurance again, and felt hope reborn in him.

Monsieur Verduret continued, "It's a matter of taking advantage of this clue that your enemies' imprudence has delivered to us. Let's begin by questioning the porter."

He opened the door and called out:

"Hey! Old fellow! Come forward a little, please."

The concierge, a very polite man, approached while twisting his cap, very intrigued with the authority over his tenant that unknown man had taken on himself.

"Who gave you the envelope that you brought up?" asked Monsieur Verduret.

"The delivery agent said it had been paid for."

"Did you know him?"

"I certainly do know him. He's the delivery man who has square brackets on his delivery cart at the wine merchant's shop on the corner of the Rue Pigalle."[30]

"Go get him for me."

While the concierge left running, Monsieur Verduret took his notebook from his pocket and was alternately consulting the bank bills spread out on the

---

[30] The square brackets were to hold delivery packages.

table and a page completely covered with numbers. When he had finished his examination, he said in a decided tone, "These bills were not sent by the man who committed the robbery."

"You don't think so, Monsieur?"

"I'm convinced of it unless, however, this thief is gifted with extraordinary intelligence and foresight. What's certain, positive, is that none of these 1,000 franc bills were part of the 350,000 stolen from your safe."

"However," said Prosper, who couldn't explain his protector's certainty, "however…"

"There's no however. Here are all the numbers of the bills in numerical order."

"What! When I myself didn't have it?"

"The bank had it, my young friend, and that's very fortunate. When you take on an affair, you should foresee everything and forget nothing. There's no excuse for an intelligent man, when he's made a blunder to say: 'Well, I didn't think about that!' I myself thought about the Bank."

If Prosper at first had some distaste in putting himself entirely in the hands of his father's friend, these feelings of repugnance vanished one by one. He understood that, alone and barely in control of himself, relying on his inexperienced ideas, he would never have had the perspicacity of this singular individual. He, however, seeming to have completely forgotten Prosper's presence, was continuing speaking to himself,

"So, not coming from the thief, the envelope must obviously have come from the other person who was near the safe at the time of the crime, who couldn't have prevented him from opening it, and who now has remorse. The probability of there being two people involved in the crime, the probability confirmed by the scratch, now changes into indisputable certainty. Ergo, I was right."

The cashier was listening with all his might, striving hard to understand something of this monologue that he didn't dare disturb.

The fat man was continuing: "Let's look for who that second person can be, whose conscience troubles him, and who, nevertheless, doesn't dare reveal anything."

He picked up the letter, and very slowly read it three or four times, scanning the sentences and weighing all the words.

"It's evident," he murmured, "very evident, that this letter was written by a woman. A man, wanting to help another man and sending him money, would never have used the word 'aid,' as wounding as it is. A man would have used the word loan, subsidy, or funds, or it doesn't matter what equivalent; but aid, never. Only a woman, ignorant of silly masculine susceptibilities, would have found very natural the idea this word represents. As for that sentence, 'There is a heart, etc.;' it could only have been thought of by a woman."

This time Prosper had been able to follow his protector's inductive work.

368

"I think you're making a mistake, Monsieur," he said. "No woman could be mixed up in this business."

Monsieur Verduret didn't pick up on the interruption. Perhaps he hadn't heard it. Perhaps it wasn't convenient for him to argue about his opinions.

"Right now," he went on, "let's try to find out where the words making up these three sentences were cut out from."

He went to the window and began to study the words glued to the envelope with the scrupulous attention of a Latin scholar trying to decipher a half-effaced manuscript.

"Small letters," he said, "very delicate, very clear, very careful printing, very thin and on strongly glazed paper. Consequently, these words were not cut from a newspaper, or even from a volume of a novel, nor from a current book. However, I've seen these characters here; I recognize them. Didot often uses similar ones, so does Madame de Tours."

He stopped, with his mouth half-opened and his eyes dilated, delving deeply into his memory, energetically concentrating his thoughts on just one point. Suddenly he slapped his forehead.

"I've got it! I've got it! How the devil did I not see that at the first glance? All the words were cut from a prayer book. What's more, as we're going to see, there's a method of verification."

Then, delicately with the end of his tongue, he wet some of the words stuck to the paper; when he saw the glue moist enough, and using a pin, he was able to detach them. On the other side of one of the words, a Latin word was printed: *Deus*.

"Ah! Ah!" he said, with a little laugh of satisfaction. "I've guessed it. Papa Tabaret, if he were here, would be happy. But what happened to the mutilated prayer book? Did they burn it? No, because a book with a binding doesn't burn that easily. They'd have thrown it in some corner."

Monsieur Verduret interrupted himself. The concierge had returned, bringing the delivery man from the corner of the Rue Pigalle.

"Ah! You've arrived at the right time, my boy," said the fat man in his most friendly way. And showing the delivery man the envelope of the letter, he asked him, "Do you remember having brought this envelope here this morning?"

"Perfectly, Monsieur, particularly since I noticed the address. You don't see many like that, do you?"

"I agree with you. And who commissioned you to bring it? Was it a man? Was it a woman?"

"No, Monsieur, it was a delivery man."

This answer, which amused the concierge considerably, didn't even make Monsieur Verduret smile.

"A delivery man," he continued. "Do you know this colleague?"

"I had never so much as seen him before."

"What was he like?"

"*Ma foi!* Monsieur, neither tall nor short; he wore a kind of greenish velvet jacket. He had his military medal."

"*Diable!* My boy, that description is vague and can apply to many delivery men. But did this colleague perhaps tell you who gave him this delivery?"

"No, Monsieur. He just told me, putting 10 sous in my hand, 'Here, take that to the Rue Chaptal, number 39. A coachman gave it to me on the boulevard.' I'm sure he made more than I did."

That answer seemed to disconcert Monsieur Verduret somewhat. That so many precautions had been taken to get that letter to Prosper, bothered him and upset his plans.

"Well," he began again, "would you recognize the delivery man from this morning?"

"That one, yes, Monsieur, if I saw him."

"Then, listen. How much do you make at your job by the day?"

"Damn! Monsieur, I don't know exactly, but you see I have a good corner. Let's say between 8 and 10 francs a day."

"Well! Me, my boy, I'm going to give you 10 francs a day just to do nothing but walk about, that is to say, to look for the delivery man from this morning. Every evening about 8:00, you'll come to the Hotel Grand-Archange, on the Quai Saint Michel, to report to me about your walks and to get paid. You'll ask for Monsieur Verduret. If you find our man, I'll give you 50 francs. Does that bargain suit you?"

"*Peste!* I certainly think so, bourgeois."

"Then don't waste a minute. Get going!"

Although he didn't know Monsieur Verduret's plan, Prosper was beginning to explain to himself the sense of these investigations. As much as to say his life depended on their success, nevertheless he almost forgot that reliance, in order to admire the unusual energy of this aide that his father had bequeathed to him. He admired his clearheaded joking, the accuracy of his inductions, the productivity of his schemes, and the rapidity of his movements.

"So, Monsieur," he asked, when the delivery man had left, "do you think you're going to find the hand of a woman in what happened to me?"

"More than ever. And what's more, in any case it's a religious woman who possesses two prayer books, because she mutilated one to write to you."

"And you have some hopes of finding her?"

"I would say a great hope, my dear Prosper, thanks to the methods I have for immediate research, methods that I'm going to use on the spot."

At these last words he sat down and rapidly scratched with pencil two or three lines on a little band of paper, which he rolled up and slipped into his waist coat.

"Are you ready, for our visit to Monsieur Fauvel?" he asked. "Yes? Then, let's go. We've certainly earned our lunch."

Chapter VIII

When he spoke about Monsieur Fauvel's extreme depression, Raoul de Lagors hadn't exaggerated anything. Since the fatal day that his cashier had been arrested through his denunciation, the banker who usually was active to the point of being restless, in prey to the blackest melancholy, had absolutely ceased taking care of his business. He, the family man par excellence, no longer met with his family except at mealtimes. He ate several mouthfuls hastily and soon disappeared. Shut up in his study, he locked himself in. His facial features contracted. His lack of interest in anything, and his constant distraction, betrayed a preoccupation with an *idée fixe* or of some secret sorrow's tyrannical control.

On the day of Prosper's release, at about 3:00 p.m. as usual, Monsieur Fauvel was seated at his desk. His elbows were on its top, his forehead in his hands, and his eyes staring into empty space, when the office boy suddenly entered with a frightened look.

"Monsieur," that man said, "it's the former cashier, Monsieur Bertomy, who's here with one of his relatives. He absolutely insists on seeing you, to talking to you."

Hearing these words, the banker straightened up quickly, more startled than if he had seen a bolt of lightning fall three feet from him. "Prosper!" he cried out in a voice strangled with anger. "What, he dares..."

But he understood that in front of an office boy he couldn't let himself show his characteristic fits of anger. He managed to control himself, and with a voice relatively calm he said:

"Have these gentlemen come in."

If that jovial fat man Monsieur Verduret had counted on a strange and emotional spectacle, his expectation wasn't wrong. There was nothing more terrible than the attitude of these two men facing each other. The banker was red, his face swollen as if he was about to be struck with a fit of apoplexy. Prosper was paler than a wounded man who had just lost his last drop of blood, immobile, shaking. Barely separated by three feet, they exchanged looks filled with mortal hatred, ready to throw themselves on one another.

Monsieur Verduret curiously examined these two enemies during at least a full minute, with the detachment and the coolness of a philosopher who, in the most violent transports of human passion, sees nothing more than a subject of study and meditation. Finally, the silence becoming more and more threatening, he decided to speak, addressing the banker:

"You probably know, Monsieur, that my young relative has just been released?"

"Yes," answered Monsieur Fauvel, who was making the most laudable efforts not to explode. "Yes, for lack of sufficient proof."

"Precisely, Monsieur. Now, considering that this 'lack of proof,' stated in the NO BILL blocks the future of my relative, he has decided to leave for America."

At this statement, Monsieur Fauvel's facial expression changed abruptly. His features relaxed as if he had been released from some terrible agony.

"Ah! He's leaving," he repeated several times. "He's leaving!"

There was no way to misunderstand the intonation. The statement 'He's leaving,' pronounced like that, was a mortal insult.

Monsieur Verduret chose not to notice anything.

"It seemed to me," he continued in a light tone, "that my relative's decision is logical. I just wanted him to come present his respects to his former employer before leaving Paris..."

A bitter smile puckered the banker's lips.

"Monsieur Bertomy," he replied, "could have spared himself that step, painful for both of us. I had nothing to hear; I have nothing to say to him."

This was a formal dismissal; and Monsieur Verduret understanding it to be such, bowed to Monsieur Fauvel and left, leading Prosper, who hadn't said a word. Only in the street did the cashier recover his speech.

"You wanted it, Monsieur," he said, in a dull voice. "You required it. I followed you. Are you happy? Am I any further along, having added that cutting humiliation to all the others?"

"You, no," answered Monsieur Verduret. "Me, yes. I couldn't go to the banker without you, and now I know all that I have any interest in knowing. I am certain that Monsieur Fauvel has nothing to do with the theft."

"Oh! Monsieur," objected Prosper, "People can pretend."

"Without a doubt, but not on this point. And that's not all I need. For my last project I needed to know if your boss would be open to certain suspicions. Now, I can strongly answer: yes, he would."

In order to talk more at their ease, Prosper and his companion had stopped at the corner of the Rue Lafayette, in the middle of a vast plot of ground opened up since the recent demolitions.[31] Monsieur Verduret appeared worried, and while talking, he looked around every few moments as if he expected someone. Soon he let out an exclamation of satisfaction. At the other side of that improvised square, Cavaillon had just appeared. He was bareheaded. He was running. He was at the same time in so much of a hurry, and so alarmed, that he thought neither to greet his great friend Prosper, nor to shake his hand. He spoke immediately to Monsieur Verduret:

"They (the women) have left," he said.

"A long time ago?"

---

[31] The story is set during the period when Baron Haussmann, with a contract from Napoleon III, was creating a new Paris, blasting through blocks of houses, straightening streets, and supplying a new water and sewer system.

"No, about a quarter of an hour ago."

"*Diable!*" said Monsieur Verduret. "That being so, we don't have a minute to lose."

And giving Cavaillon the note he had written several hours earlier at Prosper's apartment, he said, "Here, give him this and go back quickly, so no one notices your absence. To leave without a hat is carelessness which could be a warning signal."

The little Cavaillon boy didn't have to be told twice, and he left running, as he had come. Prosper was stunned.

"What!" he exclaimed. "You know Cavaillon?"

"It seems so," answered Monsieur Verduret, with a smile. "But this isn't the time to talk. Come on, let's hurry!"

"Then where are we going?"

"You'll find out. Come on, use your legs, use your legs!"

He himself gave the example, and it was almost like a gymnast that he ran up the Rue Lafayette. While walking, rather while running, he was talking, worrying very little about whether or not Prosper heard him.

"Ah! Here we are!" he was saying. "It's not in staying glued to one spot that you win prizes in a race. When you've found an opening, you shouldn't rest a minute. The savage in the virgin forest who's picked up the footprint of an enemy, follows it without stopping, knowing that a breeze or the falling rain is enough to rub out the print. It's the same for us. The least event can make the tracks we're following disappear."

Arriving in front of Number 81, Monsieur Verduret interrupted himself and stopped at the same time.

"This is it," he said to Prosper. "Let's go in."

They mounted the stairs and stopped on the third floor, in front of a door decorated with a copper shield engraved: *Fashions and Dressmaking*. A superb bell cord hung down from the door facing them, but Monsieur Verduret didn't touch it. With his fingertip he tapped very lightly in a certain fashion, and immediately, as if someone had been watching out for this signal, the door opened. It was a woman who opened the door. She could have been about forty years old. Her dress was simple, but very proper. Without any sound, she let Prosper and his companion pass into a very clean little dining room, off of which several doors opened. That woman had bowed very low before Monsieur Verduret, like a protégée before her protector. He hardly answered the bow. He looked questioningly at the woman. His look said: "Well?"

The woman nodded affirmatively.

"Yes."

"There, right?" Monsieur Verduret said in a low voice, pointing to one of the doors.

"No," the woman answered in the same tone. "On the other side, in the little sitting room."

At that, Monsieur Verduret opened the door pointed out to him, and he gently pushed Prosper into the little sitting room, whispering in his ear:

"Go in...and keep your self-control."

But what good was this advice. Thrown into that room where he had been pushed despite himself, without having been warned about anything, at the first look Prosper exclaimed loudly: "Madeleine!"

In fact, it really was Monsieur Fauvel's niece, more beautiful than ever, with that calm and serene beauty which imposes admiration and commands respect. Standing in the middle of the room, near a table covered with dressmaking fabric, she was arranging the folds of a red velvet skirt with gold lame spangles, probably the skirt of her lady-in-waiting-to-Catherine-de-Medici costume. Seeing Prosper, all the blood rushed to her face, her beautiful eyes half-closed as if she were about to faint, and she became so weak that she had to lean against the table in order to not fall.

Madeleine was not, and Prosper could not have been unaware of that, one of those strong women whose cold heart always leaves the mind free, who have sensations but never a true sentiment, heroines of novels who find something advantageous in every situation. A tender and dreamy soul, one of the special features of her personality was an exquisite, almost morbid, sensitivity. When duty spoke, she obeyed.

Her fainting spell lasted only a moment, and soon her very tender eyes expressed no more than haughtiness and resentment. She said in an offended voice:

"Who made you so daring, Monsieur, as to dare to spy on my activities? How have you allowed yourself to follow me, to enter this house?"

Prosper certainly wasn't guilty. He wanted to sum up everything that had happened. His inability to express his thoughts made him keep silent.

"You swore to me," Madeleine continued, "on your honor, never to try to see me again. Is this how you keep your word?"

"I did swear, Mademoiselle, but..." He stopped.

"Oh! Speak!"

"So many things have happened since that day that I thought I could forget that oath snatched through my weakness, if only for an hour... It's a chance. It's at least due to a will that isn't my own that I owe the happiness to find myself once again near you. Alas! Seeing you, my heart inside me is thrilled with joy. I didn't think, no, I couldn't think that pitiless, as much as or more so than everyone else, you would push me away, since I'm so unhappy."

Had he been thrown less violently outside the expected, Prosper could have followed in Madeleine's eyes, those beautiful eyes so long in control of his destiny, the trace of the combats going on inside her. It was, nevertheless, in a rather firm voice that she answered:

"Prosper, you know me well enough to know that nothing bad can happen to you which doesn't also strike me. You're suffering. I'm sorry for you as a sister is sorry for a tenderly loved brother."

"A sister!" Prosper said bitterly. "That's exactly the word you said the day you banished me from your presence. A sister! Then why, for three years, did you lull me with the most deceptive illusions. Then was I a brother to you the day we went on a pilgrimage together to Notre-Dame-de Fourvières, that day when, at the foot of the altar, we swore to love each other eternally, when you put a blessed medallion around my neck, telling me: 'For love of me, keep it always. It will bring you luck?'"

Madeleine tried to interrupt him with a gentle, begging gesture. He didn't notice it.

"That was a year ago," he went on, "and less than a month afterward you released me from my word, and you tore from me the promise never to see you again. Even now if I knew by what action or by what thought I could've displeased you... But you didn't deign to explain anything to me. You sent me away; and to obey you, I let it be thought that it was I who'd gone away voluntarily. You told me that an invincible obstacle had risen between us, and I believed you. Fool that I was! The obstacle was your heart, Madeleine. Even so, I've always piously kept the blessed medallion. It did not bring me good luck."

More motionless and whiter than a statue, Madeleine bent her head under that storm from an immense passion. Big tears rolled silently down her cheeks.

"I told you to forget," she whispered.

"Forget!" Prosper continued, as revolted as if he had heard a blasphemy. "Forget! Ah! How can I? Is it in my power to stop, by just the effort of my will, my blood's circulation? Ah! You never loved me. To forget, just as to stop the beating of my heart, there's only one way... to die."

This word, pronounced with a grim resolution, stunned Madeleine.

"Unhappy man!" she cried out.

"Yes, unhappy! A thousand times unhappier than you can imagine! You'll never understand my torture. For a year, each morning it's as if I've had to learn again my misfortune and tell myself: 'It's over. She doesn't love me anymore!' Why do you talk about forgetting! I've looked for it at the bottom of poisoned cups. I didn't find it. I tried to snuff out this memory of the past, which burns in me like a devouring flame. In vain—when the body has given in, implacable thought is still alive. You can certainly see that I have thought about repose, that is to say, suicide."

"I forbid you to say that word."

"You can't forbid anything to someone you no longer love. Madeleine, didn't you know that?"

Madeleine stopped him with a commanding gesture, as if she wished to speak, and, who knows, to explain everything, to vindicate. Yet a sudden thought stopped her. She made a movement of despair, and cried out:

"*Mon Dieu!* This is too much suffering!"

Prosper seemed to misunderstand the meaning of that exclamation.

"Your pity comes too late," he continued with heart-rending resignation. "There is no more happiness possible for someone who, like me, had caught a view of divine happiness. Nothing can tie me to life. You've killed the holiest beliefs in me. I leave prison dishonored by my enemies. What's to become of me? I vainly try to see into the future. There's no longer either hope, or promises, or smiles for me. I look around me and I see only abandon, shame and despair."

"Prosper, my friend, my brother, if you knew..."

"I know only one thing, Madeleine, and that is that you did love me, that you no longer love me, and that I love you."

He stopped talking. He was hoping for an answer. It didn't come. But suddenly the silence was broken by a stifled sob. It was Madeleine's lady's maid, who, sitting near the fireplace of the little sitting room was crying. Madeleine had forgotten her. Prosper, on entering, astounded and stunned, hadn't seen her. He looked at her. That young girl, dressed like the maids of well-to-do houses, was Nina Gypsy, there was no mistaking it. So violent was the shock Prosper felt that he neither exclaimed nor said a word. The horror of the situation terrified him. There he was, between the two women who had controlled his life, between Madeleine, the proud heiress he adored and who pushed him away, and Nina Gypsy, the poor girl who loved him and whom he disdained. And she had heard everything, that poor Gypsy. She had seen her lover's passion for another woman burst out in terrible regrets and in mad threats. Through what he was suffering, Prosper understood what she must have suffered, because she had been struck, not only in the present, but in the past. What must have been her humiliation and her anger in learning the miserable role the love of Prosper had forced on her. And he was astonished that Gypsy—violence itself—stayed there weeping, and didn't rise to protest, to curse him.

Since Prosper didn't speak, Madeleine, however, had succeeded in forcing herself to regain the appearance of calm. Slowly, with movements which she hardly seemed conscious of, she had picked up her cloak thrown on the couch. When she was ready to leave, she came forward to Prosper.

"Why did you come?" she asked. "You and I need all our courage. You're unhappy, Prosper. I'm unhappier than you are. You have the right to complain. As for me, I don't have the right to let a tear be seen; and when my heart is torn apart, I still must smile. You can ask a friend for comfort. As for me, I can have no other confident but God."

Prosper tried to stammer an answer. The words died on his lips. He was choking.

"I'd like to tell you," Madeleine continued, "that I haven't forgotten anything. Oh! That certainty can give you no hope. There is no future for us. If you love me, you'll live. You don't have the barbarity to add the sorrow of your death to my torture. A day may perhaps come when I'll be allowed to justify myself...and now, oh! My brother, oh, my only love, good-bye, good-bye!"

At the same time, she leaned forward toward Prosper. She brushed the forehead of the unhappy young man with her lips, and left quickly, followed by Nina Gypsy.

Prosper was alone. It seemed to him that he was going to faint. Only then did he force himself to become aware of what had just happened, to ask himself if he hadn't been the plaything of a dream, if he hadn't lost his reason. He couldn't misunderstand the sovereign influence of that man who had appeared to him that same morning for the first time. What mysterious power did that unknown man have at his disposal to prepare events thus at his pleasure? He seemed to foresee everything and guess everything. He was acquainted with Cavaillon; he knew Madeleine's activities; he had been able to make the independent Gypsy obey. He was suddenly so highly exasperated that the moment Monsieur Verduret came into the little sitting room, he walked up to him like an enraged man, pale and threatening, and in a hard curt voice he said to him:

"Who are you?"

The fat man seemed only slightly surprised at that excess of violence.

"A friend of your father's," he said. "Didn't you know that?"

"That's not an answer, Monsieur. I might, in a moment of surprise, give my self-determination into the hands of an unknown person, but at this time…"

"What? Is it my biography you're asking for? What I am, what I have been, what I might be? What does that matter to you? I told you. I'll save you. The essential thing is that I save you."

"Then do I have the right to ask you by what means?"

"For what purpose?"

"In order to accept your methods, Monsieur, or to reject them."

"And if I guarantee you success?"

"That's not enough, Monsieur; and it wouldn't be fitting for me to be deprived of my free will any longer, to be exposed without warning to tests like those today. A man my age must know what he's doing."

"A man your age, Prosper, when he's blind, takes a guide, and he's careful not to presume to teach the one who guides him the road to take."

Monsieur Verduret's tone, half joking, half pity, wasn't such as to calm Prosper's growing irritation.

"Since that's how it is!" he exclaimed. "Thank you for your services, Monsieur. I can do without them. If I was fighting to defend my honor and my life, that was because, even so, I hoped that Madeleine would come back to me. I know today that everything is finished between her and me. I give up the fight."

Prosper's resolution seemed so evident that for an instant Monsieur Verduret seemed alarmed.

"You've gone mad," he stated.

"No, unfortunately. Madeleine no longer loves me. What does the rest matter to me?"

His tone was so desperate at his point that Monsieur Verduret was moved.

"So," he continued. "You don't suspect anything? You weren't able to disentangle the sense of her words?"

Prosper made a terrible gesture.

"You were listening!" he cried out.

"I admit it."

"Monsieur!"

"Yes! That wasn't very delicate perhaps, but the end justifies the means. I listened and I congratulate myself since, I can now tell you, 'Take courage, Prosper. Madeleine loves you. She's never stopped loving you.'"

If he feels himself lost and near death, even though he knows it, the sick man listens to the doctor's promises. Monsieur Verduret's clear, very positive statement lit Prosper's sadness with a gleam of hope.

"Oh!" he whispered, suddenly calm. "If only I could believe that…"

"Believe me, because I couldn't be mistaken. Ah! You haven't guessed, as I have, the tortures of that young girl, struggling between her love and what she believes to be her duty. Didn't your heart beat faster at her words of farewell?"

"She loves me, she's free, and she runs from me."

"Free! No, she isn't. In releasing you from your promise she obeyed a superior and irresistible will. She is devoted…to whom? We'll soon know that. And the secret of her devotion will let us know the secret of the plot of which you're the victim."

As Monsieur Verduret went on talking, Prosper felt his resolutions of revolt melting away. Hope and confidence returned.

"If only you were telling the truth, however," he whispered. "If only you were telling the truth!"

"Unhappy young man! Why do you stubbornly close your eyes to the evidence! Then don't you understand that Madeleine knows the name of the thief?"

"That's impossible."

"It's true. But believe me, there's no human power capable of getting this name out of her. Yes, she's sacrificing you, but she almost has the right to, since she's sacrificing herself first."

Prosper was convinced, but without breaking his heart he couldn't leave the sitting room where Madeleine had appeared to him.

"Alas!" he exclaimed, squeezing Monsieur Verduret's hand, "I must seem mad, ridiculous to you, because you don't know, no, you can't know what I'm suffering."

The man with the red sideburns sadly shook his head. In a moment, his facial expression changed; his very brilliant eyes were veiled. His voice trembled.

"What you're suffering," he answered, "I suffered. Like you, I was in love, not with a noble and pure young girl, but with a girl of the streets. For three years I was at her feet. Then suddenly one day she left me, me who adored her. Then, like you, I wanted to die. Unhappy man! Neither tears nor prayers could bring her back to me. Passion isn't logical. She loved the other man."

"And you knew that other man?"

"I knew him."

"And you didn't take revenge?"

"No," answered Monsieur Verduret. And in a strange tone he added:

"Fate brought about my vengeance."

For more than a minute, Prosper was silent.

"I have decided, Monsieur," he finally stated. "My honor is a sacred trust which I must account for to my family. I am ready to follow you to the end. Do with me as you like."

True to his word, that same day Prosper sold his household furnishings and sent a letter to his friends in which he announced his approaching departure for San Francisco. And that evening he moved into the Hotel Grand-Archange, as did Monsieur Verduret. Madame Alexandre gave him her prettiest room, very ugly if compared to the very attractive sitting room in the Rue Chaptal. But he wasn't in a mood to make that comparison. Stretched out on a pathetic couch, he went over the day's events, finding a bitter enjoyment in his isolation. At about 11:00 p.m., feeling his head sluggish, he wanted to open the window. The wind made him close it quickly. But a gust of the tempest had come into the room. The drapes were blown about and a small piece of paper was spinning around in the middle of the room. Prosper mechanically picked up the paper and examined it. It was covered with fine handwriting, the handwriting of Nina Gypsy. There was no way to mistake it. It was a fragment of a torn up letter and if the incomplete sentences didn't make any satisfactory logical sense, they were enough to lead the imagination into the field of limitless possibilities.

Here is this fragment exactly:

...from Monsieur Raoul I have been very imp... ...hatched against him from whom never... ...warn Prosper and then... ...better friend, he... ...hand of Mademoiselle Ma...

Prosper didn't sleep that night.

Chapter IX

Not far from the Palais Royal in the Rue Saint-Honoré, at The Bonne Foi sign, is a small establishment, part café, part plum market, much frequented by area employees. It was on Friday in one of that modest bar/brasserie's rooms, the day after his release from prison, that Prosper was waiting for Monsieur Verduret, who had given him an appointment for about 4:00 p.m. When 4:00 p.m. sounded, Monsieur Verduret, who was punctuality itself, appeared. He was redder than he was the day before, and, just as the evening before, he had that admirable look of being happy with himself. As soon as the waiter, from whom he had ordered a steak, had gone away:

"Well!" he asked Prosper. "Have all our errands been done?"

"Yes, Monsieur."

"You saw the costume maker?"

"I gave him your letter. Everything you ordered will be delivered to you tomorrow at the Grand-Archange."

"Then everything's going well, because I haven't wasted my time, and I'm bringing great news."

The Bonne Foi market is almost deserted toward 4:00. The café's morning rush hour has passed. Time for absinthe hasn't yet arrived. Monsieur Verduret and Prosper could talk at their ease without worrying about the neighbors' indiscreet ears. Monsieur Verduret had taken out his notebook, that precious notebook, like the enchanted books of the fairies that had an answer for every question.

"While waiting here for those of our emissaries I've made appointments with," he said, "let's get busy a little with Monsieur de Lagors."

At this name, Prosper didn't protest as he had done the evening before. Similar to those invisible insects which, once they have made their way into the trunk of a tree, devour it in one night; so suspicion, once it has penetrated into our mind, grows there, and soon destroys the strongest beliefs. De Lagors' visit, and the fragment of Gypsy's letter, had raised doubts in Prosper, which had, from hour to hour you might say, enlarged and grown stronger.

Monsieur Verduret continued: "Do you know, my dear friend, from exactly what region the young monsieur who proclaims himself so strongly your friend comes?"

"He is, Monsieur, from Madame Fauvel's area, from Saint-Rémy."

"Are you sure of that?"

"Oh! Perfectly, Monsieur. Not only has he told me that very often, but I've also heard him say that to Monsieur Fauvel. I've heard him repeat it a hundred times to Madame Fauvel, when she was talking about her relative whom she loved very much, de Lagors' mother."

"So, there is neither doubt nor error possible in that regard?"

"No, Monsieur."

"Ah! Ah!" said Monsieur Verduret, "At least now we're getting to something unusual."

And he whistled between his teeth, for him a clear sign of personal and high satisfaction.

"What's unusual, Monsieur?" Prosper asked, intrigued.

"What's happening, *Parbleu!*" answered the fat man, "is what I sniffed out...*Peste!*" he continued, imitating the country fair barkers hawking curiosities. "It's a charming city, Saint-Rémy, six thousand inhabitants, delightful boulevards on the fortification emplacements, a very beautiful city hall, many fountains, great coal commerce, silk worm nursery, very famous retirement homes..."

Prosper was as if standing on hot coals.

"Please, Monsieur," he began.

Monsieur Verduret continued: "There's a Roman arch of triumph there which doesn't have its equal and a Greek mausoleum, but not a single Lagors. Saint-Rémy is Nostradamus' country, but not that of your friend."

"However, Monsieur, I've had proofs."

"Naturally. But proofs, you see, can be fabricated. Relatives can be improvised. Your evidence is suspect; my witnesses are unimpeachable. While you were mourning away in prison, I was throwing up barriers and I was gathering ammunition to open fire. I wrote to Saint-Rémy and I had answers."

"Aren't you going to tell me what they are, Monsieur?"

"Have a little patience," said Monsieur Verduret, flipping through his notebook. "Ah! Here's the first one, the number one. Admire the style. It's official."

He read:

Lagors. A very ancient family originally from Maillane. Established at Saint-Rémy for a century.

"You see!" Prosper exclaimed. "If you'd let me finish, *Hein!*" Monsieur Verduret said. And he continued:

The last of the Lagors (Jules-René-Henri), bearing the title of count without a well-established lineage, married in 1829 the young woman Rosalie-Clarisse Fontanet, de Tarascon, died in December 1848, without a male heir, leaving only two daughters. The state civil documents consulted make no mention of any person in the vicinity bearing the name de Lagors.

"Well!" demanded the fat man. "What do you think about the information?

Prosper was stunned.

"Why then did Monsieur Fauvel treat Raoul as a nephew?"

"As his wife's nephew, you mean. But let's examine notice number two. It's not official, but it lights up as bright as day, the 20,000 livres income of your friend."

Jules-René-Henri de Lagors, the last of his name, died at Saint-Rémy December 29, 1848, almost penniless. He had had a sizeable fortune. Investment in a model silk-worm nursery ruined him. He left no boy, but only two daughters, one of whom is an elementary school teacher at Aix and the other married to a small merchant at Orgon. His widow, who inhabits a farm house of Montagnette, lives in a decent fashion only through the generosity of one of her relatives, the wife of a rich banker in the capital. No one by the name of Lagors is known in the vicinity of Arles.

"That's all!" said Monsieur Verduret.

"Do you think that's enough?"

"I'll have to say, Monsieur, that I wonder if I'm wide awake." "I can understand that. However, I need to call something to your attention. Observant people will perhaps object that Madame, the Lagors widow, could have had after the death of her husband, an illegitimate child not acknowledged and bearing his name. That objection is contradicted by the age of your friend. Raoul is twenty-four years old, and Monsieur de Lagors died fewer than twenty years ago."

There was nothing to answer to that, and Prosper understood that very well. "But then," becoming thoughtful, he asked, "Who could Raoul be?"

"I don't know. Frankly, it's more difficult to discover who he is, than to know who he is not. Only one man could inform us on this point, but he'd be very careful not to say anything."

"Monsieur de Clameran, right?" "Exactly." "He's always inspired me with an unexplainable repulsion," said

Prosper. "Ah! If we could only have his dossier, that man's!"

"I already have some short notes furnished me by your father, who knows the Clameran family very well," answered Monsieur Verduret. "They're very meager, but I'm waiting for some more."

"What did my father tell you?" "Nothing favorable, of that you can be sure. In addition, for your edification, here is the summary of his information."

Louis de Clameran was born in the Chateau Clameran, near Tarascon. He had an older brother named Gaston. In 1842, following a brawl where he had the misfortune to kill a man and to seriously wound another, Gaston was obliged to flee the country. He was a loyal, frank, honest boy that everybody loved. Louis, on the contrary, had the most detestable instincts and was hated.

On the death of his father, Louis came to Paris and, in fewer than two years, devoured not only his part of the paternal inheritance, but his exiled

brother's part also.

Ruined, and riddled with debts, Louis de Clameran became a soldier and conducted himself so badly in the regiment that he was sent to the disciplinary companies. When he left the service, he was totally lost from view. The only thing known was that he lived successively in England and in Germany, where in a casino city he was involved in a terrible affair.

In 1865, we find him back in Paris. He was totally impoverished and frequented the worst society, living only in the world of crooks and prostitutes. He was reduced to the most shameful expedients when, suddenly, he learned about his brother's return to France. Gaston had made a fortune in Mexico. But still young and accustomed to an active life, he had just bought an iron works factory near Oloron when, six months ago, he died in the arms of his brother, Louis. That death gave our Clameran both a great fortune and the title of Marquis.

Prosper was thinking. During the twenty-four hours that Monsieur Verduret had been working in his presence, he was beginning to absorb his inductive method. Like him, he was trying to group together facts, to arrange circumstances into more or less probable suspicions.

"From what you're telling me, the result was that our Monsieur de Clameran was in the most profound poverty, when I saw him for the first time at Monsieur Fauvel's house."

"Obviously." "And it was shortly thereafter that Lagors arrived from his province?"

"Exactly."

"And it was about a month after his arrival that Madeleine suddenly banished me."

"Well! You're beginning to take shape and understand the significance of the facts."

He stopped talking at the entrance of a new customer into The Bonne Foi. It was a male servant from a good household, well-shaved, with well-combed hair, and wearing his black sideburns à la Bergami in a dignified way. He had beautiful high-top boots with the tops folded down, yellow knee breeches, and a long-sleeved vest with red and black stripes.

After looking rapidly but carefully around the room, he walked quickly toward Monsieur Verduret's table.

"Well! Master Dubois?" questioned the fat man.

"Ah! Boss, don't speak to me," the servant answered. "This is hot, you see; this is very hot."

Prosper concentrated all the attention he was capable of on that superb domestic. It seemed to him he knew that face. He told himself that very certainly he had already seen that receding forehead and those eyes of annoying mobility somewhere. But where? Under what circumstances? He searched and couldn't find anything.

However, Master Joseph had sat down, not at Monsieur Verduret's table, but at the neighboring table. He had ordered a glass of absinthe that he was preparing slowly, letting the water fall drop by drop from very high up, according to the accepted method.

"Talk!" Monsieur Verduret said to him.

"To begin with, Boss, I must let you know that all is not rosy in Monsieur de Clameran's valet and coachman job."

"Get to the facts, get to the facts! You can complain tomorrow."

"All right, I'm getting there. So, yesterday my lord and master left walking, about 2:00 p.m. As I was supposed to, I followed him. Do you know where he went? What a farce! He went to the Grand-Archange to meet the little lady."

"Go on. They told him she'd left. And afterward?"

"Afterward! I can assure you he wasn't happy at all. He went running back to his mansion where the other one, Monsieur Raoul de Lagors, was waiting for him. No, it's true, that man doesn't have his equal for swearing. The Raoul fellow asked him what there was new that had made him so angry. 'It's nothing,' he answered my bourgeois, 'nothing, except the little bitch has skipped out. No one knows where she is, so she's slipped through our fingers.' Then they both seemed very irritated and very worried. 'Does she know anything important?' Lagors asked. 'She doesn't know anything but what I told her,' Clameran answered, 'but this *nothing,* falling on the ears of a man with a keen nose, could set him on the track of the truth.'"

Monsieur Verduret smiled like a man who had his reasons for estimating Monsieur de Clameran's fears at their full value.

"Ah!" he said, "Do you know, he's not absolutely lacking in intelligence, your lord and master? And then?"

"When he heard that, Boss, the Lagors fellow turned green and yelled out. 'If it's serious, we have to get rid of that bitch.' He was really going on, the young one! But my boss started to laugh and shrugged. 'You're just a fool,' he answered. 'When a woman like that one gets in your way, you take steps to get rid of her administratively.' That idea made them both laugh."

"I would certainly think so!" Monsieur Verduret approved. "That's excellent, that idea. The unfortunate thing is that it's too late to carry it out. The *nothing* that Clameran was afraid of has already fallen on an intelligent ear. Nevertheless, since I don't want those fine fellows to shuffle the cards, we have to warn the authorities governing public morality."

"It's done, Boss," Master Joseph cried out joyously.

Prosper listened to this report with breathless curiosity, every word of which, you might say, shone light like a new day on the events. He could now explain, the thought, the fragment of Gypsy's letter. This Raoul, who had had all his confidence, couldn't be anything but a worthless person, he understood that. Contemptible. A thousand circumstances, unnoticed in the past, came back to him; and he wondered how he could have been blind for so long. Master Joseph, however, was continuing.

"Yesterday after his dinner, my bourgeois got dressed up like a fiancé. I shaved him, curled his hair, perfumed him, and made him into an Adonis. After that, he got into the carriage, and I drove him to the Rue de Provence, to Monsieur Fauvel's house."

"What!" Prosper exclaimed. "After his insulting words the day of the theft, he was bold enough to go back there!"

"Yes, my young Monsieur, he had that audacity; and he even dared stay there all evening, until near midnight. That was too bad for me, because I was on my seat wringing wet."

"How did he seem when he left?" asked Monsieur Verduret.

"He seemed less happy than when he arrived, that's positive. When my horse was in his stall and my carriage in the coach house, I went to ask him if he needed anything. I found his door closed, and he swore at me through it."

And to help digest that humiliation, Master Joseph swallowed a throat full of absinthe.

"Is that all?" asked Monsieur Verduret.

"For yesterday, yes, Boss. This morning the bourgeois got up late and still in a bearish mood. The other one, Raoul, arrived at noon, also furious. They immediately began to argue, but what an argument! Look, safe-crackers would have blushed to hear them. At one point, my big lout of a bourgeois grabbed the little one by the throat and he shook him like a plum tree. I really thought he was going to strangle him. But the Raoul fellow, not stupid, drew a pretty pointed knife from his pocket, and, *ma foi*, the other one was afraid and let him drop and calmed down."

"But what were they saying?"

"Ah! There's the hitch, Boss," Master Joseph said piteously. "They were speaking English, the rascals, so I didn't understand anything. What I'm sure of, however, is that they were arguing about money."

"How do you know that?"

"Because at the International Exposition I learned how you say 'money' in all the European languages, and because this word came up every moment in their conversation

Monsieur Verduret, frowning, mumbled in an unintelligible monologue. Prosper, who was watching him, wondered if by chance he could claim to recognize, just by reflection, the exact sense of the dispute which had escaped the domestic.

"At the end," continued Master Joseph, "when my rascals had calmed down, they started speaking French again. But, *Baste!* They didn't talk any more except about insignificant things, about a masked ball to take place tomorrow at the bankers. Only, in seeing the little one out, my boss said to him, 'Since that scene is inevitable, it's as well that it took place today. Stay at your place at Vésinet this evening.' Raoul answered, 'I understand.'"

As the night was coming on, little by little the bar/brasserie filled up with customers, who all yelled out for absinthe or bitters at the same time. The waiters, standing on stools, put matches to the gas lights which lit up with dull explosions.

"You need to dash off," Monsieur Verduret said to Joseph. "Your master may need you, and what's more, here's someone who wants to talk to me. See you tomorrow."

That somebody was none other than Cavaillon, more upset and more trembling than ever. He glanced around on all sides with worried looks, shaking more than a crook who knows he has all of the Paris police on his heels. He, too, didn't sit down at Monsieur Verduret's table. He gave a furtive handshake to Prosper; and it was only after having made sure that nobody was watching him that he risked giving Monsieur Verduret a little package, saying:

"Here's what she found in a closet."

It was a richly bound prayer book. Monsieur Verduret flipped through it rapidly, and he quickly found the pages from which the words stuck on the letter Prosper received the evening before had been cut.

"I had moral proof," he said, holding out the book to the young man. "Here is concrete proof which, just by itself, can save you."

Seeing this book, Prosper turned pale, because he recognized it. It was he who had given that prayer book to Madeleine in exchange for the consecrated medallion. And, in fact, on the first page Madeleine had written: *Souvenir of Notre-Dame-de-Fourvières, 17 January 1866.*

"But this book is Madeleine's," he exclaimed.

Monsieur Verduret didn't answer. He had just gotten up to go to a young man dressed like wine merchant boys, who had just entered. He had hardly glanced at a note the boy gave him than he came back to the table in a state of agitation.

"We may have them!" he exclaimed.

And throwing a 5 franc coin on the table, without saying a word to Cavaillon, he led Prosper out, dumbfounded. "We may be going to miss them. We'll surely get to the Saint-Lazare Station too late for the train to Saint-Germain."

"But what's it about, in the name of Heaven?" Prosper demanded.

"Come on, come on. We can talk on the way."

When they got to the Palais Royal Square, Monsieur Verduret stopped in front of one of the station carriages. He had evaluated the horses with a glance…

"How much do you want to drive us to Vésinet?" he asked the coachman.

"The thing is, I don't know the road there very well…"

But the name of Vésinet told Prosper everything.

"I'll show you the way," he said quickly.

"Then, at this hour," the coachman went on, "and in this wretched weather, that will be 25 francs."

"And to go fast, how much more would you ask?"

"Damn! Patron, that would be up to your generosity, but if you make it 35 francs, I believe…"

"You'll have 100," interrupted Monsieur Verduret, "if you can catch a carriage that has a half-hour's start on us."

"Tonnerre de Brest!" the coachman cried out, transported. "Get in then. You're making me lose a minute."

And cracking his whip three times over the backs of his skinny nags, he launched his carriage at a fast gallop down the Valois Road.

Chapter X

When you leave the little Vésinet railroad station, you find two roads in front of you. The one on the left, tarmacked and carefully maintained, leads to the village, whose new church you can see through the trees. The other on the right, newly laid-out and with hardly any sand, leads through an uncut forest. Along the last one which in five years will be a street, you still encounter very few houses, which are built for the most part with deplorable taste. They rise up in the distance in the middle of tree clearings, a Paris businessmen's retreat inhabited during the winter. It was at the point where these two roads met that, about 9:00 in the evening, Prosper had the carriage stopped that he had gotten into at the Place du Palais Royal with Monsieur Verduret. The coachman had earned his 100 francs. The horses were worn out, but for the last five minutes Monsieur Verduret and Prosper could distinguish the lantern lights of a rented carriage like theirs, rolling fifty meters ahead.

The first to get out of the carriage, Monsieur Verduret handed the coachman a bank bill.

"Here's what I promised you," he said. "Go to the first inn you find on the right as you go into the village. If we haven't rejoined you in an hour, you will be free to go back to Paris."

The coachman overdid it in thanks, but neither Prosper nor his companion heard him. They had started at a run down the deserted road. The weather, so detestable at the departure that it had made the coachman hesitate, was worse still. The rain was falling in torrents and a furious wind shook, so as to almost break the black tree branches, which hit against each other with a deadly noise. The darkness was profound, thick. It was made more gloomy by the twinkling of the station's street lights that you could see flickering in the distance, almost ready to go out under the wind gusts.

For five minutes Monsieur Verduret and Prosper had been running in the middle of the wet road, transformed into slush, when suddenly the cashier stopped.

"We're there," he said. "There's where Raoul lives."

In front of the iron grill of an isolated house was parked a carriage, the one Monsieur Verduret and his companion had seen in front of them. Turned around on his seat, wrapped up as well as possible in his overcoat, and despite the wind and rain, the coachman was already asleep, waiting for the return of the customer he had just brought there.

Monsieur Verduret went up to the carriage, and pulling the coachman by his overcoat, called out:

"Ah! My good fellow!"

The coachman woke with a start, automatically picking up his reins while

388

stammering:

"All right! Master, all right!"

But when he saw these two men by the light of his lanterns in that deserted place, he imagined that they perhaps wanted his purse and, who knows, his life, and he was given a terrible fright.

"I'm taken," he said, flipping his whip. "I'm spoken for."

"I know that very well, imbecile," said Monsieur Verduret, "and I only want some information from you that I'll pay 100 écus for. Haven't you just brought a middle-aged woman here?"

That question, that promise of 5 francs, far from reassuring the coachman changed his fright into terror.

"I've already told you to go on your way," he answered. "Be off; if not, I'll call for help." Monsieur Verduret backed off quickly.

"Let's leave," he whispered in Prosper's ear, "That animal would do what he says, and once that happens, it's goodbye to our plans. We'll have to get in some way other than by the gate."

Then both of them walked along the wall surrounding the garden, looking for a good place to climb over. It wasn't easy to find that place in the darkness. The wall was at least ten or twelve feet high. Fortunately, Monsieur Verduret was nimble. The weakest point found and chosen, he stepped backward, took a running start, and with a leap prodigious for such a fat man, he managed to grab a hold of the rocks set at an angle at the top. Digging in his feet and holding on with his fists, he lifted himself up and was soon astride the coping of the wall. It was then Prosper's time to climb up but, although younger than his companion, he didn't have his legs. Monsieur Verduret had to help him, not only to hitch himself up, but also to go down the other side. Once in the garden, Monsieur Verduret got busy studying the lay of the land.

The house Monsieur de Lagors lived in was built in the middle of a vast garden. It was narrow and relatively high, having two floors and some attics above them. A single window on the second floor was lit up.

"You know the house, since you've come here twenty times. Could you tell me what the room is where we see the light?" Monsieur Verduret asked.

"That's Raoul's bedroom."

"Very good. Now let's see about the arrangement. What is there on the ground floor?"

"The kitchen, the office, a billiard room and the dining room."

"And on the second floor?"

"Two sitting rooms separated by a sliding partition and a study."

"Where do the servants stay?"

"Raoul doesn't have any at this hour. People from Vésinet serve him, a husband and wife who come in the morning and leave in the evening after dinner."

Monsieur Verduret rubbed his hands together happily.

"Then, everything is going well!" he said. "It would be the devil if we didn't manage to surmise something of what Raoul and the woman who's come from Paris at this hour and in this weather are saying. Let's go in."

Prosper tried to protest. The suggestion seemed to him to be too much.

"Do you think so, Monsieur?" he asked.

"Ah! Come now!" answered the fat man in a jeering tone. "Why do you think we came here? Did you expect a party?"

"We may be caught."

"And so? At the slightest noise revealing our presence, you'll go in boldly like a friend who's come to visit his friend and who found all the doors open."

The unfortunate thing was that the door—a door of solid oak—was closed, and Monsieur Verduret shook it in vain.

"What an oversight!" he whispered in an irritated tone. "You should always have your tools with you. A cheap lock you could open with a nail, and there's not a pick, not a piece of iron wire!"

Seeing his efforts were useless, he left the door to run to each of the windows on the ground floor in turn. Alas! All the shutters were closed and solidly fastened. Monsieur Verduret seemed exasperated. He circled around the house like a fox around a chicken house, furious, looking for a way in, but finding none. Finally, in desperation, he came to stand at the spot in the garden where the lit up window could best be seen.

"If only we could see!" he exclaimed. "To think that there," and he shook his fist at the window, "is the key to the enigma and we're separated from it by only the thirty or forty feet of the two floors."

Prosper had never been so surprised before by the behavior of his strange companion. He seemed at home in this garden where he'd just climbed the wall. He came and went without taking any precautions. You'd have said he was used to such expeditions, and that he found that situation completely natural, talking about picking the lock in an inhabited house just as a bourgeois would of opening his snuff box. In addition, he was paying no attention to the bad weather, to the wind, to the rain still falling, or to the mud he was sloshing around in. He had gone back to the house, and he was calculating, and taking measurements, as if in the foolish hope of hoisting himself up that slick wall.

"I want to see," he was repeating. "I will see."

Suddenly a memory from the past crossed Prosper's mind.

"But there's a ladder here!" he cried out.

"And you didn't tell me that!…Where is it?"

"At the back of the garden, under the trees."

They ran, and, not without some trouble, found it stretched along the length of the wall. To lift it and to carry it to the house was the work of a moment. But when they had put it upright, they recognized that even when putting it more vertically upright than was prudent, it lacked at least six good feet of reaching the lighted window.

390

"We can't do it!" Prosper said, discouraged.

"We can do it!" Monsieur Verduret cried out, triumphantly.

On that, placing himself a meter from the house and facing it, he seized the ladder, lifted it cautiously, and placed the last rung on his shoulders, lifting the steps as high as possible. The obstacle was surmounted.

"Now," he said to his companion. "Climb up."

For Prosper, the situation was intense to the extreme. He didn't hesitate. Enthusiasm from the difficulty overcome, with the hope of triumph, gave him a strength and agility he didn't know he had. He lifted himself to the lower rungs without shaking and started up the ladder, which shook and wavered under his weight. But his head had scarcely gone past the window sill than he let out a huge cry, a terrible cry, which was lost amid the roaring of the storm. He slid, or rather fell, onto the wet ground crying out:

"Miserable man...miserable man!"

With extraordinary swiftness and strength, Monsieur Verduret placed the heavy ladder on the ground and dashed toward Prosper, fearing he was dangerously hurt.

"What did you see?" he asked. "What's the matter?"

But Prosper was already standing up.

If the fall had been hard, he was in one of those crises where the sovereign soul so absolutely dominates the beast that the body can't feel pain.

In a hoarse and curt voice he answered: "The matter is that it's Madeleine there in that bedroom alone with Raoul!"

Monsieur Verduret was dumbfounded. He, the infallible man, his deductions had missed the mark. He was certain it was a woman who was with Monsieur de Lagors. But according to his conjectures, after the note Gypsy had sent to him at the bar/brasserie, he thought that woman was Madame Fauvel.

"Aren't you mistaken?" he asked.

"No, Monsieur, no! I couldn't mistake another woman for Madeleine! Ah! You heard her answer me yesterday. Should I expect this foul betrayal? 'She loves you,' you told me. 'She loves you!'"

Monsieur Verduret didn't answer. Confused at first by his mistake, he was looking for the causes and his penetrating mind had already begun to sort them out.

"There is that secret Nina surmised," Prosper went on. "Madeleine, that noble and pure Madeleine in whom I had faith as in my mother, is the mistress of this forger, who has stolen even the name he carries. And I, an imbecile of an honest man, I made this miserable creature my best friend. It was to him that I told my agony and my hopes...and he was her lover! And me, I was probably the amusement of their rendezvous. They laughed at my ridiculous love, at my stupid confidence!"

He stopped. He gave in to the violence of his emotions. The ripping away of self-love adds a sharp pain to even the most atrocious suffering. That certainty of having been so unworthily betrayed and played upon brought him to the verge of madness.

"But that's enough humiliations like that," he continued. He had a tone of unbelievable rage. "It won't be said that I cowardly bowed my head under the bloodiest insults."

He was going to dash toward the house. Monsieur Verduret, who was watching his movements as much as the darkness allowed, stopped him.

"What do you intend to do?"

"Avenge myself! Ah! I'll be able to break down the door, now that I don't fear either the scandal or the gossip. I have nothing more to lose. I'm not trying any longer to slip into the house furtively, like a thief.

I want to enter as master, as a man mortally offended, who comes to ask a reason for the offense."

"You won't do that Prosper."

"Who, then, will keep me from it?"

"Me!"

"You! No. Don't think you can. To appear, overwhelm and kill them, and then to die afterward, that's what I want; that's what I'm going to do."

If Monsieur Verduret hadn't had fists of steel, Prosper would have gotten away from him. There was a short scuffle, but Monsieur Verduret came out on top.

"If you make any noise, if you raise the household, that's the end for our hopes."

"I have no more hope."

"Raoul, put on his guard, will escape us and you'll remain forever dishonored."

"What does that matter to me?"

"But it matters to me, unfortunate man! To me, who's sworn to make your innocence a sensation. At your age, you can always find another mistress. You can never recover your lost honor."

During true passion, outward circumstances don't matter. Monsieur Verduret and Prosper were there in the rain, wet to the bones, standing in the mud, and they were arguing!

"I want revenge," Prosper repeated with that idiotic persistence of the *idée fixe,* "I want revenge…"

"Get revenge, then," exclaimed Monsieur Verduret, who was beginning to get angry, "but like a man and not like a child."

"Monsieur!"

"Yes, like a child. What would you do, once you were inside the house? Are you armed? No. Would you then jump on Raoul, would you fight hand to hand with him? While this is going on, Madeleine would go back to her carriage, and after that? Are you even the stronger one?"

Crushed by the feeling of his obvious impotence, Prosper was silent.

"What good are weapons?" Monsieur Verduret continued. "You'd have to be insane to kill a man whom you could send to prison."

"What's to be done, then?"

"Wait. Vengeance is a delicious fruit that has to ripen."

Prosper was shaken. Monsieur Verduret understood that, and he threw out his last argument, the most certain, the one he was holding in reserve.

"Besides," he added, "how do we know that Mademoiselle Madeleine is here for herself. Didn't we come to the conviction that she was sacrificing herself? The superior will power that made her banish you could very well have obligated her to this evening's measures."

The voice which speaks in the direction of our dearest desires will always be listened to. That supposition, so little probable in appearance, struck Prosper.

"In fact," he whispered, "who knows?"

"I myself would certainly know," said Verduret, "if I could see."

Prosper was silent a moment without speaking.

"Will you promise me, Monsieur," he finally said, "to tell me everything you see, the truth, as painful as it might be for me?"

"I swear it to you on my word of honor."

Then, with a strength he wouldn't have thought himself capable of some instants before, Prosper lifted the ladder and placed the last rung on his shoulders, just as his companion had done.

"Climb up!" he said then.

In a second, so light, so skillful that he didn't shake the ladder once, Monsieur Verduret was up to the window.

Prosper had seen only too well. It was Madeleine who was there, at that hour, alone with Raoul de Lagors. Monsieur Verduret noted she had kept on her street clothes, her hat, and her cloth overcoat. Standing in the middle of the room, she was speaking with great animation. Her posture, her gestures, and her facial expression betrayed great indignation, held in with difficulty, and a certain contempt, badly disguised. Raoul himself was seated on a low chair, stirring up the fire with little tongs. From time to time he raised his arms shrugging, which is the movement of a man resigned to listening to everything and who responds to everything with, "I can't do anything."

Certainly Monsieur Verduret would have given the pretty ring he wore on his master finger to hear something, if only ten words of the conversation; but with such a wind, not even a vague whisper came to his ear, and he didn't dare bring his ear close to the glass for fear of being seen.

"Obviously," he thought, *"it's an argument, but it's clear it's not a lover's quarrel."*

Madeleine, however, continued talking. He hoped to find the meaning of that scene by studying Lagors' face, which he made out very well, lit as it was by the lamp placed on the chimney mantle. At times Lagors trembled, despite his apparent indifference, or he struck the hearth harder with the fire tongs. Undoubtedly, some more direct reproach had struck him.

Desperate, Madeleine was reduced to begging. She clasped her hands. She bowed. She was almost on her knees. He turned his head away. Moreover, he didn't answer except in monosyllables. Two or three times, Madeleine appeared to want to leave. She always came back, as if, asking for a favor, she couldn't resign herself to leaving without having obtained it. She must have found some decisive reason the last time, because Raoul suddenly got up, opened a little piece of furniture placed near the chimney, and took from it a bundle of papers that he held out to her.

"Ah! Look at that!" thought Monsieur Verduret. *"What the devil of a game are they playing? Is that compromising correspondence this young lady has come to reclaim?"*

Madeleine, who had taken the bundle of papers, still didn't seem satisfied. She was speaking and again insisting on obtaining something else. Raoul was refusing, and she threw the bundle of papers on the table.

These papers were of unusual interest to Monsieur Verduret. They had spread out over the table and he saw them rather well. They were in several colors, grey, green, and red.

"But I'm not making a mistake," thought Monsieur Verduret. *"I'm not blind. Those are receipts from Mont-de-Piété pawn brokers."*

Madeleine was searching through all the papers laid out on the table. She took three of them that she folded and put in her pocket, and pushed the others away with very clear disdain. This time she was determined to leave because, when she spoke, Raoul took the lamp to light her way. Monsieur Verduret had nothing more to see. While he was coming down, taking a thousand precautions, he was whispering:

"Pawn broker receipts from the Mont-de-Piété. What infamous mystery does this affair hold?"

Before anything else, it was a matter of hiding the ladder. After taking Madeleine downstairs, Raoul might decide to take a walk in the garden, and discover it despite the darkness. Set up in that way, that ladder stood out in black against the wall. Hastily, Monsieur Verduret and Prosper placed it on the ground. Without worrying about the bushes it broke, they went to hide where the darkness was the thickest, in a spot where they could watch the door of the house and the wrought iron gate at the same time.

Almost at the same moment, Raoul and Madeleine appeared on the steps. Raoul had put down his lamp on the first step. He offered his hand to the young girl, but she pushed it away with a gesture of such insulting haughtiness, that, seen by Prosper, poured balm on his wounds. This contempt didn't seem to affect nor surprise Raoul. He responded simply with an ironic gesture which meant: "As you wish!"

He went as far as the wrought iron gate, opened and closed it himself, and then went back in very quickly, while Madeleine's carriage left at a fast trot.

"Now, Monsieur," Prosper questioned, tortured by doubt. "Remember that you promised me the truth, whatever it might be. Tell me. Don't be afraid. I'm strong."

"It's against joy that you need to fortify yourself, my friend. Before a month is out, you'll bitterly regret your withering suspicions of this evening. You'll blush when thinking that you could've believed Madeleine the mistress of a man like Lagors."

"Even so, Monsieur, appearances…"

"Ah! You must beware of appearances, *Pardieu!* A suspicion, false or true, is always based on something. But we can't spend eternity here. Your scoundrel, Raoul, has closed the gate; I saw him. We'll have to go out the way we came in a while ago."

"But the ladder!"

"Let it stay where it is. Since we can't wipe out our footprints, the whole thing will be blamed on robbers."

They climbed the wall once more. They hadn't gone fifty feet down the road when they heard the noise of a gate closing. They made out footsteps, and soon a man went past them going to the station. When he was some distance away:

"That's Raoul," said Monsieur Verduret. "Our servant Joseph will soon tell us that he's gone to give an account of the scene to Monsieur Clameran. If only they're nice enough to speak French."

He walked along a while without speaking, trying to pick up the broken thread of his deductions.

"How the devil," he suddenly continued, "did this Lagors, who doesn't look for anything but society, pleasure and gambling, come to choose an isolated house in Vésinet?"

"Probably," answered Prosper, "because Monsieur Fauvel's country house is a quarter of an hour from here on the banks of the Seine."

"That's an explanation for the summer, but for the winter?"

"Oh! In the winter he has a room at the Hotel du Louvre, and throughout the year he has an apartment in Paris available."

All that didn't enlighten Monsieur Verduret. He began to walk faster.

"Hopefully," he murmured, "our coachman hasn't left. We can't think of taking the incoming train. We'd meet Raoul at the station."

Although more than an hour had gone by since Prosper and his companion had gotten off at the intersection of the two roads, the carriage which had brought them was still stationed at the inn Monsieur Verduret had pointed out. The coachman hadn't been able to resist the desire to break the 100 franc bill earned by his horses. He'd been served dinner. He liked the wine. He stayed. The sight of his bourgeois clients enchanted him. He wouldn't go back to Paris empty. However, the state in which he saw them again surprised him greatly.

"What's happened to you?" he exclaimed.

Prosper simply answered that in going to visit one of their friends, they got lost and fell in a pit—as if there were pits in the Vésinet woods!

"So that's what it was!" said the coachman.

He apparently seemed satisfied with the explanation. In reality, he wasn't far from believing that his two individuals had just tried to pull off some robbery. That last opinion must have been that of several persons present, because telling looks were exchanged. But Monsieur Verduret cut short the commentaries.

"Are we going to leave?" he demanded in his most authoritative voice.

"All right, patron, just give me time to pay the bill and I'll be with you. You get in."

The road on the return trip was deadly long and silent. Prosper had at first tried to get his strange companion to talk; but as he answered only in monosyllables, his self-esteem made him stop talking. He was irritated more and more by the absolute control that man exercised over him. The physical circumstances added more to his boredom. He was chilled, frozen right down to his bone marrow, and he felt an irresistible numbness gaining control of him which enveloped his thoughts in an opaque fog. Because, if there are no limits to the power of the imagination, physical strength has its limits. After effort comes the reaction.

Sunk into a corner, his feet on the bench in front of him, Monsieur Verduret seemed to be asleep, but nevertheless he had never been more wide awake. He was as discontented as possible. That expedition, which in his mind should have confirmed his hesitations, ended with a complication. All the strings he thought he held broke apart in his hands. True, for him, the facts remained the same, but the circumstances were changing. He could no longer discover what common motive, what moral or material complicity, or what influences pushed the four actors in his drama, Madame Fauvel, Madeleine, Raoul, and de Clameran to move in the same direction. And he looked about in his fertile mind, an encyclopedia of strategies, for what combination could throw light on the situation. Midnight struck as the carriage arrived in front of the Grand-Archange Hotel; and it was only then that Monsieur Verduret, snatched from his meditations, was aware that he hadn't had dinner. Fortunately, Madame Alexandre was expecting him and in the wink of an eye, a supper was improvised. It was more than thoughtfulness, more than respect that she showed her guest. Prosper was struck by it. She looked at his companion with a sort of amazed admiration.

Having finished eating, Monsieur Verduret rose.

"You won't see me tomorrow during the day," he said to Prosper, "but about this time in the evening, I'll be here. Maybe I'll be lucky enough to find what I'm looking for at the Messieurs Jandidier masked ball."

Prosper almost fell over. What! Monsieur Verduret was thinking about going to a party given by the richest bankers in the capital! Then that was the reason he'd sent him to the costume maker.

"Then, you've been invited?" he asked.

A thin smile passed through Monsieur Verduret's very expressive eyes.

"Not yet," he said, "but I will be."

Oh! What contradictions the human mind holds. Prosper's mind had been tortured with the most keenly distressing thoughts; and now, looking sadly around his bedroom, thinking of Monsieur Verduret's plans, he murmured:

"Ah! He's lucky, he is. Tomorrow he'll see Madeleine, more beautiful than ever, dressed as a lady-in-waiting.

Chapter XI

Located toward the middle of the Rue Saint-Lazare are the twin city dwellings of the Messieurs Jandidier, two famous financiers who would still be remarkable men, even without the prestige of their millions. That can't be said of everyone!

The two town houses, which brought cries of admiration from the press at the time of their completion several years ago, are absolutely distinct from each other, but cleverly laid out in a way so as to be a single dwelling if need be. When the Messieurs Jandidier gave a party, they had the heavy moveable partitions lifted, and their combined drawing rooms are then some of the most beautiful in Paris.

Princely magnificence marvelously arranged for comfort, and well-thought-out hospitality—everything contributed to render these celebrations the most fashionable and the most sought after. That meant that Saturday, the Rue Saint-Lazare was crowded with carriages lining up awaiting their turn.

At 10:00 p.m., they were already dancing in the two drawing rooms. It was a costume ball. Almost all the costumes were expensively decorated, some in the best taste, some truly original. Among the latter, one noticed most of all a Paillasse.[32] Oh! But a real one, having the admirable facial expression of the part, the insolent eye, a greedy and mocking mouth, brightly painted cheekbones, and a beard so red it seemed to blaze in the light of the chandeliers. The costume was exactly like that of the tradition: high-top boots with turned down tops, the hat sufficiently battered, the lace on the sleeve frill unraveled. He held in his left hand the staff of a sort of cloth banner on which six or eight scenes were designed, roughly painted like the booths at a country fair. In his right hand he was flipping a little switch with which he struck his cloth from time to time, like county fair barkers giving their spiels.

People surrounded this Paillasse, waiting to hear him pronounce some witty gibes, but he stubbornly stayed near the entry door. It was almost 10:30 p.m. when he left his post. Monsieur and Madame Fauvel, followed by their niece Madeleine, had just entered. A compact group formed almost immediately near the door. For the last ten days, the affair of the banker of the Rue de Provence had been the most tangy food of all conversations. Friends and enemies were very pleased to approach him, some to assure him of their sympathy, and others to offer him those equivocal compliments of condolences, which are the most wounding and most irritating things in the world.

Enrolled in the battalion of "serious" men, Monsieur Fauvel had not

---

[32] Grotesque character and court jester, later popularized in the Italian opera *Pagliacce* (1892) by Ruggerio Leoncavallo.

dressed in costume. He had simply thrown a short silk mantle over his shoulders. On his arm, Madame Fauvel, born Valentine de La Verberie, bowed and greeted, with the most gracious affability. Her beauty had been remarkable in the past; and that evening, with the magic of the costume lending something, and the illusion of the lights helping, she had recovered the freshness and the bloom of her youth. One would never have thought she had just completed her forty-eighth year.

She had chosen the courtly dress of the last years of Louis XIV's reign, magnificent and severe, the whole made of satin velvet brocade, without a diamond, without a jewel. And she wore it with easy nobility, having a regal air under her powder, as was proper—some charitable souls said—for a la Verberie who'd made a mistake by marrying a man of money.

But it was Madeleine that all looks were fixed on. She seemed truly a queen in that lady-in-waiting costume, seeming especially created to complement the richness of her figure. Under the heavy perfumes of the drawing rooms and under the chandeliers' rays, her beauty was in full bloom. Her hair had never been so black, her complexion had never appeared so white, and her big eyes had never shone with such luster.

Once they had entered, Madeleine took her aunt's arm, while Monsieur Fauvel lost himself in the crowd, trying to reach one of the gaming rooms, the refuge of serious men.

The ball was then at the height of its splendors. Under the baton of Strauss (Johann Strauss, the Younger) and one of his lieutenants, two orchestras filled the two mansions with their fanfares. The colorful crowd mingled together and whirled, and it was a marvelous jumble of cloth of gold and of satin, of velvet and of laces. Diamonds glittered on heads and on chests, the palest cheeks became pink, eyes sparkled, and the women's shoulders shone whiter than snow in the first rays of the April sun.

He and his banner forgotten, the Paillasse had taken refuge in the recess of a window; he was standing there, his shoulder leaning against the metal rod of the window's iron handle. He seemed somewhat affected by so much magnificence, and something of the intoxication rose to his head. However, he didn't lose sight of a couple dancing a short distance from him.

It was Madeleine, leaning on the arm of a Doge, and this Doge was none other than the Marquis de Clameran. He appeared radiant, rejuvenated. His eagerness had the appearance of triumph. In the interval of a quadrille, he leaned toward his dancer and spoke to her with flowing admiration. She seemed to listen to him, if not with pleasure, at least without anger, nodding her head at times, and at other times smiling.

"Obviously," murmured the Paillasse, "this noble scoundrel's paying court to the banker's niece. Then, I was right yesterday. But from another direction, how could Mademoiselle Madeleine resign herself to listen with such a gracious air to his dreary compliments and his declarations? Fortunately, Prosper isn't here."

He stopped. In front of him stopped a man, already old, wearing with supreme distinction the Venetian cloak.

"You know, Monsieur…Verduret," he said, half seriously, half jokingly, "what you promised me."

The Paillasse bowed respectfully, deeply, but without any appearance of lowliness or humility. "I remember!" he answered.

"Above all, don't take any risks."

"Monsieur le Comte can rest easy. He has my word."

"That's fine, Monsieur. I know its value."

The Count walked away, but during this short exchange the quadrille finished and the Paillasse no longer saw either Monsieur de Clameran or Madeleine.

"I'll find them near Madame Fauvel," he thought.

At that, he launched into the crowd, in search of the banker's wife. Made uncomfortable by the suffocating heat, Madame Fauvel had come to get some fresh air in the grand gallery of the Jandidier town houses. Thanks to that talisman that's called gold, they were transformed for the night into a fairy garden full of orange trees, laurier roses in bloom, and white lilacs, whose delicate clusters were already bending over.

The Paillasse saw her sitting near some shrubbery, not far from the door to one of the gaming rooms. Madeleine was to her right; to her left stood Raoul de Lagors, dressed as one of Henri III's pretty male favorites.

"You'll have to admit," thought the Paillasse, while looking for an observation post, *"There aren't any more handsome than this young bandit."*

Madeleine now was sad. She had picked a camellia from a nearby bush, and she was mechanically picking off its petals, her gaze lost in the distance. Raoul and Madame Fauvel, leaning toward each other, were talking. Their faces appeared calm, but the gestures of one and the trembling of the other clearly betrayed major preoccupations and a most serious conversation. From the gaming room could be seen the Doge, Monsieur de Clameran, placed so as to see Madame Fauvel and Madeleine without being seen.

"It's yesterday's scene continuing. If only I could overhear some words! If I were behind those camellias, I'm sure I could hear," thought the Paillasse.

He began to maneuver around the groups. When he came to the desired place, Madeleine rose and took the arm of a Persian, shining with precious jewels like a constellation. At the same time, Raoul got up and went into the gaming room, where he said some words in Clameran's ear.

"And there you are! Those two miserable men have a hold on those two women, and they're struggling in vain between their claws. But what hold do they have on them?" the Paillasse asked himself.

He was thinking when suddenly there was a great stir in the gallery. They were announcing a marvelous minuet in the large drawing room. Then the

Countess of Commarin had just arrived as Aurora (goddess of the dawn). Then again everyone had to go admire the Princess Karasoff's emeralds, the most beautiful in the universe.

In an instant, the gallery was almost empty; there remained only some poor unattached men, some creaking husbands whose wives were dancing, and some young men, timid and embarrassed in their costumes.

The Paillasse thought that the moment favorable for his plans had come. Suddenly he left his place, brandishing his banner, hitting the cloth with his little switch, and coughing with affectation, like a man who's getting ready to speak. He had gone across the gallery and placed himself between the armchair occupied by Madame Fauvel and the door of the salon. Immediately, all the guests who had remained in the gallery came running, making a circle around him. He had already struck a pose in the traditional attitude: his hat pushed over one ear, his body bent in the same direction as the hat.

It was with unbelievable volubility and the most emphatically comic tone that he began:

"Ladies and Gentlemen, Just this morning I solicited permission from the authorities"—he bowed—"of this city. Ah! Why? In order, gentlemen, to have the honor of exhibiting to you a spectacle which has already conquered the approval of five parts of the world and of several academies. It's inside this theatrical box, ladies. It is the representation of an unheard of drama, acted for the first time in Peking, and put on the stage by our most famous actors. People can now take their places. Gentlemen, the reservoir lamps are lit and the actors are getting dressed." He stopped, and with a perfection humiliating to the copper instruments and big drums, he imitated the ear-splitting music of the country fair hucksters.

"But Ladies and Gentlemen," he started again, "you're going to say to me *'If they're acting the play in the theatre, what are you doing here?'* What I'm doing here, Gentlemen, I'm here to give you a taste of the drama, the sensations, the emotions, the palpitations and the other distractions, in consideration for which you can pay the minor disbursement of 50 centimes, 10 écus! You see this superb tableau? Well, it represents the eight most terrible scenes of the drama. Ah! I see. You're trembling. But this is nothing. This magnificent tableau no more gives you a true idea of the play than a drop of water gives an idea of the sea, or a sparkle gives the idea of the sun. My tableau, Gentlemen, is the little trifle at the door, like, you might say, the restaurant fumes smelled by clients eager to dine."

"Do you know this Paillasse?" an enormous Turk asked a melancholy Polichinelle.

"No, but he does a superior imitation of the trumpet."

"Oh! Very superior, but what's he getting at?"

What the Paillasse wanted more than anything was to draw the attention of Madame Fauvel, who had abandoned herself to a profound and, without doubt, sad reverie, since Raoul and Madeleine had walked away.

He succeeded.

The sound of that strident voice brought the banker's wife back to reality. She trembled and looked quickly around her, as if someone had awakened her brusquely. She leaned in the Paillasse's direction.

He, however, was continuing:

"So, Gentlemen, we're in China. The first of the eight scenes of my tableau, here, above, on the left"—he pointed it out with his switch— "shows you the famous Mandarin Li-Fo, in the bosom of his family. That pretty young lady leaning on his shoulder is none other than his wife, and the children rolling around on the carpet are the fruit of this most fortunate of unions. Can't you breathe in, Gentlemen, the perfume of satisfaction and honesty which this superb painting gives off! That's because Madame Li-Fo is the most virtuous of women, adoring her husband and idolizing her children. Being virtuous, she is happy, because as Confucius says it so well, *'Virtue gives more pleasure than vice.'*"

Cautiously, Madame Fauvel had drawn closer; she had even left her chair to take another very near the Paillasse.

The melancholy Polichinelle asked his neighbor: "Do you see what he says is on his canvas?"

"Ma foi! No! And you?"

The fact is that the canvas, madly daubed with color, hardly represented that any more than something else. But the Paillasse, after having imitated the roll of a tambourine, began again, accelerating his spiel still more.

"Tableau Number Two! That old woman seated in front of a dressing table mirror, and who pulls at her hair in despair, particularly the white ones, do you recognize her? Oh! Well! Nevertheless, that is the beautiful Mandarin of the first tableau. I see tears in your eyes, Ladies and Gentlemen. Ah! She is no longer beautiful, she is no longer virtuous, and her honor has disappeared with her virtue. Ah! This is a pitiful story! One day in a Peking street, I don't know where, she met a young thief, as beautiful as an angel; and she loved him, the unhappy woman, she loved him!"

It was with the most tragic voice and with a comic expression that the Paillasse pronounced these last words. During that last tirade, he had made a half-circle. He found himself now almost in front of the banker's wife, and not losing one of his facial movements:

"You're surprised, Gentlemen," he went on. "I'm not. The great Bilboquet, my master, revealed to us that the heart has no age, and it's on a ruined stalk that the most vigorous Madagascar plant flourishes. The unhappy woman! She is fifty years old and she's in love with an adolescent! From that heart breaking scene which would pluck out the heart, is a great lesson!"

"True!" murmured a cook in white satin, who had spent the evening trying to sell a quantity of *menus*, without success. "True. I thought it was more amusing."

"But it's inside the theater that the surprising effects of the Mandarin's faults can be seen. From time to time, the light of reason lit up her sick head, and the manifestations of her agony would soften the most pitiless. Come in, and for 10 écus you'll hear sobs such as the Odeon (Paris theater) has never heard in its best days. Because she understands the stupidity, the folly, and the ridiculousness of her passion, and she admits that she was desperately in pursuit of a phantom. She knew only too well that he, in the radiance of youth, could not love her. Already an old woman, she was searching in vain to hold on to the remainder of a faded beauty. She understood that if he sometimes whispered amorous words in her ear, he was lying. She guessed that one day or the other, his cloak would remain in her hand." (Allusion to the Biblical story of Joseph's flight from Pharaoh Potiphar's wife.)

While delivering with extreme volubility this spiel, seemingly addressed to the group surrounding him, the Paillasse never stopped looking into the eyes of the banker's wife. But nothing of what he said seemed to have touched her. Half reclining in her armchair, she remained calm; her eyes kept their clarity, and she even smiled sadly.

"Ah! Well!" thought the Paillasse, a little disturbed, *"could I be on the wrong track?"*

As preoccupied as he was, he nevertheless saw a new listener, the Doge Monsieur de Clameran, who also came to be part of the circle.

"On to the third tableau," he continued, making his r's roll. "The old Mandarin said good-bye to her remorse, a bothersome tenant. She told herself that instead of love, self-interest would make the too seductive young man stay near her. It was toward this end that, having dressed him up in false dignity, she introduced him to the principal Mandarins of the capital of the Son of Heaven. Then, as a pretty boy has to keep up appearances, for his gain she stripped herself of all she possessed: bracelets, rings, necklaces, pearls, and diamonds. Everything went. It was to the lending houses of the Rue Tien-Tsi that this monster carried all these jewels, and in addition, he refused to give back the receipts."

The Paillasse had reason to be satisfied.

Very apparent to him for the last moment, Madame Fauvel had given signs of being uncomfortable and agitated. Once she tried to get up and to leave, but she wasn't strong enough. She remained nailed to her armchair, forced to listen.

"Nevertheless, Ladies, and Gentlemen," continued the Paillasse, "the richest jewelry boxes can be emptied. A day came when the Mandarin no longer had anything to give. That was when the young thief conceived the deceptive plan of stealing the Mandarin Li-Fo's jasper collar stud. It was of an incalculable value, a sign of his office, put in a granite safe, guarded night and day by three soldiers. Ah! The Mandarin resisted a long time. She knew that they would certainly accuse the innocent soldiers, and that they would be crucified, as is the custom in Peking, and that thought disturbed her. But the other one spoke in such a tender voice, that, *ma foi!*...you understand. The jasper collar button was lifted. The fourth tableau represents the two guilty ones going down the hidden stairway on tiptoes. You see their fright, you see..."

He paused. Three or four of his listeners had seen that Madame Fauvel was almost ill, and they were eager to bring her help. In addition, someone was strongly gripping his arm. He turned quickly around and found himself face to face with Monsieur de Clameran and Raoul de Lagors, one as pale and as threatening as the other.

"Do you want something, Messieurs!" he asked in his most gracious tone.

"To talk to you," they both answered at the same time.

"At your service."

And he followed them to the other side of the gallery, into the recess of a French window opening onto a balcony. There nobody would think of observing them and no one in fact saw them, except the person in the Venetian cloak to whom the Paillasse had bowed so low, while calling him "Monsieur le Comte."

With the minuet then coming to an end with the orchestras taking a half-hour rest break, and the crowd flowing into the gallery, it became in a moment too crowded. Even Madame Fauvel's sudden indisposition had passed absolutely unnoticed. Those who had seen it, seeing it so soon pass away, had blamed it on the heat. Monsieur Fauvel had been told. He had rushed in, but seeing wife chatting calmly with Madeleine, he had gone back to his game.

Less in control of himself than Raoul, Monsieur de Clameran had started talking.

"First of all, Monsieur," he began in a rude tone, "I'd like to know whom I'm addressing."

But the Paillasse had promised himself to stubbornly pretend this was a masked ball joke, until push came to shove. It was in the spirit and tone of his costume that he answered:

"You're asking me for my papers, Seigneur Doge, and you, my pretty fellow? I have the papers, but they're in the hands of the authorities of this city, with my last name, first name, age, profession, domicile, and specific information."

With a furious gesture, Monsieur de Clameran stopped him.

"You have just allowed yourself the most disgusting treachery!" he said.

"Me? Seigneur Doge!"

"You! What was that abominable story you were spewing out?"

"Abominable! You may say that, but I, who composed it..."

"Enough, Monsieur, enough. At least have the courage of your actions and admit that was a long and miserable insinuation meant for Madame Fauvel."

The Paillasse had his head turned upwards, as if looking for ideas on the ceiling. His mouth was wide open, with the dazed look of a man who, psychologically, had fallen from the skies. Those who knew him, it's true, would have seen in his dark eyes a sparkle of diabolically malicious satisfaction.

"What do you know!" he said, seeming to be a great deal less answering, than talking to himself, "What about that! This is really something. Where do you find in my play about the Mandarin Li-Fo an allusion to Madame Fauvel, whom I don't know from Adam and Eve? I have vainly looked for, examined, and scrutinized, on my honor! I don't see it. Unless…but no, that's impossible."

"Then do you claim," interrupted Monsieur de Clameran, "do you maintain that you don't know the misfortune that struck Monsieur Fauvel?"

But the Paillasse had certainly decided to let the facts come out.

"A misfortune?" he asked.

"I mean, Monsieur, the robbery of which Monsieur Fauvel was the victim, and which it seems to me had so much publicity."

"Ah! Yes, I know. His cashier made off, taking 350,000 francs with him. *Pardieu!* The accident is commonplace, and I'd almost say it happens almost daily. As for discovering the least connection between this theft and my story, that's another matter."

Monsieur de Clameran was slow to answer. A violent blow on his shoulder by de Lagors had calmed him down as if by magic. Becoming colder than marble, he looked the Paillasse up and down suspiciously and seemed to regret the telling words his lack of control had snatched from him.

"So be it!" he said in that haughty tone which was usual with him. "So be it. I could be mistaken. After your explanations, I can well admit and believe it."

But at that, the Paillasse, so foolish and humble the instant before, became angry at the word "explanation." He took a proud stance, his hand on his hip, exaggerating the attitude of defiance.

"I didn't give you—I don't need to give you—any explanation."

"Monsieur!"

"Let me finish, please. If, without intending to, I wounded in any way the wife of a man I respect, it seems to me it's up to him, the only judge and arbiter of what concerns his honor, to let me know it. He's no longer at an age, you'll tell me, to come ask me to account for an offense. That's possible. But he has sons. One of them is here. I've just seen him. You asked me who I am. In my turn I'll ask you: Who are you? By your own private authority you make yourself Madame Fauvel's champion. Are you her relative, her friend, her ally? By what right do you insult her by claiming to discover an allusion where there is only a story invented to please?"

There was nothing to say to that firm and logical answer. Monsieur de Clameran was looking for a dodge.

"I'm Monsieur Fauvel's friend," he said, "and in this capacity I have a right to be as jealous of his reputation as of my own. And if that reason isn't enough for you, let me tell you that in a short while his family will be mine."

"Ah!"

"That's how it is, Monsieur. And before a week is out, my marriage to Mademoiselle Madeleine will be officially announced."

This news was at this point unexpected; it was so bizarre, that for a moment the Paillasse remained absolutely dumbfounded and for real this time. But this was the matter of only a second. He bowed very low with a smile just ironic enough that it couldn't be noted, while saying:

"Please receive all my congratulations, Monsieur. In addition to being the belle of the ball this evening, Mademoiselle Madeleine has, they say, 500,000 francs in dowry."

It was with visible impatience and looking around anxiously in all directions that Raoul de Lagors had listened to that discussion.

"That's enough of that," he said in a curt and disdainful tone. "Your tongue is too long."

"Perhaps, my pretty young man, perhaps! But I have an arm that's even longer still."

Clameran was also in a hurry to finish.

"That's enough," he added, stamping his foot. "You can't get an explanation from a man who hides his identity under the tawdry finery of his costume."

"You're free, Seigneur Doge, to go ask the master of the house who I am...if you dare."

"You are!" shouted Clameran, "You are..."

A rapid gesture from Raoul stopped an insult on the lips of the noble master of ironworks, which was going to lead from words to action, and at the least to a challenge, to scandal and to gossip.

The Paillasse waited a moment, a mocking smile on his lips, and the insult didn't come. He looked into Monsieur de Clameran's eyes and slowly said, "I am, Monsieur, the best friend your brother had while he was alive. I was his advisor. I was the confident of his last wishes."

These simple words fell like so many sledge hammers on Clameran's head. He turned frightfully pale and recoiled a step, his hands stretched out, as if he had seen a ghost rise up there before him in the middle of that ball. He wanted to answer, to protest, and to say something. Fear froze the words in his throat.

"Let's go, come on," Lagors, who had kept his self-control, said to him. And he led him along supporting him, because he was shaking like a drunken man. He was leaning on the walls.

"Oh!" said the Paillasse, in three different tones, "Oh! Oh!"

He was almost as dazed as the master of the ironworks, and he stayed there in the recess of the window, completely motionless.

He had said that mysteriously threatening sentence completely at random, without a purpose, without a stated intention, and simply in order not to remain without a rejoinder; he had been guided unknown to himself by that marvelous instinct of the policeman, which is his strength, like the nose of the bloodhound.

"What does that mean? Why was this miserable man so frightened? What terrible memory did I stir up in his dirty soul? Then let them praise my mental acuity, the subtlety of my schemes. There's a master chess player who effort-lessly crowns everyone's pawns, who rearranges all our visions with a sudden caprice. That master chess player is luck," he murmured.

He was a hundred leagues from the present situation, from the gallery, from the Messieurs Jandidier's ball. A light tap, struck on his shoulder by the person in the Venetian cloak, called him quickly back to reality.

"Are you satisfied, Monsieur Verduret?" he asked him.

"Yes and no, Monsieur le Comte. No, because I didn't completely obtain the end I set for myself, when I asked you to get me admitted here. Yes, because our two rascals have revealed themselves in such a way that doubt is no longer possible."

"And you're complaining?"

"I'm not complaining, Monsieur le Comte. On the contrary, I'm blessing luck, or I should say Providence, which has just revealed to me the existence of a secret which I didn't suspect."

Noticing the Count, five or six guests came up to him, interrupting that conversation. The Count walked away, but not without addressing a bow to the Paillasse, more as a friend than as a protector.

Immediately getting rid of his banner, he moved into the crowd which had become so thick that you couldn't move except with great difficulty. He was looking for Madame Fauvel. She had left the gallery and he found her sitting on a bench in the grand salon, chatting with Madeleine. They were both very ani-mated.

"Good!" thought the Paillasse, "they're talking about the scene, but what has become of Lagors and Clameran?"

He wasn't long in catching sight of them. They were coming and going, moving between groups, greeting and talking to a great number of persons.

"I'd bet," murmured the Paillasse, "that they're asking about me. These honorable Messieurs are trying to find out who I am. Search away, my good friends, search away…"

Soon, they gave up the task. They were so preoccupied and needed so very much to find themselves alone, to think or deliberate, that without waiting for the evening's refreshment, they took leave of Madame Fauvel and her niece, announcing that they were leaving.

They were telling the truth. The Paillasse saw them reach the vestibule, get their overcoats, go down the grand staircase, and disappear under the porch.

"That's everything for this evening," he murmured. "I have nothing more to do here."

And in his turn he left, after having put on an immense overcoat which al-most entirely hid his costume.

There were many carriages free at the door, but the weather was beautiful; even though cold, the pavement was dry. The Paillasse decided he would return home on foot, telling himself that the open air, the exercise, and the walk would settle his still confused thoughts. Lighting a cigar, he went up the Rue Saint-Lazare and turned onto Notre-Dame-Lorette to reach the Faubourg Montmartre. Suddenly, just as he was turning into the Rue Olivier, a man, coming out of the shadows where he was hidden, jumped on him; his arm lifted, and he struck him with all his strength. Fortunately for the Paillasse, he had that marvelous instinct of the cat which, you might say, can do two things. It can simultaneously be on the look-out and take care of its safety, glancing to one side and seeing from another.

He saw, or rather he sensed, the man covered by the darkness, and felt him, in some way, jump on him. He was able to half turn backward on his strong legs, while trying to parry with his hands. This movement certainly saved his life, and it was in the arm that he received the blow of the knife which was supposed to kill him.

Anger more than pain made him cry out, "Ah! You scoundrel!"

And, immediately jumping a meter forward, he was on guard. But the precaution was useless. Seeing his blow had missed its mark, the murderer didn't try again. He continued his course and soon disappeared into the Faubourg Montmartre.

"That was Lagors, certainly, and the Clameran fellow shouldn't be far away. While I was going around the church in one direction, they went around it in the other and came to wait for me here," murmured the Paillasse.

His wound, however, made him suffer cruelly. He went to stand under a street light to examine it. It probably wasn't very serious, but it was very large and the arm had been slit from one side to the other. He immediately tore his pocket handkerchief, making four strips, and wrapped his arm with the dexterity of a hospital intern.

Chapter XII

The Drama

Two leagues from Tarascon, not far from the marvelous gardens of Messieurs Audibert on the left bank of the Rhône, there can be seen the Clameran chateau, blackened by time, neglected, and dilapidated, but still solid. There, in 1841, lived the old Marquis de Clameran and his two sons, Gaston and Louis. He was, to say the least, an unusual personage, this old Marquis. He was from that race, today almost disappeared, of stubborn gentlemen whose watch had stopped in 1789[33] and kept the time of another century. Tied to his illusions even more than to his life, the old Marquis obstinately considered the events which had occurred since '89 as a series of deplorable jokes, ridiculous endeavors by a handful of factious bourgeois. One of the first to emigrate with those following the Comte d'Artois, he didn't return to France until 1815 with the Allies.[34] He should have blessed Heaven to have recovered a part of the immense domains of his family, small, it's true, but quite sufficient to allow him to live honorably. He said he didn't think he owed God any thanks for so little. He immediately set about actively trying to obtain some position at court. At last, seeing his activities unproductive, he decided to retire to his chateau, complaining about and cursing at the same time his king that he adored and who, at the bottom of his heart, he considered a Jacobin.[35] From that moment he became easily accustomed to the expensive and comfortable life of country gentlemen. Possessing about 15,000 pounds of income, he spent every year 25,000 or 30,000 pounds, emptying the sack, claiming that he would always have enough to wait for a true Restoration, which wouldn't fail to return all his lands to him.[36]

Following his example, his two sons lived liberally. The younger, Louis, was always looking for an adventure, always taking part in the pleasures of the neighborhood, drinking and gambling for high stakes; the elder, Gaston, was trying to become part of the movement of his period, working and receiving certain newspapers secretly. Just the titles of some of these would have seemed a

---

[33] Date of the French Revolution.

[34] After the fall of Napoleon, the nations opposing him formed a coalition to occupy and govern France with a puppet king. These are the "Allies" mentioned here.

[35] Revolutionary political party supporting democracy and opposing the aristocracy.

[36] After the fall of Napoleon, the victorious Allies restored a puppet Bourbon king to the French throne, and thus it was not a true Restoration.

hangable blasphemy to his father.

In summary, comfortable in his carefree egotism, the old Marquis was the happiest of mortals, eating well, drinking even better, and hunting a great deal. He was rather liked by the peasants, but detested by the middle class of the neighboring villages, on whom he heaped sometimes witty, mocking jokes. Time never seemed heavy on his hands, except during the summer because of the terrible heat in the Rhône Valley, or when the mistral (heavy wind typical of the south) blew too strongly. However even in this situation, he had at hand an infallible distraction, always new even though always the same, always spirited, always racy. He talked about his neighbor, the Countess de La Verberie.

The Countess de La Verberie, the "*bête noire*" of the Marquis, as he called her in a not very gentlemanly fashion, was a tall and dry woman, angular in physique and in character. She was haughty, disdainful, and cold toward those she judged her equals, and hard toward lesser people. Following the example of her noble neighbor, she had emigrated with her husband; killed afterward at Lutzen, unfortunately for his memory, he was not in French ranks. In 1815, the Countess also had returned to France. But, while the Marquis de Clameran recovered a relatively comfortable living, she herself could obtain from her protectors and from the royal bounty only the small domain of the Chateau de La Verberie. From the 1,000,000 francs indemnity, she was restored only a 2,500 francs income, on which she lived.

It's true that the Chateau La Verberie would have been enough for many ambitions. More modest than the Clameran manor, the pretty La Verberie castle had a less proud appearance and less high pretensions. But it had reasonable proportions. It was convenient, well laid out, discreet and easy for those serving it, like the small house of a great lord. It was, in addition, in the middle of a vast park, while its sculpted windows opened to the rising sun. This park, which extended from the Beaucaire road right up to the edge of the river, was a marvel for the countryside—with its great trees, its hedges, its small woods, its prairie and its clear stream, which ran across it from one side to the other.

There the Countess lived, always complaining and cursing life. She had only one daughter, then eighteen years old, named Valentine. She was blonde, frail, and with great trembling eyes, beautiful enough to thrill the stone saints in their niches at the village chapel, where she went every morning to hear mass. Her beauty's renown, carried on the swift waters of the Rhône, even spread far and wide. Often the riverboat men, the strong boat haulers who drove their muscular horses half in the water, half on the tow-path, noticed Valentine. She was seated, a book in her hand, under the shade of the great trees at the edge of the water. From a distance, in her white dress, with her beautiful hair half floating, she seemed in the imagination of these rough and good men like a mysterious apparition and a sign of good luck. And often, between Arles and Valence, there was talk of the pretty little fairy of La Verberie.

If Monsieur de Clameran detested the Countess, Madame de La Verberie despised the Marquis. If he had nicknamed her "the witch," she never called him anything but "the old nincompoop."

And even so, they were born to understand each other. They had a similar opinion of the essential facts, with different ways of looking at them. That is to say, they found themselves in an admirable situation to argue eternally, without ever agreeing or ever getting angry with each other. He, behaving philosophically, made fun of everything and had good digestion. She, keeping bitter grudges in her heart, grew thin with rage and green with jealousy. That didn't matter! They spent delightful evenings together. After all, they were neighbors, very close neighbors. From Clameran, you could easily see Valentine's black greyhound running through the alleys of the La Verberie Park; and from La Verberie you could see, every evening, the lights from the Clameran's dining room windows. Between the two chateaux there was only the Rhône river, somewhat embanked at that spot, rolling its rapid current at full tide.

Yes, but between the two families there was a hatred deeper than the Rhône, more difficult to turn aside or to overcome. Where did that hatred come from? The Countess and the Marquis would have been very embarrassed to say with some accuracy. That's why what had to happen, happened, which always happens in real life and often in novels. After all, as exaggerated as they may be, novels always keep a reflection of the truth which inspired them. It so happened that Gaston, having seen Valentine at a celebration, found her beautiful and fell in love with her. It so happened that Valentine noticed Gaston and, after that, couldn't help thinking about him. But so many obstacles separated them! Each of them, for almost a year, religiously kept the secret, buried in the heart like a treasure.

Gaston and Valentine, after having seen each other one time, were already very much attracted to each other, when fate, which presided over their first encounter, drew them together again. They found themselves spending a whole day at the home of the old Duchesse d'Arlange, who had come to the country to sell what remained of her properties. This time they talked to each other like old friends, surprised to find in each other an echo of the same thoughts. Then again they were separated for months. But already, without a mutual understanding, they found themselves at certain hours on the banks of the Rhône, and they could see each other from opposite sides of the river. Finally, one evening in the month of May, as Madame La Verberie was in Beaucaire, Gaston dared to enter the park and present himself to Valentine. She was not very surprised and not at all indignant. True innocence doesn't have the pretentiousness and the frightened modesty which conventional innocence is saddled with. Valentine didn't even think about ordering Gaston to leave. She leaned on his arm a long time. They walked with little steps along the grand avenue. They didn't tell each other that they were in love. They knew it. They told each other, tears in their eyes, that their love was hopeless. They recognized that they would never triumph over the absurd hates of their families. They admitted that any attempt would be foolish. They swore to each other that they would never in their life forget, and promised each other never to see each other again, no, never…but one more time. So the second rendezvous wasn't the last. And yet, how many obstacles there were to these meetings! Gaston didn't want to trust any boatman, and it was necessary to go more than a league to find a bridge. It was then that he thought swimming across the river would be much shorter. However, he was a mediocre swimmer, and to cross the river at that spot was considered with great caution by the best swimmers. That didn't matter. He exercised in secret; and one evening, Valentine terrified, saw him come out of the water almost at her feet. She made him swear not to do that exploit again. He swore and did it again the next day and the following days. Only, since Valentine always imagined him being swept away by the rapid current, they agreed on a signal which would calm her fears. Just as he was leaving, Gaston shone a light in one of the windows of the Clameran chateau, a quarter of an hour later he was at the knees of his lover.

Valentine and Gaston thought that they alone knew the secret of their love. They had taken, they were taking, such minute precautions! They were being so very careful! They were very persuaded that their behavior was a masterpiece of dissimulation and prudence! Poor naïve lovers! As if something could be hidden from the idle-inquisitiveness of the countryside, from gossiping curiosity, and from empty and lazy minds always on the watch, always looking for some sensation, good or bad, an inoffensive or mortal scandal. They thought they were keeping their secret, but it had taken flight long before. For some time already, the stories of their love, of their rendezvous, were the entertainment of the family evening chats. Sometimes in the evening they saw a shadow, a boat gliding on the river not far from the bank, and they said: "That's some late fisherman returning home." They were mistaken. That boat held curious hidden people, spies, delighted with having caught a glimpse of them; they went in all haste to recount, with a thousand lying details, their shameful expedition. It was one evening at the beginning of November, that Gas-ton finally learned the fatal truth.

Frequent rains had swollen the Rhône. The Gardon River was feeding its waters into it, as could be seen by the color of the waters. They feared a flood. To try to swim across this enormous, impetuous torrent, would be to tempt God. Gaston de Clameran had gone then to Tarascon, counting on crossing the bridge there, and then going back up the right bank of the river as far as La Verberie. Valentine was expecting him about 11:00 p.m.

When he went to Tarascon, he always dined at the house of one of his relatives who lived on the corner of the La Charité square. Through an expected turn of events, he dined with one of his friends at the Hotel des Trois Empereurs. After dinner they went, not to the café Simon where they usually went, but to a little café situated on the fairgrounds. When they entered, the rather small main room of that establishment was full of young people from the village. The billiard table being free, Gaston and his friend ordered a bottle of beer, and began to play billiards. They were in the middle of their game when Gaston's attention was drawn to some bursts of forced laughter which came from a table at the back of the room. From this moment, preoccupied with those laughs which very evidently had a malicious intent, Gaston began to miss his shots. His lack of attention became so obvious that his friend said to him:

"What's wrong with you? You aren't paying attention to the game. You're missing easy caroms."[37]

"Nothing's wrong with me."

The game continued one more minute, but suddenly Gaston threw down his billiard cue violently on the billiard table, and dashed toward the table at the back. Five young people were there playing dominoes, and emptying a bowl of warm wine. It was the one who seemed to be the oldest, a handsome boy of twenty-six, with big shining eyes and a black mustache proudly curled up, named Jules Lazet, whom Gaston addressed.

"Repeat, then," he said to him in a voice that trembled with anger. "Dare repeat, then, what you've just said!"

"Who's to keep me from it?" Lazet answered, in a very calm tone. "I said, and I'll repeat it, that noble girls aren't any better than working girls and it isn't the particle[38] which gives virtue."

"You pronounced a name."

"I pronounced the name of the pretty little fairy of La Verberie," he said, with the most insolent smile.

All the café's clients, and even two traveling salesmen who were dining at a table near the billiard room, had gotten up and gathered around the two arguing men. From the provocative smiles he saw from those watching him, from the whispers—from the boo's rather— which had greeted him when he walked up to Lazet, Gaston should have understood. He was beginning to understand, that he was surrounded by enemies. The gratuitous meanness, the continual jokes of the old Marquis, were coming to fruition. Resentment ferments quickly and terribly in hearts and heads in Provence. But Gaston de Clameran wasn't a man to step a foot backward, even if he had a hundred, even if he had one thousand enemies instead of fifteen or twenty.

"Only a coward," he continued, in a trembling voice that the silence made almost solemn. "Only a miserable coward would have the infamy and the lowness to insult and to slander a young girl, whose mother is a widow, and who has neither a father nor a brother to defend her honor."

"If she doesn't have a father or a brother," Lazet sneered, "she has her lovers and that's enough."

Those frightful words, "her lovers," carried Gaston's scarcely controlled

---

[37] In billiards, hitting two balls with one strike.

[38] The "de" in a family name indicating land ownership and nobility.

fury to its height. He raised his arm and his hand fell, with a dull sound, on Lazet's cheek. There was only one cry in the café, a cry of terror. Everyone knew Lazet's violent character, his Herculean strength, his blind courage. With one leap, he jumped over the table which separated him from Gaston and fell on him. He seized him by the throat. There was a moment of frightful confusion. Clameran's friend wanted to come to his aid. He was surrounded, knocked down with billiard cues, kicked, and pushed under a table.

Equally vigorous, one as well as the other, young and nimble, Gaston and Lazet fought without either of them obtaining a distinct advantage. Lazet, a brave boy, as fair as courageous, didn't want any help. The witnesses are unanimous on this point. He never stopped yelling to his friends:

"Get back. Spread out. Leave this to me!"

But the others were much too stirred up already to remain simple spectators of the fight.

"Get something to throw over him!" one of them cried out, "Quick, a covering to knock the Marquis off his feet!"

Five or six young men ran toward Gaston at the same time, separating him from Lazet, pushing him up against the billiard table. Some of them tried to knock him down. Others tried to jerk him off his feet by wrapping a belt around his legs. He, defending himself with the strength of despair, gained strength that he would never have been thought capable of, from the sense that he was in the right. And, all the while defending himself furiously, he heaped insults on his opponents, calling them cowards, miserable bandits fighting twelve against one courageous man. He was backing around the billiard table, trying to reach the door, getting close to it little by little, when a shout of joy filled the room.

"Here's the blanket!" they cried out. "Wrap the little fairy's lover in the blanket!"

Gaston guessed rather than heard these cries. He saw himself beaten, in the hands of these excited men, submitting to the most ignoble of outrages. With a terrible movement to one side, he got free from three assailants holding him. A strong blow of his fist got rid of the fourth. His arms were free, but his enemies came back to the attack. Then he lost his head. Beside him, from the table where the traveling salesmen had dined, he grabbed a knife and stuck it twice in the stomach of the first man who jumped toward him. This unfortunate man was Jules Lazet. He fell. There was a stunned moment. Four or five of the assailants rushed to Lazet to help him. The woman who owned the café started screaming horribly. Some of the younger ones left, screaming "Murder!" But all of the others, still at least ten, hurled themselves on Gaston, with murderous cries.

He felt himself lost. His enemies had armed themselves with whatever they could find. He had already received three of four wounds, when he made a desperate resolution. He climbed on the billiard table and, taking a formidable leap, he threw himself out the front window of the café. That front window was solid. Nevertheless, he broke it. The pieces of glass and wood bruised and cut him in twenty places, but he got out.

Gaston de Clameran was outside, but he wasn't saved. Surprised at first, and almost disconcerted by his audacity, his enemies, quickly recovering from their stupor, gave chase. Running across the fairgrounds, he didn't know which direction to take. Finally, he decided to try to get to Clameran, if he could. He then stopped dodging; and with unbelievable speed, he went across the fairgrounds diagonally, going toward the levee, the *levade* as they called it in the countryside, which protects the Tarascon valley from floods. Unfortunately, coming to this levee, one of the most delightful promenades in Provence planted with magnificent trees, Gaston forgot that the entry to it was shut off by one of those three stage barriers that are put in front of spots reserved for pedestrians. Running at full speed, he threw himself against it and was thrown backward, not without a terrible injury to his hip. He immediately got up, but the others were on him. He had to get away or die. The unfortunate man! He had kept his knife in his bleeding hand. He struck out. Another man fell, uttering a terrible groan. That second knife strike gave him a moment's rest, as quickly gone as a bolt of lightning. But it allowed him to go around the barrier and strike out across the levee. Two of those chasing him had kneeled down near the wounded man. Five others continued the chase with more frenzied ardor. But Gaston was nimble. The horror of the situation tripled his strength. Excited by the fight, he didn't feel any of his wounds. He ran along, his elbows tight to his body, breathing deeply, as fast as a race horse. He soon outdistanced those following him. The puffs of their panting respiration got further away; the sound of their steps became less distinct. Finally, nothing could be heard.

Nevertheless, Gaston kept running for another quarter of a league. He had reached the woods, cleared the hedgerows, and jumped over the ditches; when he was totally convinced that it was impossible to catch him, he fell down at the foot of a tree. However, he couldn't stay stretched out there. There was no doubt that an armed group had been alerted. They were already looking for him. They were on his trail. Whatever happened, he must get to the Clameran chateau. Before leaving, perhaps forever, he wanted to see his father, and wanted to clasp Valentine in his arms once more. After a terribly painful journey, he rang at the chateaux's wrought iron gate. It was later than 10:00 p.m. Seeing him, the old valet who came to open the gate for him drew back terrified.

"*Grands Dieux!* Monsieur le Comte, what happened to you?"

"Silence!" said Gaston, in that harsh and curt voice which indicates imminent danger. "Silence! Where's my father?"

"Monsieur le Marquis is in his bedroom with Monsieur Louis. Monsieur has had an attack of gout. He can't budge because of that, but you Monsieur…"

Gaston no longer heard him. He had climbed the grand staircase rapidly and entered the bedroom where his father and his brother were playing trictrac.[39] His appearance startled the old Comte to the point that he dropped the dice box he was holding. And certainly that impression was explainable. Gaston's face, hands and clothes were covered with blood.

"What's happened?" asked the Marquis.

"What's happened, Father, is that I've come to embrace you one last time, and to ask for the means to flee, to go abroad."

"You want to flee?"

"I must, Father, and immediately. At this instant. People are following me; they're tracking me down. In a moment the police may be here. I've killed two men."

The shock to the Marquis was such that he tried to stand up, forgetting his gout. The pain sent him back to his armchair.

"Where? When?" he asked in a terribly altered voice.

"In Tarascon, in a café, an hour ago. There were fifteen of them. I was alone. I picked up a knife!"

"Always the pretty tricks of '93," murmured the Marquis. "Someone insulted you, Comte?"

"They insulted a noble young girl in my presence."

"And you punished those jokers? *Jarnibleu!* You did the right thing. Where have you ever seen a gentleman let some cad insult a person of quality in his presence? But who did you defend?"

"Mademoiselle de La Verberie."

"Oh!" exclaimed the Marquis "Oh! The daughter of that old witch. *Jarnitonnerre!* These La Verberie—may God wipe them out—have always brought us bad luck."

Certainly, he abominated the Countess; but the respect for his class spoke louder in him than resentment. He added:

"That doesn't matter! Comte, you did your duty."

Gaston wasn't as badly wounded as he had thought. With the exception of a knife wound, a little below the left shoulder, his other wounds were not serious. After having received the care his condition needed, Gaston felt like a new man, ready to brave new perils. His eyes were lit with renewed energy. With a gesture, the Marquis had the servants leave.

"And now," he asked Gaston, "you think you should go abroad?"

"Yes, Father."

"There's not an instant to lose," Louis observed.

"That's true," answered the Marquis, "but to flee, to go abroad takes money, and I don't have any to give him on the spot."

"Father!"

"No, I don't have any! Ah! Prodigal old fool that I am, old thoughtless child. If I only had 100 louis here!"

---

[39] A variety of the game of backgammon.

On his instructions, his second son, Louis, opened the secretary. The drawer serving as a safe held 920 francs in gold.

"Nine hundred twenty francs!" exclaimed the Marquis. "That's not enough. The elder son of our house can't flee with that miserable sum; he cannot..."

Clearly desperate, the old Marquis stayed a moment sunk in his reflections. Finally, making a decision, he ordered Louis to bring him a little case of stamped iron placed on the lower shelf of the secretary. The Marquis de Clameran wore the key to that case around his neck, suspended by a black ribbon. He opened it, not without a violent emotion that his sons noticed, and slowly took from it a necklace, a cross, some rings and various other pieces of jewelry. His face had taken on a solemn expression.

"Gaston, my very beloved son," he said, "your life at this time may depend on payment given at the right time to someone to help you."

"I'm young, Father. I have courage."

"Listen to me. These jewels belonged to your mother the Marquise, a saintly and noble woman, Gaston, who watches over us from Heaven. This jewelry has never left me. In London, in my days of poverty during the emigration, in order to live I gave harpsichord lessons. I piously kept them. I never thought of selling them. Even to pawn them would have seemed a sacrilege to me. But today...take these jewels, my son. Sell them. They are worth about 20,000 pounds."

"No, Father, no!"

"Take them, my son. Your mother, if she were still in this world, would say the same. I command it. The honor and the safety of the eldest son of the house of Clameran must not be put in danger, for lack of a little gold."

Moved, tears in his eyes, Gaston had let himself slip to the knees of the old Marquis. He took his hand and he carried it to his lips.

"Thank you, father," he whispered. "Thank you. Sometimes, in my presumptuous rashness as a young man, I allowed myself to judge you. I didn't know you. Forgive me! I accept, yes, I'll accept these jewels worn by my mother. But I take them only as a loan entrusted to my honor and which I'll one day give back to you."

Emotion overcame the Marquis de Clameran and Gaston. But Louis' soul wasn't one of those whom such spectacles could touch.

"Time's flying," he interrupted. "Time's getting short."

"He's right!" the Marquis cried out. "Leave Comte, leave my son. May God protect the eldest son of the Clamerans!"

Gaston had gotten up slowly.

"Before leaving you, father," he began, "I have to fulfill a sacred duty. I haven't told you everything. That young girl whom I defended this evening, Valentine, I love her."

"Oh!" said Monsieur de Clameran, "Oh! Oh!..."

"And I've come to ask you, father, to beg you on my knees, to ask Madame La Verberie for me for her daughter's hand. Valentine, I know, won't hesitate to share my exile. She will come join me abroad."

Gaston stopped, frightened at the effect his words had produced. The old Marquis had turned red, or rather purple, as if he were near to an attack of apoplexy.

"But that's monstrous," he kept repeating, stammering with anger. "That's madness!"

"I love her, Father. I swore to her that I'd have no other wife but her."

"Then you'll stay a bachelor."

"I'll marry her!" shouted Gaston, becoming excited little by little. "I'll marry her because I swore it and our duty demands it."

"Nonsense!"

"Mademoiselle La Verberie will be my wife, I tell you! It's too late to take back my word, because if I didn't love her any longer, I'd still marry her. She gave herself to me. Finally, understand what they said at the café this evening is true. Valentine's my mistress."

The elder son of the Clamerans had counted on the effect of that admission, which circumstances forced out of him. He was mistaken. The Marquis, so irritated, seemed relieved of an enormous weight. A wicked joy lit up his eyes.

"Ah! Ah!" he said. "She's your mistress. *Jarnibleu!* I'm delighted. My compliments, Comte. They say that little girl's very nice."

"Monsieur," interrupted Gaston, almost threatening. "You're forgetting. I've told you. I love her. I've sworn."

"Ta, Ta, Ta," the Marquis exclaimed. "I find your scruples odd. Didn't one of her own ancestors seduce one of our own ancestors from the right path. Now we're even. Ah! She's your mistress…"

"By the memory of my mother and our name, I swear it. She'll be my wife!"

"Really!" shouted the Marquis, exasperated. "You dare take this tone with me! Never, do you understand me, never will you have my consent. You know how much the honor of our house is dear to me. Well, I'd rather see you captured, judged, and condemned. I'd rather see you in prison than the husband of that pert little hussy."

These last words were too much for Gaston.

"Have it your way then, Father," he said. "I'll stay; I'll be arrested. They can do with me whatever they like. That matters little to me. I don't want to live without hope. Take back these jewels. They're useless to me from now on."

A terrible scene was certainly going to break out between the father and the son, when the bedroom door suddenly burst open. All the chateau servants had rushed into the corridor.

"The Gendarmes!" they shouted. "The Gendarmes are here!"

At that news, the old Marquis stood up and succeeded in remaining standing. So many emotions had been stirred up in him for the last hour that the gout was secondary.

"The Gendarmes!" he shouted. "In my house! At Clameran! We'll make them pay dearly for their audacity. All of you will help me!"

"Yes! Yes!" answered the servants. "Down with the Gendarmes!"

Fortunately, at this moment when everyone else was losing his head, Louis kept all his self-possession.

"Resisting would be madness," he stated. "We may throw the Gendarmes out this evening, but tomorrow more will come back."

"That's true," the old Marquis said bitterly. "Louis is right."

"Where are they?" Louis asked.

"At the gate," answered La Verdure, one of the grooms. "Can't Monsieur le Vicomte hear the terrible noise they're making with their sabers?"

"Then Gaston must escape through the door to the kitchen garden."

"It's guarded, Monsieur!" cried out La Verdure, desperate. "It's guarded! And the little door to the park also. There's a whole regiment. There are even some of them guarding the length of the park walls."

This was only too true. The noise of Lazet's death, quickly spreading, had turned Tarascon upside down. They had mounted on horseback, not only the Gendarmes, but also a squad of the garrison's Hussards to arrest the murderer. At least twenty young men from the village were leading the armed forces.

"So," the Marquis said, in the hour of danger, recovering all his presence of mind. "So, we're surrounded."

"There's no chance of escape left," trembled Saint-Jean.

"We'll see about that, *Jarnibleu!*" shouted Monsieur de Clameran. "Ah! We're not the strongest. Well! We'll be the smartest. Pay attention, everybody. You, Louis my son, you'll go down to the stables with La Verdure. You'll mount the two best horses; and reining in the horses, making the least possible noise, you'll go station yourselves: you Louis, at the park door, and you, La Verdure, at the gate. All you others, you'll go post yourselves, each one at a door, ready to open it. At the signal I give, a pistol shot, all the doors will open at the same time. Louis and La Verduret will give their horses their head and do their best to dash outside and draw the Gendarmes after them."

"I'll guarantee them a good run," La Verdure confirmed.

"Wait. While you're doing this, the Comte, aided by Saint-Jean will climb the park wall and go back up along the river, until he reaches the cabin of Pilorel, the fisherman. He's an old seaman from the Republic, a brave fellow devoted to us. He'll put the Comte in his boat, and once on the Rhône, they'll have nothing more to fear but God! You understand me, go!"

Alone with his son, the old Marquis slid the jewels that Gaston had replaced on the table into a silk purse and opened his arms.

"Come, my son," he said in a voice he forced to remain steady. "Come and let me bless you."

Gaston hesitated.

"Come," insisted the Marquis. "I want to embrace you one last time. Save yourself. Save your name, Gaston, and afterwards…You know I love you. Take back this jewelry."

For more than a minute, the father and the son, one as moved as the other, remained embraced. But becoming louder at the gate, the noise came to them distinctly.

"Let's go!" said Monsieur de Clameran.

And taking from his trophy wall a pair of small pistols, he gave them to the Comte, turning his head away and whispering:

"They must not take you alive, Gaston…"

Unfortunately, Gaston, when he left his father, didn't go downstairs immediately. He wanted more than ever to see Valentine again. He could see the possibility of saying his last goodbyes to her. He told himself that Pilorel could dock his boat along the La Verberie Park. He then took a minute, from the few minutes of respite which destiny left to him, to go up to his bedroom and put the light in the window which told his lover he was coming. He did more. He waited for an answer.

"But, come on, Monsieur le Comte," Saint-Jean, who didn't know anything about what he was doing, kept repeating. "Come on, in the name of Heaven! You're going to be doomed."

Finally, he came down, running.

He was only in the vestibule when a pistol shot, the signal given by the old Marquis, rang out. Immediately, and almost simultaneously, was heard the noise of the great gate opening, the clanks of the Gendarmes' and the Hussards' sabers, the frightened gallop of several horses. From all directions, in the park and in the great courtyard, terrible shouts and oaths rang out.

Leaning on his bedroom window with a sweating forehead, so oppressed he could hardly breathe, the Marquis de Clameran was waiting the outcome of this gamble which meant the life of his elder son. The measures he had taken were excellent. As he had foreseen, Louis and La Verdure managed to have themselves followed, and dashed headlong into the countryside, one to the right, the other to the left, each one drawing a dozen horsemen after him. With superior mounts, they should have led those following them across a lot of countryside. Gaston was saved, when fate—or was it fate?—took a hand. A hundred meters from the chateau, Louis' horse stumbled and fell, trapping his rider under him. Then, surrounded by the Gendarmes and the volunteers on foot, the second son of Monsieur de Clameran was recognized.

"That's not the murderer!" the young men from the village shouted. "Quick! Let's go back. They're trying to trick us!"

They did go back, in fact, and in exactly enough time to see, in the pale light of the moon, Gaston climbing the wall of the kitchen garden.

"There's our man!" shouted the Gendarme Brigadier. "Look out there all of you, and come ahead at a gallop!"

And all of them, lashing their horses, dashed toward the wall where they had seen Gaston climb over. On wooded land, or even on hilly ground, it's easy for a man on foot to escape from several horsemen, if he's nimble and if he keeps his head. Now on that side of the park, the land was most favorable to the young Comte de Clameran. He found himself in immense fields of madder plants, and everybody knows that cultivation of that precious root, destined to remain three years in the ground, requires furrows which attain sixty or seventy centimeters in depth.[40] The horses not only could not run, but had great trouble standing upright. That situation stopped short the Gendarmes, careful for their horses. Only four Hussards took the risk, but their efforts were useless. Jumping from furrow to furrow, Gaston had quickly reached a very wide space, still only partially cleared and dotted with spindly chestnut tree plants. The chase was then more interesting, since the fugitive had some chance. So all the horsemen became enthusiastic, encouraging each other, shouting to warn each other when Gaston left one clump of trees to run to another. As for him, knowing the countryside admirably well, he wasn't desperate. He knew that after the small chestnut trees, he would reach the fields of thistles. He remembered that the two cultivated fields were separated by a wide and deep ditch. He thought that by jumping into this ditch, he could hide and could get out of it very far away, while they were still searching for him among the trees. But he hadn't thought about the rising river waters. Coming near the ditch, he saw it was full of water. Discouraged, but not desperate, he was about to take a running jump to leap it, when he saw three horsemen on the other side. These were Gendarmes who had gone around the madder plants and chestnut seedlings fields, saying that in the level thistle fields they would again have the advantage.

Seeing them, Gaston stopped short. What was he to do? He saw the circle, of which he was the center, draw closer. Should he then have recourse to the pistols and to blow out his brains there in the middle of the fields, tracked down by the Gendarmes like a wild beast? What a death for a de Clameran! No, he told himself, that one last chance of salvation remained, weak, it was true, puny, miserable, and desperate, but still a chance. There was still the river. He ran there rapidly, keeping his pistols always cocked. He went to stand at the extremity of a little promontory, which jutted out three good meters into the Rhône. This little cape of refuge was formed by the trunk of an uprooted tree, along the length of which a thousand pieces of debris had been caught, sticks and piles of straw washed up by the current. Under Gaston's weight, the tree began sinking, shaking and cracking terribly. From there he could easily see all those who were pursuing him, Hussards and Gendarmes. There were twelve to fifteen, as many to the right as to the left, and they were shouting with joy.

"Surrender!" cried out the Gendarmerie Brigadier.

---

[40] Madder plants are frequently grown for their roots used in dying material for military uniforms.

Gaston didn't answer. He weighed—he evaluated his chances of salvation. He was well above the La Verberie Park. Could he reach it, if he wasn't immediately rolled over, drawn under and drowned? He was thinking that at this very minute, Valentine, lost, walking along the edge of the river on the other side, was waiting for him and praying.

A second time the Brigadier called out. "Will you surrender?"

The unfortunate man didn't hear him. The torrent's mighty voice, roaring and swirling around him, deafened him. With a violent motion, he threw his little pistols in the direction of the Gendarmes. He was ready. Having found a solid place for his feet, he made the sign of the cross, and head first with his arms stretched out, he dived into the Rhône. The violence of his plunge had detached the last roots of the tree. It shook for a moment, bent backward, and then was washed away in the current.

Horror and pity, much more than malice, had snatched a cry from all the horsemen.

"He's lost," murmured one of the Gendarmes. "It's over. You can't fight the Rhône. They'll take his body out tomorrow, at Arles."

True French soldiers, they were now with their whole heart on the side of the vanquished. And there wasn't one who wouldn't have been ready to attempt anything to save him, and to help his escape.

"Rotten job!" grumbled the old barracks general who commanded the Hussards.

"Baste!" said the Brigadier, a philosopher, "Just as well the Rhône, as to come up for trial! Let's all go back. What pains me is the idea of that poor old man who's waiting for news of his son. Whoever wants to can tell him the truth? I won't take it on myself."

Chapter XIII

Valentine knew that Gaston was supposed to go to Tarascon that evening, going across the Rhone on the iron cable bridge which tied Tarascon to Beaucaire. She was waiting for him on that side at 11:00 p.m., the time agreed on the day before. But well before the agreed on time, having by chance glanced toward Clameran, she seemed to see lights moving through the apartments in a very unusual way. A sinister foreboding froze all the blood in her veins, stopping the beating of her heart. A secret and commanding voice beyond herself cried out to her that something extraordinary and terrible was happening in the Clameran chateau. What? She couldn't imagine, but she was sure of it. She would have sworn that a great misfortune had just occurred. Her worry was growing, becoming more poignant and acute from minute to minute, when suddenly, at Gaston's window, she saw the dear, familiar signal which told her that her lover was going to cross the Rhone. She couldn't believe her eyes. She wanted to doubt her senses, and it was only when the signal had been repeated three times, that she answered it. Then, more dead than alive, feeling her legs give way under her, she went down to the park and reached the edge of the water. *Grands Dieux!* It seemed to her she had never seen the Rhone so furious. Was it possible that Gaston was going to try to cross it? There was no longer any doubt. Something frightful must have happened.

While the Hussards and the Gendarmes were sadly returning to the Clameran chateau, Gaston accomplished one of those prodigious feats that people would be tempted to doubt if the most indisputable testimony didn't confirm them. Immediately after he had dived in, he had been rolled over five or six times and carried to the bottom. That was because the current is not equal in a river out of its banks. The great danger is there, above all; but Gaston knew this danger. He had foreseen it. Far from using his strength in a vain struggle, he let himself go with the current, thinking only of saving his breath. A vigorous kick brought him back to the surface, scarcely more than fifteen meters from the place he had thrown himself in. Near him, with the speed of an arrow, the trunk of the tree which he had been standing on a little time before floated by. For several seconds he was entangled in all sorts of debris. An eddy swirl disentangled him. He thought of nothing but reaching the opposite bank, saying he would come to shore wherever he could. Keeping his presence of mind just as if he had found himself in ordinary conditions, he used all his strength and all his ability to travel slowly, obliquely, and without leaving the edge of the water. He knew very well he would be done for if the current flipped him backward.

That dreadful current was, in addition, as capricious as it was terrible as a result of the bizarre effects of floods. Following the meanderings of the river, it flowed sometimes to the right, sometimes to the left, sparing one bank, ravaging the other. Gaston, who had a very exact knowledge of his river, knew that a little below Clameran there was a sudden bend. He was counting on the eddy on this bend to carry him to La Verberie. He wasn't disappointed in what he had foreseen. An oblique current suddenly carried him toward the right bank, and if he hadn't been on his guard, he would have been rolled over and carried down. But the eddy didn't go as far as Gaston had supposed. He was still far from the edge when, with the lightening speed of a cannon ball, he swept past the La Verberie park. Nevertheless, he had time to see Valentine, like a white shadow under the trees, waiting for him. It was only a great deal further down the bank that, slowly approaching the edge, he tried to get to dry ground. Feeling that he had a footing, he twice stood up; twice the violence of the current forced him down. He was about to be swept away when he managed to grab some willow tree branches, which helped him hoist himself up to the river bank. He was saved.

So, without taking time to draw a breath, he dashed in the direction of La Verberie and soon was in the park. He arrived just in time. Broken by the intensity of her distress, the unfortunate Valentine lay collapsed, feeling life leaving her. Gaston's embraces brought her out of that deadly faint.

"You!" she cried out in a voice where all the madness of her passion burst through. "You! Then did God take pity on us? He really did hear my prayers?"

"No," he whispered, "No, Valentine, God has not taken pity on us."

Her foreboding hadn't deceived her. She understood that from Gaston's tone.

"What new bad luck is striking us!" she cried out. "Why did you come like this, risking your life, which is mine, too? What's happened?"

"The fact is, Valentine, our secret is no longer just ours. Our love affair is, right now, the mockery of the countryside."

She drew back as if struck by lightning, hiding her face in her hands, and letting out a long groan.

"Everything is known," Valentine stammered. "Everything is known."

In the middle of the sequence of events, Gaston had kept his cool head; but at the sound of that beloved voice, his feelings arose to delirium.

"And I wasn't able to crush them, to destroy them, these foul creatures who dared pronounce your adored name. Ah! Why did I kill only two of those miserable creatures?"

"You killed! Gaston…"

Valentine's tone of deep horror brought some light of reason to her lover.

"Yes," he answered, trying to control himself. "Yes, I killed…That's why I crossed the Rhone. It was for the honor of my name. Only a moment ago, all the Gendarmes in the country were tracking me down like some mad beast. I escaped them and now I'm in hiding. I'm running away…"

Valentine needed uncommon strength of soul not to succumb under so many unexpected blows.

"Where do you expect to flee to?" she asked.

"Ah! How do I know! Where I'm going, what will become of me, what future awaits me? Would that I could foresee it! I'm fleeing. I'm going to force myself to reach a foreign land, take an assumed name, a disguise. And I'll keep going until I find one of those countries without laws, that give asylum to murderers."

Gaston was silent. He was waiting for, he was hoping for an answer. That answer didn't come. He continued with an unusual vehemence.

"If I wanted to see you again before disappearing, Valentine, it was because at this time when everyone has abandoned me, I was counting on you. I had faith in your love. A tie binds us, oh my beloved, stronger and more indissoluble than all the ties on earth. I love you. In God's eyes you're my wife. I'm yours as you're mine, for life. Are you going to let me leave alone, Valentine? Will you add the tortures of our separation to the sorrows of exile, to the bitter regrets of my lost life?"

"Gaston, I beg you…"

"Ah! I was certain of it," he interrupted, misunderstanding the sense of his lover's exclamation. "I knew I wouldn't flee alone. I know your heart well enough to know you'd want half the burden of my misery. This moment blots everything out. Let's go! Having our happiness to protect, I don't fear anything anymore. I can face anything, conquer anything. Come, oh my Valentine. We'll perish together or save ourselves together. It's the envisioned and dreamed of future that's beginning, a future of love and liberty!"

He was mad; he was delirious. He had seized Valentine by the waist. He drew her to him. He picked her up.

To the extent that Gaston's exaltation grew, and the more he lost all self-control, Valentine managed to dominate her emotion. Gently, but with more strength than he thought she had, she withdrew from his clasp and pushed him away.

"What you wish," she said in the saddest, and yet the firmest tone, "what you hope for is impossible."

That cold resistance, inexplicable to him, seemed to confuse Gas-ton.

"Impossible!" he stammered.

"You know me well enough," Valentine continued, "to know that to share the worst of destinies with you, would be for me the height of human happiness. But beyond your voice drawing me, beyond my heart's voice, there is even so, one more powerful and more commanding which forbids me to follow you. It's the sublime voice of duty."

"What! You can think of staying, after this evening's horrible scene, after a scandal which will be public tomorrow?"

"What do you mean? That I will be lost, dishonored? Would I be it any more today than I was yesterday? Do you think that the irony and the contempt of the world would make me suffer as much as the revolt of my conscience? I have always judged myself, Gaston. And if your presence, the sound of your voice, and the feel of your hand touching mine made me forget everything, away from you I remembered and I wept."

Gaston listened, motionless, stunned. It seemed to him that a new Valentine was standing before him, and that he discovered in her soul, which he had thought he had so completely possessed, depths that escaped him.

"And your mother?" he whispered.

"Don't you understand? It's remembering her that chains me here! Do you wish me, like an unnatural daughter, to abandon her to follow my lover now, when poor, isolated, and without friends, she no longer has anyone but me?"

"But they will tell her, Valentine. We have enemies. She'll know everything."

"What does that matter? Conscience speaks. That's enough. Ah! Why can't I, at the price of my life, spare her from learning that her Valentine has failed in all the laws of honor! It's possible she'll be hard toward me, terrible, pitiless. Well! Haven't I deserved it? Oh! My only love, we've been sleeping in a dream too beautiful to last. This frightful awakening, I was expecting it. Miserable fools, poor imprudent people, we had thought that outside of duty there was lasting happiness. Sooner or later, stolen happiness grows pale. Let's bow our heads and accept humiliation."

That cold reasoning, that sad resignation, rekindled Gaston's anger.

"Don't talk like that!" he screamed. "Don't you know that just the thought of your humiliation drives me mad?"

"Alas! I must, nevertheless, expect a great deal more outrages."

"You!...What do you mean?"

"Let me tell you, Gaston..."

She stopped, hesitated a moment, and ended by saying:

"Nothing, it's nothing. I'm mad."

Even under the stress of the situation, the Comte de Clameran should have guessed by Valentine's hesitations some new misfortune, but he continued with his plans.

"Everything isn't lost," he spoke again. "My love and my despair have, I believe, touched my father, who's a good man. When I am out of danger, perhaps my letters or my brother Louis's urging will make him decide to ask Madame La Verberie for your hand in marriage."

That possibility seemed to frighten Valentine.

"May Heaven never let the Marquis attempt that!"

"Why?"

"Because my mother would refuse his request. My mother, I'll have to admit it in this extreme time, has sworn that I'll be the wife of a man with a great fortune, and your father isn't rich."

"Oh!" exclaimed Gaston, revolted. "And you would give me up for such a mother!"

"It's enough that she's my mother. I don't have the right to judge her. My

426

duty is to stay. I'll stay."

Valentine's tone announced an unshakeable resolution, and Gas-ton understood very well that all his prayers would be useless.

"Ah!" he cried out, clenching his fists in despair. "You've never loved me!"

"Unhappy man! You don't believe what you're saying!"

"No," he went on, "you don't love me. You, at this moment when we're going to be separated, have the courage to reason coldly and to be calculating. Ah! This isn't how I, myself, love you. Without you, what's the whole earth to me? To lose you is to die. Let the Rhone reclaim the life it miraculously saved, and now is a burden to me."

He was already going toward the Rhone, determined to die. Valentine held him back.

"Is this, then, what you call love?"

Gaston was absolutely discouraged, devastated.

"What's the good of living," he whispered. "What's left for me?"

"We have God, who holds our future in his hands, Gaston."

The slightest board seems salvation to the drowning man. Just the word "future" threw a light of hope on Gaston's gloom.

"You command it!" he cried out, suddenly reanimated. "I'll obey. This is enough weakness. Yes, I want to live to fight and triumph. Madame de La Verberie requires money! Well! In three years I'll have made a fortune, or I'll be dead."

Valentine had clasped her hands, and was thanking Heaven for that sudden determination she hadn't dared hope for.

"But before I leave," Gaston continued. "I want to commit a sacred trust to you."

He took the silk purse holding the Marquise de Clameran's jewels out of his pocket, and placed them in his lover's hands.

"These are my poor mother's jewels," he said. "Only you are worthy of wearing them. In my mind, I intended them for you."

And as she refused, as she was hesitating:

"Take them," he insisted, "as a pledge that I'll return. If in three years I haven't come back to reclaim them, I'll be dead. And then you'll keep them as a memento of him who loved you so much."

She burst out in tears. She accepted.

"Now," Gaston went on, "I have one last request to you. Everyone thinks I'm dead, and my salvation is in that. But I can't leave my old father in despair. Swear to me that you yourself, tomorrow morning, will go tell him I'm alive."

"I'll go; I swear to you." she answered.

Gaston's decision was made. He felt he should take advantage of this moment of courage. He leaned toward his lover and embraced her one last time. Gently, with a sad gesture, she pushed him away.

427

"Where do you plan to go?" she asked.

"I'm going to reach Marseille, where a friend will hide me, and I'll try to find a passage on a ship."

"You can't leave like this. You need a companion, a guide. I'm going to give you one in whom you can have the greatest confidence, old man Menoul, our neighbor. He's owned a boat on the Rhone for a long time."

They left by the little park door, to which Gaston had a key, and soon they came to the old boatman's house. He was sleeping by the fireside, in his white wooden armchair. Seeing Valentine come into his house accompanied by Monsieur de Clameran, he quickly stood up, rubbing his eyes, thinking he was dreaming.

"Père Menoul," Valentine said, "Monsieur le Comte here must go into hiding. He wants to reach the sea and take a boat secretly. Can you take him there in your boat as far as the mouth of the Rhone?"

The good man shook his head. "The way the water is, it's hardly possible at night," he said.

"This is an immense favor you would do me, Père Menoul."

"Then for you, Mademoiselle Valentine, it's done. We'll leave."

Only then did he think he could permit himself to point out to Gaston that his clothes were soaking wet, soiled with mud, and that he was bareheaded.

"I'm going to lend you some clothes of my dead son, for a disguise. Come with me."

Soon Père Menoul and Gaston reappeared, almost unrecognizable, and Valentine followed them to the edge of the water where the boat was docked. One last time, while the good old man prepared his rigging, the two lovers embraced, exchanging their souls in this supreme goodbye.

"In three years!" Gaston shouted. "In three years!"

"Goodbye, Mam'selle," said the old man, "and, you, my young Monsieur, hold on." And with a strong push of his boat hook, he shoved the boat into the middle of the current.

Three days later, thanks to old man Menoul's care, Gaston was hidden in the hold of the American three-masted *Tom Jones,* with Captain Warth, who set sail for Valparaiso the next day.

Chapter XIV

Motionless on the river bank, colder and whiter than a statue, Valentine watched that frail bark that carried the man she loved vanish. It glided with the current, rapid as a bird carried along by the storm. After a few seconds, it was only a black dot, hardly visible in the middle of the haze floating above the river.

With Gaston departed, saved, Valentine could let her despair burst forth without fear. From now on it was useless for her to hold back the sobs which were choking her. A total mortal collapse followed her noble valor of sometime before. She felt herself destroyed, broken, as if something in her had been torn apart. It was as if the boat, now disappeared, had carried away the better part of herself, her soul and her thoughts. But, even though Gaston kept a ray of hope at the bottom of his heart, she herself had no hope left. Overcome by the facts, she recognized that all was finished. And, questioning the future, she was seized with trembling and terror. Nevertheless, she had to go back.

She slowly returned to the chateau, passing through that little door that so many times had mysteriously opened for Gaston. It seemed to her that in closing it, she was placing an insurmountable barrier between herself and happiness. Fortunately, she was able to reach her bedroom without hindrance, and shut herself in. She needed to be alone. She wanted to think. She felt the need to strengthen herself against the terrible blows which were going to strike her. Seated in front of her little work table, she took out of her pocket the bag Gaston had given her, and mechanically examined the jewels it contained. Daylight coming, she got dressed. Shortly thereafter, when the morning Angelus rang at the village church, she told herself it was time to get started, and she went downstairs. The servants of the chateau had been up a long time. One of those, Mihonne, particularly attached to Valentine's service, was busy spreading sand on the vestibule tiles.

"If my mother asks for me," she said to the young girl, "tell her that I've gone to the first Mass."

She often went to Mass at that hour. She had nothing to fear on that count. Mihonne didn't say anything. The great difficulty for Valentine was to be back in time for lunch. She must walk more than a league before finding a bridge, and as far again to get from this bridge to Clameran. In all, more than five leagues. So, leaving La Verberie, she began to walk as fast as possible. By the realization that she was accomplishing an extraordinary action, worry and the fever of the peril confronted gave her wings. She forgot she was tired. She was no longer aware that she had spent the night crying.

However, despite her efforts, it was later than 8:00 a.m. when she came to the long alley of Azerolier trees which lined the road leading to the main gate of the Clameran chateau. She was about to take it when she saw Saint-Jean, the Marquis' valet, whom she knew very well, some steps from her.

She stopped to wait for him, and he, having seen her, hurried his steps. His face was convulsed; his eyes were red. It was obvious he had been weeping. To Valentine's great surprise, he didn't take off his cap when he neared her. With the rudest tone he asked her:

"You're going to the chateau, Mademoiselle?"

"Yes."

"If it's for Monsieur Gaston," the servant answered, underlining his odious wickedness, "your trouble is useless. Monsieur le Comte is dead, Mademoiselle, for a mistress he had."

Madeleine turned pale under the insult, but didn't react to it. As for Saint-Jean, who thought he had crushed her, he was stupefied and indignant at her cool behavior.

"I've come to the chateau," replied the young girl, "to speak to Monsieur le Marquis."

Saint-Jean seemed to sob. "Then it's not worth the trouble to go any further." "Why?" "Because Monsieur le Marquis de Clameran died this morning at 5:00 a.m." In order not to fall, Valentine had to lean against the tree she was standing near.

"Dead!" she stammered.

"Yes," answered Saint-Jean, with terrible looks, "dead."

A true servant of the Old Regime, Saint-Jean had all his masters' passions, their weaknesses, their friendships, their hatreds. He held the La Verberie in horror. He saw in Valentine the woman who had caused the death of the Marquis, whom he had served for forty years, and of Gaston, whom he adored.

Trying to make each word a knife stab, he continued:

"It was yesterday evening that Monsieur le Comte perished. When they came to tell the Marquis that his elder son was no longer alive, he, strong as an oak tree, was struck down. I was there. He beat the air with his hands and fell backward without a cry. We carried him to his bed, while Monsieur Louis mounted a horse to go bring a doctor from Tarascon. But the damage had been done. When Monsieur Raget arrived, there was nothing more to be done. However, at daylight, Monsieur le Marquis seemed to regain consciousness and he asked to be alone with Monsieur Louis. A little later, his death agony began. His last words were: 'The father and the son in the same day. They can rejoice at La Verberie.'"

With one word Valentine could have relieved the immense sadness of the faithful servant. She had only to tell him that Gaston was alive. She made the mistake of fearing an indiscretion, which might be fatal.

"Well," she said, "I must speak to Monsieur Louis."

That statement seemed to send Saint-Jean into delirium.

"You!" he shouted, "You!...Ah! Don't even think about it, Mademoiselle de La Verberie! What! After what's happened, you'd dare go see him! I won't allow it! Do you understand me? And listen, if I have any advice to give you, go back home. I can't answer for what the servants might say if they saw you."

And without waiting for an answer, he walked rapidly away.

What could Valentine do? Crushed and humiliated, she started back, dragging herself with great pain along the road she had traveled so rapidly that morning. At that hour, a great many of the farmers were returning from the town. They had learned the events of the night before and everywhere, as she passed by, the unfortunate young girl received ironic greetings and the most insulting looks.

When she came near La Verberie, she found Mihonne who had been watching for her.

"Ah! Mademoiselle," that girl said to her, "Come quickly. Madame received a visit this morning, and since then she's been shouting for you. Come, but be careful. Madame is in a terrible state."

"Miserable girl!" the Comtesse, redder than a peony, screamed wildly. "Is this how you respect the noble traditions of our house? We never had to watch over the La Verberie women. They knew by themselves how to guard their honor. It took you to abuse your liberty, to descend to the ranks of those wanton women who are the shame of their sex."

Valentine had foreseen this frightful scene. She had waited for it with a horrible tightening in her heart. She submitted to it as just, merited atonement, for guilty love. Admitting to herself that her mother's indignation was legitimate, she bowed her head like a repentant accused man before his judges. But that silence was exactly what could exasperate the Comtesse the most.

"Are you going to answer me?" she asked with a threatening gesture.

"What can I answer you, Mother?"

"You can tell me, unhappy girl, that those people who told me a La Verberie had gone astray lied about it. Go on, defend yourself. Speak."

Without answering Valentine slowly shook her head.

"Then it's true!" shouted the Comtesse, beside herself. "It's really true!"

"Forgive me, Mother," stammered the young girl. "Forgive me!"

"What do you mean, 'Forgive!' Then they didn't deceive me. Forgive! That means you admit it, impudent girl! *Jour de Dieu!* What blood flows in your veins? Don't you know that this is one of those faults that you deny, even if the evidence is clear! And you're my daughter! You don't realize that there are shameful admissions that no human power should be able to snatch from a woman! But no, she has lovers and she admits it without blushing. Brag about it. That would be news."

"Ah! You have no pity, Mother!"

"Did you pity me, daughter! Did you think about the fact that your shame could kill me! Ah! Many times probably, with your lover, you laughed at my blind confidence. Because I had faith in you as in myself. Because I thought you were as chaste and pure as when I watched over your cradle. I believed...and, nevertheless, men after drinking laughingly said your name, and then fought and killed each other over you. I had put the honor of our house in your hands. What did you do with it? You gave it to the first man who came around."

That was too much. Those words "the first man who came around" revolted Valentine's pride. She didn't deserve, no, she couldn't deserve such treatment. She tried to protest.

"I'm mistaken," the Comtesse continued. "You're right. Your lover wasn't even the first one who came around. From all of them, you went to choose the heir of our legendary enemies, Gaston de Clameran. That was the one above all you had to have, a coward, who went about publicly bragging about your favors, a miserable man who avenged himself through you and me for the heroism of our ancestors, by means of a woman and a child."

"No, mother, no. That's false. He loved me and if he could have hoped to have your consent..."

"He would've married you? Ah! Never! Better to see you roll down further and further, right to the gutter, than to know you were the wife of such a man."

So the Comtesse's hatred expressed itself precisely like the Marquis de Clameran's anger.

"Besides," she continued, with that ferocity that only a woman is capable of, "besides, he drowned, your lover, and the old Marquis is dead, from what they say. God is just. We are avenged."

Saint-Jean's words, "They will rejoice at La Verberie," came immediately back to Valentine's mind. An odious joy gleamed in the Comtesse's eyes.

This was, for the unfortunate girl, the last straw. For the last half-hour she had been making superhuman efforts to resist this atrocious stress. Her physical strength betrayed her strong willpower. She became paler, if it was possible, closed her eyes, held out her arms as if searching for something to lean on, and fell, hitting the corner of a console, making a deep cut on her forehead. The Comtesse looked with dry eyes at her daughter stretched out at her feet. All she bled was her vanity; maternal love in her hadn't been touched. She had one of those souls that anger and hatred fill so well that no tender sentiment can find room there. Seeing that Valentine didn't move, she rang, and the female servants of the chateau who were trembling in the vestibule, came running at the sound of that feared voice.

"Carry Mademoiselle into her bedroom," she told them. "You will lock her in there and bring me the key."

To keep her from leaving, because she had an insane fear of public opinion, the Comtesse was planning to keep Valentine a prisoner there for a long time. She knew the wickedness—should it be called unconscious and naïve—of the people of the countryside, where boredom causes the same scandal to live for entire months.

Nevertheless, Madame de La Verberie's reasoning was wrong. The terrible and rapid explosion of a scandal would be better than the secret and persistent rumors of scandal. However, all Madame de La Verberie's plans were going to be upset. The women soon came back to tell her that Valentine had regained consciousness, but they thought she was very sick. She began by saying that this was a pretense; but when Mihonne insisted, she resigned herself to going up to her daughter's bedroom. There she had to give in to the evidence. Valentine's life was in danger.

No alarm showed in her face, but she sent to Tarascon for Doctor Raget, who was then the oracle of the countryside, the same one who had been sent to Clameran for the Marquis, the night before.

He was, that man, one of those men whose memory still lives a long time after they themselves are no more. A noble heart and of vast intelligence, he had given his life to his art. Rich, he never asked to be paid for a visit. Night and day, he could be seen on the roads, a gray mare pulling his old cabriolet, whose storage space always held some bouillon and some wine for the poor. He was, at that time, a small man more than fifty years old, bald, with lively eyes and a clever tongue, gay, chatting easily although lisping a little, easy-going, and good to an excess.

The messenger sent had the good fortune to find him and brought him back. Doctor Raget frowned when he saw Valentine. Gifted with profound insight sharpened by practice, he alternatively studied Valentine and her mother, examining the old woman with such penetrating looks that her composure was shaken and she felt her wrinkled cheeks become red.

"That child is very sick," he finally said.

And when Madame La Verberie didn't answer, he added:

"I would like to stay alone with her for a while."

Doctor Raget, by his reputation and by his character, dominated the Comtesse too much for her to resist. She left, not without visible distaste, and went to wait in a neighboring room. Calm in appearance, she was in reality shaken with the darkest thoughts. It was scarcely at the end of a half hour—a century—that the doctor reappeared. He, who had seen so much misery, consoled so much sadness, seemed very emotional.

"Well?" The Comtesse asked him.

"You are a mother, Madame. That means your heart has treasures of indulgence and forgiveness, doesn't it? Arm yourself with courage, Madame. Valentine is pregnant."

"The miserable girl! I guessed as much."

The Comtesse's eyes had such a terrifying expression that the doctor was astounded. He put his hand on the old woman's arm, and stared at her until she shivered. He added, stressing each word:

"And the child must be born alive."

The doctor's insight was not at fault. In fact, an abominable thought had crossed Madame La Verberie's mind, the thought of doing away with that child, which would be the living testimony of Valentine's sin. Feeling she had been found out, that very hard and haughty woman lowered her eyes under the old doctor's stubborn gaze.

"I don't understand you, doctor," she murmured.

"But I'm making myself clear, Madame. I simply want to say that a crime doesn't wipe out a sin."

"Doctor!"

"I'm telling you what I think, Madame. If I'm mistaken, so much the better for you. At this moment, Mademoiselle Valentine's condition is serious but not without remedy. Too strong emotions have shaken this young being and she has fallen prey to a violent fever that I hope we can bring down quickly."

The Comtesse knew so well that the old doctor's suspicions hadn't gone away, that she tried to soften him.

She said: "At least, doctor, can you assure me there's no danger?"

"None at all, Madame, that your maternal tenderness can't take care of," Monsieur Raget answered with a fine touch of irony. "What the poor child needs most of all is mental rest that only you can give her. A few nice and gentle words from you would do more good than all my prescriptions. But, be sure of this, the least shock, the lightest mental jangle, would have disastrous consequences."

"It's true," the Comtesse said hypocritically, "that from the first moment, when learning that my dearly beloved Valentine had been the victim of a cowardly seducer, I have not been in control of my anger."

"But the first moment has passed, Madame. You're a mother; you're a Christian. You know what you have to do. My own duty is to save your daughter and her child, and I will save them. I'll come back tomorrow."

Madame La Verberie couldn't let the doctor leave like that. She stopped him with a gesture, and without thinking about the fact that she was betraying herself, that she was confessing, she exclaimed:

"What! Monsieur, do you mean you'll prevent me from doing everything in the world to keep secret the frightful misfortune which has struck me! Must our shame become public! Do you want to condemn us to become the gossip and the laughter of the countryside?"

The doctor was silent a moment without answering. He was thinking. The situation was serious.

"No, Madame," he said. "I can't keep you from leaving La Verberie. That would be going beyond my rights. But it's my duty to ask you to account for the infant. You are free, but you must supply me with proof that he's alive, or at least that nothing has been attempted against him."

With these threatening words, he left. It was really just in time, because the Comtesse was choking with rage and restraint.

"That insolent man!" she cried out. "That impertinent man! To dare lecture a woman of my rank! Ah! If I were not at his mercy!"

But she was, and she understood that this time, with no hope of going back, she had to give up all her fantasies. There would be no luxury to hope for from now on: no millionaire son-in-law, no more fortune for her old age, no more carriages, no more magnificent dresses, and no more gaming parties where they played for high stakes.

Then she would die as she had lived, poor and needy. She was condemned to a mediocrity made so much more heart-breaking, since she no longer had, to help her to submit, the prospects of a better future. And it was Valentine who had brought her to this extreme case. And at that thought, she felt stir in her against her daughter one of those hatreds which never pardons, that time rekindles instead of calming. She wished to see her, as well as that damned infant, dead. But the doctor's crushing look was too present in her memory for her to even think about trying something. She even decided to go up to her daughter's bedroom, forcing herself to smile, to say some affectionate words, then to leave her to be guarded by the devoted Mihonne.

Poor Valentine! She had been so roughly treated that she seemed to feel the source of life dry up in her. However, her suffering lessened a little. A profound numbness, almost without pain, always follows great physical or moral crises. When she was strong enough to think, she told herself: "It's over. My mother knows everything. I have nothing more to fear from her anger. I can only hope and wait for my forgiveness."

That then was the secret Valentine didn't want to reveal to Gaston, knowing very well that, if he knew it, he would never have agreed to leave her. She wanted him to save himself, and the voice of duty cried out to her at the same time to stay. And even at this hour, she still did not repent of having stayed. Her most cruel worry was the memory of Gaston. Had he or had he not succeeded in taking a boat? How could she find out? The doctor had allowed her to get up for the last two days, but she couldn't think of going out, of running to Père Menoul's cabin.

Fortunately, the old man was intelligent, as the truly devoted know how to be. Learning that the young lady of the chateau had been very sick, he thought of nothing else but some way to reassure her about the well-being of the fugitive. He found several pretexts to come to La Verberie, and finally succeeded in seeing Valentine. They were not alone, but a glance from the good man gave her to understand that Gaston no longer had anything to fear.

That certainty did more for Valentine's convalescence than all the medicine. Somewhat afterward, the doctor who had been coming for a month-and-a-half declared that the sick woman was well enough to endure the fatigues of a trip. The Comtesse had been waiting for this moment with unutterable impatience. So that nothing would slow down the departure, she had already sold half of her income, telling herself that with 25,000 francs, which was the price, she would guard against any eventuality. For two weeks she had gone about everywhere repeating that as soon as her daughter was well enough she would leave for England, where one of her relatives, very old and still rich, needed her.

Valentine only looked forward to this trip with terror. She trembled the evening the doctor released her, when her mother said to her:

"We're leaving day after tomorrow."

The day after tomorrow! And Valentine hadn't yet found any way to let Louis de Clameran know his brother was not dead. In that extreme situation, she didn't hesitate to confide in Mihonne and entrust her with a letter to Louis. But the faithful servant made a useless trip. The Clameran chateau was deserted. All the servants had been let go, and Monsieur Louis, who they now called the Marquis, had left the country.

Finally they left. Madame La Verberie, sure of Mihonne, decided to take her with them; but not without having made her swear on the Bible during the Mass, at the moment of the Elevation of the Host, to eternal secrecy. The Comtesse established herself with her daughter and her servant, in a little village north of London under the name of Madame Wilson. If she chose London, it was because she had lived there a long time, she knew its mentality and its customs, and she spoke the language as if it were her own. She had even kept up some acquaintances among the aristocracy; and in the evening she often went out, dined in the city, or went to the theater. At these times she took the most humiliating precautions against Valentine, whom she locked in with a double lock.

It was in this sad and lonely house that one night, in the month of May, Valentine brought a son into the world. He was presented to the parish priest and registered under the name Valentin-Raoul Wilson. The Comtesse had, in addition, foreseen everything and had set everything up. After searching a great deal in the village neighborhood, she had found a good, fat farm woman who, for 500 pounds (12,000 francs), had agreed to take charge of the infant. Promising to rear him with hers, she was to have him learn a trade, and even to help him rise in the world, if he turned out well. Little Raoul was delivered to her a few hours after his birth.

That woman didn't know the real name of the Comtesse. She was supposed to believe, and she did believe, she was dealing with an English woman. It was therefore more than probable, it was certain, that when he became a man, the child wouldn't be able to discover the secret of his birth.

When Valentine came to herself, she asked for her child. In her vibrated and awoke that sublime maternal love, the germ of which God put in the heart of all women. It was in this instance that the Comtesse was truly without pity.

"Your child!" she screamed. "I really don't know what you mean. I think you're dreaming. You're mad!"

And when Valentine insisted:

"Your infant is safe," she answered, "and he won't lack for anything. Let that satisfy you. You must forget what happened, as you would forget a bad dream. The past should be as if it had never been. You know me. I will have it."

The moment had come when Valentine should have, within certain limits, resisted the more and more encroaching despotism of her mother. The thought came to her, but not the courage. So much suffering with so many regrets, internal combats indeed did slow down her convalescence. Nevertheless, toward the end of June, she was well enough to go back with her mother to La Verberie. Wickedness, that time, hadn't had its usual lucidity. The Comtesse, who went everywhere complaining of her trip's lack of success, could verify that no one in the countryside had seen through the reasons for her absence. Only one man, Doctor Raget, knew the truth. But Madame La Verberie, while hating him with all her heart, gave his character enough integrity to be sure she wouldn't have to fear an indiscretion on his part. Her first visit on her arrival had been to him. She surprised him one morning, as he was getting up from the table, asking him for a moment's interview. She brusquely put under his eyes the official papers, which she had gotten just for him.

"You can see, Monsieur," she said, "the child is certainly alive, and thanks to a large sum, a good woman has taken charge of him."

"That's fine, Madame," he answered, after a close examination, "and if your conscience doesn't reproach you for anything, I've nothing to say to you on my part."

"My conscience, Monsieur, doesn't reproach me for anything."

The old doctor shook his head, and fixing on the Comtesse one of his looks which makes truth tremble in the deepest folds of the soul:

"Could you swear," he stated, "that you haven't been severe to the point of barbarity?"

She turned away her eyes, and taking on her grandest air, answered:

"I have acted as a woman of my rank should act and, I must admit, I'm surprised to find you an advocate for immoral behavior."

"Ah! Madame," the Doctor exclaimed. "Indulgence should come from you. What pity could your unfortunate child expect from strangers, if you, her mother, you yourself are without pity?"

The Comtesse didn't want to hear any more. That frank voice offended her pride. She rose.

"Is that all you have to say to me, doctor?" she asked in a haughty tone.

"All...yes, Madame, and I've never had but one thought, that of sparing you eternal regret."

Here the noble and good doctor was mistaken. He couldn't imagine that he'd encountered an exception—Madame La Verberie was not capable of remorse. But that soul, insensitive to anything that wasn't pleasure or for the satisfaction of her vanity, should suffer and would suffer cruelly. She had taken up the ordinary activities of her life; but having lost a part of her income, she could no longer manage to make ends meet. For her, that was an inexhaustible source of recriminations with which, at each meal without ceasing, apropos of everything and of nothing, she sacrificed her daughter. Because, while having de-

437

clared that the past didn't exist, she came back to it continually, as if to add new food to her anger.

"Your sin ruined us," she repeated, apropos of anything.

She said it so often that one day, Valentine, exasperated, couldn't help answering:

"You'd have forgiven me if it had made you rich!"

But Valentine's revolts were rare, even though her existence was nothing but a long series of tortures, managed with infinite art. Even the thought of Gaston, her soul's elect, had become a way of suffering.

Perhaps, discovering the uselessness of her courage and her devotion to what she had believed was her duty, she repented that she had not followed him. What had become of him? How could he not have thought of some way to get a letter to her, a souvenir, or a message? Perhaps he was dead. Perhaps he had forgotten her. He had sworn that before three years had passed, he would come back rich. Would he ever come back?

And was it even possible for him to come back? His disappearance hadn't extinguished that horrible business at Tarascon. They supposed he had drowned; but since there was no positive proof of his death, justice had been forced to satisfy aroused public opinion. The affair had been sent to the highest national court, and Gaston de Clameran had been condemned, *in absentia*, to several years of prison. As for Louis de Clameran, nobody knew exactly what had become of him. Some claimed that he was living in Paris, where he was leading a riotous life. Informed of these circumstanced by her faithful Mihonne, Valentine began to despair. She vainly looked into the gloomy future. Not one light lit the dark horizon of her life. All the inducements of the soul and the will were broken in her, and she had finally come to that passive resignation of continually mistreated beings, to that heedlessness, to that self-denial which the reasoned self-sacrifice of life had brought to her.

Time passed, and four years had gone by since that fatal evening that Gaston had been carried away in the Rhone current by Père Menoul's boat. Madame La Verberie couldn't have used these four years any worse. Seeing that she obviously couldn't live on her income, with too much silly pride to sell her land which, badly administered, didn't bring in two percent, she had resigned herself to borrow and use up the capital with the revenue. Now, following that path, it's only the first step that counts. Madame la Comtesse had walked quickly. Saying, *"Après moi le deluge,"* neither more nor less like the departed Marquis de Clameran. Madame la Comtesse no longer thought of anything but living comfortably. She had guests often, allowed herself frequent visits to neighboring cities, to Nimes and to Avignon. She ordered magnificent dresses from Paris, and gave full rein to her taste for good food. Everything that she had so long waited for from the generosity of a loving son-in-law, she gave to herself. Great sorrows require great consolation!

The problem was that this appearance of luxury is expensive, very expensive. After having sold the rest of her income, the Comtesse borrowed against the La Verberie land at first, then against the chateau itself. She was beginning not to know very well what to do. The phantom of bankruptcy stood at the foot of her bed, when luck came to her aid. For about a month, a young engineer in charge of studying repairs needed along the Rhone, had made the village adjacent to La Verberie his center of operations. As he was young, witty, and very nice looking, he had been accepted right away by local society. And the Comtesse often encountered him in the houses where she went in the evening to gamble. This young engineer was named André Fauvel.

Having noticed Valentine, he studied her closely; and little by little, he fell in love with that young girl with the reserved attitude, the great sad and gentle eyes. In that ancestral gallery, she stood out like a flowering rose bush in the middle of a winter landscape. He had not even spoken to her when he was already in love with her. He was relatively rich. A magnificent career was opening up for him. He felt he had the qualities which make millionaires. He was free. He swore that Valentine would be his wife.

It was to an old lady, a friend of La Verberie as noble as a Montmorency, and poorer than Job, that he first confided his matrimonial intentions. With the precision of a former student of the Polytechnic School, he had listed all the advantages which made him a paragon of a son-in-law.

The old lady listened to him a long time without interrupting. But, when he was finished, she didn't hide from him how presumptuous his claims seemed to her. What! He a boy who was born only a... Fauvel, a geometrician or a state surveyor, was allowing himself to aspire to the hand of a La Verberie! With a particular vehemence, she stressed the considerations due to a higher social class. Fortunately, when she had exhausted that chapter, she came to the positive.

"However," she added, "It may be that you won't be turned down. The Comtesse's situation is most embarrassing. She owes God and the Saints, the dear lady. The debt collectors visit her often, so that... you understand, if a young man, stirred by honorable intentions and having some wealth, presented himself...Ah! Ah! I don't know what would happen."

André Fauvel was young. The old lady's insinuations seemed monstrous to him. Thinking it over however, when he had considered it, most of all when he had taken the trouble to consider the mentality of the local nobility, rich utterly in prejudice, he understood that only monetary considerations would be strong enough to make the high and powerful Comtesse de La Verberie give him her daughter's hand in marriage.

That certainty cleared away his hesitations. He no longer thought of anything but of creating a way to put forward his candidacy cleverly. That didn't seem to him to be easy. To go looking for a wife with his money in his hand was strongly repugnant to his delicacy, and went against all his opinions. But he didn't know anyone in the countryside to trust, and his love was strong enough to make him disregard all his distastes, with his eyes closed.

The opportunity he was waiting for to explain himself, if not categorically, at least in a clear and transparent way, presented itself. As he entered the Beaucaire Hotel one evening to dine, he saw Madame La Verberie, who was about to sit down. Turning red right up to his ears, he asked permission to sit at her table. She granted him her permission with a most encouraging smile.

Did the Comtesse suspect the young engineer's love? Has she been told about it by her friend? It's permitted to suspect so. However it happened, without troubling André to get to the matter, to move from point to point important to his heart, she began, from the time the soup was served, to complain how hard the times were, how short in supply money was, and of the insolence of the hard business men interested only in profit. The truth was, that she had come to Beaucaire for a loan. She had found all the safes padlocked, and her lawyer's advice was to have a friendly sale of her lands.

Anger, that sixth sense, that instant secret of situations, untied her tongue; she was with this almost unknown young man more expansive than with people of her most intimate society. She told the horror of her situation, her straitened circumstances, her worries for the future, and above all, her sadness at not knowing how to provide a dowry for her dear daughter. He heard these sad stories with the proper sympathy, but inwardly he was delighted. So without letting the old lady finish, he began laying out what he called his way of looking at the situation. After having sympathized considerably with the Comtesse, he admitted that he couldn't understand her worries at all. What! She was tormented by the idea of not having a dowry to give her daughter! But Mademoiselle Valentine was one of those whose nobility and beauty are one of the most enviable assets. He himself knew more than one man who would think himself too happy that Valentine would be willing to accept his name, and who would make it his duty—a very pleasant duty—to lift from her mother all her worries. And actually, the Comtesse's situation didn't seem to him as bad as she seemed to say. What would it take to free it, to absolutely disencumber La Verberie from its mortgage? Forty thousand francs, perhaps? Actually that wasn't very much. Besides, this wouldn't be a gift her son-in-law would make to her, but a loan. Wouldn't the lands and the chateau of La Verberie revert to him, sooner or later, with the constant increase in the value of the land? And that wasn't all. A man in love with Valentine would never leave the mother of his wife deprived of the comfort due her age, her nobility and her misfortune. He took it on himself to add to her insufficient income not only the necessities of life, but abundance.

As André continued to talk, with a conviction too marked to be pretended, it seemed to the Comtesse that a heavenly dew of silver was falling on all her plagues. She brightened. Her little wild beast eyes looked softer than velvet, a provoking and friendly smile fluttered across her thin lips, usually pinched tighter than the edges of a miser's purse.

Only one thing bothered the young engineer. "Does she understand me?"

he wondered. "Will she take me seriously?"

Certainly, yes. She saw through the transparency of the allusions, and her reactions proved it.

"Alas!" she said, not without a sigh. "La Verberie can't be saved with 40,000 francs. Interest and expenses included, it would take at least 60,000 francs."

"Oh, 40,000 or 60,000 that's not a lot."

"Then, my son-in-law—this rare man of our suppositions—does he understand the necessities of my existence?"

"He would think it a pleasure, I imagine, to add 4,000 francs each year to your land's revenues."

"Four thousand francs," she finally said. "That would hardly do. Everything is outrageously priced in this land. But with 6,000 francs... Oh! With 6,000 francs..."

This demand seemed a little stiff to the young engineer; however, with the careless generosity of a lover, he answered:

"The son-in-law we're talking about would love Mademoiselle Madeleine very little if a miserable question of 2,000 francs put him off."

"You don't say!" whispered the Comtesse.

But a sudden objection came to mind.

"It would still be necessary," she remarked "that this honest son-in-law we're supposing, have enough wealth to fulfill his engagements. My daughter's happiness is too important to me to give her to a man who couldn't offer me—how do you say it—a security, guarantees..."

"Obviously," Fauvel thought, a little ashamed, *"This is a bargain we're discussing."*

And aloud he continued:

"It's clear that your son-in-law would commit himself by the marriage contract..."

"Never! Monsieur, never! And the proprieties! What would people say about me?"

"Allow me...It would be specified that your pension would be the interest from a sum that he would acknowledge he had received."

"Like that, yes, in fact..."

That evening Madame La Verberie absolutely insisted in taking André back in her carriage. Not one direct word was exchanged between them during the whole trip, but they had understood each other. They had come to a mutual agreement. They understood each other so well that, dropping the young engineer at his door, the Comtesse held out to him her thin hand, which he kissed with devotion, while thinking about Valentine's beautiful eyes, and he invited her to dine the next day.

It had certainly been many years since Madame La Verberie had been so happy, and her servants were amazed at her good humor. The reason was that

441

suddenly, brusquely, she had gone from a desperate situation to an almost brilliant position. And she, who claimed to have such proud sentiments, perceived neither the shame of that transaction nor the infamy of her conduct.

"Six thousand francs pension," she said to herself. "This young geometrician is an honest man, and 1,000 écus for the land, that's 9,000 pounds income in all. That boy will live in Paris with my daughter. I'll go visit them, these dear children, without too much expense."

Jour de Dieu! At that price she would have given not one daughter, but three, if she'd had them. But then suddenly, an idea occurred to her that turned her to ice: Would Valentine agree?

So poignant was her anxiety, that to have a clear mind about it immediately, she went up to her daughter's bedroom. She found her reading by the light of a small candle.

"Daughter," she said to her brusquely, "a young man who suits me has asked me for your hand, and I've given it to him."

At that unexpected declaration, Valentine, stunned, stood up.

"It's not possible," she stammered.

"Why, if you please?"

"Have you then said who I am, Mother? Have you told him...?"

"Past follies? God keep me from that! And you'll be as reasonable as I am, I hope, and imitate my silence."

As destroyed as Valentine's will was by her mother's crushing despotism, her honesty revolted.

"You want to test me, Mother!" she exclaimed. "To marry a man without admitting everything to him, would be the most cowardly and the most infamous of betrayals."

The Comtesse had a great desire to get angry. But she understood that this time her threats would fall apart against a resistance supported by conscience. Instead of commanding, she begged.

"Poor child," she said. "Poor dear Valentine, if you knew the horror of our situation, you wouldn't talk this way. Your folly began our ruin. It's at an end today. Do you know where we are? Our creditors are threatening to chase me out of La Verberie. What will happen to us after that, oh daughter? Must I, at my age, go from door to door holding out my hand? We're lost and this marriage is a salvation."

And after prayers, reasoning began. She had at her service, that dear Comtesse, subtle and strange theories. What she had in the past called a monstrous crime, was no longer anything but a small slip. To hear her tell it, Valentine's situation happened every day. She said she understood her daughter's scruples, if one had to fear some tale from the past. But such precautions had been taken that there was nothing to fear. Would she love her husband any the less because of it? No. Would he be any the less happy? No. Then why hesitate?

Stunned, dizzy, Valentine wondered if this was really her mother. That woman so haughty, so intractable in the past when it was a question of honor or of duty, was talking like this, all at once making a lie of the words of her entire life.

Alas! Yes, it was she. The subtle arguments, and the shameful sophistries of the Comtesse should have neither touched nor shaken her, but she didn't feel she had either the strength or the courage to resist the tears. That mother, seeing her efforts were futile, fell to her knees, begging her with clasped hands to save her. More touched than she had ever been, torn by a thousand contradictory sentiments, daring neither to refuse nor promise, and fearing the consequences of a decision thus snatched from her, the unfortunate girl begged her mother to give her at least some hours to think about it.

Madame La Verberie didn't dare refuse her these moments of reflection. The blow struck, she told herself that to insist would not be prudent.

"As you wish," she said to her daughter. "I'll go away. It would be better if your mind, and your heart, told you how to choose between a useless vow, and your mother's salvation."

And with these words she left, indignant, but full of hope. She had only too many motives for hope. Caught between two obligations equally demanding, equally sacred, but absolutely opposed, Valentine's troubled reason no longer clearly discerned where duty lay. Should she reduce her mother to the most shameful poverty? Should she unworthily take advantage of the confidence and love of an honest man? Whatever her decision, the result for her was a ghastly life and dreadful remorse. In the past, the memory of Gaston de Clameran would have spoken loudly and dictated her conduct; but this far away memory was no longer anything but a vague whisper. In novels, it's true, one finds heroines whose virtue is equaled only by their constancy. Real life seldom has any of these miracles. For a long time, Gaston had stayed dazzling and radiant in Valentine's thoughts. He had been like the hero of her dreams; but the fog of time had, little by little, hidden the idol's rays. Now he was nothing more than a cold relic at the bottom of her heart. Nevertheless, when she rose the next morning, pale and suffering from a night without sleep, she was almost resolved to speak. But when the evening came and she found herself near André Fauvel, under the eyes of her mother, threatening and begging alternately, she lacked courage. She still said to herself, "I will speak," and then she said "But tomorrow, another day, later."

None of these struggles escaped the Comtesse, but she was no longer worried. The old lady perhaps knew by experience that when you put off accomplishing a difficult and painful task, you are lost. You never do it.

Perhaps the horror of her situation gave Valentine an excuse. Perhaps, without her knowledge, an irrational hope was working inside her. A marriage, even an unhappy one, offered hopes of a change, of a new life, and of an alleviation of unsupportable suffering. Sometimes in her ignorance of everything, she told herself that, with time and with greater intimacy, the horrible admission would perhaps come out naturally, that André would forgive, and that he would marry her anyway, because he loved her. Because he did truly love her. She couldn't not see it. Certainly, it wasn't Gaston's tumultuous passion, with its terrors, its exhilaration and wild abandonment; but it was a calm, thoughtful love, deeper perhaps, drawing a kind of communion from its legitimacy and its duration. And Valentine was becoming gently used to André's presence, completely surprised by this unknown happiness, by those constant delicate attentions, by that kindness which went beyond her expectations. She didn't yet love André, but separation from him would have been sad, cruel.

During the time that the young engineer had been allowed to pay court, the old Comtesse's conduct had been a masterpiece. Calculating very accurately, she had suddenly given up all her obsessive behavior, no longer arguing, affirming instead with tearful resignation that she didn't want to influence her daughter's decisions. But she noisily talked about her poverty; she whined as if she were on the eve of lacking food. So she had taken steps to be hounded by creditors. Foreclosures and notifications rained down on La Verberie. She showed all those papers with their official stamps to Valentine, saying:

"May God will that we won't be chased out of the house of our fathers before your marriage, my love!"

In addition, sensing she had enough influence to freeze a revelation on her daughter's lips, she never left her alone one minute with André.

"Once they're married," she thought, *"They'll come to an understanding."*

Then, just as much as the impatient André, she pressed for beginning the preparations for the marriage. She didn't leave Valentine a moment to explore her feelings, or a moment to reflect. She kept her busy, flooded her and made her dizzy with thousands and thousands of details. There was a dress to buy, some trousseau objects to change, a visit to make, an outfit to buy for herself. She did this so well that she reached the evening before the big day, breathless with hope, oppressed with anxiety, like a gambler at the decisive moment of a great gamble.

That evening, for the first time, Valentine found herself alone with the man who was going to be her husband. With evening coming on, she had taken refuge in the drawing room, tormented with worry more poignant than usual. He came in. Seeing her in tears, terribly troubled, he gently took her hand and asked her what was wrong.

"Am I not your best friend?" he asked. "Shouldn't I be the confidant of your troubles, if you have any? Why these tears, my love?"

At this moment, she almost admitted everything. But suddenly she could see the scandal, André's sadness, her mother's anger. She saw her existence lost. She told herself it was too late, and with an explosion of tears, she burst out, like all young girls when the last moment is near:

"I'm afraid!"

He also tried to console her and to reassure her, explaining to himself this trouble, these vague fears, the horror of the unknown, and the revolts of modesty. He was completely surprised to see that all his kind words, far from calming her, seemed to increase her sorrow.

But Madame La Verberie had already come running. They were going to sign the marriage contract. André Fauvel must not know anything.

Finally on the next day, a beautiful springtime day, the marriage of André Fauvel and Valentine La Verberie took place in the village church.

She forced herself to remain calm, even smiling. Nevertheless, she was paler than her veil, frightful remorse tearing her apart. It seemed to her that people could read the truth on her face, that the white dress was nothing but a bitter irony, a supreme humiliation. She shivered when her best friend came forward to place the crown of orange blossoms on her head. It seemed to her that that crown was going to burn her. It didn't burn her, but one of the iron wire stems, badly wrapped, made a slight scratch on her forehead. It bled a great deal, and a drop of blood even fell on her dress. What an omen! Valentine was almost taken ill.

But the omens were liars, and the proof was that a year after her marriage, everyone was sure Valentine was the happiest of women. Happy! Yes, she would have been if she had been able to forget. André adored her. He had struck out into business, and everything succeeded for him. But he wanted to be very rich, immensely rich, not for himself, but for his beloved wife, whom he wanted to surround with all the pleasures of luxury. Finding her the most beautiful, he wished her to be the most bejeweled.

Eighteen months after her marriage, Madame Fauvel had a son. Alas! Neither that son, nor a second arriving a year later, could make her forget the other one, the abandoned one, the one a stranger had taken in for a sum of money. Passionately loving her sons, bringing them up like the sons of princes, she said to herself: "Who knows if the abandoned one even has bread to eat?" If she just knew where he was, if she dared! But she didn't dare. She was even worried sometimes about that which Gaston had left with her, those jewels of the Marquise de Clameran, that she feared she could never hide well enough.

Sometimes she said to herself: "Everything is all right. Misfortune has forgotten about me!"

Poor woman! Misfortune is a visitor who's sometimes late, but who always comes.

Chapter XV

Louis de Clameran, the second son of the Marquis, had one of those not very outgoing personalities, which, under a cold or nonchalant exterior, hide a fiery temperament, extreme passions and tremendous covetousness. All sorts of outrageous and wicked thoughts were germinating in his sick head before the events deciding the fate of the house of de Clameran. Seemingly busy with idle pleasures, this precocious hypocrite wished a larger theatre for his passions, damning the necessities which chained him to the country, and that old chateau. It seemed to him sadder than a prison and as cold as a tomb. He was bored. He didn't love his father. He hated his brother Gaston to the point of madness. The old Marquis himself, by his guilty shortsightedness, had kindled that consuming envy in his second son's heart. Observing the traditions which he declared to be the only good ones, he had declared a hundred times that the eldest son of a noble house should inherit all the wealth. Only Gaston would receive whatever fortune remained at his death. That flagrant injustice of open preference preyed on Louis' jealous heart.

Gaston had often confirmed that he would never consent to profit from the paternal prejudices. They would share everything like good brothers. Louis had not been touched by what he called the ridiculous ostentation of false unselfishness, judging everyone else by himself. That hatred, which neither the Marquis nor Gaston ever suspected, manifested itself by actions significant enough to make the servants take notice. They understood him well enough so that, the fateful evening that the fall of Louis' horse delivered Gaston to his enemies, they refused to believe in an accident, and murmured very low the word: "fratricide." There was even a deplorable scene which took place between Louis and Saint-Jean, whose fifty years of faithful service gave him a liberty he sometimes abused by his out-spoken comments, often rude and disagreeable.

"It's unfortunate," the old servant said, "that a horseman as good as you, fell just at the moment when your brother's safety depended on how you sat on your horse. La Verdure didn't fall."

The suggestion had struck the young man so much so that he turned pale, and in a terrible voice he shouted:

"Wretch! What do you mean?"

"You know very well, Monsieur le Vicomte." Saint-Jean had insisted.

"No!...Speak, explain yourself."

The servant answered only by a look, but it was so cruelly significant that Louis jumped toward Saint-Jean, his riding whip lifted. He would have given him a sound beating, without the intervention of the other servants. That scene took place just as the moment Gaston, in the middle of the madder field and the field of chestnut trees, was trying to throw those following him off the track.

446

Soon the Gendarmes and the Hussards came sadly back, very emotional, announcing that Gaston de Clameran had thrown himself into the Rhône and had certainly perished. That distressing declaration was received with a sad murmur. Among all the others, only Louis remained without emotion, not a muscle in his face trembled. His eyes even lit up, the light of triumph. A secret voice cried out to him: *"Now you're assured of the paternal fortune and the title of Marquis."* Now he was no longer the poor younger son, made poor for the profit of the elder. He was the sole heir of the Clamerans.

The Gendarme Brigadier had said: "I won't be the one to tell this poor old man that his son has drowned!" Louis had neither the scruples nor the soft-heart of the old soldier. He went without hesitation upstairs to his father, and with a firm voice he said to him:

"My brother has chosen between life and honor...He's dead."

Like an oak tree struck by lightning, at these words the Marquis had staggered and fallen. The doctor they sent for could only, alas, admit that medical knowledge was powerless. Toward daylight Louis witnessed his father's last sigh.

Henceforth, Louis was the master. But the illegal precautions the Marquis had taken to avoid the law and to assure, without contest, his whole fortune to his elder son, turned against him. Thanks to the guilty willingness of his businessmen, by means of *fidei commis*[41] tinged with fraud, Monsieur de Clameran had arranged everything so that the day after his death, Gaston could collect his whole inheritance. And it was Louis who collected it, without even needing his brother's death certificate.

He was the Marquis de Clameran. He was free. He was relatively rich. He who had never seen 25 écus in his pockets, found himself possessing almost 200,000 francs. That sudden wealth, absolutely unexpected, turned his head so much that he forgot his wise dissimulation. At the Marquis' funeral, people noticed his features. His head bowed and his handkerchief over his mouth, he walked behind the casket carried by twelve peasants; but his looks and his glowing face belied his attitude. People could discern the smile under the grimace of his fake sorrow. The sound of the last shovelfuls of earth on the casket had not yet died down, when Louis was already selling everything in the chateau that could be sold: horses, riggings, carriages.

Beginning the next day, he dismissed all the servants, poor people who had thought they would end their days under the hospitable de Clameran roof. Several of them, tears in their eyes, took him to one side to beg him to use their services, even without pay. He dismissed them brutally. He was all arithmetic at that moment. His father's notary that he'd sent for came. He gave him a power of attorney to sell all the land and received a sum of 25,000 francs as a down

---

[41] From the Latin *fides* (trust) and *committere* (to commit), meaning that something is committed to one's trust.

payment. Then one evening at the end of the week, he closed all the doors of the chateau, where he swore never to return. He gave all the keys to Saint-Jean, who, having a certain income and possessing a little house near de Clameran, could continue living in the countryside.

Finally he left! The heavy stagecoach shook and soon six horses carried it away at a gallop, digging, at every roll of the wheels, an abyss between the past and the future. Sunk in one of the corners of the closed carriage, Louis de Clameran was savoring in advance the delights, whose realities he was going to enjoy fully. At the end of the road, Paris raised itself in the purple haze, radiant as the sun, dazzling as himself. Because he was going to Paris. Wasn't that the Promised Land, the city of marvels, where each Aladdin found a lamp? There, every ambition was crowned with success, all dreams came true, all passions were indulged, and all things coveted were satiated. Everywhere there was noise, crowds, luxury, pleasure. What a dream! And Louis de Clameran's heart was swollen with desires. It seemed to him the horses were slower than turtles.

And in the evening at the time the gas lights are illuminated, when he jumped out of the stagecoach on the muddy pavement of Paris, it seemed to him that he was taking possession of the great city. She was his. He could buy her.

Full of his own importance and accustomed to the deference of the country people, the young Marquis had left his home, telling himself that in Paris he would be a person of distinction, as much as by his name as by his fortune. His coming oddly betrayed his expectations. To his grand surprise, he discovered there is nothing in a huge city that constitutes an important person. He recognized that in the middle of that busy and indifferent crowd, he was passing by as lost, as unnoticed, as a drop of water in a flood.

But the hardly flattering reality couldn't discourage a boy determined, above all and at whatever the cost, to satisfy his passions. His ancestors' name gave him only one privilege, disastrous for his future. It opened the doors to the Faubourg Saint-Germain to him. There he made the acquaintance of a rather large number of men his age, all as noble as he, whose income equaled half or even the total of his capital. Almost all of them admitted that they couldn't sustain themselves except by prodigious cleverness and economy, and by regulating their vices and their follies as wisely as a hosiery shop owner his Sunday outings with his family. These words, and a great many others, which stunned the newly disembarked man, did not open his eyes. He tried hard to copy the brilliant exterior of these economical spend-thrifty young people, without thinking about imitating their prudence.

He was the Marquis de Clameran. He presented himself as having a great fortune. He was well received. If he didn't have a friend, he at least had a large number of acquaintances. In the circle where he was introduced and invited the first days of his arrival, he found ten obliging fellows who made it their pleasure to initiate him into elegant life, and to correct what he had in his life and thought that was a little provincial. He profited quickly and well from the lessons. After three months, he was on his way. His reputation as a gambler was established, and he had nobly and gloriously compromised himself with a fashionable prostitute.

Staying at first in a hotel, near the Madeleine he rented a comfortable mezzanine apartment with a coach house and stables for three horses. He furnished that "bachelor's apartment" with only the strict necessities. Unfortunately, the necessities were exorbitantly expensive. So that the day he moved in, trying to figure out his expenses, he discovered, not without fright, that this short apprenticeship in Paris had cost him 50,000 francs, a quarter of what he had. And vis-à-vis his brilliant friends, he still remained in a state of inferiority, distressing for his vanity, a little like an owner who would break his nag trying to race with thoroughbreds.

Fifty thousand francs! Louis had half a mind to leave the game. But what! Then he would be giving up! Besides, in this charming place, his vices were growing with his comfort. He thought he had been prodigiously strong in these in the past. A thousand new corruptions were being revealed to him. Then the view of sudden success, the example of success as surprising and as unheard of as certain reversals, inflamed his imagination. He thought that in that great city, where millions walked the boulevards, he would infallibly be able, he too, to seize his million. How? He had no idea and he didn't even look for it. He simply persuaded himself that he'd have his lucky day as had many others—yet another of those errors that time would correct. There's no luck that works for the stupid. In that furious race of self-interest, it takes prodigious dexterity to be the first to mount that capricious mare called opportunity, and to ride it to the end. But Louis didn't think so far ahead. As absurd as that man who hopes to win the lottery who hasn't bought a ticket, he told himself: *"Baste! Opportunity, chance, and a good marriage, such will carry me through."* A good marriage didn't present itself, but the last bank bill did. To a pressing demand for money, his notary answered with a refusal:

You have nothing more to sell, Monsieur le Marquis, he wrote to him, nothing more except the chateau. It certainly has great value, but it's difficult, if not impossible, to find a buyer for a building of that importance in the state it's now in. Be sure that I'll actively look for that buyer, and believe, etc.

As if he hadn't foreseen that final catastrophe, Louis was absolutely dumbfounded. What was he to do? Ruined, no longer having anything to hope for, his dignity required that he imitate the poor fools who each year come forward, shine for a moment, and suddenly disappear. But Louis couldn't give up that life of easy pleasures which he had led for three years. It was said that after having left his fortune on the battle field, he would leave his honor there. He was stubborn, like the gambler who's been cleaned out, who prowls around the gaming tables closed to him, watching a game that's no longer his, always ready to ask a handout from those whom fate has favored. Louis at first lived off the fame of his exhausted fortune, off that credit which a man who's spent a lot in a short time still has. That resource played out rapidly. A day came when his creditors rose up *en masse*. The ruined Marquis had to leave in their hands the last debris of his opulence, his furniture, his carriages, and his horses.

Taking refuge in a more than modest hotel, he couldn't take it on himself to break with those rich young people, that for a moment, he had believed were his friends. He lived off them now, as he had in the past off his trades people—borrowing here and there, from 1 louis to 25, never paying back. He gambled, and if he lost, didn't pay. Half a knight of industry, half a courtesan, he showed young men around, utilizing in a thousand shameful services an experience which had cost him 200,000 francs. They didn't drive him away, but they made him cruelly atone for that favor of being tolerated. They didn't have any respect for him, and what they thought of his conduct, they said aloud.

So, when he found himself alone in his hovel, he gave vent to excesses of mad rage. He could still submit to all the humiliations, but not yet not feel them. In addition, by the things he coveted torturing him, the envy that had been gnawing at him for a long time stifled honest sentiments in him, right down to the roots. For some years of opulence, he felt himself ready to chance anything, disposed even to commit a crime. Nevertheless, he did not commit a crime, but he found himself compromised in an indecent swindling and blackmailing affair. An old friend of his family, the Comte de Commarin, saved him, hushed up the affair, and gave him the means to go over to England.

What were his means of existence in London? Only the detectives of the most corrupt capital in the universe could say. Having descended to the lowest levels of vice, the Marquis de Clameran lived in a world of crooks and fallen women, with whom he shared luck and shameful profits. Forced to leave London, he went successively throughout all of Europe without any capital except his audacity, his profound corruption, and his skill at all games of chance. Finally, in 1865, having struck a windfall in Hamburg, he returned to Paris, where, he told himself, everyone had probably forgotten him. He had left France eighteen years before.

On arriving in France, Louis de Clameran's first thought was for his birthplace, even before getting settled, even before looking for resources which he knew he could find elsewhere. It wasn't because he had any relative, any friend there, even one he could look to for help; but he remembered the old manor house for which, in the past, the notary had despaired of finding a buyer. He thought that perhaps that buyer had been found, and he decided to go to find out. Once in the region, he could always get something from this chateau, which had originally cost more than 100,000 pounds to build. On a beautiful October evening three days later, he arrived at Tarascon, where he verified that the chateau was still his property; and the next day, very early, he started walking down the road to Clameran. Soon through the trees, he could make out the bell tower of the village of Clameran, then the village itself, seated on the gentle slope of a hillside crowned with olive trees. He recognized the first houses: the blacksmith shed, the vicarage with the vine running along its roof, and further on, the inn where his brother Gaston and he went to play billiards on the immense billiard table, with corner pockets as big as baskets. Despite what he called his disdain for vulgar sentiments, an indefinable emotion clutched his heart. He couldn't control a feeling of sadness and his thoughts strayed back to the past, despite himself.

The door to Saint-Jean's house was open. He went in, and not finding anyone in the immense kitchen with a monumental chimney, he called out:

"Is anyone there?"

Almost at the same time from a door at the back, a man about forty years old, with an honest and smiling face, appeared, surprised to find a stranger in his house.

"May I help you Monsieur?" he asked.

"Isn't this where Saint-Jean, the former valet of the Marquis de Clameran, lives?"

"It will soon be five years since my father died, Monsieur," the man answered in a sad voice.

That news affected Louis painfully, as if the man he'd thought he would find could give him back something of his youth. He sighed and said:

"I'm the Marquis de Clameran."

The man, at these words, cried out in surprise.

"You! Monsieur le Marquis!" he exclaimed, "You!"

He took Louis' hand and shook it respectfully.

"Ah! If my poor father was still in this world, how happy he would be! His last words were for his former masters. Monsieur le Marquis. How many times he complained of not having news of you! He's in the ground, the poor man; but me, Joseph his son, I belong to you as he did. You, in my house, what happiness! Ah! My wife, whom I've told so much about the Clamerans, will be so happy!" He ran outside, yelling loudly at the same time:

"Toinette! Hey! Antoinette, Come hear this! Come see!"

That eager, so cordial welcome, moved Louis delightfully. It had been many years since he'd heard the expression of sincere affection and of a disinterested devotion, since the hand of a true friend had shaken his.

But already blushing and confused, a beautiful young woman with a dark complexion, with big black eyes, came in, half pulled by Joseph.

"Here is my wife, Monsieur le Marquis," he said. "Ah! Damn! I didn't give her time to go make herself presentable! This is Monsieur le Marquis, Antoinette."

The beautiful young woman bowed, completely intimidated, and finding nothing more to say, she extended her forehead, on which Louis placed a kiss.

"In a little while," Joseph said, "Monsieur le Marquis will see the children. They're at school. I've just sent for them."

At the same time, the husband and wife were pressing their hospitality on him. They told him he must need something to drink, since he'd come on foot. He must certainly accept a glass of wine while waiting for lunch, because he was going to do them the honor of having lunch at their house, wasn't he?

And Joseph went down to the wine cellar, while Toinette in the courtyard gave chase to the fattest of her pullets. In no time everything was ready, and Louis was seated in the middle of the kitchen before a table loaded with everything of the very best they had been able to procure, served by Joseph and his wife, who stood in front of him, examining him with a sort of gentle curiosity.

The great news had spread throughout the village and the door stayed open. At every moment people appeared, coming to greet the Marquis de Clameran.

"I'm so-and-so, Monsieur le Marquis, don't you recognize me? Ah! Me, I recognized you right off. The dead Marquis was very fond of me," an old man claimed.

"Do you remember the time you lent me your pistols to go hunting?" another said.

Louis accepted with inward delight all these protestations, these marks of a devotion which hadn't lessened with the years. Hearing the voices of these good men, a thousand forgotten memories were awakened in him, and he found again the fresh sensations of his youth. He, the adventurer hunted everywhere, the hero of gambling houses, the ruffian, and the abject accomplice of London crooks, delighted in these testimonies of veneration given to the de Clameran family; and it seemed to him that they had given him back something of his reputation and his self-esteem. Ah! If right now he possessed only a quarter of that inheritance thrown to the wind in absurd fantasies, with what satisfaction he would settle into this village, to end his days in peace!.

But this repose after so much vain restlessness, this port after so many shipwrecks, was forbidden to him. He had nothing. How would he live? This sad feeling of his past distress gave him just the courage to ask Joseph for the keys to the chateau, which he intended to visit.

"You need only the key to the gate, Monsieur le Marquis," answered Joseph.

It was true. Time had done its work and the heroic de Clameran mansion was no longer anything but a ruin. The rain and the sun, with the Mistral winds helping out, had rotted through the doors and carried away the outside shutters as dust. Inside, the desolation was greater still. All the furniture Louis hadn't dared to sell was still in place, but in what condition! There scarcely remained shreds of the debris of the bed trimming, only the wood had resisted. Louis, followed by Joseph, dared penetrate with difficulty the great drawing rooms where their steps made a gloomy sound. It seemed to him that the terrible Marquis de Clameran was going to rise up to throw his curse at him, to cry out to him: "What have you made of our honor?"

Perhaps his terror had another cause; perhaps he had too much reason to remember that fall, so fatal to Gaston. It was only when he found himself in full sunlight, in the garden, that he got back his assurance and remembered the object of his visit.

"This poor Saint-Jean," he said, "was really wrong not to use the furniture left in the chateau. It's been destroyed without having been of use to anyone."

"My father, Monsieur le Marquis, wouldn't have dared to move anything without an order."

"And he was very wrong. As for the chateau, if something isn't done, it will soon be lost like the furniture. My fortune, to my great regret, won't allow me to restore it. I've therefore decided to sell it while it's still standing. Would it be very difficult," Louis continued, "to sell this ruin?"

"That depends on the price, Monsieur le Marquis. I know a man in the vicinity who might be interested, if you sold it to him cheap."

"And who is that man?"

"A man named Fougeroux, who lives on the other side of the Rhône, in the Montagnette cottage. He's a boy from Beaucaire who married, about twelve years ago, a servant of the deceased Comtesse de la Verberie. Monsieur le Comte perhaps remembers a large, very dark girl named Mihonne."

Louis didn't remember Mihonne.

"When could we see this Fougeroux?" he asked.

"Today, by crossing the Rhône down there on the boat that carries people across the river."

An entire generation had disappeared since Louis had left his region. It was no longer the old sailor of the Republic, Pilorel, who "took people across." It was his son. While Pilorel the younger rowed with all his strength, Joseph tried to warn the Marquis about some of Fougeroux's tricks.

"He's a clever fox," he said, "even too clever. I've never thought much of him since his marriage. This was a good business deal only for him. The Mihonne woman was well past fifty years old, when he decided to court her, and he wasn't twenty-five. You can understand that he wanted the money and not the woman. That poor idiot believed the boy loved her, and damn! She gave him her hand and her écus."

"And, yes, they've done well," Pilorel interrupted.

"Yes, that's true. Fougeroux doesn't have his equal for squeezing money. He's rich today, but he must know that it's thanks to Mihonne that he has his money. It's understandable that he doesn't love her.

She looks like his grandmother; but it's shameful that he deprives her of everything, and that he beats her. He wants her six feet underground," said the boatman.

"And he'll put her there before very long. She's almost dead, the poor old thing, since she's become a servant to that hussy Fougeroux brought into his house."

They were coming to the shore. Joseph and the Marquis, after having asked the boatman to wait for their return, started up the road to the Montagnette cottage. It was a farm with a nice appearance, well kept up, surrounded with well-designed vineyards. Joseph, having asked for the master, a young boy answered him that "Monsieur Fougeroux" was in the nearby fields and that they were sending for him. He wasn't long in appearing. He was a very little man with a red beard and restless, shifty eyes. Although Monsieur Fougeroux claimed to detest nobles and priests, the hope of getting a good bargain made him obsequious to the point of servility. He hurried to have Louis come into his "living room" with a great many bows and no end of "Marquis le Marquis." On entering, he spoke to an old woman trembling with fever in the corner of the fireless hearth, and brutally ordered her to go down to the wine cellar to find some wine for Monsieur le Marquis de Clameran. The old woman, at this name, stood up as if shocked by an electric current. She seemed to want to speak. A look from her tyrant shoved the words down her throat. She obeyed with a wild look, and came back with a bottle and three glasses that she put on the table. Then she sat down again near the hearth, forgetting to listen, in order to look at the Marquis. However, the bargaining was still going on between Joseph and Fougeroux. The buyer offered a laughable price, buying it he said, just to tear it down and resell the material. Joseph himself listed the beams of the timbered ceilings, the floor and ceiling joists, the locks and the metal fittings.

For Mihonne, the Marquis' presence was one of those events which change existence. If, until then, the faithful servant hadn't said a word of the secrets confided to her honesty, they had nevertheless seemed to her hard to bear. Having no child, after having ardently desired one, she persuaded herself that God had struck her with sterility to punish her for having lent her hands to the abandonment of a poor little innocent. She had often thought about revealing everything. She would appease celestial anger, and bring back happiness to her household. Her attachment to Valentine had given her the strength to resist the incessant temptations. But today, Louis' presence made up her mind. Reflecting, she saw no danger in confiding herself to Gaston's brother.

The business dealings during this time were concluded. It was agreed that Fougeroux would give 5,280 francs for the chateau and the land combined, and that the debris of the furniture would go to Joseph. The buyer and the Marquis exchanged a firm handshake, pronouncing the sacramental words: "Agreed."

And Fougeroux immediately left to go himself to look for the bottle to conclude business deals, in a corner only he knew. The opportunity was favorable to Mihonne. Rising, she went straight to the Marquis, and in a low and hurried voice:

"Monsieur le Marquis, I must speak to you without witnesses," she said.

"To me, my good woman?"

"To you. It's a secret of life or death. This evening at dusk, come to the walnut trees, down there. I'll be there. I'll tell you everything."

She took her place again; her husband was coming back.

Fougeroux happily filled the glasses and drank to the health of de Clameran. While returning to the boat, Louis wondered if he would go to this unusual rendezvous.

"What the devil could that old witch want with me?" he asked Joseph.

"Who knows? She used to be in the service of a woman who was, my father told me, the late Monsieur Gaston's mistress. If I were you, Monsieur le Marquis, I'd go. You'll eat dinner with us, and afterward Pilorel will take you back over."

Curiosity decided Louis, and about 7:00 p.m. he arrived under the walnut trees. The old Mihonne had already been waiting for him a long time.

"There you are, dear, good Monsieur," she said in a tone of joy. "I was already beginning to despair."

"Yes, it's me, my good woman. Come now, what do you have to tell me?"

"Ah! Many things, Monsieur le Marquis; but first of all, have you had any news of your brother?"

Louis almost regretted having come, thinking that the old woman was in her dotage.

"You know very well," he answered, "that my poor brother threw himself in the Rhône and perished there."

"What!" Mihonne exclaimed, "What! You too don't know he was saved? He did what no other person has done. He swam the Rhône when it was out of its banks. The next day Mademoiselle Madeleine went to Clameran to tell the news. Saint-Jean kept her from getting to you. Later, I went to take you a letter, but you'd left."

These revelations after twenty years dumbfounded Louis.

"Aren't you taking your dreams for realities, my good mother," he said gently.

Mihonne shook her head sadly.

"No," she continued, "no. And if Père Menoul was still in this world, he would tell you how he took Monsieur Gaston as far as Camargue, and how from there your brother reached Marseille and left on a ship. But this is nothing yet. Monsieur Gaston has a son."

"My brother, a son? Decidedly, my good old woman, you're out of your mind."

"Alas, no, for my misfortune in this world and in the other. He had a son by Mademoiselle Valentine, a poor innocent I received in my arms in a foreign country, and that I carried to the woman who took him for money."

Then Mihonne told everything: the anger of the Comtesse, the trip to London, the abandoning of little Raoul. With that accuracy of memory of people who know neither how to read or write, not being able to commit themselves on paper, she revealed the least circumstances. Giving the most precise details, she gave the name of the village and that of the farm woman, the first and last names of the infant, and the exact dates of the events.

Then she told about Valentine's misery after her sin, the ruin of the Comtesse, and finally the marriage of the poor girl with a gentleman from Paris, rich, so rich he didn't know the total of his fortune, a banker named Fauvel. A sharp and prolonged cry interrupted her.

"Heavens!" she said in a frightened voice. "My husband is calling me." And as quickly as her old legs would carry her, she went back to the farm.

She had been gone for some time, while Louis remained immobile in the same place.

At Mihonne's story, a foul idea, so detestable that his mind, ready for anything, recoiled. And that idea began growing, like waves of tide water coming one after the other as the tide comes in. He knew the rich banker by reputation. He was thinking of what advantage he could take of what he'd just heard. There are secrets that, cleverly exploited, are worth a farm in Brie. The terrors of a miserable old age dismissed his last scruples.

"First of all, I must be sure of the reality of what the old woman said. After that, I'll lay out my plan," he thought.

That was why, two days later, having received Fougeroux's 5,280 francs, Louis de Clameran departed for London.

Chapter XVI

After more than twenty years of marriage, Valentine de La Verberie, who had become Madame Fauvel, hadn't experienced but one real sadness. Still, it was one of those sorrows which invariably come to us in our dearest affections. In 1859, she lost her mother, struck by an attack of pneumonia during one of her frequent visits to Paris. Since that time, as Madame Fauvel took pleasure in repeating, she'd never had any serious reason to be unhappy. She'd never had occasion to shed a tear. What more could she wish? After so many years, André remained for her as he had been in the first days of their union. To the love which had never lessened, was joined that delicious intimacy which came from long unity of thought, and boundless confidence.

Everything had come about as that fortunate household had wished. André had wanted to be rich. He was so, a great deal beyond his hopes, most of all a great deal beyond his desires and those of Valentine. Their two sons, Lucien and Abel,[42] handsome as their mother, with noble hearts and strong intellects, were of those elect who are the glorification of their family, and carry to the outside world a reflection of the domestic happiness. It was said that nothing was missing to Valentine's happiness. When in the hours of solitude, when by chance her husband and her sons were away for an evening, she had a companion, a young accomplished girl, Madeleine, whom she raised. She loved her as she did her own children, and Madeleine showed her the tender attentions of a devoted daughter.

Madeleine was Monsieur Fauvel's niece. She lost her parents, poor honest people, when she was still in the cradle. Valentine had wanted to take her in, perhaps in memory of that poor abandoned child in London. It seemed that God would bless her for that good work, and that Madeleine would be the guardian angel of the house. The day the orphan arrived, the rich banker had declared that he wanted to open an account for her, and, in fact, he deposited 10,000 francs for Madeleine's dowry. To amuse himself, this rich banker had increased the value of these 10,000 francs in an extraordinary fashion. He never risked a dubious speculation on his own behalf, but he took pleasure in gambling with his niece's money on the most unlikely stocks. It was only a game. He always won, so much so that in fifteen years, the 10,000 francs had become a 500,000.

Those people who envied the Fauvel family were certainly right. After a long time, Valentine's bitter remorse found rest. In that benevolent atmosphere of happiness, she had almost found forgetfulness and had made peace with her conscience. She had paid so cruelly for her sin. She had suffered so much for having deceived André, that she thought herself quits with fate. She dared now

---

[42] Gaboriau called him Albert twice previously.

to look forward to the future. Her youth, lost in a dense opaque fog, was no longer anything for her but the memory of a painful dream.

Yes, she believed herself saved, when one afternoon day in November during an absence of her husband, called to the country on serious matters, one of the servants brought her a letter left with the concierge. It had been left by an unknown person who had refused to give his name. Without the vaguest presentiment making her hand shake or tremble, she broke open the envelope and read:

Madame,
Is it relying too much on the memory of your heart to hope for a half-hour interview? Tomorrow, between 2:00 p.m., and 3:00 p.m., I will have the honor to come to your townhouse.

Marquis de Clameran

Fortunately, Madame Fauvel was alone. An agony, as terrible as the one that precedes death, clutched the poor woman's heart the instant she read the letter with a glance. She read it ten times in a low voice so as if to be fully aware of the dreadful reality, to prove to herself that she wasn't the victim of a hallucination. It was only after some time that she was able to gather together her thoughts— more scattered than autumn leaves after a storm—that she could think.

Then she began to tell herself that she had become alarmed too soon and for no reason. From whom did that letter come? Without a doubt from Gaston. Well! What reason was there to tremble? Gaston returned to France, and wanted to see her. She understood that desire. But she knew that man, loved so well in the past, well enough to know that she had nothing to fear from him. He would come; he would find her married to someone else; they would exchange memories, perhaps regrets. She would return to him what he had entrusted to her, and that would be all.

But she was assailed by frightful doubts. Should she reveal to Gas-ton that she had had a son by him? To confess? That would be to surrender herself. That would be to put herself at the mercy of a man— certainly the most honest and the most loyal, but after all, a man—not only her own honor and happiness, but the honor and happiness of her husband and children. To keep silent? That would be to commit a crime. After having abandoned her child, after having deprived him of the care and the caresses of a mother, that would be to steal the name and the fortune of his father.

She was wondering which decision to take, when she was told dinner was served. But she didn't feel she had the courage to go downstairs. To face her sons' looks was beyond her strength. She said she was very ill and went to her bedroom, happy for the first time for her husband's absence. Soon Madeleine ran in, worried; but she sent her away, saying it was nothing but a headache, and that she wanted to try to sleep. She wanted to remain alone to confront this misfortune, and to force her mind to look into the future, to guess what would happen the following day.

The following day that she both feared and wished for came. Until 2:00 p.m., she counted the hours. After that, she counted the minutes. Just at 2:30, the door of the drawing room opened and a servant announced:

"Monsieur le Marquis de Clameran."

Madame Fauvel had promised herself to remain calm, even cold. During the hard, sleepless night, she had forced herself to foresee and to arrange in advance all the circumstances of that painful interview. She had thought about the words she would say. She must say this; she must say that. But at the last moment, her strength betrayed her. A terrible emotion nailed her to her chair, without a voice, without thoughts.

He, however, after having bowed respectfully, remained standing in the middle of the drawing room, immobile, waiting. He was a fifty-year-old man, with graying moustache and hair, with a sad and severe face, looking important and wearing his black clothing with distinction.

Stirred by inexpressible sensations, trembling, Madame Fauvel looked at him. She was trying to find on his face some of the features of the man she had loved, even to the point of abandon, and that lover who had pressed his lips against hers, who had pressed her against his bosom, with whom she had had a son. And she was astonished to find nothing in this mature man of the adolescent whose memory had haunted her life, no, nothing. Finally, as he didn't move, with a shaky voice she whispered:

"Gaston!"

But he, shaking his head sadly, answered:

"I am not Gaston, Madame. My brother died from the sadness and misery of exile. I am Louis de Clameran."

What! It wasn't Gaston who'd written her. This wasn't Gaston standing there in front of her! What could he want, this other person, this brother in whom Gaston hadn't had enough confidence, she knew, to make him a part of their secret? A thousand possibilities, one more terrifying than another, came into her mind at the same time. But she was able to control her faltering so promptly, that Louis hardly noticed it. The frightful strangeness of the situation, even the immense peril, gave her mind unusual clarity. With a casual gesture, she pointed out to Louis an armchair across from her, and in the calmest voice she said:

"Well, Monsieur, will you please explain to me the purpose of a visit I was far from expecting?"

The Marquis declined to notice this sudden change. Without ceasing to keep his eyes stubbornly fixed on Madame Fauvel's eyes, he sat down.

"Before anything else, Madame," he began, "I must ask you if anyone else can hear what we say here."

"Why that question? I don't believe you have anything to say to me that couldn't be heard by my husband and children."

Louis shrugged with visible affectation, a little like a man aware of the ravings of a mad person.

"Please allow me, Madame, to insist," he said, "not for myself, but for you."

"Speak, Monsieur, speak. We're alone here, far from any indiscretion."

"Despite that assurance, the Marquis drew his chair close to Madame's Fauvel's *causeuse*[43] in order to speak low, very low, as if afraid of what he had to say.

"I've told you, Madame," he continued, "Gaston is dead. However that may be, I was the one who heard his last thoughts; I was the one he chose to be the executor of his last wishes. Do you understand now?"

She understood only too well, the poor woman, but she vainly tried to see through this fatal visitor's intentions. Perhaps he came only to claim the precious jewels entrusted to her by Gaston.

"I won't remind you," Gaston went on, "of the fatal circumstances which broke my brother's life, and destroyed his future."

Not one of Madame Fauvel's facial muscles budged. She appeared to be searching her memory for which circumstance Louis was alluding to.

"You have forgotten, Madame?" he continued in a bitter tone. "I'll try to explain myself more clearly. A long time ago, oh, that was a very long time ago, you loved my unfortunate brother..."

"Monsieur!"

"Oh! It's useless to deny it, Madame. Gaston, must I repeat it to you, Madame, told me everything, everything," he added, stressing the last word.

But Madame Fauvel shouldn't have been afraid of that revelation. What could this "everything" be? Nothing, because Gaston had left without knowing she was pregnant. She rose, and with an assurance which was very far from her heart:

"You're forgetting, it seems to me, Monsieur," she pronounced, "that you're speaking to an old woman now, married and the mother of a family. It's possible that your brother loved me; that's his secret and not yours. If, young and inexperienced, I wasn't completely prudent, it isn't up to you to remind me of it. He himself wouldn't remind me of it! After all, whatever the past you are bringing up, I've lost the memory of it for the past twenty years."

"So, you've forgotten?"

"Everything, absolutely."

"Even your child, Madame?"

That sentence, thrown out with one of those looks which reach right to the bottom of the soul, hit Madame Fauvel like a sledge hammer. She fell back on the *causeuse*, saying to herself: "What! He knows! How did he find out?"

---

[43] 19th century two-seated couch; love seat.

If it had been a matter of only herself, she certainly would not have fought. But she had the happiness of her family to guard and defend, and feeling this sacred duty, she drew on strength she would never have been thought to possess.

"I believe that you are insulting me, Monsieur!" she said.

"So, it's really true. You no longer remember Valentin-Raoul?"

"But that's indeed a strange thing to say!"

She saw very well now. In fact, that man knew everything. Where did he learn it? That mattered very little to her. He knew. But she had taken a position, very determined to deny even so stubbornly, even when faced with the most irrecusable, the most evident proofs. For a moment she thought about chasing the Marquis de Clameran away shamefully. Caution stopped her. She told herself that she should at least find out something about his plans.

"After all!" she continued with a forced laugh, "What's your point?"

"It's this, Madame. Two years ago, the hazards of exile took my brother to London. There, in a family, he met a very young man named Raoul. The appearance, the intelligence of that adolescent, struck Gaston to the point that he wanted to know who he was. He was a poor abandoned child, and when he had found out all the information, my brother became certain this Raoul was his son and yours, Madame."

"That's a novel you're reciting to me."

"Yes, Madame, a novel and the denouement is in your hands. The Comtesse, your mother, certainly took the minutest and the wisest precautions to hide your secret. But the best conceived plans always err in some way. After your departure, one of the friends your mother had in London came back to start over in the village where you'd taken up residence. That lady pronounced your real name in front of the farm woman who'd been left with the child. Everything was discovered. My brother wanted proof. He obtained undeniable, positive proof."

He stopped, watching Madame Fauvel's face for the effect of his words.

To his great surprise, she seemed neither moved nor troubled. Her eyes were smiling.

"And so?" she asked in the most unconcerned tone.

"Following this, Madame, Gaston recognized this child as his. But the Clamerans are poor. My brother died in a cheap hotel bed. I myself have only a 1,200 franc pension to live on. What's going to become of Raoul, alone without a family, without a protector, without friend? These worries tortured my brother's last moments. "

"Really, Monsieur…"

"I'm coming to the end," Louis interrupted. "It was then that Gas-ton opened his heart to me. It was then that he commanded me to come see you. 'Valentine,' he said to me, 'Valentine, will remember. She won't be able to endure the thought that our son has nothing, even food. She's rich, very rich. I die happy.'"

Madame Fauvel rose. This time it was quite obviously a dismissal.

"You will admit, will you not, Monsieur," she began, "that my patience is great."

That unshakeable assurance discomfited Louis so much that he didn't reply.

"I would wish to tell you," she continued, "that in the past, in fact, I had Monsieur Gaston de Clameran's confidence. As a proof, I'm going to restore to you the jewelry of the Marquise, your mother, which he entrusted to me at his departure."

While speaking, she had taken from under one of the cushions of the *causeuse* the purse containing the jewelry, and she held it out to Louis.

"Here's what he entrusted to me, Monsieur le Marquis," she said. "Please let me tell you I'm astonished that your brother never came to claim it."

Less a master of himself, Louis had let his surprise be seen.

"My mission," he said in a dry tone, "was not to speak of what was entrusted."

Without answering, Madame Fauvel reached for a bell pull.

"You will please allow me, Monsieur, to cut short this interview, except solely to return these precious jewels to you."

Thus repulsed, Monsieur de Clameran didn't believe he should insist.

"So be it, Madame. I'm leaving. I must only add that my brother told me something else. 'If Valentine has forgotten everything, if she refuses to guarantee the future of our son, I order you to force her to do it.' Think about these words, Madame, because what I've sworn to do, on my honor, I will do!"

Finally Madame Fauvel was alone. She was free. Finally she could, without fear, let out her despair. Worn out by the effort it had cost her to remain calm, watched by de Clameran, she felt herself broken in body and soul. She hardly had the strength to return, shaking, to her bedroom and to shut herself in there. Now, no more doubts. Her fears were a reality. She could with certainty measure the height of the precipice from which she would be thrown, and where she would drag all her family with her. Ah! Why did she listen to her mother; why did she remain silent? There was no longer any hope. That man who had just left, a threat in his mouth, he would come back. She knew that only too well. What could she answer him? It would have taken very little for her to betray herself when Louis spoke of Raoul.

At the name of this poor abandoned child, suffering for the sins of his mother, her heart had winced. At the thought that he was perhaps undergoing extreme poverty, all her being trembled with sharp pain. He, to be lacking bread, he, her child! And she was rich. All Paris envied her luxury! Ah! Why could she not put all that she possessed at his feet? With what delight she would have taken away all the most painful deprivations. But how, without compromising herself, could she get enough money to him to shelter him from the difficulties of life! Because the voice of prudence cried out to her that she should not, that she could not, accept the intervention of Louis de Clameran. To put her trust in him was to put herself at his mercy, herself and all of her family. He inspired her with instinctive terror. And she was at the point of asking herself if he was really telling the truth. Going back over in her head that man's story, she found gaps and things almost shockingly lacking in verisimilitude. Why hadn't Gaston, back in France and living in Paris, as poor as his brother said, come to ask the woman for the return of what he had entrusted to a young girl? Why, fearing the future of their child, had he not come to find her, since he supposed her rich to the point that, dying, he relied on her?

A thousand vague worries agitated her mind. She was filled with inexplicable suspicions, unaccountable mistrust. She understood that one positive step committed her forever, and then what might be demanded of her?"

One moment she thought she would throw herself at her husband's feet and admit everything. Unfortunately, she pushed away that thought of salvation. Her imagination represented to her the atrocious sadness of that honest man, discovering after more than twenty years, that he had been odiously duped. She knew André well enough to know that he would say nothing, and that he would do everything to stifle that horrible affair. But that would be the end of happiness in the house. He would desert the household. The sons would go their way. All the family ties would be broken. Fortunately, the banker was absent; and during the two days that followed Louis' visit, Madame Fauvel could stay in her bedroom and no one saw her anxiety. However, Madeleine, with her female intuition, guessed that there was something other than the nervous malady which her aunt complained of, and for which the doctor was prescribing all sorts of calming potions. She even very clearly noticed that the malady seemed to have been caused by the visit of that person with a hard face, who had remained a long time alone with her aunt. Madeleine felt so strongly there was a secret that the second day, seeing Madame Fauvel more upset, she dared say to her:

"You're sad, dear Aunt. What's wrong with you? Do you want me to have our dear priest come chat with you?"

It was with a very surprising bitterness that Madame Fauvel, who was gentleness itself, turned down her niece's suggestion.

What Louis had foreseen happened. Having thought it over, seeing no way out of her deplorable situation, Madame Fauvel, little by little decided to give in. By consenting to everything, she had a chance of saving everything. She wasn't deceiving herself. She knew she was preparing an impossible life for herself; at least she would suffer alone, and in any case, she would gain time. However, Monsieur Fauvel had returned, and Valentine, in appearance at least, had taken up her routine again. But she was no longer the happy mother of a family, the woman with a smiling and relaxed expression, so sure in her happiness, so calm in the face of the future. Everything in her betrayed horrible worry.

Not hearing from de Clameran, she as much as expected it at every moment of the day; she trembled each time the door bell rang, turning pale each

463

time the door opened, not daring to go out for fear that he would come during her absence. The man condemned to death, when waking each morning asks himself: 'Will it be today?' but doesn't undergo any more horrible agony.

Clameran didn't come; he wrote, or rather, since he was too cautious to prepare weapons against himself, he had a letter written, the meaning of which only Madame Fauvel would be able to understand. Claiming he was sick, he excused himself for being forced to give her an appointment two days later at his rooms in the Hotel du Louvre.

That letter was almost a relief for Madame Fauvel. She would have preferred anything to her worry. She was resolved to consent to anything. Then she burned the letter, telling herself, "I'll go."

Two days later, in fact at the time indicated, she put on the plainest of her black dresses, the one of her hats which best hid her face, slid a small veil in her pocket, and left. It wasn't until she was very far away from her house that she dared take a carriage, which dropped her in front of the Hotel du Louvre. The concierge told her that Monsieur Louis de Clameran's bedroom was on the fourth floor. She started up, glad to escape all the stares which seemed to her to be directed at her. But despite minute directions, she got lost in the huge hotel and wandered a long time in the interminable corridors. Finally she came to a door above which was the right number: 317. She stopped, putting both hands on her breast as if to restrain the beating of her heart, which was pounding as if it would break. At the moment of entering, at the moment of risking that decisive step, an immense fright overcame her to the point of paralyzing her movements. The sight of a hotel guest going across the corridor put an end to her hesitations. With a trembling hand, she knocked three times very softly.

"Come in," said a voice.

She went in. But it wasn't the Marquis de Clameran who was in the middle of that room. It was a very young man, almost a child, who was looking at her in an unusual way. Madame Fauvel's first impression was that she had made a mistake.

"I beg your pardon, Monsieur," she stammered, redder than a peony. "I thought I was entering the room of Monsieur le Marquis de Clameran.'

"You are in his room, Madame," responded the young man.

Seeing that she didn't say anything, that she seemed to be wondering how to leave, how to flee, he added:

"It is, I believe, to Madame Fauvel that I have the honor of speaking."

She nodded affirmatively: "Yes." She trembled on hearing her name thus pronounced. She was alarmed by the certainty that she was known, that Clameran had already revealed her secret. She waited for an explanation with visible anxiety.

"Be reassured, Madame," the young man continued. "You are as safe here as in the drawing room of your home. Monsieur de Clameran has asked me to apologize to you; you won't see him."

"Nevertheless, Monsieur, according to an urgent letter that he had sent to me the day before yesterday, I must suppose…I was supposing…"

"When he wrote to you, Madame, he had plans which he's given up forever."

Madame Fauvel was a great deal too surprised, a great deal too troubled to be able to think. She was aware of nothing beyond the present moment.

"What!" she said with certain distrust, "His intentions have changed?"

The face of the young man questioning Madame Fauvel showed a sort of sad compassion, as if he had accepted the consequences of all the unhappy woman's agony.

"The Marquis," he said in a gentle and sad voice, "has renounced what he considered—wrongly—a sacred duty. You may believe that he hesitated a long time before resigning himself to go ask you for the most painful of admissions. You have driven him away. You refused to listen to him. He didn't understand what overwhelming reasons dictated your conduct. That day, blinded by an unjust anger, he had sworn to take from you by force what he couldn't obtain from your heart. Determined to threaten your happiness, he had gathered proofs against you which would clearly support the evidence. Pardon me…an oath sworn to a dying brother bound him."

He had taken from the fireplace mantle a file of papers, which he was flipping through as he spoke.

"Here are these proofs," he went on, "flagrant, undeniable. Here is the certificate of the Reverend Sedley, the declaration of Mistress Dobbin, the farm woman, a deposition from the surgeon, depositions from people who knew the Comtesse de la Verberie in London. Oh! Nothing is missing here. It wasn't without difficulty that I constrained Monsieur de Clameran to give me all these proofs. Perhaps he saw through my intentions. And here Madame, is what I would like to do with this evidence."

With a rapid movement, he threw all the papers in the fire. They caught fire and soon were no more than a pinch of ashes.

"Everything is destroyed, Madame," he continued, his eyes shining with the most generous of resolutions. "The past, if you wish it, exists no more than do these papers. If someone, now, dares to claim that before your marriage you had a son, treat him harshly as a slanderer. There is no longer any proof. You are free."

Finally, in Madame Fauvel's eyes, the meaning of that scene became clear. She was beginning to understand. She understood. This young man who got her away from de Clameran's anger, who gave her back her free will by destroying the overwhelming evidence, who was saving her, he was the abandoned infant: Valentin-Raoul.

At this moment she forgot everything. The mother's tenderness, so long repressed, overflowed, and with a hardly distinct voice, she whispered: "Raoul!"

At this name so pronounced, the young man staggered. You would have said that he was giving way under the excess of an unexpected happiness.

"Yes, Raoul," he exclaimed. "Raoul who would rather die a thousand times than to cause his mother the slightest suffering. Raoul, who would spill all his blood to keep her from shedding a tear."

She tried neither to fight nor to resist. Her whole being vibrated, as if her womb had trembled on recognizing the one she had carried. She opened her arms to Raoul, and he rushed into them, saying in a stifled voice:

"My mother! My good mother! May you be blessed for this first kiss."

That was true, in fact. She had never seen this son. Despite her prayers and her tears, they had taken him away without even allowing her to embrace him; and this kiss she had just given him was really the first. After so much and so cruel an agony, to find this immense joy was too much happiness.

Madame Fauvel had let herself sink into an armchair, and plunged into a sort of ecstatic self-communion. She avidly looked at Raoul, who was kneeling at her feet. How handsome he seemed to her, this poor abandoned child! He had that shining beauty of love children, whose expression seems to keep a reflection of divine happiness. She ran her hand through his fine and wavy hair. She admired his forehead, white and pure as that of a young girl, his large and trembling eyes, and she thirsted for his very red lips.

"Oh! Mother," he said, "I don't know what came over me when I found out that my uncle had dared threaten you. He, threaten you! Because you see, dear Mother, I have the heart of you both, you and that noble Gaston de Clameran, my father. You see! When he told his brother to contact you, he wasn't in his right mind. I've been very well acquainted with you for a long time. My Father and I often went to roam around your townhouse, and when we caught sight of you, we returned home happy. You passed by and he said to me: 'There's your mother, Raoul.' Just to see you! That was our joy. When we found out you were going to some party, we waited at the door to see you beautiful and bedecked with jewels. How many times, in the winter, did I struggle to run as fast as your carriage horses to admire you longer."

Tears, the gentlest she had ever shed in her life, ran down Madame Fauvel's face. Raoul's shaking voice sang celestial harmonies in her ears. That voice reminded her of Gaston's, and gave her back the fresh and adorable sensations of her youth. Yes, when listening to him, she found again the enchantment of the first meetings, the thrill of her still virgin soul, the mysterious confusion of the senses. Between the moment one evening when she had abandoned herself in Gaston's arms, trembling, and the present hour, it seemed to her there had been nothing. André, her two sons, Madeleine—she forgot them, swept away by this whirlwind of tenderness.

Raoul, however, continued:

"I learned only yesterday that my uncle had gone to ask you for some small pieces of your riches for me. What was the good of that! I'm poor, that's true, very poor; but poverty doesn't frighten me. I'm used to it. I have my arms and my brain; that's enough to live on. They say you're rich. What difference does that make to me? Keep your fortune, dear Mother, but give me a little of your heart. Let me love you. Promise me that this first kiss won't be the last. No one will know anything. Don't worry. I'll know very well how to hide my happiness."

And Madame Fauvel could have doubted this son? Ah! How much she reproached herself for it. How much she also reproached herself for not having flown to him sooner. She questioned him, this son. She wanted to know about his life, to know how he had lived, and what he had done. He had nothing to hide from her, he said. His life had been that of the children of the poor. The farm woman to whom they had entrusted him had always shown him a certain amount of affection. Finding him good looking and intelligent, she had been pleased to give him some education beyond her means, and beyond his social condition. When he was sixteen, they had apprenticed him to a banker. By working, he was beginning to earn his livelihood, when one day a man came and said to him: "I'm your father," and took him away. Since that time, nothing was missing from his happiness, except the tenderness of a mother. He had truly suffered only once in his life; that was the day Gaston de Clameran died in his arms.

"But now," he said, "everything is forgotten, everything. Have I been unhappy? I no longer know, since I can see you, since I can love you."

Time was passing, and Madame Fauvel didn't notice. Raoul, fortunately, was vigilant.

"7:00 p.m.!" he suddenly exclaimed.

That exclamation brought Madame Fauvel suddenly back to reality. Seven o'clock! Would her absence for such a long time perhaps be noticed?

"Will I see you again, Mother?" Raoul asked as they separated.

"Oh! Yes," she answered with an accent of mad tenderness. "Yes, often, everyday, tomorrow."

That was the first time since she had been married, that Madame Fauvel was aware that she was not absolutely in control of her emotions. She had never before had occasion to wish for uncontrolled freedom. It was her very soul that she left in that Hotel du Louvre bedroom, where she had just found her son again. And she had to leave him. She was condemned to that intolerable torture of composing her face, of hiding this monumental event which had turned her life upside down.

Having had some trouble getting a carriage for the return trip, it was past 7:30 p.m. when she arrived at the Rue de Provence, where they were waiting for her before sitting down at the table. As Monsieur Fauvel was making a joke about her lateness, she found him common, vulgar, and even a little silly. The revolutions of passions are such that she judged him almost ridiculous, for that boundless confidence he had in her. And it was with imperturbable calm, with no trouble, that she answered these jokes. Her feelings near Raoul had been so worked up, that she was incapable of desiring anything, of dreaming about anything, beyond renewing those exquisite emotions. No more a devoted wife, no more an incomparable mother of a family. She hardly stopped to think about her two sons. They themselves had always been happy and loved. They had a father. They were rich, while the other one, the other one! How much she needed to make up to him! In her blindness, she was very near to making her family responsible for Raoul's poverty. And no more remorse, no trembling of conscience, no fear about what had happened. Her madness was complete. The future, for her, was the next day; eternity, the sixteen hours that separated her from a new meeting.

Gaston's death seemed to her to be divine forgiveness for the past as well as for the present. But she was sorry to be married. If she were free, she could devote herself entirely to Raoul. She was rich, but she would gladly have given up her luxury to be poor with him.

Neither her husband nor her sons ever suspected the thoughts which agitated her. She was not worried from that direction, but she feared her niece. It seemed to her that when she came back in, Madeleine had given her some unusual looks. Did she suspect anything? She had been asking her some strange questions for several days. She would have to beware of her. That worry changed the affection Madame Fauvel had for her adopted daughter—she so good, so charming—into a kind of hatred. She regretted having taken her in, and to have thus given herself one of those watchful spies that nothing escapes. How could she get away from that worrying devoted solicitude, she wondered, from that insight of a young girl accustomed to catching the most fleeting emotions on her face? It was with indescribable joy that she found a way close at hand. For almost two years, it had been a question of a marriage between Madeleine and the head cashier of the bank. Madame Fauvel told herself that all she needed to do was to get busy with that union, and to hurry it up as much as possible. Married, Madeleine would go live with her husband, and would leave her free to use her days as she liked. That same evening, she dared for the first time to speak of Prosper and, with duplicity which she would have been incapable of some days earlier, she got Madeleine to commit herself.

"Ah! That's how it is, Mademoiselle the Mysterious," she said gaily. "You're allowing yourself to choose among all your suitors without my permission!"

"But, good Aunt, it seems to me…"

"That I should have guessed? That's what I did."

She looked serious and added:

"That being so, nothing else remains to be done but to obtain the consent of Master Prosper. Will he give it?"

"He! Oh, Aunt! Ah! If he dared!"

"Ah! Really, you know that, Mademoiselle, my niece?"

Intimidated, confused, and blushing, Madeleine bowed her head. Madame

Fauvel drew her to her.

"Dear Child," she continued in her gentlest voice, "Why be afraid? Then you really didn't guess, you so artful, that your secret has been ours for a long time? Would Prosper have been admitted into our household as if part of the family, if it hadn't been agreed on in advance by your uncle and by me?"

Perhaps a little to hide her joy, Madeleine threw her arms around her aunt's neck, whispering:

"Thank you! Oh! Thank you. You're good; you love me..."

For her part, Madame Fauvel was saying to herself: "Without waiting, I'm going to get André to encourage Prosper. Before two months are out, these two children can be married."

Unfortunately, carried away by the whirlwind of a passion which didn't leave her a minute to think, she put off this project. Spending a part of her days at the Hotel du Louvre near Raoul, she never stopped dreaming about ways to prepare a position for him and to assure him an independent fortune.

She hadn't yet dared speak to him about anything. As she got to know him better, as he opened up himself more, she believed she discovered in him all his father's noble pride and haughty touchiness. She shuddered that she would be repulsed. She seriously wondered if he would even consent to accept the least thing from her. At the height of her hesitation, the Marquis Louis de Clameran came to her aid. She had seen him often since the day he had so frightened her, and a secret sympathy replaced her first repulsion. She liked him for all the affection he had shown her son.

If Raoul, careless about the future as one is at twenty, ridiculed the future, Louis, that man of so much experience, seemed greatly preoccupied with the fate of his nephew. That's why, one day, after some general comments, he broached that serious question of a position.

"Living thus as he does, my handsome nephew," he began, "is doubtless charming; only wouldn't it be wise of him to think about getting himself settled in some situation in the world? He has no fortune."

"Ah! Dear Uncle," Raoul interrupted, "Let me be happy without remorse; what do I lack?"

"Nothing at this moment, my handsome nephew; but when you've used up your resources and mine—and that time isn't far away—what will become of you?"

"*Bast!* I'll join the army. All the Clamerans are born soldiers, and if there's another war!..."

Madame Fauvel stopped him by putting her hand gently over his mouth.

"Wicked child!" she said in a tone of reproach. "To become a soldier! Then do you mean to deprive me of the happiness of seeing you?"

"No, Mother dear, no..."

"You see very well," Louis insisted, "that you must listen to us." "I don't ask for anything better, but later I'll work. I'll earn an enormous amount of money."

"Doing what, poor child? How?"

"Damn!... I don't know, but don't worry, I'll look around. I'll find something."

It was hard to make this presumptuous young man listen to reason. Louis and Madame Fauvel had long talks on this subject, and they promised each other to force his hand. However, to choose a profession was awkward, and Clameran thought it would be wise to reflect, to consult the young man's tastes. While waiting, it was agreed that Madame Fauvel would put at the Marquis' disposition whatever was needed for all of Raoul's expenses. Seeing in this brother of Gaston a father for her child, Madame Fauvel had rapidly come to the point of not being able to do without him. She needed to see him constantly, either to consult him about the ideas he had, or to give him a thousand suggestions.

So she was very satisfied the day that he asked her to do him the honor of receiving him openly at her home. Nothing was easier. She would present the Marquis de Clameran to her husband as an old friend of the family, and it would just be up to him to become a usual guest there.

Madame Fauvel wasn't slow to applaud that decision. Being absolutely unable to continue seeing Raoul every day, and if she wrote to him, not daring to receive his answers, she heard news of him through Louis. The news didn't stay good long, and less than a month after the day Madame Fauvel had found her son, Clameran confided to her that Raoul was beginning to make him seriously uneasy. The Marquis expressed himself in a tone and in a manner to chill a mother's heart. Still he was not without embarrassment, like a man fulfilling a duty who triumphs over great repugnance.

"What's the matter?" Madame Fauvel asked.

"The trouble is," Louis answered, "that I find in this young man the pride and the passions of the de Clamerans. Their personalities are such that nothing stops their fits of temper, that obstacles irritate them, that anything said in disapproval exasperates them, and I don't see any dike to hold back his violence."

"*Grand Dieu!* What can he have done?"

"Nothing exactly blamable, certainly nothing that can't be repaired, but his future frightens me. He doesn't yet know anything about your goodness to him. He believes he's dipping into my purse, and I see in him the prodigality of a millionaire's son."

Madame Fauvel wouldn't have been a mother if she hadn't tried to come to Raoul's defense.

"Perhaps you are a little severe," she said. "Poor child! He's suffered so much. Up until now he's known only deprivations, and good fortune makes him drunk. He's thrown himself into pleasure as a starving man does into a good meal. Is that so surprising? Come now. He'll come around promptly to reason. He has a good heart."

"He has been so unhappy!" That for Madame Fauvel was Raoul's excuse.

It was that phrase she repeated constantly to Monsieur de Clameran, every time that he complained about his nephew. And certainly, once he had begun complaining, he never stopped.

"Nothing stops him," he moaned. "A foolish idea that goes through his head becomes a foolish idea acted on."

But Madame Fauvel saw no reason to be angry with her son. That's why, seeing that his efforts didn't stop the imprudent young man on his dangerous descent, he finally called on Madame Fauvel to use her influence. She must, for her child's future, become more intimately involved in his life, to see him every day.

"Alas!" answered the poor woman. "That would be my dearest wish. But how can that be done? Do I have the right to condemn myself? I have other children to whom I must answer for my honor." That answer seemed to astonish the Marquis de Clameran. Two weeks earlier, Madame Fauvel hadn't spoken at all about her other sons.

"I'll think about it," said Louis. "Perhaps at our next meeting, I'll have the honor to submit a plan to you that will reconcile everything."

The reflections of a man of so much experience couldn't be useless. He appeared very reassured when he met her the next Thursday.

"I searched," he began, "and I found."

"What?"

"The way to save Raoul."

He explained. Madame Fauvel couldn't see her son every day without arousing her husband's suspicions. She would have to receive him at her house. Just that suggestion horrified a woman who had certainly been imprudent, even very guilty, but who was honor itself.

"That would be impossible!" she exclaimed. "That would be vile, odious, infamy..."

"Yes," answered the Marquis, who had become pensive, "but that would be the salvation of the child."

But this time she knew how to resist. She resisted with violent indignation, with a strength able to discourage a will less firm than that of the Marquis de Clameran.

"No!" she repeated. "I won't consent."

Unfortunate woman! Those who leave the straight and narrow never know what slime and quagmires will confront them! She had said "Never!" from the bottom of her soul; yet at the end of the week, she was no longer desperately refusing to consider this plan, but discussing the means for it. Here's how clever steps had brought her to this point. Lost and badgered, she vainly fought against de Clameran's politely threatening insistence, and Raoul's begging and wheedling.

"But how?" she asked, "Under what pretext can Raoul be invited?"

"That would be very simple," Clameran answered, "if it were a matter of receiving him as one receives a stranger. I'm already a frequent guest in your drawing room. It will be easier for Raoul."

It was only after having tortured Madame Fauvel a long time by continual alternations of terror and gentleness, after having broken her will and almost her sanity, that he revealed his definite plan.

"We hold the solution to the problem," he finally said. "It was a real inspiration."

She guessed by his tone that he was going to see through everything she was thinking, and she listened to him with that sad resignation of the condemned man listening to his fate being read.

"Isn't there at Saint-Rémy one of your relatives, a very old widow who only had two daughters?" Louis continued.

"Yes, my cousin, a de Lagors."

"That's the one. What is her financial situation?"

"She's poor, Monsieur, very poor."

"Precisely, and without the help you give her secretly, she would be on public charity."

Madame Fauvel was taken aback to see the Marquis so well informed.

"What!" she stammered. "You know that?"

"Yes, Madame, and a great many more things, too. I know, for example, that your husband doesn't know anyone in your family, and that he could hardly suspect the existence of your de Lagors cousin. Are you now beginning to understand my plan?"

She at least caught a glimpse of it, and she was wondering how to resist it.

"Then here is what I imagine. Tomorrow or the day after tomorrow, you'll receive a letter from your cousin in Saint-Rémy, telling you that she's sending her son to you in Paris and asking you to watch over him. Naturally, you'll show that letter to your husband. Some days later, he'll receive his rich witty nephew Raoul de Lagors, in the best fashion, a likeable charming boy who'll do everything to please him, and who will please him."

"Never, Monsieur," exclaimed Madame Fauvel. "My cousin, who's an honest woman, will never lend her hand to such a revolting comedy."

The Marquis smiled conceitedly.

"Did I tell you," he asked, "that I would take the cousin into my confidence?"

"It would certainly be necessary!"

"Oh! But no! The letter that you'll receive, and that you'll show, will be dictated by me to the first woman I meet, and mailed in Saint-Rémy by someone I trust. If I spoke about the obligations that your cousin has to you, it was to show you that in case of an accident, her interest will make us sure of her. Do you see any other obstacle?"

Carried away with indignation, Madame Fauvel had risen.

"You're not counting on my wishes!" she cried out.

472

"Pardon me," said the Marquis with joking politeness. "I'm sure you'll come around to my logic."

"But this is a crime you're suggesting to me, Monsieur, an abominable crime!"

Clameran, too, had risen. All his wicked passions coming into play gave his pale face an atrocious expression.

"I believe," he continued with restrained violence, "that we aren't understanding each other. Before talking about crime, think about the past. You were less timorous the day when, as a young girl, you took a lover. It's true that you denied that lover, and that you refused to follow him when he had just killed two men for you, and was risking being hanged. You didn't have any of these shabby intolerances when, after giving birth secretly in London, you abandoned your child. One has to render you this justice: a millionaire, you didn't even try to find out if that child you absolutely had forgotten had bread to eat. Then where were your scruples at the time of your marriage to Monsieur Fauvel? Did you tell that honest man what sort of forehead your crown of orange blossoms hid? Those are real crimes. And when in Gaston's name I asked reparation, you refused! It's too late. You lost the father, Madame. You will save the son or, on my honor, you'll no longer steal society's respect."

Vanquished, crushed, the unfortunate woman whispered: "I'll do as you say, Monsieur."

And, indeed, a week later Raoul, now Raoul de Lagors, dined at the banker's house, sitting between Madame Fauvel and Madeleine.

Chapter XVII

It wasn't without harrowing heart-break that Madame Fauvel resigned herself to submitting to the Marquis de Clameran's pitiless will. Desperate, she had gone to ask for help from her son. When listening to her, Raoul seemed carried away with indignation and he had left her, he said, to dash off and to demand apologies from the miserable man who had made his mother cry. But he overestimated his strength. He soon returned, his eyes gloomy and his head bowed, with his facial features contorted by helpless rage, saying that it was necessary to give in, to consent, and to yield. That was when the poor woman was able to measure the depth of the abyss into which they had drawn her. At this moment, she almost foresaw the crafty scheme of which she would be the victim. What horrible pangs when she had to show the work of the forger, the letter from Saint-Rémy, and when she told her husband she was expecting one of her very rich nephews, a very young man! And what torment when she had to introduce Raoul to all of her family!

However, it was with a smile on his lips that the banker welcomed this nephew he had never heard of, and to whom he extended an honest hand.

"Parbleu!" he said. "When you're young and rich you must prefer Paris to Saint-Rémy."

At least Raoul took it on himself to seem worthy of that cordial greeting. If his first education was not sufficient, that upbringing that only a family can give, it was impossible to notice it. With tact much beyond his years, he was able to understand the personality of all the people surrounding him, and to please each. He hadn't been there a week when he had managed to get into Monsieur Fauvel's good graces, to win over Abel[44] and Lucien, and had absolutely seduced Prosper Bertomy, the head teller of the bank, who spent all his evenings at his employer's house.

Since, thanks to his cousins' connections, Raoul found himself thrown into the world of rich young men, far from becoming reformed, he led a more and more dissipated life. He gambled; he ate in expensive restaurants; he showed up at racetracks and money slid like sand through his prodigal hands. In the beginning, of a delicate sensitivity almost to the point of the ridiculous, that thoughtless boy had wanted nothing from his mother but a little affection. Now, he never stopped harassing her with incessant demands. At first, she gave gladly, without counting; but she wasn't long in becoming aware that if she didn't put a limit to it, her generosity would be her downfall.

That very rich woman, whose diamonds were well known and who had one of the most beautiful carriages in Paris, understood from her most poignant

---

[44] Ditto. Called Albert twice previously.

distress the overriding necessity of not giving in to the whims of the beloved. Her husband had never thought of putting her on a budget. From the day after his marriage, he had given her the key to the secretary. Since then, freely, generously, and without limit, she had taken whatever she thought necessary, both for the considerable household expenses and for her personal expenses. But precisely because she had always been modest in her tastes, to the point that her husband joked about it, and precisely because she had always administered the household with extreme wisdom, she couldn't suddenly dispose of rather large sums without leaving herself open to upsetting questions.

Certainly Monsieur Fauvel, the most generous of millionaires, was a man to be happy seeing his wife make some silly expenditure. But silly expenditures can be explained. They can be traced. Chance might make the banker recognize the astonishing increase in the household expenditures. What could she tell him if he asked the reasons?

And in three months Raoul had spent a small fortune. Hadn't it been necessary to set himself up in a nice bachelor's apartment? He was lacking everything, like a castaway. He had wanted a horse, a brougham.[45] How could she refuse to give them to him? Then, everyday it was some new whim. If Madame Fauvel sometimes dared to protest, Raoul's face took on a grieved expression and his beautiful eyes filled with tears.

"That's true," he answered. "I'm a child, a poor fool; I'm taking advantage. I'm forgetting that I'm the son of poor Valentine and not of the rich Madame Fauvel."

The sound of his apology pierced the poor mother's heart. He had suffered so in the past! He did it so well that it was finally she who consoled and excused him. Besides, she thought she had noticed not without fright, that he was jealous of Abel and Lucien—his brothers after all. At these moments, she was ready to do anything, so that Raoul would have nothing to envy of his brothers. At least she wanted to have one thing in return. Spring was coming. She asked Raoul to move to the country, near the property she had at Saint-Germain. She was expecting some objection. Not at all. That suggestion seemed to please him; and shortly thereafter, he announced to her that he had just rented a small house at Vésinet, and that he was going to have his furniture taken there.

"In this way, Mother," he said, "I'll be closer to you. What a beautiful summer we're going to spend!"

She rejoiced, above all, because the prodigal child's spending would probably diminish. And she was so truly relieved at the end, that one evening as he was dining with the family, she dared address him, before everyone. Oh! Very gently—with some advice. The evening before he had gone to the racetrack. He had bet and lost 2,000 francs.

"Baste!" said Monsieur Fauvel with the carelessness of a man who has full

---

[45] A small closed carriage.

coffers, "Mama Lagors will pay. Mamas were created and put into the world to pay."

And not being able to see the impression the simple words produced on his wife, who had become whiter than the ruffles on her dress, he added:

"Don't worry; go on my boy. When you need money, come to me. I'll lend you some."

How could Madame Fauvel object? Hadn't she said, following Clameran's wishes, that Raoul was very rich? Why had they made her tell a useless lie? She had a rapid understanding of the trap in which she was caught, but there was no longer time to go back. Besides, the banker's words hadn't fallen on deaf ears. At the end of that week, Raoul went to find his uncle in his office, and on the spot borrowed 10,000 francs. Told of that unbelievable audacity, Madame Fauvel wrung her hands in despair.

"*Mon Dieu!* But what's he doing with so much money!" she cried out.

Clameran had scarcely been seen for a long time at the Fauvel mansion. Madame Fauvel decided to write to him to ask him for a meeting. When he learned what had happened, he maintained he knew absolutely nothing about it. The Marquis seemed worried in a different way. Above all, he was a great deal more irritated than Madame Fauvel. There was a scene of the utmost violence between Raoul and himself. But Madame Fauvel's suspicions were raised. She observed it and it seemed to her—was that possible!—that their anger was a sham, and that while they were exchanging the bitterest words and even threats, their eyes were laughing.

She didn't dare say anything; but this doubt, sinking into her mind like a drop of those subtle poisons which disorganize everything they touch, added new pain to an almost intolerable torture. She told herself that, fallen into the control of such a man, she must expect worse demands. Then she tried in vain to understand his goal. He himself soon told it to her. After having complained about Raoul more bitterly than usual, after having shown Madame Fauvel the abyss opening up under her feet, the Marquis declared that he could see but one way to prevent a catastrophe. That was that he, Clameran, marry Madeleine. Madame Fauvel had long been prepared for all the attempts from an avarice of which she was finally aware. Clameran's unexpected declaration struck her to the quick of whatever feelings she still had left after so many crises.

"And do you believe, Monsieur!" she cried out, "that I would lend my hands to your odious plans?"

With a nod, the Marquis answered:

"Yes."

"Then what woman do you think you're talking to? Ah! Certainly, I've been very guilty in the past; but the punishment, finally, goes beyond the fault. Are you the one to make me so cruelly repent of my imprudence? So long as it was a question of just myself, you've found me weak, fearful, and cowardly. Today, you're attacking my own. I'm refusing!"

"Then would it be a great misfortune, Madame, for Mademoiselle Madeleine to become the Marquise de Clameran?"

"My niece, Monsieur, has freely chosen her husband, and of her own free will. She loves Monsieur Prosper Bertomy."

The Marquis shrugged disdainfully.

"A schoolgirl's love," he said. "She'll forget him when you wish it."

"I don't wish it."

"Pardon me!" Clameran continued in that low and muffled voice of an irritated man who is forcing himself to control himself. "Let's not waste our time in idle discussions. Up until now, you've always begun by protesting, and you've then given in to the excellence of my arguments. This time, too, you'll give me the courtesy of conceding."

"No," Madame Fauvel answered firmly, "No!"

He didn't deign to acknowledge the interruption.

"If I absolutely insist on this marriage," he continued, "it's because it has to reestablish your affairs and mine, which are much compromised at the moment. The money you have at your disposal can't suffice for Raoul's prodigality. You must be aware of that. A time will come when you won't have anything more to give him, and when it will be impossible to hide from your husband your forced borrowing from the housekeeping money. What will happen that day?"

Madame Fauvel shivered. She could see the day the Marquis was talking about in the near future. He, however, continued.

"That's when you'll see the justice of my farseeing wisdom and plans. Mademoiselle Madeleine is rich, and her dowry will allow me to make up the deficit and to save you."

"I would rather be lost than saved by such methods."

"But as for me, I won't allow you to compromise all our fates. We're in business for a common purpose, Madame. Don't forget it: it's the future of Raoul."

At these words, she threw him a glance so clearly insightful that his impudence was troubled by it. At the same time she said:

"Stop insisting. My decision is irrevocable."

"Your decision?"

"Yes. Believe me, I'm resolved to do everything, everything, to get myself out of your shameful obsessions. Oh! Stop giving me that ironic look! If you force me to, I'll go throw myself at Monsieur Fauvel's feet, and I'll tell him everything. He loves me. He'll understand what I've suffered and he'll pardon me."

"Do you think so?" asked Clameran with a laugh.

"What do you mean? That he wouldn't have pity, that he would chase me away as the unhappy woman I am? So be it. I'll have deserved it. After the terrible torments that you've heaped on me, there aren't any whose prospects can frighten me."

That inconceivable resistance upset the Marquis' plans to such an extent that, exasperated, he ceased to control himself. The man of the world mask fell off. The scoundrel appeared, revoltingly cynical. His face took on the most threatening expression; his voice became brutal.

"Ah! Really!" he took up again. "You've decided to confess to Monsieur Fauvel. Marvelous idea! It's a shame it's come to you a little late. If you had admitted everything the day I came to you, you would have had some chance of saving yourself. Your husband could pardon a far away sin, hidden for twenty years by conduct beyond reproach. Because you've been a faithful wife, Madame, and a good mother. Only, think of what that dear man will say when you tell him that the pretended nephew that you had sit at his table, who borrowed money from him, is the fruit of your first love. However excellent Monsieur Fauvel's character may be, I doubt that he'll accept it as a good joke. This shows, don't be mistaken, frightful perversity, rare audacity, and superior duplicity."

What the Marquis said was true, terribly true. Nevertheless, the lightening in his glances didn't make Madame Fauvel lower her eyes.

"Peste!" he went on, "You can see that this dear Monsieur Bertomy is very close to your heart! Between the honor of the name you wear, and the love affair of this worthy teller, you don't hesitate. All right! It will be a great consolation to you, I believe, when Monsieur Fauvel separates from you, when Albert and Lucien turn away from you, ashamed to be your sons. It will be a great comfort for you to be able to say: 'Good Prosper is happy!'"

"Come what may," Madame Fauvel pronounced, "I'll do what I must."

"You'll do what I wish!" screamed Clameran, finally losing control. "An excess of sentimentality can't be allowed to plunge us all into a slime pit. The dowry of your niece is indispensable and, besides, your Madeleine...I love her."

The blow had been struck. The Marquis thought it would be wise to wait for the effect. Thanks to his surprising self-control, he returned to his usual coolness, and it was with glacial politeness that he added:

"It's up to you now, Madame, to weigh my logic. Believe me. Agree to a sacrifice which will be the last. Think of the honor of your house, and not of your niece's little love affair. I'll come back in three days for an answer."

"You will have no reason to come back, Monsieur. As soon as my husband returns, he will know everything."

If she had been cool-headed, Madame Fauvel would have been surprised by an expression of poignant worry on de Clameran's face. But this passed away quickly. He made a careless gesture which clearly meant: "As you like!" and he said:

"I believe you reasonable enough to keep our secret."

He immediately bowed ceremoniously and left, closing the door after him with a violence betraying the constraint he was imposing on himself. Clameran nevertheless had reason to fear. Madame Fauvel's strength was not feigned.

478

"Yes!" She exclaimed to herself, burning with the enthusiasm of great resolutions. "Yes, I'm going to tell André everything."

But at that same moment, just when she was sure she was alone, she heard someone walking near her. Abruptly she turned around. Madeleine came forward, paler and colder than a statue, her eyes full of tears.

"You must obey that man, Aunt," she whispered.

There were two little rooms on either side of the drawing room, two game rooms separated only by simple tapestry hangings. Madeleine, without her aunt's suspecting it, was in one of those little rooms when the Marquis de Clameran arrived and had overheard the conversation

"What!" Madame Fauvel cried out, stunned, "You know…"

"Everything, Aunt."

"And you want me to sacrifice you?"

"I ask you on my knees to allow me to save you."

"But it's impossible for you not to hate Monsieur de Clameran."

"I hate him, Aunt, and I despise him. For me, he is and always will be, the last and the most cowardly of men; and, nevertheless, I will be his wife."

"And Prosper, poor child," she continued, "Prosper, that you love?"

Madeleine stifled a sob that rose in her throat, and with a firm voice answered:

"As of tomorrow, I'll have broken off with Monsieur Bertomy forever."

"No!" Madame Fauvel cried out, "It won't be said that I've let you, you an innocent girl, carry the crushing burden of my sins."

The noble and courageous girl sadly shook her head.

"It won't be said," she continued, "that I'll let dishonor enter this house, which is mine, when I can prevent it. Don't I owe you more than life? What would I be without you? A poor working girl in my region's factories. Who took me in? You. Don't I owe my uncle for the fortune that tempts this miserable man? Aren't Abel and Lucien my brothers? And when the happiness of us all is threatened, could I hesitate!…No! I will be the Marquise de Clameran."

Then there began a battle of generosity between Madame Fauvel and her niece, so much more sublime in that each offered her life for the other, and was giving it, not in a moment of excitement, but of her free will and after deliberation. But Madeleine had to win, carried away as she was with the saintly enthusiasm of sacrifice which makes martyrs.

"I have no one to answer to but myself," she kept repeating, understanding quite well that that was the place where she must strike. "You, dear Aunt, are accountable to your husband and to your children. Think of my uncle's sadness if he ever learns the truth! He would die from it."

The generous young girl was telling the truth. Such was the fatal linking of circumstances which had always been decreed for Madame Fauvel, by the appearance of a great duty to fulfill. So after having sacrificed her husband for her mother, she was now sacrificing her husband and her children for Raoul. Madame Fauvel was still forbidding, but she was resisting more and more feebly.

"No," she said, "No. I can't accept your devotion. What would your life be like with that man?"

"Who knows?" said Madeleine, pretending a hope very far from her heart. "From what he says, he loves me. Perhaps he will be good to me. Ah! If I knew where I could get a large amount of money! It's money he wants, that man, nothing but money. Does he really need it for Raoul? Isn't it Raoul who, by his follies, has opened an abyss which has to be filled? If only I could believe in Monsieur de Clameran's sincerity."

It was with a sort of stupefied curiosity that Madame Fauvel looked at her niece. What! The young girl, so naïve and so lacking in experience, was being logical about her self-denial, while she, a woman and a mother of a family, had only obeyed the instinctive impulses of her mind and of her heart!

"What do you mean?" she asked her.

"I wonder, Aunt, if Monsieur de Clameran is really thinking about his nephew. Has he, yes or no, the formal intention of coming to his aid? When he's in control of my dowry, wouldn't he abandon you and him? Finally, there is a doubt that tortures me."

"A doubt?"

"Yes, and I would put it before you, if I dared...If I were not afraid..."

"Speak," insisted Madame Fauvel. "Tell me all that you think. Alas! Misfortune has given me strength. What do I have to fear? I can hear anything."

Madeleine hesitated, torn between the fear of hurting a beloved person, and the desire to enlighten her.

"I would like to be certain," she finally said, "that Monsieur de Clameran and Raoul don't have an understanding with each other, and are not each playing a role learned and agreed on in advance."

Passion is blind and deaf. Madame Fauvel no longer remembered the two men's laughing eyes, the day that they seemed carried away with anger in front of her. She couldn't, she wouldn't, believe in such a despicable comedy.

"That's impossible," she pronounced. "The Marquis is really indignant about his nephew's conduct, and it's not he who would ever give him bad advice. As for Raoul, he's stubborn, flighty, vain, and prodigal, but he has a good heart. Prosperity has made him drunk, but he loves me. Ah! If you could see him; if you could hear him when I reproach him! All your suspicions would vanish. When he swears to me, with tears in his eyes, that he'll be more sensible, he's in good faith. If he doesn't keep his promises, that's because his wicked friends lead him astray."

Mothers are always taken in and always blame, and will always blame, friends. The friend, that's the guilty one. But Madeleine was too kind even to try to disabuse her aunt.

"May Heaven make what you say to be true!" she whispered. "My marriage won't be useless then. We'll write to Monsieur de Clameran right this evening."

"Why this evening, Madeleine? There's no hurry. We can wait, draw things out, stall for time."

These words, these stubborn hopes in luck, in what might happen, or in nothing, told everything about Madame Fauvel's character, and explained her misfortunes. Madeleine's personality was totally different. Her timidity hid a manly soul. Having decided on a sacrifice, she wanted it to be over with, absolute. She was closing the door to deceptive illusions, and walking straight ahead without looking back.

"It's better to be finished with it, dear Aunt," she said in a firm tone. "Believe me, the reality of misfortune is less painful than waiting for it. Would you like to be free of being alternately sad and joyful? Do you know what these worries that you're hiding have done to you? Have you looked at yourself during the last four months?"

She took her aunt by the hand and led her in front of a mirror.

"There," she added. "Look at yourself."

Madame Fauvel was no longer anything but the shadow of herself. She had come to that traitorous age when a woman's beauty, like that of a rose in full bloom, fades in a day. She had grown old in five months. Worry had put its fatal imprint on her forehead. Her temples, as fresh and unlined as that of a young girl, were wrinkled, as white threads turned her thick hair silver.

"Do you understand now," Madeleine continued, "why you must have security? Do you understand that you've changed to the point that it's a miracle my uncle hasn't become worried about you?"

Madame Fauvel, who thought she had displayed outstanding concealment, made a negative gesture.

"Ah! Poor Aunt, didn't I myself guess that you had a secret?"

"You!"

"Yes! Only I thought…Oh! Forgive an unjust suspicion. I had dared suppose…"

She stopped, very troubled, and it caused her great effort to continue.

"I imagined that you were in love with a man other than my uncle."

Madame Fauvel couldn't hold back a moan. Others might also have had Madeleine's suspicion.

"My honor is lost," she whispered.

"No, dear Aunt, No!" exclaimed the young girl. "Be reassured and take courage. There are two of us to fight now. We'll defend ourselves. We'll save ourselves."

Monsieur de Clameran must have been happy that evening. A letter from Madame Fauvel told him that she consented to everything. She asked only a little time. Madeleine, she told him, couldn't break off with Monsieur Bertomy from one day to the next. Then one must expect objections on the part of Monsieur Fauvel, who loved Prosper and had tacitly settled with him.

A line from Madeleine at the bottom of her aunt's letter confirmed her agreement. Poor young girl! She wasn't very tactful. Just the next day she took Prosper aside; and taking advantage of her ascendancy over him, she tore from him that fatal promise not to try to see her again, and to take the responsibility for the rupture on himself.

He had begged Madeleine to at least tell him the reasons for that exile that would destroy his life. She had simply answered him that her honor and her personal happiness depended on his obedience.

And he went away, his soul dead. The Marquis de Clameran arrived almost on his footsteps. Yes, he had the audacity to come, in person, to tell Madame Fauvel that from the moment he had her word and that of her niece, he consented to wait. Then holding both the aunt and the niece, he wasn't worried. He told himself that a time would come when a deficit, impossible to cover, would make them wish for and hurry his marriage. Raoul was doing everything to hasten that moment. Madame Fauvel, having gone to stay at her property earlier than usual, on his side, Raoul had set himself up at Vésinet. But the country didn't make him any more economical. Little by little, he had dropped all hypocrisy. He no longer came to see his mother except when he needed money. And he needed a lot of it and often. As for the Marquis, he kept himself prudently apart, watching for the proper time, and it came by chance. Three weeks earlier he had been invited to dine at the banker's. It was a large gathering with at least twenty invited guests. The dessert had just been served and conversations were becoming animated when, all of a sudden, the banker turned toward Clameran.

"I must ask you something, Marquis le Marquis. Do you have any relatives bearing your name?"

"At least not that I know of, Monsieur."

"That's because I myself made the acquaintance of another Marquis de Clameran, a week ago."

As hardened by impudence as the Marquis de Clameran was, as armed as his mind was against the surprises of all events, he was disconcerted for a moment and turned pale.

'Oh! Oh!" he stammered, not without self-control. "A Clameran marquis…The title of Marquis is probably mine, at least."

Monsieur Fauvel wasn't displeased to find an opportunity to tease a guest whose pretensions to nobility had sometimes annoyed him.

"Marquis or not, the Clameran in question seems to me to be in a position to do honor to the title. He's rich. I at least have every reason to believe he has a large fortune. I have been entrusted on his behalf with a deposit of 400,000 francs, by one of my correspondents."

Clameran was marvelously in control of himself. He had trained his face not to betray any of his emotions. However, this time what was happening was so bizarre, so surprising, and had the possibility of such menace, that his usual assurance by his prompt recovery failed him. He found an ironic tone in the banker, an unusual air that put him on his guard. For those people who had no interest in watching him, he stayed the same. But Madeleine and her aunt had noticed his start. They had caught a rapid glance at Raoul.

"It appears," he asked, "that this new Marquis is a business man?"

"*Ma foi!* You're asking me too much. All I know is that the 400,000 francs are supposed to be paid to him by some Le Havre ship owners, after the sale of the cargo of a Brazilian ship."

"Then he's coming from Brazil?"

"I don't know that; but I can, if you wish, tell you his first name."

"Please."

The banker got up and went into the drawing room to pick up a Moroccan dispatch case stamped with his monogram. He took out a notebook and began to flip through it, muttering under his breath the names he found there.

"Wait," he said, "wait...the 22nd, no, it's later...Ah! Here we are: Clameran, Gaston. His name is Gaston."

But this time Louis didn't wince. He'd had time to compose himself, and to get together enough audacity to fend off whatever blow.

"Gaston!" He replied in a casual way. "I see. This gentleman must be the son of one of my father's sisters whose husband lived in Havana. Coming back to France, he just picked up his mother's name, better sounding than that of his father, which was, if I remember correctly, Moirot or Boirot."

The banker had put his notebook down on a piece of furniture of the dining room.

"Boirot or Clameran," he said, "I'll have you to dinner with him before long, I imagine. Of the 400,000 that I am to deposit for him, he wants only 100,000 sent to him, and asks me to keep the rest in a checking account for him, because he intends to come to Paris."

"I really wouldn't be displeased to meet him."

They talked of other things, and soon Clameran seemed to have completely forgotten what the banker had said. It's true, while talking the gayest way in the world, he never stopped watching Madame Fauvel and her niece. They were troubled in a different way than he, and their trouble was visible. They never stopped exchanging looks on the sly, the most significant looks. Evidently, the same terrible thought had crossed their mind. Madeleine seemed more moved than her aunt. Just at the moment the banker had pronounced the name of Gaston, she had seen, she wasn't mistaken, she had seen Raoul lean back in his chair and glance toward the window, like the surprised robber who looks for an exit through which to flee. And since that moment, Raoul, not as hardened as his uncle, remained abashed. Usually a shining lively talker, he had turned completely silent. He was studying Louis' behavior. Finally, the dinner over, the guests rose to go into the drawing room. Clameran and Raoul maneuvered so as to be the last ones in the dining room.

"That's him!" Raoul said.

"I believe so."

"Then everything is lost. Let's get out."

But Clameran, the audacious adventurer, wasn't the man to throw in the towel before he had to.

"Who knows?" he whispered, while the frowns on his forehead showed how hard he was thinking. "Who knows! Why didn't this miserable banker tell us where to find this damned Clameran?"

He stopped, exclaiming with joy. On the buffet he had just noticed the notebook Monsieur Fauvel had consulted.

"Keep a lookout," he said to Raoul.

He seized the notebook and flipped through it feverishly. He found: *Gaston, Marquis de Clameran, Oloron (Basses-Pyrénées).*

"Are we any further along now that we have his address?" Raoul asked.

"This means we may be saved. Come on. Our absence must not be noticed. Keep your head, *Morbleu!* Keep up appearances, be gay! I saw the moment when your looks almost gave us away."

"The two women suspect something."

"Well? So what?"

"It's not safe for us here."

"Was it better in London? Have confidence! We'll pull it off. I'm going to organize my tactics."

They rejoined the other guests. But if their conversation hadn't been overheard, their gestures had been observed. Madeleine, who had gone forward on tiptoe, had seen Clameran consult the banker's notebook. But how could looking at that notebook help the Marquis? She no longer had to doubt the infamy of that man, to whom she had promised her hand. He had firmly told Raoul that whatever happened, neither Madeleine nor her aunt could get themselves out of his control. To do so would mean they had to talk, to confess.

Two hours later, when Clameran took Raoul back as far as Vésinet, his plan was complete.

"That's he; I have no doubt," he said. "But you, my handsome nephew, have gotten alarmed too soon."

"Thank you! The banker is expecting him. We may have him on us tomorrow."

"Be quiet!" interrupted Clameran. "Does he know, or does he not know, that Fauvel is Valentine's husband? Everything is in that. If he knows that, we'll just have to take to our legs. If he doesn't know it, nothing is desperate."

"How can we find that out?"

"Simply by going to ask him."

Raoul made a movement of admiration.

"That's lovely," he said, "but dangerous."

"It would be even more dangerous to do nothing. As for skipping out because of a simple suspicion, that would be too stupid."

"And who will go find him?"

"Me!"

"Oh!" said Raoul in two different tones, "Oh! Oh!"

Clameran's audacity stunned him.

"But me?" he asked.

"You'll remain here. At the least danger, I'll send you a telegram and you can get out."

They had arrived at the gate in front of Raoul's house.

"Here's what's understood," said Clameran. "You'll stay here. But be careful during my absence. Return to being the best of sons. Take a position against me. Slander me if you can. But no stupidity! No demands for money. So, goodbye! I'll be in Oloron tomorrow and I'll have seen this Clameran."

Chapter XVIII

It wasn't without the greatest danger, without infinite trouble, that Gaston de Clameran had managed to flee when he left Valentine. He would never have been able to find a ship without the devotion and experience of his guide. Having left his mother's jewels with Valentine, he possessed as his total fortune 920 francs; and it wasn't with that paltry sum that a fugitive, who's just killed two men, pays for his passage aboard a ship. But Menoul, an old sailor, was a resourceful man. While Gaston stayed hidden in a farm in Camargue, Menoul reached Marseille. Beginning the first evening, hurrying through the cabarets frequented by sailors, he learned that a three-masted American ship lay at anchor. The captain, Monsieur Warth, a merchantman without prejudices, would consider it a pleasure to give asylum to a solid fellow who would be useful to him at sea, without worrying about his background. After having visited the ship and drunk a glass of rum with the captain, Père Menoul had gone back to get Raoul.

"If it was me," he told him, "I would do it, but you..."

"What you can do, I can do."

"The fact is, you see, you'll have to slave hard. You'll be an able-bodied seaman, for God's sake! And to tell you everything, the ship doesn't seem to me to be the most catholic, and the boss gives me the idea he's a proud rascal."

"We don't have a choice," Gaston answered. "Let's go."

It took Gaston a sojourn of only forty-eight hours aboard the *Tom Jones* to be sure, beyond all doubt, that fate had just thrown him into the middle of a remarkable collection of thieves of the worst type.

The crew, recruited a little from everywhere, was a sample of scoundrels from every country. But what did these people, among whom he was condemned to live for some months, matter to him! It was only his body the ship was carrying away toward new countries. His thoughts rested under the cool shade trees of the La Verberie Park, near his dearly beloved Valentine. What was going to become of the poor child, now that he was no longer there to love her, to console her, to defend her! Fortunately, he had neither the time nor the strength to reflect. What was the most terrible in his present situation, he didn't feel. Tied to the harsh apprenticeship of an able-bodied seaman, as one who hadn't been used to it since childhood, he hardly had enough energy to hold up under the excessive physical labor. That was his salvation. Physical fatigue calmed and deadened his moral pain. In the hours of rest, when he was allowed to stretch out on his bunk, he slept. If sometimes, with poignant anxiety, he forced himself to question the future, it was when the weather was good at night, about 4:00 a.m., when the ship had no need of any handling.

He had said he would return before three years were out, and he would return rich, to satisfy Madame de La Verberie's demands. Could he keep that presumptuous promise? If desire has wings, reality slowly drags along the ground. Now, according to what he heard those around him saying, he wasn't exactly on the road to that so much desired fortune. The *Tom Jones* had perhaps set sail for Valparaiso, but to get there it was, for certain, taking the longest route. That was because Captain Warth intended to visit the Coast of Guinea. One of his black prince friends, he said with a huge laugh, was waiting for him in the vicinity of Badagri. He would put into his care for some *pipes*[46] of rum and a hundred or so bad flint-lock rifles, and a whole cargo of "ebony wood."

To tell the truth, Gaston de Clameran was serving as a novice on one of those ships destined, at that time, for the free and philanthropic American slave trade, which each year they loaded by the hundreds. That discovery filled Gaston with anger and shame, but he was wise enough to hide his impressions. All his arguing wouldn't have disgusted the worthy Captain Warth. He was dealing in a traffic whose profit exceeded one hundred percent, despite the French and English ships patrolling the Atlantic, despite the losses in the cargo, and despite a great number of other risks.

If the men on the ship had relative consideration for Gaston, it was because Père Menoul had told the captain the story of the knife fight. To let his opinions be known would be to create, without necessity or usefulness, an impossible situation. He held his tongue, swearing he would desert as soon as a somewhat favorable opportunity presented itself. The unfortunate thing was that opportunity, like everything that's waited for with impatience, didn't come. The fact was that at the end of three months, Monsieur Warth could no longer do without Gaston. Recognizing a superior intelligence, he had made him a friend; he had him eat at his table; he took great pleasure in hearing him talk. He insisted on his taking a hand in a game of piquet. He liked him so well that, the second mate having died, Gaston was chosen to replace him. And it was in that situation that he made two successive trips to the Gulf of Guinea. It was as second mate that he helped pick up one thousand Negroes in two trips, stowing them away in the ship, guarding them during the passage of twelve thousand to fifteen thousand leagues, and finally dropping them clandestinely on the coast of Brazil.

It was more than three years since Gaston had set sail from Marseille, when the *Tom Jones* finally dropped anchor at Rio de Janeiro, before he could take leave of Captain Warth. Captain Warth was an honest man after all. He would never have resigned himself to the diabolical and repugnant commerce in human flesh, if he hadn't wanted to give his little Mary, an angel, a magnificent dowry.

These trips had at least been profitable for Gaston. He possessed very nearly 12,000 francs in savings when he set foot on Brazilian soil. However, the three years he had set for his return had passed. But perhaps Valentine had wait-

---

[46] Ancient liquid measurement.

ed before doing anything. He wrote to one of his friends who lived in Beaucaire, in whom he could have total confidence. He thirsted for news of his country, his family, and his friends. He also wrote to his father, to whom he had tried to reach by letter as often as he had the opportunity. It was only in the following year that he received a letter from his friend. With the same blow, that letter told him that his father was dead, that his brother, Louis, had left the country, that Valentine had married, and finally, that he had been condemned *in absentia* to several years in prison for murder.

That letter floored him. Henceforth he was alone in the world, without a country, dishonored by legal condemnation. With Valentine married, he saw no other reason for living. But he wasn't a man to be brought down.

"Then I'll earn money, since it's only money here below that you can count on," he cried out in rage. And he started to work with bitter activity, stirred each morning with renewed will. Gaston tried every method of making a fortune that the empire of Brazil offered to adventurers. One after the other, he speculated in the slave trade; he invested in a mine; he cleared land. Five times he went to bed rich, and woke up ruined. Five times, with the patience of the beaver whose dam is washed away by the current, he started again to build his fortune. Finally, after long years, very long years of fighting, he possessed nearly 1,000,000 in cash and vast land holdings. He had told himself that he would never leave Brazil, and that he would end his days in Rio de Janeiro. He wasn't counting on that love of one's native soil which never dies in a Frenchman's heart. Rich, he wanted to die in France. Soon he had made the preparations necessary in his situation. He made sure that, going back, he would have no reason to be worried. He turned into cash what he could of his holdings, entrusted the rest to a friend, and took a ship. It had been twenty-three years and three months since he had fled, that one beautiful day in 1866, when he set foot on the Bordeaux quays. He had left as a young man, his heart swollen with hope. He returned with gray hair, no longer believing in anything.

A factory was for sale, near Oloron, on the banks of the Gave River. He bought it, thinking of finding a way to use the immense quantities of timber which were lost in the mountains, with no methods of transport. He had already been set up there for several weeks, when one evening, his servant brought him the calling card of a stranger who wanted to see him. He took that card and read:

Louis de Clameran

"My brother!" he finally exclaimed. "My brother!"

And leaving his servant there, completely astounded, even somewhat frightened by his master's exclamation, he dashed toward the stairway. In the middle of the vestibule, a man, Louis de Clameran, stood waiting. Gaston rushed toward him; and after having hugged him in his arms, almost stifling him, he led him, or, rather, he carried him into the drawing room. There he made him sit down, and sat down himself across from him as near as possible, so as to see him better, to look at him more at ease. He had taken his two hands and kept them in his own.

"It's you," he kept repeating, speaking very loudly, as if to comprehend better, to prove the reality to himself, "You! My beloved Louis, my brother…You, it's you!"

Gaston, that man whose life had been like a continual storm, could no longer contain himself. He, the adventurer, the second- in-command of the feared Captain Warth, the searcher for gold in the mines of Villa-Rica, he cried and laughed all at the same time. "I would have recognized you," he said to his brother. "Yes, I would have recognized you. Yes, the expression of your face hasn't changed; you really have the same look; your smile is still what it was in the past."

Louis was in fact smiling, perhaps as he had smiled that fatal night when the fall of his horse had delivered up Gaston. He was smiling; he looked happy; he looked delighted. One of those agonies which would make a man's hair turn white had gone through him, when he lifted Gaston's door knocker. His teeth were chattering with fear when he said to the servant, holding out his card:

"Take this to your master."

And waiting for the return of the servant, whose absence had seemed to him to last for centuries, he asked himself:

"Is it really he? And if it is he, does he know, does he suspect?"

His anxiety was so great, that at the moment he saw Gaston coming down the stairs like a whirlwind, he was tempted to flee. Now he saw that Gaston had stayed the same—good, trusting, and credulous. Now that he was almost certain that suspicion hadn't crossed his brother's mind, he was reassured and smiling.

"Finally," Gaston went on, "I'll no longer be alone in the world. I'll have someone to love, to love me."

And then he suddenly stopped, with that lack of coherence of all strong emotions which break the mind's balance.

"Are you married?" he asked him.

"No."

"Too bad! Yes, too bad! I would've wished to see you the husband of some very devoted good woman, and the father of beautiful children. How I would've been excited to open my heart to all those people. Your family would've been mine. The family that must be so good, so sweet. To live alone, without an adored wife who would share the sadness and the joy, the difficulties and the successes, that's not to live. Having only yourself to think about, how sad! But, what am I saying? I've said enough to you, haven't I? Louis! So I have a brother, a friend I can chat with aloud, as I chat silently with myself."

"Yes, Gaston, yes, a good friend!"

"*Parbleu!* So you're my brother, Ah! You're not married! Well! We'll live together. We're going to live like bachelors, like old bachelors, happy as gods.

We'll amuse ourselves. We'll joke with each other. Think of that! What an idea! You're making me young again. I seem to feel I'm only twenty years old, that I'm as limber and vigorous as the times I swam across the Rhone. That was a long time ago, however, and since then I've fought, I've suffered, and I've grown cruelly old, changed."

"You!" interrupted Louis, "You've aged less than I."

"What a joke!"

"I swear to you."

"You would've recognized me?"

"Perfectly. You've remained yourself."

Louis was telling the truth. He himself appeared worn out, rather than grown old. But Gaston, despite his gray hair, despite his complexion which had taken on the shades of brick in the Brazilian sun, was still the robust man in the prime of life, in the full maturity of his male beauty.

"But how did you find me?" Gaston asked. "What good idea, what good fairy has guided you right to my door?"

"It's Providence you need to thank for our reunion. Three days ago in my group of friends, a young man arrived from Eaux-Bonnes told me that he had heard about a Marquis de Clameran, in the Pyrénées. You can imagine my surprise. I wondered what forger was allowing himself to carry our name. So, I hurried to the train station, and here I am.

"Then you didn't think it was me?"

"Ah! Poor brother, for twenty-three years I've thought you were dead."

"Dead!...Me! Ah! So. Then Mademoiselle de la Verberie, Valentine, didn't let you know I'd escaped? She swore to me that she'd go to my father."

Louis took on the expression of a man forced, in spite of himself, to reveal a sad truth.

"Alas!" he whispered. "She didn't tell us anything."

A glimpse of anger passed like lightening through Gaston's eyes. Perhaps he had the idea that Valentine was glad to be rid of him.

"Nothing!" he exclaimed. "She didn't say anything. She had the cruelty to let you mourn my death; she let my father die of sadness. Ah! She had a terrible fear of what people would say. She sacrificed me to her reputation."

"But, you," Louis interrupted. "Why didn't you write?"

"I wrote as soon as I could, and it was through Lafourcade that I learned our father was dead and you'd had left the country."

"I left Clameran because I thought you were dead."

Gaston got up and walked haphazardly around the drawing room. He wanted to shake off the sadness that had come over him.

"*Bast!*" he murmured. "Why worry about the past? All the memories in the world, good or bad, are not worth the slightest bit of hope. *Dieu Merci!* The future is before us."

Louis was silent. He didn't know the ground well enough yet to risk a question.

"But look how I'm going on," Gaston continued. "I talk and talk, and you may not have had dinner."

"I'll have to admit I haven't."

"And you didn't say anything! But me too, I haven't yet dined. On the first day, I'm going to let you die of hunger. Ah! I have a particularly good Cap wine…"

And he snatched all the bell pulls; in a moment the whole household was in motion, and a half-hour later the two brothers were seated in front of a table sumptuously loaded with food. The conversation between the two brothers must have been unending. Gaston wanted to know everything that had happened after his departure.

"And Clameran?" he asked when Louis had finished.

Louis hesitated a moment. Should he, or should he not, tell the truth?

"I sold Clameran," he said.

"Even the chateau?"

"Yes."

"I can understand that," Gaston murmured, "Although me, in your place…there where our ancestors lived, there where our father died…"

But seeing he was making his brother sad:

"*Bast!* It's in the heart that memories live, and not in the middle of old stones. Such as you see me, I haven't dared go back to Provence. I would have suffered too much seeing Clameran, the La Verberie Park before me. I had the only beautiful days of my life there."

Louis's expression lit up. The certainty that Gaston hadn't gone to Provence chased away one of his most pressing worries. The two brothers were still talking at 2:00 a.m. And the next day Louis found an excuse to hurry to the telegraph office and send this telegram to Raoul:

Wisdom and Caution. Follow my instructions. Everything is going well. Good Hope.

All was going well, and nevertheless Louis, despite his cleverly calculated questions, had obtained none of the information he'd come looking for. Gaston so talkative, Gaston, who had told him the entire story of his life, insisting on the least circumstances, hadn't said a word which could enlighten him. Was this chance or calculation, premeditated wisdom, or simple forgetfulness? Louis wondered about this, with the worry of perverse people, always disposed to wish off on others their own perversity. At any cost, and if it was necessary to depart from his reserve, he resolved to get things out in the open and to see clearly into his brother's mind. The moment was favorable when they sat down at the table for lunch.

"Do you know, my dear Gaston," he began, "up until now we have talked about everything except, however, important things."

"The devil! What's wrong with you that makes your expression look like a that of a lawyer?"

"The fact is, my dear brother, that believing you dead, I received our father's inheritance."

A burst of frank laughter from Gaston cut short his words.

"Is that what you call serious things?"

"Certainly. I must give you an accounting of your part of the inheritance. You have a right to half…"

"I have a right," Gaston interrupted, "to ask you to please close this chapter. What you have is yours. There is a law regarding the statute of limitations."

"No, I can't accept it."

"What! The inheritance from our father? No, not only can you, but you must. Our father wanted only one person to inherit. Let's submit to his will."

And believing he saw a cloud on his brother's brow:

"Oh, well," he added gaily, "Are you either very rich or believe I'm very poor to insist like this?"

Louis trembled imperceptibly at that question, which got to the heart of the matter. What could he answer that wouldn't commit himself?

"I'm neither rich nor poor," he said.

"Me!" Gaston exclaimed. "I'd be almost delighted to find you poorer than Job, so I could share with you all that I have."

The lunch finished, Gaston threw down his napkin and rose, saying:

"Come! I still want to show you my…that is to say, *our* property."

While following his brother, Louis was as tormented as possible. It seemed to him that Gaston was avoiding with unusual stubbornness the confidential ground onto which he was trying to draw him. Was his casual attitude then only a comedy? Louis' mistrust was again aroused; he almost regretted his telegram of the evening before. But nothing of the disturbing thoughts agitating him inside appeared on the surface. His expression was calm and smiling, his voice joyous.

He was shown everything in detail, the house first of all, then the servants' quarters, the stables, and the dog kennels, then the vast and well-planted gardens, at the end of which the Gave River on its stony bed sang its mountain song.

The factory in full operation was located at the extreme end of a pretty prairie. Gaston still had the enthusiasm of a new owner. He didn't let his brother miss either one file or one hammer. He told him his future plans, how he expected to substitute timber for coal, to improve and still take advantage of the savings by exploiting the riches of the forest, until then considered almost impossible to reach.

Louis approved everything, but he answered only with monosyllables.

"Yes! True! Very good!"

492

Because now a new sadness, which he had to hide along with the others, tormented him. That prosperity, whose evidence jumped out at him, grieved him. Comparing his brother's fate to his own, all the poisoned needles of jealousy tore into his envious heart. Seeing Gas-ton rich, happy, honored, and reaping the rewards of his courage, while he... Never had he so cruelly resented the horror of a situation which was his own creation. At twenty years distance, the shameful and vile sentiments which had made him hate his brother returned.

However, with the inspection finished:

"What do you say about my acquisitions?" Gaston asked happily.

"I say, dear brother, that you possess, in the middle of the most beautiful country in the world, the most delightful property which could tempt a poor Parisian."

"Is that really what you think?"

"Without restrictions."

"Ah! Well, brother, that property," he exclaimed, "is ours, since it's mine. It pleases you? Don't ever leave it. Do you really cling to your Paris fogs? Come establish yourself here, under the beautiful sky of Bearn."

Louis didn't say anything. These proposals one year before would have filled him with joy. With what joy he would have greeted the prospects of that beautiful and large existence! What a delightful rest after so many roads traveled! He would have been able to slough off the old man, the adventurer, and be himself again. But he couldn't accept now, and he recognized it with rage. No, he wasn't free. No, he couldn't leave Paris. There he had engaged in one of those frightful gambles, that one loses when one abandons them, and the loss of them leads to jail. Alone, he could disappear, but he wasn't alone. He had an accomplice.

"You're not giving any answer," insisted Gaston, surprised at this silence. "Can you see any obstacle to my plans?"

"None."

"Well, then?"

"The situation is, dear brother, that without the salary of a position I hold in Paris, I wouldn't have anything to live on."

"Ah, and that's your objection—you who, a minute ago, offered me half of the paternal inheritance! Louis, this is bad; it's very bad. Either you haven't understood or you are a bad brother."

Louis bowed his head. Gaston, very unknowingly, turned and twisted the knife in the wound.

"I would be a burden on you," murmured Louis.

"A burden! But you're going mad. Haven't I told you that I'm very rich? Do you think you've seen all I possess! That house and that factory don't constitute a quarter of my fortune. I got them for a song. Do you think I'd risk what I've earned in twenty years on such an enterprise? I have a good 80,000 pounds of income in Government Funds. And that's not all. It appears that my operations in Brazil will be sold. I'm lucky! My friend has already sent me 400,000 francs."

Louis trembled with pleasure. Finally, he was going to learn just to what point he was in danger.

"What friend?" he asked, looking as uninterested as he could.

"*Parbleu!* My former associate in Rio. The funds are right now available to me with my banker in Paris."

"One of your friends?"

"*Ma foi!* No. He was recommended to me by my banker in Pau as being a very rich man, prudent, and of well-known honesty. He is, wait a minute, his name is...Fauvel, who lives on the Rue de Provence."

As master of himself as Louis was, as prepared as he was for what he was going to hear, he paled and turned visibly red. But Gaston, absorbed in his own thoughts, didn't notice it.

"Do you know this banker?"

"By reputation, yes."

"Then together we'll make his acquaintance very soon, because I propose to accompany you when you return to Paris, to arrange your affairs there before getting settled here."

At that unexpected announcement of a plan, the realization of which could doom him, Louis had the strength to remain impassive. He felt his brother's gaze fixed on him.

"You yourself will go to Paris," he said.

"Certainly, what's unusual in that?"

"Nothing."

"I detest Paris, and what's more, I detest it without ever having been there. But I'm called there by..."

He hesitated. "Some serious duties. After all, I've been told Mademoiselle de La Verberie lives in Paris and I want to see her again."

"Ah!"

Gaston was thinking. He was moved and his emotion was visible.

"I can tell you, Louis," he said, "why I want to see her again. In the past I entrusted our mother's jewelry to her."

"And you wish, after twenty-three years, to reclaim what you left with her?"

"Yes...or rather, well, no. That's only a vain pretext that I try to give myself. I want to see her again because...because...I loved her. That's the truth."

"But how can you find her again?"

"Oh! That's very simple. Just anybody in the country will tell me the name of her husband, and when I know that name...So, tomorrow I'll write to Beaucaire."

Louis didn't answer. Above all, Louis was careful not to argue about his brother's plans. To oppose a man's intentions is almost always to drive them

494

deeper into his mind. Each argument has the effect of a hammer on the head of a nail. As a clever man, he changed the subject of conversation. The rest of the day there was no more discussion of Paris or of Valentine. It was only in the evening, when he found himself alone in his bedroom, that, looking the situation resolutely in the face, Louis began to study it in all its aspects. At first sight, it seemed hopeless. Cornered in a position which appeared to him to have no way out, he was close to resigning himself to stop fighting, to give up. Yes, he was wondering if it wouldn't be wise to borrow a huge sum from his brother and to disappear forever. He vainly tortured his mind. His detestable experience could show him no scheme applicable to the present circumstances. From every direction danger threatened, present, impossible to ward off. He had equally to fear Madame Fauvel, her niece, and the banker. Gaston, discovering the truth, would want to avenge himself. His accomplice, Raoul himself, in case things went wrong, would turn against him and become his most implacable enemy. Did there exist any human way to prevent the meeting of Valentine and Gaston? Evidently not. So, the instant of their meeting would be the instant of his fall.

"It's useless for me to search. There's nothing for me to do but to stall for time, nothing but to watch for an opportunity," he thought.

The fall of the horse at Clameran probably told what Louis meant by an "opportunity."

He closed his window, got in bed, and as he was so greatly accustomed to danger, he slept. In the morning, no wrinkle on his forehead revealed the agony of the night. He was affectionate, gay, and chatty, more so than he had been up to that time. He wanted to get mounted on horseback and ride through the countryside. He had suddenly become as active as he had shown himself calm. He talked of nothing but excursions in the area.

The truth was that he wanted to keep Gaston occupied, to amuse him, to get his mind off Paris, and above all, Valentine. With time, using a great deal of cleverness, he didn't despair of dissuading his brother from seeing his former lover again. He counted on showing him that that interview, absolutely useless, would be painful for both of them, embarrassing for him and dangerous for her. As for what he left with her, if Gaston persisted in asking her for it, all right! Louis intended to offer himself for that delicate step! He promised to bring it off successfully and, in fact, he knew where the jewels were. But it wasn't long before he recognized the inanity of his hopes and plans.

"You know," Gaston said to him one day, "I've written..."

Louis knew only too well what he meant. Wasn't that the constant subject of his meditations! However, he put on his most surprised look.

"Written?..." he asked. "Where, to whom, why?"

"To Beaucaire, to Lafourcade, to find out the name of Valentine's husband."

"Then you still think about her?"

"Always."

495

"You aren't giving up seeing her again?"

"Less than ever."

"Alas! Brother, what you're not thinking about is that the woman you love is the wife of another, that she is probably the mother of a family. Will she agree to see you? Do you know if you're not going to upset her life, if you aren't preparing the bitterest regrets for yourself."

"I'm crazy, that's true. I know it, but my madness is dear to me."

He said that in such a way that Louis understood very well that his position was irrevocably fixed. However, he stayed the same, in appearance busy only with pleasurable activities, in reality spending his life worrying about the letters which came to the house. He knew exactly when the mailman came. He always found himself, by chance, in the courtyard to meet him. If he was absent, as well as his brother, he knew where they put the letters which had come during the day, and he dashed there. His surveillance wasn't useless. The following Sunday, among the letters the mailman gave him, he recognized one which bore the postmark of Beaucaire. He slid it rapidly into his pocket, and although he was on the point of mounting on horseback with his brother, he found a pretext to go to his bedroom, incapable as he was to control his impatience.

It really was the expected letter. It was signed, *Lafourcade*. It was a full three pages and contained a mass of details absolutely indifferent to Louis, but here's what it said about Valentine:

Mademoiselle de la Verberie's husband is a very important banker, named André Fauvel. I don't have the honor of knowing him, but I intend to go see him on my next trip to Paris. I have conceived a project which would make the fortune of our area. I intend to submit it to him, and if he thinks it good, I'll solicit the support of his capital. You won't object, I hope, if I use your name as a reference.

Louis was trembling like a man who has just escaped great danger.

"With that letter in my brother's hands," he said, "the only thing I could do is run."

But by delaying, his downfall appeared less certain. Gaston waited for a reply for another week, and then he wrote again. Lafourcade, very surprised, answered immediately. That meant considering everything in the best light, twelve days that Louis still had in front of him.

"And here is the most immediate danger. If that imbecile goes to Paris, if he pronounces the name of Clameran before the banker, everything is finished," he told himself.

Downstairs, Gaston was getting impatient.

"Come on!" he yelled to his brother.

"I'm coming," Louis answered.

He went down, in fact, after having locked up Lafourcade's letter in a secret compartment in his baggage. From that point, he decided on a loan. Having a good sum in his pocket, added to what he already possessed, he could cross over to America, and, *Ma foi!* Raoul could get out of the business however he could. Certainly, he was saddened to see the most beautiful scheme he'd ever put together in his life fail, but the strong man doesn't get stupidly outraged against fate. He makes the best possible use of circumstances.

Beginning the next day, walking with Gaston at dusk on the pretty road leading to the Oloron factory, he set up the prologue to a little story, the conclusion of which would be borrowing 200,000 francs. They were walking along slowly, arm in arm, when, about a kilometer from the forge, they ran across a very young man dressed like the workers who travel around France, and who, passing, greeted them. Louis staggered so violently that Gaston had to catch him.

"What's wrong with you?" he asked, completely astonished.

"Nothing. I struck a rock with the end of my foot, which hurt me."

He was lying, and the trembling of his voice should have told Gas-ton so. If he was so upset, that was because in the young worker he had recognized Raoul de Lagors. From that moment, Louis de Clameran was completely shattered. The surprise, an instinctive terror, paralyzed and absolutely destroyed his audacious verve and talk. He was no longer in the conversation. He said, without being aware of what he said:

"Yes, of course, really! Perhaps."

Why was Raoul in Oloron? What had he come to do there? Why had he disguised himself as a workman? Since he had been at Oloron, Louis had written almost every day to Raoul and hadn't received any answer. This silence which at first he had found natural, he now judged extraordinary, inexplicable. Fortunately, Gaston felt tired that evening. He spoke of going back a great deal sooner than usual, and as soon as he had returned to the house, he went to his apartment.

Louis was free, finally! He lit a cigar, telling the servant not to wait up for him. He knew very well that Raoul, if that was really who it was, would prowl around the house and watch for him to come out. His expectations weren't wrong. He had hardly gone a hundred feet down the road, when a man came quickly from behind the bushes surrounding a tree, and stood in front of him. The night being very clear, Louis recognized Raoul.

"What's wrong?" he asked immediately, incapable of controlling his impatience. "What's happened?"

"Nothing."

"What! The situation there isn't threatened?"

"In no way. What's more, I'll say, that without your uncontrolled ambitions, everything would go better."

Louis shouted. It could almost be said that he bellowed with fury.

"Then!" he yelled, "What did you come here to do? Who permitted you to abandon your post at the risk of ruining us?"

"That is my business," said Raoul, in the calmest way in the world.

With a rapid movement, Louis seized the young man's wrists, squeezing them hard enough to make him cry out.

"You're going to explain yourself," he told him, in that harsh and curt voice that shows the imminence of danger. "You're going to tell me the reasons for your strange caprice."

Without any apparent effort, with a strength no one would have thought him capable of, Raoul got himself loose from Louis' grip.

"More gently, *Hein!*" he said in the most provoking tone. "I don't like to be rushed, and I have an answer for you…"

At the same time, he took a revolver half out of his pocket and showed it.

"You're going to explain yourself," Louis insisted, "or if not…"

"If not, what! Then give up once and for all any hope of scaring me. I want to answer you; but no⁺ here, in the middle of this big road, and in the light of the moon. Do you know if someone is watching us or not? All right, come on…"

He jumped the ditch which bordered the road, and started across the fields without caring about the plants he was stepping on.

"Now," Raoul began when they were a rather great distance from the road, "I can, my dear uncle, tell you what brought me here. I got your letters. I read and reread them. You wanted to be careful. I understand that, but you were at the same time so obscure that I didn't understand you. From everything you wrote to me, only one fact stands out clearly: we are threatened with great danger."

"One more reason, you wretched man, to be careful of the plants here."

"Powerfully reasoned. Only, dear, venerated uncle, before confronting the danger, I insist on knowing what it is. I'm a man to put myself in danger, but I like to know what risks I'm running."

"Didn't I tell you to stay quiet?"

Raoul made the quizzical gesture of a Paris street urchin jeering at the naïve gullibility of some nice bourgeois.

"So," he said, "I must have full and entire confidence in you, dear uncle."

"Certainly. Your doubts are absurd after what I've done for you. Who was it who went to find you in London, where you didn't know what to do? Me. Who then gave you a name and a family, to you who had neither a family nor a name? Still me. Who's working right now, after having made the present possible, to prepare a future for you? Me. Always, Me."

To hear better, Raoul had assumed a grotesquely serious pose.

"Superb!" he interrupted. "Magnificent! Splendid! Why don't you, while you're at it, prove to me that you sacrificed yourself for me. You didn't need me, did you, when you came looking for me? So, go on, show me that you're the most generous and the most disinterested of uncles. You'll ask for the Montyon prize and I'll make a note in the margin backing your request.[47]

Clameran was silent. He feared where his anger would lead him.

"So," Raoul continued, "let's stop this childishness, dear uncle. If I came, it was because I know you, because I have in you just the confidence I should have. If it seemed advantageous to you to sacrifice me, you wouldn't have a second's hesitation. In case of danger, you'd save just yourself, and you'd let your dear nephew extricate himself however he could. Oh! Don't protest. That's completely natural. In your place I'd do the same. However, and note this well, I'm not one of those who are tricked without consequences. And with that, let's stop these useless recriminations and bring me up to date..."

Such an accomplice had to be reckoned with; Louis understood that. Far from being shocked, he briefly and clearly recounted the events that had occurred since he had seen his brother. He was almost straightforward on all points except, however, what concerned his brother's fortune, the importance of which he reduced as much as possible. When he had finished:

"Well!" said Raoul, "We're in a fine mess. And do you expect to get out of it?"

"Yes, if you don't betray me."

"I've never yet betrayed anyone, you understand, Marquis. However, how do you intend to do it?"

"I don't know, but I feel I'll find a way. Oh! I'll find it; I have to. You can, you see, go back tranquil. You are running no risk in Paris as much as I do here. I'll keep watch over Gaston."

Raoul was thinking.

"No risk?" he asked "Are you very sure of that?"

"*Parbleu!* We have too tight a grip on Madame Fauvel for her ever to lift her voice against us. She could learn the truth, the real one, the one that only you and I know; but she would still not talk, too happy to escape chastisement for her past sin, the blame of society, and the resentment of her husband."

"That's true," answered Raoul, who had become serious. "We hold my mother, but she's not the one I'm afraid of."

"Who, then?"

"An enemy of your type, oh my respectable uncle, an unforgiving enemy—Madeleine."

Clameran made a disdainful gesture.

"Oh, that one," he said.

"You scoff at her, don't you?" Raoul interrupted with a tone of profound conviction. "Well, you're mistaken. She's devoted to her aunt's well-being, but she hasn't given up. She's promised to marry you. She's sent away Prosper,

---

[47] One of four prizes reinstituted by the Baron de Montyon in 1815, after the Restoration. The one mentioned here is the one for "Virtue," the most courageous act on the part of a poor Frenchman.

who's about to die of sorrow, that's true; but she hasn't given up all hope. You think she's weak, fearful, naïve, don't you? Mistake. She's too strong. She's capable of the most daring plans. Misfortune will give her experience. She's in love, my uncle, and the woman in love defends her love, as a tigress does her little ones. There's the danger."

"She has a 500,000 franc dowry."

"That's true, and at five percent, that's 12,500 francs each. That doesn't matter. If you're wise, you'll give up Madeleine."

"Never! Do you understand?" Clameran cried out. "Never! Rich, I'll marry her. Poor, I'd still marry her. It's not her dowry I want right now; it's her, Raoul, only her. I love her!"

Raoul appeared stunned by his uncle's sudden declaration. He stepped back three steps, raising his arms to heaven, with all the signs of immense surprise.

"Is it possible," he kept repeating, "You love Madeleine...You!...You!"

"Yes," answered Louis in a suspicious tone. "What do you see so extraordinary in that?"

"Nothing, assuredly. Oh! Nothing! Only that beautiful passion explains to me the changes in your conduct. Ah! You love Madeleine! Then, venerated uncle, the only thing left for us to do is turn ourselves in."

"And why, please?"

"Because, uncle, when the heart's committed, the head's lost. That's a common axiom. Generals in love have always lost their battles. A fatal day will come when, mad about Madeleine, you'll sell us for a smile. And she's our enemy, and she's subtle, and she's watching us."

With a burst of laughter too loud to be sincere, Louis interrupted his nephew.

"How you suddenly get fired up," he said. "You hate her then very much, that beautiful, that ravishing Madeleine?"

"She's the one who'll doom us."

"Be frank; are you very sure you don't love her?"

As clear as the night was, Louis couldn't see the angry movement which contracted Raoul's features.

"I've never loved anything but the dowry," he answered.

"Then what are you complaining about? Don't I have to pay you half of that dowry? You'll have the money without the woman, the benefits without the expenses."

"Me, I'm not more than fifty years old," said Raoul with a nuance of conceit.

"That's enough," Louis interrupted. "It was agreed, wasn't it, the day I went to snatch you from the most terrible poverty, that I would remain the master."

"Pardon me. You're forgetting that my life, or my freedom at least, is in this gamble. You're holding the cards, but let me advise you."

The two accomplices remained a long time studying and discussing the situation. It was after midnight when Louis thought that by staying any longer he would risk drawing embarrassing questions.

"Let's not discuss things without the facts," he said to Raoul. "I agree with you. Things are such that it's urgent to make a decision. But I can't decide on the spur of the moment. Tomorrow, at this hour, be here. I'll have completed our plan."

"Agreed. Until tomorrow."

"And no imprudence until then!"

"It seems to me, my costume ought to tell you well enough I don't intend to show myself. I've arranged an alibi in Paris so ingenious, that I defy whoever it may be, to prove—legally speaking—that I have left my house in Vésinet. I carried precaution so far as to travel in third class, and that's terribly uncomfortable. So, goodbye! I'm going back to my inn."

He went away on these words, without suspecting that he had just aroused in his accomplice a great number of suspicions.

During the course of his adventurous life, Clameran had organized enough "businesses" to know exactly what degree of confidence should be given to accomplices like Raoul. It's known that crooks have their own kind of honesty. Some put it above that of honest people, but that honesty is never the same after the "coup" what it was before. It's at the time of dividing profits that the trouble surfaces. Clameran's distrustful mind already foresaw a thousand subjects for fear and quarrels. Why, he wondered, did Raoul so carefully disguise himself to come here? What is that alibi in Paris? Is he setting a trap for me? I have a hold on him, that's true; but on my side, I'm absolutely at his mercy. All the letters that I've written him since I've been at Gaston's are so many proofs against me. Would he be thinking of revolting, of getting rid of me, of reaping the profits of our enterprise for himself?

Louis didn't close his eyes that night again; but by morning his mind was made up, and it was with feverish impatience that he waited for the evening. His desire to be finished was so great, and so strong was the tension in his thoughts, that he didn't manage that day to be what he had been on other days. Seeing him somber and preoccupied, several times his brother asked him:

"What's wrong with you? Are you sick? Are you keeping some worry from me?"

Finally evening came, and Louis could rejoin Raoul. He found him smoking, stretched out on the grass in the field where they had met the preceding night.

"Well," asked Raoul, "Have you finally decided?"

"Yes, I have two plans whose success I think infallible."

"I'm listening."

Louis seemed to reflect, like a man who wanted to present his thoughts as clearly and as briefly as possible.

"My first plan," he began, "depends on your acceptance. What would you say if I suggested giving up the affair?"

"Oh!"

"Would you agree to disappear, to leave France, to return to London, if I gave you a large sum?"

"It still would have to be known, that sum."

"I can give you 150,000 francs."

Raoul shrugged.

"Respected uncle," he said, "I see with sadness that you don't know me. Oh! Not at all! You use cunning with me, you dissimulate, and this is neither generous nor clever. It's not generous because it betrays our agreements. It's not clever, because—put this clearly into your head—I'm as strong as you."

"I don't understand you anymore."

"Too bad. I myself understand me and that's enough. Oh! I know you, my uncle. I've studied you with the eyes of self-interest, which are good. I've tapped the bottom of your sack. So, if you offer me now 150,000 francs, that's because you're certain to clean up 1,000,000."

Clameran tried to make the gesture of indignant protest of a misunderstood honest man.

He tried:

"You're out of your mind."

"Not at all. I judge the future according to the past. Of the sums snatched from Madame Fauvel—often against my wishes—what did I get? The tenth part, hardly."

"But we have reserve funds..."

"Which are in your hands, dear uncle, that's very true. In this way, if the plot were discovered tomorrow, you would save the cash; while I, with no money, would go take a turn in prison."

These reproaches seemed to sadden Louis.

"Ingrate!" he murmured. "Ingrate!"

"Bravo!" Raoul continued. "You said the right word. But stop this silly talk. Do you want me to prove you cheated me?"

"If you can..."

"So be it. You told me that your brother had only a modest living, didn't you! Well! Gaston has 60,000 francs income at the last accounting. Don't deny it. What's his property here worth? 100,000 écus. How much does he have with Monsieur Fauvel? 400,000 francs. Is that all he possesses? No, because the accounts receivable at the Oloron Bank has been charged with buying stocks for him. You can see, I didn't waste my day."

This was so clear, so precise, that Louis didn't try to answer.

"What the devil!" Raoul continued. "When someone gets mixed up in commanding, he should certainly estimate his strength. You had—we had—

between our hands the most beautiful scheme in the world. What did you do with it?"

"It seems to me…"

"What? That it's lost? That's also my opinion. And by your fault, your very serious mistake."

"You can't control events."

"Yes you can, when you're strong. Imbeciles wait for luck; the clever make it happen. That was agreed when you came looking for me in London. We were supposed to gently ask my dear mother to help us a little, and to be charming toward her, if she behaved with good grace. What happened, however? At the risk of killing the goose that laid the golden egg, you made me torment the poor woman so much that she didn't know where to look."

"It was prudent to move quickly."

"Agreed. Was it also to move quickly that you got it into your head to marry Madeleine? She had to be let in on the secret on that day. Since then, she's supported and advised her aunt. She stirs her up against us. I wouldn't be very surprised if she confessed everything to Monsieur Fauvel, or went to tell everything to the Prefect of Police."

"I love her!"

"Ah! You've already told me that. But all that's nothing. You launched us into an affair without having studied it, without understanding it. There are only idiots, my uncle, who after making a mistake, content themselves with that banal excuse: 'If I had only known!' You should have informed me. Why did you tell me: 'Your father is dead?' Not at all. He's alive, and we've acted in such a way that I can't present myself to him. He has 1,000,000 that he would've given me; I won't have a sou. And he's going to go find his Valentine, and he'll find her, and then—So long!"

Louis interrupted Raoul with a brusque gesture.

"That's enough!" he commanded. "If I've understood everything, I've a sure method for saving everything."

"You! A method! What is it?"

"Oh! That," Louis said in a somber voice, "that's my secret."

Louis and Raoul were silent for more than a minute. And that silence between the two men, in that place in the middle of the night, after the conversation they had just had, was so frightfully significant that both of them shivered. An abominable thought had come to them at the same time. Without a word, without a gesture, they understood each other. It was Louis who first broke the heavy silence.

"So," he said, "you refuse the 150,000 francs to disappear that I suggest? Think about it. There's still time."

"It's all been thought about. I'm sure now that you won't look for a way to cheat me. Between a sure comfortable living and a probable great fortune, I choose the fortune at any risk. I'll succeed or I'll perish with you."

"And you'll obey me?"

"Blindly."

It must have been very certain that Raoul had seen into his accomplice's plan, because he didn't ask him any questions.

"First of all, you're going back to Paris."

"I'll be there the day after tomorrow morning."

"You will, more than ever, be assiduously close to Madame Fauvel. Nothing must happen in the house without your being told."

"That's understood."

Louis placed his hand on Raoul's shoulder, as if to call his attention to what he was going to say.

"You have a way," he continued, "to regain all your mother's confidence. That's to blame me for all your past wrongs. Don't miss using it. The more odious you make me to Madame Fauvel and Madeleine, the better you'll help me. If they shut the door of the house to me on my return, I'd be delighted. As for the two of us, we must, in appearance, we must have had a falling out for life. If you continue to see me, it's because you couldn't do anything else. That's the theme. It's up to you to develop it."

Raoul received these instructions, unusual at least, with the most surprised air in the world.

"What!" he exclaimed. "You adore Madeleine and that's how you try to please her? That's a funny way to court her. I'll be hanged if I understand."

"You don't need to understand."

"All right!" Raoul said in the most submissive tone. "Very well."

But Louis changed his mind, telling himself that only the man who at least suspects the import of a mission can execute it well.

He asked Raoul: "Have you heard about the man who, to have the right to hold the beloved woman in his arms, set fire to the house?"

"Yes. So?"

"Well! At a certain moment, I'll command you, morally, to set fire to Madame Fauvel's house, and I'll save her as well as her niece."

With his voice and a gesture, Raoul approved his uncle.

"Not bad," he said when he had finished, "really not bad."

"So," Louis pronounced, "everything is well understood?"

"Everything, but write to me."

"Naturally, and you do the same if anything new comes up in Paris."

"You'll have a telegram."

"And don't lose sight of my rival, the cashier."

"Prosper! There's no danger there. Poor boy! He's now my best friend. Sadness has pushed him into a path where he'll perish. True! There are some days when I really want to feel sorry for him."

"Feel sorry for him. Don't hold back."

They exchanged a last handshake and separated, in appearance the best

504

friends in the world, in reality hating each other with all their might.

Gaston no longer seemed to remember that he'd written to Beaucaire, and he didn't pronounce Valentine's name even once. Like all men who, having worked a great deal in their life, need exercise and activity, Gaston was passionate about his new enterprise. The enterprise seemed to occupy him entirely. It was losing money when he bought it, and he had sworn to himself that he'd make it a fruitful operation for himself, and for the area. He had attached to himself a young engineer, and already, thanks to rapid improvements and thanks to different changes in methodology, they had arrived at the point of breaking even.

"We'll make our expenses this year," Gaston joyously said, "but next year we'll earn 25,000 francs."

Next year! Alas!

Five days after Raoul's departure, on a Saturday afternoon, Gas-ton suddenly found himself indisposed. He was sensitive to light and had vertigo, to the point that it was completely impossible for him to remain standing.

"I know about that," he said. "I've often had these dizzy spells in Rio. Two hours of sleep will cure me. I'm going to bed. Let them wake me up for dinner."

But at dinner time, when they went upstairs to tell him, he was far from feeling better. A horrible headache had followed the vertigo. His temples were throbbing with an unheard of violence. He experienced an indescribable constricted feeling and dryness in his throat.

That wasn't all. His swollen tongue no longer obeyed his thoughts and said the wrong things. He wanted to pronounce one word and articulated another, as happens in some cases of dysphonia[48] and accidental mutism. Finally, all his jaw muscles became rigid, and he could open and close his mouth only with painful effort.

Louis, who had gone upstairs to be near his brother, wanted to call a doctor. Gaston opposed it.

"Your doctor," he said, "would give me drugs and make me sick. I just have an indisposition which I know how to remedy." At the same time, he ordered Manuel, his servant, an old Spaniard in his service for ten years, to prepare him a lemonade.

The next day, in fact, Gaston seemed a great deal better. He got up, ate with a rather good appetite, but at the same time in the evening the symptoms returned, more violently.

That time, without consulting Gaston, Louis sent to Oloron for a doctor. Doctor C. owed an almost European reputation to certain cures at Eaux Bonnes. The doctor declared that it was nothing; and he limited himself to ordering the application of several plasters, on the surface of which they were to pour out some drops of morphine. He also prescribed taking some valerian.

---

[48] Disturbance of normal vocal function.

But, in the night, during the approximately three hours that Gaston rested somewhat quietly, the course of the malady suddenly changed. All the symptoms on the side of the head disappeared, to be replaced by terrible oppression, so painful that the sick man had not a minute of remission. He tossed and turned on his bed without find a position he could tolerate. The Doctor C., who came toward daylight, seemed a little surprised, even disconcerted at the change. He asked if, to calm the pain more rapidly, they hadn't exaggerated the dose of morphine. The servant Manuel, who had attended his master, answered that he hadn't. After having examined Gaston's vital signs, the doctor then examined his joints carefully, and saw that some were beginning to swell and become painful. He prescribed applying some leeches for bleeding, some quinine in high dosages, and left, saying he'd come back the next day.

Gaston, thanks to a violent effort, sat up in his bed. He ordered his servant to go get one of his friends who was a lawyer.

"And why, *Grand Dieu?*" Louis asked.

"Because, brother, I need his opinion. Let's not fool ourselves. I'm very sick. Only cowards or imbeciles let themselves be surprised by death. When I've made my arrangements, I'll be more tranquil. Let me be obeyed."

If he insisted on consulting a professional man, it was because he wanted to draw up a new will and leave all his fortune to Louis. The lawyer he had sent for—one of his friends—was a small man, well known in the area. Wily and glib, he was accustomed to the tricks of the legal profession, and at his ease in the innards of the Civil Code, like an eel in his sludge.

When he had completely understood his client's intentions, he had only one thought: to bring them about as cheaply as possible, cleverly avoiding the always considerable inheritance taxes. There was a very simple way:

If Gaston made his brother part owner of his enterprises, by a notarized document certifying he had brought in assets equivalent to half his fortune, and if he happened to die, Louis would have to pay death duties on only the remainder, that is, on half. It was with the strongest urgency that Gaston agreed to that fiction. Not that he was thinking of the savings it would bring about if he died, but because he saw in it an opportunity, if he lived, to share with his brother all he possessed, without wounding his susceptible sensitivity. An act of incorporation between the Sieurs Gaston and Louis de Cameron was then drawn up for the operation of an iron smelting factory, a document that said Louis had an investment of 500,000 francs. But Louis, who had to be made aware of this, because his signature was indispensable, seemed to strongly oppose his brother's plans. He said:

"What good are all these preparations? Why this worry about the Beyond because of an indisposition you won't remember in a week? Do you think I can agree to strip you while you're living? As long as you're alive, what you have is yours, which is understood. If you die, I'm your heir. What more do you want?"

Useless words! Gaston wasn't one of those men who have a weak will that can be changed by a negative. After a long and heroic resistance, which made apparent both his good character and his rare disinterest, Louis, out of arguments and urged by the doctor, decided to affix his signature on the documents drawn up by the lawyer.

It was done. He was henceforth, for human justice, for all the tribunals in the world, his brother's associate, the owner of half of his wealth. The strangest feelings then went through Raoul's accomplice. He almost lost his head, led astray by that passing delirium of people who, suddenly, without transition, go from poverty to opulence. Whether Gaston lived or died, Louis possessed legitimately and honestly, a 25,000 franc income, even without taking into consideration the uncertain profits from the factory. Not at any time had he ever hoped, or dreamed, of such riches. His wishes had not only been accomplished, but surpassed. What more did he need?

Alas! He lacked the possibility of enjoying that comfort in peace. It came too late. That fortune, which fell to him from heaven and which ought to have filled him with joy, filled his heart with sadness and anger. For two or three days his letters to Raoul showed very well the fluctuations of his thoughts, and reflected the detestable sentiments agitating him.

I have a 25,000 pound income," he wrote to him some hours after having signed the act of incorporation. *"I possess 500,000 francs of my own. Half of that, I might say a quarter of that sum, would have made me a year ago the happiest of men. What good is that fortune to me today? None. All the gold on earth wouldn't take away one of the problems of our situation. Yes, you were right. I've been careless, but I'm paying for my haste. We're now launched so rapidly on an incline that, willy-nilly, we must go right to the end. Even to try to stop it would be madness. Rich or poor, I must tremble so long as a meeting between Gaston and Valentine is possible. How can they be separated forever? Would my brother give up seeing that so beloved woman again?*

No, Gaston was not renouncing looking for and finding Valentine; and the proof was that several times in the middle of the greatest suffering, he called out her name. However, at the end of the week, the poor sick man had two days of remission. He could get out of bed, eat a few mouthfuls, and even speak a little. But he was no longer anything but a shadow of himself. In fewer than ten days, he had aged ten years. Sickness, taking more hold on powerful physiques such as that of Gaston, breaks them in less than no time. Leaning on his brother's arm, he went across the prairie to look in on the factory; and sitting down not far from an active furnace, he declared he was comfortable there and that he would be reborn in that intense heat. He was no longer in pain; his head was clear; he breathed easily; his thoughts of dying left him.

"I'm solid as a brick," he said to the workers surrounding him "I'm able to get over this. Old trees die when they're transplanted," he kept repeating. "It would be a good idea, if I want to live a long time, to return to Rio."

What hope that was for Louis, and how ardently he clung to it.

"Yes," he answered. "That would be good for you, even very good. I'll go with you. A voyage to Brazil with you would be a pleasure trip for me."

But what! Plans of sick men, plans of children! The next day Gas-ton had very different ideas. He maintained that he could never resolve to leave France. He made plans to go to Paris as soon as he was well. He would consult doctors there. He would find Valentine. The longer the sickness went on, the more he worried about her. He was surprised not to have received a letter from Beaucaire. That answer which was late, preoccupied him so much that he wrote again, in more pressing terms, demanding a note by return mail. Lafourcade never received that second letter. That same evening, Gaston began to complain again. The two or three better days were only a halt in the malady. It began again with unheard of strength and violence, and for the first time, Doctor C. showed his worry.

Finally, in the morning of the fourth day of his sickness, Gaston, who had remained all night plunged in the most distressing lethargy, appeared to return to life. He sent for a priest and remained alone with him for about a half-hour, declaring he would die a Christian as had his ancestors. Then he had all the doors of his bedroom opened wide, and gave an order that all his workers be brought in. He spoke his farewells to them, and told them that he had taken care of their wellbeing. When they had left, he made his brother promise to keep the factory, embraced him one last time, and fell back on his pillows. He began his death agony. As noon sounded, without shaking, without convulsions, he died. From this point on, Louis was really Marquis de Clameran, and he was a millionaire. However, two weeks later, Louis, having taken care of all his business and come to an agreement with the engineer in charge of the factory, took the train. The evening before, he had addressed to Raoul this significant telegram:

I'm coming.

Chapter XIX

Faithful to the program set out by his accomplice, while Louis was keeping vigil at Oloron, in Paris Raoul did his best to reconquer Madame Fauvel's heart, to regain her lost confidence, and, finally, to reassure her. It was a difficult task, but not impossible. Madame Fauvel had been saddened by Raoul's follies, frightened by his demands; but she had not stopped loving him. She blamed herself for his mistakes, and took it on her conscience, saying: "It's my fault. It's my very grave fault."

Raoul had seen into these feelings in order to be able take advantage of them. During the month that Louis was absent, he delighted Madame Fauvel with a pleasure she never before could have imagined. That mother of a family, a true innocent, had never dreamed of such enchantment, despite the adventures which had led her into a sin. This son's love moved her as would an adulterous passion. It had all the violence, the trouble, and the mystery. He had, for her, what her sons scarcely had, the coquetry, the consideration, and the idolatry of a young lover.

Since she was living in the country, and Monsieur Fauvel left early in the morning, leaving her days free, she spent them with Raoul at his house in Vésinet. Often, in the evening, not having seen enough of him, or listened enough to him, she required him to come to dinner with her and to spend the evening.

Living that lie didn't bore Raoul. He took to his role with the interest a good actor has. He possessed that talent which makes illustrious fakes. He was taken in by his own deception. At certain moments, he didn't know too well whether he was telling the truth, or if he was acting out a despicable comedy. But also, what a success! Madeleine, the cautious and mistrustful Madeleine. Without absolutely changing her mind about the young adventurer, Madeleine admitted that perhaps, relying too much on appearances, she had been unjust.

It was no longer a question of money. That excellent son lived on nothing. So, Raoul was triumphing when Louis arrived from Oloron, having had time to put together an elaborate a plan of action. Although very rich now, he resolved to change nothing of his way of life for the present, in appearance at least. As in the past, it was at the Hotel du Louvre that he took up residence.

Louis' dream, the end of all his ambition and of all his efforts, was to take a place among the great industrialists of France. He was aiming very high, a great deal higher than his title of Marquis, with his situation as owner of a foundry. As a result of having experienced it at his own expense, he knew that our century is not very romantic and attaches very little value to coats of arms, unless their owner can display them on a beautiful carriage. One can very well be a Marquis without a Marquisat.[49] One isn't a master of a foundry except on the condition of owning a foundry.

Louis now was thirsty for respect. All the humiliations of his existence, badly digested, sat heavily on his stomach. He wasn't taking the slightest thought of Raoul. He still needed him. He had decided to make use of his cleverness; then he intended either to get rid of him at the price of a great deal of money, or to make him part of his fortune.

The first interview of the two accomplices was at the Hotel du Louvre. Everything proved it was stormy. Raoul—a practical boy— claimed they should be very satisfied with the results obtained, and that trying for greater advantages would be foolish. But that moderation didn't suit Louis.

"I'm rich," he answered, "but I have other ambitions. More than ever, I want to marry Madeleine. Oh! She'll be mine. I've sworn it. First of all, I love her; then, becoming the nephew of one of the richest bankers in the capital, I'll immediately acquire considerable importance."

"Pursuing Madeleine, my uncle, is to run great risks."

"So be it! I'm glad to run them. My intention is to share with you, but I'll share only the day after my marriage. Madeleine's dowry will be your share."

Raoul was silent. Clameran had the money. He was master of the situation.

"You aren't worried about anything," he said in a discontented tone. "Have you asked yourself how you're going to explain your new fortune? At Monsieur Fauvel's you learned about a Clameran, whom you didn't know—you yourself said so—living near Oloron. He even had funds in the bank. What will you say when you're asked who this Clameran was, and by what chance you find yourself to be his sole heir?"

Louis shrugged.

"Trying to reach the final outcome, my nephew," he pronounced, "you've become naïve."

"Explain! Explain!"

"Oh! Easily. For the banker, for his wife, and for Madeleine, the Clameran of Oloron will be my father's illegitimate son—consequently my brother—born in Hamburg, and recognized during the emigration. Isn't it very simple that he'd wanted to enrich our family? That's what, beginning tomorrow, you'll tell your honored mother."

"That's risky."

"In what way?"

"They can go there for information."

"Who? The banker? For what purpose? What does it matter to him whether I do or do not have an illegitimate brother? I inherit; my documents are all in order; he pays me; and that's the end of it."

"From that direction, true."

---

[49] The land or rank of a Marquis.

"Then do you think Madame Fauvel and her niece are going to go looking? Why? Do they suspect anything? No. Besides, the least step can compromise them. Even if they were mistresses of our secrets, I'm not afraid of them because they can't use them."

Raoul thought a moment. He was looking for objections and didn't find any.

"All right! I'll do as you say, but now I can't count any longer on Madame Fauvel's purse."

"And why, if you please?"

"Damn! Now that you're rich, my uncle…"

"Well!" Louis exclaimed triumphantly, "What difference does that make? Haven't we fought? Haven't you said enough bad things about me to have the right to refuse my help? See! I've really thought of everything, and when I've explained my plan to you, you'll say as I do: 'We'll succeed!'"

"I'm listening."

"I first introduced myself to Madame Fauvel to tell her, not 'your purse or your life,' which is nothing, but 'your purse or your honor.' That's hard. I terrified her. I was expecting that, and I inspired her with the most profound repulsion."

"Repulsion is weak, dear uncle."

"I know it. That's when, having looked for and found you, I pushed you onto the stage. Ah! I don't want to flatter you; you had a fine success. I was present at your first interview, hidden behind a curtain. You were nothing less than sublime. She saw you and she loved you. You spoke and you were the master of her heart."

"And without you…"

"Let me go on. That was the first act of our comedy. Let's pass on to the second. Your mad behavior, your expenditures—a grandfather would say your licentiousness—weren't long in changing our respective situations. Madame Fauvel, without ceasing to adore you—you look so much like Gaston!—was afraid of you. Afraid to the point that she threw herself in my arms, that she resigned herself to turning to me, that she asked me for help and assistance."

"Poor woman!"

"I was very good in that situation. Admit it. I was serious, uncle-like, cold, paternal, and indignant, but kind. The ancient Clameran honesty spoke nobly through my mouth. As was proper, I condemned your guilty conduct. During that time, I triumphed at your expense. Reconsidering her first impressions, Madame Fauvel liked me, felt esteem for me, blessed me."

"That was some time ago."

Louis didn't deign to acknowledge his nephew's ironic interruption.

"We're coming to the third phase," he continued, "during which Madame Fauvel, having Madeleine as her advisor, has almost judged us at our true worth. Oh! Don't be mistaken, she feared and despised one of us as much as the other.

If she hasn't begun to hate you as much as she can, that's because you see, Raoul, the heart of a mother, above all in the situation Madame Fauvel finds herself, has treasures of indulgence and pardon that make *le Bon Dieu* jealous. Only a mother can despise and adore her son at the same time."

"If she didn't tell me that, she at least made me understand it in terms which moved me...me!"

"*Parbleu*! And me! Well, that's where we were: Madame Fauvel was trembling, and Madeleine, so devoted, had dismissed Prosper and agreed to marry me, when Gaston's existence was revealed to us. Since then, what's happened? You were able to make yourself as white as immaculate snow in Madame Fauvel's eyes, and you've made me, me, blacker than hell. She's started to admire your noble qualities again, and in her eyes, and in Madeleine's eyes, I'm the pernicious influence which pushed you toward evil."

"You're right about that, venerable uncle. That's where we are."

"All right! We're coming to the fifth act. Consequently a new turn is indispensable to our play."

"A new direction..."

"That seems difficult to you, doesn't it? Nothing is simpler. Listen to me closely, because the future depends on your cleverness."

Raoul, in his armchair, struck the pose of all dauntless listeners, and simply said:

"I'm all ears."

"Then," Louis continued, "beginning tomorrow, you'll go to Madame Fauvel and tell her what we've agreed on as it relates to Gaston. She won't believe you. That doesn't matter. The important thing is that you appear, you yourself, absolutely convinced of your story."

"I'll be convincing."

"As for me, four or five days from now, I'll go see Monsieur Fauvel and I'll confirm the statement our notary in Oloron must have given him, that the funds deposited with him belong to me. I'll reiterate, for his benefit, the story of the illegitimate brother; and I'll ask him to please keep the money that I don't have any use for. You're suspicion itself, my nephew. This deposit will be a guarantee for you of my sincerity."

"We'll talk about that again."

"Next, my handsome nephew, I'll go find Madame Fauvel, and I'll speak to her in something like this language: 'Since I'm very poor, dear lady, I must impose on you the obligation of coming to the aid of my brother's son, who is your son. This boy is a scoundrel...'"

"Thanks, uncle."

"'He's given you a thousand worries and he's poisoned your life, which it was his duty to improve. Accept my apologies and believe my regrets. Today I'm rich, and I've come to tell you that henceforth I intend to take on myself the present and future of Raoul.'"

"And that's what you call a plan?"

"*Parbleu!* You'll really see. At that statement, it's very probable that Madame Fauvel will want to hug me. She won't do it, however, restrained as she'll be by the thought of her niece. She'll ask me if, now that I have a fortune, I won't give up Madeleine. To which I'll answer flatly: 'No.' This will even be the moment for a nice disinterested action. 'You believed me grasping, Madame,' I'll say to her. 'You were wrong. I've been seduced, as every man must be, by the grace, the charm, the intelligence, and the beauty of Mademoiselle Madeleine, and…I love her. If she didn't have a sou, I would even more earnestly, on my knees, ask you for her hand. It's been agreed that she'll be my wife. Allow me to insist on this one article of our agreement. My silence is at this price. And to prove that her dowry is not important to me, I give you my word of honor that, the day after my marriage, I will give Raoul in writing, a 25,000 pound income.'"

Louis was expressing himself in such a tone, in a voice so compelling, that Raoul, first and foremost an artist in cheating, was amazed.

"Splendid!" he shouted. "That last phrase can create an abyss between Madame Fauvel and her niece. That assurance of a fortune for me can put my mother on our side."

"I hope so," Louis continued, with a tone of false modesty, "and I have as many more reasons to hope. I'll give the dear lady excellent arguments to excuse herself in her own eyes. Because you see, when you suggest to an honest person some little—how shall I say it?—transaction, you must offer them at the same time justifications to put their conscience at ease. The devil doesn't work otherwise. I will prove to Madame Fauvel, and to her niece, that Prosper has unworthily abused them. I'll show them this riddled with debt boy, lost through debauchery, gambling, and giving dinners, and to tell everything, living publicly with a fallen woman."

"And pretty, in the bargain. Don't forget. She is ravishing, that Senora Gypsy. Say she is adorable. That would top it all off."

"Don't worry. I'll be as eloquent and as moral as the public minister himself. Then I'll give Madame Fauvel to understand that if she really loves her niece, she should wish to see her marry not this little cashier, an underling without a soul, but an important man, a great industrialist. That man is the heir to one of the best names in France, a Marquis being able to claim the highest positions, finally rich enough to give you a position in the world."

Raoul himself was taken in by these prospects.

"If you don't persuade her, you'll make her hesitate," he said.

"Oh, I don't expect a sudden change. That's only a germ I'll deposit in her head. Thanks to you, it will develop; it will grow and produce its fruits."

"Thanks to me?"

"Yes, let me finish. That said, I disappear. I no longer show myself, and your role begins. As is expected, your mother repeats our conversation to you, and just by that we can judge the effect produced. But you, at the thought of accepting something from me, you rebel. You declare yourself ready to endure all privations as long as you live, poverty or hunger, rather than receive anything whatsoever from a man you hate, from a man who…a man that…well, you see the scene from this point."

"I see it and I feel it. I've always been good in pathetic roles, when I've had time to prepare myself."

"Perfect. But this generous disinterest won't keep you from suddenly beginning your life of dissipation again. You'll gamble; you'll bet; and you'll lose more than ever. You'll need money, and still more money. You'll be demanding, pitiless. And be aware that I won't ask you to account for anything that you grab. That will be yours, all yours."

"Diable! If you intend it like that…"

"You'll go forward, isn't that right?"

"And quickly, I can guarantee you."

"That's what I ask of you, Raoul. Before three months are out, you must have exhausted all the resources of the two women, all, do you really understand me? You must bring them to the point that they no longer know which way to turn. In three months I want them absolutely ruined, without money, without a jewel, without anything."

Louis de Clameran was expressing himself with such passion, with such passionate vehemence after having laid out his plans, that Raoul couldn't get over it.

"Then you really hate these unfortunate women?"

"Me!" exclaimed Louis, whose eyes were shining, "Me, hate them? Don't you see, blind man, that I love Madeleine to madness, as one loves at my age! You can't see that the thought of her consumes my whole being, that desire sets my head on fire, that her name, when I pronounce it, burns my lips?"

"And you are neither bothered nor moved at the idea of preparing the bitterest sorrow for her?"

"It has to be. Would she ever be mine without cruel suffering, without the bitterest disappointment? The day when you have led Madame Fauvel and her niece so near the abyss that they can see the depth, on that day I'll appear. It's when they believe themselves lost, without forgiveness, that I'll save them. Look! I've been able to keep a beautiful scene for myself, and I'll put so much nobility and grandeur into it, that Madeleine will be touched by it. She hates me, so much the better! When she really sees, when it's demonstrated to her that it's herself and not her money I want, she'll stop despising me. There's no woman that a great passion doesn't touch, and passion excuses everything. I don't say she'll love me, but she'll give herself to me without repugnance, and that's all I ask."

Raoul was silent, frightened at this cynicism, by so much cold perversity. Clameran confirmed his immense superiority in evil, and the apprentice admired the master.

"You would certainly succeed, my uncle, if it were not for the adored cashier. But between Madeleine and you there would always be, if not Prosper himself, at least his memory."

Louis had a wicked smile, which a gesture of anger and disdain made more significant and more frightening still.

"Prosper," he pronounced, throwing down his cigar that had just gone out. "I'm no more worried about him than that."

"She loves him."

"Too bad for him. In six months, she'll no longer love him. He's already morally lost. At the time it's convenient for me, I'll finish him off. Do you know where bad paths lead, my nephew? Prosper has an expensive mistress; he has his own private carriage; he has rich friends; he gambles. Are you yourself a gambler?...He'll need money after some night of bad luck. Baccarat losses are paid for in 24 hours. He wants to pay...and he has a safe."

At that, Raoul couldn't help protesting.

"Ah!"

"'He's honest!' You're going to tell me. *Parbleu!!* I certainly hope so. The day before I first cheated at cards, I was honest. A rascal would have taken advantage of Madeleine a long time ago, and we would have been forced to fold our tents. 'He's loved,' you tell me? Then what barley water flows in his veins, that he leaves the beloved woman to be carried off. Ah! If I had felt Madeleine's hand tremble in mine, if her breath, if a kiss had brushed my forehead, the entire world couldn't have taken her away from me. Too bad for whoever stands in my way. Prosper's in my way. I'll crush him. I'll take it on myself to push him into such a quagmire, with your help, that Madeleine wouldn't go near him." Louis' tone expressed such rage, such an immense desire for vengeance, that Raoul, truly moved, was thinking.

"You're saving me for a really abominable role," he said after a long moment.

"Does my nephew have scruples?" asked Clameran in a jeering tone.

"Scruples...not precisely; nevertheless, I admit..."

"What! That you want to back out? It's a little late to do that. Ah! Ah! Monsieur wants all the joys of luxury, pockets full of gold, race horses, and in short, everything that's splendid and causes envy...But Monsieur wants to remain virtuous. Then you have to be born with an income. Imbecile! Have you ever seen people like us draw millions from the pure well springs of virtue? We fish in mud, my nephew, and we clean up afterwards."

"I've never been rich enough to be honest," Raoul said humbly. "Only to torture two defenseless women, and to assassinate a poor devil who believes he's my friend, that's hard."

That resistance, which he rated as absurd and as ridiculous, exasperated Louis de Clameran to the last degree. Finally after interminable debates, everything was settled to their common satisfaction, and they separated with firm handshakes. Alas! Madame Fauvel and her niece weren't long in feeling the accord between the two wretches. Everything happened, step by step, as Louis de Clameran had foreseen and set up. Once again, and precisely when Madame Fauvel dared finally to breathe, Raoul's conduct changed suddenly. His extravagance started again even greater. In the past, Madame Fauvel had been able to ask herself: "Where does he spend all that money I give him?" This time she had no questions to ask herself. Raoul exhibited senseless passions. He was seen everywhere clothed like those young dandies who're the delight of the boulevards. He was seen at first night openings of the theatre, sitting in the most expensive seats, and at four-horse carriage races. He also had never had such pressing, so urgent a need for money. Madame Fauvel had never before had to defend herself against such exorbitant and so repeated demands.

At this rate, Madame Fauvel and her niece's available resources were quickly at an end. In one month, the miserable boy went through all they'd saved. Then they turned to all the shameful expediencies of women, whose secret expenses are the ruin of a household. They made use of all sorts of economies very damaging to their reputations. They made tradesmen wait; they bought on credit. They inflated receipts and even invented some. They both made up such costly fantasies that Monsieur Fauvel once said to them, smiling:

"You're becoming very coquettish, ladies!"

The day came, nevertheless, when Madeleine and her aunt found themselves totally out of money, one as well as the other.

The preceding day, Madame Fauvel had had some people to dinner, and she could hardly give the cook the money necessary for certain items he had to buy in Paris. Raoul came that day, claiming that he had never found himself in such financial difficulty. He positively needed 2,000 francs. They tried in vain to explain the situation to him, to beg him to wait. He wouldn't listen to anything. He was terrible, pitiless.

"But I have nothing more, unfortunate boy," Madame Fauvel repeated desperately, "nothing in the world. You've taken everything. I have only my jewels left. Do you want them? If they can help you, take them."

However great the impudence of that young bandit, he couldn't help blushing. But he had promised. But he knew that a powerful hand would stop these poor women at the edge of the precipice. And he saw fortune, a great fortune, at the end of all this infamy. Besides, he promised himself to make up for it later...So he stood firm against his softer feelings, and it was with a brutal voice that he answered his mother.

"Then I'll go to the pawn brokers, to the Mont de Piété."

And the constrained circumstances of these two women surrounded by princely luxury, whose ten servants were awaiting their command and whose team of horses snorted in the courtyard, was so terrible, that they begged Raoul to bring them something of what the pawn broker lent them, however little it might be. He promised and kept his word.

But they had shown him a new resource, a mine to exploit. He took advantage of it.

One by one, all Madame Fauvel's ornaments followed the diamonds; and her jewelry gone, those of Madeleine then parted. To defend herself against the miserable men who hounded her, she had only her prayers and her tears. That was very little. However, these revolting extortions sometimes led to such extremes that Raoul, moved and upset, was overcome with horror and disgust with himself.

"I don't have the heart for it," he said to his uncle. "I'm at the end. Armed robbery, I can do that; but to ruin two unfortunate women I like, that's too much for me!"

Clameran didn't seem at all surprised at this repugnance.

"It's sad," he said. "I know that, but necessity has no law. All right, a little energy and patience; we're coming to the end."

It was closer than Clameran thought. Toward the end of November, Madame Fauvel felt herself so near the day before a catastrophe, that she thought of appealing to the Marquis. She hadn't seen him since his return from Oloron, when he had come to tell her about his inheritance. Persuaded at that time that he was Raoul's bad genius, she had received him so coolly as to almost let him understand he was not to return. She hesitated before speaking to her niece about this project, fearing strong opposition. To her great surprise, Madeleine approved it.

"The sooner you see Monsieur Clameran," she said, "the better it will be."

As a consequence, the very next day Madame Fauvel arrived at the Hotel du Louvre, sending a note ahead about her visit. He received her with cold and studied politeness, like a man who has been misunderstood, and who, grieved and wounded, maintains a reserved attitude. He appeared indignant about his nephew's conduct. At one moment he even let out an oath, saying he would straighten out this fellow. But when Madame Fauvel told him that Raoul constantly came to her because he didn't want to ask him for anything, Clameran seemed confused.

"Ah!" He exclaimed. "This is really too much audacity! The miserable boy! In four months, I've given him more than 20,000 francs, and if I agreed to let him have them, it was because he constantly threatened to go ask you."

And seeing on Madame Fauvel's face surprise which resembled doubt, Louis got up, opened his secretary, and took from it Raoul's receipts, which he showed her. The total of those receipts reached 23,500 francs. Madame Fauvel was devastated. "He gotten nearly 40,000 francs from me," she said. "So that's at least 60,000 francs he's spent in four months."

"That would be unbelievable," Clameran answered, "if he were not in love, as he says he is."

"*Mon Dieu!* What do these creatures do with all the money men spend on them?"

"That's something that's never been found out…"

He seemed to feel very sincerely sorry for Madame Fauvel. He promised her that that very evening he would see Raoul, and that he would know how to bring him around to better behavior. Then, after long protestations, he ended by putting his entire fortune at her disposal. Madame Fauvel refused his offers, but she was touched; and upon returning, she told her niece:

"Perhaps we've been mistaken. Perhaps he's not a bad man."

Madeleine shook her head sadly. She'd foreseen what was happening. The Marquis' lovely unselfishness was the confirmation of what she'd thought would happen.

Raoul himself had gone to see his uncle for news. He found him radiant.

"Everything is going as hoped, nephew." Clameran told him. "Your receipts did the trick. Ah! You're a solid partner and I owe you the warmest congratulations. Forty thousand francs in four months?"

"Yes," Raoul answered casually. "That's just about what the pawn brokers at the Mont de Piété lent me."

"*Peste!* You must have been very economical, because the Délassement girl is only a pretext, I suppose?"

"That, dear uncle, is my business. Remember what we agreed. What I can tell you is that Madame Fauvel and her niece have turned everything into cash. They have nothing left and, me, I've had enough of my role."

"So your role is finished. I forbid you to ask for a centime in the future."

"Then where are we now? What's the situation?"

"The situation, my nephew, is that the mine has enough powder, and I'm waiting for nothing more than an opportunity to light the fuse."

That opportunity, which Louis de Clameran was waiting for with such feverish impatience, he thought his rival, Prosper Bertomy, would provide for him. He loved Madeleine too much not to be jealous, even to rage, of the man that she had chosen freely, and not to hate him with all the strength of his passion. He knew he was the only one who could marry Madeleine, but how? By outrageous violence, holding a knife to her throat. He became almost insane at the thought that he could possess her, that her body would be his, but that escaping his power, her thoughts would fly towards Prosper. So he had sworn that before being married, he would throw the cashier into some cesspool of infamy, from which it would be impossible for him to escape. He'd thought about killing him. He preferred to dishonor him. In the past he'd thought it would be easy to ruin the unfortunate young man. He supposed that he himself would furnish the means. He was wrong.

Prosper was leading, it was true, one of those foolish existences which most often lead to a final catastrophe; but he put a certain order to his disorder. If his situation was perilously bad, if he was eaten up with needs, hounded by creditors, and reduced to make-shift resources, he had taken his precautions so well that it was impossible to see it. All the attempts to hasten his ruin had failed; and it was in vain that Raoul, his hands full of gold, playing the role of tempter, had tried to prepare for his fall. He gambled for high stakes, but he gambled without passion, almost without liking it. The exaltation of winning or the disappointment of losing never made him lose his self-possession. His mistress, Nina Gypsy, was a spendthrift and extravagant; but her whims never went beyond certain limits. Examining his conduct, it was that of an unhappy man who forces himself to deaden himself, but who nevertheless, hasn't given up all hope, and who is mainly trying to gain time.

With a knowing eye, his confident Raoul, an intimate friend of Prosper, had judged the situation and penetrated the cashier's secret feelings.

"You don't understand Prosper, my uncle. Madeleine killed him the day she exiled him. Everything is indifferent to him. He takes no interest in anything."

"We'll wait."

They were in fact waiting; and to Madame Fauvel's great surprise, Raoul again became, for her, what he had been during Clameran's absence. It was just about that time that Madame Fauvel, completely rejoicing at this change, conceived the project of placing Raoul in her husband's office. Monsieur Fauvel adopted that idea. Persuaded that a young man without an occupation could only commit stupidities, he offered him a desk in the correspondence office, with a salary of 500 francs a month. Raoul was enchanted with that idea. Nevertheless, on strict orders from Clameran, he refused outright, saying he didn't feel any inclination to work in a bank. This refusal made the banker so out of sorts, that he directed some mildly bitter reproaches at Raoul, warning him he could no longer count on him; and Raoul seized this pretext to ostensibly cease his visits. If he still saw his mother, it was in the afternoon or evening when he was sure Monsieur Fauvel was out; and he only came just enough so as to keep himself abreast of the affairs of the household. This sudden respite after so many and so cruel agitations appeared sinister to Madeleine. She didn't say anything to her aunt about her forebodings, but she was prepared for anything.

"What are they up to?" Madame Fauvel sometimes asked. "Have they finally given up persecuting us?"

"Yes," Madeleine whispered. "What are they doing?"

If neither Raoul nor Louis gave any signs of life, they were holding themselves motionless like the hunter, before a flock of birds, who doesn't want to scare his victims into flight. They were on the lookout for chance. Dogging Prosper's footsteps, Raoul had exhausted all his mental resources to compromise him, to draw him into some ambush where he would lose his honor. But as he had foreseen, the cashier's indifference offered little hold. Clameran was beginning to be impatient and was already looking for some more expeditious method, when one night, about 3:00 a.m., he was awakened by Raoul.

"What is it?" he asked, very worried.

"Maybe nothing, maybe everything. I've just left Prosper."

"Well!"

"I took him, as well as Madame Gypsy, to dinner with three of my friends. After dinner, I tried to organize a little game of baccarat, but it was impossible to get Prosper to take a hand, even though he was drunk."

Louis, disappointed, made a movement of vexation.

"You're drunk yourself," he said, "since you come to wake me up in the middle of the night to tell me such blithering."

"Wait, there's something else."

"*Morbleu!* Then, speak!"

"After having played some time, we went to have a little supper, and Prosper, drunker and drunker, let slip the word he uses to close the safe."

At that information, Clameran couldn't hold back a cry of triumph.

"What's that word?" he demanded.

"The name of his mistress."

"Gypsy! That fits in fact, five letters…"

He was so excited, so agitated, that he jumped out of bed, put on his dressing gown, and began to pace up and down the apartment.

"We've got them!" he cried out with the delirious expression of satisfied hatred. "They're really ours! Ah! He won't dip into his safe, this virtuous cashier; but we'll dip into it for him, and he won't be any more or less dishonored. We have the word. You know where the key is; you told me so."

"When Monsieur Fauvel goes out, he almost always leaves his in one of the drawers of the secretary in his bedroom."

"All right! You're going to go to Madame Fauvel. You'll ask her for that key. She'll give it to you or you'll take it by force, it doesn't matter which. When you have it, you'll open the safe. You'll take out everything it contains."

Clameran absolutely beside himself, digressed for more than five minutes, mingling so strangely his hatred for Prosper with his love for Madeleine, that Raoul seriously asked himself if Clameran was going mad. He thought it his duty to calm him.

"Before singing victory, let's examine the difficulties."

"I don't see any."

"Prosper can change his word beginning tomorrow."

"That's true, but it's not very probable. He won't remember he revealed it. Besides, we're going to hurry."

"That's not all. Following Monsieur Fauvel's most positive orders, only the most insignificant sums remain in the safe over night." "There will be a very large one the evening I want it."

"What do you mean?"

"I'm saying that I have 100,000 écus deposited with Monsieur Fauvel, and if I ask to withdraw them one of these days, very early when the bank opens, they'll spend the night in the safe."

"What an idea!" Raoul, stupefied, exclaimed.

It was an idea, and in fact the two accomplices spent long hours examining it, digging into it, and studying its strengths and weaknesses. After mature thought, and after having minutely calculated the good and the bad luck, they decided the crime would be committed on the evening of the 27th of February. If they chose that evening, it was because Raoul knew that Monsieur Fauvel was supposed to dine with a financier friend, and that Madeleine was invited to a meeting of young girls. Unless there was a hitch, going to the Fauvel mansion at 8:30 p.m., Raoul ought to find his mother alone.

"Today, straightaway, I'm going to ask Monsieur Fauvel to get my funds ready for Tuesday."

"That's very short notice, my uncle," Raoul objected. "You have agreements. You must give notice in case of withdrawing your money."

"That's true, but our banker is proud. I'll say I'm in a hurry, and he will take care of it, even if he must inconvenience himself because of it. Then it's up to you to ask Prosper, as a personal favor to you, to have that sum ready when the offices open."

Raoul, once again, examined the situation, trying to see if he could discover the grain of sand that would become a mountain at the last moment. Everything went to the taste of the two miserable men. The banker, not unwilling to nullify the agreement, consented to the withdrawal at the time indicated. Prosper promised the money would be ready the next day.

Chapter XX

Clameran had told Raoul:

"Above all, be careful of your entrance. Just your look should say everything to avoid impossible explanations."

The advice was useless. Raoul, on entering the small drawing room, was so pale and disheveled; his eyes had such an expression of bewilderment that, on seeing him, Madame Fauvel couldn't hold back a cry.

"Raoul, what's happened to you?"

"The misfortune that's happened to me, my mother, will be the last!"

Madame Fauvel had never seen him like this. She rose, emotional, fluttering, and went to sit near him, as if by staring at him as hard as she could, she could read right to the bottom of his soul.

"What's wrong, Raoul, my son? Answer me."

He pushed her away gently.

"What's the matter," he answered in a stifled voice, which nevertheless shook Madame Fauvel to the depth of her being. "What's the matter is that I'm not worthy of you, not worthy of my noble and generous father."

She shook her head, as if to try to protest.

"Oh!" he continued. "I know myself and I judge myself. Nobody would be able to reproach me for the infamy of my conduct, as my conscience reproaches me. I wasn't born bad. However, I'm only a miserable fool. There are times when, struck by vertigo, I no longer know what I'm doing. Ah! I wouldn't be like this, mother, if I had had you near me in my childhood. But brought up among strangers, doing whatever I liked without any other advisors except my instincts, I gave in to all my passions. Having nothing, bearing a stolen name, I'm vain and devoured with ambition. Poor, without any other resources except your help, I have the tastes and the vices of millionaires' sons. Alas! When I found you, the evil was already done. Your affection, and your motherly tenderness, have given me my only days of true happiness here below. But they haven't been able to stop me. I, who've suffered so much, who've endured so many privations, who've gone without food, I've been made mad by the luxury so new to me that you gave me. I've hurled myself into pleasure, like a drunkard long deprived of wine throws himself into hard liquor."

Raoul was expressing himself in a tone of conviction so profound, with such force, that Madame Fauvel didn't dream of interrupting him. Mute and terrified, she listened not daring to ask questions, certain she was going to learn something terrible. He, however, continued:

"Yes, I've been insane. Happiness passed near me and I didn't know how to put out my hand to hold on to it. I pushed away delightful reality to throw myself into the pursuit of a phantom. I, who should've spent my life at your knees, finding new ways to show my gratitude, it was almost as if I tried to strike you the most cruel blows, to make you sad, to render you the most unfortunate of creatures. Ah! I was a miserable fool when, for a creature I despised, I threw a fortune to the wind. Each piece of gold cost you a tear. Near you is where happiness lies. I recognized it too late."

He stopped, as if overwhelmed by the sense of his wrongs. He seemed near to bursting into tears.

"It's never too late to repent, my son," whispered Madame Fauvel, "to atone for your sins."

"Ah! If I could," Raoul cried out… "But no! There's no longer time. Besides, how do I know how long my good resolutions would last! It isn't just today that I've condemned myself without pity. Overcome with remorse at each new fault, I swore to myself that I'd work to regain my self-esteem. Alas! How did my frequent repentance turn out? The first opportunity I had, I forgot my shame and my oaths. You think me a man. I'm only a changeable child. I'm weak and cowardly, and you aren't strong enough to dominate my weakness, to direct my changeable will. I have the best intentions in the world, yet my actions are those of a villain. Between my intentions and my desires, the disproportion is too great for me to resign myself. Besides, who knows where my deplorable character will lead me."

He made a gesture of terrible indifference and added:

"But I know how to make up for it…"

Madame Fauvel was too cruelly agitated to follow Raoul's clever transitions.

"Speak!" she cried out. "Explain to me what you mean. Am I not your mother? You owe me the truth. I can hear anything."

He appeared to hesitate, as if overwhelmed by the terrible blow he was going to give his mother. Finally, in a low voice, he answered:

"I'm lost!"

"Lost?"

"Yes, and I have nothing more to expect or hope for. I'm dishonored, and by my fault, my very grave fault."

"Raoul!"

"That's how it is. But don't be afraid of anything, my mother. I won't drag the name you gave me into the mud. I'll at least have the common courage not to survive my dishonor. So, mother, don't pity me. I'm among those destiny is set against and who have no refuge but death. I'm a person of disaster. Weren't you condemned to curse my birth? Like remorse, my memory haunted your sleepless nights for a long time. Later I found you, and as payment for your devotion, I bring a deadly element into your life."

"Ungrateful boy. Have I ever reproached you?"

"Never. So it's blessing you, and with your dear name on his lips, that your Raoul is going to die."

"Die! You!"

"It has to be, my mother. Honor demands it. I'm condemned by judges from whom there is no appeal, my will and my conscience."

An hour earlier, Madame Fauvel would have sworn that Raoul had made her suffer all that a woman could endure. Nevertheless, here he had brought a new sadness, so bitter that in comparison all the others seemed as nothing.

"What have you done?" she stammered

"Someone entrusted money to me. I gambled. I lost it."

"Then it's an enormous sum?"

"No, but neither you nor I could come up with it. Poor mother! Haven't I taken everything? Haven't you given me right down to your last jewel?"

"But Monsieur de Clameran is rich. He has put his entire fortune at my disposal. I'm going to have the carriage made ready and go to see him."

"Monsieur de Clameran, mother, will be away a week; and it's this evening I must be saved or lost. Well! I've thought about everything before making up my mind. At twenty years old you cling to life."

He took the pistol he had in his pocket half-way out, and added with a forced smile:

"Here's what arranges everything."

But Madame Fauvel was too beside herself to think about the horror of Raoul's conduct, to recognize in his horrible threats a supreme resource. Forgetting the past, without caring for the future, living entirely in the present situation, she saw only one thing: her son was going to die, and she couldn't do anything to snatch him away from suicide.

"I want you to wait," she said. "André's going to come back. I'll tell him what I need. How much did they entrust to you?"

"Thirty thousand francs."

"You'll have them tomorrow."

"It's this evening that I need them."

She felt she was going insane. She wrung her hands in despair.

"This evening," she said. "Why didn't you come sooner? Don't you have confidence in me? This evening there's no one at the safe...If it weren't for that..."

Raoul was waiting for this word. He seized it in passing. He exclaimed in joy, as if a gleam had lit the shadows of real despair.

"The safe," he said, "but do you know where the key is?"

"Yes, it's there."

"Well!"

He was looking at Madame Fauvel with such hellish audacity that she lowered her eyes.

"Give it to me, mother," he begged.

"Unfortunate boy!"

"It's life I'm asking you for."

That prayer decided her. She took one of the candelabras, passed rapidly into her bedroom, opened the secretary, and found Monsieur Fauvel's key there. But at the moment of giving it to Raoul, she came to her senses.

"No," she stammered, "no, this is not possible."

He didn't insist and even seemed to want to leave.

"You're right," he said. "Then, mother, one last kiss."

She stopped him.

"What will you do with the key, Raoul? Do you have the word?"

"No, but we can always try."

"Don't you know there's never any money in the safe?"

"Let's try it anyway. If by a miracle I open it, and if there's money in the safe, that means God's had pity on us."

"And if you don't succeed? Will you swear to me you'll wait until tomorrow?"

"On the memory of my father, I swear it."

"Then here's the key. Come on."

Pale and trembling, Madame Fauvel went with Raoul through the banker's office, and into the narrow winding staircase which linked the apartments and the offices. Raoul walked first, holding the light, holding the key to the safe between his clenched fingers. At that moment, Madame Fauvel was convinced that Raoul's attempt would be useless. She was then almost reassured about the outcome of that revolting business, and she very little feared Raoul's despair after a failure. If she lent her hand to an action, the very thought of which seemed terrible to her, if she'd given up the key, it was because she trusted Raoul's word, and she wanted above all to gain time.

"When he recognizes the insanity of his hopes and of his efforts," she was thinking, *"he's sworn to me he'll wait until tomorrow, and then I, tomorrow, tomorrow..."*

What she would do the next day, she didn't know, and didn't even ask herself. But in extreme situations, the least delay gives hope, as if a short respite were the final salvation.

They had come to Prosper's office, and Raoul had placed the light on a little table elevated enough so that, despite the shade, it lit up the whole room. He had then recovered, if not his complete self-control, at least that mechanical precision of movement almost independent of the will, and that men accustomed to danger find at their service when it's the most pressing. Rapidly, with experienced dexterity, he placed one after the other the five discs of the safe comprising the name of Gypsy.

A close friend of Prosper, having come to see him and to meet him fifty times when the offices were closing, Raoul knew perfectly well how to maneuver the key in the lock, having studied it and even tried it. He was a boy with a lot of foresight. He put it in gently, gave it a turn, pushed it in further, turned it a second time, pushed it all the way in with a shake and turned it again. His heart was beating so violently that Madame Fauvel could hear it. The word hadn't been changed. The safe opened. Raoul and his mother let out a cry at the same time, she of terror, and he of triumph.

"Shut it!" Madame Fauvel exclaimed, overwhelmed by the inexplicable result. "Quit...Come back..."

And half insane, she jumped on Raoul, clung desperately to his arm and drew him to her with such violence that the key left the lock, slid along the safe door, and traced there a long and deep scratch.

But Raoul had time to see, on the top shelf, three packages of bank bills. He seized them with his left hand and slid them under his jacket, between his vest and his shirt. Worn out by the effort she'd just made in giving in to the violence of her emotions, Madame Fauvel had turned loose of Raoul's arm. To avoid falling, she was holding on to the back of Prosper's chair.

"Please, Raoul," she said, "I beg you, put the bank notes back in the safe. I'll have ten times more tomorrow, I swear to you, and I'll give them to you, my son. Have pity on your mother."

He wasn't listening to her. He was examining the scratch left on the door. That trace of the theft was very visible and very disturbing.

"At least," Madame Fauvel continued, "don't take everything. Keep just what you need to save yourself and leave the rest."

"For what purpose? Will the theft be any the less discovered?"

"Yes, because you'll see, I'll take care of everything. Let me do it. I'll know how to find a plausible explanation. I'll tell André that I'm the one who needed money."

With a thousand precautions, Raoul had closed the safe door.

"Come," he said to his mother, "let's go back. We might be surprised. A servant might come into the drawing room, and not finding you there, wonder why."

That cruel indifference, that facility for calculation in such a moment, carried Madame Fauvel away with indignation. She believed she still had some influence over her son. She believed in the power of her prayers and her tears.

"Well!" she answered. "So much the better! If someone comes upon us, I'll be happy. Then everything will be over. André will turn me out as a worthless woman, but I won't sacrifice the innocent. Prosper's the one they'll accuse tomorrow. Clameran has taken the woman he loves from him. You yourself are trying to take his honor. I want no more."

She was speaking very loudly, in a voice so shrill that Raoul was afraid. He knew that an office boy spent the night in a neighboring room. That boy, although it wasn't late, might very well be in bed and hear everything.

"Let's get back upstairs!" he said, seizing Madame Fauvel by the arm.

But she struggled. She had clung to a table to better resist.

"I've already been cowardly enough to sacrifice Madeleine," she repeated. "I won't sacrifice Prosper."

Raoul understood that only a winning argument would break through Madame Fauvel's resolution.

"Well!" he said, with a cynical laugh. "Then you don't understand that I'm working with Prosper, and that he's waiting for me to divide this."

"That's impossible!"

"All right! Good. Do you imagine, then, that it was just luck that whispered the word to me and filled up the safe?"

"Prosper is honest."

"Certainly, and I am too. Only we didn't have any money."

"You're lying."

"No, dear mother. Madeleine chased Prosper away, and, Damn! He's consoling himself however he can, that poor boy, and consolation is expensive."

He had picked up the lamp and gently, with extraordinary strength, he pushed Madame Fauvel toward the stairway. She let herself be led now, more confused by what she had just heard, than from having seen the safe opened.

"What!" she exclaimed, "Could Prosper be a thief?"

"The key must be put back in the secretary," Raoul said, when they had returned to the bedroom.

But she didn't seem to hear him, and it was he who replaced the key in the box from which he'd seen it taken out. He then led, or rather, he carried Madame Fauvel into the little drawing room where she'd been when he arrived, and he sat her down in an armchair. The prostrations of the unhappy woman was such, with her eyes staring straight ahead and her expression revealing the frightful trouble of her mind, that Raoul, frightened, wondered if she wasn't going insane.

"Raoul," she whispered, "my son, you've killed me."

Her voice had such a penetrating gentleness, her tone expressed the most terrible despair so well, that Raoul, touched to the depth of his soul, had a movement of goodness. He wished to give back what he had just stolen. The thought of Clameran stopped him. Then seeing that Madame Fauvel remained prostrate, dying in her armchair, and fearing to see either Monsieur Fauvel or Madeleine enter, who would ask for explanations, he kissed his mother on the forehead and fled.

In the restaurant, in the little room where they had dined, Clameran, tortured by uncertainty, waited for his accomplice. Then when Raoul appeared, he stood up suddenly, pale with agony and in a barely distinct voice he demanded:

"Well?"

"It's finished, uncle. Thanks to you, I'm now the most worthless of men. Be satisfied. Here's that sum that's going to cost the honor, and perhaps the life, of three people."

Clameran didn't acknowledge the insult. He had seized the bank bills with a feverish hand, and he felt them as if to convince himself of the reality of the success.

"Now," he exclaimed, "Madeleine is mine!"

Raoul was silent. The sight of that joy, after the scenes of a while before, revolted and humiliated him. But Louis mistook the causes of that sadness.

"Was that hard?" he asked with a smile.

"I forbid you," Raoul shouted, beside himself, "I forbid you, do you understand, to talk to me anymore about this evening. I want to forget it."

At that angry explosion, Clameran shrugged slightly.

"As you like," he pronounced in a jeering tone, "forget, nephew, forget. I like to believe, nevertheless, that you won't refuse to take, as a souvenir, these 350,000 francs. Keep them. They're yours."

That generosity seemed neither to surprise nor satisfy Raoul.

"According to our agreement," he said, "I have a right to a great deal more."

"So this is only a down payment."

"And when will I have the rest, if you please?"

"The day of my marriage with Madeleine, my handsome nephew, not before. You're too precious a helper for me to dream of depriving myself of your services. You know, if I'm not suspicious of you, I'm not completely sure of your complete affection."

Raoul was reflecting that to commit a crime and not get any profit from it, would also be too stupid by far. Having come with the intention of breaking up with Clameran, he decided not to abandon his accomplice's fortune, until he had nothing more to hope from it.

"So be it," he said. "I accept the down payment; but no more assignments like the one this evening. I would refuse."

Clameran burst out laughing.

"All right," he answered. "Very well. You're becoming honest. It's the right time for it, because you're rich now. Let your timorous conscience rest easy. I have nothing more to ask of you except insignificant services of details. Go back behind the scene. My role begins now."

Chapter XXI

After Raoul's departure, Madame Fauvel remained for more than an hour, plunged into that state of numbness bordering on absolute insensibility, which follows both great moral crises and violent physical pain.

Nevertheless, little by little, she returned to the realization of the present situation. With the ability to think, came the faculty to suffer.

She now understood that she had been duped by an odious comedy. Raoul had tortured her cold-bloodedly, with premeditation, making a game of her suffering, trading on her tenderness.

But had Prosper, yes or no, seconded the theft to which Raoul had just made her an accomplice?

For Madame Fauvel, that was the whole question. What she knew of Prosper's conduct made Raoul's assertion seem likely. Still blinded, she liked to attribute to someone other than her son the initial idea for the crime.

She'd been told that Prosper loved one of those creatures who melt inheritances in the fire of strange caprices, and pervert the best natures. After that, she could suppose him capable of anything.

Didn't she know, through experience, where an imprudent act could lead!

Nevertheless, she excused Prosper, if he was guilty, and she vowed that all responsibility would fall back on her.

Reflecting, she didn't know what decision to make. Should she or should she not confide in Madeleine? Impelled toward disaster, she decided that Raoul's crime would remain her secret.

Then, when Madeleine came back from the evening party at 11 p.m., she said nothing to her. She even managed to dissimulate any trace of suffering cleverly enough to avoid questions. Her calm hadn't failed when Monsieur Fauvel and Lucien returned. Nevertheless, she had just been seized with terrible fright. The banker might take a notion to go down to his offices, to check the safe. He did that very rarely, but he had been known to do it.

As if on purpose that particular evening, he spoke of nothing but Prosper, how sorry he was to see him so unsettled, the worry he felt about it, and finally the reasons, according to him, which had taken him away from the house. Fortunately, while he was treating his cashier very badly, Monsieur Fauvel was looking neither at his wife nor at his niece. He would have been intrigued at their unusual expressions.

That night must have been, and was, a long and intolerable torture. In six hours she told herself, in three hours, in one hour, everything will be discovered. What would happen?

The morning came, the household awoke. She heard the servants coming and going. Then the sound of the offices which they were opening reached her.

But when she wanted to get up, she couldn't. A weakness she couldn't over-come, and atrocious pains, threw her back onto her pillows. From there, shiver-ing with cold and, even so, bathed in the sweat of agony, she awaited the result. She was waiting, leaning over the edge of her bed, her ears straining to hear, when the bedroom door opened. Madeleine, who had just left her, reappeared. The unfortunate girl was paler than a corpse; her eyes shone with delirium; she was shaking like leaves which tremble in the winds of a storm. Madame Fauvel knew the crime had been discovered.

"You know what's happened, don't you, my aunt?" Madeleine said in a sharp voice. "They're accusing Prosper of theft. The Commissioner is here and is going to take him to prison."

A moan was Madame Fauvel's only answer.

"I recognize the hand of Raoul or of the Marquis in this," continued the young girl.

"What! How can you explain...?"

"I don't know...What I do know is that Prosper's innocent. I've just seen him, spoken to him. Guilty, he wouldn't have been able to look me in the eyes."

Madame Fauvel opened her mouth to admit everything. She didn't dare.

"Then what do these monsters want of us?" asked Madeleine. "What sacri-fices do they require of us? Dishonor Prosper? It would be better to murder him. I would've killed him myself."

Monsieur Fauvel's entrance interrupted Madeleine.

The banker's fury was such that he could hardly speak "That miserable man," he stammered, "dares to accuse me! Me! To let it be said that I robbed myself...And this Marquis de Clameran who seems to suspect my good faith."

Then without paying attention to the effect on the two women, he recount-ed what had happened.

"I had a foreboding of this yesterday evening. This is where bad behavior leads."

That day, Madeleine's devotion to her aunt was put to a harsh test. That generous girl saw the man she loved dragged through the mud. She believed in his innocence like that of her own. She thought she knew those who'd hatched the plot that he was a victim of, and she didn't open her mouth to defend him. However, Madame Fauvel guessed her niece's suspicions. She understood that sickness was a telltale sign, and although dying, she had the courage to get up for lunch.

It was a sad meal. No one ate. The servants walked around on tip-toes, speaking low, as in houses where there's been a great misfortune.

About 2:00 p.m., Monsieur Fauvel was shut up his study, when a boy from Accounts Receivable came to tell him the Marquis de Clameran was asking to speak to him.

"What!" exclaimed the banker. "He dares..."

But he thought a moment and said:

"Ask him to come up."

Just the name of Clameran was sufficient to make Monsieur Fauvel's badly quenched anger flare up. Victim of a theft in the morning, his empty safe faced with a disbursement, he'd been able to quiet his resentment. At that moment, he promised himself, he would rejoice to take his revenge.

But the Marquis didn't want to come up. Soon the boy from Accounts Receivable appeared, announcing that for important reasons, that importunate visitor insisted on speaking to Monsieur Fauvel in his offices.

"What's this new demand?" exclaimed the banker.

And, as irritated as possible, seeing no reason to control himself, he went downstairs.

Monsieur de Clameran was standing, waiting in the first room, the one in front of the safe.

"What more do you want, Monsieur?" he demanded roughly. "You've been paid, haven't you? I have your receipt."

To the great surprise of all the employees in the bank, the Marquis seemed neither excited nor shocked by the reproach.

"You're very hard on me, Monsieur," he answered in a tone of studied deference, without humility, however. "But I deserve it. That's the reason I've come. A gentleman always suffers when he's proved wrong. That's my case, Monsieur, and I'm glad that my past allows me to admit it aloud without risking being taxed with weakness. If I've insisted on speaking to you here and not in your study, it's because, having been perfectly ungentlemanly in front of your employees, it's in front of them that I beg you to accept my apologies."

Clameran conduct was so unexpected; it contrasted so much with his accustomed haughty attitude, that the banker hardly found some of the usual words to express his astonishment.

"Yes, I admit it, your insinuations, certain doubts…"

"This morning," the Marquis went on, "I had a moment of excessive annoyance, which I couldn't master. My hair is turning gray, it's true; but when I get angry, I'm as violent and inconsiderate as when I was twenty. You're right to believe my words betrayed my intimate thoughts, and I bitterly regret them."

Monsieur Fauvel, very much carried away himself, and good-mannered at the same time, must have appreciated de Clameran's behavior more than many others, and was touched by it. In addition, a long life of scrupulous honesty couldn't be besmirched by a single ill-considered word. Faced with such nobly given explanations, his rancor didn't hold up.

He held out his hand to Clameran saying:

"Let's let everything be forgotten, Monsieur."

They talked together in a friendly way several minutes, Clameran explaining why he'd had such an urgent need for his funds, and in leaving, said he was going to ask Madame Fauvel's permission to pay his respects.

"That would perhaps be indiscreet, after the trouble she's experienced this morning," Clameran added.

"Oh, there's no reason to hesitate," the banker answered. "I even think chatting a little might distract her. I myself am forced to go out because of this deadly business."

Madame Fauvel was then in the little drawing room, where Raoul the evening before had threatened to kill himself. Suffering more and more, she was half reclined on a couch, and Madeleine was near her. When the servant announced Monsieur Louis de Clameran, they both stood up, terrified, as if by the appearance of a ghost.

While climbing the staircase, he'd had time to compose his features. Almost gay when leaving the banker, he was now grave and sad.

He greeted them. He was shown an armchair, but he refused to sit down.

"You'll excuse me, ladies," he began, "to dare trouble you in your affliction, but I have a duty to fulfill."

The two women were silent. They seemed to be waiting for an explication, so, lowering his voice, he said:

"I know everything!"

With a gesture, Madame Fauvel tried to interrupt him. She thought he was going to reveal the secret she had hidden from her niece. But Louis ignored this gesture. He seemed to be aware only of Madeleine, who said to him:

"Explain yourself, Monsieur."

"It was only an hour ago," he answered, "that I found out how, yesterday evening, Raoul, resorting to the most infamous violence, made his mother give him the key to the safe and stole the 350,000 thousand francs."

At these words, anger and shame turned Madeleine's cheeks purple. She leaned over toward her aunt, seizing her by the wrists, and shaking them:

"Is that true, then?" she asked her in a low voice. "Is it true?"

"Alas!" Madam Fauvel trembled, devastated.

Madeleine straightened up, not understanding such outrageous weakness.

"And you let them accuse Prosper!" she exclaimed. "You let him be dishonored. He's in prison!"

"Forgive me!" whispered Madame Fauvel, "I was afraid. He wanted to kill himself. Then, you don't understand…Prosper and he were in agreement."

"Oh!" Madeleine exclaimed. "You were told that, and you could believe it?"

Clameran judged this the moment to intervene.

"Unfortunately," he said in a heart-broken voice, "Mademoiselle, your aunt isn't slandering Monsieur Bertomy."

"Proof! Monsieur, proof!"

"We have Raoul's admission."

"Raoul's a scoundrel!"

"I know that only too well, but after all, who revealed the word? Who left the money in the safe? Monsieur Bertomy, without a doubt."

These objections didn't seem to affect Madeleine.

"And now," she said, not taking the trouble to hide a contempt which even amounted to disgust, "do you know what happened to the money?"

There was no way to misunderstand the meaning of that question. Given emphasis by a crushing look, it meant:

"You were the instigator of this robbery, and you received the money."

That cutting insult from a young girl he loved to the extent that he, the so careful thief, risked for her the product of his crime, struck Clameran so strongly that he turned livid. But his act was too well set up for him to lose his self-possession.

"A day will come, Mademoiselle," he continued, "when you'll regret having treated me so cruelly. I've understood the exact meaning of your question. Oh! Don't take the trouble to deny it."

"Oh, I'm not denying anything."

"Madeleine!" murmured Madame Fauvel, who trembled, seeing the evil passions of the man who held her destiny in his hands thus stirred up. "Madeleine, have pity!"

"Yes," Clameran said sadly, "Mademoiselle has no pity. She cruelly punishes an honorable man, whose only wrong was having obeyed the last wishes of a dying brother. And if I'm here nevertheless, it's because I'm one of those who believe in the solidarity of all family members."

He slowly took out several stacks of bank bills from the pockets on the side of his coat, and placed them on the mantle.

"Raoul," he pronounced, "stole 350,000 francs. Here's that sum. It's more than half my fortune. With my whole heart, I'd give what I have left to be sure that this crime will be the last."

Too inexperienced to see into Clameran's so audacious and so simple a plan, Madeleine didn't know what to say. All her expectations had been thrown off track. Madame Fauvel, on the contrary, accepted that restitution as salvation.

"Thank you, Monsieur," she said, taking Clameran's hands. "You're very good."

A ray of joy he resented lit up Louis' eyes. But he was triumphing too soon. A minute of reflection had given Madeleine back all her mistrust. She found this unselfishness too good for a man she judged incapable of a generous sentiment, and the idea occurred to her that he must be hiding a trap.

"What will we do with that money?" she asked.

"You'll give it back to Monsieur Fauvel, Mademoiselle."

"We, Monsieur, and how? Restitution means denouncing Raoul. That means giving up my aunt. Take back your money, Monsieur."

Clameran was too clever to insist. He obeyed, and seemed ready to leave.

"I understand your refusal," he said. "It's up to me to find a way. But I won't leave, Mademoiselle, without telling you how sad your injustice has made me. Perhaps after the promise you've deigned to make me, I might've expected a different reception."

"I'll keep my promise, Monsieur, but when you've given me guarantees, not before."

"Guarantees! And what are those! Please, tell me."

"Those which tell me that after my...marriage, Raoul won't come back again, threatening his mother. What would my dowry be to a man who, in four months, has gone through more than 100,000 francs? We're making a bargain: I give you my hand in exchange for the honor and the life of my aunt. Before concluding it, I then say, 'Where are your guarantees?'"

"Oh! I'll give you such good ones that you'll have to recognize my good faith," Clameran exclaimed. "Alas! You doubt my devotion— what can I do to prove it to you? Will it be necessary to try to save Monsieur Bertomy?"

"Thanks for your offer, Monsieur," Madeleine replied scornfully. "If Prosper is guilty, let him perish. If he's innocent, God will protect him."

Madame Fauvel and her niece rose. This was a dismissal. Clameran left.

"What character!" he said. "What pride! To demand guarantees from me! Ah! If I didn't love her so much! But I do love her, and I want to see that proud girl at my feet...She's so beautiful! *Ma foi!* Too bad for Raoul!"

Clameran had never been more irritated. Madeleine's strength, which his calculations had not taken into account, had just made him miss using the theatrical gesture he'd counted on, and had upset his skillful plans. He had too much experience to flatter himself that in the future he could intimidate that very resolute young girl. He understood that, without having found out what he intended, without seizing the meaning of his maneuvers, she was enough on her guard not to be surprised nor deceived. What's more, it was clear that she was going to dominate Madame Fauvel with all her firm haughtiness, animate her with some of her daring, inspire her with some of her prejudices, and in the end, keep her from any new weakness. Just at the moment Louis thought he had won by his play, he found a new adversary. The game had to start over.

It was clear that Madeleine was resigned to sacrificing herself for her aunt; but it was also certain that she was determined not to sacrifice herself except knowingly, and not on the spur of the moment on the faith of uncertain promises. Now, how could he give her the guarantees she demanded? What measures could he take to take to shield Madame Fauvel, ostensibly and definitively, from Raoul's encroachment? Actually, once Clameran was married, Raoul would become rich; Madame Fauvel would no longer be worried. But how to prove it, to show it to Madeleine? Having exact knowledge of all the circumstances of the ignoble and criminal intrigue should have reassured him on that point. But was it possible to set it up in all its details, above all, before the marriage? Evidently not. Then, what guarantees to give?

Using his craftiness, exhausting all the forces of his alert mind, Clameran studied this question from all sides for a long time. He found nothing, no possible way, not one method to his advantage. But he didn't have one of those hesitant natures that an obstacle halts for an entire week. When he couldn't unravel a situation, he cut through it. Raoul was in his way. He swore that, in one way or another, he'd get rid of this accomplice who'd become so troublesome. However, it wasn't an easy thing to extricate himself from Raoul, so mistrustful, so clever. But that consideration couldn't make Clameran reflect. He was spurred on by one of those passions that age renders terrible. The more certain he was of Madeleine's hatred and disdain, the more he loved her, by an inconceivable and nevertheless frequent aberration of the mind and the senses, the more he desired her, the more he wanted her.

However, a ray of light still shone in his sick head. He decided that he wouldn't do anything suddenly. He felt that before acting, he should await the outcome of Prosper's affair. So he hoped to see Madame Fauvel or Madeleine again. He believed they wouldn't be long in asking him for a meeting. On this last point, he was still deluded.

Judging the last acts of the accomplices coldly and logically, Madeleine told herself that for the moment, they wouldn't go any further. She understood that resistance at that time would certainly have been more disastrous than cowardly submission. She therefore resolved to assume full and entire responsibility for events, sure enough of her bravery to stand up to Raoul, as well as to Louis de Clameran. Madame Fauvel would resist, she didn't doubt that. But she decided to use, to abuse if need be, her influence to impose on her a firmer and more dignified attitude, in her own interest.

That was why, after Clameran's request, the two women gave no more signs of life, having decided to wait out their adversaries, to see them come to them. Hiding under indifference, a rather well-enacted indifference, they renounced going for information. They learned through Monsieur Fauvel, successively: the result of Prosper's interrogations, his obstinate denials, the charges brought against him, the hesitations of the Investigating Magistrate and, finally, his release for lack of sufficient proof, as well as the specified No-Bill. Since Clameran's attempt at restitution, Madame Fauvel didn't doubt the cashier's guilt. She didn't say a word; but inwardly she accused him of having seduced, led astray, and forced Raoul into crime. That was because she couldn't bring herself to cease loving him.

Madeleine, on the contrary, was sure of Prosper's innocence. So sure that, having found out that he was going to be set free, she dared ask her uncle for a sum of 10,000 francs under the pretext of a charitable work, which she sent to this unfortunate man, a victim of false appearances. According to everything she'd heard said, he must find himself without resources. If, in this letter she joined to this missive with letters cut from her prayer book, she advised Prosper to leave France, it was because she wasn't ignorant of the fact that in France existence for him would become impossible. In addition, Madeleine was then persuaded that, one day or another, she'd have to marry Clameran; and she preferred to know the man she had singled out and chosen in the past was far, very far, away from her.

Nevertheless, in the middle of that generosity that Madame Fauvel disapproved of, the two poor women were fighting against inextricable difficulties. The tradesmen, whose money Raoul had eaten up, and who had for some time extended credit, were insisting on payment for their bills. On the other hand, Madeleine and her aunt had given up going to social events all winter long, to avoid the expense of new outfits. Now they were going to find themselves obliged to appear at a ball being organized by the Messieurs Jandidier, close friends of Monsieur Fauvel. How could they appear at this ball, which, as the last straw of misfortune, was a fancy dress ball? Where could they find money for the costumes? There they were, in their inexperience with the vulgar and nevertheless atrocious difficulties of life. These women who didn't know what inconvenience was, who had always walked about with hands full of gold, hadn't paid the dressmaker in a year. They owed her a considerable sum. Would she agree to extend more credit?

A new chambermaid, named Palmyre Chocareille, who was just entering Madeleine's service, helped them out of their worries. That girl, who seemed to have great experience with small misfortunes, which are the only serious ones, perhaps guessed her mistresses' cares. Still, it happened that without being asked, she pointed out a very talented dressmaker who was just starting out. The dressmaker had some money, would be only too happy to furnish all that was needed, and would still wait for payment. She would be recompensed in advance, by the certainty that having the Fauvel ladies as clients would make her known, and bring her other customers.

But that wasn't all. Neither Madame Fauvel nor her niece could show themselves at that ball without jewelry. Now all their necklaces, without exception, had been taken and hocked at the Mont-de-Piété pawn shop by Raoul, who had kept the receipts. It was then that Madeleine decided to go ask Raoul to use at least part of the stolen money to redeem the jewelry, extorted through the weakness of his mother. She broached this project to her aunt saying to her:

"Set up a rendezvous with Raoul. He won't dare refuse you, and I'll go."

In fact, the next day the courageous girl took a carriage, and despite the atrocious weather, went to Vésinet. She didn't suspect then that Monsieur Verduret and Prosper were following her, and that, standing on a ladder, they witnessed the interview. Madeleine's courageous attempt was useless. Raoul swore that he had divided with Prosper, that his own part had been spent, and that he found himself without any money. He didn't even want to return the receipts, and Madeleine had to insist strongly to be given four or five indispensable objects of minimal value.

Clameran had ordered, imposed this refusal. He hoped that, in a moment of supreme distress, they would turn to him. Raoul had obeyed, but only after the violent altercation which Joseph Dubois, Clameran's new servant, had witnessed. That was because the two accomplices were then at their worst together.

Clameran was looking for a way, if not honest, at least less dangerous, to get rid of Raoul; and the young bandit had a foreboding of his companion's friendly intentions. Only the certainty of great danger could reconcile them, and they had that certainty at the Messieurs Jandidier ball.

Who was this mysterious Paillasse (Jester) who, after his transparent allusions to Madame Fauvel's trouble, had said to Louis in such a peculiar tone: "I'm the friend of your brother Gaston?" They couldn't guess, but they recognized an implacable enemy so well that, on leaving the ball, they tried to stab him. Having followed him, having been thrown off the track, they were terrified.

"Let's be on our guard," Clameran whispered. "We'll know only too soon who that man is."

Raoul had then tried to make him decide to give up Madeleine.

"No!" he had shouted. "I'll have her or I'll die!"

They thought it would be difficult to catch them, since they had been warned. But they didn't know what man was on their trail.

Chapter XXII

The Outcome

With knowledge almost unbelievable in investigation, such were the facts collected and coordinated by Monsieur Verduret, that fat man with a happy face who had taken Prosper under his protection. Arrived in Paris at 9:00 p.m., not by the Lyon train as he had said, but by the train from Orléans, Monsieur Verduret had immediately gone to the Hotel Grand-Archange, where he had found the cashier waiting for him, eaten up with impatience.

"Ah! You're going to hear some wonderful things," he said to him, "and you're going to see just how far, sometimes, it's necessary to go back into the past to find the first causes of a crime. Everything here below holds together and is linked together. If, twenty years ago, Gaston de Clameran hadn't gone to drink a demitasse in a little café in Jarnègue, in Tarascon, your safe wouldn't have been robbed three weeks ago. Valentine de la Verberie has paid in 1866, for the knife attack given through love for her about 1840. Nothing is lost or forgotten. In addition, listen:"

And immediately he began to recount the facts, aiding himself with his notes and the two voluminous manuscripts he'd drawn up. For a week Monsieur Verduret had not taken, in all, perhaps twenty-four hours of rest, but it hardly showed. His steel muscles held up under fatigue, and his mental resources were too solidly tempered ever to collapse. Another man would have been broken, but he held himself upright, and recited with that enthusiasm which was characteristic of him. He was participating in, it might be said, the drama's twists and turns, becoming tender or passionate—*making an entrance*— to use theater parlance, in the character of each of the personages he introduced on the stage.

Prosper was listening to him, dazzled by that marvelous ease of his storytelling. He was listening and he was wondering if this story, which explained events right down to the smallest circumstances, which analyzed fleeting sensations, which reestablished conversations which must have been secret, weren't a novel, more than a relating of exact events. Certainly, all these explanations were ingenious, intriguing as probabilities, strictly logical; but what was their basis? Weren't they the dream of an imaginative man?

Monsieur Verduret took a long time to tell everything. It was almost 4:00 a.m. when, having finished, he cried out in a tone of triumph:

"And now they're on their guard. They're clever, but I jeer at that. I've got them! They're ours! Before a week's out, friend Prosper, you'll be reinstated. I promised that to your father."

"Is it possible!" murmured the cashier, whose every idea had been upset.

"Is it possible?"

"What?"

"All that you've just told me."

Monsieur Verduret jumped like a man little used to hearing his listeners doubt the accuracy of his information.

"If this is possible?" he exclaimed. "But this is truth itself, caught as a matter of fact and still pulsating with life."

"What! Such things can happen in Paris, in the middle of us, without…"

"Parbleu!" interrupted the fat man. "You're young, my comrade. A lot of other things happen…and you're hardly aware of it. You yourself believe only in the horrors of the Investigating Magistrate's court. *Peuh!* All you see in the *Gazette des Tribunaux* in full daylight are bloody melodramas of life; and the actors, filthy scoundrels, are cowardly using the knife, or stupid with the poison they use. It's in the shadows of families, often sheltered from the Code of Criminal Justice, that real dramas happen, the poignant dramas of our époque. Here traitors wear gloves, criminals are clothed with social standing, and the victims die desperate, a smile on their lips…But what I'm telling you here is ordinary, and you're astonished…"

"I'm wondering how you've been able to discover all these foul deeds."

The fat man smiled broadly.

"Ah! Ah!" he said, seeming content with himself, "When I take on a task, I apply myself to it entirely. Pay attention to this: A man with middling intelligence, who concentrates all his thoughts and all the impulses of his will toward one single goal, almost always arrives at that end. In addition, I have my own little methods."

"Still, some clues are necessary and I don't see any."

"That's true. To guide oneself through the shadows of such an affair, it takes a light. But the flame in de Clameran's look, when I pronounced the name of Gaston, his brother, was the illumination of my lantern. From that moment, I walked straight to the solution of the problem, as toward a lighthouse."

Prosper's looks were questioning and begging. He wanted to know his protector's investigations, because he still doubted. He didn't dare believe in this happiness announced to him—a splendid reinstatement.

"Let's see!" said Monsieur Verduret. "You'd really give anything to know how I arrived at the truth?"

"Yes, I admit it. It's such a wonder for me!"

Monsieur Verduret was delightedly enjoying Prosper's amazement. Certainly, Prosper wasn't for him a well-known judge or a distinguished amateur. What did that matter? Sincere admiration is always flattering, wherever it comes from.

"All right," he answered. "I'm going to show you my system. There's not a shadow of wonder to it. We've worked together for the solution to the problem. You know how I came to suspect that Clameran had something to do with the crime. From that moment, with the things I knew for certain, the task was easy. Then what did I do? I placed my people near the people I needed to watch, Joseph Dubois with Clameran, Nina Gypsy near the Fauvel ladies."

"As matter of fact, I still can't understand how Nina consented to take on that commission."

"That," Monsieur Verduret answered, "is my secret. I'll continue. Having good eyes and sharp ears in place, sure of understanding the present, I had to learn about the past, and I left for Beaucaire. The next day I was at Clameran, and right off I got my hand on the son of Saint-Jean, the former valet. He was a fine boy, *Ma foi!*, frank and open, as unspoiled as nature, who immediately guessed that I needed to buy some madder."

"Some madder?" Prosper asked, not following the explanation.

"Certainly, that's easy to see. I must tell you, I didn't look at all as I do at the moment. He, having some madder to sell, which was also easy to see, we began to bargain. Our offers and counter-offers lasted a whole day, during which time we drank a good two dozen bottles. At supper time, Saint-Jean the son was drunk on his feet, and I had bought 900 francs' worth of madder, that your father will resell."

Prosper's look was so odd that Monsieur Verduret burst out laughing. "I risked 900 francs," he continued, "but as we kept talking, I learned the whole history of the Clameran's, Gaston's love affair, his flight and also the fall of Louis' horse. I learned also that Louis came back about a year later, that he sold the chateau to an estate merchant named Fougeroux, and that the wife of that buyer, Mihonne, had given Louis a rendezvous. That same evening, having gone across the Rhône, I went to see that Mihonne. Poor woman! That rascal of a husband of hers had beaten her so much that she wasn't far from being an idiot. I proved to her that I'd come on behalf of whatever Clameran, and she was eager to tell me all that she knew."

The simplicity of his investigative methods confused Prosper.

"From that point," Monsieur Verduret continued, "the skein came unwound. I held the main thread of the string. What had happened to Gaston remained to be found out. Ah! I had no trouble picking up his trail. Lafourcade, who is a friend of your father, told me Gaston had settled at Oloron, that he had bought a factory, and that he died there.

Thirty-six hours later I was in Oloron."

"Then you are incapable of fatigue?"

"No, but I make it a principle to strike while the iron is hot. At Oloron I met Manuel, who had come to spend a few days there before returning to Spain; and through him, I had the exact biography of Gaston and the minutest details of his death. Through Manuel, I found out about Louis' visit, and an innkeeper in the village told me about the stay at that period of a young worker, in whom I recognized Raoul."

"But the conversations," Prosper asked, "the very precise conversations..."

"You believe I put them under my hat, right? Wrong. While I was working down there, my aides here weren't letting any grass grow under their feet. Mistrusting each other, Clameran and Raoul were artless enough to keep the letters they wrote each to other. Joseph Dubois found these letters and made a copy of most of them. He had the most explicit of them photographed, and passed them all on to me. On her side, Nina spent her life listening at keyholes, and sending me a faithful summary of what she heard. And I had a last method of investigation at the Fauvel's, that I'll tell you about later."

It was clear, precise, and indisputable.

"I understand," Prosper murmured, "I understand."

"And you, my young comrade, what have you done?"

At that question, Prosper was worried and turned red. But he understood that not to reveal his imprudence would be folly and a mistake.

"Alas!" he answered. "I've been a fool. I read in a newspaper that Clameran was going to marry Madeleine."

"And then?" Monsieur Verduret insisted, becoming worried.

"I wrote an anonymous letter to Monsieur Fauvel, in which I gave him to understand that Madame Fauvel was deceiving him with Raoul."

With a strong blow of his fist, Monsieur Verduret broke the table near which he was sitting.

"Wretch!" he shouted. "You may've lost everything!"

In the bat of an eye, the expression of the fat man changed. His jovial face took on a threatening look. He got up, and stormed up and down the floor of the most beautiful bedroom of the Grand-Archange, without considering the lodgers in the floor below.

"But you are indeed a child," he said to a dismayed Prosper, "a madman, worse still...a fool!"

"Monsieur..."

"What! A brave man came along when you were drowning, threw himself into the water, and when he was about to save you, you grab onto his legs to keep him from swimming!...What did I tell you?"

"To keep quiet, not to leave."

"Well!"

Feeling his mistakes made Prosper more timid than a schoolboy, whose teacher has asked him about his hours of study, and who makes excuses.

"It was evening, Monsieur, I wasn't feeling well. I walked along the quays. I thought I could go into a café. Someone gave me a newspaper. I saw the terrible news..."

"Wasn't it understood that you were to have confidence in me?"

"You weren't here, Monsieur. The announcement of this marriage upset me. You were far away. The events might have taken you by surprise."

"There's nothing unforeseen except by imbeciles!" Monsieur Verduret declared peremptorily. "To write an anonymous letter! Do you know what you let me in for? You may be the cause that I'll break my sacred word given to one of the rare persons I esteem here below. I'll seem a knave, a cheat, a coward, me who…"

He interrupted himself as if he was afraid of having said too much, and it was only after some time that, becoming relatively calm, he continued.

"To go back over what's done is idiotic. Let's try to undo this false step. Where and when did you mail your letter?"

"Yesterday evening on the Rue du Cardinal-Lemoine. Ah! It wasn't at the bottom of the mailbox before I had regrets."

"It would have been better to have had them before. What time was it?"

"About 10:00 p.m."

"That means that your little love-letter reached Monsieur Fauvel this morning with his mail; therefore, he was probably alone in his study when he opened it and read it."

"That's not probable, it's certain."

"Do you recall the terms of your letter? Don't be upset. What I'm asking you is important. Try to remember…"

"Oh! I don't need to try to remember. I have the expression in my memory, as if I had just written them."

He was telling the truth, and he recited his letter to Monsieur Verduret almost verbatim. It was with the most concentrated attention that Monsieur Verduret listened to him, and the frowns on his forehead betrayed how hard he was thinking.

"Here we have," he murmured, "a harsh anonymous letter, which doesn't state its position. It lets everything be understood, without saying anything precisely. It's vague, jeering, perfidious…Repeat it to me once again."

Prosper obeyed and the second version didn't vary.

"It seems everything is there," the fat man went on, repeating the sentences of the letter after Prosper. "Nothing is more disturbing than that allusion to the cashier. This doubt: 'Was he also the one who stole Madam Fauvel's diamonds?' is just simply terrible. What could be more irritating than that ironic advice: 'In your place I wouldn't create a scandal; I would watch my wife?'"

His voice faded. He was continuing his monologue mentally. Finally, he came to stand right in front of Prosper, his arms crossed.

"The effect of your letter," he said, "must have been terrible. Let's leave that. He has a temper, doesn't he, your boss?"

"He's violence itself."

"Then the damage is perhaps not irreparable."

"What! Do you think…?"

"I think every man who has a violent nature is afraid of himself, and never acts on a first impulse. There's our chance of salvation. If, on receiving your letter, Monsieur Fauvel was not able to control himself, if he had dashed into his wife's bedroom shouting: 'Where are your diamonds?' Oh! No! No! Goodbye to our plans. I know Madame Fauvel; she'd confess."

"Would this be such a great misfortune?"

"Yes, my young comrade, because at the first word pronounced aloud between Madame Fauvel and her husband, our birds will fly away."

Prosper hadn't foreseen that eventuality.

"Next," continuing Monsieur Verduret, "that would be to cause someone immense sadness."

"Someone that I know?"

"Yes, my friend, and very well. Finally, I would be grieved to see these two villains make off, without being absolutely enlightened regarding them."

"It seems to me that you know what you have."

Monsieur Verduret shrugged.

"Then you didn't sense the gaps in my story?"

"None at all."

"That's because you didn't know how to listen to me. First of all, Louis de Clameran, did he or did he not, poison his brother?"

"Yes, according to what you told me. I'm sure of it."

"Oh! You're more affirmative, young man, than I dare to be. Your opinion is mine, but what decisive proof do we have? None at all. I dare believe I interrogated Doctor C. with some cleverness. He had not the shadow of a suspicion. And Doctor C. isn't a charlatan; he's a knowledgeable man, a practitioner, an observer. What poisons produce the effects described? I don't know of any. And I have, even so, studied poisons well, from the digitalis of Pommeraye, through the aconitum from Sauvresy."

"That death happened so conveniently…"

"That you couldn't help thinking of a crime? That's true, but chance is sometimes a wonderful accomplice. That's the first point. The second, I don't know anything about Raoul's background."

"Is it necessary to know it?"

"Indispensable, my friend. But we'll know it before very long. I've sent one of my men to London…Pardon me, one of my friends who's very skillful, Monsieur Palot, and he wrote to me that he's on the trail. It's true I wouldn't be unhappy to find out this young skeptical and sentimental scoundrel's epic, who, without Clameran, might be a nice and honest boy."

Prosper was no longer listening.

Monsieur Verduret's assurance gave him confidence. He saw the truly guilty men already in the hands of justice. He was delighted in advance with this drama in the National Law Courts, where his innocence would shine forth, and where he would be reinstated with brilliance, after having been loudly and publicly dishonored. What's more, he'd found Madeleine again, because he'd explained to himself her conduct, her reticence at the dressmaker's. He understood that she hadn't ceased for one instant to love him.

This certainty of happiness to come should have given him back, and did give him back, his cool head. It had been lost from the moment when, at his employer's bank, he had discovered that the safe had been robbed. And for the first time, he was astonished at his unusual situation. The events which upset human expectations are remarkable in that they turn ideas upside down, and raise them to the level of the strangest situations. Prosper, who was simply astonished at the protection of Monsieur Verduret, and at the extent of his methods of investigation, had come to ask what secret reasons motivated him. To sum it up, what were the reasons for that man's dedication, and what payment did he expect for his services?

The cashier's worry was so intense that suddenly he cried out:

"You don't have the right, Monsieur, to hide yourself from me! When someone has given back a man honor and life, when they have saved him, they let him know whom he should thank and bless."

Snatched suddenly from his meditations, the fat man started.

"Oh!" he said, smiling, "you're not yet out of this business, nor married, right? Then have patience and faith for a few days more."

It struck 6:00 a.m.

"Well!" exclaimed Monsieur Verduret. "Already 6:00 a.m., and me who came with the hope of getting myself a full night's sleep. This isn't the time to sleep."

He left the bedroom and went to lean over the staircase.

"Madame Alexandre!" he shouted, "Ah! Madame Alexandre!"

The hostess of the Grand-Archange, the voluminous spouse of Monsieur Fanferlot 'the Squirrel,' hadn't gone to bed. This detail struck Prosper. She came in a hurry, humble, smiling.

"What can I do for you gentlemen?" she asked.

"What I need, as soon as possible," Monsieur Verduret answered, "is your…Joseph Dubois and also Palmyre. Let them know that. When they arrive, wake me, because I'm going to lie down a while."

Madame Alexandre wasn't at the bottom of the stairs before the fat man had, without ceremony, thrown himself on Prosper's bed.

"You don't mind, do you?" he said.

Five minutes later he was asleep, and Prosper, stretched out in an armchair, was wondering, more intrigued than ever, who this savior was.

It was scarcely 9:00 a.m. when a timid finger knocked softly three times at the door of the bedroom. As soft as the sound was, it was enough to arouse Monsieur Verduret, who jumped out of bed saying:

"Who is it?"

But already Prosper, who hadn't been able to doze off in his armchair, had gone to open the door. Joseph Dubois, the Marquis de Clameran's servant, came in. Monsieur Verduret's helper was out of breath, like a man who'd been running, and his little cat's eyes were more shifty and worried than usual.

"Finally, I see you again, boss!" he exclaimed. "Finally, you're going to

544

tell me what to do again. When you were absent, I didn't know which saint to pray to. I was like a puppet on a stick with a broken wire."

"Who, you…you let yourself go to pieces like this!"

"Damn! Just think about it; I didn't know where to find you. Yesterday in the afternoon, I sent you three telegrams at the addresses you gave me in Lyon, in Beaucaire, in Oloron, and no answer. I thought I was going to go crazy, when someone came to get me for you."

"Then it's heating up?"

"It's more like burning up, boss, and it's no longer possible to stay in the situation, word of honor!"

While talking, Monsieur Verduret had straightened up his attire, somewhat mussed during his sleep. When he had finished, he threw himself into a chair, while Joseph remained respectfully standing, his cap in his hand, in the position of the soldier standing at attention.

"Explain yourself, my boy," Monsieur Verduret began, "and slowly, please. No long digressions."

"All right, bourgeois, I don't know what your intentions are. I'm ignorant of how you're going to do things, but you must finish it, strike your last blow, quickly, very quickly."

"That's your opinion, Master Joseph?"

"Yes, boss, because if you wait, if you hesitate, if you shilly-shally about, it's goodbye to the company. You won't find anything more than an empty cage; the birds will have flown. You're smiling? Yes, I know you're strong, but they're full of tricks too."

"Then you didn't take precautions down there, when I wrote you?"

"Yes, I did, boss, but they're people who can slip through your fingers like an eel. They know they have people on their heels."

"*Mille Diables!*" Monsieur Verduret exclaimed. "We must have done something clumsy."

That conversation was too transparent not to give Prosper a lot to think about. So he was listening with all his might, while noticing both the easy superiority of Monsieur Verduret, and the very sincere deference, you could feel it, of the servant.

"We haven't been clumsy," Joseph continued. "Our fellows' distrust, you know something about boss, dates from some time ago. They suspected something the evening you disguised yourself as a Paillasse, and the proof is the knife stab they gave you. Since then they've not slept, except with one eye open. However, I believe they were beginning to be reassured yesterday, when, *Ma foi!* the fire was decidedly fanned."

"And that was the reason you sent me the telegrams?"

"Naturally. Listen to this. Yesterday morning, when everyone was up, that's to say at 10:00 a.m., that's when my honorable bourgeois took a notion to put some order in his papers. These are shut up in a piece of furniture in the drawing room. His piece of furniture, which, I mention, has a lock that gave me a lot of trouble. Me, during that time, I pretended to stoke the fire, and I kept an eye on him. Boss, that man has a keen eye! At first glance he saw, or rather he guessed, someone had touched the damned papers. He turned white as a sheet, and he let out a curse, but what a curse!"

"Go on, go on."

"All right! How did he notice my little research? That's a mystery. You know how careful I am. I put everything back in order gently, with care! Then, to convince himself he hadn't made a mistake, there was my Marquis beginning to examine all the letters one by one, to turn them over, and to smell them. I wanted to offer him a microscope. He didn't need it, the villain. Suddenly, *Paf!*, he stood up, his eyes flashing. With his foot, he kicked his chair to the other side of the drawing room, and he jumped on me screaming: 'Somebody came in here. Somebody went through my papers. They photographed this letter!' *Brr!* I'm not any more cowardly than the next man, but all my blood stopped flowing. I saw myself dead, hacked, massacred. Then I said to myself: 'Fanfer...pardon me, Dubois, my boy, you're done for.' And I thought of Madame Alexandre..."

Monsieur Verduret had become serious. He was thinking, letting this good Joseph analyze and show his own emotions.

Finally, he said: "Continue."

"I wasn't afraid, boss. The scoundrel didn't dare touch me. It's true. For the sake of prudence, I put myself out of his reach, and we chatted with the big table in the middle of the drawing room between us. While wondering how he'd stumbled on to what's been going on, I defended myself like the devil. I was saying: 'It's not true! Monsieur le Marquis is mistaken. It's not possible!' *Bast!* He wasn't listening to me. Brandishing a letter, he was repeating to me: 'That letter has been photographed and I have the proof.'

"He wasn't wrong, the dear man. And at the same time he was showing me a little yellowish stain on the paper. 'Smell! He yelled at me, smell! It's some...It's...' He told me the name; I've forgotten it. It appears it's a drug chemical that photographers use."

"I know, I know," Monsieur Verduret interrupted. "And after that?"

"After that, boss, we had a scene. Oh! But what a scene! He finally grabbed me by the collar, and he shook me like a plum tree, to try to make me tell who I am, what I know, where I come from...Do I know what else? He made me tell him how I spent my time, almost down to a minute, since I'd been employed by him. That bandit was born to be an Investigating Magistrate. Then he had the hotel boy in charge of the apartment come up, and he questioned him, but in English, so that, you understand, I couldn't understand. Finally, however, he cooled down, and when the bell boy left, he gave me a 25 franc piece, telling me: 'Here, I'm sorry I roughed you up. You're too stupid for the job I suspected you of.'"

"He told you that?"

"In proper terms, speaking to me, yes, boss."

"And you think he believed it?"

"Positively."

The fat man whistled softly, clear indication that such was not his opinion.

"If you take it that way, Clameran was right. You're not talented."

It was easy to see that excellent Joseph was burning with desire to justify his opinion, but he didn't dare.

"In fact," he answered, very disconcerted, "it's very possible. Still, that business taken care of, Monsieur le Marquis got dressed to go out. Only, he didn't want his carriage, and I saw him take a hired carriage in the hotel court-yard. Then, frankly, I really thought I wouldn't see him for a long time, and that he was going out for a drive. Wrong. He came back to me in five hours, happy as a lark. Me, during that time, I ran to the telegraph station."

"What, you didn't follow him?"

"Excuse me, boss. One of our…friends tailed him. I made sure of that. It's actually through that friend that I know what our determined fellow did. He first went to a money changing office, then to the discount office, and then to the bank. You can see he's a capitalist! I think he's making plans for a little trip."

"And that's all?"

"From that direction, yes, boss. From another, it's good that you know our knaves tried to have Mademoiselle Palmyre locked up administratively. You know what I mean. Fortunately you'd foreseen this maneuver, and I saw to it over there. Without you, she'd have been locked up tight."[50]

He stopped, his nose in the air, trying to see if he had anything else to say. Not finding anything:

"And there you are!" he exclaimed. "I dare hope Monsieur Patrigent is go-ing to rub his hands together hard at my first visit. He's not expecting details that will make his File No. 113 fatter."

There was a long silence. So, just as the good Joseph had conjectured, the decisive moment had come, and Monsieur Verduret drew up his battle plan while waiting for the report of Nina, who'd again become Palmyre, which must decide his point of attack.

But Joseph Dubois was nervous and worried.

"What should I do now, boss?" he asked.

"You, my boy, you're going to go back to the hotel. Your master, very probably, will have noticed your absence, but he won't say anything to you about it. So you will…"

An exclamation from Prosper, who was standing near the window, inter-rupted Monsieur Verduret.

"What is it?" he asked.

"Clameran!" Prosper answered. "There."

---

[50] Locked up for prostitution, then illegal.

In a bound, Monsieur Verduret and Joseph were at the window.

"Where do you see him?" they asked him.

"There, at the corner of the bridge, behind that orange merchant's stall."

Prosper wasn't mistaken. It was indeed the noble Marquis de Clameran, who, lying in wait behind the moveable shop, was spying on the comings and goings of the Grand-Archange Hotel, and waiting for his domestic. It took a little time to be sure, because the Marquis, as an adventurer accustomed to these hazardous expeditions, hid himself very cleverly. But a moment came when, squeezed and jostled by the crowd, he was obliged to get down from the sidewalk. He was then out in the open.

"Wasn't I right?" exclaimed the cashier. "Is there doubt any longer?"

"True!" murmured Joseph, convinced. "It's unbelievable."

Monsieur Verduret himself didn't seem at all surprised.

"There's the hunted become the huntsman," he said. "Well! Joseph, my boy, do you still stubbornly maintain that your honorable bourgeois was duped by your pretending to be an idiot?"

"You've assured me of the opposite, boss," the good Dubois answered in the humblest tone, "and after an affirmation by you, proofs are useless."

"What's more," continued the fat man, "that maneuver, as reckless as it seems, was to be expected. That man knows that we're on to him, and quite naturally, he's trying to find out who his enemies are. Can you understand how much he must be suffering from these uncertainties? Perhaps he imagines that those tracking him are quite simply very hungry former accomplices, who'd like a little piece of the cake. He's going to stay there until Joseph goes out again, and then he'll come for information."

"But I can leave without his seeing me, boss."

"Yes, I know. You can jump over the little wall which separates the Grand-Archange Hotel from the wine merchant. From there you go through the basement of the stationery store, and you would get away through the Rue de la Huchette."

That good Joseph had the priceless look of a man who suddenly gets a bucket full of cold water thrown on his head, without knowing from where.

"That's really it, boss," he stammered. "They told me down there that you know all the houses in Paris like that. Is that true?"

Prosper's fat friend didn't deign to answer. He was wondering what immediate profit he could draw from Clameran's actions. As for the cashier, he was listening open-mouthed, observing alternately these two unknown men, who, apparently without anything to gain, were using their ingenuity to win the difficult game in which his honor, his happiness, and his life were at stake.

"There's still a way," Joseph, who on his part had been thinking, suggested.

"What?"

"I can leave just playing the fool, my hands in my pockets, and go back to the Hotel du Louvre, walking along the streets casually, as if I had all the time in the world."

"And afterwards?"

"Damn!...The Clameran fellow will come question Madame Alexandre; and, if you've told her what to say, you know how sharp she is, she'll confuse our fine fellow in such a way he won't know what to think."

"Bad!" Monsieur Verduret pronounced peremptorily. "You don't throw such a compromised fellow off the track and, most of all, you don't reassure him."

The fat man's decision was made. In that curt tone which did not need a reply, he continued.

"I have something better. Has Clameran seen Lagors since he's known his papers have been gone through?"

"No, boss."

"He might have written him."

"I'll bet my life he didn't. Following your instructions, having to watch his correspondence above all, I organized a little system which warns me as soon as he touches a pen. Now, for twenty-four hours the pens haven't been touched."

"Clameran went out yesterday, a part of the afternoon."

"He didn't write on the way; the man following him guarantees it."

"All right! Let's go, let's go!" the fat man said. "Go downstairs. Quicker than that! I'll give you a quarter of an hour to give yourself a disguise, a disguise for down there. You understand. Me, I won't lose sight of our villain from here."

Without hesitating, without a word, the good Joseph, light as a sylph, disappeared. Monsieur Verduret and Prosper remained near the window, observing Clameran. Following the caprices of the back and forth movement of the crowd, he appeared or disappeared, but seemed very determined not to abandon his post without having gotten some information.

"Why are you attaching yourself thus exclusively to the Marquis?" asked Prosper.

"Because, my comrade," Monsieur Verduret replied, "because..."

He was looking for a good reason to give, a plausible pretext. Not finding any, he was vexed and added roughly:

"That's my business."

They had given Joseph a quarter of an hour to metamorphose himself. Ten minutes hadn't gone by, when he reappeared. Of the good-looking servant wearing a red vest, sideburns cut in the Bergami fashion, with a demeanor cantankerous and self-important at the same time, there remained absolutely nothing. The man who reappeared was one of those whose very aspect frightens and makes the most naïve pickpockets take to flight like a flock of sparrows. His black tie, rolled into a string around a false, questionable collar, ornamented with an artificial gem tie pin, his black waistcoat buttoned very high, his greasy hat, his boots so marvelously waxed that a coquettish girl could see herself in them, and finally his heavy cane, betrayed a minor employee of the Rue de Jerusalem, as clearly as trousers dyed red with madder proclaim the soldier.

Joseph Dubois had faded away, and from his footman's livery, the crafty Fanferlot 'the Squirrel' escaped, triumphant and radiant. At his entrance, Prosper couldn't hold back an exclamation of surprise, almost of fright. He had just recognized the little man who, the day of the robbery, helped the Commissioner of Police's search. Monsieur Verduret examined his helper with an evidently satisfied air.

"Not bad," he said. "Not bad. Your whole body lets off a police perfume strong enough to make an honest man shudder. You understood me. That's exactly the way I wanted you."

The compliment seemed to carry away Dubois/Fanferlot.

"Now that I'm dressed up, boss, what do I do?"

"Nothing difficult for a clever man. However, pay attention to this. The success of my plans depends on the precision of the steps. Before taking care of Lagors, I want to finish with Clameran. Now, since the scoundrels are separated, they must be prevented from rejoining each other."

"Understood!" said Fanferlot, winking. "I'm going to set up a diversion."

"As you say. So, you're going to leave by the Rue de la Huchette, and go as far as the Pont Saint-Michel. There, you'll go down as far as the bank, and you'll very clumsily go take a post on one of the Quay stairs, in such a way that Clameran can find you and know that while he's spying from where he is, he's being spied on himself. If he doesn't see you, you're clever enough to draw his attention."

"*Parbleu!* I'll throw a stone in the water."

Delighted with his idea, Dubois/Fanferlot rubbed his hands together.

"Use a rock," Monsieur Verduret went on. "As soon as Clameran has seen you, he'll get worried and he'll make off. You, you'll follow him, apparently stupidly, but doggedly. Recognizing that he's dealing with the police, he'll become afraid, and he'll do everything he can to throw you off the track. It's at this point that you'll have to keep your eyes open. He's tricky, the scoundrel."

"Good. I wasn't born yesterday."

"So much the better! You'll prove it to him. What's sure is, feeling you on his heels, he won't dare go back to the Hotel du Louvre, fearing he'll find some curious people there. That's the main point for me."

"But if he goes back, even so?" Fanferlot asked.

The fat man seemed to evaluate this objection.

"That's not probable," he answered. "But if, nevertheless, he has that daring, you'll let him do it. You'll wait for him, and when he comes out, you'll start to follow him again. But he won't return. Instead, he'll get the idea to take it doesn't matter which train. In that case, you won't lose him, even if he should take you to Siberia. Do you have money? Good! I won't examine your travel reimbursement request too closely. Ah! Two words more. If the villain takes the train, send me word here. Next, if he's still being chased this evening, be careful in out of the way places when night comes. The scoundrel is capable of anything."

"Can I shoot at him?"

"Stop there! No childish behavior. However, if he attacks you! All right, my boy, on your way."

Dubois/Fanferlot left. Monsieur Verduret and Prosper went back to their lookout post.

"Why take so much trouble?" whispered the cashier. "I didn't have all the charges against me that overwhelm Clameran, and they didn't take such care with me..."

The fat man replied: "How is it that you still don't understand that I want to separate Raoul's case from that of the Marquis...but, *Chut!*... Look..."

Clameran had left his observation post to approach the bridge parapet, and he was walking up and down as if trying to make out something unusual.

"Ah!" murmured Monsieur Verduret, "he's just discovered our man."

Indeed, Clameran's worry was apparent. He took several steps as if he wanted to cross the bridge, then suddenly thinking better of it, he turned around and started in the direction of the Rue Saint-Jacques.

"He's trapped!" Monsieur Verduret cried out joyously. But just at that moment, the noise of the door opening made him, as well as Prosper, turn around. Madame Nina Gypsy, that is to say, Palmyre Chocareille, was standing in the middle of the bedroom. Poor Nina! Each of the days that had gone by since she entered Madeleine's service had weighed like a year on her charming head. Tears had extinguished the amorous gleam of her black eyes. Her fresh cheeks had paled and wrinkled. The smile had frozen on her lips, in the past so provocative and redder than the opened pomegranate. Poor Gypsy! So lively in the past, so happy, so restless, she was now subdued under the weight of cares too heavy for her. After having had all the overbearing qualities of happiness, she was humbled by misfortune.

Prosper imagined that, mad with joy seeing him again, totally proud of having so nobly devoted herself for him, Nina was going to throw her arms around his neck and embrace him. He was wrong. And, although belonging completely to Madeleine since he had found out the reasons for her harshness, he was affected by that disappointment. Madame Gypsy hardly seemed to recognize him. She greeted him timidly, almost as a stranger. All her attention was concentrated on Monsieur Verduret. The looks she turned on him had that fearful and loving timidity of the poor animal that had been often ill-treated by his master. He, however, behaved well toward her, paternal, affectionate.

"Well, dear child," he asked in his nicest voice, "what information do you bring me?"

"There must be something new in the household, Monsieur. I was in a hurry to warn you, but I was held back by my job. Mademoiselle Madeleine had to go to some trouble to find a pretext for me to leave."

"Please thank Mademoiselle Madeleine for her confidence," the fat man continued, "until I can express all my gratitude myself. I suppose, for the rest, she is faithful to our agreement?"

"Yes, Monsieur."

"They receive the Marquis de Clameran?"

"Since the marriage is settled on, he comes every evening, and Mademoiselle receives him very well. He seems delighted."

These assurances, which reversed all Prosper's ideas, made him angrily lose control. The poor boy, understanding nothing of Monsieur Verduret's wise maneuvers, felt himself tossed about by inexplicable wills. He suddenly saw himself betrayed, scoffed at, and tricked.

"What!" he shouted, "that miserable Marquis de Clameran, that infamous thief, that murderer, is admitted as a friend at Monsieur Fauvel's. He courts Madeleine! Then what did you tell me, Monsieur, what hopes did you lull me with to make me fall asleep?"

With a commanding gesture, Monsieur Verduret cut short his recriminations.

"Enough," he said harshly. "That's enough of that. You're far too...well-behaved, after all, my comrade. If you're incapable of trying to do anything serious to save yourself, at least let those working for you proceed without constantly bothering them with childish suspicions. Don't you think you've done enough to hinder me?" That lesson given, he turned again toward Gypsy, and in a gentler tone:

"Now, for the two of us, dear child, what have you learned?"

"Ah! Monsieur, nothing positive, unfortunately, nothing you can act on, and I'm very sorry about that, believe me!"

"However, my child, you were telling me about a serious event."

Madam Gypsy made a discouraged gesture.

"That is to say, Monsieur," she continued, "that I suspect something, that I'm guessing something. What? I don't know how to tell it, nor to express it clearly. Perhaps it's only a ridiculous foreboding which makes me see everything as extraordinary. It seems to me that misfortune is in the house, that we're approaching catastrophe. It's impossible to get anything out of Madame Fauvel. Now she's like a body without a soul. Besides, I would swear she doesn't trust her niece, that she hides things from her."

"And Monsieur Fauvel?"

"I was going to tell you about that, Monsieur. Something bad has happened to him. I'd swear to it. Since yesterday, he's not the same man. He goes, he comes, he doesn't stay in one place. You'd say he was a mad man. His voice is completely changed, so altered that Mademoiselle noticed it and mentioned it to me. And Monsieur Lucien, he too, mentioned it. The Monsieur that I've seen so indulgent, and so good, has become harsh, irritable, and nervous. He's like someone who's about to explode, and who's holding himself in. Finally, his eyes, that I've observed closely, have a strange, indefinable look, which become terrible when he looks at Madame. Yesterday evening, as soon as Monsieur Clameran arrived, Monsieur left suddenly, saying he had to work."

A triumphant exclamation from Monsieur Verduret interrupted Madam Gypsy. He was beaming.

"Hein!" he said to Prosper, forgetting his bad temper of a short time ago. *"Hein!* What did I say would happen?"

"It's certain, Monsieur…"

"This unhappy man didn't trust his first reaction. I foresaw that. Now he's watching, he's lying in wait for proofs to back up your letter. And when I say proofs…he must have some already. Did these ladies go out yesterday?"

"Yes, a part of the day."

"What did Monsieur Fauvel do?"

"He stayed home alone. The ladies took me with them."

"No longer any doubt!" shouted the fat man. "He'll have looked for and found them, *Pardieu!!* The clues were very decisive after your letter. Ah! Prosper, unhappy young man, your anonymous letter has done us a lot of harm."

Monsieur Verduret's reflections shone a sudden light on Madam Gypsy's mind.

"I've got it!" she said. "Monsieur Fauvel knows everything."

"You mean to say, he thinks he knows everything, and what he's been told is even more frightful than the truth."

"Then, I understand the order that Monsieur Cavaillon claims to have overheard."

"What order?"

"Monsieur Cavaillon maintains that he heard Monsieur Fauvel give orders to his valet, Monsieur Evariste, threatening to send him away immediately if he didn't give all the letters delivered to the house, from wherever they came and whatever the address, only to him."

"If that's how it is," observed Prosper—dominated by his very understandable egoism. "If that's how it is, everything is going to come out, and it would be better to confess…"

Once again, a crushing look from Monsieur Verduret stopped him cold.

"At what time," he asked, "did young Cavaillon hear that order given?"

"Yesterday, in the afternoon."

"That's what I was afraid of," Monsieur Verduret exclaimed. "It's clear he's made up his mind; and if he's concealing it, that's because he wants to be sure to avenge himself. Can we arrive in time to thwart his plans? Is there still time to tie a blindfold around his eyes thick enough, that he can believe that anonymous letter was false?"

He was silent. Prosper's folly—excusable, moreover—turned upside down the very simple plan he had at first conceived, and now he was searching his alert mind for a last expedient.

"Thank you for your information, my dear child," he finally said. "I'm going to think of something, because to do nothing right now would be horribly dangerous. You, return quickly. Don't be mistaken. Monsieur Fauvel thinks you're in on the secret. So be careful. At the least thing that happens, as insignificant as it may be, send word."

But Nina, thus dismissed, didn't leave.

"And Caldas, Monsieur?" she asked, very timidly.

That was the third time in two weeks that Prosper had heard that name pronounced. The first time was in the corridor of the Prefect of Police: a middle-aged man, with a respectable appearance, had whispered it in his ear, while promising him help and protection. Another time, the Investigating Magistrate had thrown it in his face when talking about Gypsy. He had searched for this name among all the individuals he had known and forgotten, and it seemed to him, that he must have found himself mixed up in some serious adventure in his life; but which one? Monsieur Verduret, himself the impassive man had, at this name, a nervous tremor, immediately suppressed.

"I promised you I'd help you find him again," he pronounced. "I'll keep my promise...*Au revoir.*"

It was noon. Monsieur Verduret found he was hungry. He called Madame Alexandre, and that powerful sovereign of the Grand-Archange soon placed in front of the window a little table, at which Prosper and his protector sat down. But neither a little lunch finely prepared with love, nor the Ostende oysters worthy of the Baron Brisse,[51] nor the excellent wine, brought out from behind the kindling where it was hidden, could cheer up Monsieur Verduret. To Madame Alexandre's eager and wheedling questions, he could only reply:

"*Chut! Chut!* Don't bother me."

For the first time since he'd met the fat man, Prosper discovered signs of worry and hesitation on his face. Prosper's anxiety increased twofold, to the point that he dared question.

"Have I put you in a terrible jam, Monsieur?" he ventured to ask.

"Yes," Monsieur Verduret answered. "Terrible is the word. What should be done? Hasten events or wait for them? And I'm bound by sacred commitments...So, I'm not going to get out of this without the Investigating Magistrate. We have to ask him for help. Come with me."

---

[51] Gastronomical historian, author of culinary guides.

Chapter XXIII

As it had been easy to foresee, as Monsieur Verduret had predicted, the effect of Prosper's anonymous letter had been dreadful. It was morning. Monsieur Fauvel had just gone into his study to open his daily correspondence. He had already broken the seal of a dozen envelopes, and gone through as many communications or business propositions, when the fatal missive came into his hand. The writing jumped out at him. That there was an attempt to disguise the handwriting was evident. And although in his situation as a millionaire he was accustomed to receiving a good number of demands or anonymous insults, that peculiarity struck him, and even—it would be childish to deny the foreboding— clutched at his heart. It was with a trembling hand, with the absolute certainty that he was going to learn misfortune, that he broke the seal, that he unfolded the heavy café paper, and that he read:

Dear Monsieur,
You turned your cashier over to the law, and you did well because you're very certain that he was unfaithful. But if he was the one who took 350,000 francs from your safe, was it also who stole Mme Fauvel's diamonds? etc., etc.

This was like a bolt of lightning for that man whose constant prosperity had drained the favors of destiny, and who, looking hard into all his past, would not have found one tear shed for a real misfortune. What! His wife was deceiving him, and among everyone, she had precisely chosen a man, vile to the point that he had taken possession of the diamonds she possessed; and he had abused his control to constrain her to become an accomplice to a robbery that would condemn an innocent man! Because that was exactly what the anonymous denunciation said.

Monsieur Fauvel was at first floored, like the unfortunate man who, at the moment he least expects it, receives a hammer blow to the skull. All his overthrown ideas whirled around in the void, haphazardly, like tree leaves in autumn at the first gusts of a thunderstorm. It seemed to him that everything around him was nothing but shadows, and that a deadly numbness was paralyzing his mind. But at the end of several minutes, reason returned.

"What cowardly infamy!" he exclaimed. "What a shameful abomination."

And crumpling the damned letter, rolling it between his hands in rage, he threw it into the fireplace, without fire at this moment, murmuring:

"I don't want to think about it anymore. I don't want to soil my imagination with this baseness."

He said that. What's more, in saying it, he believed it, and nevertheless he couldn't continue to go through his mail. Because suspicion, similar to those imperceptible worms which slip into ripe fruits without leaving a trace of their entry, and spoil them inside, suspicion, when it penetrates a brain, grows there, gets established there, and leaves there no belief intact. Leaning on his desk, Monsieur Fauvel was thinking, making futile efforts to recover his calm, his mind's lucidity. However, what if that was the truth! Anger followed the prostration of the first few minutes, one of those dangerous white angers which takes away free will, which throws a man outside himself, which makes him commit crimes.

"Ah!" He said to himself, his teeth clenched in anger, "If I knew the scoundrel who dared write to me, if I had him..."

Imagining then that the writing could tell him something, he got up and went to pick up the fatal papers from the ashes. He untwisted it, opened it, smoothed it out as well as he could and placed it on his desk. He applied himself to studying the letters, concentrating all the strength of his intelligence on a full or a thin stroke, on the shape more or less skillful of such and such a capital letter.

He thought: *"This must be the work of one of my employees whose interest or self-esteem I wounded."*

At that idea, he passed in review his numerous personnel, without discovering anyone capable of that base vengeance. Then he wondered where that letter had been mailed, thinking that that circumstance would perhaps enlighten him. He looked for the envelope, found it, and read: *Rue du Cardinal Lemoine.* That detail gave him no enlightenment. Once again, he came back to the letter, spelling out, so to speak, each word one after the other, weighing each expression, analyzing the texture of all the sentences.

It's agreed that an anonymous letter, the work of a coward, should be absolutely disdained and paid no attention to. What catastrophes, however, have no other origin! How many noble existences have been broken, blighted by some lines that a miserable person, by chance, threw on paper? Yes, people despise the anonymous letter. They throw it in the fire. It burns...But after the flame has destroyed the paper, the doubt remains; and similar to a subtle poison, it vanishes and goes into the deepest recesses of the soul, soiling and disorganizing the most saintly and firmest beliefs.

And something always remains. The woman suspected, even unjustly, if only for an hour, is no longer the woman in whom one had faith as in himself. Whatever happens, doubt leaves its traces, like sweat on the fingers does on the gilt of idols. The longer Monsieur Fauvel thought, he felt his confidence, so absolute some minutes before, changed.

"No!" he cried out, "I can't endure this torture any longer. I'm going to go show this letter to my wife." He stood up. A terrible thought, sharper than a point of red steel in the flesh, nailed him to his chair.

"What if they're telling the truth, however!" he whispered. "What if I've been miserably duped! By confiding in my wife, I'll put her on guard. I'll take away any means of investigation. I'll give up ever knowing the truth."

Thus were realized all the presumptions of Monsieur Verduret, that great analyst of passion.

"If Monsieur Fauvel doesn't give way to the first moment's reaction," he had said, "if he reflects, we have some time before us."

Indeed, after long and sad meditation, the banker decided that he would watch his wife. Yes, he, the loyal and frank man par excellence, he resigned himself to the ignoble role of the jealous man, of the domestic spy, whose sad investigations degrade him as much, or more, than the woman of whom they're the object.

He, the man of spontaneous violence, of sudden anger, soon calmed. He had just resolved to compose an impassive face, to collect one by one, proofs of innocence or guilt, to silence his resentment, not to come out into the open, finally, until he had the evidence for himself. In addition, he had a very simple method of verification. His wife's diamonds had been carried to the Mont-de-Piété pawn brokers, the letter had told him. If it was lying on this point, there was no reason to take account of the rest. If, on the contrary, it was telling the truth!

Monsieur Fauvel was at that stage in his mediations, when they came to tell him that dinner was served. It was a matter of not letting anyone see through him. Before leaving his study, he looked at himself in the mirror. He was so terribly pale, he frightened himself.

"Then are you strong enough?" he asked himself.

At the table he thought about controlling himself enough to avoid all questions, which, for the least thing, would bring on his wife's solicitude. He even talked a lot; he told stories, hoping in this way to turn away attention. But while talking, he was thinking only of ways to go through the drawers of his wife's chests as soon as possible, without her being aware of it. That idea preoccupied him to the point that he couldn't prevent himself from asking his wife if she was going out that day.

"Yes," she answered. "The weather is terrible, but Madeleine and I have some pressing errands to run."

"And what time do you intend to leave?"

"Soon after lunch."

He breathed deeply, as if he had been relieved of a terrible oppression. In a few instants he was going to be sure of his situation. Now so poignant and so intolerable was that man's uncertainty, that to it, he preferred anything, even the most atrocious reality.

Lunch finished, he lit up a cigar; but he didn't stay in the dining room, as he usually did. He went into his study, using as a pretext some urgent work. He pushed caution even to the extent of having Lucien, his son, whom he charged with an errand, follow him.

He wanted to remain alone in the house. Finally, at the end of half an hour, which seemed a century to him, he heard a carriage rolling away under the entry canopy. Madame Fauvel and her niece were leaving.

Without waiting any longer, he dashed into his wife's bedroom and opened the drawers of the chest where she kept her jewels. Many of the jewel cases that he was familiar with were missing. Those which remained—there were ten or twelve—were empty. The anonymous letter was telling the truth. That certainty burst like a bomb shell in Monsieur Fauvel's head. And nevertheless!

"No," he stammered. "That's not possible."

Immediately, with the mad desperation of agony and as if, condemned to death, he had hope of finding pardon, he began to rummage around everywhere, to search in all the furniture. He used a certain order, however, taking good care not to leave traces of his search. Madame Fauvel, he understood vaguely, might have changed where she kept her jewelry, or sent some to be repaired or reset.

Nothing. He found nothing! Then he remembered the grand ball the Messieurs Jandidier had given. He, vain, had said to his wife:

"Why don't you wear your diamonds?"

She answered, smiling, "For what reason? Everyone knows them. By not wearing them, I'll be more noticed. Besides, they don't go with my costume."

Yes, she had said that to him without any trouble, without blushing, without even her voice trembling. What impudence! What corruption was hidden under all those appearances of virginity, that she still had after twenty years of marriage! But suddenly, in the confusion of his thoughts, hope came to him, puny and hardly acceptable, to which, nevertheless, he clung as the drowning man to his ship's wreckage. Those diamonds, Madame Fauvel might have left them in Madeleine's bedroom.

Without thinking about how obnoxious his investigations were, he ran to that young girl's bedroom. There, as in his wife's, he lay his rough hands everywhere, forgetting the respect he owed to that sanctuary.

He didn't find Madame Fauvel's diamonds, but in Madeleine's jewelry chest, he saw seven or eight empty boxes. She too, she had given her jewelry. She knew the shame of the household. She was an accomplice.

This last blow destroyed Monsieur Fauvel's courage.

"They conspired to deceive me," he whispered. "They have an understanding!"

And broken, weak, he let himself fall into an armchair. Big silent tears rolled down his cheeks, and from time to time, he breathed a deep sigh. His life was over. In a moment, the structure of his happiness, of his security, of his future that he'd put twenty years into building, that he believed solid enough to withstand any vagaries of fortune, flew to pieces, more fragile than glass.

In appearance, nothing in his existence had changed. He had not been materially affected. The objects around him stayed the same, with the same appearance; and nevertheless, things had been wrecked, more unheard of, more surprising, than turning day into night.

What! Valentine, the chaste young girl so much loved in the past, whose possession he had bought at the price of his fortune. Valentine, that woman who had become more and more dear to him, as they grew old together, that spouse, incomparable in appearance, betrayed him!

She deceived him...She...the mother of his sons! That last thought above all revolted his whole being, even to disgust. His sons! Bitter derision! Were they really his! The woman who now, when her hair was already turning her temples grey, was deceiving him. Had she deceived him in the past?

And not only was he tortured by the present, but he was suffering in the past. Paying with the unheard of agony of several minutes through years of happiness, he was furious at the memory of certain intimate joys, like a man who suddenly learns that the exquisite wine he had drunk was poisoned. That's how it is, confidence has no gradations: it is, or it is not. And he, he no longer had confidence. All that unhappy man's dreams, all his hopes, rested on the love of that woman. Discovering, as he believed, that she was unworthy of him, he could see no possibility of happiness, and he wondered what was the good of living and for what purpose.

However, Monsieur Fauvel's prostration didn't last very long. The fire of anger had quickly dried his tears, and he stood up changed by revenge, deciding to make his destroyed happiness be paid for dearly. But he knew that on just one clue, the diamonds which couldn't be found, he couldn't let his resentment influence him. Fortunately, he could secure other proofs. To begin with, he called his valet, and instructed him to give all the letters which arrived at the house only to him, the master. Then he sent a detailed telegram to a notary at Saint-Rémy, his correspondent, from whom he asked exact information about the Lagors family, and about Raoul in particular. Finally, following advice concerning anonymous denunciations, he hastened to the Prefecture of Police, hoping to find a biography of Clameran there. But the police, fortunately for many people, are as discreet as the tomb. It keeps its secrets for itself alone, as a miser guards his treasure. It takes a court order to make the terrible green boxes, that it keeps padlocked like a safe, speak. They politely asked Monsieur Fauvel the reasons which impelled him to inform himself on the past of a French citizen, and as he couldn't supply them, they referred him to the State Public Minister, in the Court of Appeals. He couldn't accept that insinuation. He had sworn that the secret of his misfortunes would remain between the three interested parties. Mortally offended, he wanted to be the sole judge and executioner. He returned home more irritated than when he left, and he found a response to his Saint-Rémy telegraph.

The Lagors family, it told him, as Monsieur Verduret had learned, *is in the worst poverty and no one knows Monsieur Raoul. Madame de Lagors had only daughters in her marriage, etc.*

That revelation was the straw that broke the camel's back. The banker thought that it was up to him to measure the extent of his wife's infamy. It showed him a refinement of duplicity, more frightful perhaps than the crime itself.

"The miserable woman!" mad with sadness and raging internally, he told himself, "the miserable woman! To see her lover more freely, never to lose sight of him, she dared to introduce him to me, under the name of a nephew who's never existed. She had the inconceivable immodesty to open my house to him, to let him sit down at the family hearth, between me and my sons. And me, a stupid, honest man, trusting and credulous husband, I liked him, this boy. I shook his hand. I lent him my money."

He then imagined Raoul and his wife making merry at their rendezvous over his easy-going guilelessness; and with the sharp stings of offended egotism adding to those horrible lacerations, he underwent the most terrible torture there is here below.

Death! He saw only death to punish such insults. But just the intensity of his resentment gave him the strength to feign, to control himself.

"It'll be my turn to deceive these miscreants," he said to himself with terrible satisfaction.

He was his usual self that evening. He joked at dinner. Only, when at 9:00 p.m. he saw Clameran enter, he left, fearing he couldn't control himself, and he didn't return until very late into the night.

The next day he received the fruit of his prudence. Among the mid-day mail delivery brought by his valet, he found one bearing a Vésinet stamp. Taking infinite precautions, he broke the seal and he read:

Dear Aunt, It is indispensable that I see you right today and I'm waiting for you. I'll tell you what reasons keep me from coming to you. Raoul

"Now I've got them!" Monsieur Fauvel exclaimed, trembling with the joy of satisfied revenge. He was seeing himself so completely avenged that, opening the drawer of his desk, he took out a revolver and checked the firing mechanism. He really believed he was alone; but nevertheless, he had a witness to his smallest gestures. Her eyes glued to the keyhole, Nina Gypsy, back from the Grand-Archange, was watching and the banker's movements showed her the truth.

Monsieur Fauvel had placed his revolver on the mantle of the chimney, and he was busy readjusting the letter's seal. The operation completed, he went to take it to the concierge, not wishing his wife to know that Raoul's missive had passed through his hands. He was absent hardly two minutes; but motivated by the imminence of danger, Gypsy had time to enter the study, run to the chimney and take the balls out of the revolver.

"So," she thought, *"the immediate peril is averted, and through Cavaillon, I'm going to alert Monsieur Verdure to what's happening. He may perhaps have time to give a warning.*"

She indeed went downstairs to give instructions to the young employee, telling him to deliver the message to Madame Alexandre, to be sure of success.

An hour later having dressed, Madame Fauvel ordered a carriage and left. Monsieur Fauvel, who had ordered a hired carriage in advance, started on her trail.

"*Mon Dieu!*" Nina thought, "*If Monsieur Verduret doesn't arrive in time, Madame Fauvel and Raoul are lost.*"

Chapter XXIV

The day on which the Marquis de Clameran hadn't perceived any obstacle but Raoul de Lagors between him and Madeleine, he had firmly sworn to himself that he would get rid of the obstacle. The very next day, his measures were taken. Raoul, returning after midnight on foot to his house in Vésinet, was attacked at the detour from the little railroad station by three individuals, who insisted on seeing the time by his watch.

With prodigious strength under his apparently slim physique, agile and kept in shape by the *chausson français* exercises and English boxing, Raoul was able to throw off his attackers, without any other damage than a deep cut on his left arm. Out of danger, he promised himself that henceforth he'd take his precautions. He, who right up to that time hadn't believed he'd be stopped at night, decided he would always be armed when he returned to Vésinet. It never occurred to him then to suspect his accomplice. But two days later, in the café he frequented, a huge devil of an individual he didn't know tried to involve him in an argument for no reason. He ended up challenging him to a duel, throwing his card in his face, telling him he was at his disposition, and was ready to accord him all imaginable satisfaction. Raoul had wanted to jump on the insolent individual and challenge him to hand-to-hand fighting, but his friends held him back.

"All right," he said. "Be at your house tomorrow morning, Monsieur, and I'll send two of my friends around."

He said that on the spur of the moment, trembling with anger; but when the man who'd insulted him departed, he recovered all his coolness, reflected, and the most unusual doubts filled his head.

Having picked up the card of that individual with a big mustache and a swaggering attitude, he read:

W. H. B. JACOBSON
Former Garibaldi volunteer
Ex-Superior Officer of the Southern Armies
(Italy-America)
30, Rue Léonie

"Oh! Oh!" he thought, *"Here's a glorious military man who might have gotten all his promotions in an exercise drill hall. "*

Raoul, who had seen a lot, had retained exactly enough to know what to make of these honorable heroes who advertised their services for sale on the vellum of visiting cards. That fact didn't influence his actions. The incident having had numerous witnesses, he asked two young men he knew to please go around the next day, early in the morning, to Monsieur Jacobson's lodgings, to arrange the dueling terms with him. It was agreed that these Messieurs would give Raoul an account of the result of their mission, not at his house at Vésinet, but at the Hotel du Louvre, where he intended to spend the night. Everything arranged, Raoul left. Smelling a trap, he wanted to find out the truth of the matter.

Energetic and experienced, he began immediately to search for information. He obtained that, not without some trouble. It was neither splendid nor, above all, reassuring.

Monsieur Jacobson, who lived in a shady looking hotel, inhabited mainly by ladies of more than a little light behavior, was described to him as an eccentric gentleman, whose means of making a livelihood seemed a very difficult problem to solve. He learned that Jacobson reigned despotically at a table d'hôte, went out a great deal, and came in late. He seemed not to have any other capital, but what he gained by his services, his social talents, and a notable quantity of ways to live by his wits.

"Knowing that," Raoul thought, *"What's the purpose of that individual's trying to involve me in a quarrel?* What advantage would he draw from *the sword wound he'll give me? None, apparently, without counting on the fact that his bellicose disposition might raise the bothersome touchiness of the police, that he must have reason to handle tactfully. Therefore, he has reasons for acting as he did, that I can't discern. Therefore..."*

That little investigation briskly and cleverly conducted, these diverse considerations and their natural deductions concluded, turned Raoul so cold that, back at the Hotel du Louvre, he didn't breathe a word of his misadventure to Clameran, whom he found still up. Toward 8:30 a.m. his witnesses arrived. Monsieur Jacobson consented to fight with the sword, but on the hour in the Bois de Vincennes. Raoul was anything other than confident, but he answered very cheerfully:

"All right, I accept this gentleman's conditions. Let's go."

They arrived at the dueling field, and after a minute of engagement, Raoul was struck lightly a little above the right breast. The ex-superior southern officer wanted to continue the combat to the death—his seconds were of that opinion. But Raoul's witnesses— honest boys—declared that honor had been satisfied, and that they wouldn't let their client risk his life again. They had to be obeyed, because they threatened to withdraw; and Raoul returned, considering himself very lucky to have gotten off with that hygienic bloodletting. And he was very determined to avoid in the future that so-called Garibaldian gentleman. Because, the day before, night helping with its beneficial counsel, his alert mind had traveled a long way. Between the armed attack at Vésinet, and this evidently premeditated and wished for duel, he discovered plausible reasons for the, at least, unusual coincidences. From that, he recognized Clameran's hand in the way the two attempts appeared.

Having learned through Madame Fauvel the conditions which Madeleine made for her marriage, he understood what enormous interest Clameran had to get rid of him, without getting mixed up with the law. This suspicion in his mind, he recalled a number of insignificant facts from the preceding days. He gave meaning to certain casual remarks. He questioned the Marquis very cleverly, and soon his doubts turned into certainty. The conviction that the man, whose projects he had so powerfully aided, paid murderers and armed ruffians against him, was enough to drive him to fury.

That betrayal seemed monstrous to him. Still a naïve bandit, he believed in honesty among accomplices, in that famous honesty of crooks, more faithful to sworn faith than honest men, people like to say. To his anger, there was mingled a very natural feeling of fear. He understood that the life threatened by a scoundrel as daring as Clameran, was held only by a thread. Twice luck had miraculously favored him. A third attempt could, and even must, be fatal to him. Judging his accomplice accurately, Raoul no longer saw anything but ambushes around him. He saw death in all its forms rising before him. He feared both to go out and to stay home. He never ventured into public places, except with a thousand precautions; and he feared poison, as much as steel. He hardly dared to eat. He found bizarre tastes like the after taste of strychnine, in all the dishes served him.

It wasn't possible to live like that; and with as much a desire for revenge as the necessity of defending himself, he resolved to go on the offensive. He understood very well that in the fight thus drawn up on this terrain, between Clameran and himself, one of the two inevitably would succumb.

"It's better to kill the devil than to be killed by him," he told himself.

When he was poor, when for a few guineas he carelessly risked Botany Bay,[52] it wouldn't have bothered Raoul at all to kill the devil. With a nice little knife stab, he would have gotten the better of Clameran. But with money had come prudence. He wanted to enjoy his 400,000 stolen francs honestly, and it was important to him not to compromise his new status. He then began, on his side, to look for some discreet means of making his feared accomplice disappear. The means were hard to find. While waiting, he found it fair play to make Clameran's schemes miscarry, and to prevent his marriage. It was only up to Raoul to thwart this marriage. This way, he was sure to hit him right in the heart, and that was already satisfaction. What's more, he was persuaded that in openingly taking Madeleine and her aunt's side, he would remove them from Clameran's hands.

It was following that long thought-out resolution, that he wrote to Madame Fauvel to ask her for a rendezvous. The poor woman didn't hesitate. She hurried to Vésinet at the time indicated, trembling to have to submit again to demands

---

[52] British penal colony in Australia.

564

and threats. She was mistaken. She found the Raoul of the early days, that so attractive and so good son, whose caresses had seduced her. Before opening up to her, before explaining the truth to her in his fashion, he tried to reassure her. He succeeded. Happy and smiling, that unfortunate woman sat in an armchair, while Raoul knelt in front of her.

"I've made you suffer too much, Mother," he whispered in his most wheedling voice. "I'm sorry. Listen to me…"

He didn't have time to say any more. At the sound of the door opening, he suddenly rose. Monsieur Fauvel, a revolver in his hand, was on the threshold. The banker was frightfully pale. It was easy to see he was making superhuman efforts to show the cold impassivity of the judge, who sees and punishes the crime. But his calm was terrifying, like that which precedes the upheavals of the tempest.

He answered the cry of his wife, and Raoul couldn't hold back on seeing him, with the nervous and derisive laugh of unfortunate people close to losing their reason.

"Ah! You weren't expecting me," he said. "You thought that my imbecilic trust would mean you'd never be punished."

Raoul had at least the courage to place himself in front of Madame Fauvel, covering her with his body, waiting for—he has to be given this credit—preparing to receive a bullet.

"Believe me, my uncle…" he began.

A menacing gesture from the banker interrupted him.

"That's enough!" he said. "Enough lies and infamies like that. Stop an odious comedy of which I'm no longer a dupe."

"I swear to you…"

"Spare yourself the trouble to deny. Don't you see I know everything, understand me, absolutely everything! I know that my wife's diamonds have been taken to the Mont-de-Piété pawn brokers, and by whom! I know the author of the robbery for which Prosper, innocent, was arrested and put in prison!"

Madame Fauvel, aghast, had let herself fall on her knees. Finally it had come, the so dreaded day. Vainly, for years, she had heaped lies on lies. Vainly, she had given her life and sacrificed her own family. Everything here below comes out. Yes, always, whatever one does, a moment comes when truth throws aside the veils under which one thinks it's been buried, and shines forth brighter, like the sun after it has cleared away the fog.

She saw very well that she was lost, and with begging gestures, her face flooded with tears, she stammered:

"Mercy, André, I beg you, forgive!"

At the sound of that dying voice, the banker trembled, and was shaken to the depth of his innermost being. That was because it recalled to him, that voice, all the happy hours that he had for twenty years owed to that woman, sovereign mistress of his will. With a look, she had been able to make him happy or unhappy. All the world of the past woke with her prayers. In that unhappy woman drooping at his feet, he recognized that beloved Valentine, glimpsed like a dream under the poetic shades of La Verberie. In her he saw the loving and devoted wife of the first years, she who had almost died when Lucien was born.

And in remembering the happiness of the past, which would never come back, his heart swelled with sadness, tenderness rushed over him—forgiveness mounted to his lips.

"Miserable woman!" he whispered. "Unhappy woman! What have I done to you? Ah! I loved you too much without a doubt, and I let you see it too much. One tires of everything here below, even of happiness. The pure joys of a domestic household seemed dull to you, didn't they? Tired of the respect that surrounded you, and that you deserved, you wanted to risk your honor, ours, and brave society's scorn. What abyss have you fallen into, oh, Valentine! And why, if my caresses after a while were tiresome to you, weren't you restrained by the thought of our children!"

Monsieur Fauvel spoke slowly, with the most painful effort, as if with every word he was near suffocation. Raoul, himself, who was listening with profound attention, guessed that if the banker knew a great deal, he didn't know everything. He understood that erroneous information had deceived the banker, and that he was at this moment the victim of deceptive appearances. He thought the misunderstanding Monsieur Fauvel was a victim of could be explained.

"Monsieur..." he began, "please, I beg you..."

But the sound of his voice was enough to break the charm. The banker's anger awoke, more terrible, more menacing.

"Ah! You shut up!" he shouted, swearing, "Shut up!"

There was a long silence, interrupted only by Madame Fauvel's sobbing.

"I came," continued the banker, "with the stated intention of surprising and killing both of you. I surprised you, but...courage, yes, I lack the courage...I can't kill an unarmed man."

Raoul tried to protest.

"Let me speak!" Monsieur Fauvel interrupted. "Your life is in my hands, isn't it? The law excuses an offended husband's anger. Well! I don't want any of the Penal Code's excuses. I see a revolver like mine on your chimney mantle. Take it and defend yourself!"

"Never!"

"Defend yourself!" the banker continued, raising his weapon. "Defend yourself. If not..."

Raoul saw the barrel of Monsieur Fauvel's gun a foot from his stomach. He was afraid, and picked up his weapon from the mantle.

"Stand in one of the corners of the bedroom," the banker went on, "I'm going to stand in the other. At the sound of your clock, which is going to strike in several seconds, we'll fire at the same time."

They took their places as Monsieur Fauvel indicated, slowly, without saying a word. But the scene was too frightful for Madame Fauvel to endure. She understood only one thing: her son and her husband were going to slaughter each other, there, under her eyes. Terror and horror gave her the strength to rise, and she placed herself between the two men, her arms spread out, as if she hoped to stop the balls. She turned toward her husband:

"Have pity, André," she moaned. "Let me tell you everything. Don't kill him."

That outburst of maternal love, Monsieur Fauvel took for the cry of an adulterous woman defending her lover. With unexpected brutality, he seized his wife by the arm and threw her to one side, shouting:

"Stand back!"

But she charged back, throwing herself on Raoul. She clasped him in her arms, saying:

"I'm the one to be killed, only me, because I alone am guilty."

At these words, blood rushed to Monsieur Fauvel's head. He took aim at this despicable group and fired. Neither Raoul nor Madame Fauvel fell. The banker fired a second time, then a third. He was aiming his revolver for the fourth time, when a man burst into the middle of the room. He snatched the weapon from the banker's hands, threw him full length on a couch, and rushed toward Madame Fauvel. That man was Monsieur Verduret. Cavaillon had finally found and warned him, but he didn't know that Madame Gypsy had removed the balls from Monsieur Fauvel's revolver.

"Thank heavens she hasn't been hit," he exclaimed.

But the banker had already gotten up.

"Let me alone," he said, struggling. "I want to avenge myself."

Monsieur Verduret grabbed his wrists and squeezed, almost breaking them. He put his face close to Monsieur Fauvel's, as if to give his words greater authority.

"You, thank God," he told him, "that you were spared an atrocious crime. The anonymous letter deceived you."

Unreasonable situations are strange in this way. The excess violence that comes from them seems natural to the actors involved, whose passion has already broken through the limits of social conventions.

Monsieur Fauvel didn't think to ask that man who had suddenly entered, either who he was, or where he got his information. He saw, he retained only one thing: the anonymous letter lied.

"My wife admits she is guilty!" he whispered.

"Yes, she is that," Monsieur Verduret answered, "but not as you think. Do you know who that man is that you wanted to kill?"

"Her lover!"

"No...her son!"

The presence of that so well informed, unknown man, seemed to confuse Raoul and scare him, even more than Monsieur Fauvel's threats. However, he had enough presence of mind to answer: "It's true!"

The banker seemed near madness, and his haggard eyes went from Monsieur Verduret to Raoul, then to his wife, more sinking, subsiding, than that of the criminal awaiting a sentence of death. Suddenly it occurred to him that they were making fun of him.

"What you're telling me is impossible!" he shouted. "Give me proof!"

"Proofs you'll have," answered Monsieur Verduret, "but to begin with, listen."

And rapidly, with his marvelous ease of exposition, he sketched the main outlines of the drama he'd discovered. Certainly the truth was still terrible for Monsieur Fauvel, but what was it compared to what he'd suspected!

Through the sorrows he had felt, he recognized he still loved his wife. Could he not forgive a sin, long in the past and made amends for by a life of devotion and nobly atoned for? Monsieur Verduret had finished his story several minutes, and Monsieur Fauvel was silent.

So many happenings rapidly following each other for forty-eight hours, as unstoppable as an avalanche, and the horrible scene which had just taken place, stunned Monsieur Fauvel and took away any ability to think. Tossed about like a cork wherever the waves take it, his will floated lost, at the mercy of events.

If his heart advised him to pardon and forget, his offended ego told him to remember so as to take revenge. Without Raoul, that miserable creature who was there, standing, a living witness of a faraway sin, he wouldn't have hesitated. Gaston de Clameran was dead. He would have opened his arms to his wife, telling her: "Come, your sacrifices to my honor will be your absolution; come, and let all the past be only a bad dream that daylight will dispel."

But Raoul stopped him.

"And that's your son," he said to his wife, "that man who took all you had and stole from me!"

Madame Fauvel was too overwhelmed to be able to utter a syllable. Fortunately, Monsieur Verduret was there.

"Yes," he answered, "Madame will tell you in fact that this young man is Gaston de Clameran's son. She believes it. She's sure of it... only..."

"Well?..."

"To go through all she had more easily, they deceived her outrageously."

For a moment, Raoul had already been cleverly maneuvering, so as to approach the door. He thought no one at this moment was thinking about him. He wanted to flee. But Monsieur Verduret, who had foreseen the movement, was watching Raoul out of the corner of his eye, and stopped him the moment he was disappearing.

"So, where are you going like that, my pretty boy?" He asked, drawing him back into the middle of the bedroom. "Do we really want to give your friends the slip? That's not nice. Before separating, what the devil! Let's explain ourselves."

Monsieur Verduret's jeering attitude, his joking tones, was for Raoul like so many rays of light. He recoiled, murmuring:

"The Paillasse!"

"True!" answered the fat man, "Exactly right! Ah! You recognize me! Then I confess. Yes, I'm the happy Paillasse from the Messieurs Jandidier's ball. Do you doubt it?" He raised the sleeve of his coat, exposed his naked arm, and continued: "If you're not completely convinced, examine that very fresh scar. Wouldn't you be acquainted with the clumsy person who, one beautiful night when I was going down the Rue Bourdaloue, jumped on me, an open knife in his hand? Ah! You don't deny it? We're that much ahead. In that case, you're going to be kind enough to tell us your little story."

But Raoul was prey to one of those terrors, which constrict the throat and prevent one word from being pronounced.

"You're not talking?" Monsieur Verduret continued. "Could you be modest? Bravo! Modesty sits well with talent, and true, for your age, you're a rather successful rogue."

Monsieur Fauvel was listening without understanding.

"What abyss of shame have we fallen into!" he groaned.

"Be reassured, Monsieur," Monsieur Verduret answered, serious again. "After what I've been compelled to inform you, the rest of what I have to tell you is nothing. Here's the end of the story:

"In leaving Mihonne, who had just finished revealing to him the misfortunes of Mademoiselle Valentine de la Verberie, Clameran had nothing more pressing to do than go over to London. Well informed, he very quickly found the worthy farm woman to whom the Countess had entrusted Gaston's son. But there a little annoyance awaited him. They told him that the child, enrolled in the parish register under the name of Raoul Valentin Wilson, had died of the croup at the age of eighteen months."

Raoul tried to protest.

"They said that?..." he began.

"Yes, they said that, my pretty boy, and they also wrote it down. Do you think I'm a man to be content with empty words?"

He took out of his pocket diverse papers decorated with official stamps, which he placed on the table.

"Here," he said, "are the sworn statements of the farm woman and her husband and four witnesses; here also is an extract from the birth registry. Here, finally, is a death certificate in good and due form, the whole thing attested to by the French ambassador. Are you happy, my pretty boy, do you consider yourself satisfied?"

"But then?..." asked the banker.

"Then," Monsieur Verduret continued. "Clameran thought he didn't need the child to extort money from Monsieur Fauvel. He was wrong. His first attempt failed. What was he to do? The scoundrel is inventive. Among all the crooks of his acquaintance—and he knew quite a few—he chose the one you see in front of you."

Madame Fauvel was in a pitiful state; but nevertheless, she was reborn with hope. Her anxiety had been so atrocious for such a long time, that she experienced seeing the truth as a terrible consolation.

"Is it possible!" she stammered. "Is it possible?"

"What!" said the banker. "Can people these days put together and carry out such infamies?"

"All this is false!" Raoul daringly claimed.

It was only Raoul that Monsieur Verduret answered.

"Does Monsieur desire proof?" he said with ironic courtesy. "Monsieur will get what he wishes. I just shortly left one of my friends, Monsieur Palot, who's come from London, and who is marvelously informed. Tell me what you think of this little history he's just told me:

"About 1847, Lord Murray, who is a great and generous lord, had a jockey named Spencer he particularly liked. At the Epson races, that capable jockey unfortunately fell so badly that he died. Lord Murray was in despair, and as he didn't have any children, he stated that he intended to take charge of the future of Spencer's son. That son was then four years old. The Lord kept his word. James Spencer was brought up as the heir to a great Lord. He was a charming child, luckily gifted with an attractive make-up, with a lively and sharp intelligence. Until he was sixteen years old, James gave his protector every imaginable satisfaction. Unfortunately, at that age he got into bad company and *Ma foi!* turned bad."

"Lord Murray, who was indulgence itself, pardoned a great many faults; but one fine day, having discovered that his adopted son was amusing himself by forging his signature on bank bills of exchange, indignant, he threw him out."

"Now, James Spencer had been living in London by gambling and several other industries, when he met Clameran, who offered him 25,000 francs to play a role in a comedy which he made up...'"

Raoul didn't need to hear any more.

"Are you a Sûreté Police agent?" he asked.

The fat man smiled nicely.

"At the moment," he answered, "I'm only a friend of Prosper. According to how you behave, I'll be this or that."

"What do you want of me?"

"Where are the 350,000 stolen francs?"

The young criminal hesitated a moment.

"They're here," he finally answered.

"Good! That admission will be in your favor. In fact, the 350,000 francs are here. I know that. And I also know that they're hidden in the bottom of a wall cupboard over there. Are you returning them?"

Raoul understood the game was lost. He dashed to the cupboard and took out several bundles of bank bills, and an enormous stack of receipts from the Mont-de-Piété.

"Very good," said Monsieur Verduret, while inventorying all that Raoul had given him, "Very good, that's behaving wisely."

Raoul had very much counted on this moment, when nobody was looking. Softly, holding his breath, he reached the door, opened it quickly and disappeared, locking it after him, because the key had stayed on the outside.

"He's getting away!" Monsieur Fauvel exclaimed.

"Naturally," answered Monsieur Verduret, without bothering to turn his head. "I certainly thought that would occur to him."

"But…"

"What! Do you want all this reported? Are you anxious to tell the police what scoundrels your wife has been victimized by?"

"Oh! Monsieur!"

"Let this miserable man get away then. Here's the 350,000 francs. It's all there. Here are all he receipts for the things he pawned. Let's consider ourselves satisfied. He's still carrying away 500 francs. So much the better. That amount of money will allow him to go abroad. We won't hear any more of him."

Like everyone, Monsieur Fauvel gave in to Monsieur Verduret's strong will. Little by little, he'd come back to reality, as unhoped-for perspectives opened before him. He understood that more than his life had just been saved. The expression of his gratitude wasn't long in coming. He seized Monsieur Verduret's hands as if he wanted to carry them to his lips, and with the most emotional voice he said:

"How can I ever show you how grateful I am, Monsieur? How can I repay the immense service you've rendered me?"

Monsieur Verduret was thoughtful.

"If that's how it is," he began, "I have a favor to ask you."

"A favor, you! From me? Speak, Monsieur, speak! Can't you see that myself as well as my fortune are available to you?"

"Well then! Monsieur, I'll admit to you that I'm a friend of Prosper's. Will you not help him get reinstated? You can do so much for him, Monsieur! He's in love with Mademoiselle Madeleine…"

"Madeleine will be his wife, Monsieur," Monsieur Fauvel interrupted. "I swear it to you. Yes, I'll reinstate him, and with such public attention that no one will ever dare reproach him for my fatal error."

The fat man, exactly as if it had been a matter of an ordinary visit, had gone to pick up his cane and his hat placed in a corner.

"You'll excuse my annoying you," he said, "but Madame Fauvel…"

"André!" whispered the poor woman. "André!"

The banker resisted at first for several seconds. Then making his decision bravely, he rushed to his wife. He clasped her in his arms, saying:

"No! I'm not enough of a fool to fight against my heart. I don't forgive

Valentine, I forget. I forget everything."

Monsieur Verduret had nothing more to do in Vésinet. That's why, slipping away, he returned to the carriage that brought him, and ordered the coachman to take him to Paris, to the Hotel du Louvre... and to hurry.

At that moment, he was eaten up with worry. From Raoul's side, everything was arranged. The young crook should be far away. But was it possible to get Clameran the punishment he merited? Evidently not. Now Monsieur Verduret was wondering how to turn Clameran over to the law without compromising Madame Fauvel, and he had gone through his repertory of possible ways in vain. He saw none fitting the present circumstances.

"There is only one way," he thought. *"An accusation of poisoning must come from Oloron. I can go there to work up 'public opinion.' They'll speak against him and there'll be an inquest. Yes, but all that takes time, and Clameran has been too well alerted not to take to his legs."*

He was truly sorry for his impotence, when the carriage stopped in front of the Hotel du Louvre. It was almost night. Under the hotel porch and under the arcades, at least a hundred people crowded together, and despite the "Keep moving! Keep moving!" of the city police, there seemed to be a serious event taking place.

"What's happening," Monsieur Verduret asked one of the on-lookers.

"Something unheard of, Monsieur," replied the other man, "a type of Prudhomme.[53] Because I saw it, saw it perfectly. Look, it was in the seventh dormer window, up there, that he first appeared. He was half naked! They tried to grab him. *Baste!* As agile a monkey or a sleepwalker, he jumped to the roof, yelling he was being assassinated! The extreme recklessness of that action makes me suppose..."

The loiterer stopped short, very vexed. The man questioning him had just left.

"If that's he, if fear has disorganized that head so marvelously disposed toward crime...!" thought Monsieur Verduret.

While continuing his monologue, he had elbowed his way through the crowds and had managed to reach the hotel courtyard. There, at the foot of the grand staircase, waited Monsieur Fanferlot accompanied by three men of unusual aspect.

"Well," shouted Monsieur Verduret.

The four men, a noteworthy ensemble, came to attention.

"The boss!" they exclaimed.

"Come now, tell me what's happened," said the fat man. "What's going on?"

"The trouble is, boss," Fanferlot continued, "the trouble is, I'm unlucky,

---

[53] Joseph Prudhomme: a 19th century cartoon character created by Henri Monnier.

572

you see. The one time I fall into a real case, *Paf!* my criminal goes bankrupt."

"Then, it's Clameran who..."

"Ah! Yes! It's him. When he saw me this morning, the fellow made off like a rabbit, in a hurry. Oh! What a hurry! I thought he'd go like that right to Ivry, at least. Not at all. When he came to the Boulevard des Écoles, he suddenly thought about something, and he dashed here. Very probably he came to look for his stash of money. He entered, but what did he see? My three comrades present here. That sight for him was like a hammer blow on the forehead. He saw he was lost. His mind came unhinged."

"But where is he?"

"At the Prefecture, probably. I saw the Paris police handcuff him and take him away in a carriage."

"Then let's go..."

It was, in fact, in one of the special cells reserved for dangerous guests, that Monsieur Verduret and Fanferlot found Clameran. They had put him in a straight jacket, and he was struggling furiously with three employees and a doctor who was trying to make him swallow a potion to calm him down.

"Help!" he cried out. "Come help me! Don't you see? He's coming toward me. It's my brother. He wants to poison me!"

Monsieur Verduret took the doctor to one side to question him.

"This poor man is lost," the doctor answered. "This type of alienation can't be cured. He thinks people want to poison him. He rejects all drinks, all nourishment. And whatever is tried, he'll finally starve to death, after having felt all the tortures of poison."

Monsieur Verduret shivered in leaving the Prefecture.

"Madame Fauvel is saved, since God is taking charge of punishing Clameran," he murmured.

"With all that," Fanferlot grumbled, "me, I'm out my expenses and my trouble. What a Punch and Judy show!"

"That's true," answered Monsieur Verduret. "File 113 will never leave the clerk's office. But console yourself. Before the end of the month, I'll send you to carry a letter to one of my friends, and what you lose in fame, you'll make up for in money."

Chapter XXV

Four days later, Monsieur Lecoq—the official Lecoq—the one who looks like the head of a bureau—was pacing his office floor, looking at the clock every moment. Finally someone rang the bell, and the faithful Nanouille brought in Madame Nina and Prosper Bertomy.

"Ah! You're on time, lovers; that's good."

"We're not lovers, Monsieur," answered Madame Gypsy. "It took Monsieur Verduret's express orders to get us together again. He made an appointment for us here, in your office."

"Very good!" said the famous policeman. "Then please wait here a few moments; I'll go tell him you're here."

During the quarter of an hour that Nina and Prosper remained alone together, they didn't exchange one word. Finally, a door opened, and Monsieur Verduret appeared. Nina and Prosper wanted to rush toward him, but he nailed them to the spot with one of those looks that no one resists.

"You've come to find out the secret of my conduct," he said to them. "I promised…I'll keep my promise, whatever it costs me at this time. So listen to me. My best friend is a brave and loyal boy named Caldas. That friend was, eighteen months ago, the happiest of men. In love with a young woman, he lived only through her and for her, and, silly as he was, he imagined that she loved him above everything."

"Yes!" exclaimed Gypsy, "Yes, she loved him!"

"All right. She loved him so much that one lovely evening she left with someone else. At first, Caldas, insane with sorrow, wanted to kill himself. Then, thinking about it, he told himself it would be better to live and get revenge."

"But then!" stammered Prosper.

"So Caldas took revenge in his own way. That is to say, under the eyes of the woman who betrayed him, he dramatically demonstrated his immense superiority over the other man. Weak, cowardly, unintelligent, the other man rolled into the abyss. Caldas' powerful hand held him back. Because, you've understood, haven't you? The woman, that's Nina; the seducer, that's you. As for Caldas…"

With a violent gesture, he threw off his wig and his sideburns, and the intelligent and proud head of the real Lecoq appeared.

"Caldas!" Nina exclaimed.

"No, not Caldas, not Verduret either, but Lecoq, the Sûreté agent."

There was a moment of stupor, after which Monsieur Lecoq turned toward Prosper.

"It's not just to me you owe your salvation. A woman, having the courage to trust me, made the task easy for me. That woman is Mademoiselle Madeleine.

It's to her that I swore Monsieur Fauvel would never know anything. Your letter made my plans impossible. I said…"

He wanted to go back into his office, but Nina barred his way.

"Caldas," she was saying, "I beg you. I am an unhappy woman! Ah! If you knew, forgive, pity!"

Prosper left Monsieur Lecoq's office by himself.

The 15th of last month the marriage of Monsieur Prosper Bertomy and Mademoiselle Fauvel was celebrated at the church of Notre Dame de Lorette. The banking house is still on the Rue de Provence, but Monsieur Fauvel, intending to retire to the country, has changed the company name, which is now: *Prosper Bertomy and Company.*

CPSIA information can be obtained
at www.ICGtesting.com
Printed in the USA
FSOW01n0323030516
19943FS